An Absolute Scandal

DOUBLEDAY

NEW YORK

LONDON

TORONTO

SYDNEY

AUCKLAND

AN
Absolute
Scandal

A NOVEL

Penny Vincenzi

ⅅD

DOUBLEDAY

PUBLISHED BY DOUBLEDAY

Published in the United States by Doubleday, an imprint of
The Doubleday Publishing Group, a division of
Random House, Inc., New York.
www.doubleday.com

DOUBLEDAY is a registered trademark and
the DD colophon is a trademark of Random House, Inc.

Book design by Ellen Cipriano

Library of Congress Cataloging-in-Publication Data
Vincenzi, Penny.
An absolute scandal : a novel / by Penny Vincenzi. — 1st U.S. ed.
p. cm.
1. Financial crises—Great Britain—Fiction. 2. Lloyd's (Firm)—Fiction.
3. Nineteen eighties—Fiction. I. Title.
PR6072.I525A64 2008
823'.914—dc22
2007034495

ISBN 978-0-385-51989-2

PRINTED IN THE UNITED STATES OF AMERICA

1 3 5 7 9 10 8 6 4 2

First U.S. Edition

To Paul,
for endless support and patience
and incredible generosity

Acknowledgments

This has been one of the most demanding books I've ever written in terms of required and acquired knowledge, and I owe a huge debt to a large number of people.

The most outstanding contribution came from Gordon Medcalf, whose knowledge of Lloyd's and attention to detail was matched only by his editorial flair, and without whom certain chapters would have been sad and sorry affairs. It is with incredible sadness that I find myself unable to thank him properly, for he died just before the book was published. Therefore I would like to express my great gratitude to his wife, Julia, and his family.

Many other people gave most generously of their time and expertise, notably many Lloyd's Names: Jay and Nick Upton, Peter Carvell, John Mays, Victor Sandelson, John Rew, David Durant, Nigel Symons Jones, and James Lotery. I also received a great deal of help and information from several lawyers and bankers, who showed not only huge knowledge of Lloyd's at the time but genuine inventiveness as to plotlines. Edward Harris, in particular, alerted me to the existence of male entail. I received much help also from experts in the fields of banking, insurance, and the City of London and its banking fraternity at the time; and I was permitted to attend several Coroners' Courts and indeed study so much of their procedure that I feel I could also set up as a coroner myself.

Clodagh Hartley once again provided me with valuable inside information on the conduct of newspaper reporting, and I owe much gratitude to the staff in the archive library at the *Daily Mirror* who dug out one huge dusty volume after another.

Detective Superintendent Dermot Keating gave me a crash course in the conduct of sundry complex police procedures; and I owe a great debt to my amazingly informative and engaging guide around Harvard.

I am of course very, very grateful to everybody at Hodder Headline, who published the book in the UK; they are an absolutely amazing team.

And in the United States, great gratitude to Steve Rubin, the wonderfully inspired publishing supremo at Doubleday; to my brilliant and joyous editor, Deb Futter; to Dianne Choie for her skill in holding nuts and bolts together; and to Alison Rich, publicity director par excellence who seems to possess almost magical powers of persuasion over the media.

I owe a great debt of course to my agent, Clare Alexander, who has seen me safely across the Atlantic, and to my four daughters, Polly, Sophie, Emily, and Claudia, who manage despite demanding lives of their own to always be there when I need them.

Characters

SIMON BEAUMONT, a merchant banker
ELIZABETH, his wife, the managing director of Hargreaves, Harris and
  Osborne advertising agency
ANNABEL, TOBY, AND TILLY, their children
FLORIAN, a hairdresser, and Annabel's best friend
MADISON AND FALLON, Tilly's best friends
MARTIN DUDLEY, Simon's chairman
DAVID GREEN, an old friend and sailing companion of Simon's
FELICITY PARKER JONES, a friend of Simon's
NEIL LAWRENCE, a client of Elizabeth's, and a Lloyd's victim

LUCINDA AND NIGEL COWPER, Sloaney couple living in Cadogan Square
ERIC AND MARGARET WORTHINGTON, Lucinda's parents
LYDIA NEWHOUSE, Nigel's secretary
STEVE DURHAM, Lucinda's tough lawyer
GRAHAM PARKER, her boss

GARY "BLUE" HORTON, a market trader in the City
CHARLIE, his best friend

FLORA FIELDING, a glamorous widow
RICHARD, her son, a teacher
DEBBIE, his wife
ALEXANDER, EMMA, AND RACHEL, their children
ANNA CARTER, Debbie's boss
MORAG DUNBAR, a headmistress
COLIN PETERSON, a property developer

JOEL STRICKLAND, a financial journalist for the *Daily News*
HUGH RENWICK, his editor

CATHERINE MORGAN, a young and pretty widow, and a Lloyd's victim
FREDDIE AND CAROLINE, her children
PHYLLIS AND DUDLEY MORGAN, her parents-in-law
MARY LENNOX, her babysitter
DOMINIC MAYS, Freddie's best friend in London
JANE-ANNE PRICE, Caroline's best friend in the country and her posh
  parents, the Honourable Mark Prices
PATRICK FISHER, an admirer of Catherine's

JAMIE CARTWRIGHT, a dashing young lawyer from Boston
FRANCES AND PHILIP, his parents
KATHLEEN, his sister, married to Joe
BARTHOLOMEW ("BIF"), his brother, married to Dana

GILLIAN THOMPSON, a piano teacher, and a Lloyd's victim
MAY WILLIAMS, her neighbour
GEORGE MEYER, leader of an action group, mounting a legal challenge
  against Lloyd's
FIONA BROADHURST, a solicitor
TIM ALLINSON, man-about-town
ROBERT JEFFRIES, a coroner's officer

An Absolute Scandal

Prologue

So the person you loved best in the world had killed themselves. Had felt so desperate, so absolutely hopeless that it seemed the only option.

How could you live with yourself, knowing that even you had not been able to offer comfort of any kind?

And, even though you knew it was not directly your fault, that the blame could be very arguably laid at the door of that gleaming, futuristic-looking building in the heart of the City of London, you would still blame yourself every hour of every day for the rest of your life.

~

It wasn't the first such death of course, nor would it be the last. People had been lured by the promise of an apparently risk-free wealth by the tenants of that building, basing a lifestyle on beautiful houses, on expensively educated children, on all the powers and pleasures of wealth—only to discover the foundations of it were built on shifting, albeit golden sands. And yet the promise had been far from empty, based as it was on a background of three centuries of economic success. But for a time, in those darkly turbulent years at the end of what has now been labelled the Greed Decade, that promise seemed not only empty but also a terrifying vacuum; and it was not just the houses and the educations that were lost, but frequently the most basic of life's requirements and, for many, pride, self-respect, and, indeed, hope itself.

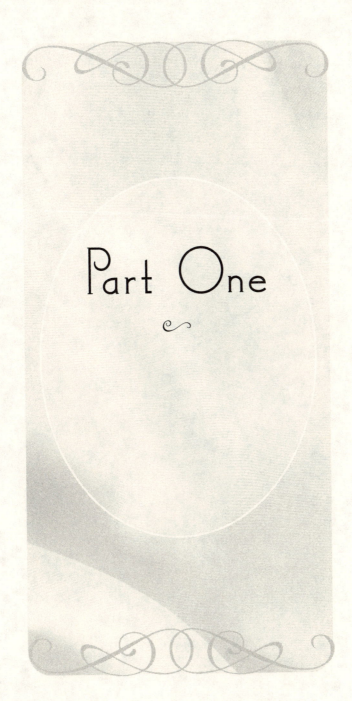

Part One

Chapter 1

She wasn't even going to think about having an affair.

It was something she totally disapproved of; it wasn't only immoral and selfish, it was deeply dangerous. She was married, very happily, to someone she not only loved but admired, and there was no way she was going to break her vows (and risk breaking Nigel's heart), and put her marriage and her very happy life at risk. So that was absolutely that. And if he phoned—which he almost certainly wouldn't, he'd been drunk and probably hadn't meant a word of what he said—but if he did, she would simply say, "No, I'm sorry, it was lovely meeting you, but I'm happily married and—well, I'm happily married." That would be enough. Surely. He'd know what she meant and he'd probably come out with some jokey reply and that would be that. And if she had to spell it out—well, she would. A fun encounter: that's all it had been. She might have been a bit silly: she *had* been a bit silly. But that was all. Blame the champagne. And luckily Nigel hadn't noticed anything . . .

He came into the bedroom now, from their bathroom, offering his wrists to her so she could put in his cuff links; as she did so, her fingers unusually fumbly—blame the champagne for that as well, she seemed to have a bit of a hangover—she suddenly found herself looking at him as if she had never seen him before. Was he really, as HE had said so rudely, a bit of a caricature? She supposed, honestly, he was: tall, blond—well, blondish, going just slightly grey now—very slim, pretty good-looking really, perfectly dressed, in his Turnbull and Asser shirt, his pinstripe suit, his Lobb shoes. (HE had been wearing Lobb shoes, he told her: "Only posh thing about me. I get a real thrill going in there, them getting the old last out.")

"Lucinda! Do concentrate, darling, I can't stand here all day."

"Sorry. There you are."

"Thanks. You having breakfast this morning?"

"Oh—no." The thought made her feel sick.

"Hope you're not overdoing the dieting?"

"Nigel, of course I'm not. I'd have thought you only had to look at me to see that."

"Well—you look pretty good to me. Anyway, I'm hungry. Not enough to eat at that thing, was there?"

"No, not really. Gosh, it's late, I didn't realise."

She mustn't be late for work today, of all days. She worked for Peter Harrison, the publishers, as secretary to Graham Parker, one of the editors, and he had an important meeting with some Americans. Being Americans, they had suggested an eight o'clock meeting; Graham had managed to persuade them forwards an hour to nine, but she'd have to be there well before then, coffee brewed, biscuits and herself ready to greet them. It would be fun.

One of the things Lucinda loved most about her job was the social aspect; there was always something going on—book launches, marketing meetings, sales conferences, press jaunts . . . She'd been working for Graham for a year now; she was hoping to be an editor herself one day, but her ambition was slightly halfhearted; she didn't intend to go on working after she'd had a baby. That was something else she disapproved of: working mothers. She intended to be like her own mother, always there, putting her children first. But—come on, Lucinda, don't start thinking about that now. You've got to get to work.

She caught sight of herself in the hall mirror and tried to see herself through HIS eyes: long-ish full-ish skirt (Laura Ashley), blue shirt with a turned-up collar (Thomas Pink), and her twenty-first-birthday pearls, of course; navy sleeveless Puffa jacket, flat shoes (Charles Jourdan), blond hair scooped back in a velvet band.

There really was no way she could possibly appeal to HIM, not really. He'd like one of those sharp eighties girls in short-skirted suits with padded shoulders, girls with big hair and big ambitions. He wouldn't even be able to remember her this morning, never mind ringing her . . . and as she stood there, checking that she had her wallet and her keys, the post came through the letter box. A couple of quite nice-looking things, clearly invitations, a bill or two, a postcard from Verbier, from the skiing party she'd wanted to join and Nigel hadn't, and a letter from Lloyd's. Lloyd's of London. One of the whiter-than-white envelopes that arrived once a year, containing a statement of their account and followed in due course by a large cheque. Nigel was a Member of Lloyd's; it was one of the things that had pleased her father most when he and Nigel had had their little chat, just before they got engaged.

"Not only all that land, down in Norfolk, but he's a Name as well; that'll stand you in good stead in the years to come."

One of her uncles had been a Name in quite a big way, apparently. When she was young, she'd heard her mother talking about it, and asked her what it meant. "Well, darling, it means you become a sort of sleeping partner," Margaret Worthington had said rather vaguely. "They insure big things, like ships and buildings, and they make a big profit on it. If you're a Name, you get a share in those profits." "What happens if the ships sink?" she'd asked, and her mother had said, well, there was more than enough money to deal with that. "They still make a profit. Ask Daddy about it, he'll tell you more, I don't really understand it. Except that it pays all your cousins' school fees," she added.

It hadn't sounded interesting enough for Lucinda to ask her father; but she did know now that there was enough money coming in from Lloyd's every year to boost their income quite a bit. Which they didn't need at the moment of course, Nigel's salary as chairman of the family business was perfectly adequate, and he had quite a big portfolio of stocks and shares, but it would be wonderfully helpful when they wanted to move to the country and buy a house.

That was the plan, to move as soon as they had children. Not to Norfolk, that was too far and the last thing Nigel wanted was to run the farm, but he didn't want to spend the rest of his life in London. Nor did she; she'd grown up in the country herself and loved it.

"Where did you live when you were a child then?" HE had asked last night. "Some pile in the country, I s'pose?"

And, "Well," she'd said, "not exactly a pile, but quite a nice house, yes, in Gloucestershire, near Cirencester."

"Oh yeah? Ponies?"

"Yes. Yes, I did have a pony. Actually."

"Very nice," he'd said, "very nice indeed. I'd like my kids to have all that, ponies and boarding school. You go to boarding school?"

"Yes, when I was thirteen."

"Like it?"

"Quite. I got awfully homesick and missed my pony. And Mummy, of course, and my brothers."

"And where were they at school? Eton or Harrow or some such?"

"Um—Eton, yes, actually."

"And hubby, he go to Eton?"

"Yes, he did."

That was when he'd said Nigel was a caricature. And— Stop it, Lucinda, stop thinking about it.

She started ripping open the envelopes to distract herself. Invitations: oh, fantastic, Caroline's wedding. And that looked like Philippa's writing (it was)—brilliant, party in the country—and Sarah's baby's christening, and— Damn! She'd opened a letter addressed to Nigel by mistake, half pulled it out. Not that Nigel would mind—at least, she didn't think so. He always said he had no secrets from her. She'd just say she was sorry and—now the letter wouldn't go back into the envelope. Lucinda pulled it out to refold it and couldn't resist reading it. The letterhead was JACKSON AND BOND, MEMBERS' AGENT, LLOYD'S OF LONDON, and the letter itself was quite brief:

Dear Nigel,
I thought I should warn you ahead of the final account that, as I

feared, you did make a loss for the year just closed. Not a big one, just a few thousand pounds . . .

A loss. How extraordinary. That had never happened before. She didn't know how many thousands of pounds Lloyd's would regard as "just a few." Maybe ten thousand, or even more? Surely not. But she did know they dealt in very big numbers. Nigel would know. They'd have to talk about it tonight.

God, she was late; she must go. She left the letters on the hall table and slammed the door behind her.

❧

Despite her resolve, she began to think about HIM again: him and last night. She'd never met anyone quite like him before. It had been at a party, to celebrate the publication of a book edited by Graham Parker about the financial markets just before and just after Big Bang—that extraordinary day in October 1986, when the stock market became totally computerised and a free-for-all, rather than the gentlemanly domain of the traditional stockbroker.

Lucinda organised and attended all the editorial department's parties; it was part of her job and she enjoyed it.

The guest list had looked like a Who's Who of the Square Mile, Nigel had been invited, not because he worked in the City—he worked for a large manufacturing company that had been founded by his grandfather—but because he had a large share portfolio and Graham had kindly suggested to Lucinda that it might be interesting for him. HE on the other hand did work in the City.

HE was one of that entirely new breed of traders, the market makers, sprung not from the great public schools but from the East End of London. "I'm one of your electronic barrow boys, so-called," he said, grinning at her, as he allowed her to refill his glass. "Not the sort the City used to give the time of day to, unless we was in our proper place in the back office." He held out his hand. "Gary Horton. Known these days as Blue. Pleased to meet you"—he peered at her name badge—"Lucinda Cowper." He pronounced it wrongly as people so often did; it always annoyed her.

"It's pronounced Cooper," she said briskly, "the *w*'s silent."

"Yeah, I see," he said looking mildly amused, and then, his dark eyes moving over her. "Are you really called Lucinda?"

"Yes, of course. Is that so unusual?"

"Well, where I come from it is. I mean, that is a posh name, isn't it? Seriously posh."

"I—I don't know," she said.

"I don't s'pose you would. Don't s'pose you know anyone who isn't posh, do you?"

"Well, of course I do," she said, rather helplessly.

"Oh, OK. What, like Daddy's chauffeur and Mummy's cleaner?"

"I think you're being rather rude," said Lucinda, "if you don't mind my saying so. Now if you'll excuse me, I—"

"Sorry," he said, putting out an arm, stopping her. "I was out of order. Sorry. It interests me, all that Eton-and-ponies stuff, not sure I know why. Probably because I can't understand how they—you've—done it."

"What do you mean?" she said, reluctantly interested.

"How you've survived so long. I mean, most dinosaurs die out, don't they? Oh, shit. Now I've been rude again, haven't I?"

"Yes. Very," she said coolly, unable to laugh it off; she looked for Nigel, went over and refilled his glass.

"You all right?" she said. "Got enough people to talk to?"

"Oh yes, of course. Jolly good party, Lucinda, well done." He smiled at her; it was one of his more endearing characteristics, that he enjoyed life enormously; his work, his social life—although he got a bit irritated with her more giggly friends—his tennis, his shooting. He was seldom out of sorts, always cheerful, almost always good-tempered. He was quite a bit older than she was, forty-two to her twenty-four, but it had never been a problem. She rather liked it; it made her feel safe.

She was in earnest conversation with one of the other editors when Blue Horton appeared at her side again.

"Look," he said, waiting patiently until the editor moved away, "I just wanted to apologise. I've got a real gift for saying the wrong thing. Can't help it, really."

"It's all right," she said. "Now if you'll excuse me, I really have to go and talk to some more—what did you call them?—oh yes, dinosaurs."

"No, don't go," he said, putting his hand on her arm, "please. One of the reasons I got carried away was because I felt—I don't know—thrown by you."

"Thrown? Why?"

"Well, because you're so bloody gorgeous," he said. "I just totally forgot myself. Looking at you."

Lucinda felt a blush rising up her throat.

"Don't be ridiculous," she said.

"I'm not being ridiculous. I'm a shy, retiring sort of a fellow."

"Now you are really being ridiculous." She smiled in spite of herself. "You're about as shy as—as"—she struggled to think of someone suitably self-confident—"Mrs. Thatcher."

"Ah, now there's a lady I admire," he said, surprising her. "She's responsible for all this"—he waved his arm round the room—"all this enterprise; she's freed up the market, she's made it possible to do whatever you want, given enough ambition and energy and that. It's getting more like the States every day here, and I like it. I think that's what I was really trying to say," he added with a grin, "when I said your lot were dinosaurs. I meant, everything's changed and you've managed not to. And still done well. Very admirable."

"Well, all right. I'll try to accept that."

"Good. So how long you been married then?"

"Three and a half years."

"And kids? Got any kids?"

"No. Not yet,"

"OK. And where'd you live? Don't tell me, somewhere not too far away from Sloane Square."

"Well, yes. Actually. In dinosaur country."

"You're not going to let me forget that, are you?"

"No, I'm not. Now I really do have to circulate a bit more."

"I'll come with you."

"Blue—" She stopped suddenly. "Why Blue, when you were christened Gary?"

"It's a nickname," he said. "We all have them and they all got some sort of reason. I mean, there's Luft, short for Luftwaffe, he's got blond hair and blue eyes and very, very right-wing views. And Croydon, because his surname is Sutton, and Harry, he's one of your coloured gentlemen, so

Harry as in Belafonte, and Kermit who looks like a frog, and Blue Buttons were the runaround boys on the old stock-exchange floor. Looked after the brokers, kept them supplied with tea and coffee—and info, of course. You'd hear people shouting for them: 'Where's the Blue? Hey, Blue, over here!' I was one of them, before Big Bang. In fact, I got to be the head Blue Button. So the name stuck. I quite like it. Don't you?"

"I . . . well, yes, I think so," she said doubtfully.

"Good. Come on, let's do some of this circulating then. You introduce me to some of these people. And your husband, if you like."

She hadn't introduced him to Nigel; it didn't seem a very good idea, she wasn't sure why. For the next half hour he followed her round the room, carrying a bottle of champagne himself to assist with the glass refilling. And then, somehow, she had found herself alone with him in the little kitchen; a lot of people had gone, the catering people were packing up glasses, and he said suddenly, "Would you have lunch with me one day?"

"No," she said, staring at him, quite shocked, "of course not."

"Why of course?"

"Well, isn't it obvious?"

"Not really, no."

"Mr. Horton," she said firmly, sorting empty bottles from full, "I'm, well, I'm married, you know that."

"And married ladies never have lunch with gentlemen? Is that right?"

"Not—well, not like that."

"Like what?"

"You know—" She stopped. "You know perfectly well what I mean. Perfectly."

"No, I don't."

"Yes, you do. Oh, this is silly."

"Yes, it is," he said, "just a bit."

And then he leaned forward and kissed her. On the mouth. Only very briefly, but it was enough; enough to create the most extraordinary sensations, somewhere deep inside her. She pulled away, stared at him; he smiled at her. He had, she noticed, even in her confusion, extraordinarily nice teeth. He wasn't very tall, only a little taller than she was in her heels; his dark hair was close-cropped, his eyes a deep, deep brown. He had long, almost girly eyelashes, a very straight nose, and quite a wide mouth (showing the very nice teeth). He wasn't fat, but he was very solidly built, broad-shouldered, with rather large hands and feet, and he seemed to emit a lot of energy; he was restless, permanently fidgeting. It was oddly attractive.

He leaned forward and kissed her again, for a fraction longer. She could feel herself responding to him, feel her lips parting, moving just a little; it was terrible, scary—

"Please stop it," she said, "I really must go."

"OK," he said, "that's fine. I'll call you in a day or so, see if you've changed your mind. I don't give up easy. Bye, Lucinda." And he was gone.

Thinking about him now, about how he had disturbed her, how funny he had been—how really rather nice—she completely forgot about the letter from Lloyd's.

$\mathcal{C}\!\!\sim$

In the trading room at McArthur's Bank, Blue Horton was telling his best mate, Charlie, over a bacon butty that he had met the girl he wanted to marry.

"Oh yeah? What's she do then?"

"Works for a publisher. And her husband's a—"

"Her husband? Blue, don't be daft, mate. You don't want to get mixed up with a married woman."

"Charlie, she was just sensational. Posh, dead posh, you know how I like all that, and beautiful. Really beautiful. Blond, blue eyes, legs like a racehorse, and really sweet. No idea how sexy she was. I reckon she's never had a good fuck, and I reckon I could give her one. Correction, I'm going to."

"You're crazy," said Charlie, "you go down that road. And if she's got any sense, she won't let you."

"She hasn't got a lot, I'd say," said Blue, "that's what I'm banking on. And she fancied me. I know she did."

$\mathcal{C}\!\!\sim$

Elizabeth Beaumont was becoming obsessed with her upper arms. It was an absurd obsession, she could see that; she had far more important things to be obsessed about, like her career and her relationship with her husband, and her eldest daughter, but she still found herself returning to the arms. They were the one bit of her body that she didn't seem able to get the better of. She could work the rest of it into submission, with the help of her personal trainer, the gym, and her own self-discipline, could make sure her stomach was flat—who would think now it had submitted to three pregnancies—and her bum taut, and her thighs cellulite-free, although several of her friends had told her that was luck rather than anything more scientific. And her bust was mercifully small and therefore pretty firm still. But her arms—above the elbows—were beginning to sag. She had worn a sleeveless top this morning, a black one under her red suit, and as she dressed after her workout in the gym, she realised it had been a mistake, that she wouldn't really want to remove her jacket during the meeting. Which was a pain, as the meeting room was always too hot, and the suit, in thick ribbed silk, was quite heavy . . .

Oh, for goodness' sake, Elizabeth, she thought, reaching for her bag, you shouldn't even be thinking about your arms, you should be thinking about the meeting. Which was going to be tricky; it was with one of the agency account directors who was anxious about a forthcoming presentation to one of their major clients, Hunter, a big-spending over-the-counter medicinal and toiletries brand. She walked out of the building, got into the cab waiting for her outside the door, and turned the full force of her formidable brain onto what lay ahead of her that morning.

Elizabeth had a very big job. She was managing director of one of London's leading advertising agencies, Hargreaves, Harris and Osborne, known in the business as H2O. Her boss had once called her the embodiment of the eighties have-it-all woman: with her gilt-edged life, her three perfect children, her handsome charming husband, her high-profile career; the compliment had pleased her immensely. She adored her work, loved urging and coercing her staff into the better-than-best work she knew they were capable of, even enjoyed the schmoozing as the essential tool it was in getting what she wanted. She appreciated her large salary, not only for what it could buy her but for what it represented: success and on a major scale in the part of the industry that traditionally had been male dominated.

Viewed from the outside, indeed, she was an absolute success; admired and feted, self-assured, in complete command of herself and her life. From the inside, a diffident, almost anxious Elizabeth looked out. From the inside, she very well knew, she was rather less of a success. And her upper arms seemed to symbolise the whole thing.

⟡

Simon Beaumont had never been remotely jealous of his wife's success; indeed, he was extremely proud of it. It helped, of course, that he was a success himself, a board director of Graburn and French, merchant bankers, and spent his days in the heady world of global stock markets, managing portfolios for private clients. He combined an ease of manner with a brilliant mind and a sharp financial instinct, and was a well-known figure in the City, much in demand for after-dinner speaking. Colleagues at a comparable level would not have dreamed of doing what he was doing that morning, which was getting his eldest daughter back to school for the summer term. Or what he had done on a hundred occasions, attending (on his own) school plays and carol concerts, parents' evenings, and, even once or twice, sitting by sickbeds when, for various reasons, neither the nanny nor the housekeeper were available and Elizabeth had a crucial meeting. For which he enjoyed, it had to be said, a great deal of cooing from various other wives of their acquaintanceship who told Elizabeth she had no idea how lucky she was. And Simon was rather afraid she did not.

He enjoyed the cooing, though. He enjoyed women altogether; they were as essential to his happiness and sense of well-being as his excellent health, his work, the fine wines with which he had filled his cellars, his two beautiful houses—one in London, one in Sussex—the long days sailing his boat, and his children, with all of whom he was besotted. He flirted with women and charmed them, and even gossiped with them—it was well known that Simon Beaumont was a fine keeper of secrets—and basked in their admiration. He enjoyed Elizabeth too: when she would allow it.

And that morning he was seeing his eldest daughter, Annabel, off to boarding school. Which he was happy to do; it provided an opportunity to admire both the girls and their mothers.

⟡

He really was a father to be proud of, Annabel thought, looking at him as he appeared in her bedroom doorway. He was very good-looking, tall and slim, with loads of hair still, even if it was going a bit grey; and he did dress well. He was wearing a great suit this morning, light grey, and really, really nice shoes.

She looked at some of her friends' fathers, paunchy and balding, and wearing really naff things sometimes, specially at weekend exeats, and wondered how they could bear it.

Her mother always looked good too; her clothes were great. Annabel thought it must be because she worked, knew what was what. Annabel was proud of her too: intensely so. When she had been little, she had wished that her mother could be at home, of course, but that had passed and their relationship was far better, she knew, more genuinely friendly and mature than those a lot of her friends had with their mothers.

"Come on, we're going to be late." Her father's voice was less tolerant than usual.

"Well, we'll have to be late. I can't find one of my essays. I know I brought it home, and now it's just vanished."

"Have you been working on it? What about your desk?" he said, carefully patient, obviously stressing. God, he stressed. They both stressed.

"I've looked there, Daddy. Obviously. And yes, I have been working on it, actually."

She hadn't, of course; she'd been much too busy seeing her friends, having fun.

"Shall I have a search? Often a fresh eye—"

"No," she said sharply. She didn't want him rummaging in her desk. She kept her pills there; of course, she'd got the current pack in her bag, but there were a couple of empty ones that she kept meaning to throw away. They weren't the sort of thing you could just chuck in the wastepaper basket.

"Well, all right. But if you can't find it, we'll have to go or you'll miss the train. I'll have a good look when you've gone and send it on to you."

"Daddy, I know it's here. Just give me five minutes. And I can always get a later train."

"Sweetheart, you have to get the school train. I've got a big meeting later this morning and—"

"I can perfectly well get myself back to school. I'm sixteen, for God's sake, I can get a cab across London and buy another ticket and read a timetable all by myself."

"You're not actually sixteen yet, Annabel. Not for another three weeks. And I want to see you safely onto that train. It's ridiculous, you should have got everything ready last night."

"Yes, all right. Sorry." She went over to him, gave him a kiss. "I was busy last night."

"Busy?" He smiled down at her, unable as she had known he would be, to stay cross with her. "Hmm. Partying until after midnight."

"Well, it was the last chance before we all go back to prison."

"All right, all right. So what do we do?"

"You wait, I'll go on looking. If I haven't found it in five minutes, we can go. Promise. Just leave me in peace, Daddy, please. I'm much more effective on my own."

She was right, of course; as soon as he had gone out of the room, she did remember where the essay was: in her bathroom, in the magazine rack. She'd been glancing at it two days earlier, as she waited for the bath to run, thinking she really must do something about it. As, of course, she hadn't. She retrieved it, pushed it into her leather Gladstone bag and rushed out into the hall.

"I'm ready."

"Good. Well, off we go then. Any more luggage?"

"No. I travel light. Apart from my trunk, and that's in the car."

"And you've rung Mum?"

"Yes, I've rung Mum. Come on then, let's go."

૯૭

There was a pile of letters on the hall table, placed there by Josie, the Portuguese housekeeper.

"Want those?" said Annabel.

"What? Oh, maybe. Grab them for me, darling, will you. I'll look at them in the car." Simon pulled the door shut behind them, ran down the steps in front of her.

"Morning, Carter. Paddington Station, please, here's Annabel's bag, and then I'm going on to the office."

Annabel sank into the corner of the car, looking back at the house briefly, then at her father as he sorted through the letters. It had been a very good holiday; they'd all had fun. Even dinner, the whole family number, had been all right. Bit of a waste of a Saturday night, but Toby had been on great form, he was an OK brother really, and Tilly was so sweet and so pretty.

"You all right, Daddy?" she said. A subdued "Fuck!" had escaped him in a tone that was half exasperation, half groan. He looked at her rather oddly, then managed a weak smile.

"Sorry, darling. Yes, I'm fine."

He didn't look fine; he looked a bit flushed.

"You sure?"

"Yes, yes, fine, just—just remembered something I should have done, that's all."

"Oh, good."

He was pushing a letter back into its envelope. She couldn't see what it said; the only words she recognised were Lloyd's of London at the top. She didn't know much about them, except that they were something to do with the City. Well, if it was only business it couldn't be that serious. She had complete faith in her father and his ability to run the world, or at least the City of London.

And then they reached Paddington Station, and she saw Miranda's mother pulling in just in front of them, and hooting, and after that in the hassle of getting her stuff out and assuring her father that there was no need to come to the platform with her, and hugging him and telling him she loved him, and saying goodbye to Carter, and waving and blowing her father kisses, she put it right out of her mind.

"Eat your breakfast, Emma, there's a good girl. Otherwise you'll be late for school."

Debbie Fielding said this every morning and at exactly the same time (8:15), just as she said, "Have a good day, both of you," to Alex and Richard, after giving them both a kiss (at 8:05), and, "Yes, Rachel, you do have to go to play school" (at 8:40).

Sometimes she thought she might as well have made a recording and just let it run each day, apart from the kissing, for all the notice anyone took of her or the response she got. Well, Richard smiled and said thanks, and plonked Alex's cap on his son's head, but Alex just heaved his schoolbag onto his back, Emma continued not to eat her breakfast, and Rachel continued to argue and say she didn't want to go to stupid play school. Just the same, by 9:30 Debbie was usually safely back at home on her own, apart from the dog and the cat.

It was her favourite moment of the day, that, the house briefly hers, nobody arguing with her or asking her for things or saying could she discuss something with him—that was Richard and usually when she was absolutely frantic and trying to get Emma off to ballet or Alex to judo or Rachel out of the bath.

What she did next was have a bath; she knew this was recklessly extravagant, in terms of time, but it helped her cling to her sanity. Quite why she found it so hard to remain sane she wasn't sure; she often said if there was a prize awarded for the most boring family in the British Isles they would win it. Three children, one cat, one dog, one car, house in the suburbs—well, she clung to the thought that Acton wasn't quite the suburbs, it had a London postcode, after all—father headmaster of the local junior school, mother full time at home, editor of the neighbourhood watch newsletter, deputy chair of the local National Childbirth Trust (NCT).

And how had that happened, Debbie wondered. How had the Debbie who had been the groundbreaker of her year at school, first to go to a music festival (Glastonbury in 1971, at the age of sixteen and without telling her parents—that had resulted in what she called house arrest for a month and which she swore was worth it), first to sleep with a boy, first to go on the pill, first to smoke pot, and who had been so excited on the morning of her first job, as runner for a local radio station, that she had been literally sick—how was it she had turned into this dull and dutiful person?

She had got two As and a B for her A levels—and moved from her grammar school in Kent to Birmingham University to read English. Where she found herself less of a groundbreaker but blissfully happy, released finally from the claustrophobia of only-childhood in her aggressively suburban home, into a paradise of like-minded, freethinking, pleasure-seeking contemporaries. She joined the debating society and several more ridiculous ones, like the Druids, partied furiously and almost failed her first-year exams. Sobered by that experience and a warning that she might lose her place unless her performance improved, she attached her nose firmly to the grindstone, and apart from a much-reduced social life, worked harder, and wrote endless pieces for *Redbrick,* the student newspaper.

And in that calmer, better-behaved phase she had met Richard Fielding, who was the antithesis of everything she liked or admired: public school, modestly good-looking, painstakingly polite, absolutely decent—it was an old-fashioned word, but suited him perfectly—bit of a swot, a reject, as he put it, from Cambridge, as if it mattered. He was reading English as well, and he was awesomely clever, regarded as a near-certainty for a First. Debbie found herself listening to him as he talked and argued in tutorials and in the student union and in debates, and gradually she became intrigued by him. He was very intense, very serious; that intrigued her too, used as she was to boys taking nothing very seriously at all, except sex and drink and various attendant pleasures, and he was able to surprise her too: a bit of a rock music buff, and the proud owner of a Harley-Davidson motorbike. Sitting behind him, holding him round the waist, as the world was reduced to a throbbing, scary blur was oddly erotic; after only the second outing she went to bed with him. He wasn't fantastic at sex, indeed rather dull compared to some of the boys she had known; but he had given the matter of her pleasure very careful attention and worked hard on it, as with everything he did, and that seemed rather engaging.

By the end of the second year they had become accepted as a couple, and he took her to meet his parents one weekend. They lived on the Gower peninsula in southwest Wales, an astonishingly lovely piece of countryside, unspoiled and untamed: where wild ponies roamed the moorland and lanes, where hawks hovered over the hills and sheep grazed the grassy cliffs high above the sea. Broken Bay House was a great heap of a place, quite isolated, high on the cliffs with an incredible view of the sea. It was large and rambling (and very cold), badly in need of painting, full of battered old rugs on stone flags, and lumpy sofas and jugs full of dried flowers everywhere, and real fires blazing, which warmed your front and left your back freezing. The kitchen was the only cosy room, because of the Aga, and they ate there, at a wooden table which was so big it could seat eight and still leave quite a long expanse at one end to be covered with letters and newspapers and books and catalogues of things like agricultural shows and art auctions. There was a vast garden with a large population of hens at the vegetable end and a stable yard with three horses: and an old Rolls tucked into one of the stables. They were obviously rich, Debbie thought, and wondered why they didn't get central heating put in. She liked William, Richard's father, he was sweet and old-fashionedly courteous, but Flora, his mother, frightened her a bit, she was so sure of herself. She wore long flowing skirts and shirts and very large sweaters, and her hair was always tumbling down from the knot she tied it in; she was nice to Debbie, but slightly patronising. Debbie could tell she thought she was common.

"How interesting you should say that," she would say when Debbie ventured an opinion on anything (which wasn't often), clearly implying it was not a view she would ever hold herself. Richard was their only child. "Do you remember so and so?" she'd keep saying to him, recalling some event. "Wasn't that fun?" And it made Debbie feel somehow excluded.

She came away freshly anxious about a relationship with a person and a life so alien to her.

By the time they graduated, they had agreed to live together; only six months into her new life with the TV company, which she had absolutely loved, she was pregnant. It was the result of a reckless weekend away when she forgot her pills, and with only a brief backward glance at her putative career in television, she declared herself astonishingly happy about it, and they agreed to get married.

And it was only now, her questing spirit tamed by family life and routine, and cast in the role of head teacher's wife, that she looked back and realised how much she had changed. She had made one very brief break for freedom when she ran away to join the women at Greenham Common with her two elder children, in order to protest about the arrival of American cruise missiles, and returned cold and filthy after four days to a rather smug Richard, but that was all.

As she lay in the bath that morning, Debbie knew exactly what she had to do that day: cooking a lasagna for an NCT quiz event tonight; writing her newsletter; collecting Rachel from play school and taking her to a party; meeting Emma and Alex from their respective schools; taking Emma to the dentist and Alex to judo—more snooty, unfriendly mothers to face down—and then tea; supervising homework (while wishing Richard could at least do that instead of disappearing into his study to do paperwork); and then the bath round, and getting Rachel into bed; and being ready, complete with lasagna, to go out, all by 7:30. And she realised there didn't seem to be a single moment in all this for attacking the high wall of ironing awaiting her.

As she pulled on her bathrobe, the phone rang; she'd been waiting for some news of a recent series of break-ins from the neighbourhood watch chairman for her newsletter.

"Hi, John," she said, but it wasn't nice John Peters, it was Flora. She still had an extremely uneasy relationship with Flora; she made her feel inadequate, and thus touchy and perverse.

Flora Fielding had been widowed five years earlier, when William had died suddenly of a heart attack, but while genuinely grief stricken, she went on determinedly and bravely with her life, refusing to move out of the house, as Richard felt she should, continuing to ride and hunt, and returning to her career as a photographer.

She worked only in black-and-white and specialised in seascapes and architectural photography. She didn't get a great many commissions, but it didn't matter, it absorbed her—along with her horses and an extremely active social life—and she certainly seemed to have no money worries. William had been a very successful accountant, as well as having family money, and he was also a Name at Lloyd's, Richard had explained to Debbie; she didn't really understand what that meant, except that it appeared to be a club for posh, rich people and was very financially desirable.

One of the things Flora insisted on was paying for the children's education. "I really want to do this," she said to them firmly, when Alex was coming up for seven. "I don't want them going to some useless place where they can indulge in free expression or whatever the latest fad is and come out at eleven with ghastly accents, not able to read."

Debbie was not even made part of this discussion, which enraged her; it seemed not to occur to Flora that Richard was the headmaster of what she would certainly consider "a useless place;" and indeed he would not have been, had he not failed to beat two other contestants at a prep school in Chiswick.

"First rejected by Cambridge, then rejected by Grange House," he said to Debbie, trying to make light of it. "What next?"

Debbie told him he would be much more use to the community at St. Luke's Junior; she would have greatly preferred Alex to be going there as well. She hated Flora paying the school fees. It meant permanent gratitude, and the right for Flora to interfere constantly in the children's progress. Not that she often did: although she did insist on doing spelling tests and tables in the car which made Debbie want to scream. Certainly they were both doing very well, roughly a year ahead of their state-educated counterparts; Debbie tried to concentrate on that and to feel genuinely—rather than resentfully—grateful to Flora.

Flora was still beautiful, tall and slim, with wild dark curly hair; the children found her huge fun to be with, playing endless games of tracking and hide-and-seek with her and clambering over rocks and up cliff paths. "You mustn't mollycoddle them," she would say to Debbie, who fretted while they climbed on a particularly hazardous pile of rocks, or waded screaming into the freezing Easter sea, their Wellies filling inevitably with water. "Children have an inbuilt sense of self-preservation."

Debbie didn't feel any amount of self-preservation could save a small child of seven from falling off a pony or getting swept out to sea in a rip, but she wasn't allowed to say so; it irritated Richard. He had grown up doing all those things, and he liked the idea of his children doing them too.

Flora did other annoying things, like keeping the children up hours beyond their bedtimes. "Rules are made to be broken," she would say, ignoring Debbie's request for a cooked tea for them, and serving dinner up for everybody at half past eight. "It does them good to eat with the grown-ups, teaches them far more than just lying upstairs in bed." She even suggested after-supper games of Scrabble to keep them up later still. Of course, it didn't matter in the holidays, but it did make the children over-tired and overexcited, made them question Debbie's own rules and argue with her endlessly.

And she just wished it could be her mother sometimes instead that they rushed to the phone to speak to, or begged to be allowed to stay with; but then her mother was a hopeless grandmother, always full of excuses about her arthritis and her husband's blood pressure preventing her from having them to stay.

❧

"Debbie, it's Flora," she said now, her plummy voice brisk. "How are you?"

"I'm very well," said Debbie, feeling instantly wrong-footed; the children still hadn't written their thank-you letters after their visit at Easter, and it was ten days since they had all got home. "How are you? Flora, I'm sorry the children haven't—"

Flora cut in. "I'm fine, thank you. Absolutely fine. I'd like to speak to Richard, please. Is he there?" There was a moment's pause, then she said, "Oh, stupid of me, he must have left for school."

"Yes," said Debbie, "yes, he has, I'm afraid. I'm sorry. You could try phoning at break, but they—"

"No, no, it's not that urgent. Perhaps you could ask him to ring me. What time does he get home? Around four, isn't it?"

"Yes. Is it anything I can help with?" Which of course it wouldn't be.

"Oh—no, thank you. No, it's fine. Thank you, Debbie. Such fun at Easter, wasn't it?"

"Wonderful," said Debbie, "and like I said, I'm so—"

But Flora had rung off.

Sometimes, Debbie thought, making a face at the phone, she really did feel like the hired help.

Chapter 2

22 APRIL 1988, EVENING

The thing to do was tell Nigel. Tell him she was going to have lunch with one of the traders at McArthur's who had phoned that day at lunchtime and issued an invitation which she had found it impossible to refuse. Which had been rather silly of her: but she could say that Blue had helped with the Big Bang book and now he—he what? Wanted to know more

· 24 ·

about publishing? Not likely. Perhaps she'd better not tell Nigel at all. The best thing would be just to have the wretched lunch and that would be that. No, the best thing would be to cancel the lunch: not go. Or—

"Lucinda, you're not listening."

"Sorry, Nigel."

He had been as near as Nigel ever got to being cross—which was more like extremely irritable—about her opening the Lloyd's letter. She wasn't quite sure why. She supposed it was the contents. They had visibly rattled him.

"It's fine, of course," he said, "we can afford it. In actual fact, it won't cost us very much at all, I can write it off as a tax loss. It's one of the joys of Lloyd's. And given how much we've had out of them over the years, it's—it's fine."

"Oh, good. Well, that's all right then."

"Yes."

She looked at him, as she ladled out the lasagna. "So why are you worried?"

"I'm not worried. Not at all."

"Yes, you are."

"Well, it's just that I've never known it happen before. I suppose it was inevitable, sooner or later, although one was rather led to believe that it never would."

"Really?" Could anything ever be that safe? Surely the whole thing about any money-making enterprise was that sometimes you did come unstuck. Otherwise *everybody* would be extremely rich. "But surely they must have warned you it might?"

"Well, they did," he said irritably. "And of course it could happen in theory, but it never has, that's the point. Well, not since the mid-sixties, anyway. They're too clever, too ahead of the game."

"Yes, but—"

"Lucinda, please. I do know what I'm talking about."

She suddenly felt fiercely cross with him. "It seems," she said, "that maybe you don't. Surely nothing can be absolutely one hundred percent certain. It can't be, you can't just know that you're going to get x thousand pounds every year, no matter what happens."

"Lucinda, you really don't know what you're talking about."

"Yes, I do," she said, stung. "Well, I don't know anything about

Lloyd's, but I haven't been listening to Daddy for years and years, talking about the stock market, without taking some of it in. You seem to think I'm a complete idiot. And how much is it anyway? Obviously enough to worry you, I can tell."

"I think we'd better stop this conversation," he said. "It's going in a direction I don't really like very much. I've been a Name for more than fifteen years, and my father was for twenty years before that, and it's served us very well indeed."

"But that's the last thirty-five years or whatever. This is now. It seems to be changing."

"Lucinda, please. Can we stop this?"

"I don't see why. You started it. I mean, you started wanting to talk about it. And I really want to know what the problem is."

"There isn't a problem. I've spoken to my Members' Agent, and he assures me it's a one-off. In fact he actually advised me to push my underwriting limit as high as I could for next year. There is absolutely—absolutely nothing to worry about."

"Well, good," she said, after a brief silence. She raised her glass and smiled at him. "And here's to next year's cheque."

He clearly was having difficulty smiling back at her. And he hadn't told her how much it was. It was definitely not the moment to tell him she was going out to lunch with another man. In fact, she'd better cancel it first thing in the morning.

"Your mother phoned," said Debbie, as soon as Richard came in. "She wants you to ring her."

"Oh. OK. Did she say what it was about?"

"No. The summer, I expect."

"Right. I'll just make myself a cup of tea and—want one?"

"Please."

He disappeared into the study; she heard the phone on the extension click as he picked it up. Twenty minutes later she needed to call Sue at the NCT about cutlery for the evening; she picked it up. She could hear Richard's voice.

"Sorry," she said, and put it down again. Twenty minutes was a long call, even for them.

Another ten minutes later, he came into the kitchen; he was looking very serious.

"You busy? I need to talk to you."

"Richard! Can't it be later, please? I really could do with some help." She was hurling spaghetti bolognese onto the children's plates; Emma was tapping her arm, asking her to test her spellings . . .

"OK. Sorry. Can I do anything?"

"You could fetch Alex. That'd be great."

"Debs, I can't do that. I don't have that sort of time, I've got a heap of marking to do and I've already lost half an hour. Sorry."

"You seemed to have plenty of time to talk to your mother," she said, driven beyond endurance.

"Oh, for God's sake," he said, and went out, slamming the door. She looked after him, surprised. He had many faults, but a bad temper wasn't usually among them.

Later, as she was changing, he came into their bedroom.

"Sorry about that," he said. "I was a bit worried. Look, do we have to go to this thing?"

"We do really, yes. I'm off to get the babysitter in about three minutes and I've cooked a lasagna for our table. We can't not go now."

"I really do need to talk to you," he said. "It's quite important."

"And so is this evening to me. I helped organise it, I have to go."

"Oh, all right," he said wearily, "but let's get away as soon as we can, maybe go for a drink?"

She looked at him; he did look drawn and rather pale. She felt a pang of concern, and put her arms round him.

"Whatever it is, it can't be that bad. And of course we'll leave the minute it's over. Promise. I'll duck out of the clearing up."

⁓

Flora had a problem, Richard said, settling uneasily into a chair in the corner of the pub. "Which could affect us. She's—well, she's made a loss at Lloyd's this year. Not much, but enough to worry her."

"Oh dear. And—what's not much?"

"About six grand."

"Six grand? My God, Richard. I'd call that quite much. But, well, I suppose she can afford it."

"She can. But she says it could leave her a bit short."

"Short?" Debbie thought of the big house, the Rolls, the new horse Flora had just bought, the portfolio of shares she was always wanting to discuss with Richard. "Can't she sell some shares or something?"

"She could. But the market's not good at the moment; she feels it would be shortsighted."

"Oh. Well, that's her decision. Obviously."

"Well, it is. And it isn't."

Debbie began to feel uneasy.

"How isn't it? Richard, you'd better get this over. You're not suggesting it might affect us, I hope?"

"Yes. It might. Not badly, but she wonders if we could take on the school fees, just for this year. It's almost exactly that sum. Six thousand, for the two lots."

"Well, we can't," she said. "We don't have six thousand to spare. Do we?"

"Well, we do," he said. "Actually. There's the money my father left me."

"The— Richard, I cannot believe I'm hearing this. We agreed that was for the future, our security, in case something awful happened, or we wanted to do something really special with it, put the children through university or—"

"Yes, well Mother says she'll pay us back when she can."

"Which is very kind of her, of course," said Debbie, thinking, *If they'd consulted me, we wouldn't even be having this conversation.* "But, Richard, it feels dangerous. Not what we thought that money was for."

"I know. But don't forget Father left the children some money in trust for things like their further education."

"Well I know. But don't forget our dream, to take the children out of school for a term, and travel with them. I think that would be much more valuable, actually. I'm sorry, Richard, but I'm just not going to give in on this. I mean, your mother undertook to pay the school fees. I never wanted her to, I was never asked about it."

"I seem to remember you being fairly articulate on the subject. At the time."

"Very briefly," she said, feeling her temper beginning to surge. "It was made clear my views were of no interest to either of you. And now, she's asking us to use up our precious savings, to do it instead. Well, I'm not going to. Sorry. They can leave those bloody schools if she's not going to pay for them, and go somewhere sensible, like St. Luke's, instead."

"You're so hostile to her, aren't you?" he said. "You don't like her, you're jealous of her, you don't understand her. Or appreciate what she does for us. For the children."

Debbie stared at him. "That is so unfair," she said.

"No, it isn't. And I happen to know she finds it very hurtful, your hostility."

"My hostility! What about hers?"

"She is not hostile to you," he said flatly.

"Well, I don't know what else you'd call it. I feel like some sort of intruder half the time. Or the hired help. And how do you know it's hurtful? Has she told you? Pretty bloody shitty of her if she has. Emotional blackmail, I'd call it. Driving a wedge between us."

"Oh, don't be absurd," he said. "She hasn't said anything. She's very loyal to you, as a matter of fact. I can just . . . just see it. For myself. And I want to help her."

"Well, I don't. Not in the way you suggest, anyway. We can go down there, talk to her about it, help her sort things out, of course. Hold her hand. But I will not agree to use that money to pay the school fees. And that's all there is to it."

"I'm afraid we have to," he said, and he looked very drawn, "some of it anyway. Or get a bank loan. Or re-mortgage."

"But why?" There seemed to be a grip on her lungs, squeezing them, making her breathless.

"Debbie, you can't just not pay the school fees at the beginning of term, take the children away. You have to give a term's notice in writing. It's a legal requirement. So at the very worst, we have to find two grand."

She digested this. "And she won't even do that?"

"No. She says she can't. She's very, very upset about it. Have you any idea," he said, his voice shaking, "how humiliating this is for me? To have my mother know that after all they did for me, all my fine education, I can't even afford to pay my own children's school fees, give them what I know they need? It's pretty bloody hard, Debbie, I can tell you."

Shocked out of her anger, her heart suddenly aching for him, for the lack of confidence that consumed him—and why, why, she often wondered, when he was so clever—and often thought too that Flora was responsible for it. And she heard herself saying that she was sorry, that of course, if that was really the only way, they would take on the school fees for the year. "But it is only the year, isn't it? You're not suggesting we do more than that?"

"Only the year," he said. "We can't do more anyway, unless I get some amazing new job. Which is—"

"Absolutely possible," she said, "in fact, quite probable. The only thing that's keeping you from an amazing new job, Richard, is that you've stopped applying for them, OK? Now I know you love St. Luke's, but if it's not really what you want, you must—*we* must rethink. You're a brilliant head, and there are lots of schools which would be just desperate for you. You start buying the *Guardian* on Wednesdays again, OK? And I'll do some applying for you, if you won't do it yourself."

"Oh, all right. Maybe." He smiled at her. He had a wonderful smile; brilliant and sudden. And irresistible.

"I love you, Debs," he said. "I'm so lucky to have you. I still think that, you know, every day of my life. And I'm sorry I said that about Mother and you. I do understand—she is quite bossy and overbearing; I can see it, you know."

"You can?" she said, astonished. She had always assumed Flora was perfect in his eyes, that the fault was all hers. She felt a rush of gratitude, and of affection for him, suddenly wanted desperately to make him feel better. She leaned forward and kissed him. "All right, ring her in the morning and tell her we'll do it. But like I said, it must only be this year, OK?"

"OK," he said. "It will be. Bless you, Debbie. Let's go home, I want to show you how much I love you."

❧

Elizabeth was talking to Peter Hargreaves in her office, dissecting the presentation of the morning—the successful presentation—when Simon rang.

"Hello. It's me. I wondered if we could have dinner tonight?" he said.

"Any particular reason?"

"Does there have to be?"

"No, not really. But I'd sort of thought I'd work on for a couple of hours. I've got a lot on—"

"Elizabeth, please. I want to talk to you." About what, she wondered with a stab of fear: surely not that again, surely— "And we might as well do it over a good dinner. It can be late if you like. Around nine."

"Oh, OK. Yes." She paused then said, almost as if prompted, "It'd be nice anyway, of course."

"Right, I'll book at Langan's. See you there."

Elizabeth was late. She often was. Simon sat waiting for her, his patience slowly fading. Why did she do this to him? When she knew he wanted to talk to her, that a table had been booked, that he might be hungry? Was it deliberate, to make her point, that she had her own life, that she was not at his beck and call—and given the events of the past two years, was that actually justified, did he deserve it? Or was it that in her hectic, high-powered schedule, time simply disappeared?

And then he saw her, walking across the restaurant, kissing him briefly before slithering into the chair the waiter had pulled out for her. She was immaculate as always, in a red short-skirted suit, with the ubiquitous padded shoulders, not a dark hair out of place in her gleaming lacquered bob, carrying the unmistakable aura of success and power.

And he remembered fiercely, briefly, the other Elizabeth, the one he had fallen in love with, so beautiful his heart had turned over the very first time he had seen her, neither successful nor powerful, a secretary indeed, at the advertising agency his bank was considering at the time; her dark eyes serious as she greeted him in reception, shook his hand, asked him to follow her to the boardroom. Even then, she had dressed the part: no seventies flowing skirts for her, but a narrow black calf-length dress and high-heeled boots, her dark hair clipped into a neat pageboy. He had liked her voice—rather low and calm, a well-educated voice—and her thoughtful good manners, taking his overcoat, offering him, as they went into the boardroom, coffee and orange juice. She said that he was the first to arrive—Simon was incapable of not being early.

"Will you be at the meeting?" he asked hopefully, and yes, she said, but in a very menial capacity, purely to take notes. "And refill coffee cups," she added with a quick smile.

"Very important," he said, "and you'll be refilling mine a lot. I run on caffeine."

"Me too," she said. "They say it's very bad for you."

"Oh, I have a lot of bad habits," he had said. "I'm awfully good at them. I like drinking and smoking too," and immediately she had offered him the cigarette box that was on the table.

The others had arrived then, and all through the meeting, he had been aware of her.

After the third meeting—for the agency had won the account—he had asked her out; she had given him the same serious look and waited for a few moments before saying, "That would be very nice, but I don't think my boyfriend would like it."

And he had said he would hate to upset her boyfriend, and that might have been that, had not Simon and his colleagues been invited to an advertising awards ceremony where their campaign was on the short list, and there she was, smiling at him across the pre-dinner drinks party.

"How nice to see you again," he said, taking a glass of champagne. "And how is the new firm? H2O, good name."

"Very good, thank you," she said, "and I'm now a junior account executive there, which is very exciting."

"Indeed it must be. We miss you a lot, though. Can I get you a drink afterwards," he said, "at the bar? Or would your boyfriend not like that either?"

"I don't think he'd mind at all," she said, "since he's not my boyfriend anymore. I'd like that very much, thank you."

The very next night they had dinner at L'Escargot in Greek Street, and after that, it was simple; they were together all the time and fell mutually and very passionately in love.

Elizabeth was only just twenty and in the style of those days, there was no question of their living together; she shared a flat with two other girls in Earl's Court, and Simon, only twenty-five himself, lived in appalling and expensive squalor with three other young men just off the Brompton Road.

He had wanted to marry her, quite badly, quite soon. "I know we're very young," he said to her, when he asked her, "but I like the idea of being married to you so much. It'd be fun. And we could buy one of those houses you were admiring the other night in the Boltons."

"Simon, you know that's nonsense. They cost about a quarter of a million."

"OK. I'm an up-and-coming young man. We'll get one next year. Or when we have our first baby."

"I don't want to have a baby," she said, "you know that, Simon, not for quite a long time. I've got my career to take care of, no time for babies."

Even then she was ferociously ambitious, determined to do not just well but superbly in the profession she loved. "I want to do the sort of thing women don't usually do in advertising, I don't want to be some dappy creative. I want to run things, have them done my way. I shall be miserable if I fail." And it was the reason she hadn't gone to university in spite of some very impressive A levels; she regarded it as a waste of time when she could have been starting on her journey in the real world.

But they did get married, six months later, when she was just twenty-one. Her father was delighted with the charming, handsome, successful young man who wanted to be his son-in-law, and they moved into a very pretty little mews house in Kensington.

Annabel was born just the same, eighteen months after they were married. There had been a scare about the pill, Simon had ordered her off it—she had done everything he wanted in those days, trusted him absolutely—and, "That seems to be that," she said to him, half happy, half tearful when she got the result of her pregnancy test.

He had been overjoyed; he loved children, loved the idea of being a father. She was less certain.

"I can't give up work," she said, "you know that. I've just got this new job."

"I do know it. We'll get a nanny, don't worry. We'll have to move, maybe not into the Boltons this time, maybe next—"

"And you'll have to help, have to support me."

"I will, I promise. I'll be the most supportive husband in London. In the world. I love you, Elizabeth, very, very much. And I'm so proud of you."

That had been the beginning of the glory years, of dizzy success for both of them. He was made a director of Graburn and French at an extraordinarily young age, her new job was at H2O, as an account executive—and account director two years later. They bought first a bigger house in Kensington and moved finally into Bolton Place just before Tilly was born. They were successful, rich, good-looking, high profile, with far more than their fair share of life's goodies. They had fun together too; wonderful extravagant holidays, sometimes with the children, but sneaking off too for long weekends on their own to Paris, Rome, the south of France—happy pleasure-drenched times, free from everything except each other, the early sexy days brought back to life.

They entertained lavishly in the splendid Boltons house, bought another in the country, gave parties that were legendary; they were sought after, admired, on every smart guest list. And he had adored her: absolutely. And she had adored him. So where—and why—had things gone so dreadfully wrong?

"Sorry, Simon." She kissed him briefly. "Had a crisis, it went on all day, and then I wanted to debrief Peter Hargreaves tonight—"

"What sort of crisis?"

"Never mind."

"I've ordered a Sancerre, all right for you?"

"Fine." She smiled up at the waiter as he poured it and then at him. "Good day?"

"Not very, no."

"I'm sorry. Annabel get off all right?"

"Yes, of course. Anyway, she should have rung you from school, I told her to."

"Well she didn't. Oh, Tilly's been made house captain, bless her. And Toby rang. I can't believe he's in his second year," she said. "He does love it."

"Just as well," said Simon shortly, "given the cost."

She looked at him curiously. "Simon! That's not like you."

"Well, I don't feel quite like me. Actually."

"Is that why you invited me to dinner?"

"Well—I wanted to have dinner with you, of course. But yes, so we could talk."

"We could have talked just as well at home."

"Except that you probably would have been about three hours late, rather than nearly one. With no table booking to put pressure on you and—" He stopped suddenly, looked at her very sadly, then said, "Oh Elizabeth. What's happened to us, why do we have to quarrel about everything?"

"I would have thought," she said, the pain hitting afresh, as it still did sometimes, "you should know that very well."

"Yes," he said quietly, "I do. But— Oh God," he said, and looked away from her. She felt alarmed.

"Simon, for heaven's sake, what on earth is it?"

"I've had a bit of bad news," he said, looking up, and his face was very bleak. "It's Lloyd's. They've made a loss on several of my syndicates this year. Including the major one."

"Oh," she said. "And—what's the damage?"

"About—about fifteen thousand pounds."

"God. God, Simon, that's a lot."

"Yes, I do know that. I mean, we can afford it, obviously, it's fine this year, but—"

"But?"

"I have a horrible feeling," he said, "that this is only the beginning."

Chapter 3

"Oh my God. Oh, God. Oh—my—God!"

She could hear herself shouting, she was somewhere outside herself, yet still there, inside it, inside the pleasure, the wonderful, soaring, bright, dark pleasure, riding it, savouring it, on and on, as long as she needed.

And then it was over. Gently, sweetly over. She collapsed slowly, back into normality: her body, fractured by delight, easing together again.

"Oh dear," she said.

"Why d'you say that?"

"You know. I mean, oh dear, that was so lovely and now it's over—our lovely little Christmas is over."

"Doesn't have to be. I'm sure they'd let us keep this room over Christmas. They're not fully booked, I asked."

"Blue, don't be silly."

"I'm not being silly, I'm being sensible. Look, you got to do it sometime. Why not now? Then we could enjoy Christmas. I'm not looking forward to it either, round my mum's with about a hundred kids."

"It sounds lovely to me," she said wistfully.

"Well, we could go there together instead. They'd be pleased to see you."

"I bet they wouldn't!"

"No, they probably wouldn't," he said cheerfully. "They'd feel they had to be on their best behaviour with a princess in their midst. No, much better stay here."

"Oh, how I'd love to," she said, "how I'd love it. This lovely place and you, and—oh dear."

She looked round the room. He had booked it for just twenty-four hours, 22 December it was; in a charming hotel in the Cotswolds, full of wood fires and leather chairs and flouncy chintz blinds. She'd invented (for Nigel) a booksellers' Christmas party that she'd had to go to; had left London very early in the morning and she and Blue had had a late breakfast, gone for a (very short) walk, come back and had champagne in bed and then a room-service lunch (smoked salmon and caviar) and then more champagne in bed and so much lovely sex. And now she had to go back to London (she probably wasn't fit to drive, although she'd only had about three glasses altogether), collect Nigel and all the presents from the flat, and be driven down to his cousins in Norfolk for a very long cold Christmas.

"Well," said Blue, "like I said. You got to do it, Lucy girl. Go on, bite the bullet."

"I can't. Not at Christmas. It would be too cruel. Christmas is special. It's about family and being together, and—"

"Yeah, well, why can't we?"

"Because we can't. It would be very wrong."

"And what you've been doing so far is very right, is it? I don't know, Lucy, seems to me you've got your morals in a twist."

"I know. I'm sorry. I'm totally awful."

"Not totally," he said, and slithered down the bed, started lazily tonguing her.

She tried to push him away, laughing. "Blue, no, no, oh God, Blue, no, I mean yes, yes . . ."

⁓

Driving very slowly and carefully on the M40, she looked down on the black Chanel box with the white ribbon he had presented her, holding a diamond-studded watch on a pink strap, absurdly vulgar and beautiful, that she could hardly ever wear: she had said that, even as she kissed him over and over again. "You can wear it when you're with me," he said, kissing her back. "It can be your fucking watch, for telling the fucking time."

She wondered, as she was always doing these days, how she could possibly have become this dreadful, deceitful, totally amoral person. Who regularly had sex with her lover, who lied to her boss as well as her husband (she had an idea that Graham suspected what she was up to and was rather amused by it), who was actually now seriously beginning to contemplate leaving her husband for her lover.

That had been quite a new thing, the contemplating; for several months she had just told herself she was having an affair, that it was terribly wrong of her, but at least Nigel had no idea, he wasn't being hurt, rather the reverse since she was so naughtily, dreadfully happy and in consequence incredibly nice to him. The only person to be hurt would be her when she ended it, which she would, and she'd deserve it and it wasn't for long anyway. She'd end it and go back to being a respectable wife and have a baby—only of course that was one of the worst things she was doing; she was taking the pill. Which she hadn't for nearly two years, ever since she and Nigel had decided to try and have a baby. "Try" being the operative word; they certainly hadn't succeeded.

She'd gone to her doctor of course: who'd examined her, got her taking her temperature, making sure she was ovulating, all that sort of thing. So they'd just started stepping up their efforts, as Nigel called it, at the right time, still unsuccessfully, when she'd met Blue. And after a shockingly short time, started to have an affair with Blue. And obviously, going back on the pill. She was so terrified of Nigel finding them that she kept them in the office.

She still wasn't sure how Blue had done it: persuaded her into bed. She'd had that first lunch, and it had been totally respectable really; they'd gone to Claridge's, "Thought I'd better bring you somewhere you'd feel at home," and afterwards he had kissed her in the taxi, but not too much, and she'd told him it had been lovely, but she couldn't possibly have lunch with him again, and he'd said bollocks, course she could, and somehow very weakly, she'd agreed to just one more. Well, it was so exciting and it made her feel so different, sort of sleek and confident and properly grown-up, and surely everyone should have one fling in their lives; in no time now she'd be living in the country with a small baby, and as flings went, two lunches weren't that serious, and she'd been absolutely resolved it would be the last.

Only he'd spent the next lunch—at the Dorchester this time—doing the most disturbing things to her legs under the table, and she'd been positively squirming with pleasure, and so she'd agreed to yet another lunch; and then the night before, she and Nigel had had a row, quite a bad one, about not going skiing, again, and she'd been really cross with him and she'd told Blue about it. "He doesn't like skiing, you see. And I love it. And he'll never ever agree to go. It's not fair, I go on his beastly shooting weekends, which I really don't like and—"

"How old is he, your old man?" said Blue suddenly.

"Oh—he's forty-four next year. Blue, please don't do that"—one of his hands was under the table, moving relentlessly and determinedly up her thigh—"but I do sometimes feel it's all give on my part and no take."

"Sounds like it," he said. "Lucy, why haven't you had no kids? I'd have thought it high on the agenda, specially hubby getting on a bit."

"We just haven't," she said, blushing. "It hasn't—well, it hasn't happened yet."

"Oh right."

"Blue, please," she said, for his fingers had now moved into her knickers. "Please don't, we'll get thrown out."

"No, we won't," he said, "but maybe we should move upstairs."

"Upstairs? What do you mean?"

"I got a room up there," he said. "Booked it."

"What for?" she said, shocked.

"What do you think?" he said, giving her his widest grin. "For us. For us to have sex in, to be precise."

"I don't believe you. They wouldn't let you book a room here for—for just the afternoon."

"I didn't—I booked it for twenty-four hours. Don't look scared, you don't have to stay the full time. Come on, finish your fish. It's good for you. Then I tell you what, we'll go up there, just have coffee and a brandy, and I swear I won't do anything you don't want. How's that? Your call, you know you can trust me."

For some reason—curiosity, a desire to appear sophisticated—she did; and discovered that she couldn't even trust herself.

"You never come before?" he said, as she lay, wide-eyed, wild-haired, sweating, almost shocked, after her baptism into pleasure, and, "Yes, of course," she'd said indignantly; but she hadn't. She absolutely hadn't. What she had known with Nigel—compared to this—was like, well, it was like pedalling earnestly uphill rather than flying down, with the wind in her hair, like—

"I don't know what you're thinking about," he said, grinning at her, "but I could tell you liked it. Am I right or am I right?"

"You're right, " she said feebly. And grinned back.

So of course she'd had to go on the pill; because obviously it was going to go on for a bit. And when it was over, as it absolutely would be, she would come off it again. She would just have this quick, wicked fling and then . . .

Only she had to go and fall in love with him. And he with her.

She really did love him; she loved everything about him and she could see that what she felt for Nigel wasn't love at all. It was fondness, a desire to be settled, a recognition that Nigel was exactly the sort of man with whom she wanted to spend the rest of her life. What she felt for Blue was wild, uncomfortable, disturbing, exhilarating—and absolutely wonderful. And it wasn't just sex; he made her laugh, and he made her feel more confident. He clearly and genuinely found her interesting, he was always asking her opinion on all sorts of things, and listened carefully to her answers—unlike Nigel, who only seemed to ask her out of politeness. Blue was a rabid Tory, found her watery liberalism extremely amusing—

and he was fascinated by her job, the people she met, the books Peter Harrison published. "I'm totally uneducated," he was always saying. "Don't know nothing. You know what Princess Diana said, about having a brain the size of a pea? Mine's a petit pois."

She had laughed at that and told him it was rubbish; and it was true. He might only have two O levels, might have left school at sixteen, but his brain was like a razor—quick, considering, uncompromising. Given an education, she told him, he could have been a professor. "No thanks. They don't make half a million a year, professors don't. Least, not when I was last looking."

"Do you really make half a million a year?" she'd said awed, and he'd said well maybe this year only a third, due to the crash, but usually, with the bonuses added in, yes, easy.

She in turn was fascinated by his work: he had told her only that he played what he called "racing demon" with the stock market every day; he bought and sold shares, and got paid a commission. "I work solo, in a manner of speaking. The bank just backs me. I make a lot of money for them, and a fair bit for me."

"And—I thought you all got sacked after the crash?"

"Some did. If you was making enough money, they kept you on. I make them a lot of money. And you know something, Lucy? For every loser there's a winner—that's my philosophy. And so far I've lived up to it."

He certainly seemed to have limitless money. He had a small house in one of the new developments near Limehouse, with pale polished wooden floors and a lot of leather-and-chrome furniture; he had a Ferrari, he went off on skiing weekends to the French Alps, and he had a Windsurfer and a Jet Ski, which he kept down at Poole, and "one leg of a racehorse," the other three being held by colleagues in the trading room. He had a roomful of incredibly expensive designer-label clothes of which he was absurdly proud: "Got this at Gucci on Saturday," he would say, doing a fancy pose in a leather coat, "and d'you like this suit, Armani, bought it twice, once in black, once in navy." He spent a fortune on drink, he and his fellow traders; where their manual-labourer or market stallholder fathers would go to the pub after work, the sons went to places like Corney and Barrow or the Colony Wine Bar and got through countless bottles of champagne and then bought hundreds of pounds' worth of wine to consume over their dinners as well. Lucinda, raised in a culture that considered the overt display of wealth not only vulgar but close to immoral, was fascinated by the whole thing.

But Blue wasn't just clever and successful, he was sweet-natured and thoughtful and insanely generous. And he loved her.

It had never occurred to her that he might be genuinely fond of her, until one early evening, when they had gone back to his apartment and were lying in his vast bed sipping champagne. They had just had some rather good sex and she was tired and a little sad, bracing herself to return to Cadogan Square and Nigel, when he suddenly said, "You know what, Lucy?" And, "No," she had said, "I don't," and he said, "I love you more every time I see you. Wouldn't have thought it was possible, but there you go."

She had been so shocked that she'd dropped her glass and the champagne went all over the bed.

"You love me?" she said.

"Yeah, course I do. Come on, Lucy! You must've realised that. Why d'you think I've been doing all this, taking me annual holiday in days off, missing out on trades—I love you more than I'd ever believed I could. Well, I hope you love me. I've been wasting me time otherwise. And quite a bit of money as well."

And, "Yes," she said, bursting into sudden, sweet tears, "yes, I suppose I do. I hadn't realised—yes, I must do."

And now, a couple of months later, being married to Nigel was beginning to seem rather pointless. Whether she had the courage though to give it all up—and it would mean all: friends, family, job possibly—she really didn't know. She'd think about it properly after Christmas.

ℰ

Elizabeth always cursed having to spend Christmas in the country: it had begun eight years earlier when Simon had bought Chadwick House, on the strength of a spectacular bonus, and had said that it was made for Christmas, with its huge fireplaces for hanging stockings, a great big hall for a really show-offy tree, and a hedge-lined drive that was made for stringing fairy lights along, and—just about everything really.

It was a beautiful house, redbrick, early seventeenth century, with an orchard and a walled vegetable garden. There was a tennis court and a swimming pool, and a stable block and paddock to house the love of Tilly's life, which at that time was a sturdy little New Forest Pony and now was a beautiful bright bay gelding called Golden Boy.

It was tucked into the South Downs, and convenient for Bosham where Simon kept his favourite toy—his sailing boat, a Contessa called the *Lizzie*. Chadwick House was a huge extravagance, as not only a housekeeper but a gardener-cum-groom had to be employed to look after it. Simon was very fond of telling people they went there every weekend, but they didn't, especially now Tilly was at boarding school, but they all moved down there for the whole of the summer holidays—Simon and Elizabeth commuting—and for Christmas as well. And sometimes even Easter.

And Elizabeth did like it and enjoyed it; especially the summer; loved giving big garden parties and barbecues, and having friends to stay. But Christmas was different: and however magical it was, it did mean, for her, doing everything twice.

The house in London had to be decorated, you couldn't live in a house through December and give a party in it, as they always did, without making it look festive, having a tree, all that sort of thing. Then on about the twenty-third, the cars had to be packed up with all the food and presents and crackers and driven sixty miles down the road to Sussex, where she had to set about transforming Chadwick House into something out of Dickens.

However much Elizabeth said every year that they would arrive for lunch, they never managed to drive away from London until after two, and so they got there as dusk was falling, and while Simon and Mr. Ford got the tree up, and Toby and Annabel strung the lights along the hedges, and Tilly had a rapturous reunion with Boy, Elizabeth unpacked the endless clothes and presents and food and wine, and tried to enjoy it too. And by the time they had eaten their first dinner, in the kitchen, in the glorious bone-warming glow of the Aga and had their first Christmas bottle of champagne, she did.

It made Christmas much more special, giving it its own setting, as it were. And there were all the lovely traditions—midnight service in the village church, the long tramp over the fields on Christmas Day, carol singing on the green, the Boxing Day meet. And this Christmas especially she felt it was wonderful to get away. It hadn't been exactly an easy year . . .

It was well known that advertising was the first budget to be cut when a company was feeling the pinch: and there was a lot of pinching going on. The economic climate was not good, whatever smooth story was being put out by Nigel Lawson. But with an agency the size of H2O you could afford to lose a bit. Just the same, everyone was on edge, every account review carrying an implied threat, and everyone told to economise where they could. Even the Christmas party had been a more modest affair than usual, held in the office rather than at their "local," as Peter Hargreaves, their very hands-on chairman, called the Ritz. "I think there are better things to spend twenty grand on than that. Especially since after an hour or so nobody can remember where they are."

And she really felt she was beginning to recover from what she had managed to think of as the other business. Painful and humiliating, far more than she would have imagined. But—she'd survived it. Hadn't she?

⁓

Thank God Christmas was over, Annabel thought; it was the first one she hadn't properly enjoyed, which seemed a bit sad, really. Her father was edgy, and kept on and on about money, it was so boring; their mother had been hyper-bossy and control-freaky—if you didn't want to play games, for God's sake, why should you, it was everyone's Christmas, not just hers—and even Toby had been kicking the furniture a bit. Only Tilly had been really happy, earnestly practising her jumping and her dressage every day on her beloved Boy.

She was just longing to see Dan. They'd had a long phone conversation on Christmas Eve, and another rather shorter one on Boxing Day, but that was about it. She was starved of him; she'd only seen him once since she'd got home from school as a matter of fact, and then only for an hour. She wanted to see him properly: all of him. She wanted to be in bed with him.

It was fantastic, having a boyfriend who was older, who had his own place. She and Dan had whole long evenings while she was supposed to be shopping or out with friends; the result was that sex was utterly wonderful. Utterly. He was terrifically good at it; of course, she didn't have any comparison, but she could just tell, from what other people said, that he was. Well, he should be, he'd had lots of practice.

He was twenty-two, and working for his father's stockbroking firm. She'd met him at a party and just fallen for him, absolutely. And tomorrow, New Year's Eve, she would see him; she had already spent hours trying on different outfits, experimenting with her hair; she might try doing it up again now, with the bits falling loose at the sides, she'd liked that best, but she hadn't quite got it right—

"Annabel! I thought you wanted to go for a walk?"

It was her mother; she'd agreed to the walk at breakfast, thinking it would pass the time, but now she'd rather stay in, in case Dan phoned. But then—he probably wouldn't.

"Yeah, I do." She headed in the direction of the utility room to get her Wellies; halfway across the hall she heard an odd sound coming from the drawing room. Going in, she found Tilly sitting huddled onto the window seat, sobbing as if she would never stop. Annabel sat down beside her, put her arms round her.

"Angel, don't cry, whatever is it?"

"I heard Daddy on the phone. He was talking about selling Chadwick, saying that it was an appalling waste of money. Just think if he did, I couldn't keep Boy in London, I'd have to sell him too. I couldn't bear it. You don't know anything about it, do you?"

"Of course not. I'm sure you heard wrong, but I'll ask Mummy anyway. She'll obviously know. He was probably just trying to get an idea of its worth or something; you know how obsessed he is with that sort of thing."

"You're not thinking of selling this place, are you?" Elizabeth had cornered Simon in his study; the children were all upstairs, watching television.

He looked awkward, then said, "I am, as a matter of fact."

"Simon! Why, for God's sake? We all love it here. And don't I have any say in it? It's mine as well, or so I've always thought." She felt a rush of anger, that he had not discussed it with her.

"I know, I know, I'm sorry. But we could all go for a holiday to the Bahamas three times a year for what Chadwick costs to run."

"Well, I'd rather have Chadwick."

"Elizabeth," he said, and his expression was very serious, "this is not a matter of either-or. I'm sorry. It will probably have to go."

"Well, thanks for telling me," she said. She felt extremely upset suddenly. "Tilly's been crying—she overheard you talking about it. I told her it must be a mistake, that you'd never do it without discussing it with me. Which you shouldn't."

"You're not exactly available for discussion," he said, "very often."

"Simon, that's not fair. You know it's not."

"It may be. It's true."

She felt near to tears herself: she loved Chadwick, and not just for itself but for what it represented, those carefree years when she had been what seemed now unimaginably happy. And thought how she longed to be back there, or at least in what they had given her, those years, the warmth, the closeness, the sense that she and Simon were at least travelling in the same direction. Now they seemed lost to each other, in some cold, uncharted territory.

"Simon, I do have time to talk," she said. "When it's important."

"Do you?"

She knew what he meant; precisely. Her lack of time for him had been the excuse. With—as she knew—a degree of justification. "And in case you hadn't noticed, I'm doing quite a big job and running quite a big family."

"Yes, and don't we all know it."

"You bastard," she said slowly, "and don't you dare sell Chadwick. I won't let you."

She went upstairs to pack; half an hour later he came into the room.

"I'm sorry," he said, "very sorry. I shouldn't have said that."

"No, you shouldn't."

"You're doing a fantastic job, and I don't deserve you. Oh, Elizabeth." He reached out and took her hand. "It's all very sad, isn't it?"

"Yes," she said, "very sad." Knowing he meant more than the loss of Chadwick, more than the distance between them. "You're really worried aren't you?" she said. "Is it this Lloyd's thing?"

"It is. Yes."

"Is it really so bad?"

"It will be," he said, "I'm afraid."

"And you can't just—just get out? Now?"

"Absolutely not," he said. "If I could, Elizabeth, I would. Believe me."

❧

The children said it had been the best Christmas ever; Debbie found that hugely annoying, thinking of all the ones she had slaved over, struggled to make perfect, consigned to a sort of "could do better" in her mothering report book.

They'd gone down to Wales, to stay with Flora. Debbie hadn't exactly wanted to, of course, but the others all had, and Flora had said she'd love to have them, it would be a way of saying thank you, and Debbie's own parents had gone on a cruise, so there was no excuse there and—no way out, really.

And it had been lovely: midnight mass at the beautiful little church above the sea at Oxwich, a Christmas-morning walk down onto the beach at Three Cliffs Bay where the children had played for hours on the stepping-stones, Christmas dinner by candlelight—and yes, all right, the children had been tired next day, but it had been rather special, something they'd remember always. Flora had sold one of her horses, the younger, feistier one.

"Well, I was getting a bit old for him," she said with a quick smile, "and I'm giving up hunting next season, it costs so much—another bit of belt-tightening, you know. Every little bit helps."

As belt-tightening went, it didn't seem too stringent to Debbie, more of a token really; but it was somehow soothing to think that Flora was prepared to do it. On the other hand, she was slightly alarmed that there was a need for further economies.

❧

It had been a very jolly Christmas indeed at the Diamond Bay Hotel in Barbados. The clientele weren't quite the crème de la crème crowd to be found at the Sandy Lane; the Diamond Bay was mostly full of the Thatcherite newly rich, survivors of the '87 crash—people who had gone public with their companies in the early to mid-eighties and walked away with millions, or ridden the wave of the property boom and then surfed off it with skill—all wearing their money in the form of cars and speed-boats and jewellery, and taking suites at the Diamond Bay for Christmas and the New Year.

Tim Allinson would probably not previously have wished to join them; Tim was old money, Harrow, Guards, a resident of Belgrave Square; tall, blond, always impeccably dressed, hugely charming. Since leaving the Guards he had worked for one of the blue-chip estate agents, mostly engaged in finding clients from his impressively large circle of friends and acquaintances in both London and the country. Finding clients or, as he preferred to express it, "making introductions" was his métier; a very pleasant second income had been earned over the past ten years by introducing people to Lloyd's. Or, to be more precise, to one of the Members' Agents. His commission on it was a very modest-sounding percentage, but the large number of new Names on which he earned it had certainly financed much of his lifestyle.

The Lloyd's shore was getting just a trifle rocky. But there were still plenty of outsiders who didn't share that knowledge, and many of the revellers at the Diamond Bay, greedy for social cachet as well as financial security, were among them.

He had gone as the guest of the hotel's owner, who had appreciated what someone of Tim's class would add to the tone of the place; thus they suited each other very well. And by New Year's Day, as he packed to go home with some relief, he reflected on at least two and possibly three new introductions.

Chapter 4

"I can't tell him this week. I just can't." Lucinda's voice was shaky on the phone. "It would be too cruel, Blue. I'm sorry. He got a letter from Lloyd's this morning. It really upset him, he—"

Blue sat bolt upright in his chair.

"Lloyd's of London? He's a Name, is he? I didn't realise."

"Yes, he is. And it all seems rather bad."

"Yeah, well, it would be—"

"Last year his main syndicate made its first loss ever. Nigel had to write a cheque for about ten thousand pounds. And this year it's about double that. He's terribly—" She paused. "Blue, what did you say?"

"I said it would be. Would be bad. It's obvious. You never heard of asbestosis?"

"No. Whatever is it?"

"Dear oh dear. Very nasty thing. Contracted by workers in the asbestos industry. Or rather, workers in the industries that use asbestos. Like construction. Cars. Furniture. Leads to cancer, all sorts of horrible things in your lungs."

"I don't see what that's got to do with Lloyd's."

"My darling Lucy, all companies insure with Lloyd's. They cover things like bodily injury, I think it'd be called. Year after year now, starting in the States, people have begun to claim huge sums of money. And the companies bloody well deserve all they can possibly get. They've acted disgracefully, tried to wriggle out of it, hush it up. Anyway, the floodgates could start to open here now. Billions and billions of pounds' worth of claims, I reckon. So course Lloyd's is affected. Horribly."

"God. So it could get worse?"

"Not could, sweetheart. It will get worse. And worse. Maybe you should get this thing over now, quickly, before it does."

"Blue, I can't. Not just . . . just yet. He's so upset."

❧

This was a terrible indictment of her motherhood, Elizabeth thought. That she'd had no idea, no idea at all what was going on, and—

She heard the front door slam. Simon. He'd been on a business trip to France for three days. She was going to have to tell him, and quickly. He'd be pretty shocked. And he'd probably cast a lot of the blame at her.

There was a pause while he checked the post. She heard him ripping open a few envelopes, heard a suppressed groan and a "Shit. Holy shit," and then he walked into the drawing room, went straight over to the drinks table without seeing her, and poured himself a very large whiskey.

"Hello, Simon," she said.

"Elizabeth! What are you doing home at teatime? Are you ill?"

"No, I'm fine. Simon, we need to talk."

"I was about to say the same thing to you. You first."

"It's Annabel. She's been expelled."

"Expelled! Annabel? Jesus. I don't believe it. But what's she done? She's only been back at school a week."

"She bunked off, spent Saturday night in London. She came up to see some boy. Who," she hesitated, he really wasn't going to like this, "who she's been seeing for a while, apparently."

"Oh my God."

"Yes. Anyway, we have to go down, bring her home."

"Why in God's name didn't they ring us? When they found her missing?"

"They didn't know about it. Her friends covered up for her beautifully, it's not difficult over a weekend. They caught her coming in last night, it seems, complete with bottle of champagne in her rucksack. Oh, and some reefers."

"Dear God! So why the hell didn't they ring us then?"

"I was told they wanted to conduct a full enquiry first. Make sure they'd got everything straight, that it really was necessary to expel her."

"Well," he said, "I can see it is."

"So come on. We're going down now."

"Now? To Somerset?"

"Yes. I . . . thought it best if we went together."

"Of course. Let me just change my shirt and I'll be with you."

As the car pulled onto the Cromwell Road, he said, "I've got some more bad news. If you can take it."

"Of course I can."

He looked at her and half smiled for the first time. "I have to say, Elizabeth, you're very good in a crisis. Always were."

This was true; she never panicked, never cried—just stayed calm and positive and clear-thinking. When Tilly had been thrown by Boy and quite badly concussed she had met the news with dignity, bravely cool. It was her way of coping; holding on to herself and her image of herself.

"Try me now," she said.

"It's—it's Lloyd's. Second year. Much worse. Chadwick *will* have to go."

"Oh Simon, no. It must be very bad. How much this time?"

"Well, about forty-five thousand."

"My God." She was stunned. "That's huge. Absolutely huge. I thought you said you'd built up a hedge fund to deal with this sort of thing."

"I—" He didn't look at her. "Not enough there, I'm afraid."

"Can't we borrow the money from the bank?"

"Well, no. I'm already quite heavily in hock to the bank. I made a loss on the stock market. In the crash. It's not good at the moment. And I put a lot of money into that overseas hotel business. Set up by Ted Rayne, remember?"

"What, in the Bahamas?"

"That's the one. It went belly-up, earlier this year."

"You didn't tell me that. Well, not that it had gone bust."

There was a silence, then: "I know," he said. "I'm sorry, I should have done. But I couldn't see much point worrying you. I thought things would sort themselves out, that the market would recover."

"Which it has."

"Not nearly enough. The country's in a hell of a mess, and Lawson seems set on taking us into the Exchange Rate Mechanism, which would be disastrous in my view. And his policy on inflation isn't helping. Businesses are going under right, left, and centre. He's at loggerheads with Thatcher over that. Anyway, I should have discussed it all with you, I know. I'm very sorry."

She was silent. Then she said, "Not a lot we can do about it, it seems. It's OK. Do you think we can squeeze one last summer in at Chadwick before it goes?"

"Yes, I should think so."

"Well, that's something. After that it won't matter quite so much. Except for Tilly, of course. Let's keep it from the children for as long as we can."

"OK." He looked at her, smiled his sudden sweet smile, reached out and briefly took her hand. "Thank you, darling."

"What for?"

"For not blaming me."

"It's not exactly your fault, is it? And don't forget, we had some awfully good years. We wouldn't have had Chadwick at all without Lloyd's. I would say," she said, realising that she felt closer to him than she had for

· 50 ·

a long time, able to comfort him rather than rail against him, "this thing with Annabel rather puts it in perspective. And it's not as if we're starving."

"Well, not yet," he said.

And in the days that followed he struggled to be his positive upbeat self; but it was hurting him badly, the erosion of his personal heritage. Simon was not old money; his father had scrimped and saved to send his bright, handsome, and already charming son to public school, wanting him to have as if by right the confidence, the accent, the manner that he himself had been at such pains to learn.

Simon had left Charterhouse and then Oxford and moved straight into the City, a shooting star; within a very few years he was making a fortune. But as a boy, he had loathed the comparison between his school friends' lavish houses and his own modest one, had been miserable at not being able to return invitations, to offer hospitality. He had loved his parents dearly, but he had suffered what all children in his position suffer: at best embarrassment, at worst shame. And the symbols of his own wealth had been doubly important, doubly precious because he had secured them for and by himself.

He found the contemplation of their loss—and the effect of it on his own children—almost unbearable.

❧

Flora sat staring at the letter. It had happened again. Lloyd's wanted more money: possibly twice as much. How could she have been so stupid, how? Why had she let William do this to her, make her a Member?

"I'm persuaded to become a Name," he had said, fifteen years ago. "It seems an excellent idea. But there are risks, and I think with your agreement, I'd rather it was you. That way, they can't bankrupt us. You've got no money and the house isn't in your name, so it'll be pretty foolproof. I'll make over just enough money to you to do it. And it'll be a nice pension for you when I'm gone. How would that be?"

She hadn't actually been very keen; she'd always been slightly suspicious of the whole Lloyd's thing, the assumption that you could get something for nothing, and her visit to Lloyd's when she'd been admitted as a Member had done nothing to make her feel better. She'd been unimpressed by Edward Trafford Smythe, the Members' Agent who had talked William into this (as she saw it); he was some kind of distant cousin to William and seemed to her very second-rate.

But, uneasy or not, she had to admit that for the past decade and more it had been an excellent source of income. Every June or July the cheque arrived; not vast, but extremely welcome. It had funded the purchase of stocks and shares, their horses, their hunting, wonderful trips to South Africa and India; and then the house soaked up money of course, they'd had dry rot one year, needed a new roof another . . .

"Good old Lloyd's will see to it," William always said, and indeed it had. And land had come onto the market, adjacent to the house, which they had bought, including one huge field sloping right down to the top of the cliffs at Broken Bay—so called, it was said, because of the way three huge, jagged rocks lay in the centre of the beach, as if they had been dropped from a great height, fracturing the smooth curve of the bay.

Flora loved that field; she called it the Meadow and she refused to put sheep on it, or graze the horses; she kept it in its natural state, filled with wildflowers and grasses. It had three dilapidated stone buildings on it, once cowsheds, but they in no way spoiled it, rather they adorned it, the flame-red climbing roses of Gower half covering one, and ivy and honeysuckle the others. When she walked through the Meadow in early summer, butterflies rose in great clouds about her, and at night she would hear the owls cry as they hunted the voles and mice that lived under the surface of the grasses. In the autumn she and the children would gather baskets of blackberries from the hedges that marked the boundaries of the field and she would turn them into jam and jelly and blackberry crumble.

But now she was a widow and the house was hers, William's pension was hers, his stocks and shares were hers, and most of his capital was hers; and they would all go into the admittedly small but unpluggable hole in the dyke that was Lloyd's. The day the letter came, that second April, she went for a long walk, making her way along the beaches as far as Tor Bay. She sat on the rocks there, looking out at the sea, and wondered how much of this treasure of hers she would have to lose. Her happiness was absolutely bound up in this place; in the roaring sea, the rolling surf, the wind, the storms, the huge brilliant skies: it was her lifeblood, she could not survive without it.

She could manage this year; she would have to renege on the school-fees agreement again, and she would have to sell all her shares, albeit at a loss, and perhaps a couple of pictures, but she could do it. But then— what of the next? And the next? How much would they take from her? The land? The house? All her money? Where would she go, what would she do?

Suddenly Flora, inexhaustible lion-hearted Flora, found herself frightened: frightened and terribly tired. She couldn't lose all this; she really would much rather die.

Chapter 5

MAY 1989

"I've decided what I want to do." Annabel smiled at her parents over the dinner table.

Simon was delighted; some positive steps at last.

"Darling, how exciting. What?"

It had been a difficult few weeks since her expulsion from school. First there had been her tantrums—anyone would have thought it was the school at fault, not her. She'd refused to accept that what she'd done was worthy of expulsion, apologising for upsetting them but insisting that the school was run by a mass of dreary old cows who had never come into the real world. "I'm seventeen, for God's sake. Why should we all live like nuns? It's pathetic."

She had been all for moving in with Dan at first. "He's got a really nice flat in Pimlico, by the river."

"Where you spent last Saturday night?"

"Yes. I did."

"And how long has this been going on?" said Simon.

"You know that, perfectly well, Miss Bollocks—"

"Don't call her that."

"Sorry, Miss Balls told you, I thought, when we all had that cosy chat."

"Annabel!" said her mother sharply. "We're trying to understand. If you're not going to cooperate at all, we really will get angry."

"How would I know the difference?" she said.

It had got better; she had tried to explain how she felt suffocated boarding at an all-girls' school, how she loved Dan, how he was really special, how she would have told them but she knew they'd disapprove, how she'd felt they didn't have enough time for her anyway, how she could never talk to either of them properly. Guilt stricken, both of them, they hadn't even tried to deny it; later she apologised, said she hadn't meant that, at least, and they told her again how much they loved her and cared what happened to her.

She'd volunteered to get a job, "Pay for my keep," and she'd actually worked in Jigsaw for a while and hated it, nearly died of boredom. They'd suggested she went to some sort of crammer, so she could take her A levels next year; she said she'd think about it, but she didn't really want to.

"I just want to get on with my life."

Simon had said rather briskly that most people had to work in order to get on with their lives, and that more interesting work was available to those with qualifications. They had reached stalemate on that one.

The relationship with Dan had fizzled out; robbed of the glamour of an illicit affair, she had begun to find him boring and even rather silly. Something at least had been accomplished, Elizabeth said to Simon.

"Well, don't keep us in suspense," said Simon now. "What is it? Do you want to go to the Sorbonne, like Miranda, or—"

"No. No, this won't cost you anything at all. The thing is, I want to be a—a . . . I want to be a hairdresser," she said, and the words suddenly tumbled out, very fast, as if she was afraid they might stop again if she let them.

"A hairdresser! Annabel, you can't be a hairdresser."

"Why not?"

"Well, you just—can't. It's not—not the sort of thing you'd— we'd . . ." Elizabeth's voice trailed away.

"Not the sort of thing you'd what? Mummy, you make it sound like I wanted to be a prostitute. What's wrong with being a hairdresser?"

"Well, nothing, darling, of course. It's just—"

"It's just what? Look, you should be pleased. I've found something I really want to do."

"How do you know you really want to do it?"

"There was a fashion show at Jigsaw the other night. I was talking to the guy who did the hair, he was great. It's such a fun thing, I know I'd like it. And I'd be good at it. I love doing my hair and Tilly's, and I used to do it for people at school—"

"Annabel, you are not going to be a hairdresser." Simon's tone was final. "I haven't spent a fortune on your education so you can spend the rest of your life brushing people's hair."

"But it isn't just brushing people's hair. It's making it look good, making them look good, making them feel good. I think it's a great job and it's what I'm going to do. It won't cost you anything, and I just can't see what's wrong with it."

"Darling," Elizabeth said again, "there's nothing wrong with it. But it's not a very—very . . ."

"Very what? Oh, I get it. Not a very socially acceptable job. Is that it? Not something you could tell your friends about. Well, you're going to bloody well have to, because it's what I'm going to do."

"Annabel—"

"You really are pathetic, you know that? You are such snobs. And I don't see that your wonderful jobs have done you much good. Daddy worried to death about losing everything. Mum worried to death about losing clients and accounts. Listen, the world's changed. There are loads of hairdressers making fortunes, people like Nicky Clarke and John Frieda. You should be pleased I'm going to get out there and do something, instead of sitting around for another four years studying a load of crap that doesn't interest me and won't do me any good at all. Anyway, I'm going to do it and that's that. I've got an interview tomorrow, and if they offer me a job I'm taking it, OK?"

And she was gone, with a slam of the door.

❧

Debbie was just loading up the washing machine with the swimming things when the phone rang.

"Debbie, hello my dear, this is Flora."

"Oh, Flora, hello. How are you? Do you want Richard?"

"If you don't mind. I won't keep him long, I expect he's very busy."

"Not really," said Debbie briskly, looking at Richard who was nodding off over the Monopoly board. "Richard, it's your mother."

He got up, took the phone from her. "Hello? Of course not, it's fine. We've just been for a picnic, I'm— Look, let me take this in the study, it's quieter there."

He was gone quite a long time, about ten minutes; when he came out he smiled at Debbie rather distractedly.

"Sorry, darling."

"What was that about then? The summer?"

"No, no, she just wanted to tell me about a meeting she's going to have. With her Members' Agent."

Members' Agent, like Managing Agent and Names and Syndicate were all words from the Lloyd's dictionary; Debbie didn't understand any of them. Richard had told her more than once that everything was better at Lloyd's now, and that was all she cared about.

"I see. Good."

"And she did mention the summer, yes, of course. Says she's looking forward to it. I said we couldn't wait either."

Flora was going to have all three children on her own for a week in August; Debbie and Richard were to have a whole wonderful seven days on their own; they were driving up to Scotland. They'd wondered about going to Florence or somewhere, but it would be terribly hot there and expensive, and if anything happened—Debbie tried not to think what that might be, drowning, broken limbs—and they had to make a dash to Wales, it would be much easier.

"She's not still worried about Lloyd's, is she?" said Debbie suddenly, pausing in her potato peeling; and there was an imperceptible pause before Richard said, "Good Lord no," and at that moment Rachel managed to fall off her chair and hit her head on the edge of the table, and Debbie forgot about that pause until much, much later when everyone was in bed; and then decided she must have imagined it and that Richard, who was the most painfully honest person she had ever met, would never be deceiving her about something so important.

Chapter 6

Annabel had never really thought about her feet before. They had been there to put shoes on, the prettier the better, to get her about; suddenly they were the dominant thing in her life. They ached, endlessly; her heels especially throbbed. They felt as if she had become extremely heavy, not the seven and a half stone of reality; she would look at herself sometimes in one of the salon mirrors, and be surprised to see herself exactly the same, rather pale and tired-looking, perhaps, deprived of fresh air as she was so much of the time, her own hair blonder by the week, as she allowed it to be used as a model for highlighting, caught back in a ponytail. She was dressed in the salon uniform of black and white, the feet, the aching tired feet in white or black jazz shoes from Anello and Davide in Covent Garden.

Her hands were terribly sore with the constant immersion in water, she could only keep a rash at bay with a steroid cream, and her back ached quite a lot of the time as well; and her head too, towards the end of her sessions—nine or ten hours long, illegally long she was sure, but who was counting or looking; she was sure she must be keeping the manufacturers of paracetamol going, she swallowed so much, and when she was really tired her ears buzzed as well.

She had got a job as a trainee at Miki Wallace, one of the top salons in London, and knew how lucky she was; some days she did love it, some days she hated it, but quitting was never an option. In the first place she knew her parents would have been delighted, and in the second, she was determined to make a success of it. She had never forgotten that heady evening at Jigsaw, watching the two stylists twisting and brushing and pushing hair into all manner of wonderful shapes, and how it had transformed the models from fairly ordinary girls into exotic creatures, works of art almost; and at a slightly less dramatic level, how quite plain girls would come into Miki's and get themselves turned into dazzling beauties for an evening, or a day, or a wedding. Hair, she had discovered, was a powerful statement about its wearer, more important even than makeup or clothes. The styles of the day were so disparate, yet as absolutely and recognisably stylish as the padded shoulders and killer heels of the age; the sleek bob of the career woman, the long layered curls of the free spirit, the big bouffant of the lady who lunches: they all walked out of the salon hour by hour, day by day, perfectly yet imaginatively exercised. One of the most important things she had learned was that a stylist first masters a style, and then personalises it.

The salon was in Belgravia, just off West Halkin Street, small enough to feel exclusive, large enough to get a buzz going, and near enough to the West End to draw its clients from the working community of London, not merely the lunching ladies. One of Miki's promises was that no one was ever kept waiting for more than ten minutes, and for the most part he managed to honour that.

He was acknowledged to be one of the greats, on a par with Michaeljohn and Daniel Galvin and John Frieda; he was clever and funny and Annabel adored him. He wasn't very tall, only a couple of inches taller than she was, with rather long dark hair and burning dark eyes, and he had a long-standing boyfriend, but he managed to project something heterosexual at the same time; conversations between Miki and the women lucky enough to be his clients were not giggly and gay and gossipy, but rather intense. The other boy stylists were more flippant and fun; some were gay, some not, but Annabel loved them all.

She was something of a curiosity in the salon, she knew; from the very first day when she had arrived, acutely nervous, and rather formally dressed in a red dress and jacket from Jigsaw, and announced herself in her unmistakably expensive voice, she had been studied closely. For the first few days, she had been sniggered at, and when she had survived that with a display of unshakable good nature, she had been teased relentlessly, called "Posho" or "Sloaney."

"You sure you're not a client got into the wrong side of the salon?" Carol, a sharp little thing from Croydon, had asked her; "Quite sure," Annabel said firmly. "My mum might come here, not me." She and Carol became best friends, sharing snatched sandwiches, swapping shifts, covering up for each other's mistakes, practising on each other's hair; a world apart in background and education, they were identical in ambition, a streak of deviousness, and a capacity for extremely hard work.

Tania, the salon manager in charge of the juniors, tall, languid, redtaloned, came forward and hustled her into the staff room that first day. She had been introduced to the others, then given a crash course in salon behaviour: "Be welcoming, smile, don't draw attention to yourself, defer to the stylists, do what they say without question," and "The client is always right and that means always: if she throws a brush at you—and that has happened—just smile and say thank you."

Tania said she should call herself Bel, that Annabel was a bit of a mouthful, and sent her to change, saying that she'd be in at the deep end, they were three juniors short that day. Dressed in her black trousers and white shirt, she was handed a broom and told to sweep the floor. "But it looks perfectly clean," she said, staring at it. "Give it ten minutes and it won't be," said Tania, and indeed, at the first drops of the waterfall of hair which flowed onto the floor every day, Annabel realised her problem would be keeping up with it, for as fast as she cleared the area round one client, another filled up.

At twelve o'clock, Tania called her over. "I'm going to give you a quick lesson in gowning up, Bel," she said.

"In what?" said Annabel.

"Gowning up. It's extremely important to get it right. Here, take this"—handing her a black nylon cape—"and imagine I'm the client. Now you greet me, tell me your name, say you're taking me to the backwash, or over to whoever the stylist is, and help me into the gown. Make me feel welcome, pleased to be here, be polite but not pushy . . ."

Annabel smiled meekly; she supposed there might be some people who needed to be taught such things, but it seemed very unlikely. But she could see also that it was absolutely essential not to say so.

Her worst moments were when her friends' mothers or indeed her own mother's friends came in and recognised her. "Annabel, darling, what on earth are you doing here?" they would shriek across the salon, often beckoning her over and occasionally and most dreadfully insisting on jumping up and kissing her. This was not only embarrassing and against the rules ("Never kiss or hug a client, even if she seems to want it"), it immediately lost her a great deal of street cred with the others.

"Annabel, dah-ling," they would chant as she went into the staff room, or "I say, yah, it's Annabel, sweetie."

But for the most part, they seemed to like her, and apart from a clear and acute curiosity about how and why she came to be there at all, accepted her. She had planned not to explain about being expelled from school but she confided it to Carol in strictest confidence, who spread it swiftly around. Annabel's reputation and popularity were immediately greatly enhanced.

⁓

Simon was at his desk, engrossed in the Nikkei—the Japanese stock market—and its seemingly unstoppable progress, when the phone rang.

"Simon Beaumont?"

"Yes."

"Look, you don't know me, but your wife said you wouldn't mind me ringing. My name's Neil Lawrence and—"

"Oh yes, of course. I remember. Nice to hear from you."

Elizabeth had told him about Lawrence. "I saw him at an advertising bash, that one at the Hilton the other night. Marketing director of Maxwell—you know, the confectionery people. Anyway, he's normally very buttoned up, but he was terribly drunk in the bar after dinner, and he mentioned that he was having 'fun and games' with Lloyd's. I said you too, and that was it, I couldn't stop him. Had to sell a lot of shares, and a house in Italy, all that stuff, scared of having to take the children out of school even. He's desperate. I told him about you and so on, and he thought he might like to talk to you. He'll ring you. He's very nice."

Simon invited Neil to have a drink. He liked him, he was quiet, almost shy, deeply embarrassed at what he had done.

"I can't believe I was so bloody stupid," he said, drinking a large glass of red wine at great speed, holding it out to have it refilled. "I came into some money, Father died, met this chap at a drinks party, we got talking, he asked me if I'd ever considered becoming a Name, I was rather—"

"Don't tell me," said Simon, "flattered."

"Well, yes, for Christ's sake. Totally pathetic."

"What was his name? Just so I can avoid him. Or alternatively, kick him in the balls."

"Allinson. Tim Allinson. Classic old Harrovian, Guards, terribly charming. Ever come across him?"

Simon shook his head.

"Well, he introduced me to someone there, I was impressed, thought it would help with the school fees, all that sort of thing—I've got four small children, and— Jesus. I don't know. My wife has no idea," he added, picking up a handful of nuts, cramming them into his mouth. He was very thin; Simon wondered if he ate enough.

"What, you haven't told her?"

"No, I can't. She's a rather anxious person, and she just couldn't handle it. I've managed to keep them at bay so far, but—anyway, I'd never told a soul about it at all until I met your wife. It was a huge relief somehow."

Simon was shocked into silence. He sat staring at Neil, wondering what on earth his midnight crises must be like. At least he could talk to Elizabeth: when she was there.

"Your wife, she's so capable and obviously a huge help financially. It must be bloody marvellous. Amanda's never worked, and—"

"But surely she'll have to know soon. I thought you'd had to sell a house in Italy?"

"Well, it's on the market, just haven't had any offers. I think I'm going to throw up every time I even contemplate the next letter. That chap Allinson has a lot to answer for. But—well, it might be all right, don't you think? My Members' Agent was very reassuring."

"Mine, too," said Simon. He ordered another bottle of wine. It seemed about the only thing he could do for Neil Lawrence.

Alan Richards had been working as a clerk at Jackson and Bond, Members' Agents at Lloyd's, for five years now; he was very ambitious and he had been told that within another year or so, he could well have his own portfolio of Members to look after. He loved his job, he loved the whole business of insurance; people thought it must be terribly boring and he tried to tell them how it felt to be there at the heart of global insurance, where you could almost smell the money summoned to staunch the ever-increasing flow of claims, drawn in from all over the world, money that no one ever actually saw, not even at Lloyd's, presenting itself only in the form of letters of credit and bankers' documents, and then materialising by some almost magical process not only to service the claims but as hard cash in the bank accounts of the people who had brought it—by way of the letters of credit—to Lloyd's in the first place. Heather, his girlfriend, failed to find it even remotely interesting and certainly not in the least exciting. She worked in a bank in Esher and said she could understand that, it was straightforward; people actually brought money in there, either in the form of cheques or quite often actual cash; the bank looked after it for them and paid them interest on it while they had it; and if they wanted it back, they got it.

"But your business, Alan, it's a bit like a conjuring trick, isn't it?"

Alan said not really, but he could see why it might seem like that. He loved going into Lloyd's; it felt a bit like walking into a history book, with brokers queuing up at the underwriters' desks to talk to them and sell them propositions, and the waiters, as they were called, in their red coats, ushering people about, and the great Lutine Bell standing on a podium at the centre of the main room. It was still rung on ceremonial occasions. "But it was once rung to alert underwriters of an overdue ship," he told the underwhelmed Heather, "once for bad news, twice for good. And losses are still recorded in the ceremonial loss book—with a quill pen." He felt a distinct pride in being associated with such an institution.

Alan never questioned the machinations of Lloyd's; he knew that things were pretty difficult at the moment, and that the Names—some of the Names—were having a bit of a hard time, but then they had had a pretty easy one for the past couple of decades, and you had to take the rough with the smooth in life.

He was beginning to develop the slightly patronising, even cynical attitude towards the Names that some inside Lloyd's had; they had come into it for profit, after all, they'd succeeded for a long time and now that things weren't quite so easy, they shouldn't complain.

He was very polite to Gillian Thompson when she came into the office, asking to see someone in authority. It was a filthy, unseasonable day, raining hard; Miss Thompson had walked to the offices of Jackson and Bond, which were just off Bishopsgate, from Liverpool Street tube station, and she was very windswept and wet, her neat brown shoes stained from stepping in puddles, and her umbrella, as she explained to Marion, the girl in reception, completely ruined. "Like my hair."

Marion came into Alan's office and said that Miss Thompson wanted to see someone about her syndicates, and that she seemed rather upset.

"Make her a cup of coffee, Marion, please," Alan said, "and I'll be out."

He came out a few minutes later, smiled at Miss Thompson who was twisting her handkerchief in her fingers, and asked what he could do to help. "I don't know," Miss Thompson said, and burst into tears. Alan was rather alarmed; he suggested to Marion that she show them into the small conference room and bring another cup of coffee.

"I don't want any more coffee," Miss Thompson said, blowing her nose. "I want to talk to someone about my syndicates."

"You can talk to me," Alan said soothingly—he had learned to soothe middle-aged women when his mother had had the change—"and we can sort something out, I'm sure. Why don't you begin at the beginning?" And he smiled at her encouragingly.

The beginning had been just a few years earlier—seven, to be precise—when Miss Thompson had been approached by the son of an acquaintance of her parents, "Such a nice young man," and he had suggested, having learned of the modest fortune bequeathed her by her father, that she became a Name at Lloyd's. "I can arrange everything for you," he said, "introduce you to someone there and he'll take care of everything for you."

Lonely and unmarried, Gillian Thompson had been grateful for such kindness, and felt the weight of her financial affairs lifting from her shoulders; three months later she was admitted as a Name. "And it was such a lovely day; I was taken up to that beautiful room, in the old building, of course, and these extremely charming gentlemen welcomed me. It was like having a sort of second family suddenly. I felt very secure. And I hadn't even had to hand over any money, apart from the deposit, of course. Sinclairs, my bank, simply provided a letter of credit and I was in. And for the first few years it was wonderful: I got a cheque every July, and I was able to do up my little house and buy a small car. And then— then . . . then it all began to go wrong. The first year wasn't too bad, they only wanted four thousand pounds. I could manage that. Of course, I was worried, but my agent told me it was simply a hiccup. The next year it was eleven thousand, which was a shock, but again I paid up, and now this year, they want forty thousand. Well, I just haven't got it, Mr.— Mr.—"

"Richards," said Alan.

"Mr. Richards. I mean, I could sell my house, but then I'd have nowhere to live, and I've sold my car, but I only got just over a thousand for it. I could sell my mother's jewellery, which is very precious to me, but of course it's all antique and what I'd get is nothing like its true worth. I just don't know where to turn. And the gentleman I saw on the first day, from this office, he was so charming and helpful and I'm sure he'd know what to do."

"What was his name?" asked Alan.

"Ferguson. Donald Ferguson."

"I'm afraid he has left," said Alan carefully. "Retired." Rather hurriedly and mysteriously, Alan just happened to know. Ferguson was now living in the south of France in a villa of considerable splendour.

"Oh dear. I was afraid of that. Well, someone else must be doing his job."

"Indeed. And I shall certainly take your case up with him."

"But—can't I see him now? I've come up from Hampshire, specially."

"Didn't you make an appointment?"

"Well, no. But I had other appointments today, with Sinclairs as a matter of fact, and my lawyers, and when I telephoned your office late one day last week, someone said if I was coming anyway, I might do best to just drop in."

Alan mentally cursed whoever that person had been—Jackie the telephonist, probably, wanting to get away quickly at the end of the day. He said how sorry he was.

"But I will look very carefully at your syndicates—I've got the numbers here—and make sure everything is in order. And then I'll write to you."

"But—I need rather more than that," said Gillian Thompson, the tears rising again. "I'm absolutely desperate. I haven't got forty thousand pounds and I can't possibly pay it. I need some kind of advice or reassurance that I won't have to, otherwise I just don't know what I can do."

"Well, the first thing to do is to make sure everything's in order," said Alan, "and I will see that your underwriters are fully informed about your case. And then I will write to you. Please try not to worry. Now can I get you a taxi or—"

Gillian Thompson suddenly became less pathetic. She stood up and faced him, the tears drying on her face.

"You haven't been listening to a word I've said, have you?" she said. "I face absolute ruin. I'm a woman completely on my own, with no assets of any kind and no support, with a demand from Lloyd's for forty thousand pounds—and you suggest getting me a taxi. I could hardly afford my train fare up from the country. Good afternoon. I have found this conversation deeply insulting and totally unsatisfactory."

And she stalked off, dumping her ruined umbrella in the wastepaper bin in the corner of reception.

Alan found himself rather bothered by the vision of Gillian Thompson: by her rage even more than her weeping. Her outburst had clearly been driven by absolute desperation. Looking up her biggest syndicate alone, Westfield Bradley, from the trend in asbestosis-related claims, it looked as if it might literally wipe her out. What was she doing in such a syndicate at all? She had trusted them completely, and they had failed her equally completely. A few years ago they could have suggested quietly to her that she start the three-year rundown and get out. Even the greediest fishermen know enough to throw the tiddlers back.

When after three days he could still see her pale puckered little face streaked with tears and hear her quiet anxious voice suddenly rising into attack, he went to see his boss, reported Miss Thompson's visit, her distress and her complete inability to pay. When he started to express his concern for her, and the duty the agency owed her, Norman Clarke interrupted him.

"Alan," he said, "everybody who comes to Lloyd's wants the same thing: risk-free investment—little old ladies included. And there is no such thing. Lloyd's is above all a repository for dreams. Rather greedy dreams. Everyone's warned, it's incumbent upon us to do so, they know perfectly well what they're getting into. Don't worry about it. Certainly don't worry about Miss Thompson. She'll be all right, I'm sure. Remember, she must have shown at least seventy-five thousand to get in, she's hardly a penniless widow."

"She's not a widow, Mr. Clarke. She's unmarried, she has no family, no one to support her in any way, and—"

"All right, penniless spinster then. They often have neurotic fantasies, spinsters, you know." He smiled at Alan, a dismissive, impatient smile. "Now I suggest you get on with your work, and leave mine to me. All right?"

Alan's grandmother had had a saying about putting something in your back tooth and chewing on it for a bit. Hardly aware of it, Alan did exactly that.

Chapter 7

Lucinda had arranged to have lunch with Blue. She was going to explain that really she couldn't go on seeing him, that it was wrong, and so unfair to Nigel, who most certainly didn't deserve it, that it had been lovely and she'd always remember Blue, and the wonderful time they'd had together. And then they could part friends instead of enemies; which was important. Then she would go back to being a good wife, and Nigel would never have to know about it, and any unhappiness she might feel would absolutely serve her right.

So she'd met him for lunch.

And been really firm about it not being any more than that . . .

❧

"I really, really will tell him tonight. I promise. Blue, don't do that, please. I can't concentrate on what I'm saying, it's important."

"Sorry. It's just that you do have such incredibly beautiful breasts. Would that be breeding, do you reckon? Are they posh breasts?"

"I don't know. I really don't know. Anyway—"

"You could get on page three, you know. No problem at all."

"Page three of what?"

"Lucy! I sometimes despair of you. You don't live in the real world at all, do you? Page three of what?! *The Sun*, girl, *The Sun* newspaper."

"Oh Blue! That's so awful. It's really disgusting, the way they do that—"

"Why? Giving innocent pleasure to millions, what's wrong with that?"

"But it's not innocent, is it?"

"Isn't it? Why not?"

"Well—it exploits women, that's why not."

There was a silence, then, "You never cease to surprise me," he said, bending to kiss the objects under discussion. "You're much cleverer than I thought, first time I met you."

"I know," said Lucinda with a sigh. "I mean, people are always saying things like that, that I'm not such a dumb blonde as they thought. I think that's how Nigel sees me though. He really doesn't think I've got a brain at all."

"Which is one of the reasons you're leaving him for someone who appreciates you. All of you. Now, you going to come straight to me tonight, or what? After you've told him?"

"Oh Blue, I suppose so. I'm so scared."

"Want me to come with you?"

"No, of course not. I'm not scared in that way. He won't do anything to me. I'm scared of what it'll do to him, that's all—how upset he'll be."

"Well, I expect he will be upset. And it's a measure of what a lovely person you are that it's worrying you so much. But he'll get over it, sweetheart. He really will. Now then, come on, what about tonight, what you going to do? I could come, park round the corner, wait for you. How'd that be?"

She considered this. "Yes. That might be good. I'll . . . I'll tell him, and then just leave. I couldn't stay anyway, not once he knows, and he won't want me to. I mean, however upset he is, he'll want me to leave. Once he's convinced, that is. Oh poor, poor Nigel. God, I feel so bad."

❧

Quite often these days, Annabel found herself thinking about Dan and marvelling that she could have ever liked him so much. Or indeed a lot of her old friends. The new world she was in now seemed to suit her much better, inhabited as it was by people who had genuine ambitions—to make money, sure, not merely to enjoy life but to carve out a way for themselves. In this they reminded her of her mother.

And they were all so funny, so irreverent, and so extremely cool. Her favourite among the stylists was a beautiful boy called Florian; he was tall and very thin, with a cap of golden-tipped brown curly hair, huge blue eyes, and an extremely full, girly mouth; he wore rather loose clothes, wide black trousers and floppy white shirts and a lot of rings. He was one of the top three stylists and Annabel assumed he must be gay, and formed a wonderfully chatty, gossipy relationship with him; she was outraged when Carol told her he was a "fantastic stud, girls lined up from here to Fulham where he lives."

"I don't believe you," Annabel said. "How do you know?"

Carol shrugged. "Ask one of the other boys."

Annabel didn't want to do that, but she found him one morning in the staff room, his head in his hands.

"Whatever's the matter?" she asked, genuinely sympathetic.

"Oh God, Bel, I've got such a hangover," he said. "Combination of red wine and other naughty stuff, never mix it, darling, very silly."

She had rushed out to the pharmacy in Sloane Street for him and bought him some Revive and fed him with that and orange juice all morning. "You're sweet," he said, "so sweet. Let me buy you a drink this evening, say thank you."

Which he had; after an hour or so, she had felt one of his long legs pressed unmistakably against hers, and shortly after that, his hand eased her face round to his and he kissed her.

"You are utterly lovely," he said, releasing her, "and I totally adore you."

Shaken more with surprise than anything, she had smiled feebly at him.

"I bet you thought I was gay," he said, smiling back.

"Of . . . of course I didn't," she said.

"Of course you did. Everyone does. Well I'm not, sweetie, not in the very least. I don't even swing both ways. My wrists are as firm as my cock is right this minute. Promise. Where would you like to go next?"

A strong instinct for self-preservation told Annabel to have an important dinner at home with her parents. She wasn't sure that she should get involved with him, much as she liked the idea. It was certainly too soon in her career at Miki Wallace; wasn't going to endear her to the rest of the staff, especially people like Tania, if she started going around with one of the senior stylists. And they would certainly all get to hear about it; Florian's best friend couldn't call him discreet.

She found herself half wishing, rather sadly on the way home, that he was actually gay. It had been less complicated that way.

This was what made her so angry, Elizabeth thought, still did; and why did he have to do it, under her nose, when he knew it upset her so much? She watched him standing in the centre of the room, listening to some woman, very carefully, smiling then laughing, and then, God, here was another, coming over, interrupting, joining the two of them, reaching up to kiss Simon briefly. And he returned the kiss, said something in her ear, clearly some small shared intimacy, and then introduced the women to each other, took a glass from a passing tray to hand to the newcomer, and then, then worse than all of it, pulled out his wallet, took one of his cards, gave it to the first woman who studied it, smiled up at him, said something, and then tucked it into her bag . . .

At moments like this, Elizabeth's success, her power, her much-acknowledged brilliance meant nothing to her whatsoever; it was simply a wife who stood there, an anxious, jealous, fearful wife . . .

"He's such a charmer, your husband, isn't he?" said their hostess, a new neighbour from the Boltons whom Elizabeth hardly knew, and turning to look at her, seeing that she was pretty too, pretty and young and beautifully dressed, and therefore yet another source of danger, further prey for Simon, suddenly she couldn't bear it any longer, thought that she might go over to the small group and throw her glass of champagne in Simon's face, just to take the smile off it, and she did indeed go over, but only to say, "Simon, darling, I'm sorry to break up the party, but we really do have to go."

And he was immediately responsive, saying yes, of course, and he kissed the first woman, and followed Elizabeth over to their hostess so that they could say goodbye, and he kissed her too, waved briefly at her husband and then they were out the door.

"What was that about?" he said, clearly genuinely baffled as they walked away.

"I might ask you the same thing," she said. "What was that about? Who was that woman, why did you give her your card?"

"She was an American who's come to live here with her husband. He's looking for a tennis partner, apparently, and I said I might just be able to fill that brief."

"And you expect me to believe that?"

"Oh Elizabeth," he said wearily, shaking his head. "Please, please don't do this."

"Do what?"

"Pursue me with that insane jealousy of yours. It's so destructive—"

"Insane! Given what happened, what you did . . ."

They had reached their own house now; he unlocked the door, ushered her in.

"Elizabeth, this isn't helping our relationship."

"We still have one, do we?" she said, stalking into the kitchen, reaching in the fridge for a bottle of water. "I hadn't realised."

"Oh, for Christ's sake. Of course we do. Well, we could if you would give it only half a chance. You've got to learn to trust me again. I know it's difficult, I know I was a bastard, but it was over a year ago—more. I promised you and I've kept my promise."

She was silent, fiddling with the top of the bottle.

"Please, Elizabeth. Otherwise there's no point our being together. I might as well clear out."

"And go back to her, do you mean?"

"No, of course not."

"It's so easy for you, Simon. Saying these things now. Telling me it's firmly in the past, when you'd been lying to me for years."

"Not years."

"Years, Simon. You don't know how much it hurt. You can't just expect someone to start believing you, when you've been lying to them for a long time."

"No, I suppose not."

"I mean, every time I hear you saying a woman's name, I wonder."

"Look," he said, "I made an appalling mistake. I'm terribly sorry. But I can't wipe it out. It's there. And really it's up to you now. To try and make it work."

"Yes, I know," she said very quietly.

"We can survive—I know we can. Other marriages do."

"Simon, you're doing it again, talking as if it was just a fling. It wasn't."

"Oh, for fuck's sake," he said. "I'm tired, I've got some work to do. Look, we've been over this a hundred times. I'm a bastard, I did you terribly wrong. But I've been eating humble pie for a long time now and the taste's pretty ghastly. I can't do more. Good night. I'll see you in the morning."

She sat there, staring at the closed door, too angry, too proud to meet him halfway.

It was quite true, what he had said: there was nothing more he could do. It was up to her now. Otherwise there was no point staying. She had to start trusting him—somehow. Or at least mistrusting him less. It was just that, well, it hadn't been just a fling. That would have been bearable. But it hadn't . . .

She had found out in the age-old way; he had told her he was somewhere one night, one of the children had been taken ill, she had phoned the hotel where he was supposed to be at a conference, and they had said, clearly embarrassed, that he wasn't there, had never been there.

Confronted, he had confessed: said he was sorry. She had said it must end, at once. He said that was impossible, he couldn't give her up.

"Then get out," she said. "Get out, now. Tonight."

He had, for a while, not to live with the other woman but to bide his time, to try to decide what to do. Elizabeth refused to learn her name even, didn't want to know who she was—"Even if she's a friend of ours."

"She's not," he said.

She said she'd never take him back, but when he asked, she did: and expecting to feel better, she felt worse.

Jealousy tore at her. What did she have, this woman, that she, his wife, had not? What had she given him?

"Time," he had said. "Time and attention. Elizabeth, when you really need me, I manage to be there for you. Somehow I don't feel you do that for me. I long to talk to you, to consult you, just to be with you, and quite often you simply are never there. And I don't mean just physically. How often have I sat talking to you, trying to discuss something important with you, and felt you were actually at the next presentation, the last sales conference."

Clear-sighted about herself, she recognised this and felt ashamed. She was prioritising her career above her marriage, above Simon whom she did—astonishingly—still love. She promised to try to spend more time at home and with him, but it was difficult; her job was not one that could be fitted into prescribed hours. But she did struggle to be more attentive, to consider his needs, to do more to please him. It seemed to have been in vain.

She sighed, picked up her glass and the bottle of water, and walked up the stairs and into her own study. Where she had work to do and where for a while she would feel in command and control once more. For a while . . .

❧

Nigel had got home early. He had some champagne on ice, and some strawberries to dip into it, and he'd booked a table at San Frediano for later in the evening. It was going to be so special and she was going to be so pleased, and relieved too: he was sure she'd been worrying quietly about Lloyd's, and then he wanted to tell her about his other decision; that would make her happy too. He knew she felt it was time, time he got himself checked out baby-wise, as she put it (although she hadn't said anything about it lately); he didn't exactly want to, but he was prepared to do it for her—and so that they could become a family, of course. She— There was the door now.

She came in looking rather strained; she kissed him briefly, put down her bag, and then said, "Nigel, could I possibly have a drink?"

This was unlike her; he really hadn't wanted to open the champagne until he'd told her what he'd done, so he got out the bottle of Sancerre they'd started on last night.

"This all right?"

"Yes, fine. Thank you." She took an enormous gulp, then as if she'd only just noticed, said, "You're very early."

"Yes," he said, "I know. I wanted to talk to you about something."

"Oh yes? Me too. I mean, I wanted to talk to you. Nigel, you have a drink too."

"I will in a minute, darling. Actually I've got something a bit special for us. In the fridge. Some Bolly. It's to go with what I've got to tell you. To celebrate it."

"Oh." She looked almost frightened. "Nigel, I think I'd better go first. If you don't mind."

"Poor darling. You're really in a bit of a state, aren't you? It's that wretched job. You've been working much too hard. Well, I think—if you want to—you can give it up."

She stared at him. "Give it up? But why should I? And I thought you said we needed my income. In case Lloyd's got worse."

"Well, darling, I've got that all sorted. It's not going to be nearly such a problem now."

"What? Really? Oh Nigel, that's wonderful news. I'm so glad. So you're feeling much better? Much happier?"

"Much."

"Right. Well," she looked at him rather nervously, "well then, my news. Nigel, I—"

"Lucinda, let me finish. I've hardly begun."

"But—"

"Please, darling. Please."

She sat down, her eyes fixed on his face. "Go on, then."

"Right. You are, from this moment—well, from this morning anyway—a much richer woman."

"Nigel, what are you talking about?"

"I've transferred all my assets to you. Well, everything I could. Into a trust fund for you. The contents of our deposit account, a few hundred thou, I've sold most of my shares and put that money in too; and the deeds of this house, and the deeds of the farm; they'll all be in your name too, once it's been legally cleared. So, you'd better not leave me, darling, all right?"

She looked a bit odd then. "But—but Nigel, why? I don't understand."

"It's quite simple. If all one's assets are held by the person in the family who isn't the Name, they can't claim them. Apparently. So—we're safe. Isn't that wonderful?"

"Well, yes." She was very white. "Is it really so bad, Nigel?"

"Pretty bad. I talked to a couple of people who were getting out, and—"

"But why can't you do that as well?"

"Darling, it's not as easy as that. In the first place, liability is unlimited—literally. It can go on when you're food for worms. And anyway, as I've told you before, the accounting is three years in arrears. So even if I resigned tomorrow, and I am trying very hard to do that, I'd still be liable for another three years' underwriting. At very best."

"So . . . how bad is it?"

"Well, it isn't anymore. But it could have been. I could literally have lost everything. I've underwritten about a million, and frankly I'd be hard-pressed to put my hands on half of that. And they'd want twice that. That's how it works. I—we—really would have been bankrupted. As it is, they can take all I've got, which is very little really, and you can look after the rest."

"But . . . but are you sure it's this simple?"

"Seems to be. Someone suggested it to me—dear old Chris Paige, remember Chris?"

Lucinda did; he was a sweet, rather jolly friend of Nigel's. She wouldn't have taken any financial advice from him more complex than not keeping money under the bed.

"Yes, well, he's doing it, seemed a brilliant idea to me."

"And what about legally? Is it all right?"

"Well," he said, looking slightly less confident, "it might be necessary if it went to court, which it wouldn't, for you to say you had no idea I'd done this. But as you didn't—that's fine. It's true. So as I say, you'd better not leave me."

"And—if I don't want it?"

"Darling, why on earth should you not want it? And please do want it, because otherwise I'm up the creek without a canoe. Now before I get the champagne out, I want to tell you something else. Something on the baby front. I think I've been rather selfish and . . ."

℮

Blue had been waiting for about half an hour when Lucinda came out of the house. She walked very slowly over to the car and got in. She seemed very calm, very composed; she turned her head to look at him.

"Hello."

"Hello, lovely. All right?"

"I . . . Blue, I'm sorry, I'm so sorry, but I can't do it. I can't come. He's—well, he's sort of trumped us."

She sat there, ice calm, being very, very careful not to touch him, and told him.

❧

In his modest flat in the less smart area of Putney, George Meyer was patiently addressing envelopes which were to contain a letter from him to everyone appearing on his list of clients of the Jackson and Bond Members' Agency. It was a long job, but George had time on his side, a lot of empty evenings.

The letter took the form of an invitation to a meeting at the Grenville Club, Pall Mall, and was, George hoped, sufficiently intriguing and attractive to ensure a high acceptance rate.

Chapter 8

AUGUST TO SEPTEMBER 1989

"Good Lord," said Simon. "Have a look at this. Very interesting." He handed Elizabeth a letter; she was reading in bed, a book for once rather than a report. They were spending a week in London, worn out by the grind of commuting in the hottest summer of the decade, leaving Tilly and Toby at Chadwick House in the care of Mrs. Ford.

She read it, then said, "Goodness. He sounds eminently sensible."

"More than that, I'd say. Impressive even. He's obviously done his homework. Do you think I should go?"

"Oh definitely, yes."

"Would you come with me?"

"Simon, I—" and then she stopped. She should go. It would be a supportive thing to do. The sort of thing that might help.

"Yes," she said, "yes, I will."

"Thank you. And I promise to stay by your side all evening and not even speak to anyone who isn't wearing a three-piece suit and stout shoes."

She managed to smile, picked up the letter and read it again.

Dear Simon Beaumont,

As a Lloyd's Name, a client of Members' Agent Jackson and Bond, and a major participant in the Westfield Bradley Group of Syndicates, I have become increasingly unhappy with what I am sure many of us regard as a deplorable state of affairs. I have been looking into the situation in some depth and I have come to three very disturbing conclusions.

The heavy losses we have all experienced recently are almost certain to get worse rather than better over the next few years. Many of us may well be bearing a disproportionate share of these losses. I have heard it estimated (though I cannot vouch for the figures) that 70 percent of the losses are being borne by only 30 percent of the Members!

I fear the possibility cannot at this stage be eliminated that as a result of (at best) bad management, there have been some serious irregularities in the way our affairs have been handled. More than this I am reluctant to commit to paper at this point, but I am inviting a number of people in a similar situation to get together for an informal exchange of views and ideas, and I would be delighted if you would join us in the large meeting room at the Grenville Club, Pall Mall, on Friday 8 September at 6 p.m.

Yours sincerely,
George Meyer

Nigel was very intrigued by the letter. He showed it to Lucinda. "Interesting, darling, wouldn't you say? Of course, I don't think we have much of a problem anymore, but it would still be a good idea to go, I think, meet some people in the same boat, have an exchange of views and ideas, as he says."

"Can I go too?"

"You? Lucinda, why on earth would you want to go? You're not a Name, I don't think you understand it very well and—"

"Nigel, I understand it perfectly well, thank you," she said, stung, remembering sharply the conversation with Blue about Lloyd's. "I know there are big problems with claims over—" She stopped.

"Over what?" he said. He looked almost shocked, as if she had shown a knowledge of sex shops.

"Oh, I've read quite a lot about it recently, as a matter of fact." Careful, he'd be wondering how she knew so much about it. "Something about asbestos—is that right?"

"Asbestosis is what you're probably thinking of. Well, you can come if you want to, but I think you'll be very bored."

"I'm sure I won't."

❧

It was getting better. She knew it was getting better. It was as if the skin had begun to grow over the gaping wound that was centred someplace where she supposed her heart to be. Day by day, she could feel herself recovering. It was a pretty feeble recovery; she still had dreadful, or rather wonderful dreams where she was with Blue and woke up smiling to the wretched reality, she still saw him on every street corner, she still half expected to hear his voice every time the phone rang, and she was very far from feeling emotionally well.

But at least she didn't want to die anymore. And Nigel had been utterly sweet, of course, and so happy, released from his own dreadful anxiety. He kept telling her she looked washed out and suggesting they take a little holiday.

"Just a few days, darling, in the sun somewhere, put a bit of colour in your cheeks—think of it as a second honeymoon. Of course if you don't want to take me, spend the money on me . . ."

This was his favourite joke at the moment and it made her want to scream: that she was the financially dominant partner in their relationship and he the poor dependent. "I'm a kept man," he told everyone. "Sort of a toy boy, if you like. Rather an elderly one, of course, but still . . ."

Lucinda found it hard to be alone with him anywhere at all, let alone on holiday, with time to think about Blue; her only salvation lay in surrounding herself and Nigel with their friends and keeping terribly busy. She entertained feverishly, one dinner party and one kitchen supper every week, in spite of feeling dreadfully tired and not actually very well; she had bought what seemed to be miles of material to make curtains for their bedroom—the torture chamber as she thought of it—and for the drawing room and the dining room as well.

The other thing she had done was take on extra work reading some manuscripts for Graham. She'd made this offer before, and it had always been refused. But this time he'd smiled at her and said yes, that would be great, and asked her to do a short report on each of them; she had felt pleased and excited and as near to happy as she had been since she had said goodbye to Blue that night. Maybe she was a career woman at heart after all . . .

And then Nigel had had a sperm test, and she knew what an ordeal it must have been for him. He had gone off to the fertility clinic alone and come back rather quiet and said that it'd been fine but that he didn't want to talk about it. "They'll let me know in a week or so. Can't think why it takes so long. Suppose they want to be sure. Too jolly important to make a mistake."

Lucinda hoped desperately that the news would be good. More than anything now she longed for a baby; a baby would make sense of life again, help to mend her heart, re-create her marriage. And help ease the misery of the torture chamber . . .

❧

Flora Fielding was quite excited by the letter from George Meyer. She sensed that he had more in mind than an evening of waffle. She rang Richard.

"I wondered if I could stay with you next Friday?"

"Of course you can, Mother, you know you're always very welcome. The children will be thrilled. And Debbie, of course," he added hastily.

"Thank you. I'm going to a meeting in the evening, in Central London. It's rather exciting: a meeting of Names in Westfield Bradley, my major syndicate at Lloyd's. I had a letter from someone called George Meyer, who sounds very interesting. I was very impressed by his letter anyway."

"Well, it'll be lovely to see you," said Richard, smiling down the phone. "Will you come here first?"

"Oh, I don't think so, darling, no. I've got a meeting with a gallery in Mumbles, they're talking about giving me an exhibition, and that's not till midday. No, I'll go straight to the meeting. And I'll leave quite early in the morning too; there's a talk at the Gower Society in the early afternoon, which I don't want to miss."

"Fine. I'll tell Debs. Oh, and Mother . . ." His voice was slightly anxious suddenly.

"Sorry, Richard, I have to go, the blacksmith's just arrived."

He put down the phone, thinking how grateful he was, they should be, that Flora led such a dynamic life, and thought that he must ring her again as soon as possible, and certainly before the next Friday.

Debbie said carefully that it would be lovely to see Flora and then added: "But I don't quite see why she wants to go to a meeting with lots of other Lloyd's people when things are better for her. It seems like a waste of time to me."

"Well, they're very complex, these syndicates," Richard said, and had she not been sorting out whites from colours she would have noticed that he flushed suddenly, then started busying himself with folding up the papers.

And all might yet have been well, had Flora not phoned the very next day before he had been able to have the conversation—which was clearly going to be difficult—with Debbie. She had answered the phone, and Flora had said that she wondered if Richard might be free to come to the meeting with her. "And you too, of course, darling, if it would interest you. See what we're all up against. I could certainly do with Richard's support and advice, and get his reaction to what's been said. The man who's called the meeting definitely sounds as if he means business."

"Well, I'm sure he'll come if he can," Debbie said. "He's very immersed in time-tabling at the moment, but there's nothing on that evening, as far as I know. I'll get him to ring you."

"Thank you, Debbie."

And then, as the proper weight of Flora's words worked into Debbie's brain, and a dreadful, wormlike suspicion began to form, she asked the question. The question—and its answer—which, as she saw it, altered her life forever.

"What I don't understand though, Flora, is why you're going to this meeting, and why you need Richard's support, when everything's so much better."

There was a silence, then Flora said, "But Debbie, it isn't so much better. I don't quite understand why you should think it was. It's worse—much worse."

℮

"You lied to me. Don't try to deny it, you did. I can't believe you could have done anything so awful. God, you're disgusting. The pair of you."

"It's got nothing to do with my mother."

"I'm sorry, but I find that very hard to believe. Don't speak to me, don't come near me. I'm going out now, to try and think what to do. You can stay here and look after the children. And maybe you'd like to sort out some more things you're going to tell me. Only don't expect me to believe anything either of you says ever again."

"Debbie, I swear to you, Mother had no idea what I'd told you. And I'd meant to tell you—"

"Tell me what? Some more lies. I don't know that I can stay married to someone who's done something so disgusting. I need to think. And you might as well start writing letters to those schools now, tell them the children are leaving. They're not getting any more of our money than I can help."

℮

Debbie was crying so hard, she didn't notice the rain for quite a long time. She walked for miles along the Uxbridge Road and then down Gunnersbury Avenue, and into Gunnersbury Park, careless that she was soaked through, that people were looking at her curiously, then past the boating lake and across to the Potomac fishpond where she and the children and indeed Richard had spent many happy hours. There she sat on a bench, staring into the water, blinded by her tears as much as the rain. How could he have deceived her like that? They were supposed to trust each other, completely; that was what marriage was about. She would never trust him again: never. It was just as bad as if she had discovered he was having an affair—worse, in fact. This wasn't just about the two of them, it was about their family. Him deciding what was best for the children and then lying about it, in case she didn't agree.

"I hate you!" she shouted into the wet grey skies. "I hate you so much!"

And in spite of the fact that she was very cold now, she stayed on her bench and buried her head in her arms and wept.

She reached home again well into the afternoon, cold and soaked to the skin; she stalked upstairs, ran herself a bath, and locked the door. The children didn't follow her, but Richard did, and started first knocking tentatively, then banging on the door.

"Debs, let me in. Please."

"No. Go away. Leave me alone."

"I'm not going anywhere. I have to explain."

"There's nothing to explain. Just—just leave me alone."

Finally she came out, walked into their bedroom; he was there, looking pale and wretched.

"Oh, just go away," she said.

"Debbie, please—" He put his hand on her arm.

"Stop it. I don't like being lied to and I don't want to talk about it now."

"Oh, for God's sake," he said, "you're overreacting. I haven't committed adultery, for God's sake, I just wanted to spare you any anxiety, and the children any distress, for that matter. It would have been dreadful for them to have to change schools now, they're doing so well, and you'd have hated seeing them disrupted and upset. And I know I can do the fees another year at least. I'll get a new job and—"

"Oh, do shut up," Debbie said. "And as far as I'm concerned, I think I'd almost rather you had been unfaithful to me. At least that's an uncomplicated situation. Anyway, I have decided one thing: I'm going to come to that meeting with you, hear it all for myself, find out exactly what is going on. I wouldn't trust a word you told me about it. Now just piss off, why don't you, and take the children to the cinema or something."

Richard did as he was told.

c⌒⊃

Very few of the Names who were to attend George Meyer's meeting at the Grenville Club slept particularly soundly the night before. George Meyer himself was very anxious; he had staked a great deal on this, invested a huge amount of time, some money—only a few hundred, but that he could ill afford—and he was nervous as well about people's reactions to what he had to say, and that he would end up back where he started. It had given him a purpose in life for a few months, as he researched his original idea, took legal advice, and then went about writing the letters, arranging a venue, and composing his speech. The uptake on his invitation had been encouraging: a very large number of the Names he approached had accepted. Among them surely he would find not only recruits to his cause but other prime movers, associates with areas of expertise other than his own, who could help him progress the whole thing. What was that quote from *Henry V* before the Battle of Agincourt? Oh, yes: "Stiffen the sinews, summon up the blood." It was hard to do much sinew stiffening on your own. Time for some companionship and some support.

A former marketing director of a medium-size company operating from Greater Manchester, Meyer had been a casualty of first the recession—"Terribly sorry, George, we're going to have to let you go"—and then of Lloyd's, and he was still reeling at the change in his circumstances from being well-heeled and successful, living in a large house in Cheshire with a rather glamorous wife and three children, to hard up and a failure, living in a small flat in Putney without his wife, who had left him. For most of which he blamed Lloyd's.

Simon Beaumont was very hopeful; apart from a natural attraction to new ideas, new causes, he could see that, without some plan such as George Meyer might be offering, he faced a future of increasing unpleasantness.

Elizabeth was rather less hopeful; she couldn't imagine what a few individuals could possibly do, pitted against the might of Lloyd's. But she was touched by Simon's excitement, she saw him more hopeful and positive about the situation than he had been for some time, and she was anxious to be supportive. Things had improved between them recently, and her accompanying him to the meeting clearly meant a lot to him. It would be boring and almost certainly a waste of time—but it was only one evening.

❦

Nigel was trying not to pin too many hopes on the meeting. He wasn't feeling quite as bullish about his situation with Lloyd's as he had been. And he felt unable to talk to Lucinda about it. She had got very thin and was certainly not eating enough; and she was working so hard which couldn't possibly help her to get pregnant. He had tried several times to suggest she give up work, but she had got quite cross and said what on earth would she do, sitting around at home all day, with nothing to do, watching the calendar.

He had been so excited about his plan, the transfer of his assets to her, that he had effected as much as he could simply by instructing his bank manager. But his solicitor, who had had to be involved in the transfer of the properties to Lucinda, had been most unhappy about it.

"The transfer of assets in the full knowledge of outstanding debts could well be deemed illegal, Nigel. I would advise very strongly against it. How far are you along this road?"

Nigel said that he had only transferred the contents of his bank account and his share portfolio to Lucinda.

"I should leave it at that, if I were you. Lloyd's aren't fools, they'll prosecute. Even money put offshore isn't safe. I really think you're on very dangerous ground, Nigel. You'd be committing perjury if you denied your knowledge of the situation a year or so down the road."

And so he had left it at that. And fallen prey once again to the dreadful anxiety that gnawed away at him in the middle of the night.

Lucinda was quite looking forward to the meeting; anything that served as a distraction was welcome at the moment. Anything that saved her from sitting alone at home with Nigel.

❦

Flora was also looking forward to it very much, but was acutely anxious about Debbie's emotional state and how it would affect their relationship. She felt furious with Richard; not just that he had told a stupid lie to

Debbie but that he had failed to think it through properly, how much it involved her and indeed, to warn her about it. She felt pleased in a way that Debbie was coming to the meeting: she might understand more clearly what they all were up against. And it would be awfully good to meet some other people in her situation; Flora had been feeling increasingly overwhelmed lately.

Richard was simply terrified of one thing: of Debbie making another scene. Which seemed to him altogether possible since, after well over a week, she was still hardly speaking to him.

And Debbie, quietly furious, was simply determined to find out the truth: and how bad for everyone the whole business threatened to be. And almost more important, for how long.

Chapter 9

"Do you mind if I sit here?"

"Of course not. My son and daughter-in-law are coming shortly, but they can sit here on my other side."

"Thank you. And I have to keep a seat for my wife. She's working late."

Flora smiled at the young man as he settled in the chair beside her, well, he was fairly young, young men were getting older these days. He was in his late thirties, early forties maybe, very well dressed, with a public-school accent: he seemed charming. William had always said that was one of the best things about Lloyd's—you knew you were with the right sort.

"Nigel Cowper," the young man said, holding out his hand.

"Flora Fielding."

"And where do you live, Mrs. Fielding?"

"I live in Wales." She smiled at him. "And call me Flora, please. Mrs. Fielding makes me feel old. Which I am, of course."

"May I say you don't look it."

"Thank you."

"And that's a long way to come for a meeting."

"Oh, I'm sure others will have come just as far, if not farther. Things are rather . . . worrying. And getting information really is the allegorical blood from a stone. I thought Mr. Meyer's letter promised at least a little blood—if you follow me. I presume that was him, greeting us at the door."

"I gathered so, yes. Well, he's got a good turnout. Ah, here's Lucinda now. Hello, darling." He stood up, gave her a quick kiss. "Come and sit down. This is Mrs. Fielding, Mrs. Flora Fielding. She's travelled all the way up from Wales. Mrs. Fielding, Lucinda. My wife."

He spoke with great pride: and no wonder, Flora thought, this really was a very pretty girl, blond with big blue yes, and her voice was pretty too, very light and attractively soft. She thought of Debbie's slightly raw voice, tinged with her London accent, then chided herself for her disloyalty. No one could help their voice.

"I love Wales," said Lucinda, shaking Flora's hand. "We used to go there quite often when I was little—to Abersoch, do you know it?"

"Oh, it's lovely," said Flora. "I haven't been there for many years though. I live in South Wales, on the Gower peninsula. Anyway, do come and join us. Oh, and there are my lot. Debbie, Richard, over here . . ."

This was even worse than she had expected, Debbie thought, absolutely full of braying posh people. Flora must be in heaven. She'd already homed in on a couple of her own; that girl was just ridiculous, an absolute cliché, more like Princess Diana than Princess Diana herself. As for that chinless wonder she was with . . .

"Hi," she said briefly to Lucinda and Nigel. "Sorry to disturb you. And sorry we're late, Flora, the babysitter let us down."

"Oh, have you got a baby?" said Lucinda. "How lovely."

"Sometimes," said Richard. "I mean, sometimes it's lovely. And actually we've got three. Well past the baby stage, unfortunately." He smiled at Lucinda; he was clearly very taken with her.

"That's a matter of opinion, Richard," said Debbie. "Personally, I'm very glad they're not babies anymore."

"No, I should think they're pretty hard work," said the chinless Nigel. "My brother's got a couple and they're permanently exhausted. Jolly little things though."

Jolly little things! thought Debbie. How was she going to get through this evening? If these were Lloyd's sufferers, they deserved all they got. And then she saw a rather pale middle-aged woman, very neatly dressed, sit down just in front of them and take her husband's hand. He gripped hers; he appeared very distressed. Debbie felt suddenly less sure of herself.

❧

The room had filled up considerably. Simon looked round, amazed and slightly comforted at the extraordinary mix of people there: representatives of the chattering classes; earnest women with no makeup and worn-corduroy-jacketed husbands; bellowing City types—he hoped he wasn't as much of a caricature as many of them—others equally near-caricatures of the huntin', shootin', and fishin' community; a few who were clearly theatricals, luvvie-ing away; and a lot of anxious middle-aged couples.

The man who had been greeting everyone at the door walked towards the platform at the front of the room. He was quite short, with neat dark hair; he was probably about forty-five, Simon thought, watching from where he was still standing at the door, waiting for Elizabeth. Couldn't she this once, just for him, be on time? And then the door opened and she slipped in. "Sorry," she whispered, "did my best. Is that George Meyer?"

"Think so. Wearing an Old Carthusian tie. Bodes well, doesn't it?"

George Meyer got up onto the platform, went through the usual rigmarole of microphone tapping and testing, and then raised his hand. Everyone stopped talking and cleared their throats. The middle-aged couple in front of Debbie grasped each other's hands more tightly.

Meyer smiled at them all.

"Thank you for coming. I'm George Meyer and I'm very pleased to see you here. I've talked to a few of you already and it's clear we've all been hit very hard financially, some of us desperately so, by the steeply escalating Lloyd's losses of the last few years."

A general murmur of affirmation ran through the room.

"Another thing we have in common is that we all share the same Members' Agent, Jackson and Bond. In my case, and I'm pretty sure in all of yours too, our problem has been greatly exacerbated by what was—with hindsight—a disproportionately heavy participation in the Westfield

Bradley Group of Syndicates, whose performance has been particularly disastrous."

Another murmur; Debbie shifted in her seat. This could get tedious. Meyer was asking questions now, requested a show of hands in answer to each one. He asked how many of them had been introduced to Lloyd's by someone they had not met before; how many got a specific suggestion from Jackson and Bond that 1986 was sure to be a very good year and that the best way to recoup any losses from 1985 (the first year there had been any, it seemed) was to increase their premium income limit—whatever that was—by as much as possible; and how many had been told by Jackson and Bond that they were recommending heavy participation in the Westfield Bradley Group, because they never took any big risks and were therefore "as safe as the Bank of England." There was some edgy laughter at this, and a great many hands went up.

"And I wonder how many of you have since had your exposure to Westfield Bradley reduced at the recommendation of Jackson and Bond? I see. None. And no doubt when you got the 'down to your last cuff link' speech, you were told that apart from two people in 1963, no one could remember any Name losing a lot of money."

More laughter; this time braver and louder.

He's good, this chap, Simon thought, really good. Better even than he'd hoped. He could see he would be good to deal with, and he could also see that Elizabeth was impressed.

"Now," said Meyer, "how many of you think that at the time you were recruited, there was no one, absolutely no one, working at Lloyd's who had any idea there was serious trouble ahead."

Not a hand went up.

"Right," Meyer said. "I'm not a lawyer, but if Lloyd's knew there were big problems looming and they deliberately withheld that information when they recruited us, then I believe we've been the victims of deliberate fraud. And therefore have some legal redress."

The silence was intense.

"I am, I suppose, raising the flag of rebellion, saying in fact that I intend to take urgent and, if necessary, drastic steps. Heaven knows how difficult it will be to collect evidence that will stand up in a court of law, but I'm determined to have a bloody good try.

"Now I'd like to hear from you. If anyone has a story which they would like to tell, please go ahead. I think it's important we share experiences, get to know what others are up against. After which I suggest a coffee break, and then we can move on to the next key question, which is: Where do we go from here? So . . . anyone want to speak?"

There was the usual awkward silence while people looked at their feet, round the room, up at the ceiling—and then Flora stood up. She would, Debbie thought.

"Yes, the lady in the blue jacket," said Meyer, smiling across at her. "Do you want to come up here, or . . ."

"Yes, if you like," said Flora, and she made her way onto the platform and stood there, looking at them all, pushing back her wild hair. She was wearing a blue embroidered velvet jacket over her long skirt, and high-heeled black boots; she looked wonderful, Debbie thought, with an unwilling stab of pride.

"Hello," she said, "and can I first thank George Meyer for having this marvellous idea in the first place. And for being good enough to contact us all. I simply wanted to tell my story very briefly; it's in no way unusual, I fear, but it will probably explain why I for one would like to explore his idea further."

And she went on to talk about how her husband had made her a Name so that their assets were limited, and then when he died six years ago, she had inherited everything anyway.

"It was a double whammy," she said with her wonderful smile. "I'm alone and I've got a lot more to lose. So, Mr. Meyer, I'm with you."

She went back to her place; after a pause a grey-haired man came up, probably in his mid-fifties, rather red-faced, dressed in a very shabby tweed suit. He was, he said, a farmer, with a "thousand acres or so in Suffolk;" he had become a Name twenty years earlier, "and I must admit, several of those years were good. But now—well, I would seem to be destitute. Almost."

Destitute, Debbie thought, with a thousand acres? Honestly . . .

"Everything I had and valued is going. The farm, which my family has owned for generations, my livestock, my horses; in theory, of course, we could keep the house, but the farm'd be worth much less without it, so my wife and I are moving into a small cottage, with no income except our state pension to look forward to. I simply don't know what we're going to do. And what angers me most is they must have known this was happening, must have seen it coming, and at no time did my agent warn me of anything. In fact, he had the gall to encourage me to increase my underwriting for next year if I could find the assets."

Nigel thought of his own land in Norfolk, very much under threat, and felt sick.

And then the line of people wanting to tell their stories grew longer: a couple in late middle age stood up. If things didn't get better in the next year, they said, standing on the platform together, they'd have to sell the family home, sell all they had; the wife actually started weeping at this point, clinging to her husband's arm. Meyer gently ushered them off the platform.

And then there was a young widow. She'd been living out in Hong Kong, her husband had died, and left her enough money to allow her to become a Name at Lloyd's, which had been suggested to her by a charming and helpful young man.

"I met him when we got home. He was connected with my husband's business in some way, and he said Lloyd's would see me and the children through. Now they're asking for more than I can possibly give them. I really don't know what to do."

And so it went on. Story after story of broken lives, of ghastly fear, of lost homes, of what had seemed secure futures wiped out. Debbie felt very shaken and oddly ashamed of herself; she avoided Richard's eyes. Finally, Meyer came back onto the platform and thanked everyone who had spoken for their honesty and courage.

"Coffee break follows. All are welcome to that, but could I ask anyone totally out of sympathy with my proposition to leave afterwards."

Coffee was served at the back of the room. Everyone moved in that direction, smiling rather awkwardly at one another. Nigel found himself in the queue behind the young widow: she was rather pretty, he thought, with light brown hair and large, anxious grey eyes. He held out his hand to her.

"Nigel Cowper. Well done for speaking. Don't think I'd have had the bottle, quite honestly."

She smiled back at him, a rather pale smile. "Catherine Morgan. I wouldn't have expected it either, but suddenly I felt I had to. People need to know. And what's the point of us all being in it together, if we're not honest?"

"You look awfully tired," he said. "Why don't you sit down there, with my wife." He waved at Lucinda, called, "We've got company, darling," and returned to the coffee queue.

"Come and join me," said Lucinda. "Jolly brave of you, that. And what an awful story. I'm so sorry, I never realised how bad things could be."

"Oh well," said Catherine, "I'm not the only one. As you heard."

"No, but . . . well, anyway, I'm Lucinda. So nice to meet you."

Nigel passed Flora Fielding on his way back to the table; she smiled at him.

"Hello. My lot are over there. Do you want to join us?"

"No," said Nigel, "but thank you for the invitation. We've set up camp on the other side of the room. With that poor girl, the widow."

"What a nightmare for her. I don't know when I felt sorrier for anyone."

"But you're a widow yourself," said Nigel, surprised at his own bluntness.

"Yes, I know, but I'm a tough old bird and I haven't got a young family. I feel so sorry for her."

Catherine smiled at Nigel and Lucinda over her coffee. "It's jolly nice to be with people, you can't imagine. It's pretty lonely, my situation. This is the most fun I've had for ages."

"Oh dear," said Lucinda, "that doesn't sound too good. I'm so sorry. How old are your children?"

"Caroline's six and Freddie's eight. Oh Lord, now look what I've done." Her coffee cup was lying on its side, the contents spilling out across the table and dribbling down onto the floor. Lucinda's bag lay in its path; she snatched it up.

"Don't worry," she said. "Nigel, why don't you go and see if you can find some paper napkins."

Nigel went obediently off; Catherine smiled awkwardly at Lucinda, and tried to dab some of the mess up with a couple of small tissues.

"Oh, I get so cross with myself, it's so embarrassing. I am just awfully clumsy. And accident-prone, come to that. My dad always said I was a walking disaster."

"Nonsense," said Lucinda. "Of course you're not. You can make wonderful speeches, for a start. And here's Nigel now, with a great stash of napkins. Well done, Nigel."

"There, that's better," he said, mopping rather ineffectually. "No harm done. And—where do you live, Catherine? May we call you Catherine?"

"Of course. I've got a flat in Fulham, but I'm afraid that'll have to go if things get any worse. It's my only asset."

"Well . . . let's hope," said Nigel without much conviction.

"Indeed."

"Tell me, Catherine," said Lucinda, "do you work?"

"Oh yes. I work part-time as a secretary at a local estate agents. It's pretty tedious, but they let me leave at three thirty each day, in time to get the children."

"And—and when did your husband die?"

"Just over four years ago. I was still getting myself sorted out, trying to cope with everything, when this chap approached me, obviously saw me as an ideal victim for Lloyd's and their merry men. I can't imagine now how I could have been so stupid, but I suppose I was still a bit shocked . . ."

"That is terrible," said Lucinda. "I think you're just so, so brave. God, they should all be strung up. More coffee, Catherine? To replace the other? I'll go, Nigel, you talk to Catherine."

She headed over to the queue; it had certainly been a very distracting evening.

Simon sought out George Meyer, leaving Elizabeth talking to some poor woman who was almost in tears.

What he had seen of Meyer, he liked very much. He held out his hand.

"Simon Beaumont. See you went to my old school."

"Charterhouse? Yes, I was there from fifty-four. What about you?"

"Bit later." Meyer was obviously older than he'd thought. "Now I just wanted to say I've been very impressed indeed by what you've had to say so far. Can't wait to hear the rest. Well done."

"Thanks," said Meyer. "And I must say I'm delighted by the uptake. I hadn't expected to get so many."

"Well, we've all got our backs to the wall. It's nice to see something that holds out some promise of a move forward. However slight."

Simon made his way after that to the coffee queue and found himself standing next to the most stunning girl. She was dressed in full Sloane regalia: white ruffled shirt, Liberty print skirt—bit too long, Simon thought, covered most of what were clearly the most glorious legs—pale beige Gucci shoes with a chain, hair held back with a velvet band. Elizabeth was very scornful of the whole Sloane tribe, said they were dinosaurs. Simon had always thought the girls at least were lovely.

"Hello," he said.

She smiled at him. "Hello."

"Have you sampled the coffee yet?"

"Yes, unfortunately. I'm having tea this time. I'd advise you to do the same." She held out a small hand, complete with gold signet ring (naturally). "How do you do. Lucinda Cowper."

"Simon Beaumont. Extremely nice to meet you, Lucinda. Er, are you here with your husband?"

"Yes. We've been fairly lucky so far, but goodness, what terrible stories we've heard. Come and meet him—we're over there, see, with that dear girl, the widow."

"Oh, thank you. Yes, I will. May I collect my wife, bring her over?"

"Of course," she said pleasantly.

She had a sweet, rather careful smile, showing very pretty teeth; there was something altogether careful about her, he couldn't quite put his finger on it, she was slightly subdued, not as bubbly as her breed usually were. But lovely and so sexy . . . Oh, for God's sake, Beaumont, get a grip.

He went over to Elizabeth.

"Come and meet some new friends," he said.

"I saw you talking to one of them. She didn't exactly seem to be wearing a three-piece suit and stout boots." But she smiled and followed him just the same.

Simon studied Nigel with some interest. Here was a classic Name, very public school, tall and slim, fair-haired, formally dressed, possibly a bit dim—a most unlikely husband for the delicious Lucinda.

He liked Catherine Morgan very much; she was rather pretty too, he thought, with her great grey eyes, and in spite of looking exhausted, she managed to chat to him quite cheerfully about what she was doing and how she was coping. Which wasn't very well, she said; she had had to make a decision to take her children out of their private schools the term before, and send them to the local state primary.

"Of course, I know that's not exactly the end of the world, but they both loved their other schools and were doing so well, and had lots of nice friends, and it's very different for them. Especially Freddie, he's quite bright and wants to do well, and he's constantly teased for being a swot. I feel so guilty."

Simon said he couldn't imagine anything worse. "And at that age, it's so hard for them to understand. God, what a mess. Do you work?"

"Well, I do. But it's very, very low-calibre work, I'm afraid. And terribly badly paid. It was the only job I could get that let me be home after school. But at least it's something. It gets me out of the house, and it helps a bit."

"How old are your children?" asked Elizabeth.

"Freddie's eight and Caroline's six."

"How lovely. Perfect ages, I always think. They must be such a comfort to you."

"Yes, they are, of course. Er . . . what about you, what do you do?"

"Oh, I work in advertising."

"Goodness, how interesting."

"Yes, it is sometimes," she said, and Simon loved her in that moment, for making it sound nothing special in front of this sweetly unfortunate girl.

"And Lucinda, what do you do?"

"I work in publishing. I'm just a PA, nothing the least bit clever."

"Oh, come on, darling, don't put yourself down," said Nigel, adding rather pompously, "she's always doing that."

"I'm not," said Lucinda, and her voice was intensely irritated suddenly. "And don't talk about me as if I wasn't there."

Ah, discord in paradise, thought Simon.

"Sorry, darling. Sorry."

"And where do you live?" said Catherine.

"Oh, Chelsea. Yes. Cadogan Square."

Simon couldn't remember when he had met anyone quite so delicious.

☙

Debbie was sitting with the nice hand-holding couple from the row in front. They had remained in their seats at the start of the coffee break, looking quite shell-shocked. It was Flora who had smiled at them, invited them to join their party for coffee; the woman had been pleased and said how nice that would be, but her husband said nothing, simply followed her.

Flora and Richard went off to get the coffee; Debbie smiled rather awkwardly at the couple.

"Hello, I'm Debbie Fielding."

"Mary and Michael Gardner," said Mary.

"So—what did you think?"

"About going to court, do you mean? Oh, we were quite impressed by Mr. Meyer, weren't we, dear? But we don't think we'd contemplate any further risks. Trouble enough already."

"Yes, I can understand that," said Debbie.

Michael stood up. "I'm just going to the cloakroom, Mary. Won't be long."

"All right, see you later." She looked after him anxiously, then confided in Debbie: "He was very reluctant to come, but I said we should. See if we could gain anything from the evening."

She certainly wasn't what Debbie had expected; her voice was pleasant, but in no way posh, and she wore a twinset and a pleated skirt, and rather old-fashioned, highly polished court shoes.

"And you?" she said to Debbie. "Are you and your husband Names?"

"Er, no," Debbie said. "We're here with my mother-in-law, Flora Fielding, the first to speak."

"Yes," said Mary. "You must be very proud of her."

Debbie longed to say that she wasn't, but it seemed necessary to be polite.

"Yes, of course," she said.

"Well, you're very fortunate," said Mary, "not to be directly involved.

It has been so dreadful for us. And the worst thing— Oh, I do hope you don't mind my talking to you, but I've been bottling it up for so long— Michael won't let me talk about it."

"No," said Debbie. "No, of course I don't mind."

"The worst thing of all has been his pride. The loss of his pride, rather. He was so proud of being invited to become a Name. His parents were quite—quite modest people. For him it was a great honour, a bit like getting his Member of the British Empire . . ."

"Oh really?" said Debbie politely.

"Oh yes. Perhaps not quite as good; that was really wonderful, going into Buckingham Palace, sitting in that wonderful room, watching Michael actually being spoken to by the Queen, and you know, she pins on the medal herself. I always thought some—some lackey would do that. Anyway, Michael was invited into Lloyd's when his firm went public. He was managing director, you see, and there was a lot of publicity in the paper about it, and someone who'd known someone on the board had rung him up and said he was a Members' Agent at Lloyd's and had Michael ever considered becoming a Name. Oh, he was so excited! The day he joined, he came back terribly impressed. He said they'd really made him feel like someone, and he'd seen the underwriting room, and Lord Nelson's telescope, and then they served him lunch and congratulated him on becoming a Name. They gave him a certificate and, oh dear, he was so proud of that, he hung it on the wall of his study. I don't need to tell you it's not there anymore."

"No, I'm sure not."

"And of course they told him the risks were negligible and for several years, we did get quite a lot of money. And Michael liked to boast about it a bit. I'd hear him saying, 'Oh, I'm a Name at Lloyd's, you know' when we were entertaining and it seemed quite harmless to me. But that's what I mean about his pride. When they started demanding money—oh, two years ago—he didn't even tell me at first."

"He didn't tell you!"

"No. He couldn't bring himself to. It wasn't just that he thought I'd worry, he thought he'd look foolish. I only found out when he was ill and I discovered he'd cancelled the medical insurance. By which time he owed a lot of money. Almost as much as our house in Guildford is worth. It was a dreadful shock. But that didn't matter to him nearly as much as having to confess to me. And he won't talk about it to anyone else, he won't even tell our children. I had a terrible time getting him to come here this evening."

"So what are you going to do?" asked Debbie. She felt genuinely sympathetic.

"Well, we can sell the house and buy somewhere much smaller. But that will only be this year's debt. Goodness knows how we'll manage next time."

"It's awful. I'm so sorry."

"Thank you, dear, that's kind of you. Oh, I see your mother-in-law coming back now. She's more the sort of person I think you'd expect to be a Name—but you know, there are an awful lot of people like us, much more ordinary people, who should never have been brought in in the first place, but who were, well, dazzled by it all. As Michael was."

"Yes," said Debbie. "Yes, I hadn't realised that."

George Meyer was back on the platform. He smiled into the room; he had a very nice smile, Elizabeth noticed.

"Right. Back to business. I can see almost no one has gone, which means that everyone wants to explore the fraud possibility. Our very first task must be to find a good solicitor, preferably with a sound knowledge of Lloyd's, who can confirm whether or not we have a case.

"Now, as far as I can see, there is one very difficult decision to be taken. Who, precisely, do we sue?"

He had everyone's attention. Looking round, Flora was impressed that she was the only person doing so; everyone's eyes were fixed on Meyer. She felt profoundly glad she had come to the meeting; if nothing else, it had created a camaraderie in a shorter time than she would have believed possible. And it was a very positive, almost excited camaraderie.

"Anyway," Meyer was saying, "I discussed the problem with my accountant, who came back to me with an interesting idea. 'I don't think you should sue Lloyd's as a whole,' he said. 'The law protects the Council and all the others are like stallholders in a marketplace. Your best bet is to concentrate on the specifically named companies which have let you down.' And that, of course, is what we should do—in my view. Step forward, therefore, Members' Agents, Jackson and Bond. I don't know if we could ever prove conclusively that they knew there was big trouble brewing yet failed to warn us when we joined. But it's worth a damn good try. They certainly piled us recklessly into the Westfield Bradley Group. And unlike some other agents, they did little or nothing to switch us out of WBG into syndicates with a better track record, which I believe it was their duty to do.

"Now there is clearly much more to be said; but there is one other crucial thing. This is going to cost us a great deal of money. But in my view, if the lawyers don't get our money, then sooner or later Lloyd's will. So to all intents and purposes it will be Lloyd's money we are spending, which I find a comforting thought. Anyway, that's quite enough from me; you are invited to stay for further refreshment and I shall be delighted to talk to anyone personally. Thank you all so much again."

There was a spontaneous burst of applause. Simon stood up and said, "I'm sure you would like to join me in thanking George Meyer for all his hard work, and for a most inspiring evening. I for one will undoubtedly be signing up."

He might have asked me, Elizabeth thought. It wasn't actually Lloyd's money that he'd be using, whatever Mr. Meyer might say; it was his—theirs—and she felt suddenly and fiercely angry.

"We're going," whispered Lucinda. "Lovely to have met you both. I think your husband and Nigel have swapped cards. Bye!"

"Bye," said Elizabeth, forcing a smile, and then she caught up with Simon in the queue to talk to Meyer and said she was sorry, but she had to go; she had a lot of work to do still, and she'd get a cab home.

"Fine," he said, clearly unaware of the edge in her voice. "See you later, darling, thank you for coming."

"Oh, it was nothing," she said, and left. Had she stayed she would have been still more annoyed, for Simon, having talked very briefly to Meyer, was now pushing his way through the crowd, trying to catch up with Catherine Morgan. He had been very moved by her story and her obvious loneliness, and he had been impressed by her courage in getting up to speak. He felt that here was one victim at least he could help. He tapped her on the shoulder; she turned round, flushed as she saw him and dropped her bag—the contents went all over the floor.

"Oh gosh, I'm so sorry," she said, as Simon dived down to recapture lipsticks, Biros, a diary. "Thank you very much."

"That's perfectly all right. Think I've got everything. There you are. Look, here's my card. I was thinking, I might well be able to find you a job. We employ a large number of secretaries and two of the girls are leaving next week. Come and see me if you're interested."

"Golly," she said, "how terribly kind. Of course I'd be interested. But I don't think you realise, I can only do school hours."

"Yes, I realise it very well. I'm sure we can work something out. I'd like to help. As one Lloyd's victim to another."

"Well, thank you," said Catherine, her big grey eyes brilliant as she looked at him, "that is extremely kind. I—well, I don't know what to say."

"You don't have to say anything now," Simon said. "Oh, God, I must go back, I've left my scarf on my seat. Bye, Catherine, see you again, I hope."

⁓

Debbie and Richard had gone home; Flora had been delayed talking to the nice Mary Gardner; she was buttoning up her coat and found herself near to Simon as they made their way to the door. He held it open for her.

"Thank you. Quite an evening, wasn't it?" she said.

"Extremely interesting, I thought."

"Me too." She held out her hand. "Flora Fielding. Are you on your own?"

"Yes, I am, as a matter of fact. My wife's just left—she had some work to attend to. How do you do, Mrs. Fielding. Simon Beaumont."

"Flora, please. My family have left too."

He smiled at her; he was very attractive, she thought, with his thick greying hair and smiling brown eyes.

"Now tell me," he said as they headed for the main door. "What did you really think? Will you be joining him?"

"Yes, I'll come on board. For a while at least."

"Oh, I'm delighted. Me too. I was pretty impressed by him, I must say. And I enjoyed your little speech."

"Thank you."

"Where do you come from? Are you a Londoner?"

"No, thank God. I live in Wales. Wet Wales."

"You're not going back tonight, I hope?"

"No, I'm staying with my son and his family. In . . . in Ealing." She could never quite bring herself to say Acton, it sounded so dreadful. He looked at his watch. "Bit of a trek to Ealing. Have you got a car?"

"Yes, but I don't know if I'll ever find it again. I left it in a multistorey car park near Leicester Square."

"Mine's there too," he said, smiling at her again. "Look, why don't I escort you there, make sure you do find it. I hate to think of you wandering those dangerous streets on your own."

"That's very kind of you, but—"

"No buts," he said. "I never leave a damsel in distress."

"I'm far from being a damsel, I'm afraid."

"Nonsense. So—impertinent question, but it's been a night for truth-telling. How bad are your losses?"

"Well, I'm doing pretty nicely so far. At losing, I mean. Where do you think it will end?"

"God knows," Simon said.

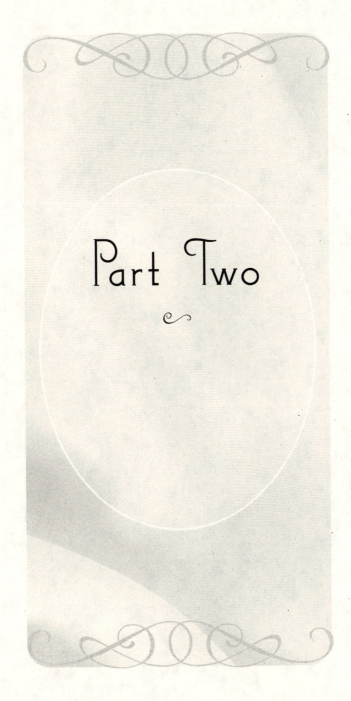

Part Two

Chapter 10

It seemed to go on all night, the crying. He got up three times to try and comfort her, to take her in his arms; she shook him off, told him she hated him, buried her head in the pillow and wept on. Finally, somewhere near two o'clock, it stopped; in the silence he lay and hated himself.

How had it happened, that with the very best of intentions he had brought this upon her, his beloved youngest daughter, forced her—as she saw it—to bid farewell to a pony that was more dear to her than anything else in the world. Simon's remorse and guilt were huge; he would have taken and borne all her grief if he could.

"Can't I keep him in London?" she had said. "There are livery stables here, aren't there? I could see him more probably than now."

And he had said, yes, she could; but asked her to consider how would he feel, her beautiful, free-spirited Boy, used to the hills and valleys of Sussex, of going out hunting on frosty mornings, taking fences, half flying across fields; how would he be, confined to a stable yard in Kensington, say, and limited to a neat and tidy canter across Hyde Park? They had investigated livery stables in the country too; less expensive, but how could she ride him without a home to go from, without the means to get there?

It was terrible, the creeping tentacles of this thing: the unhappiness taking hold of more and more people, innocent people. So he had only been acting for the best, a decade ago, thinking to improve his lot and the lot of his family, to bring happiness, security, pleasure to all of them.

Of what value was that to them now?

⌇

"I'm going back to work," Debbie said. This was something of an exaggeration, but she wanted to upset Richard as much as she possibly could.

"Debbie, you can't do that. You know we agreed—"

"We agreed lots of things, Richard. Like we'd always be honest with each other."

"Debbie, please. It really doesn't help, raking that over endlessly. I've told you so many times how sorry I am."

"Yes, you have. Funnily enough, I don't seem to feel much better about it. Anyway, don't you want to hear about my job?"

"What about the children? Who's going to look after them?"

"After school, you can. You're here, aren't you, and it's not rocket science. Rachel's at school now, and you can pick her up quite easily, before you get the others. That's what I do. After that, it's pretty straightforward, just giving them their tea and making sure they do their homework. And then bathing them, of course. I'll be home long before supper and I can still do that. I think you're getting off pretty lightly really."

"Debbie, I can't do all that! I have work of my own to do, you know that."

"Yes, well, you'll have to do it later in the evening." He looked so alarmed, she suddenly gave in and grinned at him. "Oh, and I did say, didn't I, it's only two days a week. Monday and Wednesday. So that really won't be too difficult, will it?"

They had settled into a truce; like all truces it was uncomfortable, but it was either that or leaving him. She was still desperate about the school fees; she had told Richard to make sure the children could leave their schools as soon as possible; he hadn't argued, but when Emma came back on the first day appointed form captain and Alex had won a place by the end of the week in the under-tens rugby team, he had asked her if she was quite sure that leaving would be best for them.

"I really can do at least two terms, and I know I'll have a new job by the summer, so for their sake, Debbie, couldn't you—"

And of course she had given in; the only concession she won was that Rachel at least would start at the local primary with all her friends from play school. But she was left hurting, and very badly; she had not been exaggerating when she had said she would never trust Richard again. Something had been broken between them, and nothing seemed quite right anymore.

"It's a bit like having permanent indigestion," she confided to Jan, "but all over. And especially when Richard wants to have sex. I just lie there seething and willing him to stop."

Jan said she did that most of the time anyway. "Well, willing Mike to stop, so I can go to sleep. Honestly, Debbie, remember when we couldn't get enough? What happened? Babies, I suppose."

"Babies and housework," sighed Debbie, "and predictability. Sometimes I think if Richard says what I know he's going to say just once more I shall scream. And especially in bed. My God, how do we let them get away with it?"

"So what does he say?" asked Jan with interest.

"He says 'I hope you've got a bit of energy left for me' when he puts the light out. I mean, how erotic is that?"

"Better than Mike. He says, 'How are you feeling?' One of these days I shall tell him."

"No, you won't," said Debbie.

The job Debbie had got was with a PR company. They did a lot of book promotion, but they had recently moved into the health and fitness area, and as well as a couple of health clubs and a range of dance wear, had taken on a line of what they called "body cosmetics"—shower gels, body lotions, scrubs, and some special shampoos. The new venture wouldn't pay for a full-time person, but two days a week was just about affordable.

It wasn't exactly her ideal job, but it meant two days a week out of the house, getting dressed up, going into the West End—well, Earl's Court— and actually being with grown-ups. She was very excited. Equally important, it would pay her £8,000 a year, which was almost as much as she had been earning when she had given up last time.

"OK, it's not a king's ransom, but it'll help, won't it?" she said to Richard. "Oh, and not one farthing of it is to go towards the school fees, OK?"

Richard was silent.

The company, Know How Promotions, was run by a husband-and-wife team, Anna and Peter Carter; Peter stayed in the back room and did the hard slog, and Anna went out and got the business. Debbie, who was uneasy with any kind of hard sell, was nevertheless terribly impressed by her. Anna was tiny, with cropped dark hair and large brown eyes, and an energy that seemed to explode out of her. Her voice, which was swift and clipped, would fly through presentations, blinding prospective clients with facts and figures, finishing by telling them they couldn't afford not to employ Know How. Peter was much more laid-back and apparently rather slow on the uptake, but painstaking and astonishingly efficient; they made a formidable team. They employed four other full-time people. "We've never tried part-timers before, never quite believed in it," Anna said to Debbie, "and I'm still not sure, to be truthful with you. You've got to prove me wrong."

Debbie was determined that she would.

e⁓

"Mrs. Fielding, isn't it? Are you all right?"

Flora had been hurrying through Leadenhall Market, anxious to get to Monument tube station; she had caught her heel in the cobblestones and it snapped. She was standing balancing on one leg, trying to work out what she could do to effect a temporary repair, muttering furiously under her breath. She looked up and for a moment couldn't think who it was.

"It's Simon Beaumont. We met at the Lloyd's meeting, nearly a month ago."

"Oh—yes. Yes, of course. I'm so sorry."

"That's quite all right. Is there something wrong with your shoe?"

"Yes, I broke my heel on the stones in the market. That'll teach me to dress unsuitably. I should be in grandmotherly lace-ups, not tottering about two and a half inches above the ground."

"I can't think of anything less suitable for you than lace-ups," he said. "Here, let me see. Ah, yes, completely snapped. Oh dear. Where are you heading for?"

"The tube station and thence to Paddington. I'll just have to hop. Bloody stones. They're very picturesque, but—"

"They are, aren't they? You know, this is where all our troubles started, just about three hundred years ago."

"What do you mean?"

"This was coffeehouse country. And Mr. Edward Lloyd had the initiative to open one near Tower Wharf. All the shipowners used to go there, as did the merchants who dabbled in marine insurance. That was the beginning of Lloyd's." He smiled at her. "Look, I've got an appointment in Park Lane in half an hour's time. My driver's got nothing to do this afternoon except wait for me. He can take you on. And you could buy some slippers or something on the way."

"I couldn't possibly. It would be much too kind."

"Now how could something be too kind?" he said. "Too cruel perhaps, but—anyway, come along. My office is a hundred yards away, so if you can just hobble there . . . I'd offer my arm if it wouldn't seem a little forward of me."

"It wouldn't," she said, taking his arm gratefully. "So where is your office? And what does it do?"

"It's a small merchant bank. I'm one of the directors. Here it is. Now if you wouldn't mind just waiting down here in reception a few minutes . . ."

❧

"Fascinating place, that market," Simon said as the car passed it. "Do you know, every so often they release a falcon into it, very, very early, to catch the pigeons. The tourists don't want to be showered with pigeon sh—poo. What are you doing here anyway? Why aren't you in Wales?"

"I came up to have lunch with my Members' Agent."

"Did he have anything cheerful to tell you?"

"Of course not. Another difficult year, he said."

"Mine too. Oh well. Have you heard anything from George Meyer?"

"Not really. Have you?"

"I had a very good lunch with him, and I've volunteered to help him look for a likely solicitor, but he was waiting to get some more firm responses in before we went on. Everyone might have expressed great interest that night, but a lot of it has evaporated. People are scared of further risk. So if you haven't written yet, do. I don't want to influence you, but it is at least something we can do."

"Yes, I know. And I have been meaning to write. I will."

"Good for you. I think it's worth a shot. Although I'm a bit disappointed there's no action yet. I wouldn't mind if it was just me, you know, but it's hurting the family now. My twelve-year-old daughter, Tilly she's called, isn't speaking to me. Our house in the country has to go and her pony with it. We've had our last summer there, it's on the market."

"Where is it?"

"West Sussex. Lovely place. And I keep a boat near Chichester—my wife calls her the love of my life."

"My husband used to sail," said Flora. "I could never see the fun of it myself."

"Oh, some of my happiest hours are out there with the *Lizzie,* that's her name, the nearest thing to flying on this earth."

"Why Lizzie?"

"It's my wife's name. Well, she's Elizabeth, but . . . Anyway, back to Tilly and the horse. She adores that animal. And I feel utterly wretched about it. She cries herself to sleep every night."

"That is very sad," said Flora, and meant it. "Have you considered livery?"

"Yes, but London would be ghastly for him, and—well, it's just not very practical, I'm afraid."

There was a silence, then Flora said, quite casually, "Well if it's a matter of not having anywhere for him to go, I have a couple of empty stalls at the moment. I've had to sell one of my hunters—thanks again to Messrs. Lloyd's. I'd be very willing to have him. How big is he?"

"Fifteen hands. He's an eventer."

"He sounds lovely. And I could ride him for her, keep him exercised. Your daughter could come down in the school holidays. It's quite a big house. The riding's a bit rough, but at least it wouldn't be that awful agonising farewell. Think about it, I really mean it."

"Daddy, oh Daddy, I love you so so much. Thank you, thank you . . ." Tilly was home at Chadwick House on a weekend exeat.

"Darling, don't thank me. Thank this very nice lady. It's she who's going to have Boy."

"And this very nice lady is—who?" said Elizabeth when Tilly had gone off to get herself a drink. Her voice was rather cold.

"She's called Flora Fielding. Remember? She was the first to speak on the platform at the Lloyd's meeting, and I got chatting to her later. After you'd gone off early."

"It seems an awful lot to do for a complete stranger," Elizabeth said.

"Do you know," he said, "she doesn't feel like a complete stranger. It's a very strong bond, this business. We're all in it together. It's the one good thing about it."

"Yes, well, you certainly seem keen on sharing it with George Meyer."

"Oh for heaven's sake. It's something I might be able to do, Elizabeth, rather than just chewing my nails to the quick and staring into the darkness."

"Yes, but—" She stopped. They had had one row about his not consulting her; and he had been completely incapable of understanding her anger.

"It's my money, I'm not asking you to contribute."

"Simon, any money you don't have, I have to find."

"That's a filthy lie," he said. "I'm probably going to have to sell the *Lizzie,* and that would support me through this lawsuit. Oh, for God's sake, what is the point of this discussion! I thought you'd be pleased about Flora Fielding having Boy. Obviously I was wrong."

She felt remorse suddenly.

"I'm sorry. I am really. And it is very good of her. I just feel—well, we should be giving her something for it. Towards Boy's keep."

"I offered, obviously. She said at the moment it wouldn't be much—apart from vet's bills, of course. He'll be out a lot of the year. And she seems to have a fair bit of land."

"And when can he go down there? Boy I mean?"

"Probably at half term." As their daughter came back into the room:

"Now, Tilly darling, you do realise, don't you, that you won't be able to see nearly so much of Boy? Wales is a lot farther away."

"Yes, of course. But at least he won't have to be sold, and he'll be happy and I can see him every holiday."

"Tilly, not every holiday, darling," said Elizabeth.

"Why not? Daddy said Mrs. Fielding said I could go and stay in the holidays."

"Yes, well, that won't always be easy. And you might not like her. She might not like you. I really think, Simon, we should perhaps take Tilly down to meet Mrs. Fielding before we even accept this offer. And then we could check the place out. I mean, it might be some fearful dump, you don't know."

"I think I do know," said Simon, "but yes, I agree that she and Tilly should meet. We could go down next weekend even, if it suited her. And if we could take Tilly out of school again."

"Oh, they won't mind," said Tilly blithely.

"Well, I'll ask. Toby's home next weekend, we could make a family outing of it. Anyway, what I think you should do first, Tilly darling, is write Mrs. Fielding a very, very nice letter saying thank you. And maybe send her some pictures of Boy, so she—"

"—can see how beautiful he is. Yes, I will. I'll go and write to her now. Oh I'm so happy. I can't believe how happy I am."

❧

It was on 10 October that it happened. Lucinda would never forget the date: 10.10.89, so easy to remember, it seemed somehow gouged out in her brain.

She had actually had a good day. Graham had been very pleased with a report of a manuscript she had done, said she had made some really good points that he had missed; and Justin, the art director, told her she was looking particularly tasty. She was wearing a new pale-pink V-neck sweater she'd bought herself as a present—she was buying herself a lot of presents at the moment, she felt she deserved them—and a much shorter skirt than she usually wore (another present). This made her think of Blue, who was always telling her she had the best legs he'd ever seen, and why did she keep them hidden under a series of tablecloths; but she managed to push that thought down and concentrate on Justin's compliment instead.

And then she had met her friend Katy for lunch. Katy worked for a small art gallery in Cork Street and had just become engaged.

"So when's the wedding? And where?" Lucinda said, surprised to find she could actually whip up a degree of interest at least.

"Oh, in the country. Mummy would die if it wasn't. And next June—how corny is that? But it is the perfect month, don't you think, roses everywhere, and it might even be nice weather, you never know. And Lucinda, please please will you be matron of honour?"

Lucinda flushed with pleasure and said she'd love to, and thought how amazingly lucky she was to have such good friends, and how without even knowing it, they were all helping her get through her misery; and after an hour of discussing the wedding and its date, she returned to the office feeling almost happy.

She and Nigel were going out that evening to see *When Harry Met Sally*. Going to the cinema was one of the things that worked best for Lucinda at the moment; a total absorption in the experience, an evening taken care of with no need to talk much, and then straight home to bed. Quite late: which meant Nigel usually went straight to sleep. That was a big help as well.

He came to collect her from the office. She was still clearing up and told reception to send him along to her office; he came in looking very happy and kissed her.

"Something to celebrate," he said, shutting the door and then lowering his voice. "I got my results today. Of the, you know, the test."

"And?" said Lucinda, suddenly nervous.

"And it's not too bad. I don't exactly have a high, you know, high sperm count, apparently, in fact, it's a little low—but there's no reason why we shouldn't be able to have a family. Isn't that wonderful?"

"It is, really wonderful," said Lucinda, and meant it. It would be wonderful for her too she thought.

"Yes. So we just have to keep working at it, darling. Be fun, won't it?" He blushed.

"Nigel, I'm so, so happy," said Lucinda, shrinking slightly from the thought of working at it. "Now look, I just have to go to the loo, make myself look a bit more presentable."

"You look pretty presentable to me," he said, "but then you always do. OK, I'll wait for you here."

"I won't be a minute. Help yourself to a book, there's that new one on the ancient Egyptians you were interested in."

She took her time in the loo; putting on some fresh lipstick, spraying herself with perfume, even gingering up her hair with her tongs, humming under her breath.

She walked out, after smiling at herself in the mirror, thinking that things really were getting better, thinking that even the sex would be more bearable now, with the thought of a baby to help her along, and she did a little skip as she walked along the corridor into her office.

"Sorry I was so long, darling, I—"

And stopped. For he was standing with his back to her desk, white-faced and almost hollow-eyed, one hand in his pocket, looking at her with such intense hostility she was quite frightened.

"Nigel," she said, "whatever is it? What's the matter?"

"What the fuck are you doing with these?" he said, shaking something at her; he never swore, the strongest word he ever used was "shit," and that only in the most dire situations. "What the fuck have you been up to?"

She couldn't see for a moment what it was he was holding. And then she realised. It was what she had kept so carefully, so fearfully, in her desk drawer, only taking them into the house singly at the weekends, tucked into her wallet, wrapped in tissue: her contraceptive pills.

At the very first, he had assumed she had been taking them simply to avoid pregnancy, had been lying to him, had not wanted a child at all, had accused her of the ultimate selfishness. "What were you worrying about, Lucinda? Ruining your figure? Giving up your job?" But even as she protested, tears of panic streaming down her face, the second horror hit him.

"You've been having an affair, haven't you? That's what you've been doing. All that working late, having to go away, I thought it seemed odd—you know, I'm not quite the simpleton you clearly think—but I kept telling myself you'd never do that, it wasn't in you. I thought you were incapable of it. That's it, isn't it, you've been having an affair?"

And yes, she had said finally, calm suddenly; and he became calmer too, said who was it, that he had to know. Was it someone at work, was it one of their friends . . . ?

They were home now; after a totally silent cab ride.

"No, Nigel, it isn't one of our friends, it's no one you know," she said.

"So who then? I would rather know, Lucinda. I shall go mad otherwise."

"Really," she said, "there's no point telling you. Leave it, please."

"Are you still seeing him?"

And, "No," she said, "I'm not," thankful for that at least, that she could claim it was over, that she had decided not to stay with him.

"And why was that?"

"Well, I—" She couldn't give him the real reason, that it was because of the money; it would sound terrible, so open to misinterpretation.

"When did it end then? Perhaps you'd be good enough to tell me that? It seems odd that you're still taking those—those things."

"I'm not," she said. "I stopped the moment I ended the affair. I felt I had to give our marriage every possible chance, and obviously having a baby, or trying to have a baby, was a huge part of that."

"How good of you."

She was silent.

"I do want to know," he said, "when it ended. I really feel I have a right to know. To know everything. I'm not sure why," he added. He sounded bewildered, the old Nigel, gentle and good. "It wasn't the money, was it? You didn't stay with me because of the money? I did wonder where on earth you disappeared to that night, rushing out like that, coming back without the coffee."

"What coffee?" she said.

"The coffee you said you were going to get. So was that it? When you decided to stay with me?"

"Well . . . yes," she said, watching herself walking into his trap, absolutely unable to prevent herself. "Yes, it was."

"So it wasn't loyalty that drove you back to me, or a desire to keep your marriage vows, or even love. It was money—"

"Nigel, please. You don't understand."

"You are disgusting," he said, and his pale, decent face was suddenly flushed and ugly, distorted with pain and rage. "You are utterly disgusting. I cannot imagine how I could ever have loved you. Just get out, would you? I don't care where you go, you can sleep in the street for all I care. Just get out."

"Yes, all right," she said, her voice very low, and she picked up her bag and walked towards the door.

"Of course, you could go and stay at Claridge's or the Savoy with the money I gave you. And take your fancy man with you. Why don't you, Lucinda, why don't you do that?"

And then he put his head in his arms and started to sob; and she looked at him, and thought she could hardly endure having put him in such pain, and she went over and placed her hands on his shoulders.

"I'm so sorry," she said, "so very, very sorry. I do hope one day you'll be able to believe it."

And she walked out, pulling the door to behind her.

Chapter 11

Debbie was trying very hard to be a good wife. She knew Richard deserved it, because he was being so great about her working; of course he still felt guilty about lying to her, but just the same, it wasn't exactly easy for him, having to leave all his marking and organisational work until she got home, making sure he wasn't late to collect the children, and that there was something for their tea, and OK, it was only what she did, what most mothers did, but it didn't come so easily to men. And it meant she could have this wonderful time, for two days every week when she was doing something so well that someone was paying her for it. It made her feel sleek and cool and clever, far from the dithery Debbie who had become so familiar to her, always late, the house always in chaos. She was still like that at home, of course, but in the office she was a byword for efficiency, with a slickly neat desk, a perfectly planned diary. She got more done in her two days, Anna often told her, than most people did in five.

"Well, it's so mind-concentrating," she had said. "I know I can't waste a minute, from the moment I hit the desk."

She loved it, loved the work; she enjoyed presentations and was going to be extremely good at them, Anna had said, having allowed her to assist on a couple; sensing when a cool prospective client became enthusiastic, picking up on what they liked and running with it. "It's taken me years to learn to do that," Anna said, slightly ruefully, after one particularly successful pitch for a series of books on finance for women. "Who taught you?"

"My husband," said Debbie briefly, and in a way it was true. She had learned to read Richard's mind and capitalise on the knowledge very early in their marriage.

And so she had suggested half term in Wales, and of course everyone had been thrilled, especially Richard.

"I know I was against you working," he said carefully, "but I think I was wrong. It suits you."

And she had been really nice to Flora, and found it surprisingly easy. And they had all been having a lovely time until . . .

"We have some visitors coming the day after tomorrow," Flora said. "I do hope you'll like them." The visitors were the Beaumonts. "He was at the Lloyd's meeting," Flora said. "I met him after you'd gone. Charming, absolutely charming."

Debbie knew what charming meant. Posh. Smooth. Public school. She managed to smile.

"And he's bringing his wife and family. I've offered to have the daughter's pony here, they've got to sell their country house and . . ."

They arrived about midday, the man, yes, oh so charming, with his perfect haircut and smile and his Barbour and green Wellies, and his wife, who was actually rather beautiful, and turned out to have an incredibly high-powered job; in fact, she was exactly the sort of person Debbie would have liked to be. But the child, she was really ridiculous, a simpering, irritating little thing, with her long blond hair and her big blue eyes and a voice so plummy you practically needed an interpreter; she could see Flora thought she was absolutely wonderful, that she'd grow up into exactly the sort of girl Richard should have married, if Flora had had her way. And the boy, he'd just been a joke; he'd stayed in the Land Rover at first, had sat there listening to his Walkman until the man called him from the doorway, said, "Come on, Toby, come along in," and he'd reluctantly got out of the car and walked across the yard and into the house;

and then shaken hands with Flora and everyone in sight, saying how do you do.

"And where are you at school, Toby?" Flora had said, and "Eton," he'd said (of course). Debbie studied him, with his floppy haircut and his blue-and-white striped shirt and blazer—a blazer, for God's sake, what sort of a boy these days wore a blazer?—and thought how much she'd hate it if Alexander turned out like that.

And they'd all stood there in the kitchen, drinking sherry, apart from the children who'd been given lemonade. "Homemade, hope it's all right," Flora had said, with her most annoying smile, while the visitors blah-blahed away, and the girl, Tilly—Tilly, what a name—brought out some pictures of her pony to show them.

"Oh, he's such a gorgeous chap. So beautiful," Flora had said, gush-ing, "sweet face"—as if a horse could have a face that was sweet or sour or anything really.

Sherry finished, they all went out to inspect the stables; Debbie said she'd make the salad for lunch and was furiously chopping cucumber when Toby, the boy, came back in.

"Hi," she said. "Finished viewing the accommodation?"

"What? Oh yes, thanks." He grinned at her, rather shyly. "I'm not very horse-minded. Don't like them that much, to tell you the truth. In fact, I hate riding. How about you?"

"I've never tried it, but I'm sure I'd hate it too. Too far from the ground. What do you like doing? Want some more lemonade?"

"Thanks. Well, I like skiing." He would, Debbie thought. "And rugby. Oh, and tennis. I love tennis."

"I like tennis," said Debbie, "but I never manage to play enough to get good. Only at uni, really."

"Well, I play at school, of course. And rugby. I'm hoping to get in a team, but I'm a bit small."

"And do you like school?"

"Yeah, I love it. It's great."

"You don't get homesick at all?" she said.

"No way." He looked quite surprised. "I've been away since I was nine, so I'm quite used to it. It's fun, your friends around you all the time."

How odd they were, these upper-class people, she thought, sending little boys of eight or nine away from home when they didn't have to. What was the point of having them at all?

"This is really kind of Mrs. Fielding," said Toby, "having Boy."

"I think she wants to," said Debbie. "She doesn't like the stables being empty."

"No, maybe not. Still, jolly nice of her. Tilly is just so happy about it. She was crying herself to sleep every night."

"Poor Tilly," said Debbie politely.

"So, if she can still get to see him in the holidays, that's the answer," Toby said. "She can't take him to school with her, anyway."

"I shouldn't think she could," said Debbie, laughing. "What school would take a pony?"

"Oh, some do," said Toby earnestly. "I have one friend, he plays polo, and he takes his ponies to school. He's at Millfield, they have a polo team, you know."

"No," said Debbie, "I didn't know that actually. Pass me those tomatoes, would you, Toby, please."

There was a lot of noise in the yard; and then everyone came back into the kitchen, talking and laughing.

"Let's have lunch then," said Flora. "Hope nobody minds the kitchen. Oh, Debbie dear, how sweet of you to do the salad. Now Tilly, would you like to help Emma lay the table and Simon, you give Elizabeth another sherry and have one yourself. And Richard, you could open that wine."

Debbie had to admit by the end of lunch that she quite liked Simon Beaumont. He was incredibly relaxed and easy to talk to. He flirted with her just enough to please and not embarrass her, and made her feel much more interesting than she really was. He asked her about her work, said it must be very difficult to combine it with running a family, and she'd taken a huge breath and said she couldn't possibly do it without Richard's help—while smiling across the table at Richard, who was clearly pleased by this acknowledgment—and then Elizabeth Beaumont had said rather unexpectedly that she could never have done her job without Simon's help when the children were young.

"He was marvellous, well ahead of his time; he could change a nappy when most men hardly knew which end of a baby it should go on, and he'd go to plays and concerts at school if I absolutely couldn't get there."

"Very ahead of his time," Debbie said, grinning at Simon; and then

Elizabeth started asking Debbie about her job, which she found almost embarrassing, given Elizabeth's own awe-inspiring status, but she seemed genuinely interested and said her agency had considered having a PR wing, but she'd given up the idea because she'd never found anyone of sufficient calibre to run it. "Maybe you could do it for me in a few years' time," she said to Debbie, and Simon said from what he'd seen of Debbie, she'd be running her own agency by then; and it was all rather fun in the end. And then Emma, who was clearly completely captivated by Tilly, as small girls tend to be by their just-slightly elders, asked her if she would come and see Flora's horses with her and Tilly was endlessly patient and led Emma up and down the yard on Becky, Flora's gentle old mare, for about an hour, while they continued to talk; and it wasn't until they had all gone and Flora had taken the children for a walk, that Debbie realised that Richard was looking very dark and brooding.

"What on earth's the matter with you?" she said.

"Oh, nothing. You seemed to be enjoying yourself."

"Well, I was. What's wrong with that?"

"You don't usually like those sorts of people."

"I know, but I liked them. I thought they were interesting."

He was silent; then he said, "I suppose that's the sort of setup you'd like. Big smart house, with staff"—the existence of Josie had emerged—"rich successful husband, so you could pursue your own career . . ."

Debbie stared at him. "Richard," she said, "I don't know what you're talking about."

"Yes, you do. You'd like all that and you've got me. Not rich, not successful, and a rotten little house in the suburbs."

"Richard. Honestly. You are so very silly. You are not a failure and it is not a rotten little house, it's home and I love it. Except I wish you wouldn't call it the suburbs, it's West London. It's as bad as your mother calling it Ealing. And I've got you—do you really think I'd be happy with that smoothie?"

"You seemed to be pretty happy at lunch."

"OK, I was happy at lunch. But lunch isn't a marriage. Is it? A marriage is what we've got and it's working pretty well, specially lately. I think we're doing pretty good."

"Do you?" he said, and he put his arms round her waist, rested his head on her breast. "Do you really?"

"Yes," she said, "I really do. And if you come upstairs with me now, I'll show you."

He looked up at her, clearly half shocked, half tempted.

"But Debbie, they might come back, then what would we do?"

"What we used to do, get dressed mega-fast and one of us dive into the loo. Come on, it'll be fun. I really, really want to. Don't you?"

"Well . . . yes. Yes, I do. But—"

"Richard," she said, pulling him up from his chair, slithering her fingers into his fly, "Richard, I do really want to." And it was true, she did, excitement rising into her for the first time in ages. "Come on, then, what are you waiting for?"

But he shook his head, drew away from her, said, "No, no, I wouldn't enjoy it, I'd be worrying all the time. Sorry. Maybe later, tonight?"

But later her desire was stilled, disappointed, and although she let him make love to her, she was haunted by what might have been a few hours earlier and thought that it was not Richard's failure in his work that troubled her but his failure to recognise what she really wanted.

❦

Lucinda supposed a lot of people would have expected her to go back to Blue. This seemed to her absolutely unthinkable. She had entered into a relationship with him, let him fall in love with her, and then broken his heart. According to Lucinda's code of conduct, it was simply unfair to then return to him because it suited her and expect him to be grateful. It would be monstrously selfish and indeed arrogant of her to say, "OK, Blue, bit of a to-do with Nigel, I'm free now, come on over."

The only good thing about the whole mess was that at last she could wear the pink Chanel watch. All the time.

Her parents had been predictably horrified by her separation from Nigel. She had gone down bravely for the weekend following the dreadful Tuesday to tell them; at that point she was staying in a boardinghouse in Victoria. It had been even worse than she feared; her mother had burst into tears and her father had stalked out of the room without a word and shut himself in his study, slamming the door.

"You're making the most terrible mistake," her mother had said, wiping her eyes. "He's such a dear, and so devoted to you. Men like that don't grow on trees, Lucinda. What is it? What's gone wrong?"

"I . . . don't really know. It's impossible to say. The marriage just isn't working."

"Marriages can be made to work," said her mother, "with a bit of determination on both sides. Of course, I always thought you should have started a family sooner. Children cement a marriage. A career isn't everything, you know."

Her father stalked back into the room, glass of gin and tonic in hand, and glared at her.

"I really think you must have taken leave of your senses, Lucinda. You won't find another husband as good as Nigel in a hurry."

"No, I'm sure you're right."

"He hasn't been playing around, I presume? Because if he has, I'll speak to him myself."

"No, Daddy, he hasn't. And please, whatever you do, don't speak to him. He's terribly upset and—"

"I expect he is. Well, in that case, you just go back to him and tell him you want to work things out. I daresay you think it'll be rather exciting, living in London on your own, a single girl again. Well it won't. You'll be lonely and miserable."

"Truly," she said, "truly, I don't like the idea of being on my own."

"Then why—"

"I told you. It just isn't working anymore."

"Well, I think it's a pretty poor show," said her father.

From her sister, Susannah, came much the same. "You're quite mad, Lucinda. He's such a sweetheart, and he adores you. So unless he's actually knocking you about, I think you should go back to him PDQ. Work it out. Marriage isn't always easy, I should know. But it's better than not being married."

Her brothers were slightly more sympathetic. John, the baby, just gave her a hug and said he was very sorry for her and Anthony, always her favourite sibling, said, "I did always think Nigel was a bit—well, you know, not terribly exciting. But such a nice chap, Lucinda, and he seemed absolutely devoted to you."

"Yes, he was."

"Don't let the parents bully you into something you don't want. I'm just afraid you'll be lonely, that's all. Wish I lived in London, then I could keep you company." Anthony was in the army, currently based in Shrivenham, about to be posted to Northern Ireland.

"Well, thanks, Anthony. You're the only person who's even tried to see it my way."

And so it went: on and on.

℮

"Shall we leave this lot, go and have a quiet drink in the bar?"

Elizabeth had been planning on sneaking off herself, going up to bed. She smiled rather cautiously at John Martin, worldwide president of Hunter Pharmaceuticals. The sales conference had gone well; she had sat with Peter Hargreaves watching it, proud of the creative team. It was the big one: the annual Hunter sales conference. Held at Boyle Park, the huge country-house hotel on the Gloucestershire and Warwickshire border, that provided not only accommodation for the entire sales force and top management, and a magnificently equipped conference centre, but also a spa and swimming pool, a nine-hole golf course, and a boating lake.

John always came over from the States for the conference, and Peter and Elizabeth always made speeches. It took place over two days, with one afternoon set aside for the delights of Boyle Park. The advertising work had gone down well; the sales figures, despite the economic downturn, were good; and morale was high. Elizabeth looked around her; the evening had moved into chaos phase, the pre-dinner flirty drinks and the four-course meal over. The men stood in groups, still serious, looking suddenly more handsome in their dinner jackets, and the girls began to join them, smiling and self-conscious, emerging like so many butterflies from their sober suits and neat shirts into brightly coloured silk and chiffon, their legs and bosoms well on display, their sleek hair teased into chignons and ringlets, and everywhere a myriad of bracelets and necklaces and earrings, dangling and swinging and teasing in a cloud of over-heavy perfume. In another hour or two, Elizabeth thought, the hotel would be rocking on its foundations. What exactly was it about conferences that suspended normal moral judgement, that saw otherwise devoted and dutiful young husbands moving into beds and bodies where they had no business to be, and normally well-behaved and self-respecting young

· 121 ·

women encouraging them, luring them even, on their way? It wasn't just the alcohol—in fact, it was hardly the alcohol at all—it was a kind of moral moratorium, a sense of reckless freedom and sexual greed, created not so much by an absence from hearth and home, as by a presence in a shared and oddly isolated country that offered, or rather almost demanded, as full an exploration as possible. And a return from which could be easily and safely accomplished, with the unspoken promise that no mention or even acknowledgment of it need ever be made.

Sitting at her table, watching girls weaving their way rather unsteadily towards the dancing, dreading that someone would feel duty-bound to invite her to dance, Elizabeth was surprised as well as relieved by John's invitation. The previous year he had been a most vigorous member of the disco team; she reminded him of it now as they settled in the comparative quiet of the main bar.

"Oh, don't," he said. "I can't bear to think what a complete moron I must have looked. My fourteen-year-old daughter explained to me in words of very few syllables how obscene it was for anyone over twenty to dance in public. What would you like? Brandy? Whiskey?"

"Oh, more champagne, I think. It ends the evening on such a high."

"I hope it's not over yet. But—fine. I'm a bourbon man myself. I never can quite see the point of wine. I like my stomach lined and warmed and then kept that way. But I expect your husband is a great wine buff?"

"Well, he likes it. And takes a bit of interest in it, I suppose. Not as much as he did," she added, thinking of the fast-emptying cellar in London, the decimated one that had left Chadwick House.

"Oh really? Why is that?"

"It's an expensive hobby."

"So?"

"Oh well, you know. Inflation, children to educate, all that sort of thing," she said quickly. She certainly wasn't going to air their financial troubles with John Martin.

"Right. Well, how do you think it's gone?"

"Very, very well. There's a terrific spirit in the company. And this is a great venue—I really like it."

"Me too. I almost brought my wife—but, you know, I don't really believe in mixing business with pleasure."

This was not what Elizabeth had heard; John took a great deal of pleasure along with his business. And he was actually very attractive; tall and heavily built with a shock of blond hair and startlingly dark-blue eyes beneath a thatch of thick blond eyebrows. And he dressed well too, in cutting-edge suits. He wasn't old money, indeed he had come up the hard way, but he enjoyed what he could buy of the old-money life, a house on Long Island as well as an apartment in Manhattan, a yacht (motor variety, Simon had been deeply disapproving), and an impressive golf handicap. He was also on his third wife. "Classic, she is," Peter Hargreaves had said, "blond, big blue eyes, Permatan, extremely deep cleavage . . . and quite young."

"They seem to be having a great time at the disco," John said now. "Good to see them all letting their hair down. Helps."

"Helps what?"

"Oh, you know. With company loyalty, that sort of thing. They'll all go back to their desks now, feeling good about us. Wouldn't you say so?"

He obviously required her agreement. "Of course."

The waiter arrived with the drinks.

"Cheers," he said.

"Cheers, John. Thank you."

"Your team's presentation was very good," he said. "I like the new corporate campaign. Not sure about fannying around with the logo, but—"

"I wouldn't call it fannying around," she said. "I'd call it a strong new branding statement."

"Yes, I know, I was listening. Don't look so indignant, everyone likes it except me, but it'll happen. I do occasionally bow to pressure, you know."

"I didn't, no," she said, smiling at him. "I've never seen you even dip your head, let alone bow."

"Well, you haven't known me long enough then," he said. "I know enough about running companies to give the experts a say now and again. And I'd call your agency experts."

"Well—thank you."

"That's all right. Tell me, Elizabeth," he said suddenly, "are you happily married?"

"That's an extremely impertinent question," she said, trying both to keep her voice light and not to let herself consider it seriously. It was too dangerous, too destructive . . .

"No, it's not. I find you interesting. I want to know."

"Well, I don't think you're going to find out," she said, smiling.

"OK." He smiled back. "That means no, I would suggest."

"It doesn't actually," she said coolly. "It means I don't want to tell you, that I don't think it's relevant to the occasion."

"Well, I think it is," he said, and, "Why?" she said and was annoyed at the irritation in her voice; she should be keeping cool.

"Elizabeth, Elizabeth," he shook his head at her, "there's no need to be so edgy. You interest me, that's all. What makes you tick, what drives you."

"Do you know," she said, suddenly less annoyed with him, feeling this was safer ground, "I often wonder that myself. I really have no idea. It's just—there. I was born with it. It's certainly not the money, or anything. In the beginning I worked for nothing. Well, I mean there wasn't any profit, after paying the nanny and so on. I was an only child," she added. "I often think that has something to do with it. My father was incredibly proud of me, urged me on, and I so wanted to please him. He desperately wanted a son, and my mother couldn't have any more children."

"I was an only child too. The centre of my parents' world. Interesting, isn't it? I've heard that theory before, as a matter of fact. About only children. We're high achievers. Well, whatever does it for you, it makes you very attractive."

"Oh," she said, suddenly confused. "Oh—well, thank you."

"No need to thank me. It's a fact."

She was suddenly aware that one of his legs was pressing against hers; she moved, as subtly as she could, just slightly away from him.

"You are an extraordinarily fascinating woman," he said, "as well as successful and clever. I hope your husband appreciates you." She felt him move nearer to her again, felt the heat of him, smelled the whiskey breath. "You're very sexy, Elizabeth, you know that? Sexy and beautiful. How about we go and hit the dance floor?"

She looked at John and she quite literally longed not only to dance with him but to talk to him some more, drink with him some more, possibly even go to bed with him, for she had no doubt that that could happen too, at the end of her little adventure. How wonderful to return to Simon, knowing she was still desirable, still desiring.

But: "I'd love to, John, and thank you for the invitation. I really am tired—I'm sorry. I've enjoyed our talk though. Very much. And thank you for the champagne. It was lovely. I'll see you in the morning."

He was arguably the most powerful man she knew, and however attractive that made him, it also made him dangerous; she had seen too many such liaisons and the quicksands they created. She couldn't risk it. It would be an act of infinite folly.

He smiled at her, regret in the astonishing blue eyes, and she could see he understood. All of it. Which made her at one and the same time want him even more and yet be absolutely sure that she had done the right thing.

Chapter 12

CHRISTMAS 1989

Simon was dreading Christmas: the first time they wouldn't be at Chadwick. The rest of the family, apart from Tilly, were quite looking forward to it: Elizabeth because it would be easier, Annabel and Toby because they would be nearer their friends.

But for Simon it was yet another mark of a very public and high-profile failure: having been the golden boy all his life, successful at school, successful with women, immensely successful at work, he was having to watch as the symbols of that success—the lovely houses, the horses, the spectacular holidays—slowly but steadily whittled away. They were all going skiing early next year, at half term. It might be the last year, he warned them, "But let's bloody well make it a humdinger."

And what he saw coming now, as they moved with sickening inevitability towards the next year, the third set of losses, was a reckoning of such vast proportions it was all he could do, especially in the middle of the night, not to panic totally, pull out, and run away. It was very frightening indeed: and it was an absolutely lonely terror that he found it hard to share, even with Elizabeth. Only his fellow sufferers provided proper comfort, only they understood the predawn terrors, the sense of dreadful impotence. Although the lawsuit promised some relief from that: if it ever happened. He was beginning to despair of that as well; there had been no further word from George Meyer.

And then, just before Christmas, he got two calls that cheered him immensely. The first was from Catherine Morgan: Could she come and see him, if his offer was still open? Her voice was very tentative.

"Of course you can. It'd be lovely to see you."

He invited her up to his office; she came in, clearly impressed by its grandeur, the deep leather sofas, his huge desk, the books lining the walls, the rather fine black marble fireplace. She looked tireder than ever; she was wearing exactly the same skirt and sweater as she had at the meeting. He wondered if she possessed anything else. He sat her down, asked for some coffee for them both.

"How are the kids getting on at school?"

"Oh, just about all right," she said, but her eyes were shadowy. "That's why I'm here. Caroline isn't doing too badly, there are a few what you might call nice little girls there, but for Freddie it's pretty miserable really. He gets teased endlessly about his accent, and about being rather bright academically. He often comes home looking very upset and even with a few scrapes and bruises, but he's so brave and he refuses to admit there's anything wrong. I could kill those boys: I feel absolutely desperate about it. I just don't know what to do."

"And you don't have any family?"

"No. Both my parents died while we were in Hong Kong and their legacy has gone to Lloyd's as well. And my in-laws are . . . well. Not very approachable. Anyway, that's why I've come to see you. I thought if—well, if you were mad enough to take me on, then I could perhaps put Freddie back in the independent sector. But then is that fair to Caroline? And I certainly can't pay two lots of school fees."

"Well, if she's doing all right, I shouldn't fret about that, not at the moment anyway," said Simon. "Now, tell me about yourself—professionally, I mean. How up on all the new technology you are, that sort of thing."

It transpired that she was very up on it—and she began talking about spreadsheets and documents. "I'm a very good typist, and I can do short-hand, and, well, I'm quite a good secretary although I say it myself. But I am tied to school hours, I can't possibly pay anyone to look after the children. The other thing I've thought of is selling the flat, moving into rented accommodation, that would provide a few terms' fees, but I worry all the time about next year and how much money I might have to find then."

"Catherine, don't sell your flat, whatever you do," said Simon. "The market's on the up again, it'll be worth more soon. I think your working is the answer. All you need is an enlightened boss. Like me."

"Yes, well, it does seem pretty lucky. You've got children of your own, of course?"

"I have. Two still at school and one out in the big wide world, working."

"Oh really? What does he do?"

"She. She's a hairdresser. Not what I'd have chosen for her, I have to say, but—"

"Why not?" asked Catherine. "I think it's a really good job for a girl. You spend your days making people look better, which must be very satisfying, and then when you're married and have babies, you can still do it, working from home."

"I suppose so," said Simon. He felt rather ashamed of himself suddenly, presented with this blindingly sensible view of Annabel's job. All right, she might not be getting a degree, but what good had his fine degree and his high-profile job done him, now the chips were down. It was a genuinely good and useful career, and he resolved in future to say so.

"Right then," he said to Catherine, "I have a personal secretary and she works pretty long hours, but we do need someone to help my assistant's PA; the current incumbent is leaving to have a baby. I'll call her in, in a minute, and you can have a chat with her."

"It sounds too good to be true," said Catherine, "but won't she mind about the hours I can do?"

"No, she won't. Provided you can come in fairly early, make up the time a bit there—banking's an early-start business, or the sort we do—she'll thinks it's fine." In fact, the secretary in question didn't think it would be fine at all, but she was rather dazzled by Simon Beaumont; all the secretaries were. Together with most of the female staff.

"Yes, I do think I could manage that—getting in early, I mean."

"Good. Now, I don't know what you're earning at the moment . . ."

"Nine thousand. I know it sounds a lot, but it doesn't seem to go anywhere and—"

"It doesn't sound a great deal," said Simon, thinking that this was roughly what Boy's vet's bills came to. "How does twelve sound to you? Twelve and your season ticket? There now. Take it or leave it." He smiled at her. "I think you'd suit us all very well."

Catherine said she would take it, and had great difficulty restraining herself from hugging him.

And then, three days before Christmas Eve, he got another call.

"Simon Beaumont?"

"Yes."

"Simon, it's George Meyer."

"Oh, hi. I was beginning to wonder when I'd hear from you."

"Yes, I'm sorry. The thing is, I felt we had to get the solicitor absolutely right and the first one I approached fell by the wayside. As did yours, I seem to remember. And then I had to go to the Gulf for a month—"

"Yes, your office did explain. Doesn't matter."

"Anyway, are you still with me?"

"Absolutely. Especially as I reckon I'll be in for well over half a million next year. The house'll have to go. I'm just bracing myself to contemplate putting it on the market, buying something smaller."

"You should be grateful you've got a house. Mine is long gone. There's something very . . . seminal about having to sell your house. Everything becomes very shaky without it. I don't mind admitting I shed a few tears the day mine went. Beautiful place it was, in a lovely part of Cheshire."

"Well anyway, I do now have a solicitor for us. Absolutely top-notch, reputation as a fighter, wants to meet as soon as possible."

"Fine. Count me in. When do we see this chap?"

"Well, as I said, the sooner the better. Get your diary out. But—there's one thing, and I don't know how you'll feel about it."

"What's that?" said Simon, reaching for his diary.

"It's not a chap."

⁓

Alan Richards and Barry Grove were having lunch in the George and Vulture, a favourite bar with the City boys as well as the serious bankers and the Lloyd's people. The long bench tables, always cosy, were packed so tightly that it required a certain dexterity to move hand to mouth. The noise level was also considerable; a newcomer to the scene would have considered speech out of the question. Alan and Barry were not newcomers.

"What you doing for Christmas then?" asked Barry, taking a large swill of beer. "Spending it with Heather?"

"Splitting it," said Alan. "Her parents for lunch, mine for the evening. And then Boxing Day I'm taking her to the races at Sandown Park. You?"

"Oh, going round my brother's. Him and his wife, they really know how to do Christmas. First bottle opened straight after breakfast and then it's nonstop till bedtime. Pretty good day on the whole. I've never been to the races, though. I envy you that. Do you put a lot of money on the gee-gees?"

"Not me. Maybe a tenner each way on the George the Sixth—that's the big race of the day. Hey, why don't you come with us? Heather won't mind—the more, the merrier."

"Cheers, mate, I might just do that," said Barry. "But I like a certainty, myself, with my money. Premium bonds, that sort of thing. Or Lloyd's. I mean, that's what they all thought; poor buggers."

"Yeah. Incidentally, I meant to tell you I heard someone talking the other day, round in the Jam Pot it was, saying that there are those that think it wasn't just bad luck got all those people into trouble. The word is that there's a sort of conspiracy going on."

"What sort of conspiracy?"

Alan looked around, and then thought no one could possibly hear a word he said. "Lloyd's needed more money and sharpish. So they hauled in a lot of new people, blinded them with science, didn't look too hard at their equity and bunged them in the dodgiest syndicates. Reckoned they'd never know the difference. Well, no one does, do they?"

Barry shook his head. "Certainly don't. Most of them are like me at the races—don't have a clue, poor suckers."

"But it is only a rumour," said Alan again, "and you didn't hear it from me—right?"

"Heard what?" said Barry. He grinned at Alan, then went on more soberly: "But if it is true, then it's pretty bloody rotten, I'd say. You up for another one of those?"

"Yeah, why not," said Alan. He pulled his handkerchief out of his pocket, wiped his forehead. As he put it back, he knocked the arm of the man sitting next to him. "Sorry, mate."

"No, that's OK," said the man. "Wonder you can breathe at all in here. Someone's gone to get me a pint as well. If he's back before teatime I'll be impressed. You work in the City then?"

"Well, sort of. For Jackson and Bond, underwriters—you know them?"

"Yeah, course. At Lloyd's."

"You in the business? S'pose you must be, or you wouldn't be here."

"In a way. I'm a hack," said the man, "work for the *Daily News.* On the City pages."

"That interesting, is it?" said Alan.

"Sometimes. Look, I couldn't help hearing what you were saying just now. About Lloyd's. I'd be really interested in hearing a bit more—if you felt you could talk. It sounded quite—well, it intrigued me. Let's just say that."

"Sorry," said Alan shortly, feeling a rush of panic rising in his throat. "Never talk to the press. More than my job's worth. And I don't know what you heard, but—"

"Let's just say I've heard something a bit like it before," said the man. "About Lloyd's pulling a few fast ones on people. Well, if you ever did want to talk to me—in the strictest confidence, of course—just give me a bell. Here's my card."

"Thanks," said Alan, taking it gingerly, as if it might burn him. "No offence or anything, but I don't think I'll be using it."

The man shrugged. "Fine. But you never know, there might be another story, one that you were less worried about . . ."

"Who said I was worried?" said Alan.

"I did. Look, I'm going to cut and run, my friend's got my pint and he's waving me to move outside. Nice to talk to you. Merry Christmas."

"Merry Christmas," said Alan.

He smiled rather warily at the man. He was quite young—no more than thirty—and Alan had an idea Heather would have considered him a bit tasty. He was dark, with fairly close-cropped hair, and he was wearing quite a sharp suit. He looked at the card: Joel Strickland, it said, City Editor, *Daily News,* Butts Wharf, E.1., direct line 01–271–7913. Well, that was one number he wouldn't be ringing. Just the same he put the card carefully in his wallet. You never knew.

Lucinda was to spend Christmas with her parents, together with her sister, Susannah, and her extremely pompous husband and rather dull children. It was not an attractive proposition. She hadn't even spoken to Nigel; he had sent her a note, giving her some times when she could go and pick up her things, and asking her to leave the keys on the hall table. At least after that she had some clothes, and a few photographs, although most of them were of the two of them together. She had left her keys with a note, saying once again how sorry she was; there was no reply.

She felt totally ashamed; horribly remorseful at making him so unhappy, and very depressed. She seemed to herself a worthless, useless creature. She couldn't sleep, couldn't eat, lacked the energy even to read.

Blue Horton supposed he was dreading Christmas. He certainly ought to be, it was going to be pretty bloody awful, although his vast family did manage to make quite an event out of it, lot of eating, awful lot of drinking, and his mum did the best Christmas dinner in the world, and his dad always dressed up as Santa Claus for the kids, and in the evening they all got completely hammered and the males tried to get a poker school going only it never lasted long because the girls rolled back the carpet and they had a good old knees-up. Twenty-four of them last year there'd been, counting the kids; they all went to his parents' house in Chelmsford, not because it was the biggest in the family but because they knew no one would ever be able to do it half as well. From time to time, during what he thought of as the Lucinda period, Blue tried to picture her joining in; bit of a worry, but she'd probably get used to it. But he wasn't actually dreading it too much, because he was so bloody miserable all the time he couldn't imagine ever feeling any worse. Every day was horrible, and this would be another one exactly like it.

Two months it was now, just over actually, since that awful night, and he didn't feel the slightest bit better.

He'd loved her so much, so very, very much—no, more than loved her, he'd bloody well worshipped her, he'd have died for her if she'd asked him, chucked himself out of the window of McArthur's without a moment's hesitation.

He'd told her that once and she'd sat looking at him, very seriously as she did, with her lovely eyes wide, and then she'd said, "But Blue, if you did that, what would be the point of my living either? I'd just have to jump out after you." And then she'd giggled and said, "Bit of a waste, really, both of us gone." God, he missed that giggle. And those eyes. And—well, there was nothing he didn't miss really, it was horrible.

℮

Debbie and Richard always had a row on Christmas Eve; Debbie said it was part of their Christmas tradition. It seemed funny afterwards too; at the time, with emotions running high anyway, due to the stress of Christmas, it seemed more serious.

This year was no different. She went into the study to get some more Sellotape and found Richard looking morose, staring out of the window.

"What's the matter with you?" she said briskly.

"Oh, nothing you'd sympathise with."

"OK. Let me be unsympathetic. Just tell me."

"I'm worried about Mother. If you really want to know."

"Richard, I'm sure she's fine."

"No, Debbie, she's not. She's been very upset by our not going down—she loved last Christmas and so did the children. As did I."

"We all did," said Debbie carefully. "I just thought this year it would be nice to be on our own as a family. We did invite her here, you know. And she refused."

"Yes, I know."

"So—"

"Debbie, we've been through this. She has the animals and so on to look after. And she likes to do Christmas her way, dress up the house, follow her own traditions . . ."

"Well that's very unusual isn't it? So do I!"

"We don't have traditions in the same way, you know we don't."

"Yes, because we always have to follow hers."

He ignored this. "And the children love it there, you know they do. It just doesn't seem much to ask really, to make her happy."

"It seems a lot to me. Packing everything up, trailing down there in a huge traffic jam, missing things here; the children might like midnight mass at Oxwich, but they also like going to our church for the crib service and seeing all their friends. And I like seeing all our friends. I'm looking forward to going to Jan's tonight and Sarah's on Boxing Day, instead of trailing round all those big houses, trying to make conversation with people I don't know and don't want to know."

"Well, I can't help worrying about her," he said. "She's been very brave, telling us about all the parties and so on she's going to, but the fact remains she'll wake up alone on Christmas morning and go to bed alone on Christmas night. And have her friends wondering why she isn't at least coming up here to be with her grandchildren, if we can't go down there."

"Richard, I just said she could have been up here. Oh, this is a ridiculous conversation. I haven't time for it, anyway. Have you got any more Sellotape? I have about a dozen parcels still to wrap up and we've got to go to the church in an hour."

There was a long silence, then he said, "I would not have believed you could have become so hard, Debbie. So hard and so—so aggressive. It makes me very unhappy." And he walked out of the room and slammed the door.

Soon after, he reappeared. "Now the children are upset," he said. "You know how they hate us quarrelling at Christmas."

"Richard, I'm sorry, but I seem to remember it was you who started this, you who slammed the door, when all I wanted was a bit of Sellotape. For God's sake, why don't you help instead of picking on me?"

"Oh, just shut up," he said. "I really have had—"

And then Emma appeared in the doorway, her eyes full of tears. "Just stop it!" she said. "It's horrible, you shouldn't be quarrelling at Christmas; it's a time for being happy, loving one another, doing what Jesus would want."

"Oh, darling," said Debbie, remorse flooding her, "darling, I'm sorry. It wasn't a real quarrel, just—"

"Yes, it was. I heard Daddy shouting at you. So—make up friends. Now. Say you're sorry, go on, both of you, in turn, and then Daddy, give Mummy a kiss and then Mummy give Daddy one."

Debbie looked at Richard and felt suddenly overwhelmed with mirth. It was a bit like the marriage service, she felt, being told what to say each in turn by a third party; and then being told that the groom might now kiss the bride.

She managed not to laugh—just; and then said dutifully, "I'm sorry, Richard."

"Good. Now Daddy . . ."

Richard remained silent.

"Daddy. Go on."

"Go on, Richard," said Debbie. "I did."

"I'm sorry," he said very quickly.

"Right. Now Daddy, kiss Mummy. Go on . . ."

Finally satisfied, Emma left the room; Debbie started to laugh. Richard stared at her, then reluctantly smiled too.

"Come on now," she said, "do it again. I wasn't very impressed with that kiss. I didn't feel you meant it."

"Of course I did."

"No, you didn't. Come here, Richard. This is a kiss. In case you don't remember. Bit of a while . . ." She started to kiss him; and as so often, her emotions heightened by the row, she began to feel sexy. And felt him, with great unwillingness, start to respond.

"Lock the door," she said.

"Debs! No, the kids are all over the house."

"They can manage without us for a few minutes. I heard Emma telling the others we were making up friends. I really think we should, don't you?"

"Debbie—"

But she had already started pulling up her skirt, slithering out of her pants; she pushed him against the desk, started unzipping his fly—and suddenly, with a rather awkward grin, he reached for her.

It was over in minutes; excited, joyous, half-guilty sex. Afterwards, flushed, breathing hard, pulling her clothes into order, feeling absurdly happy, she smiled at him and said, "You can still do it, Mr. Fielding, still show me a good time. Right, what's next? Oh, yes, the nativity service. How appropriate. Poor old Mary didn't know what she was missing."

"Debbie!" said Richard, his voice shocked. But he smiled back at her just the same.

"I'm off to the shower," she said. "Oh, and I tell you what, how about we all go down to Wales for New Year?"

This was a considerable sacrifice as her new friends at Know How were having a party, and it would have been fantastic, lots of media and publishing people.

"I think that would be very nice," he said. "Thank you. And for the early Christmas present. Much better than the CDs I found hidden in your drawer."

"Richard! That's not very nice, poking around in my drawers."

"But I thought that was what you wanted," he said, "to have me poking around in your drawers."

It was quite a long time since he had made her laugh, she thought; or made her come, for that matter. She suddenly felt very happy.

"Happy Christmas, Richard," she said.

e⌒

Lucinda had offered to go into the office on Christmas Eve. She had nothing better to do, she certainly didn't want to get to her parents' any sooner than she had to, and working was the only thing that soothed the dreadful aching misery that seemed to be getting worse rather than better.

e⌒

Blue was trying to enjoy the customary Christmas Eve piss-up at McArthur's. Apart from anything else, he thought that a few glasses—just a few—would help to cure his hangover. They did, briefly, but then he started feeling drunk again: drunk and absolutely miserable. He left the group and went and sat by his desk, staring at the empty screen; if someone had offered him a gun, he thought, he would have held it to his head and fired it.

"Blue!" It was Stella, one of the receptionists; the girls didn't usually venture onto the trading floors as the welcome they got, although enthusiastic, was not exactly subtle or gentlemanly. "Blue, you OK?"

"No, not really, Stella love, I'm not," said Blue. He reached out an arm, put it round her without looking at her; the screen blurred. She stood there, and then suddenly bent down and kissed the top of his head.

"What is it? Girl trouble?"

"Girl trouble, Stella. Got it in one."

"Oh, I'm sorry. Well, all I can say is she must need her head examined. No one in her right mind would turn you down, Blue. I certainly wouldn't."

"You wouldn't?"

"Course not."

He turned his head and looked up past her considerable breasts to her concerned face. She had very large blue eyes: a bit like Lucinda's, he thought. They were regarding him with an almost maternal sympathy.

"You should try again," she said.

"What—even if the situation was totally hopeless?"

"Course. Always worth another try. She might just be playing hard to get," she added helpfully.

"I don't think so."

Stella bent down and kissed him again; her breasts, richly perfumed, moved into view. Christ. He'd almost forgotten what breasts could do to you. Apart from anything else, he was bloody sick of being celibate.

"Look," she said, "what you got to lose? It's Christmas." Blue couldn't quite see what that had to do with it, but a surge of recklessness suddenly rose up from somewhere. From between Stella's breasts, probably.

"All right," he said. "I will. Right now."

"Well done," she said, straightening up. "You do that and I'll go and get you another glass of bubbly. All right?"

"All right," said Blue.

He picked up the phone and dialled Lucinda's office number. She probably wouldn't be there, but he certainly couldn't ring her at home.

It was nearly lunchtime; the office was dead. There was no point staying any longer. She was the only person there, apart from the doorman. She might as well go and do a bit of last-minute shopping. She still hadn't got anything for her sister. And then she could join the car park that would be the M4 on a Christmas Eve evening.

She walked down the corridor, pressed the button to call the rackety old lift. God, her head hurt. The sooner she got out in the fresh air, the better.

No answer. He'd hung on for ages. She'd obviously left. Well, he'd tried. He almost felt better; quite pleased with himself, in fact. He could see Stella coming back now with the champagne. He'd drink that, and then he might even ask her out. She was sweet. And those breasts; you could drown in them. That's what he needed: breast engulfment . . .

"She wasn't there," he said, "before you ask."

⟳

Lucinda reached the ground floor and looked out at the street; it was teeming with people, noisy, laughing, happy people. She really couldn't go out there and join them, not with this headache. She might have to give in and take a couple of aspirin . . .

⟳

"She might have gone to the toilet," said Stella helpfully. "You can't just give up that easily, Blue. She got her own office, has she?"

"Yes."

"Well then. Try again. Just once more, go on."

"Will you hold my hand?"

"My pleasure," she said brightly.

⟳

Lucinda went back up to the office, unlocked the door, sat down at her desk, opened a drawer. She certainly had some painkillers in there. Quite strong ones that Blue had given her after one of their more spectacular lunches.

"Buck-up pills these are, Lucy. Take two and think of me."

Don't think about Blue, Lucinda, don't. It won't help. It won't do any good at all. She pulled out the packet, got up again to fetch a glass of water. The phone rang.

"Go away," she said to it. "Just go away."

And then thought that it might perhaps be Nigel. You never knew.

He might just want to make peace: given that it was Christmas. She picked it up, hoping. "Hello?" she said.

It wasn't Nigel.

"Lucy? It's me, Blue. I—er—I just phoned to say Happy Christmas. Hope that's all right."

"Oh Blue," she said. "Oh Blue, please . . ." And burst into tears.

"Stay there," he said. "I'm coming over."

He arrived within twenty minutes; she didn't have the strength to move, to run away, to tell the doorman not to let him in, any of the sensible, right things. She just sat at her desk, staring at the phone, still holding it, where she had placed it back on the base, contact with him of a sort at last. She would just see him and chat to him for a bit and convince him somehow that everything was all right and then—

"Hello, Lucinda."

He was standing in the doorway.

Lucinda felt faint; faint with shock, with love, with grief.

"Oh," she said, as if she was surprised he was there. "Oh Blue, hello."

He didn't move: nor did she.

"You all right?"

"Yes, I'm perfectly all right, thank you."

"Because you were crying."

"Yes, I know. Silly. Couldn't help it. Sorry."

"Why were you crying, Lucinda? Is something wrong?"

"No," she said. "No, of course not. Well, obviously I'm a bit—emotional. At hearing from you, and—and—but no, everything's fine. Yes, I'm just off to the country, you know."

And then it was all too much and she started crying again. And reached out to the box of tissues at the back of her desk and her sleeve slipped up her arm . . . and he saw.

"Lucy," he said, his eyes fixed on it.

"Yes, Blue?" she said, blowing her nose, unaware of what miracle she had worked. "Yes, Blue, what?"

He moved round the desk then, tipped up her head, made her look at him.

"If everything's so absolutely all right, perhaps you'd like to tell me why you're wearing that fucking watch."

Chapter 13

Ms. Fiona Broadhurst. Age probably mid-thirties, Simon would have said: tall and very slim, with light-brown hair caught back in a ponytail, and brilliant probing blue eyes in a pale and rather emotionless face. She wore a black suit and a white shirt, and black shoes, and she had extremely good legs. Her voice was quick and clipped, as if she didn't want to waste any more time than was necessary on speaking—and she had (Simon inevitably noticed such things) very pretty hands and nails. Unpainted, of course. She was, in a rather cool way, extremely sexy. Which would make meetings more pleasant, he thought, smiling at her; she didn't smile back. So—maybe not.

She was a partner in Evans Dixon Campbell, a medium-size setup near Charterhouse Square; they were in the boardroom, which was as plainly decorated as Fiona herself, at half past ten in the morning.

"Good morning," she said, shaking hands with each of them in turn. "Very nice to meet you all. I'm Fiona Broadhurst, this is my assistant Clare Lomax. Mr. Meyer, perhaps you could go first."

They went round the table; Simon, who had got to know the other two during the first abortive attempt to find a solicitor, wondered how many would stay the undoubtedly tough course. There was a rather thuggish Northerner, called Terence Cunningham, and a clearly formidable lady, Anne Rudyard. And of course Flora Fielding.

"Right," said Fiona, smiling briefly at them all, "let's get down to business, shall we? Perhaps you'd like me to summarise the case as I see it.

"As I understand it, your case rests on whether the inducement to you to become Names was reckless or not; whether it was fraudulent or not. If it was fraudulent, then that would remove all liability from you. Of course, fraud is the highest burden of proof, it's almost criminal, up in the ninety percent league. It's beyond reckless; reckless is not caring, fraud is mens rea. I presume you all know what that means?"

Simon was brave enough to say he did not; Fiona Broadhurst gave him a patient look and said, "It's literally criminal intent, the knowledge of wrongdoing; it's what distinguishes murder, for example, from manslaughter. In this case, what you are seeking to prove is that Lloyd's, or to be more precise your Members' Agents Jackson and Bond and/or your main syndicate group Westfield Bradley knew this very large swathe of claims was coming their way, mostly for asbestosis or pollution, that they didn't have the funds to meet them and were seeking further investment from people without examining the latter's resources sufficiently carefully, and without warning them of the possible consequences. Would you say that states your case clearly?"

George Meyer said it did.

"So what you are saying is that you have been fraudulently induced into becoming Names, that you want your money back, plus some costs, you want interest on the money you have disgorged, and you don't want to pay any more."

"Yes," said Meyer, "that's about the size of it."

"Well, that's pretty straightforward."

"Is it?" said Simon hopefully.

"Mr. Beaumont, when I say straightforward," said Fiona Broadhurst severely, "I mean your aims are pretty straightforward, I don't mean a settlement will be. And of course in this country you won't get anything for pain, aggravation, and suffering, all that sort of thing. The Americans are very keen on that, but it won't happen here, so I hope you're not expecting it."

"No, of course not," said Simon, anxious to distance himself from such self-indulgent nonsense.

"But your case is complex. And I can't say yet if I can take it on. At this stage. I need a great deal from you first, and I need to do a lot of work of my own. That said, litigation is teamwork and we will need to work together from start to finish."

"What sort of work and what would you need from us?" said Cunningham. "I must say, I'd always thought lawyers took whatever they could get. I've never heard of this sort of auditioning business."

Fiona Broadhurst looked at him very coolly.

"Then clearly you've never been involved in a case of this kind," she said. "I, and the other partners here, assess cases very carefully before committing prospective clients to heavy expense and high risk. As to the second part of your question, or rather the first, if we are to be pedantic, I would require each of you to come to me and say, 'This is the situation, this is my contract, this is what induced me, these representations in this brochure, this is what I've paid already, this is what my balance is.' I need to know what you're upset about, apart from the obvious which is that you don't feel you should have to pay. I need to know where you feel you've been misled. If you feel there has been a cover-up, if you feel the people in Jackson and Bond or Westfield Bradley knew, if the market knew, if those who were dealing with Lloyd's knew, if those who had a vested interest in Lloyd's knew, and didn't properly disclose it. I need to know all these things. I would like each of you to drop me a line, giving me a statement of what you owe, whether it's increased, whether you agreed at any stage to write more business and why. I shall then look at that and give you my decision as to whether I think you have a case. And I should tell you, of course, at this stage, that going to law is a massive decision; it's terribly expensive and you must know there are no guarantees that you will win."

"Could you give us some idea of costs?" said Meyer.

"Not at this stage, because I don't have any real idea of how long it will take, but I do anticipate it would be very expensive. We would get a top Queen's Counsel, a top junior, our fees here are between two hundred and fifty and three hundred pounds an hour, less of course for assistants. But you're certainly looking at several hundred thousand pounds. A comparatively simple case, lasting six or seven days, can cost in the order of a hundred thousand, and a case like this, with this type of complexity, you could be looking at a lot more. We'd need experts of every kind, experts on the state of the market, experts on asbestosis, and it would be very expensive. And we would want money on account, paid in advance, something like fifty thousand pounds. So I would advise you to think about it all very carefully before you come to see me again. More coffee, anyone?"

Nobody wanted more coffee.

"Now Bel darling, what do you think you're going to be doing tomorrow?"

"Oh, can't imagine," said Annabel. "I mean, not shampooing, or gowning up, or sweeping up, or even blow-drying Carol's hair if I'm really lucky. Nothing like that, obviously."

"Darling! So bitter. Let me cheer you up. I'm doing a session for *Seventh Day,* the magazine for the *Sunday News,* and guess who's going to come with me as my assistant?"

"Me?" said Annabel. Her voice came out sounding slightly squeaky.

"The very one. Merle's got a stomach bug, poor darling, and I thought, well, why not? You've been a very good girl lately and—"

"Oh Florian! Oh, thank you so, so much!" They were in the staff room; Annabel hurled herself into Florian's arms, kissed him rapturously.

"Sweetie! If I'd known it would have this effect on you I'd have done it sooner. So, Saville Studios, that's in Whitechapel, at eight. Eight as in a.m."

"I'll be there," she said.

She was actually there at seven thirty, so frightened was she of being late, complete with a vast bagful of rollers, dryers, brushes, pins, and tongs; at five to eight a girl arrived, pulled out a great bunch of keys from her pocket. She was so tall and thin that Annabel thought she must be the model, but, "Hi. I'm Elise, studio dogsbody. Come on in, you look frozen."

"Thanks. I am a bit."

"I'll get you a coffee. You Florian's assistant? We love working with him, he's such fun and so brilliant. But God, this is going to be a long day. Six shots. Probably still be at it at midnight."

At eight thirty Florian arrived. "This is going to be one hell of a day," he said, throwing his coat over a leather sofa, taking the mug of coffee. "The combination of Effie and our Sandra—God help us."

"I like Sandra, Florian," said Elise. "I think she's really nice, terribly professional."

"Yes, but darling, all the more reason for her to get cross with Effie. You know how otherworldly she is, never knows what way she's up . . . I blame the dope myself."

"You're a fine one to talk," said Elise briskly.

"Now that is so unfair," said Florian. "I never smoke on the job. Well, not this sort of job anyway. Do I, Bel, sweetie?"

"Um—no, of course not," said Annabel.

Florian did a lot of drugs, it was one of the things that worried her about him. Not only did he smoke dope constantly (although not at work, that at least was true), he took Ecstasy which she could just about accept, after all everybody did, but also cocaine. He had tried to encourage her to try it; so far she had resisted (apart from the occasional spliff, obviously), but Florian's powers of persuasion were scarily strong. If anything was going to end their rather odd relationship, it would be that.

❦

They were going to be a good team, Simon thought: a bunch of really solid people, and he'd even liked Terence Cunningham, the Northern industrialist, belligerent bugger as he promised to be. They'd gone for a drink after the meeting. Cunningham, like Meyer, had seen his wife walk away with a new man.

"She started out all sweetness and light, swore she'd stand by me, but after a bit she couldn't cope with the reality. Losing the golf-club membership, seeing her friends in new frocks while she had to wear the old ones, it was all too much." He glared into his beer. "Frailty, thy name is woman, my dad used to say. Too bloody right."

Simon was silent; he thought of Elizabeth, 101 percent behind him, resolutely keeping their ship afloat, and thought too of Neil Lawrence, who felt unable still even to tell his wife; and thought then how he'd betrayed Elizabeth, and felt desperately remorseful. Neil had called him the day before in an appalling state.

"I just can't cope with this," he said, "I can't. I had lunch with my Members' Agent yesterday and I sat up all night literally just staring at the wall, thinking: What have I done? How did I get into this?"

"How much this time?" said Simon.

"Over three hundred thousand at least. Simon, both my houses together aren't going to meet that. I just feel violently sick, all the time. I can't think about anything else. Can't work, can't sleep, it's literally hell. I know how people feel now, when they say they wish they were dead. I view that as a very attractive option."

"No, you don't," said Simon. "Er . . . what does your wife say?"

"I still haven't told her," said Neil.

They had all been excited by the meeting, they agreed, in spite of Ms. Broadhurst's rather daunting prognostication, and indeed daunting presence. "I thought she was marvellous," said Flora, "didn't you, Simon?"

"She seemed very capable, yes," he said, and then saw Flora looking at him with a certain humour in her dark eyes. Clearly she had observed his reaction to Fiona Broadhurst; no point trying to deceive her about anything.

"She'll do, I reckon," said Cunningham. "Let's hope she thinks we will."

❧

Elise had been right; it was proving a long day. Annabel felt quite sick with tiredness: they had only done four of the six shots, and it was already half past five.

Sandra, the fashion editor, and Florian were having a mild tiff over the hair for the next shot, a dazzling summer ball gown, when a man walked into the studio. A distinctly attractive man, Annabel thought, studying him: bit old, probably over thirty, but still . . . He was quite tall, with close-cropped hair and brilliant dark eyes, and he was wearing a dinner jacket; she wondered if he was another model.

But, "Joel, oh my God, how frightful. Is it really that sort of time?" said Sandra. "I'm not nearly ready."

"Don't worry, you've got at least another hour. I had an appointment at the NatWest Tower, thought I'd come up here and collect you, rather than go back to the office. Find out what really happens at a photographic session. Looks like fun to me."

"An hour won't be enough," said Sandra. "Come on, guys, for God's sake! This is Joel Strickland, everyone, our City editor; we've got an awards thing this evening—we're both up for a gong—and we've been summoned to cocktails with the proprietor first, so we absolutely have to leave at six thirty—"

"Darling, don't fret," said Paolo, the photographer. "If we haven't finished by then, we'll see it all through without you. You just tell us what you want, and you'll get it."

"Well, OK. Joel, there are lots of magazines over there, and probably some wine."

"No, no, I'll just have coffee, thanks," said Joel Strickland. "It's going to be a long night, better not start too early."

"I'll make you some coffee," said Annabel, jumping up from the sofa. She had had nothing to do for the past hour, and was feeling distinctly spare; Jonty, Sandra's assistant, seemed to have taken over her role as Florian's assistant.

"That's very kind of you," said Joel. He had a very nice smile. "And who are you?"

"I'm Annabel, I mean Bel."

"Aren't you sure?"

She smiled back. "Well, my real name is Annabel. They call me Bel in the hairdressing salon where I work. I'm assisting him." She gestured at Florian. "But I think Jonty's doing a better job."

"Well, I know who I'd rather have as my assistant," he said, smiling at her again. "Come and sit with me and entertain me. How long have you been mixed up with all these terrible people?"

"Only since this morning," she said, and then, realising what she had said: "Only they're not terrible, they're all very nice. But I've been training as a hairdresser for about—goodness, eight months now."

"And—do you like it?"

"Yes, I absolutely love it."

"Good. That's what I like to hear, people enjoying what they do. More important than anything, really."

"Do you enjoy what you do?"

"I certainly do. Best job in the world, journalism. You get to go anywhere you want, meet anyone you fancy—I mean, how else would I be sitting here, talking to you?"

"And you're up for an award. How exciting."

"I won't get it, though. Much too much competition. Still, it'll be a fun evening."

"What was your story about?"

"Fraud," he said. "Juicy little number, but not strong enough to win. Guy from *The Times* will probably win, he wrote about Afghanistan and the drug kings. More of a proper story."

"And— Sorry, do you mind answering all these questions?" She was genuinely interested. And he really was rather sexy.

"Of course not. God, what are they doing in there?"

"I think," said Annabel, "they're making the hair a bit bigger."

"My word. That does sound serious. Go on."

"I was going to ask if journalists worked on one story at a time, or lots."

"Well, it depends. Reporters usually work on one at a time, but sometimes more than one in a day. On the City pages there's lots of short, everyday stuff and then there might be one big story which can go on for weeks. Or even months. And you need to be very patient, putting bits and pieces together. It's fun. Now, do you think we could share a glass of that nice wine Sandra mentioned? I think I want to get into the party mood after all."

"Well, I'd better not. But I'll get you one."

"This really is very nice," said Joel, setting down his glass. "You're missing quite a treat. Now you mustn't let me bore you rigid. Tell me about you."

"Oh, I'm not very interesting," she said. "Left school last year. Doing this now. Still live at home with my parents."

"Do you mind that?"

"Not really. It's quite a big house. And my parents are very good, really. They mostly leave me alone. Don't interfere. They're not too keen on me doing hairdressing, but—"

"Why not?"

"Oh, they're disappointed I didn't go to university. It's practically a religion for my father. He went to Oxford, and he was longing for me to go. But my brother will, I'm sure, and my little sister."

"Well, I went and it didn't do me an awful lot of good. My brother didn't and he's got a very successful little building company, makes about three times as much money as me . . . You could tell your father that. What does he do?"

"He works in the City. He's on the board of a bank."

"Which one?"

"Graburn and French."

"Very good outfit. I sat next to the chairman at some PR dinner just before Christmas. Nice man. The bank's doing rather well—not easy in this financial climate."

"Is it? That's good. Poor old Dad needs some luck at the moment. He's just lost an awful lot of money at Lloyd's."

"Has he really?" said Joel Strickland.

In her pretty cottage in Hampshire, Gillian Thompson drank a cup of tea, very hot and strong, the way she liked it, and then picked up her beloved tabby cat, Mustapha, put him in his carrying basket and took him to her friend, May Williams, who lived just down the road. May was also very fond of Mustapha, and had once or twice looked after him when Gillian had gone on holiday.

"I'm sorry it's such short notice, May, but I've been called away. Would you mind looking after him for a while? I so hate to think of him in that cattery."

"Of course," said May, scooping Mustapha out of his basket. "I always love to have him, you know that. He'll never lack for a home while I'm around."

"Good," said Gillian. "That's very comforting, May, thank you. I'm not quite sure when I'll be back, is that all right?"

"Of course. Would you like a cup of tea?"

"No, thank you, I've just had one and I ought to be getting along. I'll— Well, thank you, May. Goodbye then."

And she was gone, her small feet in their nicely polished shoes tap-tapping down the brick path.

Gillian went back to her cottage, carefully closed all the windows and put a rolled-up blanket along the bottom of the living-room door; she took a couple of aspirin and switched on her gas fire. Then she lay down as close to it as she could and started to inhale very deeply and slowly.

Chapter 14

He looked awfully fierce. His eyes had that sort of hard, shiny look to them that she didn't like, making them unreadable. And his mouth was narrower, tighter—he was obviously very cross. Oh God. Now what was she going to do?

"I'm sorry," she said again. "Really sorry."

"Yes, all right," he said.

"I know I should have told you before."

"Probably you should. Well—" And then he smiled suddenly, his face appearing to crack almost in two, his widest, most glorious grin. "Say it again. Go on. I want to hear it again."

"I'm going to have a baby," she said. Breathing more easily, feeling less frightened.

He shook his head quickly several times as if he thought his hearing might be affected. "You're not having me on?"

"Well, no. I'm sorry if it's a shock, but—"

"It is a bit," he said. "Pretty shocking. I'm not sure why that should be. We've been doing all the right things. God in heaven, Lucinda, a baby. You and me. Yours and mine. Jesus. Are you quite, quite sure?"

"I'm terribly sure, yes," she said. "I've missed my period—well, nearly two now . . ."

"You know, I did wonder," he said, "then I thought, no, I never could count. Go on—"

"And I've had a test done. At the doctor—I don't trust those things you buy."

"God," he said again. "This really is quite monumentally good news. Wouldn't you say?"

"Well, I think so, yes. So you're not cross?"

"Cross? No, Lucy, I'm not cross. Why should I be cross, for pity's sake? Whatever made you think that?"

"Well . . . I don't know really. We didn't exactly plan it. And it's my fault, entirely. I got behind with my pills. I left it too late to get another prescription, and then I—well, I thought supposing I was pregnant, I didn't want to take the pill if I was, it might harm the baby in some way, you know, so I thought I'd better wait till the next time, and—"

"You haven't got much common sense, have you, Lucinda?" he said.

"I suppose not," she said humbly. "Not a lot."

"Well, thank God for it," he said. "I don't know when I was so pleased about anything. Except when I saw that fucking watch on your wrist. A baby. My God. Here, come and give your old man a kiss.

"You know what we've got to do next, don't you?" said Blue.

"Um . . . tell our mothers?"

They were lying in bed, Blue drinking champagne and Lucinda a mug of hot milk.

What they really had to do, must do, he told her, cradling her in his arms, was get the divorce going.

"I'm not having my son born out of wedlock," he said, "and that's that."

"Oh, now Blue, that's just silly."

"Why?"

"Well, in the first place, we'll never get it all over and done with and us married by November."

"Is that when it is?" he said, sounding startled. "Blimey. You sure?"

"November, yes. It usually takes nine months, I believe. And in the second place, it might be a girl."

There was a long silence, then: "No," he said, "not possible. Out of the question."

"OK. Well, anyway, I can try with Nigel. Try again. But I don't hold out a lot of hope. He just acts as if I don't exist."

e⌒

It had been a very exciting four months, she thought, lying awake staring happily into the darkness while Blue slept. Starting with Christmas, with telling her parents she couldn't come after all. They'd been predictably sniffy; her mother said it would mess up all sorts of arrangements.

Blue had taken her to meet his family on New Year's Day. "Now they are a bit much," he said, "I warn you. Not too much like your folks, I'd say."

"That's good news," she said.

She had fallen in love with them, the whole noisy, cheerful, over-the-top lot of them; she could see they found her very strange, and Blue's choice of her even stranger. It had been hard at first, she had been trying to play down her background, and had been feeling very tense and shy, trying not to say anything that could be remotely interpreted as snooty; the day was made even odder by the fact that Blue was Gary at home; it was oddly disconcerting. She was beginning to feel slightly desperate, when Blue's nine-year-old nephew, a bullet-headed replica of his uncle, had fixed her with beady dark eyes and said, "Gary says you're well posh. We never met anyone posh before—what's it like then? You met the Queen and that?"

"Jason," said Margo, Blue's mother, "that's no way to talk to Lucinda."

"Of course it is," said Lucinda, relaxing suddenly, "and actually I'm really not very posh as you call it, Jason, not at all."

"Oh no, I don't think so, not actually," whispered Holly, his ten-year-old sister, in a parody of Lucinda's accent.

Her father gave her a smart clip round the ear. "I don't want any of your cheek, Holly. You be polite to the lady. I'm sorry, Lucinda."

"Honestly, please, please don't be polite," she said, "I'd much rather they weren't. Anyway, Jason, no, I haven't met the Queen. But I have been to Buckingham Palace."

"And was Princess Diana there?" said Holly, curiosity getting the better of her.

"Very sadly, no. I was with my father, he was getting a—a sort of medal. I think Diana was in her own palace. She's beautiful, don't you think?"

"Yes. You look a bit like her," said Holly consideringly. "Not as pretty, but a bit the same."

"Well, thank you," said Lucinda. "I call that a huge compliment."

"And what a good mother, isn't she?" said Margo. "Lovely they are, those boys. I think she's wonderful, I really do. I don't reckon Prince Charles appreciates her properly, you know."

"No, I think that's probably right," said Lucinda.

"And her clothes. Really lovely. She makes the rest of them look pretty frumpy, doesn't she?"

"She certainly does. I like her hair a bit longer too."

After that, things got easier very quickly.

For Blue, meeting Lucinda's parents, things were more difficult. He could have been an alien landing on Earth from another planet for the violence of their reaction to him. They stared at him, transfixed, their smiles chilly, their faces frozen, through the longest lunch Lucinda could ever remember; her father only addressed him directly to ask him if he would like some more wine; her mother, clearly at a complete loss to understand the relationship, struggled to be more friendly, asking Blue about his work, about where he lived, about his own family, but it was painfully awkward. Quite apart from anything else, they had trouble with his name, ended up calling him Mr. Horton. As soon as coffee was half drunk, Lucinda stood up and said they must go.

"I'm so sorry, Blue," she said, almost in tears as they drove away. "They're just—just rather stupid."

"It's OK."

"It's not OK at all. They were rude—rude and insulting. And what for?"

"Well, I s'pose we've broken the number-one rule: stick to your own tribe."

"Your family don't mind me."

"They do a bit. I mean, they like you and that, but they think it's well odd. Oh, except for my dad. He thinks you're wonderful. Calls you the princess. I didn't tell you that, did I?"

"No," she said, "you didn't. Blue, I do apologise."

Blue pulled into the side of the road. "Lucy," he said, "it's you I love. Not them. In fact, I love you more than ever."

"Why?" she said curiously.

"Well, to have managed to have turned out so extremely well. I'd say it was a considerable achievement, myself. Now give me a kiss and let's stop worrying about them, OK? If I can live with them, then you can."

"Not literally, please God," she said, and shuddered.

Her friends she told gradually; a lot of them took Nigel's part and stopped seeing her. She was hurt; she hadn't expected that. It seemed terrible that a rift in a marriage should have to gape so widely and so relentlessly. Some people did take her side, though; she was grateful, and then introduced them to Blue rather nervously. On the whole it was the men who took to him more.

"Bloody clever," said Katy's fiancé, Hugh. "Fantastic what he does every day. Millions of pounds go through his fingers. Don't know how he does it without having a heart attack."

Others said much the same thing. Lucinda felt a bit silly; she had always thought what Blue did must be clever, but she had never really understood it and certainly hadn't realised how extremely difficult it must be. She looked at him almost awed, newly and deeply impressed by him. He was very amused.

"You see, Lucinda, it's possible to be quite clever, do fairly well even, without ever having been to one of those schools of yours."

They were living in his little house in Limehouse; she was still working at Harrison. Graham Parker twinkled at her when she told him what was happening to her.

"I'm glad it's all worked out so nicely," he said. "I was a bit . . . concerned."

"Thank you," she said, and then, staring at him: "What do you mean, it's worked out?"

"Lucinda," he said, "you must think I am very stupid. It's quite hard not to notice when someone working for you is having an affair. All those long lunch hours? And what a lot of dental appointments you had."

"Oh," she said, blushing furiously. "Oh no, I mean yes, I mean—well, thank you for putting up with it."

"That's all right. I was more impressed than anything. Bit of excitement in my middle-aged life."

But she continued to worry about Nigel until Katy told her he was surviving quite well.

"Honestly, Lucinda, you don't have to worry about him. All his friends are looking after him beautifully. I saw him at two dinner parties last week alone."

She felt a stab of hurt, then of relief. But he still wouldn't reply to any of her phone calls or letters.

"Well, he'll have to now," said Blue. "We got to get this thing sorted. Including the money."

"Yes, I know—but how, without it all going to Lloyd's?"

"God knows," said Blue. "You need to ask a lawyer."

❧

Now what had she done, Debbie thought. Without consultation too. God, she'd be in trouble. Terrible, awful trouble. Maybe she should backtrack, say she must think about it. But why on earth should she? It was entirely good, what she was doing. Contributing hugely, financially—and anyway, she was much better-tempered, much happier altogether, really. Certainly felt less mad. And no one was suffering, and—

Her door opened again. It was Anna.

"Sorry. Should have asked you. How soon can you start?"

"Well . . ." The Easter holidays were about to begin. She didn't think she could possibly spring this on Richard, tell him he was committed to another whole day of childminding a week until they were all back at school. "In about four weeks? That soon enough?"

"It'll have to be. If you could shave a week off . . ."

"Leave it with me, Anna, I'll try. But I can't promise."

"Fine," said Anna.

*   *   *

"Easter in Wales with Granny then?" she said to the children, three days later. "That be fun? She just invited us."

And, "Yes!" they all yelled; she would have been irritated, if it hadn't been part of her plan. For Flora had not exactly invited them. Well, she had, but only in response to a hint heavy enough to stun.

*   *   *

"Right," said Fiona Broadhurst. "I've had a look at everything you've given me, and the implications. And I think you have a case. If you're right about what you've said here, and if we can find any evidence of a cover-up, of knowledge of what was going on, while they continued to promote Membership—and I appreciate you're not the first to have made this claim—then I think there is a reasonable prima facie case and we can go on, if you still wish. I have to say, however, that what you've given me here is almost certainly not enough. I think we need to find the smoking gun."

"What does that mean exactly?" said George Meyer.

"It means we need something much closer to proof. We need to find someone who has said something, or done something, that can be seen as at least fairly conclusive. I think we all need to do more work on the extent of your knowledge. There's still a very long way to go. Now, I think you should discuss what you can afford, and I would urge you to put a limit on the cost, because that helps me as well in planning the case. And I would like to say at this point that if you do run out of money and can't afford to go on, then please don't think you can come crying to me because I've got bills to pay."

There was a long silence while she looked at them; then Simon Beaumont said, "Well, thank you for your time, Ms. Broadhurst. And for considering the case so carefully. Speaking for myself, I feel I would definitely like to go on."

"Good." For the first time she smiled at them properly. "I hope your colleagues will feel the same way."

God, she was sexy, thought Simon.

"And if we do, if we're all in agreement, what would be the next step?" said Meyer.

"The next step would be that we would go to Counsel. Who, I hope, would say I'm right. Let us say that yes, he agrees there is a case or might be a case, then I would invite you to meet him. I feel you're paying for the show, and you should hear what he has to say. And I also want him—or her—to share your passion about it, to know how you feel. It won't necessarily be an easy conversation, but I would hope then that he would say yes, and then I would expect him to say what work we all have to do. I want precise information, the people who told you what a great club this was, and exactly how they told it, the language used, and when. We'll need chapter and verse; hearsay is no good to me. Litigation is teamwork—clients, solicitor, barrister, we've all got to do our share. I hope that's clear."

"It is clear," said Meyer, "and I have to say to you I like it. I like this idea of our having such close involvement, some kind of control."

"Good," said Fiona. "We do find it a far more pragmatic and indeed useful way to proceed. Now I would suggest that you go away and discuss the matter and then come back to me with your decision. In writing, obviously. Is that all right?"

They stood on the pavement outside, hardly looking at one another, Meyer and Terrence Cunningham slightly sheepishly lighting cigarettes.

"What I need is a drink," said George. "Shall we go and get one and see what we think?"

But they actually knew what they thought; and half an hour later, Simon agreed to draft a letter officially instructing Fiona to take their case.

It was as well the family were coming this year, Flora thought. The next year's results had arrived and next year there might be no house to come to. Correction. Would be no house to come to.

It had actually been a physical shock, reading the results; she felt faint, breathless, had to close her eyes. And then she opened her eyes and forced them onto the piece of paper again. It informed her she owed £275,000. A sum she most assuredly had not got, would not have even if she sold everything she possessed.

She gazed around her in a kind of desperation, seeing what she must lose to feed the monster: the house, the beloved house, of course; she had almost faced that, knowing only a miracle could save her from it, but suddenly she saw the other things that she had not properly considered that must go with it. The stables, and thus the horses: gone the long days of riding over the moors in the hot sun, in the company of the wild ponies and the hawks, surrounded with skylark song, and she would lose Tilly too, and Boy would have to go, and all these lovely easy holidays with the children. She would lose her Meadow and the rest of her land, lose the particular views of Gower they offered; would lose the sweet summer darkness filled with owls hooting and foxes screeching, and the lovely dawns, drenched in birdsong; would lose the wild winter landscape, the towering black cliffs above the raging seas, the sound of the wind hurtling round her house.

It was wicked, it was monstrous, it was absolutely and totally unjust, the result of a small, foolish act of generosity on the part of her husband.

And there was absolutely nothing she could do about it.

"You buggers!" she shouted, standing in the yard, holding the letter, waving her fist at the stormy sky. "You absolute bastards!"

Boy, Tilly's pony, and her own beloved Prince Hal looked at her in surprise. She was enjoying having Boy immensely, and enjoying her relationship with Tilly too. She was a sweet child, perfectly mannered, and a hugely talented rider. She and Boy could have made a pretty impressive mark on the eventing circuit, had the money been still there. But it wasn't . . .

They had come down after Christmas as promised, she and her father; they had stayed in the B&B for a couple of days and then, when

Richard and the family arrived for New Year, perfect chaperones for Tilly, it had seemed very silly for her not to move in with them and for Simon to leave. Emma adored Tilly, followed her about everywhere, mucking out the stables, sweeping up the icy yard uncomplainingly while Tilly encouraged her, gave her lessons, patiently answered her endless questions and not even Debbie could dislike her. Why was her daughter-in-law so awkward? Flora often wondered. It would be so nice if she could be sweet and pliable, like—well, like Tilly. Of course, Richard had his faults, and she was far from blind to them; and as the years went by he seemed to her to become increasingly like his father.

On the other hand, Flora thought, she wasn't too much like Debbie. And crushed the rider to that thought that she hoped not . . .

⁀

"Is that Simon Beaumont?"

"Yes, speaking. Who—"

"Mr. Beaumont, my name's Joel Strickland, I'm a financial journalist, work on the *Daily News*—"

"Oh yes?"

"I believe you're a Name at Lloyd's."

"Correct," said Simon shortly.

"Mr. Beaumont, I'm investigating some of the—the events at Lloyd's. For a piece I'm writing."

"Right," said Simon slowly. "What sort of piece?"

"Oh, pretty broadly based—history, financial analysis, all that sort of thing. I personally think there's rather more going on than meets the eye. Plus, you know, there is the human element, the stories behind the facts."

"Well, I certainly don't want to be part of some bleeding-hearts story, sorry. How did you get my name anyway?"

"It wouldn't be bleeding hearts, as you put it. I can guarantee that. And I met your daughter at a photographic session. Oh, she was very discreet, but she thought you might like to talk about it."

"No, I don't think so. I'm sorry if she's wasted your time."

"She hasn't. Following up leads is part of the job. But if anything changes your mind—ring me. Here are my numbers . . ."

Simon put the phone down. He'd have to speak to Annabel; he couldn't have her talking about the family affairs to complete strangers. Especially if the strangers were journalists. Even so, interesting what the guy had said . . . very interesting. He could even be useful.

∾

"Wow. Get him. Totally gorgeous. Shirt-soaking time, Bel. My turn." Annabel looked; an Adonis had just walked into the salon. Young, but not too young, probably about twenty-three, she decided, blond, tall, wearing a light camel-hair coat over jeans and very nice brown cowboy boots. Totally, totally gorgeous, as Carol said. But Carol wasn't going to have him. She pushed her mane of hair back and walked purposefully towards him.

She had actually made eye contact with him, was congratulating herself that he'd clearly noticed her, when, "Carol, take Mr. Cartwright's coat, would you?" Susan the receptionist said, with a tart smile. "And then tell David his client is here. Bel, I think the floor could do with a little sweep, dear."

"Bitch!" hissed Annabel into Carol's ear. Carol flashed Annabel her sweetest smile as she walked towards Mr. Cartwright and held out her arm for his coat.

"Good morning," she said, redirecting the smile. "I'm Carol, your junior. Would you like to follow me over to the dressing table. David will be with you in just a moment."

"Temper temper," said Florian as Annabel swept round his feet just a little too vigorously. "Honestly, darling, he's not for you, much too much of a baby, it's men of the world you need."

Annabel, seeing that Mr. Cartwright was momentarily not being taken care of, pushed her broom purposefully over to his dressing table. Or rather work station as Miki now liked them to be called.

"Er—can I get you a coffee or something? While you're waiting?" she said. Mr. Cartwright directed a pair of rather intense blue eyes at her and smiled.

"That's really nice of you," he said, in an accent that Annabel recognised as old-money American, "but I think the other young lady is bringing me some."

"There we are." The other young lady set down a tray of coffee on the table with a slight, Playboy Bunny–style bob. "Can I get you some magazines? Bel, I think Florian's looking for you."

Annabel gave up.

She was walking wearily past the Carlton Tower Hotel that evening, looking longingly at the cab rank, when she heard a voice. An American old-money voice.

"Hello. Isn't it Cinderella?"

She spun round; he was emerging from the hotel. Miraculously alone.

"Well, yes. Yes, it is. I'm just looking for my pumpkin coach." He grinned. Showing the inevitably perfect American white teeth.

"Haven't seen one. Well—look, I don't have a coach or anything, but I'm taking a cab down to Fulham Road. Could I offer you a lift? Or is that totally the wrong direction?"

Annabel would have said it was the right direction if he had been going to Birmingham, but, "It is totally the right one," she said, "thank you."

"That's OK." He ushered her into a cab, then held out his hand to her. "James Cartwright. Usually known as Jamie."

"Hi, Jamie. I'm Annabel. Annabel Beaumont."

"And you work in that place full-time, Annabel?"

"Oh yes. I like it," she added firmly. She could feel the usual puzzlement coming. "Except the sweeping. It's fun."

"I felt kind of like an idiot in there," he said, "with all those women, but my mother said I absolutely had to get a haircut and the hotel recommended your place." It was almost seven; the traffic was bad. "This is terrible," he said, "I'm going to be so late."

"For?"

"Oh, drinks with friends of my parents. My mother's already there. She's going to be so annoyed."

"Well, you could call her. In about five minutes we'll be at my house. You can come in, use our phone if you like."

"That's so nice of you. Are you sure you don't mind?"

"Of course not. Anyway, my dad pays the bill."

"Great. Well, thank you. So how come you work there?" he said, visibly more relaxed. "You just don't seem quite . . . quite . . ." He stopped, obviously afraid of committing a gaffe.

"The sort of girl you find in a hairdressing salon?"

"Well, yes. Sorry, does that sound rude? Or too personal?"

"Not rude. A bit personal. Anyway, whether I am or whether I'm not that sort of girl, I'm to be found there, and I really, really like it. Honestly. I know it looks like shit and it is a lot of the time, but it's also fun and it's what I want to do, and when I'm a stylist, which I will be in another year, life'll be a lot better. And even if I didn't like it," she added with a grin, "I could never admit it to my parents, so I'm stuck with it anyway."

"Your parents aren't into the idea?"

"They're coming round. And at least I'm earning something. However pathetic." They pulled into Bolton Place. "That one, down at the bottom," said Annabel.

"Is this where you live?" he said, looking up at the house.

"This is where I live. Come along in," she said, rummaging in her bag. "I don't seem to have my key, but Josie will let us in."

"Josie?"

"Our housekeeper."

"Oh OK. Would you wait right here?" he said to the cabdriver. Annabel listened, half amused, as he made his phone call; he was clearly terrified of his mother. "Yes, Mother, I know, I know, and I'm sorry. But the traffic was just . . . What? Well, I know I should have, but . . . Yes, anyway. I'll be about . . . Just a minute." He put his hand over the receiver and turned to Annabel. "How long from here, do you think?"

"Oh, the way things are going, about fifteen minutes max."

"Fifteen minutes max," he said. "Anyway, tell Deidre I'm so sorry . . . Yes, OK, I will . . . Yes, sure. Bye, Mother. Phew," he said, putting the phone down. "She wasn't very pleased with me. Can I buy you a drink or something tomorrow, to say thank you? Maybe lunchtime?"

"Lunchtime?" she said, grinning at him. "What's lunchtime?"

"Well, OK, evening then. Around six thirty? Come to the hotel, why don't you?"

"OK. Six thirty it is. Um—why don't you buy your mother's friend some flowers? There's a lovely flower shop in the Fulham Road, near the cinema; the driver'll know it."

"That's a fantastic idea," he said. "Well, I'll see you tomorrow."

"Tomorrow. Have a good evening."

She waved the taxi off, went back inside, and shut the door, smiling. Prince Charming had finally happened along, it seemed.

Alan Richards was extremely upset when he heard about Miss Thompson. Her death made a small paragraph in most of the papers; apparently she'd once been a modestly successful concert pianist and had given piano lessons to local children in the Hampshire village where she lived, completely free for those whose parents couldn't afford to pay.

"Musical philanthropist found dead in cottage," it said, continuing that the whole village mourned her passing; he'd spotted it in the *Sketch* as he travelled to work one morning. She had been such a pathetic old bird, all alone in the world, obviously terribly upset and frightened—and what had they done to help her? Nothing, nothing at all. He kept thinking about her, about how desperate she had been; a neighbour had found her apparently—another old lady, who'd been looking after Miss Thompson's cat. What must that have been like for her as well, the poor old soul? There was to be an inquest; there had been no suicide note left in the cottage, but the neighbour had said that in her view, Miss Thompson had definitely killed herself.

"She'd been very depressed recently and she had money worries, I think, quite serious ones."

He suddenly remembered Joel Strickland and his conversation with him in the George and Vulture. Maybe he'd get in touch now; he felt that he owed it to Miss Thompson. And bugger Norman Clarke.

He looked in his wallet; yes, Joel's card was still there . . .

Chapter 15

People were so complex, Debbie thought. You just never knew. Here she was, ready to fight for her professional life, proclaiming her rights both as an individual and a woman, and ready to argue that Richard should be recognising that rather than crushing her into submission—she'd been rehearsing the arguments for days—and instead he was smiling at her, telling her it would be fine if she worked another day, that he was quite enjoying being with the children more and that he was very proud of her success.

"I've told you, being at work suits you. You seem happier. It's working out very nicely, I think. And the house certainly looks tidier."

"Oh," she said. "Oh I see. Well—that's great. Fantastic. Thank you, Richard. So much."

"No need to thank me," he said. "I was wrong the first time, and I don't mind admitting it. Although I do think three days is enough. I wouldn't be happy with any more. And maybe a little bit of the extra money could go towards a cleaner. Just once a week, say?"

Debbie said of course it could, and kissed him and thanked him again, and then thought that there had been no need to arrange Easter in Wales after all. And then thought what a truly awful person she was, told Richard she'd like to go to bed early—thereby inducing the sheepish smile she'd once thought so sweet and now found so irritating—and set about tidying up the kitchen.

Anyway, it had been fine so far. Flora was throwing herself into grandmothering with her usual enthusiasm which meant that she and Richard could actually have some time to themselves, go for walks, read, and even have some uninterrupted discussions.

She helped him with his CV—"Don't mind me wanting to, I see so many coming into the office, and of course while that's a completely different world, you're still trying to grab people's attention"—acted as sous chef as he prepared an Easter cake as a surprise for Flora, and generally felt rather surprisingly content. Although she could have done without the arrival on Saturday of the Beaumonts. The daughter, Tilly, was all right, but the conversation would be so boring, all about horses and saddles and girths and feed and absolutely nonstop, right through most meals, with Emma listening shiny-eyed.

They arrived at about lunchtime; Tilly tumbling out of the Range Rover and across the yard, taking Boy's head in her hands and kissing his nose rapturously. Flora hurrying out to welcome them, giving Simon a quick kiss and then hugging Tilly. Simon was staying for twenty-four hours and then leaving Tilly until the end of the week; even though he'd lost weight, Debbie thought he still looked like a Ralph Lauren ad, what with the inevitable polo pony on his sweater and the new-looking tweed jacket.

They had lunch in the kitchen and then Flora suggested that she and Tilly go riding. "You can go off on your own with Boy, darling, if you like, but I'd love to come with you."

Tilly said nothing could be nicer, and that when they got back, she'd give Emma a lesson; Emma went red in the face with excitement.

"How long are you down for?" Simon said; and, "Just till Tuesday," Debbie said.

"That's a shame," said Tilly. "I'm here for a whole week and I could have given Emma lots of lessons."

"Well, she could stay," said Flora, "even if you've got to go back. And is there any rush?"

"Yes, there is, I'm afraid," said Debbie. "I've got to go back to work."

"Oh yes, of course. Well, just leave Emma, then—it's fine by me."

"Oh Mummy, please say yes, please . . ."

"We could bring her back," Simon said. "I'm coming down to get Tilly on Sunday, I could easily drop Emma off with you. No problem."

"Well, Richard, what do you think?"

Richard had clearly taken against Simon Beaumont; Debbie had watched, half amused, half sympathetic, as Simon joked and chatted and flattered Flora, and teased the children, holding the table with his easy charm in exactly the way she knew Richard would have loved to do himself. Although he would die rather than admit it.

"Well, I don't know," he said, "isn't it a bit much for you, Mother?"

"Of course not. Don't talk like that, Richard, you make me feel like an old lady."

"What absolute rubbish," Simon said. "I've never known anybody with quite such energy as you, Flora."

"Please, Mr. Fielding," said Tilly, smiling at him, "I'd love Emma to stay. We'll take great care of her, won't we, Flora?"

In the end, Richard gave in.

⟍⟍

"Alan, I really think you should ring that journalist," said Heather. "What harm can it do? It might in fact do some good, not for that poor lady, all right, but maybe some of the others. Go on, give him a call. You could make it anonymous, if you liked. If you're worried."

"Yeah," said Alan. "Yeah, I hadn't thought of that."

"And from a public call box. Then there'd be no trace."

"Blimey, Heather," said Alan admiringly, "you ought to work for MI6."

⁓

Nigel read Lucinda's letter twice before the full meaning of it sank in; then he put his head in his hands and started to weep. He would never have believed anything could hurt so much. Lucinda was having a baby: the baby he had wanted to give her. It was all terribly unfair.

"And so," the letter had ended, "as I am sure you will understand, I do now want a divorce, fairly quickly. I will obviously do everything I can to make it as painless as possible for you. Perhaps you could talk to your solicitor and let me know what you would like me to do."

He'd like her to come back to him, that's what he'd like her to do. Not as she was now, of course, but as she had been, sweet, pretty, loving Lucinda, who had made him so happy and looked after him so well. Why had she gone, for God's sake, why?

"I have no excuse whatsoever," she had said that dreadful night when he had found out. "You've been a perfect husband, Nigel, and I don't deserve you."

Should he perhaps have tried harder then, to make it work? Let her stay, have forgiven her? But he knew it was impossible. He couldn't love someone who had deceived him as dreadfully and as relentlessly as she had. He couldn't imagine now how he had got through those first few awful months: but somehow he had. Work had immunised him against the pain and the humiliation. While he was there he felt safe; worked doggedly for long hours and told no one that Lucinda had left him. The only person he confided in was his secretary, Lydia Newhouse. Lydia had worked for Nigel for almost ten years, and absolutely adored him. She was completely at a loss as to how Lucinda could have done such a dreadful thing: or such a stupid one. Her outrage was immensely soothing to Nigel; he imbibed it with every cup of coffee she made him, every perfectly typed folder of letters she laid in front of him, every gentle enquiry as to whether she could get him anything else before leaving for the night.

But by that spring he was feeling a little better: was growing accustomed to his solitary state, was reverting, slowly if not pleasurably, to bachelorhood, and while he was often lonely and the sense of absolute foolishness that Lucinda's adultery had bestowed upon him still woke him up in the smallest of the small hours, he could begin to contemplate at least a time when he might enjoy himself once more.

Until now: when he felt he had reached a new level of raw pain. And by a most cruel piece of juxtaposition on the part of Fate, the day before the arrival of Lucinda's letter, the next year's results had arrived. With horrifying implications.

Lucinda had been instructed by his solicitor to transfer all the assets into a holding account, where they were frozen while he worked out what to do. But the fact remained that her defection had inflicted another, terrible blow: his assets were no longer safe from the predators of Lloyd's if Lucinda actually returned them to him. The dreadful irony of the situation was not lost on his lawyers; the errant wife holding the key to his financial salvation, or indeed the reverse.

It was Lydia who found him weeping at his desk, over Lucinda's letter—she had been instructed to write to him at work, rather than at home—and over a cup of very sweet coffee, she asked him if there was anything she could do. Emotionally weakened by being caught in such disarray, Nigel found himself telling her the latest sad chapter in his saga. "I can't see her, Lydia, it would be more than flesh and blood could stand."

Lydia thought for a while and then said she thought it was essential he agreed to the divorce.

"You can't go on like this, Mr. Cowper. Things must be properly resolved. For financial reasons as much as anything else. And I think if you could bring yourself to meet her, face-to-face, it would all be so much simpler."

Nigel blew his nose, took another mouthful of the coffee. "Very well, you'd better set up a meeting with my solicitor. I'll start with them and then maybe it won't be necessary for us to meet. Here is Lucinda's telephone number and address; perhaps you could write to her and tell her I'm seeing my solicitor, and that I'll be in touch. I don't think I could bear to speak to her until it is absolutely necessary. Just the same—the sooner the better, if you please."

He means before the baby starts to show, Lydia thought, her heart constricting with sympathy. Heavens, she'd like to give that girl a piece of her mind.

 ☙

Richard had gone for a walk in Richmond Park when Simon arrived with Emma and Tilly. Debbie had a feeling he'd gone there on purpose, in order not to see him, which really was a bit pathetic.

Emma bore Tilly up to her bedroom to show her her collection of Julip horses, and Debbie invited Simon into the kitchen, wishing she'd thought to tidy it up first. His house would doubtless be a model of neatness.

He wandered round it, admiring all the things she liked best herself—her collection of old jugs, the jumble of photographs, the children's paintings she'd had framed—then sat down and drank the mug of tea she had given him.

"Sorry, I don't have any wonderful homemade cakes like Flora's."

"I'm not allowed cakes, wonderful or otherwise; my tailor's forbidden it. So how are things with you, Debbie? I think you'd got a new job last time we met. Do you enjoy it?"

"I love it. Too much, really."

"You can't love anything—or indeed, anyone—too much," he said. "And anyway why shouldn't you love it?"

"Well, I feel a bit guilty, you know, leaving the children and so on."

"Oh, now that is ridiculous," he said. "Tough little things, children, and anyway, as I used to say to Elizabeth, when she said the same, it's not as if you'd sent them out to live on the streets."

"No, of course not. Um . . . did she really say the same, Elizabeth?"

"She really did. But I encouraged her to work anyway, she'd have been miserable at home. It's all very well, this ideal of Mum being at home, baking cakes and making finger puppets. It's a different world now, and people like you and Elizabeth aren't bred for domesticity. You don't fit the mould, and it's unfair to try and force you into it."

Tilly and Emma appeared in the doorway. "Tilly says I must go down to Wales next time she's there," Emma said, beaming.

"Well, that's very kind," said Debbie, "but I'm sure Tilly would like a bit of peace and quiet with her horse."

"Tilly?" said Simon. "She wouldn't know peace and quiet if it came up and hit her. Would you, darling?"

"Daddy, that's so silly. How could peace and quiet come and hit you?"

"OK, sneaked up on you then. Anyway, we should go home, poppet, and see Mummy. She's missed you."

"Well, thank you so much for bringing Emma home," said Debbie, "and for playing with her all week, Tilly. It was very kind indeed."

"Mummy! We weren't playing. Horses are hard work."

"They certainly are," said Simon.

"Daddy! You don't know. All you ever do is look at them."

"True. And I've had some very happy days doing that. Now Debbie, any time you want Emma driven down or brought back, just ring me. Here's my card." She looked at it. Simon Beaumont, it said. Director, Private Clients Division. Graburn and French.

"Thank you," she said, pinning it up onto the board. "I really appreciate it."

He walked out into the hall, bent and kissed Emma, and then, clearly on an impulse, leaned down and kissed Debbie too.

"I've enjoyed our chat," he said. "Bye, Debbie."

"Bye, Simon. So have I."

When Richard got back, she saw him peering at Simon's card. "What on earth is that doing there?" he said.

"Simon gave it to me. In case we wanted him to drive Emma down again. Or bring her back. Wasn't that kind of him?" she said, well aware of what she was doing and unable to resist the temptation.

"Not particularly. If he's driving down anyway . . ." He was clearly jealous; it was rather nice, Debbie thought; she couldn't remember when she'd last been able to do that.

The first date had been perfect: he'd bought Annabel champagne cocktails at the Carlton Tower and then said would she like to have dinner, and was there anywhere she'd like specially to go; she'd suggested Rumours in Covent Garden, because she'd thought he'd find it fun, and it wouldn't be too expensive if she had to pay for herself: although she didn't think she would, he was too much of a gentleman and clearly very well-off. Or at any rate, his parents were.

They were over on a fortnight's trip; his father had business in London, he said, and his mother liked to shop, and he'd had some vacation owed to him, so he'd come along too. He was a lawyer, "just a trainee, actually," pretty fresh out of Harvard; his father was also a lawyer, and had his own firm in Boston, where they lived, and which Jamie had recently joined. He loved the law; he said it fascinated him, creating order out of chaos, making people's lives better. He spoke about it rather as if it was something very noble, and didn't mention the considerable rewards it clearly brought the family.

They seemed to be extremely rich. They lived just off Beacon Hill, which was the very best area in Boston, her father said. He'd met Jamie on their second date when he came to call for her and had been rather taken by him. Jamie was the youngest in the Cartwright family; there was an elder brother called Bartholomew (known as Bif) and a sister called Kathleen; they were both married. Bif was also a lawyer with the family firm. "He's so great," Jamie had said, "such a perfect big brother. All my life he's looked out for me, still does; don't know what I'd do without him. And his wife, Dana, she's very, very beautiful. She works in real estate, makes a lot of money. And Kathleen works in an art gallery. She's an agent for the artists."

"Do either of them have children?"

"Not yet. My mother worries that they're both waiting too long."

"How long have they been married?"

"Oh, Dana and Bif three years, Kathleen almost two."

"But that's nothing," said Annabel, adding, "is it?" not wishing to sound rude or in any way possessed of the sort of opinions Kathleen—or more possibly, her mother—might consider unsympathetic.

"Well, I think Kathleen feels a little torn. She loves her job, and she's really good at it, but I guess for a girl the whole point of getting married is to make a family."

"I think it's much more to be with the person you love," said Annabel, "and to enjoy life together. You're a mother for a long time. That's what my mother says anyway."

"Your mother sounds amazing," said Jamie, "doing that job and raising a family at the same time."

"Yes, she is, although my dad did a lot. I don't mean he changed nappies and stuff, we had nannies, but if my mum couldn't get to a school thing, for instance, then he would come along."

"He seems to be a pretty special guy altogether," said Jamie. "I really like him."

"I like him too," said Annabel. He was actually a bit like her father, Annabel thought: charming, easy to be with. She felt happy with him, really happy. When he took her home that night in a cab (having paid for dinner), he kissed her nearly all the way. It was extremely nice.

"You are really, really special," he said to her, as she finally and reluctantly got out of the cab, driven by the cabbie's rather determined throat-clearing and coughing, "and I can't wait to see you again. Tomorrow?"

"Tomorrow—yes, please."

There was still over a week to go. It was absolutely brilliant.

⸎

"Hello! Isn't it Mrs. Cowper?"

Of course it was: looking more beautiful than ever, and dressed a lot more sexily, in an above-the-knee skirt—more of those incredible legs on display, that was good—and quite a sharp little jacket in brilliant pink. She looked puzzled for a moment.

"We met at the Lloyd's do, that legal-ish meeting."

"Oh—of course. Yes." She smiled at him, that wonderful half shy, half flirtatious smile. "And you're Mr. Beaumont."

"Simon, please. How are you?"

"I'm fine. And I'm Lucinda." Lucinda. He remembered now. What an absurdly perfect name for her. "It's lovely to see you. Whatever are you doing in this part of town?"

"It's nice to see you too. I was . . . um . . . well, having lunch with someone."

"Right. Good lunch?"

"Yes, it was lovely, thank you. I'm haring back to work now, bit late."

"I've been trying to get hold of your husband. To discuss something. But he hasn't returned my calls. I wonder if you could jog him? It's quite important—to do with Lloyd's, actually."

"Well . . . well, the thing is . . . we're—we're not together any-more . . ."

"Oh. Oh, I'm sorry. How sad."

"Yes. Yes, it is."

Not for her, obviously; it explained a good deal. And not too surprising, really.

"But I will be seeing him, quite soon, so I'll try and get him to call you. But—but he might not. I . . . well, I don't have much influence over him, I'm afraid."

"No, of course not. But that would be very kind. Tell me, where's work?"

"Oh, Bloomsbury. I work for a publisher, Peter Harrison."

"Oh really? Didn't you publish that biography of Soros? I've put it on my birthday list. Look—let me give you my card. I did give it to your husband, but he might have lost it. Would that be all right?"

"Yes, of course. Well, it was really nice to see you again. Bye now." And she was gone, with another dazzling smile. He stood looking after her, drinking her in as she disappeared into the throng of people.

Catherine Morgan, who had been hurrying out of the Graburn and French building, saw him chatting to Lucinda and felt a pang of jealousy. Only a very mild one; and obviously she couldn't possibly compete with Lucinda's starry glamour, but after four months of working for Simon Beaumont, she was definitely slightly in love with him. Not enough in love to make her unhappy, or to cause him a moment's unease; just enough to make going to work pleasantly exciting. She didn't see him every day; but when she did, he always smiled at her, asked her how she was, and if there was time, like before a meeting where she was taking the minutes, or in the lift, how the children were, how they were getting on, particularly Freddie; and when he smiled at her, that extraordinarily easy, charming smile, she felt like skipping or singing. She knew it was silly, a grown-up version of a schoolgirl crush, but it still made life more fun. And her life had been pretty short on fun the last few years.

In fact, everything seemed better; Freddie was terribly pleased to be back at Lynton House, and Caroline seemed not to mind in the very least that she was still at St. Joseph's Fulham. She managed to meet Caroline only occasionally a little late, and they usually got to Lynton House just before the boys all came out; apart from the mercifully rare nightmare days when one or other of them was ill it worked brilliantly. And for the holidays, she had found a very nice woman, Mrs. Lennox, who lived a few doors away and who was happy to look after them.

Her life, Catherine thought as she walked through Leadenhall Market, really had improved dramatically. And it was all down to Simon, to charming, handsome, kind Simon Beaumont, who was, she saw, gazing at Lucinda as she got into a taxi, patently wishing he was going off in it with her . . .

℮

The more Joel Strickland heard from the players in this Lloyd's drama, the more he thought it would make a brilliant article. But God, it was hard getting it together. That phone call from that poor terrified bloke—what did he think was going to happen to him, for God's sake, that he'd be put in the Tower?—had put quite a bit more of the jigsaw in place. And although he was very sorry for the old lady, a death always brought a story alive. Gave it a heart. His editor had been very lukewarm, had said what everyone said: that nobody was going to care very much about a whole lot of rich spoiled people crying because they were going to be a bit less rich. Initially Joel had agreed with him, but a little homework had revealed something rather different.

Gillian Thompson, for instance, hadn't been rich or spoiled. And from what the bloke had said, a fairly recent recruit to Lloyd's. Poor old soul. Who had done that to her? Who had suggested she became a Name? And how had it been allowed to happen, when the minimum capital requirement was £75,000, and that was supposed to exclude your main residence? And according to that young man, she'd been put in the wrong sort of high-risk syndicate, along with a lot of other people. Joel decided to go and visit May Williams, the unfortunate woman who had discovered her body.

Chapter 16

"Darling, whatever is it? Look, you know we don't allow tears here. Far too self-indulgent. And you'll turn that blond solution brown if you're not careful and then all the clients will sue. Come on, sweetie, nothing's that bad. How about I take you out for a really glamorous cup of cocoa after work, no expense spared . . . here, wipe your eyes on this—no, not that, you silly bitch, not my foils . . ."

In spite of herself, Annabel half smiled, rubbed her fist across her eyes. "Sorry."

"I should just think so, and you should see yourself now—you look like something out of the *Black and White Minstrel* . . ."

"Well, thanks!"

"That's all right. Oh God, here comes the Virgin Queen. Miki, darling, just leave us for two minutes, that's all I ask, just a tiny little upset here, and then I'm all yours—if you'll only have me."

"Florian," said Miki, "in two minutes, Mrs. Alexander will have left the salon for good. She's furious. Get upstairs and start calming her down right now. And Bel, if you have to cry, please do it in your own time. You've got two clients waiting to be shampooed. I will not have this sort of nonsense in the salon, it is so absolutely unprofessional. Now wash your face and get back to work at once, please."

Annabel really hadn't expected to feel this bad. She'd only known Jamie for two weeks, and here she was acting like they'd been together for years. Maybe that proved how important it was. And at least she'd passed the biggest test of all: meeting his parents.

They'd had a totally perfect weekend, a lovely afternoon and evening in London—lots of cocktails at the Criterion in Piccadilly (fun), then dinner at Daphne's (divine), and then—then champagne and endless wonderful snogging in Jamie's room at the Carlton Tower. His parents were away for the night, he'd said, so he felt very relaxed. She couldn't quite get over a man of twenty-four feeling inhibited by his parents' presence several rooms along the corridor in a hotel, but still . . .

He told her he didn't want to have sex yet; he said it was too soon. She was half disappointed, half pleased by this; having grown up in a culture where sex had moved so far up the dating agenda that it was regarded by many as the norm on the second date at the latest, such modest behaviour seemed rather odd. But it made her feel quite special. She wondered if it was shyness on his part, or even fear, but as they lay on his bed, watching the dawn come up, he said he had had two quite serious relationships before, and that he simply thought that you should be very sure of yourself and your feelings before you asked someone to go to bed with you.

"It's a huge commitment, as far as I'm concerned. I don't think it should be like—well, like just kissing."

She fell asleep contentedly in his arms, still half dressed; she was sure the waiter who brought them breakfast in bed would never have believed the innocence of the night they had spent.

And then, on the way back from Bath, from another perfect day together, driving through the endless golden midsummer evening, he suddenly said, "Stop the car, I want to tell you something."

Half frightened, she had pulled onto the hard shoulder and sat, heart thumping, waiting for some kind of harsh judgement or final farewell.

"I want you to know I'm in love with you," he said. "I know it's all been fast, but I'm totally sure. And I need to know how you feel about me."

"I feel the same," she said, "darling Jamie. Just the same. So that's really good, isn't it?"

"Really good. And so I thought, we could go back to the hotel and—well, prove it to each other. Now that we're both sure."

They drove the rest of the way with his hand tucked companionably between her thighs; by the time they got back to the hotel, Annabel was in such a state of acute sexual excitement she could hardly sit still, and her pants were uncomfortably damp: so damp indeed that she feared her fine voile skirt might reveal the fact.

And then, as they hurried into the foyer, hand in hand, giggling like guilty children, and went over to the desk to get his room key, they heard a voice. A low, drawling, slightly hard-edged voice: "Jamie, darling, there you are. We wondered. Good weekend? Are you going to join us for dinner?"

It was his mother.

She was all right, Annabel supposed, shaking Mrs. Cartwright's hand, keeping her back to the reception counter, smiling dutifully, wishing she'd at least had time to comb her hair, still extremely ruffled by some heavy-duty snogging in a cornfield just outside Bath, and for all she knew, containing lots of ears of corn. Mrs. Cartwright was polite and gracious if a little chilly; she was certainly beautiful, in a blond Grace Kelly sort of way, perfectly dressed and pressed and coiffed, and although she obviously wasn't very pleased to find her son in the company of this strange girl, and one moreover he was clearly very taken with, she made a good attempt at disguising it, urging Annabel to join them for dinner. Which of course she accepted; she could hardly claim a prior engagement when she and Jamie had been so unmistakably going up to his room together and as good as neon signs on their heads saying Orgasms Imminent.

And it had been agony in a way, trying to calm down, pretending everything was really cool, not being able to get him to tell her over and over again that he loved her, not being able to tell him the same thing, not being able to have sex, for God's sake. But precisely because she did love him so much and she wanted to please him, and wanted his parents to like her, she managed it, listened politely to details of a night in Stratford, and a visit to Shakespeare's birthplace and inevitably (they being Americans) to criticism of their hotel and comparisons with ones they had stayed at in the States, like the Bel-Air in Los Angeles.

When Mr. Cartwright joined them, it was better; he was just an older version of Jamie, and she had a lot of fun comparing them; he was also quite flirtatious in a very upper-class way, and she liked that. And when finally the endless evening was over, she knew that she would have to go home, on her own, and there would be no sex that night, or even for many, many nights, as the Cartwrights were leaving the next evening. But it was all worth it, because Jamie suddenly appeared in the salon at lunchtime next day, and she somehow persuaded Tania to let her out just for ten minutes; and there, standing out in the street, he told her he loved her, and that he would see her soon; somehow, he'd be back, and if not she had to come over and stay with them in Boston, "Because my parents both loved you, my mother particularly. She said you were absolutely de-lightful, and I don't remember her ever saying that before about any of my girlfriends."

And then he gave her a kiss, a quick, light, lingering kiss, and he was

gone. Leaving Annabel not sure whether to laugh or cry. Within the space
of the next twenty-four hours, she had done a great deal of both.

Chapter 17

MAY 1990

Lucinda hadn't been sick at all during her pregnancy until the day she and
Nigel were to meet to discuss the divorce. She woke up feeling absolutely
dreadful, sobbing, her nightdress drenched with sweat, to find Blue shaking her; she clung to him, refusing to speak and then, suddenly overcome
with nausea, had to rush to the bathroom where she threw up repeatedly.

"Sweet, what is it? For God's sake, you got to tell me. Get back to bed,
I'll call the doctor." He had come in after her, was standing looking down
on her as she knelt by the lavatory, a ghastly colour himself. She blew her
nose, managed to stand up, even to smile at him.

"It's OK, I'm OK, I've only been sick, for heaven's sake, there's nothing wrong. I just had some bad dreams, and you know it's today, with
Nigel and—"

"Course I know it's today. I didn't expect you to be in this sort of state
though. I think I'd better come with you."

"No," said Lucinda wearily, "no, Blue. It's going to be bad enough for
Nigel without you being there."

"Well, thanks for that. I don't like it, Lucy, not one bit. I just don't
like you going off on your own, facing him and all, and now if you're
ill . . ."

He had been totally horrified by the suggestion when it came from
Nigel; it had taken days to persuade him.

"I'm not having it and that's that," he kept saying. "You're not seeing
him, not without me."

Lucinda had been rather shocked by this; in fact, it led to one of their
rare but colourful rows.

"It's not a question of you having or not having anything," she had
said. "It's my decision, and I've made it. And I'm going. There's nothing
more to discuss."

In the end, he had agreed; but with extreme reluctance.

"I just don't like it," he said now. "I think it's wrong. He might do anything to you."

"Blue, of course he won't do anything to me. I simply feel awful about it all. You must see that."

"You have to get rid of some of this guilt, Lucy," said Blue, "otherwise you're going to drive yourself mad. There's a long tough road ahead of you—"

"I don't see why it has to be long or tough. I'm not going to argue about anything. I want to do everything for him that I can."

"You know," said Blue, "this is not the way to approach divorce, Lucinda. His solicitor's going to take you to the cleaners if you're not careful."

"But he's welcome to. He can take me to all the cleaners he can find. I don't want anything from Nigel, anything at all. I want to help him. Anyway, I've got nothing to give him, that's half the trouble, why I feel so bad." She started to cry again.

"I really think I'd better come with you," Blue said. "Lucinda, you ever had any dealings with lawyers?"

"No. Except when we bought our flat. Oh, and when Nigel made over all that money to me; we had to go and sign some stuff about the more complicated things."

"Thought not. They're fucking villains. Every minute you spend with them, that's money in their pockets. So the more minutes the better. You can see them watching the clock, adding it up. So just you be careful. And I wish you'd let me find you someone, someone shit hot, not this dickhead who looks after your dad."

"He's not a dickhead," said Lucinda, "and don't talk like that. I keep telling you— Oh God, I think I'm going to be sick again."

℮

It was truly shocking news. Elizabeth phoned after an early meeting, her voice sober: Neil Lawrence had taken an overdose, was in intensive care. Simon stood in the hall, feeling shaky and oddly frightened.

"Is there anything we should do?" he said.

"I don't know, Simon. His wife's with him. It's touch and go, apparently. She found him, poor girl. Someone called the agency, he was coming in later today."

"Oh, Christ. Look, I'll speak to you later. Keep me posted."

He walked back into the kitchen, still feeling sick, sat down at the table. Annabel was there, drinking orange juice.

"You look awfully pale, Daddy." She put her arm round his shoulders. "What's wrong?"

"Oh, nothing that need trouble you."

How could he tell her, tell this beloved child, or indeed the other beloved children, that a man faced with the same problems as his own, the loss of everything he had, had attempted suicide, had been so deranged with terror and shame that he had not even properly considered the effect of that on his wife and children . . .

Later, when she had gone, he called George Meyer.

"A friend—no, an acquaintance tried to kill himself last night. Took an overdose— He's up to his neck, half a million's worth of debt, no hope of paying it, had kept it from his wife, obviously finally cracked. Nice chap, I really liked him."

There was a silence, then George said, "Could you ever imagine doing that?"

"No, not in a million years. You've let them win then, haven't you? Christ, I keep thinking, could I have done something for him, helped in some way . . . When's it going to end, George?"

"God knows," said George, "and I actually doubt if He's very interested."

"You know something?" Simon said suddenly. "I'm going to talk to that journalist I told you about. People need to know just how bad this fucking business really is."

❧

Tim Allinson had decided: it was time to get out and move to the south of France. He'd almost decided that before, but he'd thought one more summer season, and then he'd sell up. There was plenty to sell; the flat in Pelham Crescent was worth a bit, and there were a few paintings, and some very nice furniture, and he had Lloyd's, or to be precise the Westfield Bradley Group of Syndicates, to thank for all that. He'd always loved

Nice: or perhaps Antibes, that was so beautiful, fish restaurants to die for and there was the Hotel du Cap, best Bellinis in the world, in his opinion. And he could afford to retire, pretty well. He had some investments, and you never knew, there were lots of rich widows down there. But—it was getting dodgy in England now. He hadn't liked being told, very nicely of course, to stop working a house party, as his host had put it, the weekend before.

"All very well, old chap," his host had said, "singing the praises of Lloyd's, but it just isn't the safe bet it was. I wouldn't touch it these days— few nasty stories coming out."

Tim had said, only mildly indignant, that Lloyd's was as safe as the Bank of England and he'd only been talking about it to Mick Bridgeman, not trying to suggest he joined—which of course he wouldn't have done, he always made the formal approach on his own patch, but just the same it had shaken him. He didn't want to get caught with his very expensive trousers down. Best find something else to do. Like wooing widows.

⁊

Michael Booker, one of the Members' Agents at Jackson and Bond, was delighted to accept a lunch invitation from Simon Beaumont.

"Just wanted to talk a few things through with you," Simon said, "given the time of year and the approach of the results. And I've asked George Meyer along."

"Fine. Splendid."

Simon had booked a table at Simpson's in the Strand. He was well-known there, they'd get good service and at worst a very good lunch; he and George were there before Booker, drinking neat tonic water with ice and lemon.

"We need very clear heads," Simon had said.

Michael Booker walked in; he was tall and dark, just slightly overweight, and dressed in a superbly cut suit that almost but not quite concealed the fact. He came over to the table, smiling, hand held out.

"Jolly nice to see you both."

God, these people are incredible, Simon thought. Skins like four-ply rhino hide.

"And you, Michael. We're on gin and tonic—suit you?"

· 177 ·

Booker said it would suit very well. He ate heartily—oysters, beef and ale pie, and a wonderfully Bunter-ish trifle. He talked on unabated, glimpses of his meal constantly on show as he chomped. Finally as he waved away the cheese trolley—"Supposed to be watching my weight"—he said, "And what about you chaps—everything all right with you? Any particular issues you wanted to discuss?"

Simon, who had resisted more than one glass of a very fine Merlot with great difficulty, said there were a few. "And when do we get next year's results?"

"Ah," said Booker, "yes. Well, good old Lloyd's"—God, thought Simon, maybe he's going to tell us it's better, maybe we can all begin to breathe a bit more easily—"punctual as usual."

"And—what news might you have for us?"

"For you? Well, not entirely good, I'm afraid. No. No, indeed." His face, flushed with the Merlot, had become rather sweaty; it was not an attractive sight. "No. 'Fraid Westfield Bradley in particular have taken a bit of a pasting. This year."

"Not like last year," said Simon drily.

"What? Oh, yes. Yes, quite true. Bit of a bad patch altogether. Yes."

"Michael," said George, "this is more than a bad patch. It's gone on and on."

"Indeed. But—well, that's why I was glad to come today, have a chat. I didn't want you rushing off to sell your houses, do anything hasty."

"Unfortunately you're a little late to prevent that," said Simon. "We've both done some house-selling. I still have my main residence—"

"Oh, good man. Want to hold on to that."

"Yes," said Simon, "I do actually. But it looks a bit more difficult. I am actually wondering what to do."

"Well, you know, you can always speak to me."

"That's very good to know, of course," said Simon, "but to be perfectly honest, I don't feel we can talk frankly without there being a risk of your coming up against a clash of interest or divided loyalties."

"There is no way that can happen, Simon. I don't quite follow."

"Well, just for example, in a letter to me last November you showed how support for the Westfield Bradley Syndicate over the period 1986–87 dropped by about seventy percent—more than £300 million. But you only reduced my participation by about ten percent. Why didn't you take me right out of them?"

"Simon," said Booker, a note of near-indignation in his voice, "we were seriously concerned that if everyone pulled out, the syndicates would go down the pan. It's absolutely crucial that syndicates remain operative. For all our sakes."

They sat staring at him in silence for about twenty seconds; then Simon spoke.

"Michael, I am speechless. I think you've just made my point."

Booker left quite shortly; when he had gone, Simon ordered another bottle of Merlot.

"Well, what do you think?" he said. "Was that gun smoking or not?"

"I'm not sure," said George, pulling a notebook out of his pocket. "I take his point about keeping the syndicates going. But let's write down every bloody word and pass it into Ms. Broadhurst's tender keeping."

❧

They had agreed to meet in the lounge of the Selfridge Hotel at teatime. It was ideal for their purpose, Lucinda said, having proposed it; it was very quiet, it was about halfway between both their offices.

Four o'clock saw them walking up the stairs at the same time: recognising each other, smiling faintly and saying hello, and then being led to one of the low chintz-covered sofas and ordering tea.

"And scones," said Lucinda, smiling at the waiter, "scones, oh and Little Scarlet strawberry jam if you've got it. He loves scones, don't you, Nigel?"

He managed to nod.

The pain was so awful he thought he might pass out from it. Sitting there, looking at her, so lovely, her fair hair scooped back in a ponytail, her large blue eyes fixed tenderly—if rather nervously—on him; it was like a form of particularly awful torture. Nothing showed, thank goodness; she was thinner, if anything. That helped—a bit. The alternative would have been unbearable.

"You look . . . well," he said. Simply speaking was an effort.

"Thank you. So do you."

"Yes, well. I've been to Norfolk a lot at the weekends. Country air, you know."

"Good, I'm glad. Oh, and before I forget, I don't suppose you'll want to, but Simon Beaumont, you know that nice man from the Lloyd's meeting, he wants you to ring him about something."

"Why have you been talking to Simon Beaumont?"

"Oh, I bumped into him last week. In the City."

And he knew why she had been in the City: meeting HIM. He winced. "Well, I don't want to talk to him," he said. "That lawsuit against Lloyd's, is the last thing I can be doing with at the moment."

"Of course, I understand. I'll . . . I'll call and tell him. Don't give it another thought."

She smiled at him: her sweet perfect smile . . .

"Lucinda, we have to talk."

"Yes, Nigel, I know. You're not eating your scone."

"I don't want the bloody scone," he said, and his voice sounded quite violent even to him.

"Sorry," she said. "Sorry, Nigel."

"It's OK. Let's just get on, shall we, with deciding what we're going to do. How we're going to play it. The thing is," he said, "my solicitor says that we have to decide who's going to petition whom."

"That means who's going to divorce who. Is that right?"

"Yes, that's right . . . I presume you've talked to someone about it."

"No, I haven't actually. Except, well, except my . . . my family."

She meant HIM: the person he couldn't bear to think about. "Right. So—no one legal."

"Well, no. I thought you should tell me what you want first, and then I'll just go along with it. I want to be helpful, Nigel, that's the very least I can do for you."

"Indeed," he said coldly.

"I'm so sorry," she said. "So sorry. You do know that, don't you?"

"So you keep saying."

"I know it's awful. Awful for you."

"Oh, I don't know."

"Well—good. Maybe not quite so awful then."

"It's been totally fucking awful," he choked out, "more awful than you could possibly imagine. Why did you do it, Lucinda? How could you do it? Why didn't you stop, right at the beginning, before—before any-thing— Oh shit!" The tears had begun: he could feel one running down his nose, and the shame of that was intense. He was sitting here, suppos-edly cool and in control, sorting out the details of their divorce, and he was blubbering like a baby. He fumbled in his pocket for his handker-chief, blew his nose, wiped his eyes.

"Sorry," he said. "So sorry."

"Oh Nigel," she said, and he looked up at her then, at the break in her own voice, and saw that she was crying too, tears spilling out of her eyes, trickling down her cheeks. "Nigel, don't say you're sorry. I feel so ashamed, so dreadfully ashamed, making you so unhappy, oh dear, dear Nigel," and she moved nearer to him, put her arms round him, and he clung to her, useless as he knew it was, feeling just for a moment the briefest sensation of happiness as he felt her warmth again, smelled her, loved her still, so, so much.

"I'm sorry," he said again, pulling back quickly, wiping his eyes again. "No, really, I'm fine. I—I wonder if you can get a drink here, this time of day."

"Of course you can, of course, it's a hotel, for heaven's sake." She waved at the waiter. "Could we have—what do you want, Nigel? Whiskey?"

"No, I'll have a brandy," he said. "Make it a double, would you? What about you?"

"No, I won't. I'm not—I don't want one, thank you," and he thought she was going to say, "I'm not allowed to," and he wrenched his mind with such effort from the reason that he felt quite dizzy.

"I—Nigel, before we start talking about the divorce, what about the money? What about Lloyd's? It's been worrying me so much, now that it's back in your court, so to speak . . ."

"Me too," he said, taking an enormous slug of the brandy. "And you know, what I discovered, I really think my solicitor should have told me: had I gone bankrupt two years after I made over that money to you, the transfer would have been null and void anyway. So it wasn't so clever."

"Oh, that's terrible. God, they're awful, those people, aren't they? Sup-pose I claimed all the money, and then gave it back to you. How would that be?"

"Don't be silly," he said, "they'd work that out in a trice. Anyway, I don't want to be offensive, Lucinda," and for the first time that day he managed a real smile, "but I really don't think you would be able to. You are the guilty party, after all."

"Yes, of course. I do know. Just joking. Well . . ." She was silent for a moment, thinking of Blue, of his words that morning. "There might be something. Lawyers are very, very clever, you know. They can do all sorts of things the rest of us might never think of."

"Mine isn't," said Nigel gloomily. "What about yours?"

"I was going to use Daddy's, but maybe I can find a really clever person and see if there isn't a way round it all."

"Lucinda, there can't be. I've made a frightful hash of it, and now I've just got to pay up. If I end up bankrupt, which I very well could, I'll have to put up with it. Get a job in a shop or something. Go and live in a council flat."

"You wouldn't lose the house, would you?"

"I could, apparently. I could lose everything. Down to the last cuff link, that's what they say to you at Lloyd's when you become a Name. So even Grandpa Cowper's gold-and-diamond ones would go."

"No, they won't." Those cuff links epitomised Nigel in a funny way: they were his heritage, the symbol of his family, his roots. She had put them on for him so many times before they went out; he loved them, was intensely proud of them. "You are not losing those cuff links, Nigel," she said, suddenly fierce, "nor the house, nor the farm. We'll work something out, I promise you. I have no idea how, but . . ."

She went straight home after their meeting; she was tired. Blue was waiting for her there, drinking whiskey, white-faced.

"You all right?" he said. "Feeling OK, no more throwing up, how was he, what did he say, he'd better not have been difficult—"

"Oh Blue, do shut up," said Lucinda wearily, "and—look, I was wrong this morning. I think I'd like to talk to a shit-hot lawyer. As soon as possible. Will you help me find one, please?"

Chapter 18

Richard had announced that he was going off on a teaching conference for three days. "It sounds very interesting, and I think it's the sort of thing that would make my CV look a bit better. As you pointed out, it's not great in some ways. Of course I realise it's half term and it will make things difficult for you, but I'm sure other working mothers manage. They can't all have teacher husbands."

He had smiled at her but there was an edge to his voice. There was no way she was going to ask him not to go, Debbie thought, no way he could claim her job put obstacles in his path.

"Of course. No, it's fine. There's lots of people I can ask. I might even get one of our babysitters to do it."

"I don't think I like that idea," he said. "I can't think some half-baked schoolgirl could possibly cope with them full-time, it's a bit different from an evening, Debbie."

"Richard, I was thinking of one of the sixth formers, they're not exactly half baked. Anyway, don't worry about it."

"I'll try not to," he said, and turned to walk out of the room.

But they were still happy; the extra day didn't seem to be causing any problems and she'd even found a cleaner. She wasn't much good, but it seemed to be the principle that counted.

Flora offered to have the children for half term. "It must be so hard," she said, "managing while you're working, and of course with Richard doing this course . . ."

"Well—yes." Was there anything he didn't tell his mother? God, it was annoying.

"And what about the summer holidays?" Flora went on. "Even if you do go camping in France for some of the time—"

"I didn't know we were going camping in France," said Debbie briskly.

"Oh darling, I'm sorry. Richard just said it was a possibility—perhaps he wants to surprise you . . . Oh, how stupid of me."

"No, Flora, it's fine. We may well do that. But yes, half term would be wonderful. Thank you. One of us will bring them down."

"Splendid. And hopefully stay a day or two. Tilly will be here too, and Emma adores her, doesn't she, so we shall have a full house. Which will be very nice for me. Goodbye, Debbie. Let me know when they'll be coming."

Debbie put the phone down, and instead of feeling relieved and happy, she felt cross and miserable. Courses, summer holidays—what else did he talk to his mother about? Their finances? Their sex life? Nothing would surprise her.

℮

"Goodness." Lucinda had been looking for the address of a literary agent; a manuscript had come in, completely hopeless, like so many of them, and it had to be sent back with one of the charming and regretful notes that were her specialty. Other people sent printed cards; Lucinda, with her tender heart, felt that rejection of what represented at the very least a great deal of hard work should be softened. Only she couldn't find the address. She couldn't find a lot of things these days; her brain seemed to be shrinking as her uterus grew. But it didn't seem to matter; she had never been so happy. Every time she thought about caring for their baby, hers and Blue's—and Blue as well, of course—she felt as if she was looking at some wonderful, warm, sunlit meadow.

The only darkness cast over the meadow was Nigel; Nigel and his dreadful, patent misery. And it was quite a big darkness, for it was her fault.

Blue had said he really couldn't quite see that Nigel needed any help, but that he was fixing for her to see a solicitor mate of his: "Not quite your idea of one, Lucy, went to the same shit-awful—"

"Blue, don't use that language, you've got to start thinking of the baby."

"Sorry. Same bloody-awful comp as I did, dragged hisself up from there, but my God, he's got a brain and a half. Three-quarters, actually. OK?"

"Yes, OK. But bloody isn't much better than shit."

She was off to see him that afternoon, actually, which was probably why her brain was so feeble; she was very nervous. She finally found the agent's address tucked into a pile of reviews, waiting for filing. Along with Simon Beaumont's card.

"Goodness," she said again now, talking to herself, for Graham was out at lunch, "I promised to call him, completely forgot." She'd better make amends—do it at once.

He was very pleasant, of course, said it didn't matter in the least—"But sweet of you to ring at all."

"Yes, well, I think it's so awful not to do what you say. And I've not done about a hundred things today, I shall get fired if I'm not careful. I tell you what," she said suddenly, looking at the row of books on her shelf, "I can ship over a copy of that Soros book you were talking about, if you haven't got it yet. It's the least I can do, after forgetting to ring you."

"Don't be silly, it's only been a few days and I told you it didn't matter. I wouldn't dream of accepting the book."

"Well, you should dream of it. I've got at least a dozen here. Take it off your birthday list. When is it?"

"Next week, actually. May the twenty-fifth."

"I'm coming into the City that very day to, well, to see someone—so I could drop it into your office. I'm looking at your card now, you're in Threadneedle Street, aren't you, and I'm meeting my friend in Cornhill."

"That's astonishingly kind. You wouldn't like to have lunch with me, I suppose, instead? Really make my birthday?"

"No, sorry," she said, and giggled. "I don't think my fiancé would find that very amusing. But I'll leave the book in reception for you, shall I?"

"Absolutely not. I'll come down and get it. Or give you an after-lunch coffee, how about that?"

She hesitated, then said almost regretfully, "No, I'll be dashing back to work. Sorry again."

"Never mind. Bye, Lucinda."

She sat smiling at the phone rather foolishly. He was quite dishy. Then she shook herself. Honestly, Lucinda, whatever would Blue say?

❧

Debbie had agreed to take the children down to Wales on the Saturday; this had caused major ructions from Emma. "But Mummy, there's a horse show on Saturday, Granny says, and she and Tilly are going—can't we go on Friday? Oh, please please, we'll be finished at school by three and—"

"No," said Debbie, "we can't. I'm working on Friday, and Daddy's off on his course . . ." It seemed a bit odd that, a course starting over a weekend, but she didn't press him on it, she knew it would be interpreted as awkwardness.

"So? We could get there late. Granny always likes that, and—"

"Emma, no."

Emma jumped up, rushed out of the room, slammed the door. "I hate you!" she shouted, from the top of the stairs.

Richard's eyes met Debbie's. "She's starting early," he said, and grinned. She grinned back. He seemed much happier suddenly. Maybe he'd just begun to accept that things had changed.

A compromise was finally reached; the cross-country event was being held at Margam Country Park, which was near Swansea. Debbie and the children would meet Flora and the Beaumonts there.

"It'll be so much fun," said Emma, her eyes shining. "There's a course with lots of jumps, and Tilly and Boy have a really good chance of doing well, Granny says. We can follow them round—"

"What, over the jumps?" said Alex. "I can just see you doing that, Emma, making that stupid trotting noise—"

"Oh, shut up," said Emma. "You don't know anything!"

☙

"Well, this is fun." Debbie stood in the sunshine, smiling at Flora, surprised to find she meant it. Here she was, surrounded by people in Wellingtons with Labradors and shooting sticks, yelling at one another in what seemed pretty well a foreign language, and yet she was really enjoying herself.

"Isn't it? When the weather's good, a day of horse trials is unbeatable. Even if you don't like horses, Debbie, which I know you don't."

"It's not the horses I don't like, it's the—" and then she stopped, horrified at what she had nearly said.

"Horsey people," Flora finished for her. "Don't look so upset, nor do I—well, not some of them. Dreadful insensitive lot, they can be. But they can be fun, and there is one quality they nearly all share, which is courage. They're mostly very brave—like the horses they ride. Which is a nice quality, I think," she added. "Right, come on, everybody, time to move on."

They had spent about ten minutes at the jump; watched three horses take it, seen one rider come off, one horse stumble and then recover, and one soar over it. Debbie was beginning to get the hang of the whole thing; you moved from one jump to the next, stood patiently at the back as the first horse approached, unable to see much, then shuffled forward for the second, pushing the children in front, and then got a front-row seat—or rather stand—for the third. A few people even carried small stepladders round, which they stood on. She would never have believed she would find it fun, or even remotely interesting, but here she was, clapping and shouting "Oohh!" and "Ahh!" and "Hurray!" in the prescribed manner.

"When will it be Tilly?" asked Emma. "Please say she's soon, I can't wait much longer."

"I think she's next but one," said Flora. "I honestly don't think she'll do very well," she said under her voice to Debbie, "not her fault, she and Boy just haven't had the time to practise, but she's very talented, she might come in moderately well. Ah, here's Simon, did you find her?"

"Yes. She's a mass of nerves, poor child. We shouldn't have let her do it, Flora, she was sick last night you know, and I—"

"Oh, nonsense," said Flora. "She'll have a marvellous day's riding, meet some of the other young people from round here, and at worst, it's a wonderful experience. I mean, just being here taking part is a privilege. Look at it, all of you."

Debbie looked: at the graceful parkland of Margam, the ruined abbey below them, the blue sky above studded with seagulls, and all around them, the golden gorse of early summer on the endless rolling green of the hills. And at the horses, beautiful, gleaming, perfectly schooled, so brave as Flora had said as they took the sometimes impossible-seeming jumps, their riders so absolutely at one with them that they hardly appeared separate beings; she closed her eyes for a moment and heard her children all laughing, and she felt briefly and absurdly happy and wished that Richard was there with her.

And then they heard, "Number seventeen, Miss Ottilie Beaumont, on Golden Boy," and everything was blotted out and they stayed where they were, afraid that if they moved they might miss her. The jump was a horror, two almost at once, set in a zigzag.

Debbie found herself digging her nails into her palms as they saw the bright blur that was Boy and Tilly a few hundred yards away, soaring over the first two jumps, heard the applause, watched them go out of sight for a while, and then reappear, clearing the water jump that preceded the zigzag, saw them coming towards it now, stood totally silent, all of them equally terrified, as she drew near enough for them to see her face, white and absolutely set in its concentration, her eyes fixed on her own personal horizon, and then she was there, upon them, taking the jump; Debbie felt first one hand grabbed suddenly by Emma and then another by Simon. Amused and touched, she glanced up at him; he was pale, his eyes fixed on his daughter as if he could take her over by sheer willpower. Tilly cleared the first fence, turned Boy neatly, and dug her heels hard into his side; he seemed to hesitate for what felt like minutes and "Go on, go on," groaned Simon, and then, then it was all right, and Boy seemed to take heart, jumped again, a little late it seemed to Debbie; he cleared it, but then clipped it with his hooves, stumbled slightly, and then recovered. Tilly pulled him up, and they were off again on their way, disappearing into a thicket.

"Water next. She'll be fine there," said Flora. "God, she did well. They both did. Oh, I'm so proud of her."

"Me too," said Simon, and he released Debbie's hand suddenly, as if he had only just realised he had been holding it. He grinned at her. "Sorry," he said, laughing, "got a bit carried away."

"I don't mind," she said, laughing back at him. "Goodness, that was wonderful. How do you think she's doing, Flora?"

"We won't know for a bit. She's not going very fast, so——"

"Granny!" said Emma. "She was going like the wind."

"I know, darling, but some of the others were going faster than the wind. And he'll lose marks for clipping that fence. But she should get round now. This is definitely the worst jump and she was looking very comfortable . . ."

Comfortable was the last word Debbie would have chosen: how odd they were, these horsey people, she thought.

In the end, Tilly came in at seventh place, and they all went back to

Broken Bay for a triumphant supper, Emma as flushed with triumph as if it was she who had ridden Boy to glory, not Tilly. Halfway through the meal the phone rang; it was Richard, to make sure they were all right and had arrived safely, and Emma spent about twenty minutes talking him round the entire cross-country course—"and then it was the water jump and she cleared that easily and then she did really well at the brush"—until, mindful of Richard's hotel phone bill, Debbie interrupted her and spoke to him briefly. He sounded very happy and almost excited. "I might have a bit of good news by the time I get home," he said, refusing to say more; Debbie had had quite a lot of Flora's wine and said she couldn't wait for him to get home and that she'd wished he'd been at the trials.

"Did you ever ride in anything like that?" she asked.

"Good Lord, no," he said, "no good at all," and she asked Flora later if that had been true.

"Well, he wasn't much good, no. Bit of a wimp when it came to horses," Flora said slightly dismissively; and, Debbie saw for the very first time that Richard was not entirely perfect in his mother's eyes, and felt oddly soothed by it.

After supper they started to play Scrabble, but Simon, who was rather drunk, began doing unsuitably rude words and Debbie took the opportunity to get the children off to bed. Tilly was dropping with exhaustion, and by the time Debbie came back to the kitchen, Flora had disappeared too.

"She said to say good night to you," Simon said. "She's very tired."

"Oh, right. She doesn't often admit to that. Well, I might follow her myself."

"Debbie, don't go," he said. "Stay and chat to me. I'll find some more wine."

"Well . . ." Suddenly it seemed a rather nice idea. "Just for a bit."

"Good. Thank you." He disappeared down the cellar steps, came back grinning. "Here we are. That was a fun day, wasn't it?"

"Great fun, yes."

"It was lovely for Tilly. After all her heartbreak. And she did pretty well too."

"She did. And she's so kind to Emma, I really do appreciate it."

"As long as horses are involved, Tilly will do anything. She'd scrub out a stable quite willingly. Ask her to unload a dishwasher and you get a rather different reaction. Anyway, jolly little thing, your Emma. Good fun." He topped up her glass.

"Don't give me too much, I don't want a hangover."

"Oh, nonsense. You seem to be getting on better with Flora," he added unexpectedly.

"Yes, I think I am."

"Good. And how are things with you then?"

"Um—fine," she said. "Thank you."

"Good. So, where is hubby? I wasn't really listening."

"Oh, he's on a course. And it's half term, so Flora's having the children."

"Isn't she wonderful?" He rubbed his hand across his eyes. "Christ, I'm tired. So—what sort of course?"

"Oh, a teaching one."

"Has he got a new job yet?"

"No, no yet."

"I'm sure he will soon," he said easily. "And what about your job? How's that going?"

"You don't want to hear about my job," she said, and, "Yes, I do," he said. "I want to know all about you, as a matter of fact. I find you very interesting, Debbie. Go on, tell me about your job."

So she did, trying to make it sound entertaining, while at the same time not exaggerating what she did. He listened intently, asking the occasional, totally relevant question; she found it oddly refreshing. There wasn't anyone she could talk to about her job; not Richard, not Flora, not her parents, they all disapproved; nor most of her old friends, for apart from Jan, they were jealous and clearly felt she had set them and the life they had all shared aside in order to pursue something more interesting.

"So—is PR your forte, do you think? Or do you feel you might like to do something different one day?"

"I think most of all I'd like to be a journalist," she said. "I love what I see of their jobs. Of course it's tough, and terribly hard work, but . . ."

"Well, you clearly don't mind that," he said. "What do you think drives you, Debbie?"

"I'm not sure," she said. "I just think you ought to do everything you can while you can. But it's hard on the children, I do realise that."

"Oh, they survive surprisingly well. Tyrants, children are, bit like husbands."

"I'm sure you're not a tyrant," she said.

"Oh, but I am, in my own way. You'd be surprised."

"Yes, I would. You told me you were very proud of Elizabeth last time we talked."

"And so I am. For most of our lives, I've been bloody proud of her, and she wouldn't have been the person I loved otherwise. I could see that. But if Elizabeth could hear me talking now," he said, his mood suddenly changing, "uttering all these fine words, she'd kick me in the balls and with good reason. I've behaved very badly, Debbie, very badly indeed."

"I'm sure you haven't."

"I'm afraid I have. And look at what else I've done, landing my family in the most appalling financial mess . . ."

"If you mean Lloyd's, as far as I can make out, no one could possibly have known what was going to happen. I went to that meeting, don't forget; I'm sure all of you were acting for the very best."

"I'm afraid that's rather arguable." He drained his glass again. "Give me some more, there's a good girl."

She filled his glass again, knowing that she really shouldn't, that he was getting very drunk, and at the same time not wanting the conversation to end. He looked at her over the wine and tried to smile. "I've done some pretty terrible things, you know, really pretty terrible. And Elizabeth is terribly angry with me and hurt and—oh God." He dashed his hand across his eyes; when he looked up at her again, she saw there were tears in them. "I'm a grade-A shit, Debbie, that's what. I deserve everything that's coming to me."

Debbie felt a wave of such sympathy she could hardly bear it. She put her hand out across the table, took his.

"Simon," she said, "Simon, it's simply not true. You do your absolute best for everyone, I'm sure you do."

"No," he said, shaking his head. He put his hand over one of hers, held it against him. "No, Debbie, that's not true. I've failed her horribly, and I'm failing them all horribly and—oh God." Tears were actually falling now. "What am I going to do, Debbie, what in the name of heaven am I going to do?"

Debbie reached out, stroked his cheek, wiped away some of the tears. "It'll be all right," she said, as if he was one of the children. "It'll be fine, I'm sure."

"No," he said. "No, it won't be all right, it can't possibly be. Only the other day a chap I know, in this like the rest of us, nice chap, he took an overdose, couldn't cope anymore. And you know, I was thinking, I can see why he did it—"

"Simon, please, please don't talk like that."

"I can see it very clearly, he'd be safe now, away from it all, the shame and the misery, and you know that really is the only sure way . . . I'm frightened, Debbie, do you know that? Absolutely shit terrified."

She got up and went over to him; he turned on his chair and she drew his head towards her, onto her breast, stood there, stroking his hair and his arms went round her then, and she felt strange—strange and disoriented—as if she hardly knew who she was, or what she was doing. And, "Simon, dear Simon, don't . . ." she said. And then, quite suddenly, the door opened and Flora came in.

Chapter 19

MAY TO JUNE 1990

"Right, then, Lucinda." Steve Durham smiled at her. "You don't mind if I call you Lucinda, I hope?"

"No, of—of course not."

"Good. And you call me Steve. So let's have a little chat about this marriage of yours, Lucinda, shall we? And see what we're going to do about it."

She didn't like Steve Durham one bit. Blue had told her she wouldn't. "But he's what you—we—need, Lucinda. I'm afraid he's not really your sort of person. Which is fine—you don't have to ask him to a dinner party or anything." Lucinda didn't say that she never asked anyone to dinner parties anymore. It was one of the things she missed.

She felt uneasy in Durham's rather flashy office, all black leather and chrome, in a building just off Regent Street. Durham was flashy too and also dressed in black leather, or at least his upper half was; he wore a very fine black leather jacket over a bright blue shirt and white silk tie. Lucinda had the rather wild thought that her mother would not have had him in the house and then mentally shook herself. Nor would Mrs. Worthington have had Blue in the house, were there any choice in the matter.

"Now, I don't want you to be nervous about any of this," Durham said.

"I don't feel in the least nervous," said Lucinda rather stiffly.

"Good. So let's get down to business. Your husband's name is Nigel. Nigel Cowper. Quite a name that, spelled that way—does he come from some terribly ancient English family?"

"Well, quite ancient, yes. I think they go back several hundred years."

"Very nice. I can only trace my family over a few hundred months. Then it gets very muddy. OK. So you were married—how long?"

"Four years."

"I see. And—no children?"

"No," she said quickly.

"And you lived—where?"

"In our house, in Cadogan Square."

"Very nice. And your husband lives there still, does he?"

"Oh, yes."

"And have you remained on good terms with him?"

"Yes. Very," she said firmly.

He sighed and shook his head.

"And would you say the marriage was happy? Until you met Mr. Horton, of course."

"Yes. Very happy."

"And . . . Mr. Cowper treated you well?"

"Terribly well. He was very—very kind and generous."

"So until you did meet Mr. Horton, you had no complaints?"

"No. I still don't. None at all."

"Right. Now Lucinda, forgive me, but I'm not sure we have much of a case here. Or that you need someone like me. There you were, happily married to a kind and generous man, against whom you had no complaints. You aren't going to find many judges to take your side." She was silent. "I mean, it looks quite bad—on your part. You run away and leave him, for no reason whatsoever, set up home with Mr. Horton, and now you're pregnant with Mr. Horton's baby. I'm afraid that makes you very much the guilty party."

"Yes, I suppose it does."

"A short marriage, with no children—that doesn't earn you a huge amount of assets that weren't yours in the first place. Mr. Cowper is pretty well-off, I gather?"

"Well, yes. But that's—"

He interrupted her. "Is that mostly in liquid assets?"

"I'm not sure what you mean."

"Well, is it cash sitting in the bank, or in stocks and shares, or tied up in property, or what?"

"Oh, I see. Well, he does have some stocks and shares, and quite a lot of cash. At least, he did. But most of his real wealth is in land. He's got about two thousand acres in Norfolk, for instance."

"And property?"

"Well, there's a farmhouse there, and some cottages. It's a working farm, you see."

"Ye-es. And in London?"

"There's the house in Cadogan Square."

"Right."

"Oh, and then I suppose you could count the income from the family business. It's a manufacturing company, still privately owned. It's quite small, but Nigel's the chairman and he owns the majority share. But Mr. Durham—"

"Steve, please."

"Steve. There's something I want to explain—"

"We'll come to that in a minute. I'd rather get the facts sorted first. Were any of these things acquired after he met you?"

"Oh, goodness no."

"So there's nothing you've contributed to, financially?"

"Well, no."

He was silent, then he said, "Of course. Now—there was no baby for you and Mr. Cowper?"

"No."

"Was that—forgive me for asking this, Lucinda—was that agreed between you?"

"Oh, yes." She wasn't going to get into discussing that; not with him.

"So you did want to have a baby together?"

"Well, we did one day, yes. But—there was plenty of time, we felt."

"And yet you and Mr. Horton are having a baby pretty soon after you began cohabiting."

"Well, yes."

"So you must have been pretty keen on the idea?"

"Oh, I was. Yes."

"So it was Mr. Cowper who didn't want children?"

"I didn't say that."

"OK, we'll leave that for now. Now I understand there has been a trust fund set up for you."

"Yes, that's right."

"In a very generous settlement, by Mr. Cowper."

"Yes."

"Which of course will now probably be redistributed at the discretion of the courts."

"Yes, I suppose so."

"Look," he said, "I don't often say this, but I'm not sure there's a lot I can do for you. You have a pretty weak case. This is a short marriage, you made little or no contribution to it, and you're now living with another wealthy man and having his child."

"I know, I know. But—but can I explain now?"

"Yeah, OK. Go ahead."

He sat back, looking at her with what she could only describe as disdain.

"There's something I don't think you realise," she said. "I thought Blue had told you."

"He didn't tell me anything," said Steve Durham. "Mind if I smoke?"

"Yes," said Lucinda firmly, "I'm sorry, but I do. Now please, let me finish. Nigel's about to lose almost everything he's got to Lloyd's."

"Oh yes? Well, that settles it. He certainly won't have anything for you in that case."

"I know," said Lucinda. "That's the whole point."

"Sorry? I don't get it."

"Mr.—Steve, if you'd just listen to me for a bit, you will get it. I have had an idea, and I think it's quite a good one. But I'm really going to need all your—your experience to even remotely bring it off. Can I go on?"

"Go ahead." He was looking slightly more interested.

"Well, you see . . ."

It didn't take long; and when she had finished, he stood up and walked over to the window looking down at Regent Street. Then he turned round and grinned at her.

"It's going to be tough," he said, "but I like a challenge. I reckon we can do it somehow. Somehow or other. I must admit, Lucinda, you're a lot cleverer than I thought you were. Very impressed I am. Very impressed."

"Oh good," she said. "I'm so pleased."

℮

She thought they had got away with it. That Flora actually hadn't seen them, not in flagrante as it were. Not that it was in flagrante, of course, but who could have blamed Flora for thinking it was, rather than an innocent—well, nearly innocent—comforting embrace.

Simon had reacted with incredible speed, pulling away from her, reaching for the wine bottle and making a great thing of pouring yet more; and she had gone equally fast over to the sink and made a great thing of washing glasses.

"You've caught us at it, Flora, I'm afraid," Simon had said, and she had turned in horror, but he was grinning up at Flora ruefully—and Debbie had never known quite what rueful was until that moment—"getting drunk together. I've been boring the pants off poor Debbie, and she's been really gallant, letting me run on and on."

"I see," said Flora briskly, and Debbie felt her stomach heave with fear; but then, "Well, I just wanted a cup of tea. Can I interest either of you in something so wholesome?"

"Absolutely," Simon said, "do us both good. Here, Debbie, could you rinse these cups out as well?"

And keeping her back still carefully turned to Flora, she said, praying her voice would sound normal, "Sorry, Flora, did we wake you up?"

"No, no, I couldn't sleep. Often happens these days."

"It's a symptom of our common disease," Simon said to Debbie, smiling. "Lloydsitis, very nasty. Others include nausea, headaches, nightmares. Oh, and loss of appetite."

How did he do that, she wondered. How could he switch from wretched to lighthearted at the click of a switch—or rather the turn of a door handle? It was a great gift.

Debbie lay awake for hours, staring into the darkness, suffering from intermittent tremor just about all over, wondering what on earth Flora might have thought: and indeed what she might do, had she thought it.

It was truly hideous: here she was, Flora's daughter-in-law, married to her only son, and apparently behaving like a trollop in her house. But then, Debbie thought, Flora had seemed fine, not really suspicious; although obviously a bit surprised. And anyway, what exactly would she want to tell Richard? Well, and here the waves began to rise again, well, that Simon had had his arms round Debbie and she had been bending over him, clearly about to kiss him; and Flora didn't like her, never had, and would be delighted to blacken her in Richard's eyes . . .

At six, having slept about two hours, woken by the sound of horse's hooves, she went downstairs and out into the garden, bathed in mist; and saw Simon sitting on a low wall.

"Hi," he said. "You all right?"

"Not really," she said, "bit—you know—worried."

"About last night? No need. She's fine. I was just chatting to her—she's gone out riding. I kind of dug a bit and she couldn't have been easier or more relaxed. I'm sure she doesn't suspect a thing. Not that there was a thing to suspect."

"Simon, there was. And I'm married to her son. Don't be ridiculous, please."

"Darling—"

"And don't call me darling. I don't like it."

"Sorry. But you really are worrying about nothing. Promise. You'll see."

And indeed when Flora got back she seemed very happy and they all had breakfast in the kitchen and Flora proposed a picnic and was actually very warm towards Debbie. So perhaps Simon was right. But she continued to worry, just a little; and also to remember the sliver of attraction and wonder what exactly might have happened, had Flora not come down.

*

Lucinda swallowed hard.

"I just don't understand," Blue said, "why you won't talk about it. It's ridiculous!"

"Because—well, because I need to think about it."

"Think about what? Lucinda, I've been very patient for a long time, listening to you fretting over that overaged schoolboy of a husband of yours, saying how sorry you are for him, how worried about it all, and I've had enough. You get rid of him, and fast; I want to get married, before the boy's born—"

"Blue, that really won't be possible. Divorce can't just be done in five months."

"That's bollocks," he said. "It's uncontested, for God's sake. You're supplying the grounds, no one's arguing about it, it could be done in no time, no time at all."

"That's not what Steve Durham said. Blue, please. We have to be very . . . careful about all this."

"Careful? What have we to be careful about, for God's sake? What's the matter with you, Lucinda? This bloke seems to have affected you very badly."

"He didn't. He just made me . . . think. That's all."

"Think about what? Us? Because I'll have his balls off if that's the case."

"Blue, stop it! You just don't understand. I—"

"You're too right I don't," he said. "I'm going out. And when I get back, I'd like a bit more of an explanation, all right? So you'd better be ready with it."

He stood up and stalked out of the door, slamming it hard. She looked after him, near to tears, wondering if she was in fact brave enough to go through with what at best would be terribly, terribly difficult. And then she thought of Nigel, dear, dear Nigel, living in a council house and forced to sell his diamond cuff links, and she knew she had to be.

℮∽

"And this is Flora Fielding. Flora, Colin Peterson. Flora has one of the most beautiful houses on Gower, Colin. You'd give your eyeteeth for it, I'm sure."

"Oh really? Are you looking for a house on Gower?" said Flora, as politely as she could. She didn't feel very polite. She would have much preferred to be at home, where a very self-important Tilly was acting as babysitter, with Mrs. Connor in the cottage five hundred yards down the lane on call and Mr. Connor popping in regularly throughout the evening. But Philippa invited her to dinner at least once a month, determinedly kindly, and it was impossible not to like the Webbers; they had moved to the area ten years earlier, and William in particular had tried and failed to dislike them, and the Fieldings had entertained them occasionally and Flora became deeply ashamed of herself after William died and they phoned, once or twice a week, to ask if she'd like to go for a walk with them; they brought her flowers, and in the early days, Philippa had delivered her some soup from time to time, or a quiche that she had made, saying, "I know how easy it is not to bother," and just very quietly and sweetly kept an eye on her.

And so it was that, from time to time, Flora gritted her teeth and drove along the South Gower Road with dread in her heart for an evening of admittedly very good food and to meet the Webbers' friends who were rather alien to her, living as they did in large modern houses in Swansea, or even Cardiff, and who drove flashy cars and went on holiday to places like Gran Canaria and Florida.

It transpired that Colin Peterson, a widower, Philippa rather archly announced as she guided them into the dining room, was not looking for a house on Gower, or not personally at any rate; he was a property developer and responsible for several of the flashier developments on the outskirts of Swansea. Since property developers would have been prominent among those Flora would have compulsorily ejected from this world and into the bowels of hell, she was fairly appalled to find herself placed next to him; he had other vices too, in her book, he wore a Ralph Lauren shirt complete with polo emblem, a matching Christian Dior tie and silk handkerchief, and had nails that looked to her suspiciously manicured.

On the other hand, he was rather good company. And disarming. He told her he would no more touch Gower with a single new brick than throw himself off the Worms Head, and that although he made his crust putting up modern houses, he was in fact a member of various Victorian societies and spent a lot of time getting up petitions to save terraces and other antique structures. His passion in life was actually sacred music, and she left the Webbers' dinner party a great deal later than she had planned, feeling warmed and almost happy. Not least by Colin Peterson's suggestion that they might perhaps attend a forthcoming concert in Cardiff Cathedral.

And after all, wearing clothes covered with those dreadful trademarks—or logos as you were supposed to call them, Tilly had told her—wasn't exactly a capital crime. She had managed to overlook Simon's.

℮

Annabel really, really couldn't believe it. Half of her had expected never to hear from him again. It had only been just over a week, after all, and OK, he had said he loved her, but that often happened with holiday romances, which is what it was in a way, and America was a long, long way away, and he had a whole life there, and he was young and gorgeous and . . . and . . .

"And he's asked me to go over and stay with them," she said.

"Who, darling?"

"Dad! You haven't been listening. Jamie, you know that gorgeous American boy."

"Oh, yes. And you really like him?"

"I really like him, Dad. And he's asked me to go over to Boston and stay with him and his family. For a few days."

"Well, that sounds great. And—do you think you'll go?"

"Well, of course I'll go!"

"Didn't you meet his parents?"

"Yes, I did."

"And?"

"And they were great. Well, his dad was great. His mother was a bit terrifying. Jamie seemed to find her quite terrifying too."

"My darling, never have anything to do with a man who's frightened of his mother. Not a good scene."

"You're joking, aren't you?"

"Only partly. Anyway, when does he want you to go?"

"Sometime in July. God, I hope I can get the time off. Oh, it's so exciting, Daddy, isn't it? I must ring him right now—or would it be better to write, do you think? Cooler?"

"Definitely cooler. He wrote to you, after all."

"Yes, I know, but— Yes, you're right. I'll write today, when I've asked for the time off. Oh, wow, I really can't believe it! It is just so wonderful—wait till I tell Carol . . ."

e

Joel Strickland was just filing a rather mediocre story on negative equity—the new buzzword in the property business—and wondering if he could cut and run after lunch (well, it was Friday) when his phone rang. It was Simon Beaumont. "Look," he said, "if you're still interested in talking to me, I could spare you half an hour next week. I don't know how much use it would be, I imagine my story's pretty much like everyone else's, but you're welcome to it."

Joel said he would be very interested in talking to him.

"Right then. Suppose we say Thursday, around seven? Royal Garden Hotel suit you?"

"That's great," said Joel. "I'll be there. Thank you. Er . . . anything in particular change your mind?"

"Yes, as a matter of fact. Friend of mine, another victim, tried to kill himself recently. I think this is a story that needs to be told."

"Well, I agree with you," said Joel, "and thanks very much."

e

Simon sat staring at the phone, feeling nervous and almost excited, as if he had done something rather momentous, without being sure why. He was easing up the lid of Pandora's box, and God knew what demons would be released. Well, someone had to do it.

e

"Freddie, where's your lunch box?" said Catherine.

"Um, don't know. Must have left it at school."

Freddie's normally pale face had become slightly rosy and his big brown eyes were firmly fixed on the cereal packet he was reading.

"Darling, that's two this term already. You must be more careful, Freddie, lunch boxes cost a lot of money."

"Sorry."

"And now what am I going to put your lunch in?"

"He can have mine," said Caroline helpfully.

"What? That pink thing—My Little Ponies all over it?" said Freddie. "No thanks. I'll just take a plastic bag, Mummy, it'll be fine."

"Well, it's not really allowed. But we don't have much option, do we? Now I must go. See you this afternoon. Have good days. Love you."

"Love you," they said in unison. She left them, worrying as she always did, praying silently that they'd be all right, and hurried down the street towards the tube station. It wasn't ideal, but it did mean Freddie was happier. So much happier. And doing well. So it really was worth it.

"Right," said Freddie, ten minutes later after they had cleared away their breakfast things, and picked up their school bags. "Let's go. Get it over with."

"Freddie," said Caroline. "Don't you think we ought to tell Mummy?"

"Why do you have to ask me that, every day? We can't tell her, she's got enough to worry about. I'll be all right." He looked at the clock. "If we leave now, we can go the long way round. Come on."

Caroline looked at him rather sorrowfully. "You really are ever so brave," she said.

ᑫ

Debbie could never remember being so frightened. Or so shocked. She sat staring at Richard, as if willing the words back into his mouth, safely unsaid.

"So that's what she said." Richard was beaming. "And what do you have to say about it?"

"Well, I . . . well, obviously it's amazing. Absolutely amazing. Yes."

"Isn't it? And if I hadn't gone on that course, I'd never have found out about it. To think I nearly didn't go. Of course, it's not settled yet . . ."

"Oh, it's not?" Don't sound too hopeful, Debbie, just don't.

"No. There has to be an interview, but it's purely a matter of form, Miss Dunbar—Morag—assured me. She had to get the approval of the board of governors, and so on. But she'd want me there in Scotland for the autumn term, and she's already advertised it, I can't think how I missed it, and actually done some interviews, so she can tell the governors that she's not just giving it to the first person who's come along."

"No. No, I see. But—it's only deputy head? Isn't that a bit of a backward step?"

"Oh no, not in this case. It's a very famous school—Morag Dunbar has told me, confidentially, that she's up for the top job at the senior school, and, well, she didn't exactly promise anything, but she made it pretty clear that I'd be head designate."

"Well, that is fantastic, Richard. Congratulations. I'm so proud of you."

"Thanks." He looked suddenly ten years younger, his eyes shining. "I'm pretty proud of me too. And of course, it being a boarding school, we'll be incredibly involved with the boys. We get a house in the grounds—"

"A house in the grounds?"

"One of the best. It goes with the job, but a very pretty one, and quite big. I can show you a photograph."

"You mean we won't have our own house?"

"Well, no. Of course we can buy one anyway, either up there or nearby, as an investment, or we can keep this one and let it, but they'd want me on the spot. It's very much part of the job. And you'd be very much part of the team, of course. It's something we can do together, Debbie—you know how much I've always wanted that."

"Me!"

"Well, yes. Deputy headmaster's wife—pretty important, you know. Not just helping me with running the school but right in there with the boys and their lives. Don't look so scared, darling, you'd be brilliant."

Don't mention your job, Debbie, just don't. Don't even think about it. It's important not to panic. This is just conference chitchat. Keep calm.

"And what about the children?" she asked. "They'd have to move schools, would they?"

"Well, obviously. But Alex can go there, of course, to St. Andrews. It'd be the most marvellous opportunity for him, it's such a brilliant place. And the girls—well, there's a very good girls' prep very nearby, apparently. Almost a sister school. The girls can both go there."

The outrage was beginning to surface.

"You seem to have made an awful lot of decisions without me," she said. "I might not think it was right for them."

Just for a moment he looked taken aback: very slightly. "Well, of course you must go and see it," he said. "Obviously, you've got to be happy about it. But you will be, I know. Morag Dunbar has invited us all up to stay for the weekend in a couple of weeks' time. I know you'll like her, Debbie, she's very—very warm. She's so looking forward to meeting you. She does see you as a very important part of the package, of course. I know you'll be marvellous, take to it all like a duck to water. Come here, darling, and give me a hug. I know I'm always saying this, but I mean it: I could never have done this without you, your support."

She resisted the hug.

"You know, Richard, I'm really not sure about it," she said. "I mean, I've never done anything like that in my life."

"Darling Debbie, you'll be wonderful. Children always love you. And you're so organised—"

"Richard, I am not organised."

"Yes, you are. Look how well you've managed with your job and everything."

"I know, but—"

"Of course, that would have to come to an end, but—well, this is so much better for everyone, isn't it?"

She couldn't help it then. It came out, in spite of herself, in spite of willing it back so hard it hurt physically.

"Everyone but me," she said.

It was a very big mistake.

℮

Flora hadn't intended to come to London; she liked it less and less. But she had a few remaining stocks and shares and felt that a personal conversation with her stockbroker was essential; and there was a very good lunchtime concert at St. Martin-in-the-Fields that day which she could go to first. Flora, like Debbie, preferred her days crammed full. And then she found another concert at the Wigmore Hall in the evening, and decided to go to that too, and to stay with Richard and Debbie instead of going back to Wales as she had planned. And then Simon just mentioned casually on the phone, while thanking her for having Tilly, that Friday was his birthday and she felt that she could cram in a visit there as well. She changed the appointment with the stockbroker to half an hour later and arrived at Graburn and French just after three, with a copy of the new P. D. James book. He'd never read P. D. James; Flora had told him quite severely he should. "She combines superb plots with superb writing. Quite rare, in my opinion."

She was sitting in the marble-floored atrium of Graburn and French, waiting for his secretary to come down and collect her, when a dazzlingly pretty girl walked up to the reception desk, holding a package. She looked vaguely familiar to Flora. "Hello," she said, "I've got something here for Mr. Beaumont. Mr. Simon Beaumont."

"Fine. If you'd like to just leave it with me, I'll see he gets it."

"Well, that'd be terribly kind, but he did say to tell you he wanted to come down and get it himself."

"Oh, all right. I'll give him a call. What name is it?"

"Cowper, Lucinda Cowper. Thank you." She looked round the hall, saw Flora and smiled at her. "Hello! We've met, haven't we? At that Lloyd's meeting, wasn't it? I remember your lovely blue jacket."

"Oh, of course!" said Flora, standing up, holding out her hand. "Flora Fielding."

"He'll be right down," said the man. "Popular today, Mr. Beaumont—two beautiful ladies waiting to see him."

"Oh really?" Lucinda smiled at Flora again. "You too? Well, lucky him."

The lift doors opened, and Catherine Morgan emerged; she came across to Flora.

"Mrs. Fielding? He says he's on his way down, and— Oh, hello," she said to Lucinda. "How lovely to see you."

"Lovely to see you too," said Lucinda. "Catherine, isn't it? How are you? And you're working for Simon, how nice."

"Yes, he's been terribly kind, gave me a job here."

"Not just kind, I'm sure," said Lucinda. "And how are your children?"

"Fine. Yes. How clever of you to remember."

"Well, I do remember some things," said Lucinda. "The others seem to drop through the rather wide mesh that my brain's turned into." She patted the small but unmistakable bump of her stomach. "This is what I blame. Anyway, I've come to see Simon too. I've brought him a book for his birthday. I work for a publisher."

"I too," said Flora, "have brought him a book. Not the same one, I trust. Mine is— Oh Simon, hello. Happy birthday."

"And from me," said Lucinda.

"Lucinda! How lovely to see you. How lovely to see both of you. I'm having a wonderful day. And Catherine's children have made me cards. I am very spoiled."

"I so believe in spoiling," said Lucinda. "Well, on birthdays anyway."

"I'm glad you do. Well well well, what a pulchritudinous gathering. A birthday party, you might almost say. Why don't you all come up to my office?"

"No, I must fly," said Lucinda, "I'm so late already. But I hope you like the book."

"I'm sure I will. Flora, some tea? Come on, just a quick one. Bye, Lucinda, thank you again." And he ushered Flora into the lift, followed by Catherine.

"Such a sweetie," said Lucinda absently, to nobody in particular.

Chapter 20

JUNE 1990

Debbie had thought things couldn't get any worse. Not since she had made what she had mentally labelled the Killer Remark. But they had just got worse. And in front of Richard's mother. Richard had hardly spoken to her, apart from essential conversations about arrangements, since . . . She could still hear herself saying it, still found it hard to believe she had been so stupid. And so cruel. He was obviously incredibly hurt, and rightly so; she knew it had been horrible of her. It had just—just come out. He had told her that all the pleasure and excitement of the job had been destroyed for him.

"I don't even want to go now," he said, glaring at her across the room that evening. "Can't see the point."

"Richard, of course there's a point. Don't be silly, I didn't mean—"

"What you meant was it would be crucifixion for you. Well, I'm not going to be the one to hammer the nails in, Debbie, and be blamed for it for the rest of our lives. I suppose I could go on my own, that's an option."

"Of course it's not. I'll come. I was just—just a bit taken aback, that's all. Surely you can see—"

"What I can see, Debbie, is that your life, your job, come first and mine an inconvenient second. Well, that's not what I call a marriage."

Debbie said, rather boldly, that a marriage was something where the two people involved tried to compromise and move along together.

"I totally agree. And for the last few months it's been all about you, your job, your child-care arrangements, your future. Mine didn't seem to be getting much of a look-in. I'm here, providing a very useful resource for you, and the fact that I'm doing a crappy soul-destroying job that doesn't even supply me with adequate funds to do what I want for my family is neither here nor there to you. Well, you'd better do some very hard thinking, Debbie, because something's got to give."

He had gone down to Wales alone to get the children; he had said it would be nice to spend some time with them on his own. She had mooched about the house, hoping that when he returned, he might feel better. He didn't.

And now Flora was here.

Only for the night; she had come in quite late, full of talk about the concerts and some impromptu birthday party Simon Beaumont had held in his office.

And then it happened.

They were having breakfast; Debbie had dutifully cooked mushrooms and scrambled eggs because that was what Flora liked best; the children had said how lovely to have a yummy breakfast, usually they just had rotten muesli; she had thought Richard might be pleased too, but he chomped gloomily through his meal, not speaking unless he had to.

And then Flora said, "Now, Richard, what was this exciting news you told us about, when you phoned from Scotland."

"Oh, it was nothing."

"Really?"

"It was," Debbie said. "Richard's been offered a new job, up in Scotland, as deputy head of a really good prep school."

"Really?" Flora said. "How exciting! Why on earth didn't you tell me?"

"Because I'm not going to take it," Richard said, standing up, gulping down what was left of his orange juice.

"Not going to take it? Why ever not?" Flora said, and he replied, with a look at Debbie of such intense dislike that she winced, "Because Debbie and I have discussed it, and we don't feel it would be in the family's best interests."

"What?" said Flora. "But—" and then stopped, because Debbie's eyes filled with tears and she stood up, her chair scraping on the floor and said, "Excuse me, please," and rushed out of the room. Flora looked at Richard rather hard and then said, "Well, that sounds like a pity. But I'm sure you know best. Now I must go. Richard, would you drive me to the station, please?"

And Debbie had come down and kissed Flora goodbye and tried to pretend everything was all right and that she wasn't crying at all, and waved them off, and eventually Richard came back and said he was going into school as he had a lot to do and needed some peace and quiet.

And came home that afternoon clearly still hating her. And so it had gone on.

Later, she had tried again.

"Can we please, please talk about this. Properly, without all the emotional garbage. I really can't say I'm sorry again—"

"You don't have to. In any case, I don't want you saying things that aren't true."

"It is true, for fuck's sake!" She was shouting, desperate with frustration and anger.

"Don't swear."

"I'll swear if I want to. Look, Richard—"

"Debbie, you said you didn't want to go to Scotland, and as far as I'm concerned, that is that. Unfortunately."

"I didn't say that, it's so unfair. I simply said it wasn't ideal for me. I regret that very bitterly, I shouldn't have said it. But I've said I'll go, said I'll give up my job. What more do you want—blood?"

"I want a wife who's behind me," he said, "properly, not grudgingly."

"I am not grudging. Oh, this is hopeless. What have you done about the job anyway? I really think I have a right to know."

"I've turned it down," he said. "I've told Miss Dunbar that we can't come, that you don't want to, that it's wrong for the family."

She felt ice cold and then violently sick; her head swam, she felt she might faint.

"You've actually done that? Formally? Without discussing it any further?"

"Yes."

"Richard," said Debbie, "you had absolutely no right to do that. You're mad."

"Well, that's great. I do what you want and then you tell me I'm mad."

"It is not what I want," she said, her voice very low now, shaking with emotion, "and you know that perfectly well, underneath all your wretched pride and self-importance. You've done it to hurt me, God knows why."

"Perhaps you should look at your own behaviour," he said, standing up, walking over to the door. "I really don't think there's any future in this discussion, Debbie."

He shut the door very carefully and quietly after him; she sat staring at the chair where he had been sitting. Feeling really very frightened.

❧

"So, that's about it, really," said Lucinda. "That's what we're going to do. Isn't it clever? Aren't you pleased?"

Nigel looked at her, sitting there on the big sofa—they had agreed to meet at the Selfridge Hotel again—looking so lovely, so sweet and earnest, smiling at him gently, her blue eyes shining, and felt a slight sense of unreality. Was she really saying all these things, making these suggestions, without any great difficulty, with apparent relish even? This was not the Lucinda, surely, that he had fallen in love with and married; she had changed, changed a lot, and it must be that man, brutalising her, distorting her sense of honour, of what was right and wrong. And trying, as far as he could see, to distort his.

"Of course, you'll have to back it all up," she said, "the story. Which is true, obviously."

"Well . . ." He hesitated. "Well, Lucinda, is it?"

"What do you mean? Nigel, we're not going to get very far with this if you're going to be difficult. It's all for your benefit, you've got to remember that. So—what isn't true?"

"Well . . . well, I don't really remember that stuff about the gallery."

"Don't you? Well, that just goes to show how very unselfish I was about it. Not making a fuss. I mean, surely you remember that I was working for the gallery when you met me?"

"Yes, of course."

"But you don't remember anything about them asking me to go to New York?"

"Not really, no, I can't say I do."

"Oh dear. Well, I'll have to remind you. So that Grandfather Cowper's cuff links stay safe. So try, please try to do your bit."

"And remember things that didn't happen?" He sounded bitter, even to himself.

Lucinda sighed. "Nigel, they did happen. I'm going to talk to Virgil Barrymore myself, and I'm sure he'll be able to convince you. Honestly. They asked me to go to New York and I didn't. It's terribly simple."

"And what about the other stuff? Leaving you with the money in the trust fund because I'm worried about you?"

"Well, aren't you?"

"Of course I am."

"Well then."

"And how do you think your Mr. Horton will feel about that? And . . . and the other thing you said."

"Oh, he won't mind," said Lucinda. "He'll be fine. Now, about the house and how we're going to deal with that . . ."

Nigel gave up and tried to concentrate on what she was saying. The plan was very clever. Very clever indeed. And it would certainly be an answer—of sorts. But one thing he was quite sure of, however confident and sharp Lucinda might be. Horton wouldn't like it; he wouldn't like it one bit.

꙳

Catherine had reached such an extreme of worry now about the money that it had, in a strange way, become unreal. She knew she could do noth-

ing about it; therefore it seemed the only thing to do was to take no notice of it. It was like some extremely severe pain that somehow she had got
used to living with; she took painkillers in the form of her work and her
children and her very few friends, and they allowed her to get on with her
life to a large extent. It was only at night, when the painkillers wore off,
that she had to face it all: the letters—increasingly pressing—from her
Members' Agent, the gnawing indecision over whether she should sell the
flat, the horror of having once more to remove Freddie from his school,
where he was clearly now so happy, and the absolute terror of what might
happen to a lone and penniless mother with huge debts she was completely unable to pay—the children taken into care, her begging in door-
ways. But in the office and at the school gates she seemed cheerful,
competent, brave, and to a certain effect felt all those things; she surprised
herself. Perhaps, she thought, she should have been an actress. She would
surely have won an Oscar.

She looked up one afternoon from her word processor to see Simon
smiling down at her.

"Hello, Catherine. I want to ask you a favour."

"Of course."

She had expected him to give her some extra work to do; what he actually wanted was for her to join the Graburn and French box at Ascot "to
help look after some of our lady guests." She said it sounded wonderful,
but she couldn't possibly; that she had nothing to wear, that she was
bound to drop and spill a great many things, that she would have nothing to say, that he was being much, much too kind, that— And he had
interrupted this torrent of self-denigration to say that, on the contrary, he
was not being much too kind, rather the reverse; he was planning to make
her work very hard. She would be of inestimable value to him, "just looking after people, quietly and nicely."

"I need someone keeping an eye on things in the box, making sure
glasses are topped up, that everyone's had enough to eat, that people know
where the loos are, especially the wives, that nobody's being left out, all
that sort of thing. You've no idea how easily it can go wrong; some quiet
little person isn't properly introduced, gets left in a corner while hubby
goes flashing his money around at the Tote. You'd be ideal. It's the week
after next—Wednesday, if that's all right. And if you're worried about
clothes, go and get yourself an outfit on expenses. I'll sign the chit. Oh,

and if you're worrying about them," he said, indicating the photograph on her desk, "we can easily cover any expense there."

"No," she said, "I've got this nice woman, Mrs. Lennox, who helps in the holidays. I'm sure she'd take care of them."

She asked Mrs. Lennox, who said that she would be happy to look after the children. It would be a pleasure. Catherine, relieved and excited, and, feeling increasingly like Cinderella suddenly granted an invitation to the ball, went shopping. She bought her outfit at Fenwick: Simon had given her a budget of £200 which seemed like a queen's ransom to her. She'd got a dress and jacket similar to one of the outfits Princess Diana had worn the year before, which made it absolutely safe, style-wise, she decided. It was very simple, in brilliant pink silk, the jacket lapels trimmed in black; and then she bought a very plain black straw hat and fairly low-heeled black court shoes. She would be on her feet all day long, Simon kept telling her, and she wanted to be comfortable.

The children seemed perfectly content at the idea of Mrs. Lennox looking after them: well, Caroline was. Freddie didn't seem quite himself; he was rather pale and tired-looking, but whenever she asked him if he was all right he told her not to fuss.

"I'm fine," he said, "honestly. Don't worry about me."

Elizabeth had planned to leave the agency early; she knew Simon wanted to talk to her about the lawsuit, but just after lunch the client services director came into her office and said there was a problem with a presentation the next day to a hugely important new business pitch. It was going to take a lot of sorting out. She called Simon.

"Sorry. I'll do my best to be back by nine. That won't be too late, will it?"

"I suppose not," he said. He sounded tired and deflated.

"Sorry, Simon. But it's really important."

"Of course."

It was half past ten when she got home.

Simon was sitting up in bed reading; he looked at her, his face expressionless.

"Good of you to come home."

"Simon! I was working."

"Of course. As always. Important client, no doubt."

"Important would-be client. Presentation tomorrow, last-minute hitch. God, I'm tired." She kicked off her shoes, rubbed her neck.

"Really? I'm so sorry. Well, I'm just the unimportant husband, of course. It's one law for the rich in this house, isn't it, another for the poor. Me being the poor. Obviously."

"Simon—"

"You can stay out all hours, go to dinners, cancel evenings with me, that's all fine. God help me if I step out of line."

"How dare you," she said, slightly breathless with her rage. "How dare you compare your behaviour with mine! Let me remind you, Simon, I have not been having an affair, I have not announced that I am in love with someone else, I have not threatened to leave. I just get on with my job. Trying to keep things together, you know. Before we go bankrupt."

"Oh, for fuck's sake, I have had it up to here with my bad behaviour. How much longer do I have to drag myself round in sackcloth and ashes. It's nearly two fucking years ago now, Elizabeth. For Christ's sake, give me a break. What do you think it's like for me, living in this Lloyd's nightmare? I'm doing my best, just as I'm doing my best for you and the family. And everything I try to do, to make things better, I get pilloried for—selling Chadwick, selling all our pictures . . . Christ Almighty, I decided tonight I really have got to sell the *Lizzie*. It's bloody terrifying, Elizabeth, and I know it's my own fault, but I need you with me, supporting me, not dragging me constantly through the mire, reminding me of my shortcomings . . ."

He stopped, and she saw with a sense of shock that there were tears in his eyes; he dashed his hand across them. "Oh, just fuck off, why don't you? Get some sleep, ready for another important day tomorrow."

A long, long silence; then she sat down suddenly, put her hand on his arm.

"Simon, I'm sorry. So, so sorry. I—I didn't think. Didn't realise how badly you felt, how worried you were. I should have done."

"Yes, you bloody well should. I've never felt so alone."

That was it, she realised, staring at him, that was what had gone wrong; they both felt alone. Were alone. They were separated by a vast abyss of recrimination and rejection, and how were they ever to cross it now? And she felt absolutely terrified suddenly that it was gone forever.

"I think I'd better go," he said.

"Go where?"

"I don't know. Just—leave here. This house—you. I'm clearly no use to any of you. I mean it, you'll be better off without me. I'll get out, Elizabeth. We've lost one another, there's no way back."

She stared at him.

"Don't you feel that?" he said. "Honestly? Don't you think it's time to give in? Because I do. We've fought this for a long, long time and we're not winning, are we?" He stared back at her, his face heavy with despair. "God, I used to love you so much. And you loved me. But it's gone. I really think that it's gone. I've tried, Christ knows I've tried, to get back, to get you back, but I can't. We've gone too far."

Elizabeth sat on the bed, knowing that he had indeed done all he could; and knew she must—somehow—try to explain. Which would require a brand of courage she wasn't sure she was capable of; the courage to let down her guard, to be no longer cool and self-sufficient, but frail and weak and dependent.

"It's . . . not . . . you," she said, dragging the words out slowly and painfully. "It's me. I feel so . . . despairing of myself. Being unable to . . . to manage it."

"Manage what?"

"Manage living with it. It's so . . . so hard." She felt her eyes fill with tears. "I just feel I'm not what you want anymore. That I can't be."

"You were always what I wanted."

"But I wasn't, was I? You wanted her too. And now . . . well, all the time, all the time we're together, whenever we get close, whenever we make love, I think of her. Or rather of you and her. What did she do? To please you? Was it different from me? Did she know how to arouse you, did she do things I never discovered you like . . ."

"Elizabeth—"

"No, listen to me. You've got to understand. It's why I'm so jealous. So afraid. I . . . I watch myself in bed with you, and I can't . . . can't . . ." Tears began to fall on the bedclothes; she brushed them angrily away. "How hard do you think it is, admitting this? That I feel inadequate, when I'm with you. Of course it's hard. It's horrible. I—I'm in despair. Despair about myself."

Simon reached out and touched her face, very gently. "Well, now you know how I feel. All the time. In despair about myself. My darling Elizabeth, I have never wanted anyone as I want you. Ever. After all these years, I still want you, desperately. What happened was a kind of—of lashing back. Of course, there was more to it than that, I don't pretend that was the only reason." He smiled at her. "I'm not a fine example of the husband breed, I know. But you seemed to put me last, always. No, that's not right. You just dumped me emotionally while you got on with your important life. I was too demanding, took too much time from you. That's hard to live with. And someone else put me first for a while and that was very pleasant. But—God, it wasn't enough. It was you I really wanted. If you only knew how much I want you. Still. And, yes, how much I love you."

"Do you?"

"Of course I do. And I can see how you can wonder how, when I betrayed you so completely. But actually, it wasn't so complete. It was only because I couldn't have you. In the way I wanted, the way I did have once. Now I know that's a feeble excuse, and it isn't even meant to be one, and Christ we've been over this so many times, and I'm so ashamed of myself, and shocked at the way I behaved, but just this one last time, let me tell you it's you that I wanted and loved and needed, and you that didn't seem to want or love or need me. You may tell me that is not right, but it's what I felt, Elizabeth. And I still feel that. I really do. That you've removed yourself, from my life. You've been marvellous and taken me back and carried on being the wonderful wife everyone so admires, but I've lost the essential you. The you that was really close to me."

"But you haven't, you see, that's what I'm trying to say. The essential me is still here. But I hid her. It was the only way I could cope, by pretending, staying cool, saying, 'Look, everybody, look at me, still smiling, still succeeding, still in control. It didn't really matter, Simon's little fling, it's fine, I'm not the sort of woman who can't deal with a little infidelity.' "

"Well, you did a pretty good job," he said. "And I began to think: If she can deal with it this well, maybe she didn't care that much—and what does that say about her and me and our relationship?"

She sat there, staring at him, shocked and frightened.

"Oh dear," he said, "what dangerous territory we stray into, in our efforts to exalt ourselves. I stray into infidelity, you into rejection of a different kind altogether. One emotion following another. But at least I understand now, and I can—just possibly—draw you back to me. I know how hard it must have been for you to tell me that, and I know it means you do indeed still love me. And do you know what that makes me want to do?"

"No," she said, almost irritably, and she looked at him, and saw he was smiling his most infectious, glorious smile.

"It makes me want to shout out of the window, take space in newspapers, hire a plane with a banner behind it saying 'Elizabeth Beaumont loves me, and that makes me the luckiest man in the world.' And if you'll come and sit a bit nearer to me—yes, that's right, and take those silly shoes off, and maybe the jacket . . . I'm going to try and persuade you I mean it."

It was very good sex: quick, urgent, violent. It was the first time she had wanted it, really wanted it since . . . well, since then. And the first time she had felt confident enough to release herself, and that there hadn't been some dark anger and misery hanging over their bed. She felt loved, truly loved and totally engaged by him, she had almost forgotten that, in her long grief and anger, forgotten how sex could consume everything but itself, time and place and other concerns lost in its intense rituals and delights. She came, more than once, crying out, her body arched with pleasure, willing it to go on and on. And afterwards, lying on the bed, still half dressed, almost surprised at the depth of her desire, her body eased, stilled, her mind released of tension, she said, "I've missed that so much, Simon. So much."

"Me too. But it seems we can still do it. We just have to practise a lot."

"I'd like that."

"I have never loved anyone as I love you, you know. In every way. Try to believe it. Try to go on believing it."

"I will."

She laughed and realised she felt quite different. Stronger. And very much happier. She was a realist, she knew she would return to the jealousy and the rage every so often, but she also felt, for the first time since it had happened, that she might be able to survive it.

"I love you," she said suddenly. She hadn't said it for a long time; it was very sweet and very good to be able to do so.

"I love you too," he said.

Chapter 21

"And perhaps I could buy you a drink after the meeting?" Was she really saying this?

"That would be very nice."

She was going to buy a man—not a particularly attractive man, but a very nice one and quite important—a drink. On expenses. On her expenses.

"The Royal Garden would be quite near. Would that suit you?"

"It would, yes, thank you." Derek Earnshaw clearly found the idea almost as exciting as she did. She would be in the bar of a smart hotel. At teatime. Well, high teatime. Fish-finger time. Only it wouldn't be fish fingers for her, it would be olives and those extra-thin crisps. Washed down by some extremely cold Chardonnay.

She had given up on Richard: there simply seemed no point. Life was altogether horrible. Until today. Somehow she had gone back to work and summoned up the other Debbie, the cool, efficient, clever Debbie, who was a success at her job and who everyone seemed to approve of. And the contrast was so great that she felt even more the other Debbie; she felt sexy, larky, a bit of a witch.

This was her first proper account: one she was handling all on her own. A small publishing company producing personalised books for children: where the hero—or heroine—could bear the name of the child who was to receive it.

"I think you should handle this one," Anna had said. "You've got kids—you'll have lots of ideas."

She had: several. The one she was proudest of was that every child receiving the book could enter a competition to write a short story of their own: the winning entry would then be properly printed and presented to its new author.

"And the panel of judges could include a well-known children's author. Maybe the child could even meet him or her."

"I like that," Derek Earnshaw said, "it's very clever. Yes. Well done." He had liked her other ideas too; walking into the bar at the Royal Garden Hotel with him, Debbie felt absurdly excited and pleased with herself; rather as if she was walking into a theatre on the red carpet, or—

"Debbie! Hello. How lovely to see you."

It was Simon Beaumont, looking extremely smooth and handsome. And somehow younger. He stood up and gave her a kiss; she felt starrier still.

"Lovely to see you too, Simon," she said. "This is Derek Earnshaw, a client of mine. Derek, this is Simon Beaumont."

"Who would dearly love to be a client of hers," said Simon, smiling, holding out his hand. "Lucky man. Well, I won't keep you. Enjoy your drink. Nice to have met you," he added to Earnshaw. If she had written the script herself, Debbie couldn't have done it better.

As they settled at a table at the far end of the bar, she saw Simon had been joined by a man. A young, rather tasty man, with dark, slightly spiky hair and a very sharp suit. Pity he hadn't been there a few minutes earlier . . . Debbie, concentrate. You're a professional woman, not a bimbo. You have a client to look after.

"Nice chap," said Derek Earnshaw. "What does he do?"

"Oh, he runs a bank," said Debbie airily.

⌁

Simon liked Joel Strickland: very much. He hadn't exactly been expecting a hack in a beer-stained jacket, but a bright and personable young man with a clear grasp of his subject seemed too much to hope for. Nevertheless, that was what he had got.

"Now what can I tell you," said Simon. "I haven't got too long, I'm taking some clients out to the White City, to the dogs. You ever do that?"

"Yeah, I've been with the boys at the sports desk once or twice. Good fun." He grinned at Simon. "Can I say first of all that I'm so grateful to you for seeing me. And I simply want your story, everything you can tell me about the Lloyd's experience. As it affected you, obviously."

The interview ran along fairly predictable lines; when had he first considered becoming a Name, who had introduced him, how much business had he written; had he been encouraged to increase his underwriting; had he had any say in which syndicates he went into.

"Sadly not. Although how could I have known, anyway, that Westfield Bradley was one of the less scrupulous groups. And yes, I'd been advised that I'd always make money on marine and motor. I said I'd like to be in those. They said fine. Which I was. But a few other things as well. Like non-marine. Only much later did I learn that was a holdall which included asbestosis."

He had felt absolutely no suspicion, he said. Lloyd's record was impeccable, a lot of his friends did very nicely out of them. "I thought I was pretty lucky to have been invited in."

"And—good years followed?"

"Very good. Ten of them. Can't deny it. But then the rumours began towards the end of eighty-seven, I'd say. I remember sitting at a lunch and someone saying he thought there'd be enormous calls on Names soon and that Lloyd's was in debt to the tune of a billion or whatever. And we said, almost cheerfully, you know how one does, 'Well, nothing we can do about it.' We were all confident our particular syndicates would be all right, that our Members' Agents would look after us—and it's always the other fellow, isn't it, who gets caught."

"And you can't get out, of course, can you?"

"You can resign in theory, but that only lets you off the hook with any new business they write. For everything you've signed up to, it's the grave and beyond. The whole thing is an absolute scandal. They can come after your executors if they think it will do them any good. So to an extent it was head-in-the-sand time. Until I got what you might call the first minus accounting. In eighty-eight."

"And how did you feel?"

"Absolutely sick. Terrified. I was shitting myself. Almost literally. And this year, worse still. I may have to sell the London house. But I'm going to law, planning to sue them . . ."

"Really?"

"Yes. Lot of us, all with the same Members' Agency. We'll be suing them, incidentally, not Lloyd's as a whole. That really wouldn't wash."

"And who's masterminding it, so to speak?"

"Oh, a chap who might well talk to you, very nice indeed, used to have it all, big house, kids at public school, only difference is his wife's left him. I've been lucky there. Very lucky. Anyway, we've decided it's the only thing to do. We're just not prepared to lie down and tell them to take it. And one of the reasons I decided to talk to you was that a friend of mine recently tried to kill himself. Nice chap, in total despair, hadn't even told his wife. Took an overdose. They saved him, but I'm not sure he was very grateful for it. It doesn't bear thinking about. And he's not the only one, of course."

"I know it," said Strickland soberly. "I interviewed the neighbour of some old lady who did exactly that. Ghastly. Tell me, does the name Allinson mean anything to you?"

"Don't think so. Why?"

"Oh, got a bit of a lead from someone. You don't think your friend would talk to me, do you?"

"I'm not sure. I can certainly ask him. He'd be very happy to see the whole of Lloyd's cast into the fiery furnace."

"Thanks, I'd appreciate it. Very brave of you to sue them. How's it going?"

"Oh, slowly. We haven't even got a barrister yet, but we've got a very impressive solicitor. We're enrolling as many as we can, to help bolster the fighting fund. I'd be pleased with a hundred or so; some of these cases have thousands of protagonists. Anyway, I think that's about it. I'll speak to both these chaps, see how they feel about talking to you."

"Tell me, can you remember which year they suggested you increased your underwriting?"

"Oh, eighty-three, eighty-four, I think."

"Well," said Strickland, "as far as I can make out, claims were being made as far back as the 1970s by persons suffering from asbestos-related diseases. Presumably that's the basis of your case against them—that they must have known."

"Broadly speaking, yes. But I don't think we should discuss that now. Probably against the rules. I'll check with the solicitor."

"Fine. I'd be very grateful."

"To be honest, I've enjoyed it," said Simon, "and now— Ah, Debbie. You leaving?"

"Yes, 'fraid so. Mr. Earnshaw has a train to catch."

"I see. Can't tempt you to join us then? I hope she's looked after you nicely, Mr. Earnshaw."

"She has. Very nicely, thank you. Bye now."

"Who was that?" said Joel when the two of them had disappeared; he was staring after them. It was fairly obvious his interest wasn't in Earnshaw.

"Oh, young friend of mine."

"She's very attractive."

"Yes, she is. Bit troublesome though."

"In what way?"

"Oh, hard to say. I always remember Roald Dahl saying that sharing a house with his daughters was like living with a lot of unsettled heifers. Debbie is a very unsettled heifer."

"She seemed to like you."

"Only in a daughterly way," said Simon.

❧

They were standing waiting for the lift when Debbie realised she had left her scarf behind.

"I'm sorry," she said to Earnshaw. "Stupid of me. You just go. It's fine."

"Sure? I really am running a bit late."

"Perfectly sure."

"Thank you again. I feel very excited about the whole project."

"Good. Me too."

She supposed a psychiatrist would have said she left the scarf deliberately. So she would have to go back into the bar. And pass Simon Beaumont and his tasty companion. And be drawn into further conversation with them. But she wasn't dappy, not in that way anyway, and she might not be speaking to her husband at the moment, or rather he might not be speaking to her, but there was no way she'd be going to such lengths to meet some complete stranger just because she liked his haircut. Those days were long gone. Sadly. She walked back into the bar, trying to look relaxed. "Hi," she said as they both looked up at her. "I left my scarf behind. Stupid of me."

"Well, your loss is our gain. Want a quick drink with us? Go on, spoil yourself. You could even call it work. Joel here is a journalist, could be an important contact for you."

"Well . . ." It would be the end of a perfect day really. And she just felt so—so soothed by it all. After days of Richard treating her like a piece of dog poo that had found its way onto his shoe, here she was being flattered and sought after, it was—well it was irresistible really . . .

Simon bought a bottle of champagne for the three of them. She sat next to him and opposite Joel, and watched him watching her, admiring her and smiling at her as she chattered and joked and teased Simon about Flora. "She's my mother-in-law, totally beautiful and wonderful in every way," she said to Joel.

"Except that she annoys Debbie to death."

"No, she doesn't. Well, not to death. Anyway, Simon is rather taken with her—"

"I am not. But I am very fond of her and I do admire her. She might be someone you could talk to," he said to Joel. "She's in this thing too—that's how we all met."

"She sounds like quite a mother-in-law," said Joel.

"She is. Hard to live up to. Do you have a mother-in-law?" God, why had she said that? How awful, how embarrassing, how crass . . .

"No, thank God." He looked amused, recognising her confusion. "I've been spared that so far."

"Let me top you up, Debbie," said Simon, "and then I must go."

"No, no, don't give me any more—"

"Why not? It suits you. The last time we were together, Debbie and I," he said to Joel, "we'd both had rather too much, hadn't we, darling? And talked a bit too much."

"Just a bit."

"That was in Flora's kitchen, in case you get any funny ideas, Joel. Oh Lord, look at the time. I must go. You two finish the bottle, I'll take care of the bill—"

"No, no," said Joel, "that's ridiculous, the *News* will pay. Please, Simon, I insist."

"OK. Well, nice talking to you. I'll get back to you about those people. And the lawsuit."

"So, are you doing a piece about Lloyd's?" said Debbie when he had gone.

"Trying to. Most of them won't talk, but Simon's opening a few doors."

"Good. You're the City editor of the *News*, did Simon say?"

"That's correct. Now tell me, what's a nice girl like you doing in PR?" The dark brown eyes were thoughtful as he looked at her.

"I like it," she said defensively.

"Really?"

"Yes, really. It's fun. And it means you can meet journalists," she added. She smiled at him, but her voice was just slightly barbed.

"Well, obviously that's a very important bonus." He grinned back at her. God, he was so sexy. "And what does your old man do?"

"He's headmaster of a school in Ealing."

"And he enjoys that?"

"No, not much. He's frustrated. He's been offered a new job," she added, "up in Scotland."

"So, you'll be moving up there, will you?"

"I'm . . . I'm not sure," she said carefully. "We're thinking about it."

"Well, it's a long way away," he said. "Big move. Away from all your friends and so on."

"Yes. But it's important for him . . ."

"Well, I've certainly got you wrong," he said, smiling at her again. "Thought you were a go-getting girl about town. And what do I find? A dutiful wife."

"And what's wrong with that?" said Debbie.

"Nothing at all. It's very impressive. I would say you're a dying breed." He raised his glass to her. "To wifehood."

"Don't say that," said Debbie. "Now you've made me feel dull and dreary."

"Oh no," he said, and his expression was quite serious now. "You could never seem dull and dreary. Quite impossible." She felt herself blush, unable to think of anything to say. He did it for her. "I must go," he said.

"Me too."

"It's been really nice meeting you."

"Thank you. I've enjoyed it too. Very much." She looked at her watch. "God, it's late. Goodbye, Joel."

"Goodbye, Debbie. And if you're ever in the *News* offices, come and say hello."

❧

"I think we should move," said Blue.

"Move! But why?"

"Well, this is hardly a family home, is it? No room for a nursery, no proper garden, terrible pollution. The country's the place for children to grow up."

"The country!"

"I thought you'd like the idea, Lucinda. Thought you was a country girl at heart. You said yourself, you wanted ponies and that for our kids."

"Yes, I do. So where were you thinking we might go?"

"Chislehurst," said Blue, without a moment's hesitation.

"Chislehurst! Where's that?"

"Kent."

"Oh. Oh, I see. But I don't know anybody in Kent. I think I'd rather go where I have a few friends already. Old ones. Like—like Gloucestershire, for instance."

"No, don't think so. No offence, Lucy, but your parents have tended to put me off Gloucestershire. No, Chislehurst's the job. Beautiful properties, easy run into London Bridge for me. And anyway, Luft lives out there and so does Harry; you'll find yourself with loads of friends ready-made."

"Well, maybe we could have a look," said Lucinda. "Can I have some more coffee, Blue, please?"

"Course you can. God, it suits you, being pregnant. You look absolutely gorgeous this morning."

"Thank you. I feel quite gorgeous. Actually."

"Well, seeing as it's Sunday, maybe we should pop back into bed. Just for a little while."

"Yes, let's," she said, smiling at him. It was funny, but being pregnant made her feel even more sexy, she thought, as she took his hand and let him lead her into the bedroom. She'd have thought it would be the reverse, but . . .

Afterwards, when she was settling into herself again, no longer fractured with the violent piercing pleasure, languorously, warmly peaceful, Blue curled up behind her, rather absentmindedly playing with her breasts—her wonderfully full breasts, the sort she had always dreamed of having—she said, "Blue, I would love to move to the country, of course. But maybe not yet. Not till I've had the baby, and I can give it my full attention. It's a lot of work, moving."

"Yeah, all right," he said, already half asleep. "Whatever you want." It was the first time, she realised, quite shocked at her own ability to do so, that she had been anything other than entirely honest with him. But it really would have spoiled the lovely Sunday to have to go any further into why she didn't want to move yet.

Chapter 22

There really was still something special about Ascot, Elizabeth thought, looking down from the agency box on the sixth floor, in spite of the vulgarity, the drunkenness, the overt commercialism. It was, if the sun shone, a wonderful spectacle—the blue sky, the green ribbon of the course, the pastel shades of the hats, and the vivid colours of the jockeys' silks moving in a kaleidoscopic pattern; the beautiful gleaming animals, so clearly out to enjoy themselves, to show off; and an almost tangible sense of enjoyment settling over the whole thing to create a glorious tapestry. And the sun was shining today.

She was very pleased with what she was wearing: a cream silk suit, very simple, and a wide-brimmed black straw hat with a cream ribbon. And very high-heeled shoes with fine ankle straps which she'd regret, she knew, by the end of the day. But they were lovely—what Annabel called fuck-me shoes. She'd been very shocked when her daughter had first said that; Annabel had simply giggled and said, "Mu-u-um!" (turning the word into three syllables in the way she had).

Of all the corporate entertaining the agency did, she enjoyed Ascot most. It was such fun, a kind of charming carnival that took a miserable spirit to resist. And it still had a huge cachet; clients seldom refused an invitation to Ascot. Her agency took a box for one day, Simon's bank for two; sometimes they overlapped. This year was one of them. They had never managed to actually go together and for pleasure; they certainly never would now. The extravagance was unthinkable.

They arrived that day, in the same hire car, kissed, parted, made their way to their respective boxes (half an hour before their earliest guests), agreeing to try and meet in the paddock, but otherwise at home very much later, all their attention and loyalty now turned to their clients; and what an illusion they presented, she thought, glossy, good-looking, moneyed, and giving absolutely no hint of the financial nightmare that stalked them.

∞

Lucinda had always enjoyed Ascot, loved the dressing up, the way you could be really excessive without it seeming vulgar. This year's hat was one of the best. She had chosen it with great care, a wide-brimmed, beribboned thing from Harvey Nichols; smaller, chicer styles didn't really suit her changing shape; the traditional sort balanced it better, somehow. She was quite pleased with her dress as well, pale-blue silk, like the hat, gently high-waisted with narrow sleeves. At least one bit of her could look slim. It was certainly going to be different. McArthur's were taking a large party, but she couldn't help feeling that Ascot in a pair of corporate boxes on one of those top floors wouldn't be quite the same as being in the Royal Enclosure with lots of lifelong chums, and she had so loved the picnics and then meeting everyone in the evening in a great mob in Kensington.

She'd been to the Derby with Blue—he liked to do the big ones, as he put it—and that had been huge fun; she did love his friends, they all made such a fuss of her, treated her as if she was royalty, even though they did tease her a lot as well, and she supposed a couple of the girls were a bit less friendly. Blue had put some enormous sum of money on a horse, and lost it; he'd just laughed and said he could take a hiding as well as the next man. His generosity was one of the things she loved most about him.

Everything seemed to be all right again; she had managed to explain a bit about the divorce, about what Steve Durham had said they might be able to do. Of course she hadn't gone into the details, because Steve was still fine-tuning them, as he put it, and one or two of them might be a bit upsetting for Blue, she could see, until he really understood, but he seemed perfectly happy about everything so far.

℮

Joel Strickland was going to Ascot; it wasn't exactly within his brief as City editor, but several press tickets had arrived and he loved the races. He actually found flat racing slightly boring, he preferred the jumps, but a load of *News* writers were going together in a minibus: Sandra Keswick and a photographer to cover the fashion, Suzy Jameson to do the gossip, as well as the sports guys. They'd have a laugh. And he always enjoyed being with Suzy, who was pretty and sassy with extremely good legs; she was also brilliant at her job. She was cunning in her pursuit of gossip; manicurists, florists, and chambermaids were her favourite sources of information: she knew they were far more likely to spill spicy beans than the friends and relations of her prey. Her finest hour had been when she managed to prise out of a laundry deliveryman details of a well-known socialite (married) who suddenly started sending twice the number of sheets for laundering every week. "And to pay me with cash; that seemed a bit funny," he said to Suzy, over a third whiskey and soda. "I mean, always suspicious, cash, wouldn't you say?"

Suzy agreed.

Suzy was one of the reasons Joel wasn't taking his girlfriend, Maggie, with him; he and Suzy tended to work together to a degree on such occasions, but she was overtly flirtatious and Maggie was intensely jealous. She was jealous not only of the other women in Joel's life, even the working colleagues, but of the job itself, the way it took him to parties and smart hotels and on the odd overseas binge. Working in the City herself, she knew how it ran on social contact, and she knew how much Joel enjoyed it; she pretended not to care, but she always grilled him after a dinner or a conference. He was going to have to do something about her soon; it simply wasn't working. He was terribly fond of her, but he didn't want to spend the rest of his life with her: which was patently what she wanted.

Meanwhile, the immediate future was today at Ascot. And his presence there was not entirely self-indulgent. You could always pick up a good financial story—or at any rate, some good financial gossip—at Ascot, crawling as it was with the great and the good, or rather, the great and the wealthy. One occasion had provided him with the first straws in the wind of a big money-laundering operation: nowhere better to quietly hide a few grand than at a race meeting. And maybe today he'd get something for his Lloyd's story. Which was very slow in coming together. And his editor wasn't keen, said who was going to care about a lot of rich greedy people getting their just deserts. He'd been much more interested in a story about Gordon Brown and John Smith agreeing to support the Exchange Rate Mechanism.

❦

"I'm so sorry."

"No, no, it was my fault. The sun's so dazzling coming out of that tunnel— Simon! Hello!" He was looking pretty dazzling too, Lucinda thought; he really was amazingly good-looking. Well worth bumping into.

"It certainly is," he said. "Wonderful day, isn't it? And you look gorgeous, if I may say so. That's a lovely hat."

"You certainly may. Thank you. Isn't it beautiful here today?"

"It is. Can't beat it when the sun shines." He stood back, smiling at her. "So, where's your—your . . ."

"My fiancé? He's in a box with lots of his cronies. None of them were very interested in the horses, which seemed a bit of a shame, so I came down. It's my favourite part of Ascot, visiting the paddock."

"Mine too. I had a similar experience with my guests. If you like, we could take a turn together."

"That would be nice."

They walked in silence, easily companionable, watching the horses beginning to form into a line for the next race, dancing and skitting about, eyeing one another up, like so many models backstage, preparing to walk down the catwalk.

"So are you up with the corporate lot then?" he said.

"Yes. It's a new experience actually. Blue—that is, my . . . my fiancé—he works for McArthur's. He's a market maker."

"I see. Amazing creatures, aren't they?" he said, breaking off, studying the horses. "Those beauties, I mean, not market makers. Much smaller than you'd expect, somehow."

"Yes, I always think that. Do you like horses?"

"Oh, they're all right. My younger daughter would like to be one. Or marry one."

Lucinda laughed. "How old is she?"

"Thirteen."

"And she has a pony?"

"She does. We can't house him anymore, thanks to Lloyd's; he lives farther away than Tilly would like now, but at least she still has him. He's down in Wales with Flora Fielding—can't remember if you met her or not—another Lloyd's victim."

"Yes, I did. She was rather lovely, I thought. So are you up there with the corporates as well?"

"I am indeed. Another bank—merchant variety. I should be getting back to them really. But if you want to look in at my box later, it's number 502, and bring your fiancé, we'd love to see you both. Catherine is here."

"Catherine! How nice."

"Yes, she's working rather hard up there. So she'd particularly love to see you—have an excuse to stop for a moment."

"Then we'll most definitely come. And I'm sure Blue would love to meet you. Thank you."

❦

He was on his way to the press tent when he saw Simon Beaumont waving at him. Simon was clearly in an extremely cheerful state of mind, and had undoubtedly had more than one glass of champagne.

"Just won three hundred quid. Won't solve all my problems, of course, but—how's the story going?"

"Oh, slowly. But thanks a lot for all your help. And your friend Neil Lawrence called me, said he'd be happy to talk."

"Good. And did you have a nice chat with Debbie after I'd gone?"

"Oh—yes, thanks," said Joel. "Yes, she's—great fun." He had actually felt Debbie was more than great fun; he had been what he called "bothered" by her for several days; she had stuck in his head, and he wasn't sure why. She wasn't particularly pretty—although she had those amazing brown eyes, and actually, yes, a completely sexy mouth—and her figure wasn't exactly sensational, she was small and rather skinny. But she was very attractive, no doubt about that, and amusing in a rather quirky way; had she not been married he would probably have asked her out.

"Anyway," said Simon, "come up for a drink a bit later. Girl in my box, works for me, horribly affected by it all, she'd probably like to talk to you. And my wife'll be there by then, she wanted to meet you too, not sure why. Or was that my daughter? Can't remember."

"Is your daughter here?" asked Joel. He still remembered Annabel in all her engaging beauty: much too young for him, of course, but . . .

"No, no, she's working. Big day for hairdressers, I'm told. Anyway, you come up around four thirty or five, when things are winding down a bit, box number 502, have a drink, meet Catherine."

⁓

"Simon, hello. This is my fiancé, Blue Horton. Is this really all right, Simon?"

"Absolutely! How do you do, Blue, very nice to meet you." So this was the Adonis who had persuaded Lucinda away from her dull husband: interesting. It wasn't his looks, that was for sure. He looked a bit of a thug, with close-cropped hair and a rather thick neck. A working-class thug, moreover. Extraordinary.

Blue held out a hand to Simon. "Pleased to meet you at last. Lucinda never stops talking about you."

"Oh really? I find that a little hard to believe. Glass of champagne?"

"Won't say no, although Lucinda tells me I've had quite enough. I personally don't think you can ever have enough champagne, but there you go. Had a good day?"

"Pretty good, yes. Won a bit."

"Lucky you. I've lost a lot." He smiled at Simon; and suddenly Simon could see it. What this man had was charm: in lorryloads. He was easy, and at the same time possessed of huge energy; he almost crackled, standing there, his dark eyes roaming the box, following Lucinda as she embraced Catherine, smiling fondly at her, then coming back to Simon.

"Your wife here?"

"Oh no. She's entertaining on her own account."

"Oh yeah?" He looked genuinely interested, wasn't merely being polite. "She got her own business, has she?"

"Well, almost. She's MD of an advertising agency."

"Blimey. I've heard of these superwomen. Never met one in the flesh, though."

"Well, you can," said Simon, "if you hang on a bit. She's promised to come up at about five."

"Well, we could do that, yeah. Thanks very much."

"Blue, this is Catherine," said Lucinda, leading a rather weary-looking girl over. "I told you about her, remember?"

"Lucinda, if I remembered everything you told me, my head would burst," said Blue.

❧

Catherine was beginning to feel very tired. It had been a long day and a huge strain. She hadn't been able to eat anything; whenever her hand stretched out to take a smoked-salmon sandwich or mini-quiche, someone would put a glass of champagne or a plate of petit fours into it, to take to somebody else. She would have given anything just to have been able to take in the scene properly for five minutes, to actually see a race. She could have been anywhere at all, she thought wearily.

The mood in the box was jovial; everyone seemed to have won something, or were eager to relate what a lot they had lost; indeed, that seemed to be almost more enjoyable.

"Yes, damn near a grand altogether," said a red-faced man, and: "You're doing well," said another. "I did the fatal thing, you know, got the winner in the first race and then spent most of the day losing it twice over. Not a word to the wife, though."

And had they any idea at all how lucky they were, Catherine thought, to be able to regard the loss of what would have paid Freddie's school fees for more than a term with such absurd equanimity?

"Here, why don't I hold that plate for you for a minute so you can eat some of it yourself. I've been watching you—you look very hungry."

Catherine turned and saw a young, rather dashing-looking man, with very dark hair and eyes, grinning at her. "Joel Strickland," he added, holding out his hand for the plate.

"How very kind," said Catherine gratefully, seizing a couple of fondants and (she was afraid) literally shovelling them into her mouth. "It is very nice to meet you, Joel. And how do you know Simon?"

"I'm a journalist. I interviewed him not so long ago."

"What paper are you on?"

"The *News*. I'm the City editor."

"Gosh. I don't think I've ever met a journalist. Not a real one. I did some work experience once for the local paper, but I wasn't much good at it," she added.

"I can't believe that. So what's your role here?"

"Oh, general dogsbody. Making sure everyone had enough to eat and wasn't being neglected, that sort of thing."

"I can see you've been pretty effective. Nobody is close to starving—apart from you, that is. Why don't you sit down for a bit, enjoy that food."

"Oh no, I couldn't possibly," said Catherine. "I'm not here to sit down. Let me get you a drink." She signalled to the waitress.

"OK. Well, tell me, how have you found Ascot?"

"Oh, wonderful," she said brightly—and then meeting his sharp, amused eyes, blushed and said, "It wasn't quite how I expected."

"Really?"

"Yes. I thought it would be much more about the racing—the horses, you know."

" 'Fraid not," he said. "Most of the people who come for the racing aren't up here. This lot just want to drink, show off their hats, and tell everyone how much they've lost. And—"

"Catherine, how lovely to see you." It was Lucinda. "Simon said you'd be here."

At which point, someone jogged Catherine's arm, and the glass of champagne she was taking from the tray went all over Joel's shirt and tie.

"Oh dear, let me—"

"It's all right. Please don't worry. Occupational hazard, I'd say."

"Catherine, stop fussing," said Lucinda. "He's right, you expect to get showered with champagne here, don't you?" she added to Joel. "Can I find you some tissues or something? Or replace that drink?"

Simon, who had been watching this scene out of the corner of his eye, thought what a treasure Lucinda was, and hoped her charming fiancé realised it. Simon was pleased with the day. People had appreciated it, seemed happy, a great many male egos had been stroked and female ones flattered, the atmosphere was easily relaxed; the sun had been warm, the champagne cold, the food delicious, and the view of the course—for those who had wished to admire it—breathtaking. And many business relationships had been strengthened by the sharing of the day's pleasures—which was, after all, the whole idea . . .

"Simon! Hello, darling. I've come for a quick visit, as promised. How's everything?" It was Elizabeth: looking stunning. God, he was proud of her. He kissed her.

"I'm fine. Except I'm even poorer."

"Me too. Lost lots."

"Mrs. Beaumont? Blue Horton. You're the superwoman, I understand."

"On a good day, perhaps."

"Well, I wish our managing director looked like you. Can I ask you a question about your business?"

"Of course."

"What I can never understand, some of those ads, those really good ones—take the Cinzano one for instance, with Joan Collins and that Rossiter chap—everyone knows the ads, says how bl—how marvellous they are, then you ask them what the product is and they say Martini. Or Campari, or something like that. So what's the point? Seems like that's a bit of a wank—"

Lucinda had come over, tucked her arm through his. "Blue," she said warningly.

"Sorry, bit of self-indulgence anyway on the part of your industry. I mean, the whole point of an ad surely is to sell the product?"

"Well, yes. You're right. And it's very clever of you to make that point. But you know, the real trick is to register the brand and what it has to offer in a distinctive and memorable way. And—"

And the argument might have gone on for some time, had not

Catherine slowly and very gracefully slithered to the floor of the box in a dead faint.

"She looks to me as if she doesn't have enough to eat," said Elizabeth severely to Simon, as if it was his fault. Various people helped Catherine to a chair, fetched water, pushed her head between her knees.

"Quite possibly," he said. "I worry about her a lot."

"Look, I'll take her home," said Lucinda. "I'm actually very tired—no, really Simon, I am, ask Blue. Didn't I just say I was tired, Blue?"

"Yes, you did."

"And Blue's got to stay and take his clients out to dinner," said Lucinda. "But I was never going to do that anyway, being . . . well, you know."

"She's in the family way," said Blue, and the infinite pride with which he spoke was hugely touching; Elizabeth felt like hugging him.

"Yes, and I'm not supposed to get too tired. So why don't I take the car and drop Catherine off? Blue, you can go up to town with someone else, can't you?"

"Oh no," said Catherine, who was so embarrassed she felt she might faint again. "There's no need, honestly."

"It's quite all right," said Lucinda, "it's a big car. You can lie down in the back, if you like. Blue, darling, I'll see you later. Try not to get too drunk. Come on, Catherine. Now are you sure you're all right to walk to the car park?"

"I think I'll come with you," said Blue. "Make sure you're OK. Everything's breaking up now, anyway, and we're having dinner in the West End, at Langan's. I'll meet up with everyone there."

"Well, if you're really sure, it's terribly kind."

"We're really sure," said Lucinda.

"Lovely, isn't she?" said Blue to the room in general, watching Lucinda as she helped Catherine into her jacket. "Heart of gold too. Can't believe she's mine."

Even from a man with at least two bottles of champagne inside him, it was a very touching tribute.

The box emptied quite quickly after that. Joel went first, and the others followed. It had been, they all agreed, a wonderfully successful day.

But when Catherine, Lucinda, and Blue reached Fulham, they found

Mrs. Lennox and Caroline both white-faced and fighting down hysteria. Freddie had disappeared.

Chapter 23

It was when the policeman asked Catherine whether Freddie was a trusting sort of child that she became visibly frightened. Until then, she had forced back the tears and remained calm, for Caroline's sake as much as anything: Caroline, who had sat wide-eyed and white-faced, utterly silent while Mary Lennox choked out her story; while the school was rung, neighbours contacted; while Blue knocked on door after door in the area, asking if anyone had seen him, if they could look around their gardens, their garages, their houses, in the absolutely unlikely event of Freddie hiding there.

But at that question, with its sinister, scarcely hidden agenda, Catherine cracked and began to sob, quite loudly, cradling Caroline in her arms, and the sturdily kind policewoman who had been standing until then, simply observing the scene, ordered the young constable, who looked hardly old enough to have left school himself, to go and make a nice big pot of tea.

"It's all right," said Catherine, wiping her eyes. "I'm sorry, of course you must go on. It doesn't matter about me, what matters is finding Freddie."

They had been fantastic, the police, from the moment Blue had rung them. "We're just wasting valuable time now," he had said. "Let's get the professionals in."

The officers had arrived in ten minutes, four of them, calm and capable. Two were dispatched to do a proper, systematic search of all the houses in the area, while the questioning went on and on. How long had Catherine known Mary Lennox, who else did she know in the area . . . It was all nicely done, very straightforward with no hint of reproach, but it inevitably made her feel irresponsible. They asked for a photograph; she gave them the one she carried in her bag, a school photograph of a smiling, pretty little boy; both Mary and Caroline confirmed that he had been wearing his school uniform when they had last seen him, that he hadn't changed into his jeans when he got home. That was when the police asked if he was trusting.

"Perhaps we could talk to you again, Mrs. Lennox," the officer in charge said. "Will you tell us once more exactly what happened this afternoon, after you fetched Freddie from school."

And she went through it again: how they had come into the flat, how she had given the children some milk and biscuits, and how after they had done their homework she had settled them down in front of the TV while she went to cook their tea. When it was ready, she had gone to fetch them and Caroline had been sitting there on her own, and had looked faintly surprised when Mary asked her where Freddie was.

"He went to the toilet and then he said he was going to find you." Mrs. Lennox had telephoned Lynton House, while knowing it was very unlikely that Freddie would have gone back there, and a friend of Catherine's whose number she had been given to use in "a real emergency." "And then, I was just wondering if I should call the police, when Mrs. Morgan arrived home with her friends here."

Blue and Lucinda were now sitting drinking tea, determined not to leave until they felt that the situation had somehow been resolved. Catherine was questioned repeatedly. Was Freddie happy at home and at school? Did he have much freedom? What did he like doing—what were his hobbies? Might he suddenly decide to go to the cinema?

"No, I don't think so. We never go to the cinema, he's not a cinema sort of child . . ."

"And would he have had any money on him?"

"Well, I did give him a bit for today, just in case something happened, as an emergency, you know. Just a couple of pounds."

"But he hadn't spent it? As far as you know, at any rate, Mrs. Lennox, seeing as you picked him up from school."

"No, no, he had no reason to, no opportunity," said Mary Lennox. She seemed to have aged twenty years.

"That could be important," said the policeman. "If he's got a couple of quid, he could go on a bus or something," and then everyone looked at Caroline as a sound escaped her that was a mixture of a whisper and a squeak.

"What, darling?" Catherine said sharply. "What is it?"

"Some boys took it," she said. "They took his money."

"What boys?"

"From school."

"I don't understand—do you mean his old school? Your school?" Reluctantly, Caroline nodded.

"But when? How?"

It turned out that "some horrible big boys," met Freddie every morning. "They turn out his pockets and his school bag, take what they want. They say they'll beat him up if he tells."

"Oh no!" Catherine thought of all the occasions when she had rebuked Freddie for losing things. "Why didn't you tell me, Caroline, if he felt he couldn't?"

"They said they'd beat me up as well."

"Oh, God." She clutched Caroline to her, wondering how she would ever be able to let her out of her sight again, wondering how children could be capable of such things.

"Well, it's one good thing," said the police sergeant. "It means he didn't have any money after all, so he can't have gone far. Not under his own steam anyway."

⁂

"No news yet," said Lucinda the next morning, putting the phone down. "Poor, poor Catherine. How on earth do you think she got through the night? And is there anything we can do for her?"

"Nothing," Blue said. "The police are doing what they can. Bloody impressive they are, I asked them on the QT what about perverts and that, and the sergeant said they were already doing a search, any known ones in the area . . ."

"Blue, that's so horrible."

"Yes, I know, but it's got to be faced."

"I wonder if I should go over there or something—"

"No, don't," he said. "We're not family, we're not even close friends. We just happened to be there."

"Yes, and it was so kind of you to stay, be so late for your dinner. She's lovely, Catherine, isn't she?"

"Yeah, she's OK. Poor cow. Just think about it—no husband, no money, hardly any friends, far as I can make out, those fuckers after her—"

"Blue . . ."

"Well, they are. I'm sorry. And now her kid's gone missing. Bloody awful. I hope those coppers question the other kids."

"Yes, she said they were going to the school today."

"God, children are evil. Poor little sod, being bullied on top of everything else."

"Yes, I know. But at least he's back at his nice little school now; he must be all right there."

"Lucinda," said Blue, "do you really think nobody gets bullied at 'nice little schools' as you call them? Children are savages, all of them, and being pushed into some poncey uniform and taught to speak nicely don't make no difference at all. Believe me. Luft went to one of those schools, got bullied so badly, and by his housemaster an' all, he says he'll never get over it."

"Yes, I see," said Lucinda meekly.

                        ❧

Simon felt, absurdly he knew, guilty about Freddie. God, poor woman. What a nightmare her whole life was. He phoned Elizabeth to tell her about Freddie; she was very upset. "Simon, how dreadful. I'm so sorry. Poor, poor Catherine. I can't think of anything worse. I still dread it daily, you know—something happening to one of the children. So much more terrible than it being us."

"It rather puts everything into perspective, doesn't it? Which reminds me—I'm asking a couple of agents to come and have a look at the house. Value it, you know. Hope that's all right."

"Yes, of course," said Elizabeth.

"Good. Thanks. I know—well, I know how much you mind."

"Oh, I know you do. And it's all right." She was so much happier suddenly, so astonished by the way they seemed to have moved together again, that nothing seemed quite so serious. And certainly, compared to the loss of a small boy, the sale of a house, however beloved, could not seem remotely important.

"Now, I just got a call from the solicitor. She wants to have a meeting this Friday afternoon with the barrister. Flora will be coming. All right if I ask her to stay the night with us?"

"Of course," Elizabeth said. "It would be nice to spend a bit of time with her."

"Good. Thank you."

"No need to thank me. Oh, and Simon—"

"Yes?"

"Simon, lots of love."

"And to you," he said.

e ∽

Catherine couldn't imagine wanting to live any longer, unless Freddie were found. Somehow, she felt oddly hopeless. There was something about this whole thing that forbade positive thinking. It was the way Freddie appeared to have vanished from the face of the earth, the way no one had even seen him walking along the road . . .

e ∽

"Um, is Joel Strickland in today?" Debbie tried to sound casual. Really, really casual. As you would if you were in a newspaper office, doing your job, and had a friend who worked there.

"Not sure." Nicky Holt, assistant fashion and beauty editor of the *News,* looked at her coolly. Debbie had come in to tell her about the new body range with built-in deodorant that one of their clients was launching, and Nicky had clearly been underwhelmed by it. "He a friend of yours?"

"Sort of—yes."

"Well, want to go along to his office? He might be there. Keeps funny hours, our Joel."

"Oh, OK." She was beginning to regret ever mentioning him. He probably wouldn't remember her properly if he was there, and then she'd look really stupid.

"Know where his office is?" Nicky asked, and feeling even more stupid, she said no, she didn't.

Nicky gave her a funny look and said, "Straight down through the news room, turn left, first office on the right."

"OK, thanks."

She managed to find the office without asking anyone else, and peeped in; he wasn't there. It was an interesting office for a newspaper, quite different from the chaos of the fashion and beauty department, with its heaped-up sweaters and shoes and rails of clothes and mountains of bags. Joel's office was very neat, with a computer screen showing City prices, and stacks of files and framed copies of various successful stories he'd done on the wall, including one that simply said WIPE OUT, in enormous red letters on the front page from the Monday after the crash and the great storm of '87. She waited a moment or two in case he was with someone else and came back, but he didn't.

She left then, feeling this was a clear sign from Fate that she was never destined to meet him again. And really, what would be the point if she did?

❧

"Right then," said Sergeant Lockyer, looking at the five boys: big, all of them, tough and aggressive, two of them quite spotty, grown out of their junior school and its gentle ways. "Which of you shall I talk to first?"

It was the usual story: they hadn't meant any harm, Freddie should have been able to take a bit of teasing, they hadn't realised they were upsetting him. They displayed a degree of bravado at first, then crumbled when Lockyer said he was going to get their parents in. That was when one of them, the biggest and spottiest, said, "If you really want to know who else was upsetting him, you might try the other lot. Those poshoes up the road, the ones Freddie went running back to."

Chapter 24

Catherine wasn't sure what would be the worst of the things that might have happened to Freddie: she forced herself to face them one by one, feeling that since he might be enduring them, then so must she. Abduction, abuse, murder—each one worse than the last. She kept thinking of her son as she had last seen him, before she left for Ascot; he had been smiling, so cheerful—and so brave, as she now knew, having learned of the bullying. How could her beautiful, clever, courageous little boy have suffered this awful thing? How could the life she had made for him so carefully, filled with the things that she felt mattered, with books, with music, with friends, with fun—and they had managed to have fun, in spite of everything, the three of them—how could that life have turned so ugly, so treacherous?

As the second ghastly night finally ended, Catherine began to lose hope. And running through her fear was an ongoing seething rage at Lloyd's. Whose fault she felt the whole thing undeniably was.

Sergeant Lockyer didn't like Donald Archer, the head of Lynton House. He was rampantly complacent. "I don't know where you got this story from, but it can't be correct. We simply don't tolerate bullying here," he said, peering over his half-moon glasses at Lockyer. "It's one of the reasons for our success, why parents choose Lynton House above most of the other private schools in the neighbourhood. And our academic record, of course."

"We got it from a child at St. Joseph's who has a brother here. It was confirmed by Freddie Morgan's younger sister. And I might add that the boy had been driven to calling ChildLine about it."

Donald Archer looked very shocked. "I don't know what to say," he said finally.

"What I'd like you to say, and to Freddie's class initially, is that he has disappeared, possibly run away, that you have been informed of bullying by members of the school which could have been a factor, and it is essential that we are able to talk to those responsible."

"I don't know that I could agree to that. I don't get the connection, to be frank with you."

"Really? The bottom line of the connection, you might say, is that your boys would be treated as suspects."

"What—in Freddie Morgan's disappearance? But that's absurd!"

"It might seem absurd to you, Mr. Archer, but that is how we have to proceed with cases like this. So could you call them together. Oh, and please stress that covering up for friends and so on is not an option. This is a matter of life and death. Or," he added, "we could say it for you."

℘

Nigel was doing some fairly ugly calculations when Lucinda phoned. It was becoming perfectly clear that he was going to have to sell the farm—or most of it. And having done that, he would remain in desperate trouble. If he still owned it, he would have had to sell the house in Cadogan Square as well, just to have some money to live on: but that was in trust for Lucinda. For the time being. And anyway, what would he be able to buy? God, he felt as if he was being sucked down into a whirlpool of panic and fear, and slowly drowning.

"Nigel, hello. It's me."

"Oh—yes. Hello, Lucinda." He wasn't sure he could bear to talk to her at the moment.

"How are you?"

"Bit worried, actually."

"I'm sorry. What about?"

"Oh, nothing much. Just a few hundred thousand pounds to find, you know the sort of thing." His voice sounded bitter even to himself.

"Well, that's exactly what I'm ringing about. My solicitor has written a brilliant letter and he's sending it to yours, OK? Stating what I—we—need."

"Oh yes?"

"And you've got to stick to the plan, Nigel. No weakening. All right?"

"Have . . . have you told your Mr. Horton about this?"

"Of course I have. He's perfectly happy with it."

"Really? All of it? Even the . . . well, you know, the difficult part?"

"Well—yes. I mean, he's agreed in principle and honestly, the rest is just small print, isn't it?"

Nigel agreed it might be called that; while thinking that Horton was exactly the sort of person to read small print very carefully. And not be entirely pleased with what it said.

"So, just sit tight, all right? Everything's going to be absolutely fine."

"Yes, all right," he said. He was hating this whole thing, so deeply did it go against his instincts.

"Good. Now Nigel, such awful news. Do you remember Catherine, Catherine Morgan? She was at that Lloyd's meeting, the first one that we went to, pretty girl. She spoke—she was the widow, with two young children. Had lived in Hong Kong."

"Um . . . yes. What's happened to her?"

"It's not her, it's her little boy, Freddie. He's disappeared."

"Disappeared? How terrible. Where?"

"Well, from his home in Fulham. The day before yesterday, after Ascot. The police are involved and everything, but there's been no sign of him at all yet. I feel so desperately sorry for her and I just wish there was something I could do."

"What a ghastly thing," said Nigel. "I'm so sorry. If you're in touch with her, do please give her my—my sympathy, will you?"

"Yes, of course. I'd suggest you rang, but I suppose every time the phone rings she thinks it might be news, so best not to really."

"Yes. Probably. Anyway, I don't really know her at all and it's a very private situation, I'd have thought. Oh dear. What a rotten world."

"Totally rotten," said Lucinda.

Nigel had never known the joys and anguishes of parenthood, but suddenly even losing his farm didn't seem quite so important.

❧

In a scene which Blue Horton would have delighted in playing before Lucinda, three boys from Lynton House had been brought to the headmaster's study. ("Appalling," Donald Archer said afterwards. "Some of my brightest boys—scholarship to Winchester, one of them.") One, the smallest, had owned up of his own volition, and then his best friend had sneaked (as he put it) on the other two.

"It was only teasing," said the oldest boy defensively, "that's all."

"And what form did this teasing take, exactly?"

"Well . . ." The small one blushed violently. "Well, it was mostly about—about money, actually. He had to leave Lynton, you know, because his mother couldn't pay the fees anymore, and he went to the state school down the road."

"And you teased him about that? Doesn't sound very amusing to me," said Lockyer.

"No, no, of course not. We were jolly sorry for him, anyone would be. But then when he came back he was a bit—different. Sort of—boastful. Said his mother was working for a big banker chap in the City, that everything was all right now."

"Oh yes?" God, children were complex creatures. "So . . ." Lockyer turned to the biggest boy. "What happened next?"

"Well, it was all a bit odd really. I mean, there obviously wasn't any money, he was still living in the same grotty little place and he didn't have much of the proper kit for anything and he couldn't come on the trip to France we were all going on."

"So you teased him about that?"

"Well, we didn't exactly tease him."

"Were you nice to him then?"

"Yes. Sort of."

"You were nice to him. Funny he should have run away then. I fear we might have to involve your parents in this, if you can't cooperate a bit more. This is very, very important you know, it isn't some game."

Silence.

Lockyer turned to Donald Archer. "Perhaps you could call the boys' parents."

"No, don't do that." It was the third boy. "OK, we did rag him a bit, but it was his fault. We wouldn't have if he hadn't been so full of himself."

"You ragged him, as you put it, about not having what the rest of you had got. I see. Anything else?"

"Well, he was a bit of a goody-goody. Toadied up to the masters, that sort of thing. So—yes, there was that. And then he was always arriving at school without his packed lunch and stuff like that. He really was pretty hopeless."

"Right." Lockyer looked at Donald Archer then back at the boys. "It didn't occur to you, obviously, that he'd been trying to tough it out, that he was ashamed of not having the proper kit as you call it, of having to leave for financial reasons?"

Silence.

"I'd have thought it would be better to try to help someone who was having problems, who was 'pretty hopeless' as you put it, not . . . er . . . rag them. I'm sure your headmaster would agree with me."

"Er, yes," said Archer. "Yes, absolutely. Those are the values we do encourage here. Naturally."

"Well, that's good. I'm pleased to hear it. Anything else?"

"Not really. Except recently, he started saying he'd liked it at the state school, that the boys had been quite good eggs, that we were a load of snobs, sort of thing, so we said, 'Bug off back there then.' "

"I see," said Lockyer. "Did you know he was so desperate he was calling ChildLine?"

"ChildLine! No," said the biggest boy. "Of course we didn't."

"Well, I suppose that's something. So do any of you have any idea at all where he might have gone? Know anyone he knew, either inside or outside school, that we should talk to?"

They all shook their heads; they looked very uncomfortable. "Honestly, sir," said the biggest boy. "Honestly, if we knew, we'd tell you."

Reluctantly, Lockyer was forced to believe them.

Chapter 25

JUNE 1990

Simon sat staring at this person who quite literally held his fate in his hands and hoped Fiona Broadhurst knew what she was doing. He had not expected this tall, blond patrician, with that odd mixture of clipped and drawling accent that characterises the Old Etonian. He had somehow expected Fiona to produce something rather different, a bit of an oddball even, after all her protestations of wanting them to work as a team and not regard the barrister as the member of some superior race. Lindsay-Cowan QC did not seem to him a team player at all. He smiled at them all, rather graciously, indicated to them to sit down on the shabby leather sofas that lined his chamber walls, and asked them if they would like China or Indian tea. That settled, he spoke. And Simon immediately felt better.

"Right," he said, "now the first thing I want to say is that we may get these bastards and we may not, but if we don't I shall certainly enjoy trying. Although I can see it may be rather less enjoyable for you. Especially if we don't win. But if we do win, of course, we shall be making history. There are literally hundreds of these cases being prepared even as we speak. Or rather as I speak. I'm sure you are aware that seventy percent of losses have fallen on thirty percent of Names. I think those figures speak for themselves. They cannot be attributed to coincidence.

"Now one of three things will happen. We will win outright. Unlikely. We will lose. Very possibly. We shall get settlement. Moderately likely. Although not as likely as that we shall lose."

"So what the hell are we here for?" said George Meyer.

"We are here because we have a chance. And we will at least tweak the tiger's tail. That will be very pleasant. They are not enjoying this, you know, the tigers. They have not experienced a total deficit as they are doing now for twenty-one years. They have their backs to the wall. Unfortunately, they hold many of the cards. Strictly speaking, and within the letter of the law, they have right on their side. You underwrote the losses which they have sustained. You signed documents, you neglected to research the situation thoroughly, you were not, so far as I can see, very proactive in taking out reinsurance. Not that it would have done you a great deal of good in certain cases. I understand stop-loss policies are extremely costly and with a very large excess. And, of course, you took their money during the good years. Many people would say you have very little to complain about, that you are crying over some rather sour spilled milk."

The group was silent. It was a bit like getting a wigging from the headmaster, Simon thought.

"Now, as I understand it, the main thrust of your quarrel with Members' Agents Jackson and Bond, or the Westfield Bradley Syndicates—or possibly both—is that they were continuing to press people into membership, people they well knew could not afford the massive risk they were being exposed to, and in the full knowledge of that exposure. That would be a strong case indeed if it could be proved, but I fear that would be extremely difficult. You would need witnesses from within the organisation, prepared to admit that this was the case, copies of incriminating documents, notes, and written accounts of conversations. All highly unlikely, I fear, although not impossible. I know that you also feel the undoubted existence of the so-called baby syndicates—these syndicates within syndicates—could be incriminating, if proven. Very tricky. You would need to produce a Members' Agent who would admit to it in court, or certainly in a sworn statement. Even more unlikely."

"What about a tape-recorded statement?" said Simon.

"If they knew you were recording them, then yes. If not, then no. But if you can persuade someone into talking, discussing their situation, it would be very valuable. A lot of the work, as Ms. Broadhurst will have told you, is down to you. I need help, suggestions, leads, witnesses. Ms. Broadhurst will give you further guidance on the sort of thing I'm talking about, but basically your most useful function will be to get witness statements. Talk to everyone you can in your syndicate, not just those of you involved in this case. Supposing a Name increased his premium income limit at the year end from £150,000 to £180,000, ask exactly why he did so, who he talked to, who encouraged him, ask for any relevant documents. We have a right to disclosure of all documents that touch and concern the case, and that touch and concern all the issues in the case. Both of our claim and whatever defence they put forward."

"I have a question," said George. "How accessible will you both be? Because I can see many occasions where one of us will want clarification on whether a line of enquiry we're pursuing might be relevant and indeed, the sort of thing Simon asked, whether tape-recorded conversations are admissible evidence. So how often and how easily can we contact you? I think that's very important."

Fiona Broadhurst gave him one of her coolest looks and said, "I can't speak for Mr. Lindsay-Cowan, but you may call me as often as you like. I would only remind you that any time spent on the case will cost money. It goes without saying that talking to my assistant will be more economical."

"I have a very important question. What happens next?" asked Flora. "I'm interested in time span here. Are we talking about months, years, centuries . . ."

"Many months, certainly," said Lindsay-Cowan. "Let me outline the probable sequence of events. We issue and serve our writ and serve our statement of claim. We receive their defence and, if necessary, seek further clarification of the defence by serving a request for further particulars. We then have a pretrial review at court and receive a timetable. We prepare our list of documents and they do the same, and we then exchange lists and call for copies of relevant documents, review these, and prepare our witness statements. Experts will be instructed to review all this. My junior will be available to review everything and we will work together with Ms. Broadhurst. That will take several months. After that, providing it is all satisfactory, we exchange with the other side: we get their witnesses, their documents, their experts' reports. They get ours. More time will pass. Finally, we'll decide to get on with it. We then have a pretrial review, to fix a date for trial. Which will include the length of time we think we will need in court, depending upon the number of witnesses and documents. We agree some dates with the court—what's called a window—for the trial, anything from three months to a year hence, and then we write to all the witnesses, find out which dates suit them best, which suit you, suit me. And we need a judge, of course; the dates need to take that into consideration. And then we'll be told we can have our trial in, let us say, nine months from then. So I would say we're looking, at the very least, at two years from now."

"Two years!" said George.

They looked at one another. It sounded a desperately long time. How could they all survive it?

❧

"If you don't mind," Lucinda said to Blue on the phone, "I think I might go and visit Catherine this evening. I know she's not a close friend, but just having someone to talk to might help. It's three days now . . . Well, this is the third night. Although I'm sure she knows that."

❧

Catherine's ravaged face greeted her at the front door of the flat in Fulham. "Hello, Lucinda," she said, and her voice was heavy and lifeless.

"Hello. Can I come in?"

"Of course. Caroline's asleep, thank God. Being brave for her sake is the hardest thing of all."

"Oh Catherine." Lucinda put a tender arm round her shoulders. "I'm so, so sorry."

Catherine managed a half smile. "It just gets worse, you know? Every hour. I look back to when I first heard and it didn't seem quite so terrible then. I mean, it was terrible, of course, an awful shock, but there seemed . . . hope. Now that's gone. It's just completely—over. I can't believe I ever had him with me, warm and alive and breathing, instead of—instead of . . ."

"Catherine, he's not dead. I'm sure he's not."

"You're not sure," Catherine started to shout. "You're not sure about anything of the sort, so don't be so bloody stupid. If he was alive, someone would know; and if someone knows and hasn't said, it's because they're . . . they're . . . Oh my God, when I think of what might be happening to him, what might be being done to him, all these awful perverts about, hurting him, frightening him . . . Oh God, Lucinda, I can't stand it, I just can't stand it any longer. If it wasn't for Caroline I'd kill myself, I really would, it would be a relief."

She dropped her head into her hands; she was shaking violently. Lucinda sat there, holding her, crying herself now, wondering what she could possibly say or do that might help.

"I'm sorry," said Catherine, looking at her through watery eyes. "Sorry, Lucinda. I shouldn't have shouted at you."

"Don't be silly. If it helps, shout some more."

"It doesn't. Nothing helps. It's literally unbearable. Oh God, Lucinda, why did he do it? Why did he go? What did I do? Oh Lucinda, when you have that little baby," she nodded in the direction of Lucinda's stomach, "just never let it out of your sight, never ever."

❧

It was absurd, this, Simon thought; here he was, acting like some sentimental girl, as if she was a person, a person with feelings, rather than a boat. It was just that, well, they were as one on the water, he and the *Lizzie,* taking on the sea and the wind, everything else wiped out in the glorious and absolute concentration of sailing. He could set out feeling wretched, anxious, or tired, as he felt today after the gruelling interview with Lindsay-Cowan, and come back restored, exhilarated. Or he could set out feeling joyful, triumphant, or sweetly happy and return even more so. The *Lizzie* had no negative associations for him; even danger, even fear, became things to laugh at, to boast of when they had overcome them together; she was absolutely intrinsic to his happiness. And now she had to go. This was their last day together, he had found a buyer for her, she was to be taken off, away from him, she was about to become a memory. And even the famous Beaumont ability to be upbeat, positive about it, was being severely challenged.

❧

It had been a very good evening with Flora; Elizabeth had made a huge effort with the food, having acquired some Welsh lamb, and although they ate in the kitchen, she had dressed up the table with candles and flowers. Simon had been very touched.

Flora had admired the house and sympathised with the prospect of having to part with it—"Don't tell me about selling lovely houses; sometimes I wonder if I can bear it; sometimes I know I can't"—and they had sat up late, the three of them discussing the lawsuit.

Simon had left London at the same time as Flora; the day was too lovely to lose and he wanted as long as possible with the *Lizzie.* As he walked down to the *Lizzie's* moorings, looking up at the blue, mist-streaked sky, he heard his name.

"Simon! Hi. You going to France?"

He turned. "Felicity! Hello. Lovely to see you. That's my plan."

"Me too. To Saint-Valéry. Let's meet there for lunch."

"Great idea. Whoever's first, order the wine. See you there."

Felicity Parker Jones. He had known her a long time, had sailed with her, raced with her even. She was the one person he might have wanted to be with that day: cool, unsentimental, brave herself. There would be no tedious questions, no sympathetic comments. But she would understand, she would know how he felt, and then see no need to express it. She was also extremely attractive: about Elizabeth's age, tall, slim, blond, and very funny. That would help too. He waved to her and jumped down into the *Lizzie,* feeling suddenly better.

❧

Catherine was trying to force herself out of the chair where she sat hour after hour, and get some kind of lunch organised for Caroline when the phone rang.

"Hello," she said dully.

"Mrs. Morgan? It's Sergeant Lockyer."

"Yes?" She could hear her own voice, torn with fear. And then there seemed to be an interminable silence, while she waited for the news she knew had to come: that Freddie was dead.

And then: "It's all right, Mrs. Morgan. I've got Freddie here. He's alive and well."

❧

Never underestimate a child, thought Sergeant Lockyer, never. They are so much cleverer, and more capable, than adults give them credit for. He looked at the pair of them, one slightly wearier and scruffier than the other, both half-defiant, half-sheepishly relieved that they had been caught.

"Well well well," he said. "What a lot of trouble you've caused."

Such a brilliant hiding place: a pool house. Providing shelter, tap water, a toilet—most of the necessities of life, apart from food. And where, as long as the owners of the pool house and indeed the house were not likely to be present for a few days, a small boy with a willing accomplice could be perfectly safe, and even comfortable. It explained quite a lot: explained how the small boy in question had managed to vanish into thin air for three days, how he hadn't been spotted anywhere, looking scruffy, buying food . . .

Indeed, had the weekend not arrived, and had the weather not been so beautiful, and the pool looked so inviting, he might well have remained undiscovered for a great deal longer.

"What you did was extremely stupid," Lockyer said severely to the pair of them, to Freddie and his best friend from school, Dominic Mays, as they sat in the kitchen of the house in Chelsea, waiting for Catherine to arrive. "Extremely stupid. You've caused a great deal of anxiety, and a great deal of work; you've cost and arguably wasted a lot of police time, Freddie's mum has been off her head with worry— Ah, here she is now. Just saying how worried you've been, haven't you, Mrs. Morgan?"

Catherine, gaunt and white-faced, accompanied by a wide-eyed Caroline, nodded feebly and sat down. Freddie stared at her across the room, smiling rather uncertainly. She stared back, unable even to smile, so violent were her emotions; it was all she could do simply to look at him, as she had not thought to do again, drinking him in, alive, safe, unmolested.

"Sorry," he said. "I'm very sorry. I thought—"

"You thought what, Freddie?"

"Oh, doesn't matter." He still sounded odd, almost detached. Well, it wasn't so surprising.

"So what do you have to say for yourselves?" Paul Mays, Dominic's father, and in charge of him—together with the au pair—for a few days, while his ex-wife, Denise, went to Paris with her new boyfriend, looked only a little better than Catherine. Guilty conscience, thought Lockyer, and good reason; should have picked something up, surely. And then thought probably not, and went back to contemplating the cleverness of children. And the comparative foolishness of adults.

"We are very sorry," said Dominic, "but it seemed such a good idea to us. And Freddie was so miserable, weren't you, Fred? I just wanted to help."

Freddie nodded silently.

"Dominic," said Paul, "didn't you think for one moment that if it had been you, I would have been worried to death?"

"No," said Dominic, with all the devastating honesty of childhood. "I'd have thought you'd be glad to be able to stay at work a bit longer." Denise Mays's expression at this point was an interesting mixture of amusement and contempt.

"And why didn't you come forward when the police asked?"

"They said Freddie had been badly teased and they wanted to talk to anyone who might have been involved. I was being nice to him and I knew he was perfectly safe."

Dominic was also at Lynton House; like Freddie he was unhappy there. He was fat; he was being teased mercilessly, in fact, which was what had drawn him and Freddie together. He had begged to leave, but his parents, guiltily aware that he was eating himself out of his misery at the divorce, had told him that he should ignore the teasing, that his tormentors would get tired of it and find another victim. All the usual platitudes, in fact; the usual, easy platitudes.

"He was really unhappy," said Dominic, "just like I was. And then one day he was crying, said he had to run away, it was the only thing to do, but he didn't know where he could go, had I got any ideas? I said he could stay in the pool house for a bit, at my dad's new house; no one would know, and he'd be really safe. Which he was. Anyway, how did you find out?"

"One of your classmates rang up this morning. Or rather, his father did. He'd had an idea Dominic might have been in cahoots with you, and he was right. Bit more sense than you two."

"Well, words fail me," said Denise. It was clear they did nothing of the sort. "I cannot believe, Paul, you could have been so unaware of what was going on, right under your nose. I shall think very hard about leaving Dominic in your care in future. Were you out? Did you go away? I mean, how could this have possibly happened?"

"I was working," said Paul, looking at her with intense dislike. "Working late. Leaving early. This is what I do. As you may remember."

"Unfortunately, yes. As for you, Dominic, how could you be so self-ish, so absolutely stupid—"

"He's not," said Freddie. "He's a really, really good friend. And clever. It wasn't his idea, we worked it out together. Please don't be cross with him, it's not fair."

"So how did you get here? From home?" said Catherine. It was the first time she had spoken. "It's quite a long way."

"I walked."

"You walked!"

"Yes, I gave him a map," said Dominic. "It only took him about half an hour. And it was just lucky everything worked out, him being looked after by that lady, and Mum being away that week, and me being there with Dad."

"Very lucky," said Lockyer.

"It was all right at first, quite fun, specially before Dad came home; if

· 253 ·

the au pair was snogging her boyfriend we could even swim or play table tennis, and there was masses of food."

"Oh Dominic," said Paul, and he buried his face in his hands.

"And how long did you think Freddie could stay there?" said Lockyer.

"Well, we weren't sure. It was going to be more difficult at the weekend, especially if Dad didn't work on Saturday."

"Do you often work on Saturdays, Mr. Mays?"

"Quite often, yes."

"He's a workaholic," said Denise witheringly.

"And then Mrs. Patton—"

"Who's Mrs. Patton?"

"The housekeeper. She said she'd booked someone to clean out the pool house next week, ready for the summer holidays. So we weren't quite sure what to do next."

"I see," said Lockyer. "Well, you know now. You, Dominic, you must never do anything like this again. And you, Freddie, you say sorry to your mum. You should both be very ashamed of yourselves. Very."

They said they were. Very.

Eventually, Catherine and Caroline and Freddie were driven home. The nightmare over.

For a while, at least.

Chapter 26

None of it had been quite how Catherine would have imagined, had she been brave enough to imagine it. There was no joyful, hugging, kissing reunion; no ebullient little boy hurling himself into her arms with cries of "Mummy."

Rather, a subdued small stranger, awkwardly polite, kissing her briefly, saying he was fine and sorry to have worried her and then—nothing. "How about going to the Pizza Express?" she said. "For supper?"

An unimaginable treat. He shrugged. "OK."

"Yes, please," said Caroline.

They ate their pizzas in a strained silence; in spite of herself, by the time they reached home again, a certain rage was building up. Surely he was old enough to realise what agony he had put her through, how much she must have worried, how terrifying it had been. An explanation would have done; but none was offered.

"He's being weird," said Caroline, restored to complete normality with the blinding resilience of children. "Can I go and play with Katy, Mummy?"

Catherine had managed to stay calm, to get him to have a bath; he was surprisingly dirty, considering he had spent four days virtually in a swimming pool. She offered to read to him—he still liked that even now—to take them both to the zoo next day. But Freddie remained silent, uncommunicative, and had taken himself to bed early. When she looked in, terrified he would have run away again, he was sucking his thumb as she had not seen him do for years, and fast asleep.

And by Monday, he was still not saying anything.

〜

"Look, Nigel . . ." Douglas Wilson's voice was quite indignant. "I've had a letter from your wife's solicitor about the divorce. And I must say it's really rather extraordinary, what's being suggested by way of a settlement. But he says that you and your wife have agreed to it, in broad terms. Is that right?"

"It is, yes."

"I can see why she's agreed to it, but are you really happy with all of this? It's extraordinarily generous. You were only married for four years or so, she made virtually no financial contribution, and you have no children."

"I know all that, and yes, I'm perfectly happy. I . . . I want her to be well provided for."

"But—look, my dear chap, she left you. With no provocation whatsoever, as far as I can make out. I mean, you were a most generous husband. I presume you weren't knocking her about—"

"Of course not!" said Nigel.

"Sorry, I have to ask. Or, forgive me, playing away."

"Playing away?"

"Well yes. I mean, of—of any adultery on your part?"

"Absolutely not."

"And as far as you were concerned, the marriage was perfectly happy."

"Yes," said Nigel, and his voice was very sad.

"Then why this absurdly generous offer? You really don't have to do this." Douglas Wilson sounded almost impatient. "You don't have to give her anything like this. Certainly not the money in that trust fund and most certainly not the house. It's ridiculous."

"It's not ridiculous. I want her to be well provided for."

"But she is well provided for. And what's all this about the gallery in New York—is that right?"

"Oh yes. Absolutely right. Yes. She was very—very cut up about it. I'd like to make it up to her."

"To the tune of a hundred thousand quid? It's sheer madness!"

"I—suppose you could say that, yes. But she might be a rich woman now in her own right, if it hadn't been for me—look at it that way."

"Well, it's your money. But I'm still not happy about it. I'm going to write to her solicitor as a matter of principle—with your agreement, that is—pointing out, as I said, that it was a short marriage, and she is now living with and is pregnant by a wealthy lover. And I don't think she has any claim on the house at the very least. Certainly not its full value. And the cash settlement over the New York gallery is simply absurd. I don't think we should just lie down and take it."

"But—"

"Trust me, please. I do know what I'm doing. A good divorce settlement is a compromise. I don't see much evidence of that on their side. In fact, none at all. So let's at least make a bit of an effort."

"Yes, all right. If you think we should."

"I do."

Nigel put the phone down; he didn't like this one bit. It went against everything he saw as right. And he couldn't really believe they were going to get away with it. But—all the alternative routes seemed closed. And if it only saved Grandfather Cowper's cuff links it would be better than nothing.

ℯↃ

As the early-July dawn broke, Catherine couldn't take it any longer. She knew he was awake, she'd heard him moving around. She knocked very gently on the door.

"Freddie! Darling, it's Mummy, please let me in."

Silence.

"Freddie. Please. I so want to talk to you. Please let me in. Tell me what's wrong, I need to know, so I can try to put it right."

Another shorter silence, then very reluctantly: "OK." He opened the door and let her in; he was very pale and there were deep shadows under his eyes. He looked at her solemnly, didn't smile, didn't speak.

"Sweetie. Please. I want so much to find out what's wrong. I love you so much, Freddie, you've got to believe me."

He shrugged. "Why do you want to get rid of us then?" he said, and with each word his voice got louder, until he was screaming, high spots of colour on his face, the eyes still huge and strained.

"What do you mean? Of course I don't want to get rid of you."

"You do. You wish we weren't here. You said it yourself, I heard you. That's why I went—I thought it was what you wanted. I thought it would make things easier."

"I don't understand," said Catherine slowly, "I really don't. Of course I didn't say that. I would never have said it. You and Caroline are the only things that make my life worthwhile. Honestly."

"I heard you myself with my own ears. On the phone to someone."

"Freddie, please tell me exactly what I said. I need to know."

"You said, and I don't know who it was to, 'If it wasn't for the children, especially Freddie, I wouldn't mind. Without them, I could cope with it easily.' Don't tell me that doesn't mean you wish we weren't here. I'm not that stupid."

"Oh my darling," said Catherine, and she was crying herself now. She picked up her son's hand and he pulled it away. "I was talking to some old friend of Daddy's. We were talking about, you know, this awful business that's taken all our money away—"

"Lloyd's?"

"Yes, Lloyd's. And—I did say that, and what I meant was that all I cared about was you two having to go through such a horrible time. I don't mind one bit. It's you who get the worst of it, having to keep changing schools and you two who can't go on school trips and who have the wrong games kit. I do have to worry about it all, of course, and I don't like living in this funny little flat, although I think we've been quite happy here at times. But it doesn't matter to me one bit. What matters to me is you being unhappy and not having all the things you should have, and having to look after Caroline for me if I'm late. Don't you see? Oh Freddie, you silly old thing. Is that why you went? Because you thought it was what I wanted?"

He nodded; his eyes fixed on her face as if he would never look away from it again.

"Oh darling. I'm so sorry you thought that. Because if it wasn't for you and Caroline, I would just . . . well, I really wouldn't be able to bear it. Including being without Daddy. You're all I care about; and if you'd listened a bit longer to that conversation you'd have heard me say that too. Do you believe me?"

Gradually, very slowly, the stony little face softened; and he smiled, a small, quavery smile; and then he moved nearer her, and let her put her arm round him; and then suddenly, in a huge rush, he hurled himself at her, threw his arms round her neck so tightly she could hardly breathe, and said, his voice muffled against her, "I love you, Mummy. I'm sorry you were worried. So sorry. I thought—I thought I was being helpful."

He started to cry then; she felt his skinny little body heaving, felt his tears trickling down her neck, felt his breath warm as he sobbed, on and on, and she sat there stroking his hair, kissing his head, and thought of all the times she had thought she would never know any of this again, that she would never be able to hold him again, never comfort him again, never laugh with him again—and she felt so weak with the relief of having him close to her, safe and sweetly loving, that she began to cry again as well.

Annabel was so excited she could hardly breathe. In just three days' time she would be on the flight to Boston; Jamie was going to meet her at Logan Airport and take her into Boston by the water shuttle: "It's the scenic route, really the best way into Boston for the first time." They were all so pleased she was coming, he said, and it sounded wonderful, what had been arranged for her. Every day there was something special: a tour of Boston, a party so she could meet all Jamie's friends, a concert by the Boston Pops ("They're amazing"), a shopping trip with his mother and sister ("We have the equivalent of your Bond Street here"), and then for the second week, a trip down to Cape Cod to the family house there ("It's by the ocean, you'll just love it").

Carol had done her hair beautifully, highlighted it and cut it just a bit into really long layers; and Annabel had treated herself to a manicure and pedicure and a sun-bed session. Jamie was about to see the whole of her, and she didn't want his ardour dimmed by a lot of pallid skin. She could hardly remember what he looked like now; she knew he had wonderful blue eyes and floppy blond hair and a really, really good mouth and that he was tall and quite athletic-looking—but she couldn't quite remember how he smiled and what his eyes went like when he was gazing into hers, and all that sort of thing. Florian had been teasing her a bit inevitably, singing "The Battle Hymn of the Republic" very loudly whenever she came into the staff room; but also advising on the exact right length for her hair, and on her last day he gave her a present—an absolutely beautiful tortoiseshell-and-silver comb for her hair. "Well, darling, we want you looking classy. I can't have you letting the salon down, and those scrunchie things you've taken to wearing are just too suburban for words." She was so touched, tears filled her eyes. "Now, darling, no sex on the first night, remember."

"Why on earth not?" she said, laughing.

"Oh, overenthusiasm is just so common. His mother won't like it."

"His mother won't know."

"I know her type. She'll be listening, you mark my words, and examining the sheets in the morning."

"Florian!" said Annabel. "You are just so awful." But she had been wondering about precisely what sleeping arrangements the daunting Mrs. Cartwright might have made, and how easy it might be to breach them if they were unfriendly.

"Sweetie, it's true. She'll be less foxy after that. So—just lie there, OK?"

"OK," said Annabel.

℘

On the very day he was going to meet Joel Strickland again, it happened.

"Quick word, Simon," the chairman had said to him in the lift, as he came back from lunch—a ridiculously expensive lunch—and, "Of course," he had said, "I'll be right up, give me five minutes," and five minutes later exactly he had walked into the large, wood-panelled cliché of an office with its leather chairs and sofas and portraits of William Graburn and Theodore French; he was slightly surprised to see two of his fellow board members in the room, but presumably they were going to discuss some important deal. He smiled at them, said, "Hi," and they half smiled back and said nothing. It was . . . slightly odd.

"Drink, Simon?" Martin Dudley said, and Simon shook his head, saying, "Got work to do," and sat down comfortably in one of the leather chairs, smiling expectantly at the three of them, thinking that when Dudley had said whatever he wanted to say, then he must talk to them about Lloyd's too . . . And Dudley did actually say, "Tell me about this Lloyd's business," and he had begun to tell him, said, yes, it wasn't very funny—in fact, it was perfectly awful, but he was pretty confident that he could survive at least another year, and he was going to law and—

"Yes, but what are your debts? That's what I'd like to know."

"Oh, about . . . about half a million," Simon said, feeling just slightly less sure of himself.

"Half a million? You have personal debts of half a million?"

"Well, yes, give or take a few thousand."

"And—do you have half a million pounds? That you can put your hands on?" The other two seemed to be finding the carpet particularly interesting.

"Well, not precisely, no." Why were his guts lurching in this unpleasant way? "In fact, I'm putting our house on the market. Although I've actually decided to take Lloyd's to court. With a few other like-minded people."

"You're taking Lloyd's to court? Yes, I thought that was what you said."

"I am, yes. Our solicitor thinks we have a case."

"And does this mean you won't be paying your debt to them?"

"Well, I suppose it does, yes. If we regard them as debts. Which actually we don't. We think they've acted fraudulently, and—"

"You consider Lloyd's have acted fraudulently?"

"Yes, we do. As a matter of fact."

Martin Dudley sighed, then said, "I see. I find that extraordinarily hard to believe."

"I'm sure you do," said Simon, trying to keep his voice light. "We all did at first. But if you look at the facts—I could take you through them if you like . . ."

"I think not. Certainly not at present. You say others are taking this route?"

"Oh yes. There are scores of lawsuits being prepared. We're a small group, but growing in number as people gain confidence in what we feel certain is a case. And—"

"Simon. Simon, I'm extremely sorry, but I simply cannot contemplate having one of our main board directors involved in litigation against Lloyd's. It's out of the question."

There was a complete silence in the room. A pin dropping would have been an appalling intrusion.

"Lloyd's is one of the prime institutions in the City of London. Many of our clients have connections with them; some are managing agents there." Dudley paused, then said, "Tell me, if you met your debt this year, by selling your house, would you then be in the clear?"

"Well, of course not," said Simon. "The whole point about the Lloyd's liability is that it's unlimited. It's there until death, quite literally, if you get involved with a long-tailed syndicate—that's one where claims may arise long after the period of cover has expired—and they can be coming after you for fifty years. It's hideous."

"Nevertheless, you signed up to this arrangement, I imagine?"

"Well, of course I did. Yes."

"Without a great deal of thought, it seems. And there were good years, I believe. So let's just go over this again. You owe them half a million at the present time."

"Yes. That's correct."

"What about next year? What will you do then?"

"Well, as I say, I would hope we'd have won our lawsuit."

One of the others cleared his throat then said, "Leaving that aside for the moment, it does seem to us, Simon, that there's a possibility of serious financial embarrassment here."

Looking back afterwards, he could define that as the moment when he stopped hoping. He knew what they were doing now; acting as a team.

"Right," said Dudley. "Now, I've been looking at your contract. There are some very clear references in that to your being subject to a bankruptcy order. Which seems to me a possibility. Or that you are unable to compound with your creditors. Equally so. Or indeed that you are acting in a way that brings discredit to the bank. Any of those would necessarily result in your offering your resignation."

Simon felt as if he was going to vomit. "Surely nothing we've been discussing this afternoon would justify such a thing," he said, struggling to keep his voice level and composed.

"I'm afraid it would. Certainly taking legal action against Lloyd's would qualify. Your financial embarrassment likewise. And I'm sure you are aware of clause twelve, point three in the contract."

"Not precisely, no."

"Then I think I should read it to you." He opened a drawer and pulled out a document. It had clearly been placed there for the purpose, for this moment. The whole thing was like a bad play. Dudley was reading aloud. " 'Nothing in these terms and conditions of employment shall prevent the Bank from terminating your employment without notice, or salary in lieu of notice in the event of gross misconduct'—well, of course, no one is suggesting that, Simon," he gave him a sweaty smile, " 'or if you are subject to a bankruptcy order . . .' "

"But I'm not."

"Well, I think we are agreed you are in grave danger of it, or have a receiving order made against you. And then of course there is clause twelve, point seven, which states that the same conditions apply 'if you conduct yourself in a manner prejudicial to the Bank.' "

Simon was silent.

"Well, look, Simon, I'm sure we can work something out here. Dropping your lawsuit would be a start. I would like to suggest that the bank makes you some kind of loan—"

A lurch, of a more pleasant type. A hopeful lurch.

"But I'm afraid it would be completely against company rules. Perhaps you have sources who could do that for you personally?"

"I don't," said Simon simply.

"Right. Pity. Well—look. Give it some thought. I would hate to lose you, Simon. You've been a marvellous asset to the bank—and over many years. But I'm sure you must see I can't fly in the face of bank regulations.

It would simply be unfair to the other directors. Most unfair. Now look, I'm sorry, but it's getting late and I've actually got to see someone at four. Have to prepare for it. Thank you for your honesty, Simon, much appreciated. I'm sure we can work something out. Perhaps you could come back to me in, what shall we say, ten days? That seem fair to you?"

"Oh yes," said Simon, "after twenty-five years' service and bringing countless millions into your wretched coffers. Perfectly fair. I mean, if that's what the contract says, you must abide by it. Of course. Certainly not try to find a way of working round it. You bastard—you miserable, mean, cowardly bastard."

Then he turned and walked out of the room, shutting the door very carefully after him.

Everything seemed very quiet; except for a heavy thudding noise. It took a while for him to realise it was his heart. He leaned against the wall for a moment and closed his eyes, then walked towards his office. He had been fired as if he was the meanest office boy, told he was no longer of any use, his nose rubbed in the dirt as he went. In response to a non-crime, a trumped-up felony. He felt at once outraged and completely vulnerable, and if he had been asked to say his name, or where he lived, he would have been hard-pressed to do so.

He opened the window of his office, his office on the sixth floor, looking down at the street far below him, and seriously considered jumping out of it. Then he picked up the phone and called Joel Strickland . . .

Chapter 27

Joel had been very shaken by his evening with Simon. He sat in his office the next day, feeling depressed and impotent. He had seldom seen anyone in such patent distress. It was dreadful; Simon had sat there, emotionally naked, stripped of his confidence, his humour, his charm, talking intermittently and drinking endless brandy and sodas until Joel finally suggested it was time to leave, and poured him into a cab in the courtyard of the Savoy.

At first, he hadn't told him anything; he had come in looking ghastly, white, and drawn, but clearly struggling to appear normal. Finally, Simon blurted it out.

"Fired?" Joel said. "Simon, surely not. I'm so sorry."

"Yup, that's about the size of it," Simon said, "for doing absolutely fucking nothing. I didn't abscond with the company's money, I didn't upset any clients, I didn't give away any secrets, I didn't even fiddle my expenses. I just wanted a bit of justice for us all, you know. Tell a few home truths about those fuckers. It's not right, is it, not fair. Now I want you to write about this, Joel. About this injustice. People ought to know. People have to know."

"Sure. Of course."

"It's just not fucking fair. Is it?"

"No, it isn't."

And then he looked at Joel and said, "Christ, Joel, what am I going to do all day? Can you tell me that? Eh? Because no one else'll give me a job now."

And that, Joel thought, as the cab pulled out of Savoy Court, was perhaps the worst thing for him of all.

He wondered if Debbie knew, whether she would want to know, and having decided she would, whether he should ring her and tell her. They seemed to be quite good friends, she and Simon, and it would be one call Simon wouldn't have to make. Unless he'd made it already. And, well, and it gave him an excuse to ring her.

There was clearly no theoretical point in that—she was married, she had children, he could hardly ask her out—but he couldn't quite put her out of his head. And who was to say she wouldn't be up for a quick fling? She'd tried to see him the other day, Nicky Holt had told him, so the interest was obviously reciprocated. He might ask her out for a drink, at least; get to know her a bit better. No harm in that. And— "Oh fuck it," Joel said, and dialled her number.

She was very upset indeed to hear about Simon. "That's dreadful, Joel. Awful. Oh, poor Simon. I'm so sorry. I just can't imagine him without that job. It's as much a part of him as the colour of his eyes. Or those perfect suits of his. D'you know what I mean?"

"Of course. Very well expressed. Well, I thought you'd want to know."

"Yes. Thank you, Joel, for telling me. I might try and call him. I wonder if Flora's heard?"

"Is that your exotic mother-in-law? Debbie, do you think she'd talk to me, about this Lloyd's piece? Simon was going to ask her, but I can't really bother him now. And I feel more than ever that I want to write it."

"Well, she might. Do you want me to ask her?"

"It would be great if you could."

"OK. I'll ask her and call you back."

"So that's the whole story," said Flora. "You can see why I'm feeling depressed."

She was sitting in a restaurant in Cardiff with Colin Peterson, having agreed, very much against her better judgement, to go to the concert, and then to have dinner with him afterwards. And was surprised to find herself not only enjoying the experience but telling him her troubles. Her financial troubles.

"I can indeed," he said. "I'm so sorry. And you say you have to give them this next sum of money pretty soon?"

"Yes, in theory. I believe they'll stretch it a bit, if you plead hardship. They're very gentlemanly, in their conduct."

"I'm sure. I believe being gentlemanly has done them a great service."

"Indeed. I remember William being very impressed by it, by the fact that they were such decent chaps, as he put it. Including his own cousin, who actually got him in. It's hard to believe, isn't it?"

"How did you feel about it, at the time?" asked Colin.

"Oh, I didn't feel anything much. I would never have questioned that sort of decision anyway. It wasn't in my domain." She laughed suddenly. "That sounds terribly old-fashioned, doesn't it? But we had a very old-fashioned marriage. He had an extremely clear idea of what my boundaries were and I really didn't question it. He gave me an allowance for the housekeeping, and a second one for clothes, and that was that. I didn't have any money of my own, well, very little from my photography, and in an odd way very little status. But I didn't question that either."

"But that's how it was then, wasn't it? My wife and I had very much that sort of marriage. I saw to the financial side of things, to earning the money, to sorting out things, major things, when we needed a new roof or a new car. She was concerned with the children, the housework and the cooking, schools, holidays. Arguably much more important, of course. It made life very simple, in retrospect. There was no overlap of tasks. Of course we discussed things, but we each knew where our priorities lay."

"When—when did she die?" asked Flora.

"Oh, quite a long time ago now. Five years. I'm getting quite good at living on my own. Still don't like it, mind."

"I do, you know," said Flora, "in a way. Of course I miss William dreadfully, but he was a bit of a . . . fusspot. I have to admit I like being able to make decisions, act on them, and I'm pretty good at being on my own. I always was. I'm an only child."

"But you were . . . happy? Oh, forgive me, I shouldn't have asked."

"Not at all. Yes, we were perfectly happy. When he died, part of me did too. But I don't approve of people who give in. I'm a fighter. And I still have a great deal. My family, my work, living in that glorious place. Only . . ." and she heard her voice shake, suddenly, "only I won't. Much longer."

"No?"

"No. I'll have to sell it. And pretty soon. I don't know how I'm going to give them this next lot of money—"

"Could I be extremely ungentlemanly," he said, "and ask how much it is."

"Two hundred and seventy-five thousand pounds," she said, so quietly she could hardly hear it herself.

He stared at her, clearly shocked.

"And unless I sell the house, I can't pay it. Can't pay it if I do sell the house, but it'll help."

"Have you tried discussing it with them?"

"Of course. And they're always very kind, very polite. Very gentlemanly. But they always finish by pointing out that I do owe it to them, that I signed the contract with them, that I have to pay that debt, just as I shared in the money in the good years. Oh God." Horrified, she felt her eyes fill with tears; impatiently she brushed them away. "Sorry."

"Don't be silly. It's completely understandable. Er, forgive me, but do you really have no other assets?"

"Not now. I've sold all my shares, a couple of paintings—"

"What about mortgaging the house?"

"I can't service the loan. I have very little income left, now the shares have gone, just a bit of capital."

"Sell some land?"

"Colin, land on Gower isn't worth much. I've only got about ten acres—that's not going to save me. And besides, if I still own the house, they can come after it. They say you don't have to sell your main residence, but obviously they can see if it's much too big for you. You can't say 'Right, I've given you all I can' when you patently haven't. And every year the debt goes on, even though I've obviously resigned my membership. You're never safe, you know. It's unlimited liability, that's the whole point."

"It sounds quite criminal. But you know . . ." He hesitated. "Your land would be worth quite a lot, to someone like me."

"No, it wouldn't. This is mostly greenbelt, not available for building on. The planners are incredibly strict, and thank God for it. Oh, I'm sorry, that must sound very rude. I know that's what you do . . ."

"Now I did tell you," he said, "that I wouldn't want to build on Gower. I think it would be a crime. But if you have to sell your beautiful house anyway . . ."

"Yes, I know, I know. But at least if I can leave it intact, leave the land intact, I could look myself in the face."

"And where would you live? If you had to sell?"

"Oh, I don't know," she said. "This is where I come back to, day after day, night after night. I know that they'd probably take the proceeds of the house in settlement, if I really didn't have anything else, and leave me enough for some little hole somewhere. They don't like seeing old ladies tipped destitute onto the street; it's bad for their image."

"And this wretched little hole you see yourself living in, would that be here? Would you stay in the area?"

"I can't see myself anywhere else. I don't really like anywhere else. I love the sea, I love the moors and the cliffs and the Gower skies, it's all a part of me. But you know, something's happened just these last few days that's changed the way I see things. Made even losing my house seem less important."

She told him about Freddie; he seemed quite upset.

"How dreadful. And you know this girl?"

"Yes, I've met her. She's very sweet, but another victim—that's how it happened. She had to take the little boy away from his prep school, then he was being bullied . . ."

"Oh dear, how sad. But at least he's been found. Now . . ." He hesitated. "Flora, will you allow me to put my mind to this for you? I'm quite financially ingenious, you know. I've had to be, doing what I do. I probably can't come up with anything, but—well, two heads are notoriously better than one. Now what about another glass of wine, or even a brandy? I imagine you as a brandy girl."

"What about your driver? Won't he be getting tired?"

"I pay him to be tired, and he's a very patient fellow."

Debbie was watching *Play School* with Rachel, who had a stomach bug, when the phone rang. She ignored it; the answering machine could pick it up. Rachel was drowsy; if she dropped off now, it would do her so much good.

Rachel did go to sleep; Debbie eased her onto the sofa, fetched a pillow and a duvet, and went to make herself a cup of coffee and to check the answering machine, to see who had called. The voice was pleasant, with a Scottish burr, and asked for Richard.

"This is Morag Dunbar," it said. "I wonder if Mr. Fielding could give me a call. Nothing very important, just to get a date in the diary for the next visit, and to say that the house is ready for inspection, if Mrs. Fielding would like to come up with him. I think she'll be quite pleased with it."

Chapter 28

She stood there, staring at the answering machine, feeling an odd mixture of hope and fear. Nothing could save them now, her or the house. But— she pressed the button, listened again.

"Flora, this is Colin Peterson. Look, I wonder if I might come and see you. I've done some thinking, as I promised, and I have a bit of an idea. Give me a ring. Here's my home number."

How sweet he was, she thought, and how rotten she had been, looking down—well not looking down exactly but— Yes, Flora, looking down. Shame on you.

She picked up the phone and dialled the number: his answering machine cut in. Well, he'd be at work, of course. She left a message, thanking him for his kindness and asking him to ring her: "Perhaps you'd like to come for kitchen supper one night next week. It all sounds very intriguing. I'll look forward to hearing from you."

He rang her within the hour; they fixed a date for the following Monday.

"I won't say any more now, except that I think I just might be onto something," he said.

℮

"Joel, it's Debbie. Debbie Fielding."

"Oh—hi. How are you?"

"Fine. Now, I haven't been able to get hold of Simon, but I did ring my mother-in-law for you. She's happy to talk. She didn't know about Simon, she was very upset."

"I'm sure she was. Thanks, Debbie. That's really great."

"Here's the number. She said to tell you evenings were best."

"OK. Thanks very much. So—it's Mrs. Flora Fielding, is that right?"

"That's right." The mother of my husband, Debbie thought. My appallingly badly behaved, mean-spirited, devious husband. Who still doesn't know I know how devious he is.

Joel hesitated. Then he said, "Debbie, I don't suppose you'd like to come for a drink one night?"

There was a very long silence; he could hear her considering his invitation, hear her being tempted by it—and then deciding against it.

"I'm sorry, Joel, it'd be great, but I really can't. Thanks just the same."

An observer watching them put their phones down would have found it difficult to say who was the more regretful.

℮

Richard had taken to eating his supper in complete silence. It would have been better, Debbie thought, if he'd looked at the paper or read a book, but he just sat there, refusing to meet her eyes, chewing—she really hadn't noticed before how thoroughly he chewed everything, since they had always talked a lot over meals; Flora, she supposed, would have insisted on it, saying it would help his digestion—and then saying, "Thanks," before taking his plate over to the dishwasher and rinsing it carefully, putting it in, and walking out of the kitchen.

Tonight she had decided not even to bother to cook. She gave the children their tea, ate some of it herself—fish fingers, she had forgotten how delicious they were with lots of tomato sauce—and when he came out of his study at half past seven, their usual suppertime, she just looked at him disinterestedly and then back at the television.

"Are we not eating tonight?" he said, his voice very cold.

"I'm not," she said, and smiled at him, knowing that would annoy him more, "but you do go ahead."

"Is it ready?"

"No, it's not. Sorry. I'm sure there's something in the freezer though. Have a look."

She returned to *EastEnders;* she heard him moving swiftly across the room, didn't realise what he was doing until the television was switched off. She looked at him, quite shocked; he stared back at her, his face white with rage.

"How dare you behave like this?"

"Behave like what? I've been trying very hard, actually. Cooking your supper, ironing your shirts, all that crap. And checking you could cope with the kids the days I was working. I'm sick of sitting opposite you every night while you concentrate on not communicating with me. Oh, and chewing your food really carefully. I'm sure your mother would be proud of that."

He waited, then he said, and he sounded very tired, "We can't go on like this, it's ridiculous. I'm beginning to wonder if there isn't someone else in your life."

She stared at him, her heart thudding violently. Had Flora—might Flora . . . no. Surely not. He would have reacted before this. Wouldn't he?

"What an extraordinary thing to say."

"It may be extraordinary but it's what I feel."

"Well, you're mad. Completely mad. Of course there isn't."

"Well, I have to take your word for it, I suppose. Anyway, we can't go on like this."

"I quite agree."

"So what are you going to do about it?"

"I really think that's up to you, Richard—up to you to do something."

"And I think rather differently. I didn't start all this—this miserable business," he said. "It's been you that's caused all the trouble."

A small explosion took place somewhere. Debbie contemplated—and it seemed quite a slow process, she could feel herself carefully considering each option—slapping his face, boxing his ears, kicking him in the crotch, even spitting at him. None of them seemed quite appropriate to the situation, offensive enough, hurtful enough. And then inspiration came.

"I do hope," she said, and even managed to smile, a cool, polite smile, "I do hope you've been in touch with Morag Dunbar. About the house, about our visit up there. It must be nearly a week since she called. It really does seem a bit rude to ignore her."

She knew he'd got the message; she'd heard him checking it, listening to the machine when he got in.

She saw Richard apparently cease even to breathe, saw his eyes fix on hers, every facial muscle motionless, saw one of his hands pause on its way to push back his hair the way he did when he was nervous or upset, one foot slightly behind the other. He looked like a shop-window dummy; absolutely absurd. She wanted to giggle.

A long, long time later he released a breath; then said, "How do you know that?"

"Richard, I heard the message. It was on the answering machine."

"And you didn't tell me."

"No, I didn't tell you. But I knew you'd got the message, I heard you listening to it."

"And you still didn't say anything."

"No, I didn't say anything. I can't think what I would have said. Actually."

Another silence, then: "That was a filthy thing to do. Keeping that to yourself. Filthy and devious."

"Oh, really? Not as filthy and devious as telling me you'd turned the job down when you hadn't. Making me feel as bad as you knew how. I call that really filthy. Actually. So have you been in touch with her, Richard, or have you not? I really would rather like to know. For obvious reasons. Arrangements and all that sort of thing."

"Any arrangements I might make," he said, "certainly won't include you. Be quite sure of that, Debbie."

Joel switched off his tape recorder feeling rather depressed. His Lloyd's feature was shaping up at last, but Neil Lawrence's story had been truly dreadful. He'd lost everything, his house—well, two houses actually—his car, his job, and now his wife. Not surprising the poor sod had tried to kill himself.

That had been before the wife had gone—but she had, taking the children with her. Neil said it really seemed the only thing to do.

"Whatever way I turned, I came to the same dead end."

That was a rather good phrase: he might even call the piece that. And what was it Simon had said? Oh yes, that it was "an absolute scandal," the whole thing. He liked that too.

And then Neil said that he hadn't wanted to be rescued, that coming round had been one of the worst moments of his life. "This was not a cry for help. It was an escape bid."

His wife had called him a coward, apparently: that was one of her reasons for leaving him. Poor bugger. He was living in a bedsit in Camden Town now, on benefits of some kind or another.

"How did you get into it?" Joel said.

"It was a bloke I met playing tennis. At Queens, you know. Nice chap, we played a few times, and then he asked if I'd ever considered becoming a Name. It was in the early eighties, money still growing on trees, we were all getting a bit reckless; you bought shares, they doubled in value overnight; you bought a house, it had put on twenty grand before the ink dried on your signature. It sounded like another good idea, and I was rather flattered, to tell you the truth. It was a bit like being asked to join the Reform, or Wentworth Golf Club."

"And what was his name?"

"Allinson," said Neil. "Tim Allinson."

"My God!" said Joel. "Do you know, you are the second person I've interviewed who's been led to the slaughter by that bugger."

"I'm not surprised. It was a sort of job for him, as far as I can make out. I'd nail the bastard to a tree if I could get hold of him."

"And have you tried? To get hold of him, not nail him to a tree."

"I have, yes. Since things went belly-up, he appeared to move. Certainly changed his phone number. Funny, that."

"God, I'd like to track him down," said Joel. "Well, thanks so much, Neil. You've been terrifically helpful. And you don't mind my using all this?"

"God, no," said Neil. "What have I got to lose?"

That was what had depressed Joel. It was so patently true. He bought Neil another beer and left.

❧

There he was, leaning on the rail in Arrivals. Then when he saw her, holding out his arms, and she left her trolley and just ran into them. And oh God, he was so gorgeous. So totally, unbelievably, wonderfully gorgeous.

"Hi," he said, smiling at her, standing just slightly back, studying her.

"Hi, Jamie." She smiled back, thinking how much she had missed him, how odd it was that he had become, so quickly, the most important person in her life.

"You look lovely," he said.

"Thank you."

He gave her a quick kiss. "I can't believe you're here."

"You can't? Neither can I!"

He retrieved the trolley, pushed it along with one hand, his other arm round her. "We're not going on the water shuttle after all. It's really crowded when you get to the other side. You can see all that tomorrow. Dad's driver's here; he'll take us home."

Annabel wouldn't really have minded if he'd said they had to walk. She was here. He was here. She wouldn't have minded anything.

Two hours later, she was beginning to mind just a bit. Everything was lovely, of course, but rather formal. The car was huge and the driver equally so, huge and very black; his rearview mirror was vast too, and every time Annabel looked into it, he seemed to be watching her, so there wasn't the opportunity she had hoped for, for a good, ice-breaking snog. As it was, Jamie sat rather carefully away from her, although he did reach out after a bit to hold her hand. She saw the driver, Tony, watching this too.

The drive from the airport wasn't exactly long, but it was very slow; the traffic was awful, "Rush hour, I'm sorry," said Jamie, adding that it was mostly awful all day long anyway.

They hit the city at about five; Annabel was beginning to feel terribly tired—well, it was already around ten London time by her calculation—and to her horror as she heard Jamie say, "Here we are," she realised she'd been asleep. God, supposing she'd snored. Or dribbled.

"Sorry," she said to Jamie, who just smiled and said, "That's OK, you must be exhausted," but he was so polite, he'd never have told her if she'd been doing anything disgusting. Or even unladylike.

The Cartwright house, which she stood blinking up at, was not in the least how she had expected. It was on a square that could easily have been in London, tall, perfectly proportioned, bow-fronted; it was beautiful. She said as much to Jamie; he smiled and said, "We like it." And his voice was filled with pride. "And here's Mother. Mother, hello. She's arrived, safe and sound."

"Annabel, my dear." Mrs. Cartwright was wearing immaculate white trousers and a blue-and-white striped shirt. She kissed Annabel—or rather, sent a kiss winging into the air somewhere past Annabel's head—and then stood back smiling at her. She had a particularly strange smile; Annabel had noticed it before in London. It was situated entirely in her mouth, revealing a row of perfect and very neat teeth, and made no connection with her eyes whatsoever. "How wonderful to have you here. How was your flight?"

"Oh, fine, thank you. Yes. I'm a bit tired, but—"

"Of course you are. Come along in, let me show you straight up to your room. I expect you'd like a rest before dinner."

Annabel followed her, feeling suddenly nervous. Inside, the house was also strangely familiar: tall graceful windows, elaborate fireplaces, flowers in huge vases on polished tables, wooden floors, beautiful Oriental rugs. For a wild moment Annabel wondered if she'd managed to leave England at all. Her bedroom was charming: the wallpaper blue and white, with a pretty white fireplace and a white iron bedstead; the carpet was pale blue, the curtains white muslin, the quilt pale blue. A bookshelf was filled with children's classics, *Little Women, What Katy Did, Anne of Green Gables, Alice in Wonderland.* A posy of blue-and-white flowers stood on the bedside table and two embroidered samplers hung on the wall on either side of the fireplace. It sent a very clear message. This is a young girl's room: no sharing.

"I do hope you'll be comfortable. Regard the bathroom next door as your own; towels in there for you. Is there anything you would like now, Annabel? A cold drink—I'm afraid it's awfully hot here—iced tea or homemade lemonade?"

"Lemonade sounds lovely."

"I'll send some up. Now do take your time, have a bath if you like, no hurry at all, drinks downstairs at six thirty in the drawing room. All right?"

"Wonderful."

"And just family supper, no need to dress up. Kathleen and Joe will be joining us and Bif and his wife, Dana. They're all longing to meet you."

"I'm longing to meet them too."

Where was Jamie? Why wasn't he with her? Who had she come to visit? Something resembling ice-cold water seemed to be creeping slowly down her spine.

Jamie was waiting for her in the hall when she came down; not sure what to wear for what Mrs. Cartwright (who had now instructed her to call her Frances) called family supper, she had put on a flowered crêpe dress, mid-calf length, cut on the bias, with cap sleeves; it was what she called her tea-dance dress.

"You look lovely," he said, and gave her a kiss—on the cheek.

She grabbed his hand. "I want to be alone with you," she hissed.

Jamie looked almost shocked. "Not now. Maybe later. Now come into the drawing room . . . Annabel, this is Kathleen and her husband, Joe."

"Hello, Annabel," Kathleen said. "How wonderful to meet you." She was very pretty, with impeccably styled blond hair exactly like her mother's and Jamie's blue eyes; she was wearing a red silk suit with wide shoulders and elbow-length sleeves, very high heels, and a heavy gilt link necklace, which seemed to Annabel much too old for her; but her smile was warm and friendly.

"Lovely to meet you too."

"Hi, Annabel," said Joe. He shook her hand; his was sweaty. She wasn't so sure about him. He looked just slightly sleazy. He was wearing a dark suit buttoned over a burgeoning stomach, and his dark hair was already receding. "Welcome to Boston. You ever been before?"

"No. It seems lovely."

"Glad you like it."

"Duck Tour tomorrow," said Jamie. "First thing."

"Oh no! Poor Annabel."

A maid dressed in black with a white apron appeared with a tray of champagne glasses. This was ridiculous, Annabel thought. What family supper?

"Annabel, how lovely you look." It was Frances Cartwright, dressed in a suit almost identical to Kathleen's, in brilliant peacock blue, the lacquered helmet of fair hair clearly re-glued for the occasion.

"Thank you."

"I love that natural English style. Tell me, is that Laura Ashley?"

"No!" said Annabel, unable even to try to sound polite. "Miss Selfridge." Laura Ashley! As if she'd be seen dead in the stuff.

"Now have you had some champagne?"

"Yes, thank you." She had; half a glass already. It was cold and fizzily perfect and exactly what she needed. She had felt her spirits lift.

"Bif! I didn't hear you come in!"

"Sorry, Mother. Now you must be the delectable Annabel."

She smiled at him. "Hope so."

He was exactly like Jamie, same colouring, same lovely smile, just slightly more heavily built. And more sensibly dressed certainly than Joe, in a linen suit and open-necked silk shirt.

"This is Dana, my wife."

Dana was a Kathleen clone, only dark-haired; she too was wearing the Suit, in black, with a huge pearl choker.

"It's lovely to meet you," she said, her smile much warmer than Frances's. "I hope the flight was all right."

"It was fine. Thank you." She allowed the maid to refill her glass.

She noticed that everyone else's was still full. Well, what the hell. She needed it.

"Daddy's going to be a little late," said Frances to Jamie, "so we'll give him half an hour and then go in. Big deal going through, apparently. I'm so sorry, Annabel."

"That's perfectly all right. Of course."

The maid brought a plate of canapés round; Annabel shook her head and drained her second glass, smiling hopefully at Jamie; he was looking at his mother, not her. The icy trickle started again. Why was she here? Why had she come?

By the time they sat down to dinner—without Mr. Cartwright—the combination of an empty stomach, an eighteen-hour day, and three glasses of champagne had made Annabel rather drunk. She was next to Jamie—that in itself seemed rather amazing—and Joe on her other side. She put her hand under the table and groped for Jamie's; it didn't come to meet hers. What was the matter with him?

"So, what do you do, Annabel?" asked Dana. "Jamie said it was something rather glamorous."

"I'm a hairdresser," she said.

"A hairdresser!" said Frances. Her tone outdid Lady Bracknell.

"Oh." The silence was frozen: just for a moment. Then Dana rallied. "What fun."

"Yes, it is. And it's terribly hard work. And actually very creative. And what I want more than anything is to have my own salon."

"And where do you live?"

"Well, with my parents at the moment. In London."

"Oh yes. And your father is a banker, I think Mother said."

"Yes, he is." No way was she going to tell them what had happened to him. "And my mother is managing director of an advertising agency." It seemed important she got that in quickly; she wanted them to know her mother was a person in her own right. It would tell them a lot about her family, a lot that she wanted them to know.

"Oh really?" said Dana, her dark eyes thoughtful. "How wonderful. She must be extremely clever."

"Yes, she is. She's totally brilliant at it. And she worked so hard to get there."

"And how many of you are there?" asked Kathleen. "Do you have brothers and sisters?"

"One of each. Both younger than me. Toby's fifteen and Tilly's thirteen."

"Quite a young family, then. So when did your mother return to work? Quite recently, I imagine."

"She never stopped," said Annabel firmly. "We all grew up accepting that she worked. We liked it. It was just—how things were."

"Good gracious, how impressive," said Frances, making it clear that she found this totally unacceptable. "Jamie, dear, give Annabel some water. And some wine, of course." But water first, more important: she'd noticed. Oh God. Oh God. She wanted to go home. Or to bed. With Jamie.

The evening got worse. She managed to sober up a bit, but the meal was endless, four courses, and it seemed terribly hot. She found it harder and harder to sound interesting or even remotely intelligent; glancing at her watch which was on English time, she saw that she'd been up nearly twenty-four hours. They must realise. How could they do this to her? How could they?

Mr. Cartwright arrived home at ten, clearly in a bad temper; he came into the dining room, managed to smile at her and welcome her, and then told his wife to have dinner served in his study.

"I have to send some faxes, make some phone calls. Bif, you might come with me for a moment, just want to check a couple of details with you."

Bif rose from the table at once, followed his father out of the room. Dana smiled at her mother-in-law.

"This one's been a brute, hasn't it?"

"A complete brute," said Frances. "I'm so sorry, Annabel. This must seem rather rude."

"No, no, not at all. But—"

"Now what plans do you have for tomorrow, Jamie?"

"Well, we're doing the Duck Tour in the morning, as I said."

"The Duck Tour! Jamie, you can't take Annabel on that. It's appalling." She said to Annabel, "A trip round the town on some sort of old military tank and then it takes to the water. Terribly touristy and really rather vulgar—the guides are all out-of-work actors."

"I think they're rather fun," said Dana.

"It sounds like that to me," said Annabel staunchly. She smiled at Jamie. He was looking at Frances.

"I really think she'll like it, Mother, but if you—"

"Jamie, I want to go," said Annabel firmly.

"Well, you'd better go then," said Frances. She sounded almost cross. "But don't say I didn't warn you."

"I promise I won't," said Annabel. At least she'd get Jamie to herself for a bit.

"And we'll want to be settled at the Hatch with our picnic by five," said Kathleen. "Don't you dare be late for that!"

"Of course not. It's the Fourth of July celebrations," said Jamie to Annabel. "I told you about it, it's absolutely wonderful—a concert by the Boston Pops and a huge firework display over the Charles River. We're all going—we take a picnic, sit on the grass and listen to the music. You'll love it."

"I'm sure I will," said Annabel. She felt like crying. All of them going. All of these awful people.

"Do have a truffle," said Kathleen.

"Thank you." It might help, the sugar, keep her awake. She ate two in swift succession. And then realised, to her horror, she was feeling nauseated. Really, really nauseated. And swimmy and sweaty and . . . "I'm sorry," she said, pushing her chair back, standing up. "Could you show me where the bathroom is, please, Jamie. I feel—I think—"

She rushed from the room, followed by Jamie; just reached the cloakroom in time, didn't even have time to shut the door . . .

Later, lying on her bed, being offered cold water by Jamie, feeling more wretched in every way than she could ever remember, some words of Florian's swam into her head.

"I hate being sick," he'd said. "It's so common." Common indeed; as was getting drunk, getting drunk in your new boyfriend's parents' house. How could she have done that?

"I'm so sorry, Jamie," she said, pushing the water away, "so terribly sorry. Whatever will they think of me?"

"I'm sure they'll just feel sympathetic," he said. "It was obviously something you ate on the plane."

"Jamie, it wasn't. It was champagne and truffles, too much of both. Oh God, I'm so ashamed."

"Don't be silly. I think you should try to get some sleep now; you'll feel much better in the morning."

"I won't," she said, "not unless we get to spend some time together, just the two of us. That's what I've come for, Jamie, to see you. Your family are lovely, but I kind of thought we'd be alone together this evening." She patted the bed beside her. "Come and lie down with me, Jamie, please."

"Annabel, not here." He looked shocked and embarrassed in equal proportions. "We can't—Mother's waiting to hear how you are; she's so worried about you."

"Yes, all right, but please come back later."

"Annabel, you don't understand. Their room is right along the hall-way."

"Jamie, I don't get all this. What are we supposed to be, a pair of virgins or something?"

"Well, no, of course not." He looked wretched. "But you're a guest in their house; we have to follow their rules."

A wave of rage swept over Annabel: rage and strength. She sat up suddenly. "Well, I'm sorry," she said, "but I didn't come all this way to be with your mother. Either we spend some time together, on our own, or I'm on the first plane back to London tomorrow, OK? Now if this room is along the corridor from your parents, where's yours?"

"On the next floor," he said, still looking wretched.

"Right. Tell me exactly and I'll be up later. OK? I mean it, Jamie, this is horrible. I love you, I've missed you, please, please try to understand."

"Well, I've missed you too," he said, "but—"

"But nothing. Look, all right. I'll stay here tonight." ("Wait till the second night"—Florian.) "I still feel a bit rough. But tomorrow—just you and me, all right? Except for this pop concert in the evening, maybe?"

"It's not a pop concert," he said wearily.

"Well, whatever sort of concert. I want to see the city and I want to be alone with you, preferably in a bed. God, Jamie, we're talking about loving each other, and we've never had sex; it's ridiculous. I mean don't you fancy me or something?"

"Yes, of course I do. But—"

"No buts. That's the deal. Gosh, I feel better already. Tell you what I'd love, do you have any Diet Coke?"

"I'm not sure," he said.

"Well, go and check it out. Then I'll leave you in peace. Until tomorrow."

He stood up, looking down at her.

"Go on. It's not a lot to ask."

"I know. Sorry." He looked more like a frightened little boy than a lover. "It's all right. And you'd better bring me a bowl as well. I do feel better, but . . . it might happen again."

When Jamie came back, bearing the bowl but no Diet Coke, just a jug of iced water, she was fast asleep. He breathed a sigh of immense relief and tiptoed out, shutting the door behind him, smiling nervously at his mother who was hovering in the corridor.

"She's asleep," he said. "Good night, Mother."

"Good night, Jamie. Sleep well. I do hope she'll be all right. Something she ate on the plane, no doubt."

"No doubt."

Chapter 29

It was very odd, Simon was discovering, not to be in the office every day. His life had revolved around it for almost thirty years; he had had dreams of becoming chairman one day, at very least managing director, but he had awoken now to the harsh reality of, at very best, some nonexecutive directorships, and at worst the half-life of early retirement and some meaningless consultancies.

The perks of his job—the first-class travel, the car, the driver, the easy acquisition of tables at fashionable restaurants, the best seats at theatres, the best view at sporting events—he could live without. It was the other, much more important things that his job gave him that he would miss: the things that made it challenging, difficult, that pumped out the adrenaline and speeded up the clock, that created the sense of being not personally but professionally important: those were the things that he knew he would look back on and long for. And he owed Lloyd's and would for the rest of his life.

God, it was unfair, so dreadfully desperately unfair. All his life he had worked and fought and schemed and manoeuvred and been rewarded for it; and now nothing could ever see him rewarded, see him safe. And all he had done, to find himself in this helpless, hapless situation, was make one piece of fatally bad judgement, in the very best of faith. Other mistakes could be rectified, but not that one; and at the end of that first, awful day, he could see that the Simon Beaumont he had been, that he had wanted to be, might as well have died for all that his future could possibly offer.

℃

"I've decided to bite the bullet," said Catherine. "In fact, I don't feel I have any choice anymore."

Blue and Lucinda had invited her and the children to tea; she had revealed that it was her birthday. Lucinda had gone to enormous trouble, ordered a cake from Fortnum, made piles of smoked-salmon sandwiches, and given her a pink cashmere sweater; and Blue had decorated the front of the house with balloons and a banner that said HAPPY BIRTHDAY CATHERINE and bought musical candles for the cake. They all sang "Happy Birthday" and Catherine was so touched she cried. Blue had then taken the children to see what would be the Marina, and Lucinda and Catherine were sitting in the kitchen, pretending not to be eating any more cake, while actually picking at it constantly.

"What bullet?" said Lucinda.

"I'm going to ask for help. From Frederick's parents."

"But I thought they were vile. I thought you said you'd rather die than go to them?"

"Even if I'd rather die, the children wouldn't. I'll almost certainly lose my job. Simon's secretary, who's never liked me, called on Friday and said he'd gone, and that personnel want to see me. Which means they're going to tell me to leave. I knew it would happen. I was very much in Simon's personal gift, so to speak. Anyway, I can't manage anymore. I can't earn enough to pay Freddie's school fees, and I'm not having him going back to that terrible place, it's too cruel."

"No, I can see that."

"The worst aspect of this whole thing is that none of us have done anything wrong," said Catherine. "We're being punished just for trying to do the right thing for our families. We haven't stolen anything, or embezzled any funds, or—well, or done anything really. I was saying that only yesterday morning to Nigel."

"To Nigel!"

"Yes. Oh gosh." Catherine blushed suddenly, looked at Lucinda. "I hope it's all right, talking about him and to him, and so on. I hope you don't mind."

"Catherine, of course it's all right. Why ever shouldn't it be?"

"Well, I don't know. He was your husband and I know you're still friends . . ."

"Friends, yes. And he was my husband, but he's about not to be anymore. Don't be silly. Where did you see him?"

"Well, we were in Peter Jones—you know, I've still got an account there, and I never use it and our bath towels are just threadbare, and I thought, golly, why not. I can pay it off at five pounds a month for the next twenty years, so in we went and bought them, huge great fluffy things, so lovely, and then the children wanted to ride on the escalator and we were going up and he was coming down and—well, we all had coffee together. I was jolly surprised he remembered me actually, as we only met once."

"Of course he would have remembered you," said Lucinda.

"Well, anyway, we had a super chat. He was rather good with the children, kept asking them silly riddles and things. They thought he was wonderful."

"He would so have loved children," said Lucinda, rather sadly. "But—well, I'm sure it's not too late."

"I hope not. Anyway, that's what we were talking about, how blameless we'd all been and how this great thing had come along and knocked us right off our perches—"

"Exactly. Oh, I'm glad you had coffee with him, it would have cheered him up; he's awfully lonely, poor lamb."

"Anyway, back to my in-laws. I'm throwing myself on their mercy. And I can tell you, merciful is the opposite of what they are. They're really horrible, although they were very supportive and concerned, I must say, when Freddie was missing; kept ringing me and asking if there was any-thing they could do."

"Well, they are his grandparents."

"Yes, I know. But not exactly interested ones. He's a bully and she's just totally mean-spirited. How they produced Frederick, I'll never know. But they have got lots of money and even if they'd see me starve—which they would, quite happily—they won't let that happen to the children."

"But what could they do for you?"

"Oh, they told me before, when I first came home. They've got a huge house. Well, it seems huge to me. It's not specially nice, it's a sort of two-storey bungalow in the depths of Somerset. Anyway, they've offered to put me and the children up there until we get ourselves sorted out. I know it sounds kind, but I can tell you it will be dreadful. I'll be made to feel like Jane Eyre or something, completely the poor relation, and Mrs. Morgan actually said I could claim benefits and give it to her in return for board and lodging."

"What?"

"Yes. But Freddie and Caroline will both be secure, not latchkey kids living in a poky flat. Lots of fresh air, room to run about and play—so good for them, don't you think?" She smiled bravely at Lucinda.

"Well, yes, of course. But won't Freddie have to move schools again?" asked Lucinda. "I thought—"

"Lucinda, I can't keep him at Lynton House. And he'll go somewhere similar. They'll be so much better off. And in due course, maybe I can get a job down there and even a place of our own again."

"You're very brave, you know," said Lucinda. "They wouldn't do some-thing really helpful if they've got all that money and pay your debts? Or buy you a little house?"

"No, of course not," said Catherine. "They see it as absolutely my fault, signing all the money over to Lloyd's, and it is a bit. I shouldn't have been so gullible."

"Catherine, stop being so totally ridiculous. Oh hello, Blue darling. Nice walk?"

"Yes, thanks. Your Freddie's very bright, Catherine, asking me about what I did—said it sounded like a game of poker. How does he know about poker?"

"Freddie!" said Catherine. "That wasn't very polite."

"Sorry. Daddy used to play sometimes, out in Hong Kong. He explained it to me a few times."

"Perfectly polite," said Blue. "I'm impressed. It is exactly like poker, what I do. Well, almost exactly. He can come to me for a job anytime."

"You don't employ minors, I suppose?" said Catherine.

It was very clever, Colin's plan, Flora thought. And she could see it was just about feasible. It wouldn't exactly save the house for her—and certainly not her Meadow—but it would leave her far from destitute, with Lloyd's neatly done down. She smiled at him.

"Thank you so much. I really do appreciate your devoting so much thought to my problems. I'm deeply touched. And I do see that it could work . . . Look, let me have a think about it, would you? And then we can proceed to the next stage."

"Of course."

"And meanwhile, will you have some more cottage pie?"

"I certainly will. It's absolutely delicious. Is it made from salt-marsh lamb?"

"Is there any other sort?" said Flora, and smiled at him. "Now—some more wine to go with it? I presume your driver's coming for you."

"He is indeed. So yes, please. And maybe we should change the subject. There's another lovely concert in Cardiff Cathedral in two weeks' time. Would you like to go?"

"I'd love to," she said.

After he had gone, she went outside and sat on the stone garden bench with another cup of coffee. It was a beautiful night and the moonlight on the calm sea was almost daytime brilliant. She put her cup down, walked to the gate of the Meadow, and, after hesitating for a moment, opened it and set off down the path to the sea, shining her big torch in front of her. A heavy scuffling fifty yards ahead startled her for a moment; then she smiled. She knew what it was. Mr. Badger as William had called him—or to be precise Mr. Badger's great-grandson's great-great-grandson—setting off across his run. He followed exactly the same route on his hunting expeditions, as all badgers do, and always used the same place, just above the ditch to relieve himself; his run was as clearly marked across the Meadow as any man-made footpath. He froze briefly in the beam, then scuttled firmly across, his big heavy body moving the grass on either side of him. She switched her torch off; the moonlight, brighter without it, shone down on what looked like scores of rabbits: good pickings for the foxes and their young families. If there was a heaven, she thought, it must be very like this. And if it wasn't, she didn't want to go there.

There was nowhere she could imagine loving like this: not even the wilds of the Scottish Highlands, or the rocky coast of the Algarve, both of which Colin had suggested as possible new homes for her. And if she adopted his plan, would she not be betraying it, this place and its beauty? But then she would have to leave it anyway, and who knew what the new owner might do? And if she was far away, at least she wouldn't have to see it.

She stood for a while, looking at the sea, then turned and walked back up the Meadow towards the house. The lovely grey stone house that had been home to her husband's family for more than two centuries. Everything she cared about was held in those walls; leaving it would be like dying, having her heart removed from her. How was she going to bear it?

As she had borne other griefs and hurts, she supposed: William's death, the endless miscarriages she had suffered; because she was her, because she was strong. It was just that she didn't feel very strong at all. She was beginning, in fact, to feel rather feeble. Defeated, even . . .

~

"Hello, Debbie."

"Simon, hello. How lovely to hear from you." It was; it always was.

"How's things?" he asked.

"Oh, you know. Much the same. How are they with you?"

"Oh, fine," he said, and she could hear the effort in his voice. "It's wonderful, not being chained to the office and the diary."

"So what are you doing?"

"Oh, I'm very busy. At the moment. Truly. Loads of loose ends to tie up. House to sell, all that sort of thing."

"Yes, I see. Well, is there anything I can do for you? Because—"

"No, no, not really. Just wanted to bring you up-to-date, see how you were, give you my home phone number—that is, my personal one. You never know, you might want to talk to me again."

"Simon! I'll always want to talk to you, don't be silly. Look, can I buy you a drink? It's my turn. Then we can chat a bit more. And I promise I won't even mention my husband."

"How sweet of you. I . . ." He hesitated. Then: "Well, that would be very nice. Yes, thank you. Where would you like to meet? Your end of town?"

"It would be easier. What about the Royal Garden again?"

"Fine. So when and what time? Your call. I have all the time in the world."

"How about Wednesday evening? Richard's taking the children to some film, as an end-of-term treat. They won't be home till eight at the earliest."

"You're on. Bless you, Debbie. I'll look forward to it. Bye, my love." It seemed ages since anyone had used a term of endearment to her; absurdly she felt her eyes filling with tears. Get a grip, Debbie, for God's sake!

The Fourth of July concert had actually been rather wonderful. A sort of cross between Glyndebourne and the Last Night of the Proms; they had sat on the grass by this thing called the Hatch Memorial Shell, which was a vast red-and-gold shell-shaped concert platform, and drunk champagne, being very careful of her consumption, and Frances had produced a suitably grand picnic, and Dana and Bif had laughingly provided a silver candelabra, and they listened to the Boston Pops playing all sorts of familiar classics. The finale was the 1812 Overture; and then there was a spectacular and very long firework display, set off over the Charles River, lighting up the sky and the water. Annabel had always loved fireworks, they affected her emotionally, tended to make her cry; the whole family teased her about it. She sat there, on the grass, gazing at them, her head still filled with the music, and tears began to roll down her cheeks; Bif noticed and nudged his younger brother.

"Annabel's crying—what have you done to her?"

"Nothing," said Jamie indignantly, and put his arm round her shoulders. "What is it? What's the matter?"

"Nothing," she said. "I always cry at fireworks, they make me feel so happy, and these are just so wonderful." Nothing could have endeared her to the Cartwrights more; they all laughed and made a great fuss of her and suddenly it was all right for Jamie to have his arm round her, she didn't feel they were at all disapproving, rather the reverse, and when they finally reached home, walking through the warm smiling crowds, greeted constantly by friends, she realised he had been holding her hand all the way.

Later, much, much later, as the household fell silent, she left her pretty, virginal room and crept up the stairs to his. "This is as much a little boy's room as mine is a little girl's," she hissed at him, and indeed it was; she had seen it earlier, a big rectangular room, with dark green curtains and cream walls, and bookshelves filled with things like *Huckleberry Finn* and *The Man in the Iron Mask,* and a fantastic display of lead soldiers on a large table, and to bring it into the twentieth century, a computer, a fantastic music system, a television, and a sleek-looking video player. But it was very much a bedroom, not a bed-sitting-room, as she had at home—there was no sofa, no coffee table; clearly no question of him having any privacy. His life was lived with the family; it was as simple as that.

But they had privacy now; she abandoned her bathrobe onto the floor and slithered into bed beside him. She was naked, but he was wearing pyjamas.

"Jamie," she said, "take them off. At once. Let me help you." She tugged at his trousers, giggling; and felt his erection. "And I don't want to hear even a syllable of any words like 'mother' or 'parents,' " she said. "Their light is out, and your dad's snoring, if that makes you feel any better. Oh Jamie, I do love you. I really, really do. And that was such a wonderful evening."

He began to kiss her, sweetly and slowly; his hands moved on her, over her, a little hesitant, but then with more confidence. She felt the first real shoots of desire, began to squirm, to breathe more quickly; he stopped suddenly, moved away from her and said, "Should I . . . that is, do you want me to . . ."

Briefly puzzled, then amused, she said, "Jamie, I'm on the pill, don't worry. All I want is for you not to stop."

"I won't," he said. "I can't." And then he moved onto her, and into her, and began to move and she with him, and her memories of the evening, the music, the fireworks, the happiness all merged together with her body and his, and it wasn't just sex, it was absolute happiness and pleasure as she closed round him, and melted and sank and rose and climbed into the brightness, and finally came gloriously and triumphantly, the pleasure as vivid, as violent, as piercing as the fireworks she had watched and wept at with him, what seemed like another lifetime ago, and, "I love you," he whispered as he came too and they lay there together as the pleasure slowly eased and ebbed away, and for the first time since she had arrived she felt properly happy.

❧

If Frances had heard them, or indeed inspected the sheets, as Florian had predicted, she gave no sign of it. She greeted Annabel at the breakfast table quite warmly, offered her hash browns and mushrooms and orange juice, and said she hoped she had slept well.

"Very well, thank you," said Annabel. "That was a wonderful, wonderful evening. Thank you so much. I shall never forget it."

"Good. I'm so glad." The smile came, the awful, chilling smile. How did she do that?

"And today we're going to just wander around," said Jamie, who had come in, sitting down beside Annabel, "take it easy. I thought this evening, Annabel and I would go out for dinner on our own, if that's all right. We could go to Legal, the one down by the Aquarium."

"Legal?" said Annabel.

"Yes, short for Legal Seafoods, probably the most famous seafood restaurant in the world."

Not more than Wheeler's, that's for sure, thought Annabel, but she smiled and said, "How lovely."

"What a good idea," said Frances, "and you know, Bif and Dana love it there, maybe they might join you," and just as Annabel's heart was doing a combination of sinking and raging, Mr. Cartwright said, "Frances, leave them be. They want to be alone, for God's sake," and she restrained herself with great difficulty from going over to him and kissing him.

And as they left the house, walking through the cobbled streets with all the pretty little shops and cafés that marked out Beacon Hill, and down across the Common into the town, she felt she was seeing the real Boston, stylish and charming, and she loved it. They walked down Newbury Street, where the posh shops were, Chanel and Gucci and Ralph Lauren. "Mother and the girls are planning on bringing you here tomorrow," Jamie said. And he showed her a jewellery shop on Boylston Street called Shreve, Crump & Low where, it seemed, all the very best diamond rings for the very best people's engagements were to be bought. "Dad bought Mother's ring here, and Bif bought Dana's, and Joe Kathleen's," said Jamie. She wondered why he was showing her; but she admired it and said it reminded her of Tiffany's.

"You know New York, do you?" said Jamie and seemed surprised; she felt mildly irritated that he might see her as a sort of naïve traveller, dazzled by being in the States at all.

"Jamie, I've been to New York, several times," she said, "and L.A. and San Francisco. And Disneyland when I was little," she added. "Where you must have been lots of times," and was shocked when he said he never had. "Mother didn't think it was somewhere she wanted to go," he said without a hint of resentment.

It was very hot when they got back and the garden, with its big trees, looked inviting. But Frances was there, and so was Kathleen: Kathleen looking flushed and rather agitated.

"Kathleen has some wonderful news. She's going to have a baby. She's just had it confirmed by her doctor. Isn't it exciting?"

"Kathy, that's great news," said Jamie. He went over to her and gave her a hug. "Congratulations."

"Thank you, Jamie."

"How lovely," said Annabel. "Congratulations, Kathleen."

"Thank you. I didn't want to say anything until the test results were in. But there's no doubt about it, it seems." She looked down at her stomach and smiled rather foolishly. "I can't quite believe it."

"She's feeling fine, apparently," said Frances. "No sickness, not tired—you're very lucky, Kathleen. Well, we must drink a toast. Only I suppose we should do it in something nonalcoholic. I'll ask for some fruit punch. My goodness, a grandmother at last! I thought it would never happen. I must tell Daddy. He'll be very excited."

"I'll come and help with the drinks," said Jamie.

Frances walked briskly into the house, Jamie following her; Annabel smiled at Kathleen.

"Joe must be thrilled."

"Yes, he is. He's coming over later. Mother's already arranging something special for dinner, asking Dana and Bif over. I know you were going out, but I hope you'll stay. It would be nice to have you and Jamie here."

"Yes, of course we will," said Annabel. "I feel very honoured to be part of it." And she did; she really liked Kathleen.

Jamie reappeared with a tray of drinks. "Here we are. Mother is already on the bush telegraph. Dad's coming right home, and Caroline and Jerome are coming over too."

"Caroline and Jerome?"

"Yes, well, Mother felt they must be part of the evening. She is your godmother, after all."

"Yes. Yes, I suppose so."

"Only thing is," Jamie said, lowering his voice, "this is going to make things a little difficult for Dana."

"I know it. I thought of that. It will increase the pressure on her a lot."

Frances had reappeared, she was smiling radiantly. "Caroline and Jerome are on their way. They're so thrilled. I knew you'd want them here, Kathleen."

"Yes, of course."

"And I've sent a fax to Grandma Cartwright. She'll be over the moon; she's always said it was her one remaining ambition, to be a great-grandmother. My goodness, I feel quite overcome with the whole thing. Such a lot to plan and to think about, isn't there?"

Anyone would think, Annabel reflected, sipping her fruit punch, that it was Frances's baby.

❧

It had been a very nice evening; Richard felt suddenly more cheerful. They had gone, he and the children, to see *Teenage Mutant Ninja Turtles,* and then, as a really special treat, to tea at McDonald's in Kensington

High Street. Richard knew he shouldn't approve of McDonald's, but the children loved the novelty of eating with their fingers and the little cardboard containers of chips and the sickly sweetness of the milk shakes. When they had finished, he said, "Right, home. The tube's just over the road. One stop to the Central Line."

They were waiting to cross the road, when an open-topped tourist bus pulled up by them. Rachel gazed at it, transfixed.

"Can we go on that?" she said. "Oh please, please, Daddy, please! Up on the top, please!"

"It's going the wrong way, Rachel."

"Doesn't matter, does it?" said Emma. "Doesn't matter if we're late, it's the holidays. Oh please, Daddy, it would be fun. Please!"

"I don't suppose they'll let us on," said Richard, but luck was not on his side: it was one of the stops on the circuit where people could get on and off.

They got on.

The evening sun was very warm and the plane trees practically brushed their heads as they drove along. And there was Kensington Gardens, on their left and— "Look, there's Mummy!" shouted Emma suddenly. "Look, in front of that hotel. Look, there, with that man, see? Mummy, Mum, Mum! Oh and look, it's Simon, it's Tilly's dad. Mum, look up here, on the bus!"

And they all started shouting, shouting and waving; but Debbie neither heard them, through the thick noise of the traffic, nor saw them, for she was reaching up to kiss Simon, and as they all watched and waved, they saw him put both his arms round her and give her a hug; and then they began to walk slowly down the ramp, his arm round her shoulders, hers round his waist.

The children, faintly anxious by now, looked at their father, who was very white. Emma moved closer to him, slipped her hand through his arm.

"They've probably been doing some work together," she said, some deep precocious instinct telling her that such comfort was necessary.

Chapter 30

Thank God for the *Daily Mail,* Joel thought. That small miracle, worked for him by Nigel Dempster with an item headed TROUBLE IN PARADISE? The paradise referred to was Paradise Island, just off Nassau, and the trouble upon it was the failure of a building company to complete the renovation work on one of the private homes on the island, owned by one Mick Bridgeman.

> Multimillionaire British industrialist Bridgeman is furious at being forced to entertain a party of guests at the Ocean Hill Hotel, rather than at his home. Bridgeman's lawyers have been instructed to sue if the house is not finished within the next two weeks. The persistent frolicking of Bridgeman's stunning young wife, Thandie, with another guest, rock musician Nelson Crewe, has not improved Bridgeman's mood. Other guests include Italian supermodel Bibi, the fashion designer Giles Courtney and his friend Dick "Tracy" Lord, and Irish charmer Tim Allinson, walker to the stars. Watch this space for further fireworks.

"Got him!" Joel shouted, and punched the air, and then rushed out of the office.

Hugh Renwick, the *News* Editor, was extremely unimpressed. "Course you can't go swanning off to the Bahamas. It's a wild-goose chase. I just don't buy this story anyway. Lot of rich spoiled people who can't take their medicine when they clearly have to."

"But it isn't like that," said Joel, thinking of Catherine, of Gillian Thompson, of Neil Lawrence, of Simon Beaumont. "There's much more to this story, I swear to you. People are in complete despair, actually topping themselves—I've got a lot of stuff now, from people who've talked to me, stories that would really touch the readers' hearts."

"Well, none of it touches mine. Sorry, Joel. Just drop it, would you. I need you for good solid stories, not this fancy crap. Like that piece on educational trusts I asked you for. How's that going?"

"Oh, I've got a few leads," said Joel impatiently. He thought of Tim Allinson, sitting out there, juicily ripe for plucking; in a few days he could be gone and so would any chance of getting his story. He could hardly bear it.

"Well, get on with it. Otherwise you're going to find yourself in Shit Street rather than Fleet Street, I warn you."

"Yes, OK," said Joel, "but you could be sorry."

❧

"We saw you, we saw you!" The children came into the kitchen where Debbie was sitting, checking the post. She had got home five minutes before them.

"Saw me where? What are you talking about? How was the film?"

"Great," said Alex.

"Lovely," said Rachel. Emma was rather quiet, looked at her mother awkwardly as she poured herself a glass of squash.

"Where did you see me?"

"Coming out of the Royal Garden Hotel," said Richard. His voice was very cold. "With Simon Beaumont."

"Oh did you?" She felt herself flush; and cursed it. As if she had any reason to. "Yes, we were having a drink. He's been fired, you know, from the bank and I—"

"I don't think we should talk about it now," said Richard.

"Richard, there's nothing to talk about."

"Good. Well, come on, children. You did promise straight upstairs. And then I want to ring Granny, see if you can go down to stay with her a bit sooner."

"Ye-es! Could we?"

"I'm not sure I want them to," said Debbie. "I've got things arranged for the end of the week."

He looked at her with such withering dislike she felt sick. "Really?" he said, and walked out of the room, shutting the door behind him.

❧

"Well, at least I know the real reason why you don't want to go to Scotland," he said. It was much later; Debbie was in the sitting room, ironing and watching Wimbledon highlights.

She stared at him. "What did you say?"

He switched the television off. "I said I know now why you don't want to go to Scotland. It would put an end to your relationship with Simon Beaumont."

Her stomach lurched. Had Flora . . . ? No, no, surely not. "Richard!" she said, struggling to sound calm. "You're going mad. Of course I'm not having a relationship with Simon Beaumont."

"Is that so? Is that why you were coming out of a hotel with him, kissing him, carrying on—"

"Please don't be so ridiculous. I was not carrying on. We'd had a drink, he's been fired, I wanted to cheer him up."

"Oh, I'm sure you did. Lucky man. It's a long time since you wanted to cheer me up."

"That is so untrue," she said in a low voice.

"It is not untrue. I can't remember when we last had sex. Anyway, let's not argue about that. We have to decide what to do."

"What on earth do you mean?"

"I mean about our marriage"

"Our marriage? I don't understand you— What is all this about? I am not having an affair with Simon Beaumont, nothing could be less likely, he's just been rather kind to me and—"

"Debbie, I'm not stupid. I've observed you with him. You're obviously obsessed with him. Tell me something, truthfully please: Was that the first time you've met him in London?"

"Well, no." It seemed better to tell the truth; lying was dangerous.

"I see. More drinks in other hotels?"

"You've got this so wrong, I can't begin to tell you. I don't fancy him. Get that into your skull, would you? I do not fancy Simon Beaumont."

"Oh, shut up," he said wearily. "Anyway, I'm going to take the children down to Mother's tomorrow. I don't want them upset by all this, and we really do have to get things sorted out. Not just our marriage, but what I'm going to say to Morag Dunbar, and—"

"Yes, I wondered when we were going to get round to her. What did you think of saying to her? 'My wife was kissing a man on the steps of a hotel in broad daylight and I'm going to divorce her.' She'll think you're insane. You *are* insane."

"You're entitled to your opinion," he said, "but I'd like the children's things packed, please. I've spoken to Mother and she's happy to have them tomorrow. She's expecting us around teatime."

There was clearly nothing she could do about it; he seemed absolutely determined. She nodded and said quietly, "Yes, all right." But she felt sick. What if Richard asked Flora if she thought there was anything between her and Simon? What might she say? What in God's name might she say?

℃∽

Lucinda opened the letter.

> *Darling Lucinda,*
> *How wonderful to hear from you. My life has not been the same without you. In fact, I can't imagine how I've survived. I'm intrigued by your request. I'm happy to help if I can, but I think I'd like to know a little more. I'm coming to London en route to France in the last week of July. I'll be with Greg, my partner—you'll love him, Lucinda, and he'll love you. Let's meet then and you can tell me all about it. Longing to make the new man's acquaintance.*
>
> *All love, Virgil*

"Damn," said Lucinda. "Damn damn damn." It was getting tougher; she was tempted to give up on this one. And Blue was pressing her harder and harder about moving; she just didn't know how much longer she could hang on. But if she didn't—well, that would be Nigel done for. She really needed to talk to someone about this. Someone with lots of common sense. But they'd need to know Blue as well as Nigel. Like—well, maybe like Simon. Yes, she'd talk to him about it. Take him out to lunch. See what he thought.

She reached for the phone.

℃∽

"Debbie, dear, it's Flora."

"Hello, Flora," she said carefully. She was sitting in her office at Know How Promotions.

"I haven't heard from that young man yet, the journalist. If he wants to talk to me, it had better be today. Once the children are here, it will be very difficult to find the time."

"Oh, OK. I'll call him. Sorry, Flora."

She rang Joel, too weary and miserable to feel even remotely awkward; told him what Flora had said.

"Oh sorry. Yes, I was going to call her. But—well, to be honest, Debbie, I don't think I can do this story after all. The editor's more or less told me to spike it. But I will ring your mother-in-law. It would seem rude not to. Thanks, Debbie."

❦

Flora was a fantastic interviewee; she didn't waffle on, didn't get emotional, just gave him the facts—which were pretty dramatic, losing first her husband and then everything she had as a result. He thanked her and then sat thinking for a while, replaying bits of the recording. And in a rush of reckless courage, decided to finance the trip himself. Some stories were too good to be missed. And then he rang Debbie back. "Just to let you know, I've spoken to your mother-in-law. She was just ace. Thanks so much."

"Don't be silly. I didn't do much."

"You led me to her. And I've been thinking: I know this is a good story. I'm going to do it anyway. I've got this incredible lead, bloke out in the Bahamas—"

"The Bahamas? You going there? Doesn't sound as if your editor's spiking it."

"He's not paying my fare—I am."

"Gosh. That is quite a gamble."

"I know. But I think it'll pay off."

"Great."

She was taking this call in her office, feeling totally wretched. The children had hardly said goodbye to her, they were so excited about their extended visit to Gower. Richard had said he would be staying down there himself until Saturday; and every time she thought of him talking to Flora about her and Simon—surely, surely he couldn't be that mad?—every time she thought about it, she felt she was going to throw up.

She was horrified to feel a sob rise in her throat. She swallowed hard. "Well, have fun. I must go. Bye, Joel." She slammed the phone down, threw her head back and fought down the tears. This was ridiculous! The phone rang again.

"Debbie? It's me. Are you all right?"

She was not going to tell him about her troubles. She just wasn't. "Yes. Yes, I'm absolutely fine. Thanks."

"Oh, good. I thought you sounded a bit down."

"No, no, not at all. Couldn't be higher actually," she said. Only on the word "actually" her voice wobbled.

"You're not, are you?" he said. "What is it, what's the matter?"

"Oh, nothing. Nothing serious anyway."

"Good. Well, I'll call Simon now and get a bit more of a lowdown on his situation."

"Great. Well—" And then she thought of how extremely unlikely it was that she would speak to Simon ever again, and that made her feel terribly sad too, and this time the tears did start, and there was no stopping them, and no stopping Joel hearing them either.

"Hey," he said, "there *is* something wrong. Want to tell me about it? I owe you, that's for sure. I'm free after work. Or do you have to get home?"

"No," she said, sniffing loudly, misery making her horribly truthful. "I don't have to get home. There's nobody there."

"Great," he said. "Criterion suit you? At about six thirty?"

"I really shouldn't," she said.

"Nor should I. So let's. Bye, Debbie. See you later."

Now why in God's name had he done that? Very, very silly. Getting involved with a married woman. A not entirely happily married woman, if Simon was to be believed. Not that Joel was getting involved; he was just having a drink with her . . .

Debbie spent most of the afternoon picking up the phone to cancel the arrangement, and then putting it down again.

Chapter 31

Annabel and Jamie were sitting on the beach in front of the Cartwright house on Cape Cod. Annabel loved Cape Cod, loved everything about it, its great stretches of white beaches, and long-grassed dunes, the woods, the cranberry swamps, the fishing villages, and the wild salty wind that filled the air. The house was charming, all sanded floors, white walls and brick fireplaces and French windows everywhere, opening onto the lovely air.

It was "furnished comfy" as Jamie put it, lots of wicker chairs and low tables and carefully casual painted furniture; a verandah ran round three sides of it, there was a deck at the front, right on the beach, and a lush garden, with hammocks slung between the trees.

"If I die and go to heaven, I shall expect it to be just like this," Annabel told Frances, wandering round, her eyes shining; Frances smiled at her graciously and said she was glad she liked it.

"Of course, the area's not what it was, so touristy now, and the marsh-lands are constantly under threat; my husband gives a lot of money every year to the grass-planting project."

"This is where the Pilgrim Fathers first settled, you know," said Jamie. "Well, not exactly here, of course, up there on the northernmost tip, near Truro. We can go there tomorrow if you like."

"I would like," said Annabel.

It was a different world down here; the Cartwrights all became easier, less watchful of one another. Even Frances's hair seemed to relax a little. The days slipped by in an easy, sunlit chain, each one as happy as the one before. Hugely and happily energised, Annabel demanded Jamie took her everywhere; they rode the cycle trails, wandered the villages, walked through the dunes and the salt marshes, went on a whale-watching cruise, and crewed for Dana and Bif for two wonderful days.

"This is the nearest to flying you'll get on this earth," Bif shouted at her, as they leaned backwards over the side of the boat, hanging onto the sail sheets, and indeed it was exactly like that, she thought, looking up at the tall sails and the blue sky and the clouds scudding beyond them. She suddenly thought of her father selling the *Lizzie* and realised how dreadful a loss it was.

By the end of the week, she had eaten so much seafood in the endless fish restaurants and bars that she said she would turn into a fish. "A mermaid would be nicer," Jamie said. That was at lunchtime though—even here there were strict Cartwright rules. Philip cooked every night on the barbecue; there was no question of going to a restaurant except on the last night.

She didn't mind that so much; it was very different from the formality of the dining room in Boston; they sat at a long table on the verandah, or the beachside patio, and felt the warm wind grow colder and then went inside and played games—Scrabble and backgammon—before being allowed up to bed. Even that was easier here; Frances seemed to have accepted their relationship: their rooms were side by side, with only a bathroom dividing them. And besides, she had grown used to the family by now. Being with them was like belonging to a club, and you knew you had to keep to its rather archaic traditions and customs, otherwise there was no point joining. And it was actually a nice club, close and rather protective; members were watchful for one another, wary of strangers, generous to those they had accepted.

And she had been accepted, in spite of the terrible first night, and she felt almost one of them by that last evening, as they sat at a long table in one of the endless local seafood restaurants, laughing, teasing one another, tired out by the fresh air and the sun; she was between Bif and Jamie, and Philip twinkled across the table at her.

"We shall miss you, Annabel. Shame you can't stay."

"I wish I could," she said, and meant it from the bottom of her heart. She had to leave at midday, to catch her flight from Boston in the evening; the last night with Jamie was sweetly sad. They made love rather quietly and gently, their bodies now easily familiar, and then lay in each other's arms, and the last thing she heard him say as she drifted off to sleep was, "How am I going to get through the rest of the summer without you?"

She remembered thinking it would be easier for him, with the cool white beaches and brilliant skies to console him, but was too sleepy to say so; she slept dreamlessly and woke up to find him sitting up looking at her.

"You're so beautiful," he said, "so lovely. I'm going to miss you so much. Look at what colour you are, pale honey," and he picked up a tress of her long sun-streaked hair and kissed it, kissed her hands, her breasts, her flat brown stomach. She felt something close to grief. Jamie had become part of her, part of herself.

"Oh Jamie," she said, "I can't bear it, I can't be without you, it's horrible even to think about. We've been so happy and now we're going to be so unhappy." And she looked at days, at weeks, at months without him, without him holding her hand and kissing her and making love to her and talking to her and laughing with her, looked at being alone and lonely and it was impossible to see any point in any of it.

"Let's go for a walk," he said, and they got dressed and walked down the garden and onto the beach. It was very early—"Only six o'clock," she said, surprised, and she gazed into the distance across the water, the distance that was another place in every sense, where she had to go, where she would be so very alone, and she started to cry. That was when Jamie said he wanted to ask her something.

He had even bought a ring, a diamond ring, from Shreve, Crump & Low, he told her, and indeed gave her the box; she sat staring at it, on her finger, on the proper finger, laughing and crying at the same time.

"I can't believe it," she said. "I can't believe I'm engaged to you, that you know you want to marry me."

"Of course we have to wait a while," he said. "You're so young, your parents don't even know me, I'm only just qualified. It will be at least a year, probably two, but I wanted to get it settled. I wanted to know I had you, that you were really, really mine."

"I'm really, really yours," she said, smiling, kissing him. "Make no mistake about that."

And then thoughts began to come into her head. "Jamie," she said, and she felt oddly frightened suddenly, "have you told your parents?"

"Not yet," he said. "I wanted to make sure you wanted it first. But they'll be so pleased, they love you, they all love you, and—"

"Could you not tell them? Could it be our secret—just for now? I want to go away from here today with only us knowing. It will help me, help me not mind so much. I don't want fuss and celebrations today; it would be too much, too difficult. This is our day, our very own; and it's not so sad now, it's a special, special day. Let's keep it that way, can we?"

He was clearly disappointed. "I wanted us to tell them together," he said.

"But are you sure they'll be pleased? Won't they think we're too young and all that?"

"No, no," he said, "we have a tradition in our family for marrying young. Bif was only twenty-two when he and Dana got engaged, and Kathleen only twenty. And Father was only twenty-two when he married Mother. Who was only twenty. So they'll think it's totally normal. I'm not worried about that at all."

She digested this for a moment, this dutiful following in the Cartwright family tradition, and her being an appropriate part of that, and then said, "Maybe we can tell them together, but another time, another day. Please, Jamie. It's about us, isn't it? Just us?"

"Well, not really," he said. "It's about our families too."

"Yes. But it's us who love each other, us who are going to get married. My God. I can't believe that. You and me, getting married. How very grown-up."

"Very grown-up, yes," he said, and laughed. "My lovely Annabel. You are just so perfect. The perfect Mrs. James Cartwright."

Just for a second then, the sliver of a second, she felt—what? Alarm. No, not alarm, but nerviness. Not at the thought of being Annabel Cartwright, but of being Mrs. James Cartwright. And of having to be a perfect Mrs. Cartwright, like Frances, like Dana, like any of them. A perfect member of this perfect clan. Because that is what she'd have to be. And it might be . . . difficult.

And then it passed, as swiftly as it had come.

❧

Flora and Richard were just finishing supper when the phone rang. "Do you mind, darling, if I take it? I think I know who it is."

"Of course not."

"Ah," he heard her say, "Edward. Yes, thank you, how nice of you to call . . . Well, as I said, anything you could do . . . Oh. Oh, I see. Well, even advice would be helpful. Yes, very. I mean, do I have to sell the house, for instance, or . . . look, I'm busy at the moment, but I'm coming up to town again next week, probably on Wednesday. Maybe we could meet then. I could even buy you a return lunch, to show my gratitude . . . What? . . . Oh well, that's very kind. Look, I'll call you after the weekend, when my plans have firmed up a little . . . Yes. Fine. Thank you, Edward."

"So was it who you thought?" said Richard.

"It was indeed. Nasty little rat, responsible for all my troubles."

"You weren't talking to him as if he was a nasty little rat."

"No, I know. I'm being a bit devious. Think I might be able to get some information out of him, which might help Simon Beaumont in this lawsuit he's mounting."

"Oh yes?"

"He was William's cousin. If he was a relative of mine, I'd disown him. Dreadful man. Oily, self-satisfied little creep."

Richard had avoided so much as mentioning Simon; had simply told his mother that Debbie was working all week and it would be immensely helpful if the children could come down two days early. But now . . .

"You seem to know Beaumont rather well," he said.

"Quite well. I'm very fond of him. He's been a tower of strength through this whole thing, and not just to me. Nothing gets him down, it seems; although he's been fired now from Graburn and French—the bank he works for. Very harsh, that. Poor Simon. Something to do with his contract and bringing the bank into disrepute."

"Shame," said Richard. He sounded singularly unsympathetic, even to himself.

Flora looked at him. "He's not really your sort of person, I know. Your father wouldn't have liked him very much. Bit flashy, he'd have said. But as I say, I have grown fond of him. And he's helped many people. Given that poor girl Catherine Morgan a job at his bank, advised another man who'd tried to kill himself, can you imagine. And of course he's Tilly's father, so I would feel fondly towards him. And he is very charming, very good company."

This was more than he could bear, having to listen to praise being heaped on Simon Beaumont's head.

"I'll just—just go and see the kids," he said, "make sure they're OK. If you don't mind."

"Of course, darling."

"And then I'll come and help you clear up."

"No need. You look tired. Have an early night, why don't you?"

He did feel tired. He wasn't sleeping, and a terrible paralysis seemed to have overtaken him. He had to phone Morag Dunbar, say something; if only that he wasn't coming. Or that he would be coming up alone. Or . . .

"No. No, I'll come down again in a minute." He did; she had made him some of the hot chocolate he loved.

"There you are. Lots of sugar in it. Like your father didn't allow. I do lots of things he didn't allow these days. It helps."

"Do you still miss him so much?" he asked.

"Yes, of course."

"Oh Mother." He looked at her, his grey eyes so exactly like his father's, very concerned. "You shouldn't be so—so brave. It makes us forget. Well, no not forget, but forget to worry about you."

"Richard, I'm fine. You know I am."

"You're not really though, are you?" he said. "You've got this awful thing to cope with, all on your own. I'm so sorry. I wish I could be with you more."

"Oh Richard, don't be ridiculous. You have your own life. And I'm very happy, really I am. Apart from all this wretched business, of course. Now look, would it be OK with you, and Debbie of course, if I get Mrs. Connor to look after the children just for one day next week? She's very firm with them, I promise, and she knows them all. And Tilly will be here, she's very sensible, and extremely grown-up. It really is important to me, this meeting."

"Yes, of course," he said. "Of course it is. Do you really think you'll have to sell the house?"

"Oh, without doubt, I'm afraid. I'm so sorry, I had hoped it would be yours one day. And I love it so much, as you know. But—needs must and all that, while the devil drives. And the devil is certainly driving."

"He does seem to be."

Richard was in something of a state, Flora thought: both edgy and down. And he'd lost weight.

"Richard, darling, would you like some more wine? I can easily—"
The phone rang again. It was Simon.

"Sorry, Richard, won't be long. How are you, Simon?"

"Oh, not great. Discovering what boredom's about. And loneliness—that's been hard, not being surrounded by people all day."

"Of course," said Flora, "but it will be all right. You'll make it so. Now I mustn't be long, sorry, got Richard here, we're chatting. I've spoken to William's cousin, and he's still a Working Name. Yes. And do you know, he had the gall to tell me to trade through—said it was like the races, run of bad luck."

"And what was his explanation for your troubles?"

"Oh, he said he couldn't understand it. I asked him if he'd put me in the same syndicates as himself, as William had requested, and he said yes, of course. I asked him if he was still in the same ones, and he became a bit shifty, said he'd had to move some of the money around, but generally speaking, yes, he was. Simon, I know there's something going on. There must be. He's living in Chelsea, he's got a couple of racehorses, and a villa in some dreadful place in Spain. If he really was in the same syndicates as me, he wouldn't have any of that."

"Baby syndicates," said Simon, "must be. Buggers. What's his name?"

"He claims it's Edward Trafford Smythe."

"What do you mean, 'claims'?" said Simon, laughing. "God, you're like a tonic, Flora. I feel better already."

"What I mean is, I'd bet anything he's called just plain Smythe and some uncle or other was called Trafford. So common, that sort of thing. Anyway, I've arranged to have lunch with him next week. On Wednesday, at the Savoy. Are you free?"

"Free every day, unfortunately. Something for me to look forward to."

"So what do you want me to do?" asked Flora.

"I want you to act totally dumb, act like you're really impressed by him. I'll be there, apparently lunching with someone, and you can introduce us. Very casually. Ask me to join you. I'll take over after that see if we can trick him into saying something damning. It's worth a try, anyway."

"Fine. How exciting. I shall feel like Miss Moneypenny."

"Well, I don't feel too much like Bond, I'm afraid. So who's there with you—Debbie?"

"No, no, Debbie's in London. Working. But Richard's here. Going back on Sunday, I think."

Great, thought Richard. She was only telling Debbie's lover her husband was away and for how long. Although surely he'd have known. It was probably a clever ruse on Beaumont's part, to appear totally innocent in front of Flora. Debbie might even be with him now, egging him on, the pair of them laughing at him. A sudden lump rose in Richard's throat; he felt rather sick and very, very sad. He got up, turned away, started loading up the dishwasher. He was dangerously near tears.

"Sorry, Richard." Flora put the phone down. "But our solicitor says we have to find a smoking gun if we're to have a hope of bringing these people to justice, and Simon and I think we might be able to, with the help of Trafford Smythe. Oh, and a tape recorder."

"A tape recorder!"

"Yes. We think he's running some of these baby syndicates and we're going to try and trick him into saying so."

"What on earth are baby syndicates?"

"Usually they're little self-contained cells, inside the main syndicate, created for the underwriter's friends and relations. So they're nominally still in the Bloggs Group, or in our case Westfield Bradley, but when a particularly attractive bit of business comes along, they write it into the baby syndicate. It's absolute skulduggery. Richard, are you all right?"

"Yes, yes, I'm fine."

"Good. Yes, poor old Simon, he's taken a terrible pasting. It's so hard, having held a prominent position as he did—"

"Could we just stop talking about bloody Simon Beaumont?" Richard said, and he was almost shouting at her. "I don't want to—to—" he stopped.

Flora stared at him. "Yes, of course," she said calmly, "if you like. Sorry." A few seconds went by, then she said, very gently, "Is there some problem between you and Simon?"

"I . . . don't know," he said, and then the tears came. It was terribly embarrassing; he sat at his mother's kitchen table and buried his head in his hands. "I really don't know. I'm sorry."

"Don't apologise," said Flora. "Don't be silly. Do you want to talk about it?"

"No. Well—yes. Mother, you know him pretty well. Have you ever thought—had reason to think—there was something going on between him and Debbie?" There was a silence that seemed rather long to him, then; "Let's have a drink, shall we?" she said.

⁓

It had been her suggestion that they should meet at Fortnum's Soda Fountain: "I'll buy you tea. Lots of crumpets and things. In return for your advice."

"Nothing I like better than lots of crumpets. I'll be there."

Lucinda saw him coming in; got up, went over to him, and hugged him. "Darling Simon. So sweet of you to come. How are you?"

"Oh, not too bad considering. A lot better for seeing you."

"I can't believe that. I'm beginning to feel a bit portly."

"Well, you certainly don't look portly. Never was an adjective less suitable. Let's order, shall we, and then I can concentrate."

"I don't quite know where to begin," she said, shortly. "Milk in your tea?"

"A bit, please. What about the beginning?"

"Well, the beginning is me leaving Nigel. No, it's not, it's Lloyd's. As you know, Simon, he's going to be horribly badly hit, poor angel."

"Indeed."

"Steve Durham and I have put our heads together and come up with something quite clever."

"Who's Steve Durham?"

"My solicitor."

"Right. Go on."

"Well, we thought—Simon, you won't talk to anyone about this, will you? It's a bit . . . delicate."

"Of course I won't."

"Anyway, what we thought was that I should get as much from Nigel by way of a settlement as I possibly could."

"Difficult, I'd have thought. You're not exactly the innocent party, my darling, are you?"

"No, of course not. But Steve has managed to make things look a bit more as if I am. And he thinks I can get the house, because Nigel made it over to me anyway, and he's said he wants me still to have it."

"Nigel! Is he involved in this deception?"

"Oh yes, very much so. He's finding it all very difficult, of course, because he's so terribly upright, but I've managed to persuade him. Anyway, he's saying things like he's worried the relationship might not last, that he feels I'm in a very vulnerable position, being pregnant and not married, and he wants me to be financially secure. And that he wants me to have the house at least. And then he put a lot of money in trust for me and Steve is arguing that it would be unreasonable to take it back at this stage. When I could be relying on it."

"I see. He's going to come over as a bit of a patsy, isn't he?"

"Maybe, but it'll be worth it. And then there was another angle Steve thought of—that maybe I'd given things up when I married Nigel, a job, for instance. And of course I did. I was working for an artist, as his sort of PA. Sweet man, called Virgil Barrymore. Anyway, he did ask me to go with him when he moved to New York and I didn't because I was marrying Nigel."

"Ye-es."

"And the thing is that Virgil's paintings sell for squillions now, and I could have been working on a percentage, earning ten percent of a squillion. And been financially independent. Virgil's coming over to London next month, and he's going to—well, I hope he's going to—agree to say that."

"Lucinda," said Simon, "this is rather incredible. You're a very clever girl."

"No, I'm not. Steve thought of most of it. I'm just—well, maybe a bit ingenious."

"Very ingenious. So let's say you win, and you get all this money, and the house—then what?"

"Well, then, first of all, we set up some kind of educational trust. A charity that benefits poor deprived children. And some of the income will come from property which the trust owns. Including the house in Cadogan Square. I'll borrow against it and put all the money into that. And Nigel will be able to get at it, you see; he'll be one of the major trustees . . . It will have to be quite a complex process, but Steve is sure it can be done and Lloyd's won't be able to touch it. And Nigel will have lost everything—on paper. To me."

"Christ," said Simon, "I wish this man Durham was my lawyer."

"I'm sure he would be if you asked him. But yes, it is clever, isn't it? I mean, even if I don't get everything, Steve really thinks I'll get a lot. Which means Nigel will get a lot." She looked smug and started on the pile of smoked-salmon sandwiches.

"Hmm." Simon studied her. "There's only one thing that I don't get about it all. I mean, it's all very well Nigel saying he's worried the relationship won't last, but here you are, bursting with happiness, so why should any divorce judge believe all this guff about Nigel being afraid the relationship won't last."

"Well . . . oh dear, this is the difficult part, Simon. I've got to say I'm a bit worried about it too. About the relationship. Say I do feel insecure. I've got to put that in a letter. And also I certainly can't be living in some mansion that Blue's bought, because Nigel's also going to say that the little house where we are is most unsuitable for a baby. So we'll have to stay there until the thing's gone through. It has to look really good on paper, you see. I'm sure Blue won't mind, not really, that he'll go along with it if I explain properly. Well, I thought so at first. Now I'm not quite so sure."

"So he doesn't know anything about all this?"

"Well, no. I'm beginning to wish I'd told him about it in the first place, so he could get used to the idea slowly. But it's a bit late for that now. So I wondered what you thought about it, exactly how I should play it, so to speak."

"I think," said Simon carefully, "you have to tell him just the minute you can. Be completely honest. And I also think you have to be prepared for him minding quite a lot."

"Oh dear, do you?"

Simon thought of Blue, his pride in and love for Lucinda, his driving, pugnacious energy, his old-fashioned, working-class proprietary attitude and tried to imagine his reacting sympathetically to Lucinda's plan.

"I do, my darling, yes. I should get it over just as soon as you can, if I were you. Really soon. Before it's too late."

Chapter 32

"Oh God," said Debbie. "Oh God, oh God, oh God." She felt—what did she feel? Scared. Very scared. Shocked at herself, at what she had done. Disbelieving of what she had done. Excited, of course. Emotionally and sexually. And happy. Brilliantly, feverishly, shakily happy.

She was at her desk; the same desk she had been at twenty-four hours earlier, in the same office, and that in itself was hard to believe, that she was still sitting there, working, or supposedly working; that the world had not dropped from its axis, time had not speeded up nor stood still; that all around her people were working and chatting and laughing and fret-ting, doing the same sort of things in the same sort of way, as she was pre-sumed to be doing. And she looked the same—she kept checking that, for reassurance, getting the mirror from her drawer, looking at her face, scared of what it might show.

And she sounded the same; she kept hearing herself saying things like, "I'm fine, thanks," and "I'll get that release off today," and "Yes, of course I can run off that presentation document."

And yet, everything had changed.

She was no longer nice—or quite nice—respectable Debbie Fielding, married happily—or quite happily—to Richard, mother of three chil-dren, struggling to keep her family and her job and her husband all going in the same direction. She was Debbie Fielding, adulteress; she had a lover, a man who was not her husband, who she had been to bed with, and she couldn't wait to do so again, and she felt really bad and really wonderful in equal proportions and at the same time . . .

He had been waiting for her at the Criterion. Careful not to appear wretched, she had put on lots of makeup, rushed out and bought herself a new shirt at Next, rather than the shabby T-shirt she'd pulled over her tear-stained face, been ready with a lighthearted version of her story. He'd asked her what she wanted to drink: "White wine spitzer, please," she said (it took a lot of those to make her drunk), and after ordering it and a beer for himself, Joel had sat just looking at her for a minute and then said, "You look great."

"I don't think so."

"No, you do. I mean it. So want to talk about it? Whatever's upsetting you so badly?"

"Not . . . not really."

"In that case," he said, grinning, "you've got me here under false pretences, Mrs. Fielding—"

"Don't call me that. Mrs. Fielding is my mother-in-law."

"Sorry. OK, what shall we talk about instead?"

"Um . . . not sure." This was awful; her mind was a blank, she couldn't think of a word to say; she stared into her glass, feeling hot and cold and thoroughly miserable. She should never have come, she'd just drink the spritzer and then go, and—

"Mind out what you're bloody doing."

It was Fate: Fate in the form of a man, slightly the worse for the hour or so he had already spent in the bar, pushing past them, knocking Joel's arm, and thus the contents of Joel's bottle of beer over Debbie. Over quite a lot of her, but most markedly, her chest.

"Oh God, I'm so sorry," said the man. "God. Here, let me get a cloth from the bar, wait there . . ." He disappeared.

Joel sat looking at Debbie rather ruefully, and then pulled a handkerchief out of his pocket and started dabbing at her jacket. "I'm sorry. How awful."

"Oh, doesn't matter. Honestly. It's an old shirt." About three hours old; nicely ruined. The man reappeared, with two clean tea towels.

"Give those to me," she said, and made for the ladies', where she applied lots of cold water, but the stain was quite bad. And the smell. Well, best thing was to make her excuses and leave. She went back to the bar, to where Joel was sitting, looking rather depressed.

"Look, I think I'd better just go home. I can't sit here, smelling of Budweiser or whatever it was for the rest of the evening."

"Oh, OK." He was clearly miserable about the way the evening was turning out. He drained his glass. "I'll escort you to the tube."

They walked out into the evening sunshine; or rather the petrol-induced haze that was Piccadilly Circus at the end of a hot day.

A bunch of girls walked past, giggling and chattering, carrying Miss Selfridge bags; Joel looked after them. Debbie felt irritated and still more depressed; they were all young, pretty, clearly unencumbered by husbands or babies.

"Nothing like a bit of retail therapy," Joel said.

"Well, no," said Debbie.

"You know, I don't mind shopping. Maggie—she's my girlfriend—says it's one of my few virtues."

OK, he had a girlfriend. Well. Of course he would have done.

"But I mean—what bloke wouldn't like it?" he said. "Hanging around with crowds of women, preferably near the changing room. Great."

"I don't think my husband sees it quite like that," said Debbie. And thought how wholesome the conversation had become, him talking about his girlfriend, her talking about her husband.

"In fact," Joel was looking at her now and smiling, "it's Thursday, isn't it? Late-night shopping. Let me buy you a new shirt."

"Oh Joel, no."

"Oh Debbie, yes. Come on, it'll make me feel better, less guilty. What's your favourite shop? I'll enjoy helping you choose. And hanging round the changing room." Suddenly she felt more cheerful. It would be fun. *He* was fun.

"All right," she said, "you're on. But you're not paying for it."

"I am. But we can argue about that later."

They went to Miss Selfridge, the big one inside Selfridges itself. It was full of lovely sexy tops, strappy T-shirts, denim shirts, boned corselettes; none of which remotely replaced the shirt. It was also full of young girls, with their bosoms breaking out of their tops and their long legs bare. Joel began to feel slightly dizzy.

"That's nice," he said, pointing at a strapless, clingy dress, very, very short.

"It is," she said, "it's totally gorgeous, but I don't see it in the office."

"I don't know. Might get the clients pouring in even faster. Try it on. Go on." She came out of the changing room smiling. She had an amazing smile, it was that big mouth of hers and those perfect white teeth. She was a bit like Julia Roberts . . . Joel! Come on! The dress looked incredible on her. She was very skinny, and it only came about a quarter of the way down her thighs, so that he was able to see more of her legs. Her really rather amazing legs.

"You should get it," he said.

"You think?"

"Sure. Turn around. Give us a twirl."

She twirled, laughing, and then it happened: the dress, which really required more of a bosom than she possessed, slipped, and for a moment, maybe five moments, Joel found himself staring at her breasts. Which were small, OK, but absolutely perfect: firm, dark-nippled . . .

Joel had never liked big breasts. Well, not as much as he liked small ones. He swallowed, felt a response, a very strong response, it threatened to become embarrassing, and tried to tear his eyes away. And then she hitched up the dress, and her eyes met his, half startled, half amused, and—something else? what? something slightly carnal—she disappeared into the changing room. She reappeared, wearing a white cotton shirt, slightly oversized, the sort Princess Diana had worn and made famous last year, photographed with the princes.

"I think this is a bit more suitable," she said.

"Well, it's great," Joel said, "but I still think you should buy the dress."

"Well, I don't," she said firmly. "That is no dress for a—a mother."

"But Debbie, you don't look like a mother."

"I *am* a mother. I'm not ashamed of it."

"I know you're not. But mothers look mumsy. You look—well, like a very sexy girl. Who should be wearing that dress. Go on, get it."

"Joel, I'm not buying it."

"OK. Let's get the shirt. I'll pay."

"You won't."

"I will. I really do want to. Now are you going to leave it on?"

"Yes, I am. Get rid of the smell of bitter or whatever it was."

"It was not bitter," he said. "I have my pride. It was Michelob."

"Is that a trendy beer?"

"Very trendy. Ask your husband."

"He wouldn't know a trendy beer if—if it was chucked all over him," she said, and then, "I didn't say that."

"Yes, you did. Sorry."

She was happy and easy now, an intimacy forged by the shopping experience.

"Come on," he said, "let's buy ourselves a picnic and go up to the park." He watched her struggling with this, knowing that he shouldn't have asked her, and half hoping she'd say no.

She didn't: she grinned at him. "OK," she said.

So they went back into Selfridges and bought some French bread and pâté and strawberries and a bottle of white wine and got a cab up to Regent's Park. Where they settled on the grass, near one of the ponds, and Joel opened the wine and the sun was warm, slanting through the trees, and they set out their picnic, chatting easily about work and colleagues and films they had seen and their ambitions and even those of their partners, and he thought how lovely she was and what fun—interspersed with thoughts of how lovely her breasts were, and how good her legs, and how much he would like to see the bit in between, only clearly he wasn't going to. And thought that really the evening should end like this: happy, flirty, quite safe.

And then she lay back on the grass, clearly just slightly drunk, flung her arms out to the sides, and said, "Oh, this is such fun."

And he suddenly wanted to know a bit more about her. He leaned over her, smiling down at her, and said, "S-o-o . . . what was the matter? This afternoon?" She shouldn't have told him that either; she shouldn't have become so relaxed, so happily reckless.

"Oh, it's totally silly," she said. "I can't go into it all. But we fell out weeks ago, over his new job—he got one in Scotland."

"And let me guess, you didn't want to go to Scotland."

"Well, not terribly. And unfortunately, I sort of said that. And then the other day he saw me leaving a hotel with Simon—"

"With Simon?"

"Yes."

"What hotel?"

"The Royal Garden. And—and he decided we must be having an affair. It's just ridiculous!"

"Is it?"

"Well, of course."

"I'll tell you something," he said, "if I saw you leaving the Royal Garden Hotel with Simon Beaumont, I'd probably think you were having an affair as well."

"But why?"

"You can't be that dumb," he said.

"But he's miles older than me, and he likes things like horses and drives a Range Rover and—"

"Dear God," said Joel, and he started to laugh. "If that was your defence, I really am beginning to feel very sorry for your husband."

"But why?"

"Debbie, Simon Beaumont is extremely charming and incredibly good-looking, added to which he's a smooth bastard and—"

"No, he's not," said Debbie heatedly.

"He must seem so, to your husband. And he's successful—"

"Not anymore."

"No, OK, not anymore. Nice set of knives to twist in a husbandly wound though."

"But it was broad daylight, and we'd only had a drink."

"Did you know that fifty percent of adulteries are committed at lunchtime? In hotels. When it's usually broad daylight, it must be said. Dear oh dear. Poor old Richard. There you are, so lovely and sexy and funny and fun—of course the poor chap's jealous. Of any man who comes near you. You must see that. I mean, there you are coming out of a hotel with a particularly fine example of one. Man, I mean, not hotel. Give the poor guy a break."

She felt rather odd suddenly. Odd and very disturbed. But more than anything, cross.

"Joel, I'm afraid you don't understand at all," she said, trying to sound cool. "And it's not really anything to do with you. As far as I can see. Look, we'd better go, it's getting very late and—"

"It is something to do with me," he said. "Because you did, at some stage, agree to tell me about it. Because you were crying this afternoon, so you're obviously upset. And I like you enough to mind about that. Because I think you've been quite foolish. Actually."

"Just shut up, will you. I don't want to listen to a lecture from you, I have quite enough of those already. Everyone does it—"

"Well, I'm not surprised," he said, "actually. When you're so—so dense."

"I am not dense!"

"Yes, you are. Irresistibly, sexily, gloriously dense."

Debbie scowled at him; he looked at her, his dark eyes snapping with amusement. "You are so . . . so . . ." she said.

"What? So what?"

"Rude," she said. "Really, really rude. I don't know what I'm doing here. Why I came out with you at all."

Joel began to laugh; then he reached up and caught her hand.

She tried to pull her hand free. "Don't."

He hung on to it, still laughing, then said, suddenly more serious, "I'll tell you what you're doing here, and why you came out with me. Because you bloody well wanted to. You wanted to be with me, like I want to be with you. You may not have wanted it quite as much as I did, but I think you knew exactly what you were doing—shit, Debbie, stop glaring at me like that."

"What do you expect me to do?" she said furiously. "Smile dotingly at you?"

"You could try," he said, and then he leaned forward and kissed her. On the mouth. Quite hard.

And she sat there and wanted to push him away, to slap him, to stalk off to the road and into a cab—but she couldn't. Because his mouth, working on hers, his tongue, seeking out hers, was having an extraordinary effect on her. She felt it, that mouth, felt it in her whole head, which was throbbing suddenly. And in her breasts now—how could a kiss, a kiss on the lips, reach your breasts, but it had, it was making them desperate for touching, for caressing, for kissing too, and it was all she could do not to reach for one of his hands and place it there. And then the sensation moved on, lower, lower, somewhere in the region of her stomach, or even, oh God, yes, even there, and she felt herself grow sweetly soft and liquid and still the darts of pleasure moved on, travelling as if on fine, piercing threads, broadening now, making their way through her, pushing, reaching, parting her on their way, until she was entirely consumed by them and all she could think of was how quickly she might be able to answer them, to respond, and when Joel said, "Shall we go back to my place then?" any other answer but, "Yes," was unthinkable. Absolutely, gloriously, emphatically unthinkable.

Chapter 33

She really hadn't wanted to tell anyone yet; she wanted to keep it safe, safe from everybody's eyes and opinions; she didn't want it discussed and pronounced upon, she didn't want to be warned about it, told it was too soon or too much, didn't even want to be congratulated. It was nothing to do with anybody else, when the next step was so far into the future; it was her treasure, to be locked safely away for her eyes only, a source of happiness to be drawn on when she needed it.

She didn't say anything to her parents; simply that she had had a lovely time, that Jamie had been totally wonderful, that his family was great (although his mother could be difficult), that she had loved Boston and adored Cape Cod, and that she couldn't believe it was actually over.

Two days later, Annabel couldn't bear it any longer. She'd had a phone call from Jamie.

"Please, please let me tell the family. They haven't stopped talking about you since you left, how much they loved you, how right for me you were."

She hesitated, then: "All right, but not till I've told mine. I'll fax you when I've done it."

Her parents were having a drink together in the garden; Annabel went out to them. She had her ring on, her hands in her pockets.

"Hi. Mind if I join you?"

"Of course not. Don't be silly."

She sat down, took a glass of wine. "Thanks. How's it going, Dad?"

"Oh, you know. Fine. Lot of people inviting me to lunch."

"Good. You'll be back in work in no time then."

"Could be." He grinned at her; his usual confident grin. She was comforted. In spite of her total faith in him, she had been worrying.

"And then we won't have to sell the house?"

"Possibly not."

"Great. Um . . . I want to tell you something."

"Ye-es?"

She took her left hand out of her pocket, held it out to them. "Do you like that?"

They looked at it in silence; then: "It's lovely, darling," her father said, "absolutely lovely. Er . . . any significance in the finger?"

"Just a bit," she said. "Jamie's asked me to marry him." There was another silence; then her mother went over to her, hugged her.

"Darling," she said, "how absolutely lovely for you. I'm thrilled. Congratulations."

And her father said, "Sweetheart, that's wonderful news. Lovely. I'll get some champagne. Pity the others aren't here."

That was all they said about it, either of them; they just sat there in the lovely warm evening drinking champagne, and let her talk endlessly about Jamie and how much she loved him and how happy she was.

"I know you'll think we're too young, but we're not. I just know it's right. He's so—so perfect and it's perfect. I do hope you're happy about it."

"Darling, of course we are," her father said, kissing her.

"It's lovely to see you so happy," her mother said. "Now tell us more about the family, they obviously made a big impression on you."

Days later, when Jamie phoned to say how thrilled his parents had been, how his mother wanted to know when Annabel could come over for an engagement party, that they assumed it would be quite a long engagement ("At least two years, Mother thought, and I guess that's about right"), that they loved the thought of having her living in Boston with them, that of course she must bring her parents when she came over for the party, and her brother and sister too, and when might the party in London be, what London papers were they announcing it in, they thought they'd put it in *The Boston Globe* and maybe *The Washington Post*, and that his mother was writing to Elizabeth "right now" . . . all through that phone call, almost against her will, she kept contrasting the reactions of their two sets of parents and thinking how lucky, how very lucky she was.

℘

The air was soupy with warmth: that was Joel's first impression of Nassau; it was like a warm cosh as you got off the plane. The second, as he trav-

· 318 ·

elled through it in a cab on his way to Paradise Island, was of a kind of charming toy town, with its packed streets and sudden squares, its wonderful colonial-style buildings and its policemen dressed in gold-braided white uniforms with white pith helmets and white gloves, constantly and rather ineffectually blowing whistles and shouting at traffic; and endless horse-drawn carriages painted in a rainbow of different colours, driving tourists round the city. The noise was astonishing: car horns set on permanent "go," roaring motorbikes, shouting children, and an incredible mishmash of music—reggae, rock, and the native soca—coming not only from the cars but from the stereo systems carried on the shoulders of teenage boys, the grinning, cheerful teenage boys.

He had tried and failed to book into the Ocean Hill Hotel on Paradise Island where the Bridgeman party were staying; having discovered the cost for even two nights, he was quite relieved. All the hotels on the island had been fully booked; he had had to settle for the Palace, in Nassau itself. It was hardly slumming it; it was pink-and-white and colonial in concept, although its 170 rooms (as against the Ocean Hill's mere 70) spoke for its lower caste. But it would provide him with a base from which to inveigle himself into the Ocean Hill; and if he failed to collar Allinson, he would have the very slight consolation of knowing he had saved several hundred pounds.

Even so, the investment in the trip had been considerable; he had bought some extremely expensive clothes—a linen suit from Armani, some shoes from JP Tod's—befitting of a guest at one of the most expensive hotels in the world, and some horrendously expensive leather luggage from Mulberry. It had better be worth it as he was paying for it all himself.

That was before he had discovered he couldn't get into the Ocean Hill. Bit of a waste, he supposed: but it would last him a lifetime. And in his pocket a new leather wallet, also from Mulberry—a present from Debbie.

"That's to make sure you think of me at least every time you spend any money. Which I daresay will be quite often."

"I'll think of you all the time," he said, kissing her. "I don't need a wallet to make me do that."

He checked in, established that the hotel ran a limo service—he could hardly arrive at the Ocean Hill in one of Nassau's rackety taxis—booked one for the evening and another for the following day, and went down to the palm-lined pool for a swim. He longed to go to bed, but he had to survive until the cocktail hour at the very least. He'd decided that would be the easiest way to collar Allinson. He was still there; Joel had phoned and checked before even leaving London.

"God, you must have fun doing your job," said Debbie enviously. "It's like a James Bond movie."

"Oh, it is. Especially when I'm in bed with very beautiful girls, which I am all the time, of course."

He was worried about Debbie; he knew he had walked into quicksand. It had to be stopped: now. Before he got in any deeper. He'd call her when he got back and they could part, friends still, loving, sexy friends after a sweet but very short adventure. He was good at those sorts of partings: always had been, seemed to have the knack of keeping emotions at bay. Probably because he'd been doing exactly that all his life. It had been sweet though, and the sex had been amazing. She had been extraordinarily . . . driven. That was the only word for it. Fiercely determined to give—and to get—pleasure. And pleasure there had been, in abundance.

Chapter 34

"I really liked that house," said Blue. He was sitting at the table, drinking whiskey; he smiled at her, patted the chair next to him. "Come and join me. You never settle these days."

This was the time to tell him: to explain why they couldn't move. And if he was really angry, well, that was her own fault. But . . .

"Which house?" she said, playing for time.

"The one in Weybridge—the one we saw this afternoon."

"What, the one without a swimming pool? But I thought you wanted a pool."

"We can install a pool, Lucinda. It's not very difficult."

"But is there room?"

"Of course there's bloody room. That garden is almost two acres.

Now I know I said Surrey wasn't ideal and it isn't, not for me, worse journey, but I liked the area and I think it'll be good for you and the boy."

Come on, Lucinda, say it. Get it over. He can't kill you.

"I think we should put in an offer straightaway. Then we can move in, hopefully, in a couple of months. Three at the latest."

"Blue, I'll be having the baby in three months. I really won't want to move then. I do wish you'd agree to let us wait. And Blue, there's something—"

"Lucinda, this is beginning to get on my nerves. I'm fairly patient but you are testing me rather."

Now she'd missed her chance; he was irritable already. So—not just now. Wait for the next good mood.

"What on God's earth is the point in waiting? It's not as if the house is in a bad state, it seems fine to me. Just needs redecorating. It's even got a nursery."

"With Peter Rabbit wallpaper," said Lucinda witheringly.

"What the fuck's wrong with Peter Rabbit? Thought you liked all that sort of thing. And I just said redecorate, didn't I? Or did I not? Bloody change it before you do anything else."

"Oh, stop swearing!" cried Lucinda. "You know I hate it. And I hated that house and I don't want to move into it."

"Lucy, you said you loved it. At the time. What's the matter with you?" Lucinda hesitated. She had actually liked the house rather a lot. It was big and rambly, with huge sunny rooms, gorgeous parquet floors, a massive ranch-like kitchen with an Aga in it, and a wonderful garden, with an almost wild woodland area, furthest from the house. She could already see herself and a little two-year-old person, holding her hand, toddling through the long grass. It was perfectly lovely. But she couldn't have Blue buying it before the divorce went through. She really couldn't.

"I don't want to move yet. I just don't."

"OK. We'll buy it and move in after the boy's born. Have our first Christmas there. How would that be?"

It was hugely tempting: but Steve Durham would be furious. "No," she said, "no, I can't, Blue. I don't want to even think about moving until after I've had the baby. I wish you could get that into your head."

"Oh for God's sake," he said, "I give up. I just bloody give up. I've never heard such fucking rubbish. I'm going out."

And he was gone, slamming the front door behind him. Lucinda looked after it, quite frightened. She did seem to have made a mess of things . . .

❧

"This is an amazing place," said Joel.

"Isn't it? Never been here before then?"

"No."

"Of course, it's even better in the winter. When it's less humid, slightly cooler. And—it must be said—a little chicer. But, well, our host wanted to bring us here now. And who am I to complain?"

He grinned at Joel; Joel grinned back. He could see how Tim Allinson had done so well; he was charming, easy to talk to, amusing, self-deprecating. He could hardly believe how simple it had been, making contact with him. He'd arrived at the hotel, just as the rich darkness was falling, made his way to the cocktail bar, ordered a Bellini, and asked the barman if he knew a Mr. Allinson. "In Mr. Bridgeman's party," he added, handing the man some credentials, lest he think Joel was some kind of fraudster, trying to muscle in on the guests.

"Yes, sir, I do. He usually comes down around now."

"Good."

He settled in a corner with his Bellini, enjoying the sunset, watching the flow of people into the bar. The drink made him sleepy; he swallowed a handful of nuts, desperately trying to pump up his energy level. Half an hour, three-quarters went by, the Bellini long drunk; he asked for a Virgin Mary, afraid of what further alcohol might do to him. A waiter brought it over; then he noticed the barman saying something to some-one, pointing him out. And Tim walked over to him, smiling. It was as simple as that.

"Sorry," said Joel pleasantly holding out his hand, "Joel Sherlock. You probably want some peace and quiet, after a long hard day here."

"No, no it's fine. I'm sorry, I'm not sure . . ."

"I think you knew my uncle," Joel said, "Peter Sherlock. He's a banker, with Chase, in New York. He said if I ran into you here, to say hi." He thought of his real uncle, Mick Strickland, white-van man and occasional wife beater. What would Tim Allinson make of him?

· 322 ·

Allinson frowned briefly. "Oh—possibly. Does ring a faint bell. How is he?"

"Pretty well, thanks. Yes."

"Give him my best wishes, won't you?"

"Of course."

He obviously left no contact unturned, real or otherwise.

"Anyway, nice to meet you. You staying here?"

"Sadly not, couldn't get in. Staying at the Palace. It's not too bad—and I'm only here for forty-eight hours."

"Oh, really? You working?"

"You could say that. I'm in the export business; my company's got certain interests out here."

"Oh, OK. Well, not a bad place to find yourself. Where do you live?"

"Oh, London—Kensington. And I've got a house in Berkshire." Allinson turned just imperceptibly towards Joel, and at the same time sat back in his chair. He clearly found him worth a little time and attention.

"So—working holiday?"

"Indeed. Monday I'm off to San Francisco. But I'm taking tomorrow off, exploring the place. That's why I came up here tonight, see if it was worth spending it here, or whether I should stay in downtown Nassau."

"Oh, here, I'd say. Definitely. It really is marvellous. Not just the hotel, that is, but the whole island. You should go out to Paradise Beach, do a bit of parasailing. It's a bit naff, but great fun. And—" A noisy group had come into the bar, two men of about fifty, and two extremely well-endowed and well-tanned blondes; they waved at Tim. He waved back. "Be over in a minute." A pause, then: "Mine hosts. Very nice, very nice indeed, but . . . well, you know. Quite exhausting." His eyes met Joel's in the flattery of conspiracy: "we know, you and I, what's what," that look said. "I'd ask you to join us," Tim said, "but—"

"No, no, I'm having dinner with someone at my hotel. In fact, I must get back there now. Now that's what I call impressive," Joel added. An extremely tall and beautiful girl had walked into the bar; she was tanned deep olive, not the slightly bright brown of the other two, and she was wearing a long, brilliant print silk dress, modestly cut at the front, outrageously low at the back and slit up the sides. A gleaming dark rope of hair hung over one shoulder in a plait; she was a class act if ever Joel had seen one. She waved at Tim and walked over to him.

"Hi, Tim."

"Hello, my darling. Come and meet a new friend. Joel Sherlock. Joel—Bibi, star of *Vogue, Harper's Bazaar,* and God knows what else. Joel's just visiting. Slumming it at the Palace."

"That's a shame." Bibi smiled at him. She had a low, slightly husky voice, with the obligatory American overtone to her Italian accent. She was gorgeous.

"Yes. Well, I'm thinking of spending tomorrow up here."

"Oh, really? Well, it's pretty nice. Isn't it, Timmy?" Her eyes met Tim's. "Although I'm a little tired tonight. I thought I might take tomorrow off, not go out on the yacht."

"Do you know, my darling, I thought the same. A little of our young rocker friend goes a long way."

"Although not as far as Thandie would like, I think. Anyway, I'd better go and join them. Nice to meet you, Mr. Sherlock."

"I'd better be off too," he said. "Maybe I'll see you tomorrow then? This is a great place for cocktails."

"You might well. In fact, if you're at a loose end at lunchtime, come and find me. They do a marvellous poolside buffet."

"Thanks. Very good of you. Nice to have met you anyway." He shook Tim's hand, waved at Bibi, and then went out to his limo. Fate seemed not only to be on his side but to have picked him as her only teammate.

Debbie was hanging out the washing when Richard arrived home. She had spent the whole weekend in an orgy of housekeeping, had vacuumed and polished and dusted, washed paintwork, changed all the beds—and even done some weeding. She wasn't sure why, since she had no interest in pleasing Richard; she supposed it was so that he would have less to berate her with, when and if he came home.

It was a bit like being in a film; she kept looking at herself in various mirrors as she went around the house, and thought she looked much too ordinary to find herself in such a situation; she needed to look interesting, glamorous, mysterious, with a suntan and big hair . . .

"Hello."

She jumped, dropped two of the pegs. It was Richard; he had come through the French windows that led from the kitchen. She looked at him and struggled to appear at least politely pleased to see him, while wishing desperately he was going to be away another five days. Or five weeks. Or five years. How could you live with a person who made you feel like that?

"Hi. Good journey?"

"Yes, it was OK, thanks. I was going against the traffic, of course. Terrible going the other way. Especially at the M5 turnoff." He yawned.

"Were the children all right?"

"Yes. Let's go inside, shall we."

"Must we? It's lovely out here."

"Yes, we must. I want to talk to you."

"We can talk out here."

"Debbie, I want to go inside, all right?"

She followed him, wondering, half hoping indeed, if this might be the beginning of the end.

℮⁊

"Richard has got it into his head that you and Debbie are having an affair," said Flora.

They were sitting on the stone bench in the Meadow; below them the sea was calm, brilliantly smooth, and blue. Simon felt quite dizzy.

"He what?"

"Yes. He's very upset."

"Christ," he said, staring at her. "Christ Almighty, how—how absurd."

"It is a bit."

"But—why? I don't understand."

"Apparently he saw you and her coming out of a hotel last week. And she was kissing you and you were hugging her."

"Flora, that's insane. I hug and kiss everybody—it's what I do. I've been known to hug and kiss you—would you like to suggest you're having an affair with me? Maybe that would distract him."

"I know that. Of course. But Richard doesn't. He's a very, very jealous person, Simon. Like his father. And he was saying how much you obviously liked her, right from the start, how he noticed some sort of chemistry between you."

· 325 ·

"What!"

"Anyway, I did my best. Told him it was absurd. But I think he thought I was holding something back."

"Flora! For Christ's sake. What was there to hold back?"

"Nothing, of course," she said. She didn't meet his eyes.

"Bloody right there's nothing. Unless you are thinking of that moment in the kitchen a few months ago. In which case, let me tell you I was extremely upset and Debbie was . . . well, simply trying to make me feel better."

"Which is precisely what I thought. I did see you, of course, but I can recognise incipient sex when I see it."

"Good phrase, Mrs. Fielding." Simon smiled for the first time. "And the other night, she'd heard about my being fired and offered to buy me a drink. That's all. So what did you actually say?"

"That I was sure nothing could be further from the truth and that I had never been given any cause to think it."

"Well, thank you for that."

"But I'm not sure he believed me. Altogether. The thing is, Simon, you and Debbie are quite close, there is some chemistry between you—he's right in that."

"So what do you suggest?" he said. "Any denial would be incriminating. He's obviously mad, I know he's your son, but—"

"I don't think he's mad," said Flora. "I think he's very unhappy. I think Debbie hasn't been as supportive as she might be, although I can see she's having a very difficult time."

"What, over this Scottish business? Yes, she told me about that. Bit of a mess."

"There you are, you see," said Flora. "You seem to know a lot about each other. I agree he's leaping to absurd conclusions but I do have to say, I can see—just about—how that has happened. Maybe that's what he's picked up."

"Dear sweet Jesus," he said, "and I thought you were my friend."

"I *am* your friend, Simon. I feel desperately sorry about the whole thing, and I wish I could help more."

"So where is Richard now?"

"On his way back to London. To see Debbie."

"Oh God," said Simon wearily. "What a fucking mess."

That he didn't apologise to Flora for his language showed her how extremely upset with her he was.

❧

Joel had never tried parasailing; it was fantastic, rather like flying very slowly through the warm air. After that he went out on a Jet Ski a couple of times, snorkelled for half an hour; and then changed into shorts, polo shirt, and deck shoes, put his wet swimming shorts into his rucksack, and made his way up to the Ocean Hill. It was still only half past twelve, far too early to appear for lunch. The rich lunched late. He went into the bar, got himself a glass of ice water, and wandered outside to explore the grounds. They were spectacular, terraced gardens, complete with statues, lush green lawns, brilliant flowers, a great swathe of tennis courts, a large lake, and what looked like a chapel.

"Incredible, isn't it?" It was Bibi. "Hi. I saw you wandering round the courts. Tim and I were contemplating a game, but the standard seemed a little high. McEnroe was the last person to play here."

"Sounds challenging," said Joel, laughing.

"Just a little bit. What are you doing now? Timmy's gone to change."

"Oh, just exploring."

"Oh, OK. Well, I'll maybe see you by the pool. That'd be nice."

"Indeed."

She smiled at him. Her eyes lingered, rather pointedly, on his mouth. Confusing. Very confusing.

"I'll see you later then," she said. "Oh look, there's Timmy coming now." And she leaned towards him and kissed him briefly, but quite firmly, on the mouth.

"Tell me," said Joel to Allinson when he had greeted him, "what on earth is that place over there? That looks like a chapel."

"A chapel, my boy. Genuine late twentieth century."

Joel nodded. If nothing else came of this trip, it would make a fantastic travel piece. They walked across the drive to the chapel: it was purest kitsch, complete with stained-glass windows.

"Big favourite for Nassau brides," said Allinson. "Can you wonder?"

They strolled back to the hotel, changed, and then went down to the pool, which was set in the heart of the gardens. Waiters scuttled about ready to do their masters' bidding.

"Right. Buffet's over there, or you can order off the card. I usually have a club sandwich, they're excellent. And what about a beer?"

"Good idea," said Joel. "This is very kind of you."

"Oh, not at all. Nice to have you to talk to."

"Is Bibi around?"

"She's gone to have a nap. She doesn't eat."

"Today I do." Bibi flopped down on a lounger next to Joel, removed her bikini top, and started to apply sun lotion to her breasts. They were incredible: full, but very firm. Joel tried not to stare at them, but she saw him trying and smiled, before closing her eyes and surrendering herself to the sun.

"So, what exactly does your company do?" said Allinson.

"We import glass and fine china. Which I'm sure you know have a huge sale here."

"Oh right. Interesting. And where do you manufacture?"

"Mostly in the north of England, but we also have a factory in Limoges." Joel had just happened to read an article in one of the in-flight magazines about the pottery and porcelain of Limoges, and had added it to his story. "And then we have another line, completely different—linen. We buy a lot from Russia, sell it to hotels, mostly American."

"Uh-huh. Family company, is it?"

"Yup. My grandfather started it. I enjoy it, but it's hard work."

"Most ways of making money are. Mine host now, he works like the proverbial black. One mustn't say that anymore, of course. But eleven months of the year, pretty well eighteen hours a day, he's at his desk."

"What does he do there?"

"He manufactures nuts, bolts, screws, and so on. Supplies firms like that new IKEA place."

"I see."

"And the voluptuous Thandie is the third wife. She's very sweet, but a little exhausting."

"And where do you live?"

"I'm in the throes of trying to decide that. I'm contemplating Jersey or Guernsey, possibly New England."

He was obviously very rich then, Joel thought. Bastard. He'd been sinking beneath Allinson's charm; he remembered Gillian Thompson and Neil Lawrence and hauled himself briskly to the surface.

"And what do you do? God, this sun is hot, must find some sun lotion. Excuse me a second . . ." He rummaged in his rucksack, found the Ambre Solaire, and managed to switch on his tape recorder. He lay back again, smiled at Allinson. "Sorry. You were saying?"

"I wasn't. But I think you'd asked me what I do."

"Yup."

"Oh, a bit of this, bit of that. My family owned a textile company, which I inherited and then sold a few years ago. Invested the money in stocks and shares, which have more or less stood the test of time. Although Black Friday didn't do me much good."

"My uncle said he thought you worked for one of the banks."

"No, not really."

"Or was it Lloyd's? Lloyd's of London. Or was that wrong?"

"No, not entirely wrong. I wasn't a Working Name. I introduced people to Lloyd's, people I thought would benefit. Increased a lot of people's incomes for them."

"But you weren't a Name yourself?"

"Oh, I was, yes. For a while."

"I'd heard they were having a rough time."

"Who, Lloyd's? A little, yes. Nothing serious."

"I read something the other day about—what was it called?—asbestosis."

"You don't want to believe everything you read in the newspapers, dear boy. I can show you a great many people who are still making a lot of money from being Members of Lloyd's."

"I'm sure. God, this is nice. I'm in danger of drifting off. And I have to leave in about an hour. Might take a quick dip."

"And I'm going to find some cigarettes. See you later."

It was a risk; Allinson might find someone else to talk to. But he didn't want to appear as if he was interrogating him. He swam a couple of lengths, then paused, hanging on to the side at the deep end, breathing heavily. God, he was unfit. He was suddenly aware of a hand slithering into his trunks, caressing his buttocks.

"Hi," said Bibi. "Nice bum."

"Well, thanks."

She moved slightly, and moved her hand too, so that it was at the front of him, probing his pubic hair, seeking out his cock. His inevitably flaccid cock.

"Sorry," he said. "Cold water. Not a great aphrodisiac."

"That's OK," she said, and laughed. "Do you normally need aphrodisiacs?"

"Absolutely not."

"I didn't think so. It's very nice to see someone young here. A young man, anyway. They all seem to be a hundred. Except our friend the rocker, of course. How old are you, Joel?"

"Thirty-four."

"Uh-huh. Good age."

"I'm glad you think so. Er, here's Tim back again. I think we might get out."

"He's not my keeper," she said, and added, "or yours."

"No, of course not. But—"

"Go on then," she said. "I'll see you later." She set off towards the steps, pulling a sarong round her.

"That was great," Joel said, settling down again beside Allinson. "You going in?"

"No, too soon after lunch. Mind if I smoke?"

"Of course not."

Allinson produced a pack of cigarillos, lit one, inhaled deeply.

"So no truth in the rumours about Lloyd's then?" said Joel.

"None that troubled me," said Allinson easily.

"Now come on . . . Don't tell me you didn't know about it at all. I mean, why did you get out?"

"Well, there's no doubt it's going through something of a bad patch," Allinson said. "But you have to look at the big picture. Last bad patch was 1961. That's not a bad record."

"But you still encouraged people in? As did Lloyd's."

"Well, yes. It's a business, for God's sake. And it needed further investment. My job was to help them find that. Look, I don't know how you run your company, but I imagine you don't go round telling your customers about the mistakes you've made. That, let's say, several consignments of porcelain get smashed every year. You tell them you have a very small percentage of breakages."

"Correct."

"Well then. Lloyd's weren't about to tell a whole lot of prospective investors that they might get their fingers burned. That's not good business practice. They told them the truth—that the last time anyone lost a lot of money was twenty-five years ago."

"Oh, OK," said Joel slowly. "Very good."

"They took the view that any problems could be solved by substantial further investment, as I said. More Names, spread the risk. Which is where I came in."

"Excellent," said Joel. He grinned at Allinson. "I really admire that. Good presentation, as you say. Tell me, is it true you have to be superrich to be a Name?"

"It used to be. Lately they've lowered the bar considerably. Allowed much smaller people in. Who, of course, were delighted to join such a prestigious club . . ."

"Of course. Lot of snobbery there, I imagine. Which you could presumably cash in on."

"Indeed."

"Must have been fun."

"It was, actually. There is no doubt I brightened a lot of people's lives, and their bank accounts." He smiled at Joel.

"But have they continued to be brightened?"

"I hope so. I really don't follow them all up, you know." He paused. "You seem very interested in all this. Any particular reason?"

"Well, yes, to be honest. I had been considering joining myself, as a Name. Would you recommend it?"

There was a long silence; then Tim said, "Possibly not. Just at the moment. Give it a year or two, then talk to me. I'll give you my card."

"Great. But I thought you weren't involved anymore?"

"Not officially, no. But I can certainly put you in touch with the right people there."

"Thank you. I'd really appreciate that. In the fullness of time. So are you saying it's not true about the asbestosis?"

"My dear boy, I've told you. I don't worry about the detail."

"Of course not. Do you think they suspect it?"

"Who, the Lloyd's people? Some of them may, I suppose." He lay back, pulled his Panama hat over his eyes. "It's quite a strong rumour."

"But they need to keep the money coming in?"

"Absolutely. Only way to get by."

"And is it working?"

"Oh, too early to say. I hope so."

"And—you never find yourself lying awake at night, any of you?" Joel sat up now, moving in for the kill. Ready to run.

"Why should we? We've helped a lot of people make a lot of money."

"But not the ones you've hauled in over the past—what—seven years? They must be losing it now."

"I don't know that I like the phrase 'hauled in,' " said Tim rather stiffly. He was sitting up, looking at Joel.

"But that is what you've been doing, surely . . . And now it's all gone wrong and they're hopelessly in debt; people have actually killed themselves, you know. In despair. People who simply can't afford to meet the claims."

"That's ridiculous!" said Tim.

"It's not ridiculous. People whose lives have been ruined, completely ruined. Like—well, let's just take one person, shall we? Does the name Gillian Thompson mean anything to you?"

"It does not. And I think this conversation has gone on a little too long."

"Gillian Thompson was a nice old lady, Mr. Allinson, who gave piano lessons free and who baked you cakes when you went to see her about her investments. She killed herself in January—because there was nothing else for her to do. She was completely penniless, thanks to Lloyd's. She'd sold everything she had and it still wasn't nearly enough."

"I told you, I've never heard of Gillian Thompson."

"OK, so what about Neil Lawrence? Bankrupt, four children, attempted suicide. He was one of your imports too. Into the same syndicate, I understand. Obviously you have connections there. You don't remember his name?"

"Of course not."

"Well, he remembers yours. It's all right, I'm going. Immediately. But just before you drift off to sleep tonight, after another excellent dinner, spare a thought for those two, would you? And possibly the hundreds more you've duped. Here's some money—I think it will more than cover my lunch. Goodbye, Mr. Allinson. It's been very interesting talking to you. I can't say I've exactly enjoyed it, but I've certainly learned a lot."

Safely in a taxi, he pulled out the tape recorder. It was nearly all there, albeit rather crackling and muffled, Tim Allinson's complacent public-school tones providing the heart of his article. A devastating article. It had been worth all that money.

He went back to the Palace, showered, had a drink, and then ordered dinner in his room. He heard the trolley coming along the corridor before he had dressed; he was still naked under his bathrobe. That had been quick.

There was a knock on the door; he opened it. It was, indeed, room service, a nicely laid trolley, with a bottle of claret as he had requested. But the person pushing it was not one of the friendly waiters. It was Bibi.

"Hi," she said, "I see you're ready for me." And she shut the door behind her and started pulling his robe off; she stood looking at him, smiling, studying his body. "I see you weren't lying then," she said, her hand reaching out for his cock which was already—well, already appreciating her. "No aphrodisiacs necessary."

Chapter 35

The first thing he'd said, after sitting her down and making her a cup of tea, and while she was bracing herself to hear that he wanted a divorce, was, "I'm sorry." She was so surprised she knocked over her tea. By the time she had mopped the table, made another mugful, she had composed herself, felt able to cope with whatever he might say next.

"Start again."

"Yes, OK. I . . . I said I'm sorry. I think I overreacted. My mother helped me to see that. She said she was absolutely sure there was nothing going on between the two of you. She said she thought you and Simon were very fond of each other, but it was no more than that."

"I see. I did tell you that, Richard."

"Yes, I know you did. And I apologise. It was very . . . very wrong of me."

"I see," she said again. Thinking how wildly, absurdly ironic all this was. Because had he not accused her of the affair, had he not gone rushing down to Wales with the children, she would never have gone out with Joel that night. And their affair would never have begun . . .

She sat silent, wondering what on earth she could say.

"I know I haven't behaved entirely well," said Richard. "It was very wrong of me, lying about the job in Scotland. I'm sorry."

"It's all right," she said. "I've never stopped feeling bad about how I behaved either. I didn't want to go, but I knew how important to you it was, and I would have come. I really would."

"Really?"

"Yes."

"Then perhaps there is a way forward."

Panic hit her. "How?"

"Well, maybe we could still go. I want it so much, and I'm sure you'd love it. I know we've started badly with it, but . . ."

"I'm aware how much you want it," she said. "But . . . but I'd just like a bit of time. You know."

"What for?"

Could he mean that? Could he not realise how upset she'd been, how miserable. How he'd hit her below the belt again and again?

"I—" she said, but at the same time he spoke.

"Sorry. Of course I can see that you need time. I can wait, Debbie, try and make it up to you. And I was thinking maybe you could get a job up in Scotland. So you don't have to devote all your time to the school and everything. I mean, that was a bit unrealistic of me. I can see that. I know how much it matters to you, your job. I really do."

"Yes," she said, feeling still worse. "Yes, it does. Well, thank you. Um—another cup of tea?"

"Actually, I think I'd like something a bit stronger," he said. That was quite unlike him too.

"Debbie, my darling, it's Simon. Are you all right?"

"I'm fine, yes, thank you. It's very nice to hear from you."

"And can you talk?"

"Oh yes. Richard's gone for a job."

"Look, Flora told me about this absurd idea of your husband's—that we were having an affair. Are things any better?"

"Yes," she said after a pause. "He seems to have decided he's wrong about it all. In fact, he's apologised to me. For accusing me."

"Oh, really? Good."

"Yes. Flora seems to have been really fantastic. I can't quite work out how to thank her. I mean, she could have said . . . well, you know. Couldn't she?"

"She could. But she wouldn't have. Too sneaky. She's a class act, your mother-in-law."

"Yes. I don't quite know what to do though. It seems a bit odd to ring her up and say, 'Thank you for not telling my husband you found me and Simon snogging late one night.' But I'd like to say something."

"Darling! Not quite snogging. Although of course I wish we had been."

"You know what I mean," she said firmly.

"Yes, I do. And I think you should say absolutely nothing. Flora would consider it rather—what shall I say—rather suburban, making a big thing about it."

"Suburban?"

"Suburban."

"Oh God, she's such a snob," said Debbie.

"She is. And something of a time warp. But you can't help admiring her for it. I think she's rather wonderful."

"Yes, but she doesn't think *you're* common," Debbie said emphatically, "or suburban."

"Well, I should certainly hope not. I'm sure she doesn't think you are, either. So, what happens next—in the Debbie Fielding soap opera?"

"Don't call it that," she said sharply.

"Sorry. But do you and Richard disappear into a Scottish sunset together?"

"I don't know," she said, and her voice sounded very sad. And then, "Simon, it's lovely of you to call, but I'm terribly busy, I'm sorry."

That hurt; that hurt a lot. He'd been going to offer her lunch, a drink, hear how things were, advise her. But his role of confidant for her, which he'd rather enjoyed, seemed to be over. She was terribly busy, and he wasn't. Not at all.

"Of course," he said. "Well, just call me if you want to chat. About anything. I'll be very much around. As always. Maybe next week?"

"Yes, course, Simon. Thank you. I will."

But he knew she wouldn't. He couldn't quite work out why; but something had changed. Everything seemed to have bloody changed.

⁓

"You what!"

The roar was so loud the entire editorial floor heard it.

"You bloody arrogant little shit. Who the fuck do you think you are, taking it upon yourself to decide what stories you'll write! And against my explicit instructions. I told you, I don't want any bloody stories about Lloyd's. I told you several times."

"Yeah, I know. Hugh—"

"You can get out, all right? Today. Now."

"Yes, all right. But could you just read the first two hundred words, would you?"

"No, I will fucking not. Why should I read two hundred words on a subject I know will send our readers straight to sleep?"

"Because it won't. Because it really is hot stuff. Trust me."

"Why should I bloody trust you?"

"Because I'm telling you to. Go on. Two suicides and a con man. And a supermodel. In the Bahamas."

That was pushing it, but it might persuade him. Joel could see curiosity shifting his outrage—just a bit.

"Well, you can give it to me. But don't think it's going to change my mind."

"Of course not. Here you are."

He held out a page of copy. Renwick snatched it from him, stalked out, slamming the door behind him.

"Joel, it's me. Debbie."

"Oh—hi."

"I just wondered how it had all gone. If you got your story."

"Oh—yeah. Yeah, I did. It went really well. Got a lot on tape."

"Great. Well done."

"Thanks."

He sounded extremely distant and cool; she felt sick. Could this really be the same Joel she had been in bed with, gloriously in bed, only—what?—seventy-two hours ago? Best just finish the conversation as soon as possible.

"Good, I'm pleased. So, has the editor bought it?"

"I don't know yet. The early signs are that he hasn't. If being fired is anything to go by."

"Fired! You've been fired?"

"Yup. Supposed to be packing right now."

"Oh Joel. I'm so sorry."

"Thanks. Look—I don't want to sound rude, Debbie, but I have got rather a lot on my plate at the moment. Maybe later, yeah?"

"Yes, of course. Sorry."

"That's OK. Bye for now."

Debbie could never remember feeling so completely crushed. Or so stupid, Or so miserable. She put the phone down and, determined not to cry, addressed herself to a press release about a self-tanning lotion. It didn't prove much of a distraction.

❧

"Simon! Whoever would have thought I'd see you here! How are you? This is Edward Trafford Smythe. Great friend of my late husband's. Edward—Simon Beaumont."

"How do you do," said Trafford Smythe. He was rather florid, and he was wearing a striped shirt with a white collar. Very naff, as Annabel would say.

"How do you do," he said.

"Are you meeting someone, Simon?" asked Flora. "I suppose you are."

"No, I've met them and they've gone. Market makers," he said to Trafford Smythe, "busy afternoon ahead, playing with the Dow."

"Ah yes."

"Well, we've only just had our main course. Why don't you join us?" said Flora. "You wouldn't mind, would you, Edward?"

"No, of course not."

"Well, that's very kind. Let me at least pay my way, buy another bottle of wine. That one looks quite—tired. You look like a claret man to me," he said to Trafford Smythe. "Am I right?"

Trafford Smythe said he was.

Flora turned the conversation to horses for a while; Trafford Smythe was a great racegoer and he owned a couple of horses himself. By the time the second bottle of claret had disappeared—three-quarters of it into him—he was relaxed, slurring his words, inviting Simon down to the yard where he kept his horses.

"I'd love that. Thanks."

"And what do you do?"

"Me? Oh, I'm a banker. Yes. Work for Graburn and French."

"Very nice. They surviving the recession?"

"More or less. It's not easy of course, but—"

"Edward and my husband, William, were great friends," interrupted Flora. "He used to take William racing, didn't you, Edward? And he got me into Lloyd's. Which I'm trying to forgive him for. No, seriously, I can't possibly blame you."

"Oh really? You a Working Name?" said Simon.

"Absolutely. You had anything to do with them?"

"No, no. Bit too cautious."

"Ah well, things aren't too good at the moment, of course. But they'll pick up again. I told Flora she should be trading through, not pulling out. Increasing her underwriting, if anything."

"I've told him that's out of the question. Sadly. That I've got to sell the house."

"You know," said Trafford Smythe, "you shouldn't have to sell your house, Flora. Lloyd's don't want people out on the street, so to speak. Any more than they want them bankrupt."

"Is that so?" said Simon. "Well, Flora, maybe you'll be all right after all."

"Indeed," said Trafford Smythe. "You'd do far better talking to the hardship committee. See what they can suggest."

"I'll certainly try. And Edward is being very patient with me, Simon, explaining things about Lloyd's I still don't understand. I was just asking him why my biggest syndicate, Westfield Bradley, and, I believe, some of the others, has two marine and two non-marine syndicates and not just one of each, like all the rest. What was it you called them, Edward?"

Right, thought Simon, here we go: please God. He reached into his breast pocket, pressed the record button on his tape recorder. He had been practising it for the last few days, and he did feel a bit like James Bond. Here it would come: how they had accomplished all this skulduggery and double-dealing, spelled out in this ghastly character's plummy tones; really, Flora was a genius, she'd handled it so well. And then he could give it to Fiona and get lots of brownie points for it.

"Ah . . ." Trafford Smythe said, leaning back in his chair. "Baby syndicates, I imagine you mean. Such an interesting idea. Well, it's very simple: they enable a successful underwriter to expand without diluting the profits of the main syndicate. By careful management of the best business."

"Oh really? I'd understood they were a bit—suspect," said Simon.

"No, not at all. They're not corrupt and they're not illegal. Otherwise I do assure you I wouldn't have anything to do with it."

"So how is it that you and I are in the same syndicate and you're a millionaire and I'm going bankrupt?" said Flora. "That's what I still don't understand. I mean, how do you get to be in one of these profitable divisions?"

"Ah, now that comes down to where your Members' Agent put you in the first place. Generally he would spread your risk, of course. And in a large syndicate group there are many subdivisions, as you might say. I'm afraid you have found yourself in one or two of the weaker ones. That, I must admit, may not have been reinsured adequately. And of course I did urge William to take out stop-loss. For some reason he didn't do that."

"Well, I've obviously had it all wrong," said Simon. "I thought it was a case of the underwriters making sure their friends and relations were getting all the good business, sitting on a raft if you like, and everyone else sinking or swimming furiously about with the bad. Is that not right? Not ever the case?"

Go on, say, "Yes, that does happen sometimes, that does go on." Give me a break, Mr. Trafford Smythe, please, for the love of God, that claret cost £27 a bottle.

But, "No," said Trafford Smythe, meeting his eyes with a certain disdain. He seemed perfectly sober suddenly. "No, that's a complete myth. Put about by all those people who can't handle their losses. I don't know who's been telling you all this, Mr. Beaumont, but whoever it was, they were extremely wrongheaded. Or thinking very wishfully indeed. Now I must go. Thanks for the wine. Very good. And don't forget, I'd be delighted to show you my yard. Anytime that suits you."

They stared after him in silence, then Flora said, "I'm sorry, Simon."

"Don't apologise," he said. "Don't be silly, it wasn't your fault. You were marvellous."

"So were you. Damn. Dreadful little man. I really can't believe he was related to William. So common. Did you see he was wearing a tiepin? A tiepin! Really."

"No," said Simon, and started to laugh. "Flora, you are the most terrible snob."

"I prefer to think of it," she said almost sternly, "as having standards."

"I see. All right. Let's have another drink, Flora. Here's to standards. It's not the end of the world. Serves us right for trying to be too clever. Bastards, aren't they? The reason they don't want people selling their houses is because it leads to bad publicity, and the reason they don't like people going bankrupt is that there's no more money for them. These hardship committees exist not to get you off the hook, as far as I can see, but to keep you on it, do deals with you to get regular payments from you out of future earnings. Oh God."

They ordered coffee, sat chatting for a bit. And then she said rather quickly, clearly hating having to say it at all, "Simon, if—when I sell the house, then I'm afraid that Boy will have to go. Hal as well, although a friend will probably take him on. I'm so sorry."

"Oh, that's all right," he said. "And of course I've thought of it." He hadn't, actually. The prospect of having to break that piece of news to Tilly was so awful that his eyes filled with tears. He blew his nose, forced a smile at Flora.

"We'll think of something," he said, "don't worry."

"Yes, I'm sure you will," she said, and then, looking at him curiously: "Does anything ever get you down, Simon?"

"Not often. Which is just as well at the moment."

*

They'd probably been as nice as they could be, Catherine thought, which wasn't very nice at all. But at least they were trying. Lucinda had lent her her little Peugeot 204 to travel down in. It had been better than travelling by train, but it was a long drive to Somerset; the children were hot and fractious by the time they arrived. All they needed was to run around unfettered for a while; Phyllis Morgan clearly couldn't see this.

"Come in and sit down quietly, children," she said, "and you'd better have a drink. I've made some lemonade for you. Here you are. Catherine, will you have some?"

"Please!" said Catherine. But the lemonade wasn't properly cold and very bitter; she could see Caroline struggling with it, and shot her a sympathetic glance.

"Dudley will be in soon, he's coming back specially to see you. Although he's terribly busy."

"That's very kind," said Catherine.

"And I had a golf match which I cancelled."

"Well, thank you," said Catherine.

"It's a pity you don't play," Phyllis said. "You'd make some friends that way."

"Maybe I could learn."

"Well, I doubt it. Golf lessons are very expensive." She was laying down markers already.

Lunch was not nice, fatty lamb chops, which the children could not force down, pushed to the sides of their plates. "I do hope they're not fussy eaters," Dudley said, noting this. "When I was a child we had to sit at the table until everything was gone. Never did me any harm."

He said this a great deal. Catherine wondered, as she had so often, how these people could have produced her beloved Frederick. Over a trifle, which bore a strong resemblance to the ones served at motorway service stations, the move was discussed.

"It won't be easy," Phyllis said, "but we've discussed it and we feel that we have to offer you a home. It would be extremely uncharitable not to; you are our son's wife and these are our grandchildren. Our friends are all filled with admiration."

"Yes, it's very, very kind of you," said Catherine.

"Can we get down?" said Caroline hopefully.

"Not until I say so, dear. Now we thought we could convert part of the top floor into a sort of flat for you. So that you can be self-contained. We don't want to be living in one another's pockets all the time."

"That would be marvellous," said Catherine. "Would it have a kitchen?"

"Not as such," said Dudley. "The cost of that would be prohibitive. But we thought we'd put in a gas ring and a point where you could boil a kettle, make yourself a cup of tea, that sort of thing. We imagined you'd make the children's tea there, and so on, although of course you're welcome to use our kitchen. As long as you give Phyllis plenty of notice."

"And of course you're welcome to eat with us if you want to," said Phyllis, "but we thought you'd rather cater for yourself most of the time. Perhaps Sunday lunch we could eat together as a family."

"Yes, that would be nice."

"The children may play in the garden, of course, but they must treat it with respect. No bikes or footballs, young man."

"Could we have a swing?" Caroline asked.

"It might be possible, I suppose, if we could find somewhere where it was out of sight. I'll have a think about that."

"Thank you."

"I imagine you'll be doing your own shopping," said Phyllis. "I'll keep a section of one of the fridges clear for you. So that we don't get into a muddle. I presume you're getting some kind of National Assistance money."

"A bit," said Catherine.

"And I'm very pleased to see you've got a car. You'll be rather cut off here without it."

"Oh, it's not mine, I'm afraid. A friend has lent it to me for a while."

"He or she must be a very good friend," said Dudley.

"She is indeed," said Catherine, thinking longingly of Lucinda, sweet generous Lucinda.

"Well, I don't know what you'll do down here without one. There is a bus, but only twice a day, morning and evening."

"I—daresay you could give me a lift from time to time. Or maybe I could drive one of your cars occasionally." There were three in the drive: a flashy new Jaguar, a Ford Escort, equally new, and a rather older, battered Polo.

"Well, I don't know. Possibly the Polo. We keep it for emergencies though; I wouldn't want it gone for long at a time."

"What about things like the school run?" said Catherine, rather desperately. "How will I do that?" This was worse than she had expected.

"Ah, yes. Schools. Now, as I said in my letter, we are prepared to take on the school fees. It's a great deal of money but—well, hopefully it will be worth it."

"I hope so too. That's terribly generous of you. I really do appreciate it."

"And then, as a quid pro quo, we would want complete control over their schooling. We would expect to choose the schools, to be very involved in their progress. We don't want any bad reports," said Dudley, looking rather sternly at the children.

"Well, of course. But I'd like to have some say in the choice of school."

Dudley looked at her. "I suppose that's reasonable," he said, after a moment's consideration. "But Phyllis and I have discussed the whole thing and we feel that Freddie should go to boarding school."

"Boarding school!" Nothing could have prepared her for this horror. "What—straightaway?"

"In the autumn term, yes. There's an excellent prep school near Shaftesbury, only about thirty miles or so away. Gets boys into all the major public schools. I imagine he's very behind, all the upheavals he's been through, not to mention that stint in the state system. We went to see this place the other day and it seemed excellent. They could take him, provided his present school gives him a good report."

"But I don't want—" Catherine looked at Freddie, who was wide-eyed with misery. "Er . . . Dudley, could the children go outside to play, please? It's been a long drive down here and they do need to work off a bit of steam."

"Well, I suppose so. Mind the flower beds, both of you. And no climbing the trees."

"I really don't want Freddie to go away to school," she said, when the children were safely outside. "He's not ready for it."

"Nonsense. He's nine years old. I went away at seven, didn't do me any harm."

"Well, I think it would harm Freddie," said Catherine. "He's just had this very bad bullying experience at school . . ."

"Yes, but that was at the state school, surely," said Phyllis.

"It was, but his prep school in Fulham was just as bad, it seems."

"Catherine, you can't wrap children in cotton wool," said Dudley. "He has to grow up, learn to cope. And for Caroline, there's a very nice girls' prep school about five miles away."

"And that's another thing, they'll miss each other," said Catherine. "They're always together, terribly close. They'll be terribly unhappy, they'll—"

"Oh nonsense," said Dudley. "Half Freddie's problems, I'd say, not enough male influence in his life. Now I'm going to leave you girls to have a chat and get back to the office. Bye, Catherine. You can sort out exactly when you move in with Phyllis, but the conversion could take a couple of months."

And he was gone.

<hr />

"It was ghastly," she said to Lucinda on the phone, "and I just don't know what to do. Freddie's really upset. But we've got absolutely no money, and we've got to live somewhere. Oh dear."

"Catherine, I'm so, so sorry." Lucinda's voice was heavy with sympathy. "I wish I could help, I really do. But our house is so tiny, and—"

"Yes, I thought you were going to move?"

"Oh, don't. So did Blue. So does everyone And we will, after—well, after the baby."

"But why not now, when it's easier?"

"Oh, don't you start," said Lucinda, and her voice wobbled. "Sorry, bit of a row last night. Blue really wants to move."

"And you don't?"

"Oh Catherine, it's terribly complicated. I can't explain."

Chapter 36

"Joel." Hugh Renwick walked very fast into his office. Fast was good; slow was bad. "Joel, get it finished, let me have the rest. Not more than fifteen hundred words. Then I'll decide."

"Yes, OK. Thanks. Shouldn't take too long." He wasn't going to tell him he'd actually finished the piece.

"Better not. If I do decide to run it, it'll be Thursday's paper. Maybe Friday."

"OK."

"But I probably won't."

"No."

"And I want it pretty damn quick, as well. Don't start wanking over it."

"No, OK."

Joel took his story into evening conference, handed it to Hugh at the end. He read it in silence.

"OK, it'll do. We'll shoehorn it into tomorrow's paper."

Tomorrow! That was better even than he'd hoped. It must be good.

"Have you called Allinson yet?"

"No, not yet."

"Do it, soon as you can. And Lloyd's as well—they'd better be given the chance to respond."

"Sure."

Hugh picked up his phone, then put it down again, and said, "So you paid your own expenses on this, did you?"

"Yup."

"And what would you have done if I hadn't run it?"

"I thought someone else would," said Joel.

"Arrogant little bugger, you are, Strickland. Anyway, you can put a chit in, if you like. Just the airfare and the hotel—nothing else, mind."

"Thanks."

"And next time, you're out on your ear—understood?"

"Understood."

The accent that had become familiar to him came down the phone. "Ocean Hill."

"Oh, good—good morning," said Joel, looking at his watch, doing a quick calculation. "Is Mr. Allinson there, please? He's in Mr. Bridgeman's party." It was around lunchtime there; with luck, he'd catch the bugger by the pool. He hoped Tim hadn't gone out on the yacht.

It felt like forever. It actually was quite a long time, at least five minutes. Thank God the *News* was paying.

Finally: "Hello, Timothy Allinson. Who is this?"

"Mr. Allinson, sorry to disturb your day. Joel Strickland here, *Daily News*,"

"Oh yes? What can I do for you?"

"I just wondered if you'd like to comment on a story we're running in our paper, about Lloyd's of London."

"What sort of story?"

"It's about the considerable hardship endured by people who were Names and really couldn't afford the risk."

"How extraordinary. That certainly isn't a picture I recognise. Complete drivel, I assure you. I don't know where you got your facts from, but—"

"Well, the thing is, Mr. Allinson, you have already contributed in some measure. You gave me some very interesting quotes yesterday. By the pool. About the way certain syndicates operated, how you operated on their behalf. Saying, for instance, that they had 'lowered the bar' as you put it, deliberately inviting people with quite modest incomes to become Names because they needed to keep the money coming in; only way they could cope with the rising spiral of claims."

"What on earth are you talking about? Who did you say you were?"

"Joel Strickland. Oh sorry, I think I introduced myself to you as Joel Sherlock. It's one of my pseudonyms. Confusing for you, I can see that. Anyway, I'm sorry you don't recall it. I have it all on tape. Would you like me to read it over to you? It really is rather interesting."

"This is outrageous! And let me tell you, if any of that appears in your newspaper, I shall sue."

"That's your prerogative, Mr. Allinson. Meanwhile, would you like to comment further on what you said?"

"Certainly not. Except to say that it is clearly a complete fabrication. I have always behaved with the utmost integrity."

"So you would deny saying that, despite knowing Lloyd's were 'going through a bad patch,' as you put it, you were still inviting people to become Names?"

"I have nothing more to say to you. Except to warn you once again that I shall sue if this story and its absurd claims gets into your paper."

"Very well. Thank you, Mr. Allinson."

Joel put the phone down and smiled at it. "That was for you, Miss Thompson," he said.

Now he must ring Lloyd's. Give them the right to reply too. And then maybe, just maybe, he should ring Debbie.

He didn't actually ring her until the next day

"Hi. You OK?" He sounded more friendly now. Less cold, less distracted.

"Oh yes, fine. Thanks. What—what happened? About the story?"

"Oh, we're running it."

"Fantastic. I'm so pleased. When? And you haven't been fired?"

"I haven't. Well, not yet. And tomorrow. Hubby back?"

"Yes. Yes, he is."

"And—"

"Oh, it's fine. Well, you know. Fine as it could be."

"Great."

Go on, for God's sake say something, she thought. Say something that means something. That might help. He didn't. "How was it, in the Bahamas? Is it lovely there?"

"Yeah, it's great. Really beautiful."

"Good. Well, I can't wait to hear about it." There was a pause then; she felt more frightened than she'd ever been in her life, more than when Flora had found her and Simon in the kitchen . . . just sheer, gut-tearing terror.

And then he said it. Said he'd missed her, said he wanted to see her. Asked when could that be.

She said she'd have to check a few things out and that she'd call him back. And then sat staring at the phone wondering what on earth she was going to do.

℮↝

Joel was looking very pleased with himself. "I just wanted you to know I got a lot of good stuff from our friend Allinson."

"Did you now? Well done you. Did he confess to anything?"

"Enough to make a story, and it's going in tomorrow's paper."

"Great. Worth the trip, eh?"

"Very much so. God, it was tough—five-star hotels, fantastic food, beautiful women—"

"Wish I'd been with you," said Simon, laughing.

"You'd have loved it. Anyway, you're very welcome to the tape, or at any rate a copy of it. What I got might not be enough to help you, not for a court of law, but it's good background information at the very least. I really want to help you with your case, Simon. I owe you a lot."

"OK. That's very good of you—I appreciate it. Especially as I've just drawn a spectacularly blank card myself. I was feeling a bit downhearted. You've actually got some stuff on this tape, have you?"

"You bet. Our slimy friend Allinson saying all sorts of stuff about huge losses on the horizon which Lloyd's knew about and how they'd felt the only way was to pull more people in, without actually being up front about it. It's jolly good."

"Joel, that sounds incredible. Fantastic. Thanks so much. God, maybe I've found the smoking gun."

"The what?"

"What our very sexy lawyer calls the smoking gun: an admission by someone that something slightly dirty was going on. Very hard to come by."

"Well, I should say this gun is definitely pretty smoky."

"Good. Well, bless you. I'll buy you the most stupendous lunch sometime. Now tell me, where did you go exactly? I love the Bahamas. Once stayed at the Cotton Bay Club, on Eleuthera. Glorious. Wonderful sailing. Very romantic too. Elizabeth and I were on our second honeymoon—or was it our third? Can't remember." He grinned at Joel. "It

· 348 ·

might amuse you to know I've been accused of having an affair with Debbie Fielding. By her husband."

"Yes, I heard," said Joel. He spoke without thinking. Simon stared at him. "I didn't think anyone else knew. Who told you?"

"Er, can't remember."

"Joel! Come on. It's important—this is my reputation at stake."

Joel was silent; Simon sat watching him, reading his body language, working things out in his head.

"It wasn't Debbie, was it?"

"It was, yes," Joel said. Very reluctantly. Simon sat digesting this piece of information. Then he said, "You're not having a thing with Debbie yourself, are you?"

"No, of course not. Well, not actually a thing, no."

"Look, it's nothing to do with me, Joel, but that girl is dynamite."

"I know it," said Joel, clearly trying to appear lighthearted, amused.

"No, seriously. She's quite . . . dangerous, I'd say. Not in herself, but she's not very happily married. And she's very emotional. Reckless even."

"I daresay she is," said Joel. He pushed his hand through his hair. "Honestly, Simon, can we just forget this conversation?"

"Well," said Simon, "I know you probably see me as older than God, but affairs with married women—not a good idea. In my experience."

"Look," said Joel, "sorry and all that, but I really would rather not talk about this. In fact, I haven't even said I'm having an affair with Debbie: you did. So let's leave it, shall we?"

Simon looked at him; then he sighed, a heavy, almost despairing sigh. "All right, I'm sorry. But—just know that you're playing with fire. Sorry about the cliché."

"I'll remember," said Joel.

ℰↄ

Simon left quite soon after that. He felt very optimistic suddenly. At this rate, they might even win. They would win. Lloyd's would lose. He'd get his job back, buy another boat, stable Boy . . .

He could hardly sleep that night for excitement, made a very tired Elizabeth listen while he told her about it.

"I really think this could be a bit of good luck at last. What do you think, darling?"

"I think," said Elizabeth sleepily, giving him a kiss, "that you should send Joel Strickland an enormous bottle of champagne."

⌇

Early next day, Simon appeared on Catherine's doorstep with a large bunch of white roses.

"Simon! Come in! That's jolly naughty. Thank you so much. But—?"

"They're to say sorry," he said. "For failing you. Getting you into such a hole. I feel dreadful."

"Simon, you did not get me into a hole. You gave me six super months. Golly, without that I'd be in a bin by now, I should think. Please, please don't feel bad about it."

"Well, I do. Can't help it."

"Try to help it. You look very smart, where are you off to?"

"Le Caprice. For lunch."

"Sounds very glamorous."

"Well, you know me," he said with his broad grin. "My life is one long glamorous event after another."

"Well, it does seem that way a bit. Who are you lunching with?"

"Oh, rather frightening lady. Who I quite fancy actually. She has a certain dominatrix charm."

"Crikey," said Catherine.

"Now tell me about the in-laws. How was that?"

"Awful," said Catherine, and then realised he would worry about her even more if he knew the truth, and managed somehow to make the story sound amusing.

"So there I'll be, up in the attic, like Mrs. Rochester . . ."

"Sounds more like Jane Eyre to me. God. They seem to be terrible people."

"Oh, they're OK. Hearts in the right place and all that." She smiled at him determinedly. He smiled back.

"Don't you dare go off to Somerset," he said. "I'll miss you far too much. I must go."

On the doorstep he bent, gave her a kiss. "Look after yourself," he said, "and don't forget, you can always call me if things get really tough. Don't know what I can do, but I'm quite a good listener."

"You certainly are."

"I'll say one thing about this wretched business, it's given me a whole lot of awfully nice new friends."

"It's done that for all of us," said Catherine, "and you're the most awfully nice of all."

"Bless you," he said, and kissed her again.

Fiona Broadhurst rarely accepted lunch invitations. She felt the time was far better spent working. But Simon Beaumont had been rather pressing on the phone, said he needed to talk something over with her. She wore her red shoes in honour of the occasion and a new black suit from Armani with a rather shorter skirt than usual.

"Here's to the case then," she said, raising her glass, looking round her. Le Caprice seemed to be filled with women in red suits. She felt rather pleased she was in black.

"Indeed. And thank you for all your help so far. Now, I've got what I think is some pretty good news. Although not quite as good as I'd hoped . . . big disappointment yesterday." He told her about the lunch with Flora and Edward Trafford Smythe, how he had admitted to nothing.

"He wouldn't. None of them would, not wittingly. Certainly not with a victim present. Have you not heard of closed ranks, Mr. Beaumont?"

"Simon."

"Have you not heard of closed ranks, Simon? I'm afraid they don't come much more closed than Lloyd's. So was the lunch good at least?"

"It was. But here comes the good news. Friend of mine, journalist on the *News*, he got something approaching a confession from one of the Lloyd's pimps."

"Not an expression I'd advise you to use in court."

"I'll try and remember. Anyway, it's all on tape, apparently and—"

"And how did he obtain this recording?"

"Oh, he was staying at the same hotel, they got chatting—apparently innocently—by the pool one afternoon."

"So the Lloyd's representative knew he was being recorded, did he?"

"No," said Simon. "No, of course not. He wouldn't have talked if he had." She looked at him carefully, then she said, "I'm afraid that wouldn't be admissible in court."

"Why?"

"Well, because of the danger of tampering. Think about it." He thought about it; she watched his buoyancy slowly collapse.

"So not a lot of good then?"

"Not really."

"Pity," he said finally. "I really thought I'd found our smoking gun."

"I'm afraid," said Fiona, "it's got to be a lot bigger and smokier than that."

"Oh. I see." He looked stricken now, white-faced, and infinitely sad. She felt very sorry for him.

"But," she said quickly, "it still might be of use. Even though it's inadmissible, a judge could still be interested in hearing it. It might help sway his view of the case in our favour."

"I think you're just trying to make me feel better," he said.

"Simon, I'm not in the business of making people feel better. Except by actually winning their cases for them."

The maître d' approached the table. "Call for you, Miss Broadhurst. Behind the bar."

"Oh—yes. Sorry, Simon, I have been waiting for some important information about a case. Please excuse me a moment."

As she talked, she watched a woman stop by Simon's table, stand there talking to him. She was very tall and blond, and she was wearing a cream-and-blue printed silk dress and jacket; she stood out in the roomful of power suits. As Fiona got near to the table, the woman bent down and kissed Simon quickly, then moved away. No introductions then: interesting.

Simon smiled at her, half stood as she sat down. He had amazingly good manners, she thought: a bit old-fashioned, but very nice. "Great suit, that. And I love the shoes."

He poured her another drink; they sat there for quite a long time chatting. He was dangerously easy to talk to; despite it being one of her sacred tenets never to reveal any personal details about herself, by half past three when they left the restaurant, Simon Beaumont knew rather more about her than she would actually have chosen to tell him. The blonde was long gone, had smiled briefly as she passed them.

"It's been fun," Simon said, "I've really enjoyed it. Loved talking to you. And I feel very sad for all those chaps out there."

"Which chaps?" she said, smiling, eased by two glasses of champagne and one of Sancerre—Simon Beaumont certainly wasn't behaving like someone about to go bankrupt.

"The ones who aren't going to be your husband. Shame."

She flushed. "I've talked too much."

"Not at all. I've enjoyed it. Very much."

He kissed her on the cheek, smiled, and handed her into her taxi; she drove off feeling sleek and rather pleased with life. She wondered if he had that effect on all women. And felt rather sorry for his wife. Or possibly even jealous of her. She couldn't decide which.

"Daddy! Hi. You look a bit tired. Shall I fix you a drink?"

"No, darling, I've had quite enough to drink for one day."

"Well—nice sparkly water then? With ice and lemon? I want to talk to you about something."

"All right. I'll be in the garden."

"Mummy said to tell you she'd be back around ten. And to call her if you want."

"OK. I will. . . . Elizabeth? It's me."

"Oh—hello, Simon. Good day?"

"Yes, pretty good. Tell you about it later."

"Be quite a bit later, I'm afraid."

"Annabel said ten-ish."

"More like eleven-ish, worst luck. Did you get my message about the house?"

"No."

"Oh. Well, those Americans came back with a better offer: two point two. Which would pay off Lloyd's just about . . ."

"For this year."

She sighed. And then he could hear her being positive and brave.

"Well, anyway, it would pay them off for this year, and buy us quite a nice house somewhere like Fulham."

"Sure. Great. So—"

"And then there are some Arabs."

"Ye-es?"

"They are offering a bit less, but the agent said he knew he could push them up. What do you think?"

"I don't know." He suddenly felt exhausted. "Let's talk about it when you get home."

Annabel came out with a tray: ice, lemon, and a bottle of water. "There you go. Full kit. Anyway, I had a long chat with Jamie today. He wants to come and see you."

"Really? Why?"

"He wants to ask you formally for my hand in marriage. Isn't that sweet? I mean, a bit old-fashioned but—sweet."

"It's not really old-fashioned," said Simon. "I think it's simply good manners."

"Yes, of course." She smiled at him. "That's what he says. Normally he wouldn't have asked me without speaking to you, but, well, things got a bit out of our control. Anyway, he's coming later in the month, just for a few days, so he can ask you, and maybe get a few things sorted out. I know you'll both love him, he's so adorable. And so nice."

"I'm sure we will."

"And . . . this is a bit difficult, a bit delicate even, but Daddy, do you think you will be selling this house?"

"I'm afraid so."

"Well—well, Jamie said his mother had made a suggestion."

"Oh yes?" Already he disliked Frances Cartwright. Quite a lot. He felt he was about to dislike her more.

"Now this is really up to you, I promise. Really, really. She—well, she suggests we might get married over there. You know? Not in Boston, but down at Cape Cod. The house is just so gorgeous, and right on the sea, I really, really loved it. And the garden is huge and would take a ginormus marquee and . . . well, I would't have even considered it if we were staying here, but as we'll be somewhere much smaller, I can't see it working. And you know I've always wanted to be married at home, not in some horrible great hotel, and the weather is so reliably wonderful, whereas in England—"

"But Annabel, this is your home, England is your home—" He stopped; he felt very upset. He had always loved the idea of bringing Annabel down the aisle in Chelsea Old Church, where all three children had been christened, and then of having the reception at home, in the Boltons, in the great green garden, with its tall ivy-covered walls, and where there was also plenty of room for a marquee. Where so many parties had been held, where the ghosts of long lovely days, of warm flower-scented evenings would always remain. That was what all weddings should be, family parties, held in the family home. Only—only he was being robbed of it, of his dream, for they wouldn't be here, not by then; it would be home to strangers who would never have, or so he felt, any real right to it. The family house would be some rotten little place in Fulham. And his daughter, his beloved daughter, would be getting married in another country, in the home of people he didn't even know.

"Daddy, I promise I won't do it if you don't like the idea," she said. "I promise! But, well, it is so lovely there, and I know you'd love it too, and—"

She was flushed now, anxious at his reaction; he made a Herculean effort to smile at her, to dissemble.

"I'm sure I would. And I'm very, very happy to consider it, if it's what you want. But hey, who knows where we'll be living then? In—what is it? Two years?"

"About that. Maybe a bit sooner. We did—well, wonder. You and Mummy can talk to Jamie about it when he comes."

Don't go, he wanted to say, please don't go. Don't go and live in Boston, don't get married in Cape Cod; stay here with me, in England; stay in the place that made you, and where all your friends are, and everyone who loves you. But of course he didn't say any of it. He smiled and said, "It sounds as if it could be huge fun. We'll have to hire a jumbo jet to transport everyone over there . . ."

Elizabeth was much later than she had said; it was almost midnight when she got in. He was half asleep by the time she slithered into bed beside him.

"Sorry," she whispered.

"It's all right." Silence, then: "I love you, Elizabeth," he said, "very much."

"I love you too."

And then he made love to her, very sweetly and tenderly, and afterwards he said again, "I love you," and fell asleep, holding her in his arms.

And in the morning he was gone.

Chapter 37

"Daddy's gone sailing apparently," said Elizabeth. "He went early, left me a note. I'm glad, it'll do him good. He's missed it terribly, and it's been such an awful strain for him, all this."

"Where's he gone?"

"Oh, to the club in Chichester. David Green's lending him his boat. He said they might even go over to France together, take a couple of days."

"Did he say anything about the wedding last night when you came in?"

"The wedding? No," said Elizabeth, smiling at the thought of the very short, sweet conversation she and Simon had had. "No, he didn't. Why?"

"Oh, tell you another time. Got to go. I was late yesterday, Tania was not pleased. You in tonight?"

"Think so."

"Well, we can talk then. Bye, Mum."

❧

"Elizabeth, I'm planning a dinner party." Peter Hargreaves put his head round her door. "Early next month, hopefully the first Thursday. I'd like you and Simon to come. I'm inviting a couple of long-service clients and a handful of good, long-suffering friends."

"Which am I?"

"You're both. Which is why I'm keen to know about Simon. Could you let me know ASAP?"

"Of course," said Elizabeth. "He's gone sailing, but he's bound to check in towards the end of the day. I'm afraid it's very unlikely that he won't be able to come. I don't mean that the way it sounds," she added smiling. "I mean, I'm afraid he won't have anything else on. His life's taken a bit of a dive."

"Poor chap." He hesitated, then said, "But you seem rather happy."

"I am happy, Peter. More than I've been for a long time. Whoever said money wasn't everything was right."

Her phone rang.

"Mummy? Mummy, it's me! You must get a copy of the *News*. Joel's piece is in. Daddy's in it, and Mrs. Fielding, and that poor girl whose little boy went missing, and—well, just about everyone really."

"My secretary's got a copy—I think she always buys it—yes, oh, my goodness! I wonder if Daddy's seen it?"

He had, of course seen the reference to him, to Simon Beaumont:

. . . successful City banker, who has lost almost everything, including his job. "I was too trusting," he says, "some would say naïve." Beaumont is lucky, he still has his beautiful, high-earning wife and his happy family. Others have been less fortunate, their marriages broken by the strain of facing bankruptcy, of having to remove children from schools, leave much-loved family homes . . . I have heard of several cases indeed of suicide . . . one elderly lady, who had handed over her father's entire fortune into Lloyd's tender keeping found herself unable to pay her debts, and was discovered by a neighbour, lying dead by her own gas fire.

"Flora, you're in the papers!" Colin sounded quite excited on the phone. "Have you seen it, the *Daily News*?"

"No, I have not," said Flora crisply, more troubled by the thought that Colin expected her to be a *Daily News* reader rather than anything the article might say.

"Well, I'll read it to you."

Widowed Mrs. Flora Fielding is one of many who face considerable hardship and may be forced to sacrifice her beautiful eighteenth-century house in order to meet debts. "Lloyd's appeared to be run by gentlemen," she said, "and foolishly, I trusted them. As did many others, misled by the sense that we were fortunate to be joining a rather exclusive club . . ."

"Goodness," she said. "I must go out and buy a copy for myself."

❧

Catherine, alerted to the story by Lucinda, went out to buy a copy of the *News* and promptly spilled her coffee all over it as she read about the beautiful young widow (could that be her?), who had had to take her vulnerable little boy out of his school where he was so happy and doing well and put him in another, where he was bullied so badly that he ran away from home. For some reason she wondered if Nigel had seen it.

❧

Nigel had; the article had been placed on his desk by the devoted Lydia, and while he was enjoying it very much, he did reflect with deep gratitude on the fact that he had not been asked to participate in any way. It just wasn't—wasn't very seemly somehow.

❧

Lucinda was very excited. Blue had called her at the office and told her to go and buy a copy of the *News,* which of course she hadn't had to, since the PR Department got all the papers every day. She rang him back.

"Blue! So many of our friends, isn't it wonderful? And did you see they described Catherine as beautiful? So nice for her—and of course she is."

Blue said there were two or three inaccuracies in the story as far as he could see, but that that was the most serious.

"You are just so beastly," said Lucinda.

"No, I'm not. Just truthful."

Debbie was reading the article for roughly the fifth time when Richard phoned her.

"There's an article about Lloyd's in the *Daily News*," he said, "with my mother in it."

"Really?"

"Yes. By someone called . . . let's see, Joel Strickland. It's rather good. You don't know him, do you?"

"Um, I've met him once or twice. Yes."

"Very well researched. So did you put him onto her?"

"No, of course not. How could I?"

"Must have been Beaumont then. Anyway, she seems quite chuffed about it."

"Good, I'm pleased to hear it. I must—I must have a look at it."

She did, for the sixth time and then the seventh; and then decided to ring him, and tell him how great she thought it was.

"Thank you. Yes, I'm quite pleased. Just waiting to hear from our friend in the Bahamas."

"Oh, yes. Do you think you will?"

"His lawyers, more likely."

"Will they be able to sue?"

"No, they won't. I've got him on tape. There's not a word there that he didn't actually utter."

"Oh, right. And what did Lloyd's say?"

"They had no comment to make, beyond that they'd always acted in good faith. Anyway, glad you liked it. I must go, it's spawned rather a lot of work, I'm afraid. See you soon."

"Yes, hope so." Shouldn't have said that: might have sounded too keen. Pathetic? Clinging?

"Very soon," he added. "I'll call you. Promise."

Not too keen then.

She rang off, put the article in her bag, and tried to concentrate on her work.

Blue had cancelled lunch with Lucinda. "Sorry, Lucy, got to do a bit of schmoozing. Another day."

"Blue, it's fine. Honestly."

She smiled at him; he grinned back, came over to where she lay in their bed, and gave her a kiss.

"Love me?"

"Of course I do. You know I do. I was proving it like anything last night, remember?"

She smiled at him, snuggled down again under the duvet. It was one of the best things about Blue's early starts; she could go back to sleep for a whole hour afterwards. But now maybe she should fix that lunch with Simon. He had seemed at a bit of a loose end, poor darling. It must be so awful for him, not having a job anymore. She'd ring him when she got into the office—it was too early now—and suggest it.

℮∽

It had been a particularly busy morning at Jenkins and Jenkins, insurance brokers, the phones ringing nonstop. Maurice Crane, one of the executives there, took off his spectacles as lunchtime approached, rubbed his eyes, and thought that he really was getting too old for all this.

He sent up a small prayer of gratitude that retirement was now only a few months away and made his way to the gents' before going out for his customary roast-beef sandwich.

As he pushed open the door, he felt suddenly rather dizzy and put out his hand to steady himself on the doorframe; felt a little better and stepped forward. And slipped on a patch of water on the tile floor and fell heavily.

He was found only a few minutes later, and half an hour after that he was lying on a trolley in Casualty at St. Thomas's Hospital. Shortly afterwards he was diagnosed with a fractured femur. His leg was put in plaster and he was sent home in an ambulance, and told he would need several weeks off work to recover.

Maurice Crane, looking out of the window at his sun-filled garden, felt that this was not an entirely cruel blow on the part of Fate.

℮∽

· 360 ·

"Debbie, it's Joel. Sorry about earlier."

"That's OK."

She'd just been deciding to finish whatever it was she had with him. It was too dangerous, it was foolish, he clearly didn't care about her in the least—and why should he?

"How are you?"

"Oh, fine. Yes, thank you." She was trying very hard not to think how sexy his voice was.

"How are things at home?"

"Oh, you know. All right. Bit strained. He's trying really hard to be nice. Joel—"

"Sorry. Look, I don't know when we can meet. I—I'd like to though. Of course."

"Yes, me too. But Joel—"

"So when?"

"Well," she said—now come on, Debbie, this is the moment, just tell him, tell him there's no point seeing him. "Well, Richard's going to go down to Wales again next week. So that's a possibility. Although Flora's got some agricultural show she wants us to go to. Exciting, huh?"

"You could make anything exciting, Debbie. So next week's a possibility, yes?"

"Oh yes. Definitely a possibility. Or definitely hopefully as they say in Wales."

He laughed. "I like that. OK, well definitely hopefully next week then."

And maybe by next week she'd feel clearer about what she wanted to do.

"You haven't heard from Simon today, have you?" he asked.

"No. Why?"

"Oh, I just wanted to get hold of him. There's no reply at home. If he rings you, could you ask him to call me?"

"Yes, of course."

"Bye, Debbie. Definitely hopefully next week then."

"Definitely hopefully."

"Elizabeth?" It was Peter Hargreaves on the internal line. "Any news from Simon yet?"

"No." She frowned at her watch. "He should have called by now. It's nearly five. I'll give him another thirty minutes and then ring the Yacht Club. He's probably propping up the bar, forgotten the time."

It was after six when Elizabeth finally got hold of David Green. "Sorry, Elizabeth, no news from the old bugger yet . . . No, he went out on his own in the end. I had too much to do here. I've been trying to radio him, but the bloody thing seems to be switched off . . . Yes, of course I'll ring you the minute I hear . . . What's that? . . . No, no, he didn't take his mobile phone. Said it would sink the boat . . . Sorry? . . . No, the weather's been OK. Well, bit of a squall mid-Channel this afternoon, but nothing Simon couldn't handle. Good God, he's been sailing all his life."

That phrase haunted Elizabeth all that long, terrible night: until reports came in early next day of a sailing boat found drifting mid-Channel, its boom flapping and no sign of anyone on board.

Simon had indeed been sailing all his life. All his life, right up to the moment it ended.

Part Three

Chapter 38

Elizabeth had always said that she would be able to bear anything except the loss of one of her children. She was discovering she was wrong. She couldn't bear the death of her husband, either.

There was no happiness, no comfort, no pleasure, no relief from the pain. It was so agonising that she quite often found herself fighting for breath, as if it was physical, boring into her body instead of her heart or her head or wherever the grief was precisely felt.

The body—how could it have happened that her brilliant, handsome, charming husband had become a body—had been washed up on a beach near Gravelines, just north of Calais in the afternoon of 26 August. They knew it was Simon because his passport was still in the pocket of his jeans.

After three more days, endless, hideous days, Simon's body was taken to the mortuary in the Kensington and Fulham Hospital and she was asked to go and identify it formally. By now, friends had been notified, and they had formed a sort of rota, made sure that she had someone on call night and day.

David Green went with her to the mortuary where they were shown into a waiting area. A man came in, holding out his hand to her. "Robert

Jeffries. I'm the coroner's officer. I'd like to pretend I was in charge, but I'm afraid I'm not."

Elizabeth smiled at him obediently while marvelling that her facial muscles would do anything so extraordinary.

Robert Jeffries explained that there was no need for her to actually look at the body, he would be satisfied if she identified Simon from some photographs.

When the photographs were brought, the effort required to lift her eyes and to look at them was so stupendous that for quite a while she simply couldn't do it. And then although it was totally horrible and nauseating and she wanted to be sick, because of what the body was like, bloated and frigid, it wasn't actually quite so terrible, because it wasn't Simon lying there. All the clichés about empty shells and the lights being on but no one at home were absolutely true.

This . . . this body in the photographs had Simon's hair and Simon's face—just—but it had nothing to do with the warm, charming, loving man she had been married to . . . It really wasn't the worst thing: not by a long way.

The worst thing was not knowing. Not knowing if he had chosen to kill himself, if he had been unable to face life any longer. Or if it had indeed been an accident, that he had been knocked overboard, possibly by the untethered boom, and had desperately tried to get back on board. That was a dreadful thought, of course: but not as dreadful as that he had deliberately turned his back on her, on all of them, found them wanting, unable to give him sufficient hope and courage to carry on.

She just didn't believe he could have done that to her, to their children, shown them such dreadful wilful cruelty.

When she felt a little better, Mr. Jeffries took them to a café for some tea, which to her amazement she did seem to want, and said that he wondered if she realised that there would be an inquest.

"The purpose of which is to establish who the deceased is, and when, where, and how he came by his death. The how and when a person died, but not why. There is no question of apportioning any blame on any individual. It's important you understand that."

She nodded feebly and said she did.

"Good. Now it's my job to investigate the death rather than the cause of death, which will be the postmortem result, and then to present the evidence in court."

"Yes, I see."

"There has been a postmortem performed in France. I can give you the details of that, if you would like."

She said she felt she had to know as much as she possibly could, however much it hurt.

There had been no evidence of anything suspicious going on, Mr. Jeffries said, of a fight or anything like that; no injuries to the body, except a bruise and swelling to the back of the head, presumably caused by the swinging boom which had possibly knocked him into the water. He had been wearing a life jacket but it was not inflated; but this would not have been for any sinister reason, Elizabeth explained. There were two types of life jacket: one which inflated automatically on contact with the water, and one which required a tug of its cord to inflate it.

"The thing is, you see, the automatic sort are more cumbersome; a lot of people don't like them, there's been considerable debate about them."

Mr. Jeffries nodded and made further notes. "And then toxicology has revealed the presence of some alcohol, not an inordinate amount, perhaps the equivalent of two or three glasses of wine, and also the presence of some analgesia. Again, nothing excessive, possibly a couple of paracetamol. But of course, those would interact with the alcohol.

"He wasn't on any medication permanently? Was his health good?"

Very good, she said, and he wasn't on any medication.

What about his state of mind? Jeffries asked. Had he been depressed about anything? She denied the depression, simply said that he had considerable financial worries, that he had lost a lot of money to Lloyd's, and his job as well, that he was very worried.

"But he was fighting back; he was in the throes of taking out a lawsuit against Lloyd's. He was being very positive, he was like that."

"I'm sure," Jeffries said gently, and then asked what Simon had been doing the day before he went off. Had he seen anyone who might have heard him say something, or . . .

"He saw lots of people," she said, and said she would try to make a list of people he might have contacted.

"Thank you, Mrs. Beaumont, that would be very helpful." He hesitated. "It's usual to talk to the GP, the bank manager, people like that, if you could add those names to the list."

She got the impression he saw suicide as a very real possibility, which made her more inclined to think it too. But—that was no good; she had to believe in him, in his absolute determination to win, whatever life threw at him. That had characterised him all his life; she would not allow herself to think it had changed.

Mercifully the children took this view; it didn't seem to occur to them that their father might have taken his own life, although Annabel was beside herself, afraid she had made his last hours unhappy.

"I went on and on about my stupid wedding! God, I'm such a stupid selfish idiot." She cried for hours while Elizabeth tried to comfort her, to reassure her; where she got the strength from, she had no idea.

At first, the official view seemed to be that it had been a dreadful accident; but when they knew more about his financial situation, the sky darkened further; the debt to Lloyd's, his having been fired, made suicide seem increasingly likely. They took statements from his doctor, from colleagues, from friends, from Elizabeth herself; she supplied them with a list of everyone he had seen, or might have seen in those final few days.

"And before you dare to ask me about our marriage," Elizabeth said, a rush of hostile emotion focusing against the extremely pleasant young man who was questioning her, "let me tell you it was happier than it's ever been."

But some frightened and remorseful part of her still felt that Simon might have decided that enough was finally more than enough. In which case, she surely must bear some of the blame.

Chapter 39

It was, everyone said afterwards, a very splendid funeral. Simon would have loved it, lots of them also said. Elizabeth felt vaguely comforted. Organising it had somehow removed her from the grief and anxiety of the rest of her life and gave her a focus. She was determined that it would be as colourful, and as musically diverse, as she could manage.

Simon was a sworn agnostic, but he had always rather liked churches, insisted on visiting any he came across on their holidays. He was enchanted by them all, as much by the tiny village churches of the Cotswolds and of Sussex as by the vast sky-brushing vaults of the cathedrals of England and France. He loved the small whitewashed churches of the Greek islands, the gilded mosques of India, and the gloriously ornate duomos of Italy: and perhaps most of all the small clapboard, tin-roofed churches of the Bahamas and Key West.

He loved music too, although, "I'm a bit Radio Two," he would say apologetically, and he liked the more popular operas *(La Bohème* never failed to make him cry) and the more popular composers. "I'll go up to Mozart soon," he would say to Elizabeth. "Just one more year of Beethoven first." And he loved singing, his easy baritone voice joyfully loud at carol concerts and weddings. And even other people's funerals. "I think we owe it to them to do our best," he had once said to Elizabeth before the funeral of an old school friend who had died of cancer. "He deserves a jolly good effort, send him on his way," and sang "To Be a Pilgrim" staunchly to the end, tears streaming down his face. And he loved the music of words, loved the poets, loved Shakespeare and what he called "the proper words" of the Bible, the King James version. The children had all said they would like to read; and Tilly, who was the most musical, had helped draw up a short list. The church was to be Chelsea Old Church, and, absurdly, she gave a lot of thought to what she would wear; it seemed to matter that she would look right, that Simon would have liked it. She settled on red, her favourite, and the colour Simon had always loved her in: a dark red jacket over a black skirt and black camisole, and her favourite high-heeled Manolos, and she had gone to Harvey Nichols for a new hat, a wide-brimmed straw with black feathers wrapped around the crown.

She asked the children what they would like to wear. Annabel said could she wear the drifty chiffon she had bought for America: "I don't want to look dreary for Daddy." Tilly chose a simple cream linen shift, and Toby said he'd wear his Eton uniform. "Dad was so proud of me being there," he said. "I think he'd have liked that."

"I think so too."

It might look a little odd, she thought, but what did it matter?

The night before the funeral, she fell asleep in the garden; it was a beautiful night, the country was still going through one of its rare heat waves, the air heavy and scented. She felt restless and anxious, knew she wouldn't sleep; Annabel was out with Florian, who she said had been fantastic—"He wants to come to the funeral, is that all right?"—and she had shared a rather silent supper with Toby and Tilly who were now struggling to distract themselves by watching a week's recording of *Neighbours*. Simon had often said that the programme wielded enormous force for the good. "It's all that sitting down and discussing issues, as they call it. And they all wear cycling helmets. What more can you ask?"

And so she sat in the garden, under the chestnut tree and looked up at the stars and thought about Simon, and hoped that she would do well enough for him next day; and as much as she was able to do, sent up a small prayer to the Being beyond the stars, who she didn't really believe in, that all would go well . . .

❧

In there is my husband, Elizabeth thought, looking at the coffin in church, lying silent and still, as he never was in life, lost to me now, locked away from me in there. There were two bouquets on Simon's coffin; one of red roses, one of white. The red was from her, and said simply "Simon, from Elizabeth with all my love" and the white from the children, saying more poignantly still, "Daddy, with our love." She sat staring at it, trying to feel something and couldn't. It frightened her; she should be sobbing, inconsolable, instead of sitting here, cool and calm with her children; and worried that people would be noticing, would be thinking she was unfeeling.

The church began to fill up: friends, relatives, business associates. There was a large contingent from Graburn and French, including Martin Dudley the chairman; that was brave of him, Elizabeth thought, and then realised the true reason: Simon had been so popular, the outrage at his firing so great, that Dudley would have had a full-scale rebellion on his hands had he not been there. Sarah, Simon's chilly and devoted secretary, was there, very red-eyed.

Almost everyone from the agency had come. Peter Hargreaves sat in the pew behind her, with his wife; had greeted her with a kiss and then to her great surprise, sank onto his knees in prayer. She would never have thought of him as religious; looking round, she realised that many other people were doing the same thing. She wished she could find the comfort in prayer and God and the vision of everlasting life that the vicar had so clearly imagined she would.

The new friends were all there, the Lloyd's friends as she thought of them, including a rather cool-looking girl with brown straight hair, wearing no makeup, sitting next to George Meyer. Could she be the sexy lawyer, who she had been worried about? Hardly Simon's type.

And there was Florian, dear Florian, dressed in a dark suit, his wild curls neatly tamed, and a few other people from the salon. Florian had been a tower of strength to Annabel, and who would have thought that? More than anything this week, she had learned how unpredictable people were.

Neil Lawrence was there, glassy pale, and Flora, of course, in a black flowing skirt and lace-up boots, but rather surprisingly a wonderful aqua-coloured embroidered silk jacket. She was sitting with Richard and Debbie—who was looking particularly dreadful, white and drawn—and their two older children.

There were two other children, she couldn't think who at first and then realised they were Catherine's. Catherine who looked terribly pale, biting her lip. And the lovely Lucinda, quite pregnant now, very sober and still, and beside her—what was his name? oh yes, Blue—looking very fierce, scowling into the aisle. And there was that nice, rather attractive journalist, Joel something or other and . . . who was that tall, thin man, walking rather nervously down the aisle, trying to find a seat in the now-packed church? Lucinda half rose to greet him, while looking nervously at Blue, but then she saw Catherine smile at him and move her children up and create an empty seat beside her.

The organ was playing, lovely, lovely Handel and Bach, and the sun was streaming in and it all seemed rather joyful and Elizabeth wondered wildly, briefly, where she was and what she was doing there. And then she stiffened, for the church fell silent, and the rich voice of the vicar rang out into it, saying, "I am the Way, the Truth and the Life . . ." and Annabel was sobbing quietly, and huge tears were rolling down Tilly's face as the organ broke into her choice for her father, "Lord of All Hopefulness."

Annabel was reading first, the twenty-third Psalm, and she couldn't imagine how she could possibly get through one line of it, let alone twenty. She felt her mother nudge her gently, and whisper, "Good luck, darling," and she walked to the lectern and looked at them all and took a deep breath and began, heard her voice shake, stopped, thought she couldn't go on, and then saw Florian smile very briefly and sweetly at her, and that got her through, even though her voice continued to shake at times and when she finally reached, "And I will dwell in the house of the Lord for ever," she heard someone begin to cry very quietly and realised it was her, and she went back to her mother's side, tears flooding now but no longer important, because she had done what she had to do for both her and for her father.

Catherine had continued to hold her children's hands throughout the service. She felt a great need for human contact, for reality in this nightmare that made no sense at all. She recognised that she had—like so many women, she felt sure—been half in love with Simon, and it wasn't just because of his kindness to her, or even because of his charm and his gift for making her feel important. He had been that rare thing, a joy to know; he had made everything sweeter, funnier, warmer just by being there.

His children; those poor children. She, more than anyone, knew what it meant to children to lose their father. These were older than hers, but still so vulnerable . . . She saw Toby, dressed in the absurdly idiosyncratic uniform of Eton College, mount the lectern and read with extraordinary maturity the very piece she had chosen for Frederick's funeral, Canon Henry Scott-Holland's lovely "Death Is Nothing at All," and sat listening to this light, adolescent voice telling them what his father would have wished them to think, had he had any choice in the matter: "I have only slipped away into the next room . . . Call me by my old familiar name . . ."

"Oh dear," she whispered, trying not to cry for she felt dreadfully and freshly alone: and then realised that Nigel was looking at her over the heads of her children, looking at her with great concern, and then he half smiled at her, and she smiled back, and suddenly felt a little better.

Toby had finished reading, and suddenly he felt the need to say something else, and he took a deep breath and said, "I expect many of you will be wondering why I'm wearing my school uniform in the middle of the holidays." He even at this point managed a smile. "My father was incredibly proud that I got into Eton, and incredibly proud that I was there. I think today is about doing what he'd like, and I thought he'd like me to be wearing these ridiculous clothes."

Everyone smiled; there was even a light wave of laughter. And then Toby went and said, "Budge up" to Tilly, and sat down very quiet and still, his head bowed, and then, as the organ rose again, he reached across Tilly for his mother's hand and held it as if he would never let it go again. And when Tilly got up to read, he moved closer still to Elizabeth and he looked up at her and smiled and then, big boy that he was, put his head on her shoulder and stayed there, unmoving, for a long time.

Tilly read beautifully, her voice calm and confident. "This is a poem my father and I both loved, it's by Gerard Manley Hopkins and it's called 'Heaven-Haven.' "

Flora sat listening to her, thinking of her friendship with Simon, the friendship that had become so important to her, and thought too, that he had exactly arrived "Where no storms come, Where the green swell is in the havens dumb, And out of the swing of the sea," and in spite of her sadness, of the tears and sorrow in the church, the sad droop of Elizabeth's lovely head, of Annabel's fresh tears, she felt they were all briefly comforted.

Just the same she felt very much afraid that, in spite of his brave words, his refusal to accept defeat, it was likely that in the end it had all become unbearable, though she would have died rather than admit it.

They all stood now to sing the last hymn, "Jerusalem," and as the organ drenched the church in wonderful, inspirational sound, Debbie felt she would be crying forever. It wasn't just Simon she had lost, her friend and guide through nearly two years now, it was the previous years, the innocent happy-family years, that had ended as she had met him. Just now she felt absolutely lost and afraid; with no idea what might happen to her.

And then, as the choir sang "God Be in My Head," the coffin was borne from the church, followed by the family and closest friends, bound for the crematorium and the fearsome, final goodbye.

Joel, surprised at his misery, had been sitting at the back of the church, carefully far from Debbie and her family, waiting for it to be all right to leave. And then, as if it was the most natural thing in the world, the organ stopped playing Bach and moved into Simon's favourite song—"Your Song," by Elton John. Joel would have expected it to sound inappropriate, cheap even, but it seemed to suit that moment of that day to an extraordinary degree. People were eased into smiling, moving, greeting one another, saying how lovely it had been, the Simon they had all known brought in some odd way back into their midst.

His desire to escape quite gone, Joel sat there, listening, not thinking very much at all; and then he stood up, turned to his left—and found himself staring straight into Debbie's large brown eyes. And then he was struck by a great blow of emotion, emotion for her. He wasn't quite sure what it was even, but love, tenderness, concern, they were all there, and he wanted to tell her, to show her, to make sure she knew.

And Debbie, staring back at him, felt it too, and acknowledged it; and she knew quite clearly, they both did, she and Joel, that this was a new and important thing between them, only just beginning, and it had only a little to do with what had happened before.

The party, for such it became—and to which Debbie went, but Joel did not—was surprisingly splendid, held in the garden of the house. There was champagne, there was sunshine, there was a jazz band, people talked and laughed and regaled one another with stories about Simon, and the children felt briefly better, released from the formality of the morning and the horror of seeing their father's coffin slide through the curtains in the crematorium chapel.

Only Elizabeth remained absolutely unhappy through it all; and even she, as the shadows crept into the garden and lengthened, felt at the very least a satisfaction that she had done her best and that Simon would have been pleased.

Chapter 40

Morag Dunbar was a pretty woman, blond and blue-eyed, in her mid-forties, Debbie thought, dressed exactly as she would have expected in a pale-blue twinset, tweed skirt, and navy leather loafers.

"I can't tell you," she said, "how thrilled I am that you and your husband are going to join us. And your delightful family, of course. Alexander seems to like what he's seen of the school and I can tell you the school will certainly like him. A cricketer! We're rather short of them. Now for the girls, I'd suggest St. Margaret's, in Calderigg; it's only about ten miles away, a delightful school, quite academic, and very caring. I know the head very well and—"

Debbie shot a beseeching glance at Richard. To her immense relief, he responded. He really was trying; she had to give him that.

"Well, the thing is, Morag, Debbie has her job in London, and needs to give them proper notice, and we don't want to rush the decision about the girls' school."

"Oh dear." Morag's face was sterner suddenly. "I thought you had made your minds up. That is certainly what you led me to believe."

"I've made my mind up," said Richard, smiling slightly nervously, "and indeed we will be coming, but Debbie and the children possibly not until next term. I can do a term here solo, as it were, and then—"

"That won't be nearly as satisfactory," said Morag. "I need a wife who can provide the pastoral care the children need: that would be very much your role, Mrs. Fielding—"

"Debbie," said Debbie politely.

"Debbie. Very much your role. And I'm sure your employers would understand that you need to be here for the beginning of term. That is just over four weeks away now, so they would have a little time to replace you. What is it you do, Debbie? I'm sorry, your husband did tell me, but I've forgotten."

"I'm in public relations," said Debbie.

"Really? My goodness, we can put you to work on the school's behalf; we desperately need our profile raised—is that the right expression?"

"Yes, it is. Yes, but you see—" Don't get excited, Debbie, don't get aggressive. Just stay calm.

"I'm sorry, Morag," said Richard. "I'm afraid that we do have to ask for this term's grace for my wife. She's hoping to continue working for her firm on certain projects, you see, much easier now with this wonderful new e-mail—and then we have to sell our house, which won't be easy long distance, with the property market in disarray. I'm very sorry." Richard smiled at Morag. "It's my fault for not—not planning it all properly. But there is one other thing: my mother has lost all her money at Lloyd's and she's got to sell the family home, and I think one of us should be near her while she's going through that."

"Of course," said Morag. This seemed to be a far more reasonable excuse for Debbie's delayed arrival. "How dreadful. I've got friends in her situation—I think we all have. Well, it's far from ideal. But I've made my decision that you are the perfect candidate, and the governors are in agreement. We'll just have to muddle along for the first term."

"Well, that's wonderful." Richard was flushed with relief and happiness. He grinned at Debbie and he suddenly looked young again, young and happy, the person she had fallen in love with. And then out of love . . .

She was trying very hard indeed not to think about Joel. It wasn't easy. She seemed to think about him all the time. But if Richard ever found out, it would be the end of their marriage, it was as simple as that. And she had realised, in the dreadfully sad, difficult days after the funeral, that he might be boring and fussy and demanding, and he might have done some fairly mean things recently, but he was basically kind and good, and he loved her. And she loved him. Of course she did.

She would be a good wife and mother, and plan her life around Richard and the children, which was quite easy a lot of the time, especially as Richard was being so extremely nice still . . .

There was a short paragraph in the *Telegraph* about the funeral and about Simon, describing him as a successful and popular City figure.

Maurice Crane's wife, Daphne, brought the paper out to him as he sat in the sun, drinking his coffee.

"You knew him, didn't you, Maurice?"

"Who?"

"Simon Beaumont."

"Yes, I do. He does all his personal insurance through us. Why, what's happened to him?"

"He's dead," said Daphne. "Drowned in a sailing accident."

Maurice was very shocked; he took the paper from her and read the report three times.

"What a terrible thing," he said. "What a really terrible thing." And wondered if he ought to get in touch with Mrs. Beaumont, whom he had spoken to once or twice, to say how sorry he was; and decided that it might be better not to.

Jamie had arrived three weeks after the funeral. "Just for a few days, is that all right, Mummy? I'd so love to see him, it would help, and I don't want to go over there."

Elizabeth had said of course it was all right, and anyway, it would do them all good to have to make an effort for someone, talk about other things.

He really was very sweet, Elizabeth thought; she liked him a lot. Extremely good-looking too, and with the most perfect manners. And he adored Annabel, and was endlessly considerate of her, even if she was being a bit difficult. Which was quite understandable. Apart from the grief which was still awful, they were all on edge. The inquest would be months ahead apparently, because of the French police and their enquiries, and it was going to be hideous. Whatever the outcome.

Toby was particularly haunted by the whole thing, not only that his father might have killed himself but that everyone was about to be told that his father had killed himself.

"I mean, Dad had lots of reasons to do it, didn't he? Losing his job, losing all the money."

"He did, darling, yes, I'm afraid."

"But it's such an awful thing to do. So cowardly. So . . . so kind of giving in. And so awful for us. He must have thought of that!"

"Of course he would have done. And I don't believe he would have hurt us like that. He would just have stuck it out."

Tilly was outraged at the very suggestion, said she knew he wouldn't have done such a thing, that he was too brave, too positive, "Just too happy. He stayed happy through it all. Everyone said so."

Just the same, the whole process of the inquest haunted her; and she had the ordeal of going away to a new school.

Elizabeth was planning to go back to the agency in another week. She asked the children if they'd think it very bad of her, that she might seem uncaring, and they'd all stared at her as if she'd suggested joining a nunnery.

"Of course we wouldn't mind," said Tilly. "You need your work, Mummy, and it needs you. It'll help you, I'm sure."

And then Tilly asked if, for the same reason, she might go and stay with Flora for a few days, see lots of Boy, before she went off to school. A little anxious, for the question of Boy's future had occurred to Elizabeth as it didn't seem to have occurred to Tilly, she had said yes.

"I'll drive you down this weekend—I'd like to see Flora, anyway. She's been a good friend to this family."

And she'd like to say so to Flora's face, Elizabeth thought; she knew she had been less than friendly to her.

❧

"Work seems to cheer Annabel up," Jamie said to Elizabeth. "She really seems to love it." He sounded slightly surprised; Elizabeth smiled at him.

"I know you probably think it's a funny job for a clever girl like her. We did too, at first. But she's very good at it and you know, Jamie, being good at your job and enjoying it is the most wonderful thing. Having fun with it—that's really lucky. Do you enjoy your work?"

"Well, yeah, I guess I do. But law's pretty dry and dusty, and because

Dad runs the firm and tells us all what to do, I don't feel like that too much."

"Yes, I see," said Elizabeth.

"But I mean I'm really glad Annabel has her job, if it makes her feel better. Um . . . did you feel like that when you were young?"

"I did indeed, and I still do. I started work really young—I was only nineteen. I decided, rather like Annabel, not to go to university. I had this chance to go to an agency as a PA, and I just knew I could work my way up. You could then, you can't now—you need degrees and so on."

"Yeah? And when did you have Annabel?" said Jamie.

"Oh, I was twenty-one."

"But you went on working?"

"I did indeed. It was that important to me. And it was very hard sometimes and I'm sure for her as well, and the others when they came along. But I was me, and Simon was Simon, and for both of us that was how we liked—well, me to be. Working, passionate about something. And good at it, which is where we came in."

"Yes, I see." He clearly didn't.

"Your mother didn't work, I know."

"No, she didn't."

"And what about your sister? She's having a baby, I believe?"

"Oh, yes. Well, she'll give up work, pretty soon now. She'll be like my mother. Dana, she's my sister-in-law, she's more like you. She just loves her job. She's a lawyer and she's very successful. But the—the what-do-you-call-it, the clock . . ."

"The biological clock?"

"Yeah, that's it, it's ticking away. And Kathleen being pregnant makes the pressure on her harder. And Bif wouldn't want her to work, if she had a baby, so they're kind of trying to work things out. Mother says she knows she'll come round in the end," he said, clearly unaware of the irony of what he was saying.

"Right. Well, it's a difficult one. And there isn't a right answer. You just have to find your own way."

"I guess so. Er . . . Mrs. Beaumont, my mother is still keen for us to have an engagement party—over in Boston—so that all our friends can meet Annabel. Not yet, of course, but maybe in the New Year. And of course she'd want you and Tilly and Toby to come. She's really looking forward to meeting you all."

"And I'm looking forward to it too. Well, it's a little hard to think about just yet."

"Of course. Now . . . I was going to speak to Mr. Beaumont about all this, of course." More unconscious irony. "But I . . . well, I take it you're happy about our engagement. And I'm very sorry I didn't ask him—and you, of course—before. I got a little carried away. I do love Annabel very, very much. I promise you I'll do everything in my power to make her happy."

"I know that, Jamie. And of course we're . . . that is, I"—how long was it going to be before she ceased to think of herself as herself and Simon—"am very happy about it. But I do have to say, I think she is very young. I imagine you won't think of getting married too soon?"

"No, no of course not. But Mother was only twenty when she married Father. She thinks that would be OK for us. I don't know what you'd think," he added quickly.

"How can I argue? I was only twenty-one when I got married. But what about Annabel, what does she think? She's the important one, surely."

"Yes, of course. I think she agrees that would be about right."

"Good."

"Anyway, we won't be taking her away from you just yet, I promise." Now why did that strike such a chill around her heart, Elizabeth wondered. And then knew. It wasn't that Annabel would be moving to Boston—she was prepared for that. It was the "we." She really didn't like that "we."

❧

Sitting on the verandah of her father's beachside house in Barbados, Felicity Parker Jones was reading a clipping she had been sent from *The Times*, about the tragic death of the prominent City banker, Simon Beaumont.

"Damn shame," she said aloud; and when her father came out to join her for breakfast she showed it to him.

"Good God," he said, "poor chap. How dreadful. You'll miss him,

Flick, won't you? In more ways than one. Have to make a few adjustments."

"I will indeed," she said.

Chapter 41

"Joel, go away. Just go away. Please."

He had arrived at her office, just as she was leaving, bearing a large bunch of roses. Which was hugely romantic, of course, but wasn't helping her in her resolve.

"Please go away," she said feebly again.

That first time he was waiting outside when she left for the day, blinding her with the sweet shock of it.

"Joel!"

"That's me. Where can we go?"

"Nowhere. I mean, I'm going home. I'm late already and—" And then she looked at him, looked properly at him, and absolutely unable to resist him, said, "Well, maybe just a coffee or something. But only so I can explain."

She really had tried, so hard. She told him how she felt deeply ashamed of herself. "It was awful, terrible of me; and I shouldn't have done it."

"I'm glad you did."

She sighed and tried to explain how loyal and supportive Richard was being about going up to Scotland, how he had risked losing the job altogether, to give her some time. "I really can't go on seeing you, Joel."

"Don't you want to?" She hesitated; he pounced on it. "There you are, you do want to."

"Joel please stop it. I—I might want to, but I can't. It was just a . . . a fling, and OK, it was great, but—"

"That's exactly what I thought," he said, "that it was just a fling. But it wasn't. Not for me. It was a shock, that—I'm rather good at flings, I've had lots of them, and don't think I'm proud of that either. But when I got back from the Bahamas, I realised you'd meant a bit more than that. A lot more. I . . . I seem really to care about you, Debbie. I almost wish I didn't, it would make life much simpler, but I do."

And Debbie sat there, looking into his dark eyes, and she could hardly bear it, she wanted him and what he was offering her so much; and then she took a deep breath and tried once again to explain. Which was obviously not very effective, since here he was again, two days later.

Catherine couldn't ever remember being so unhappy. Well, of course she could—when Freddie had run away, and when her husband had died, but even those dreadful events hadn't wiped out her existence as a fully operating human being. Now she seemed to have been completely taken over by the Morgans, and she had no option but to do what they said. Even down to when they would all eat, what times they could leave the house, where the children went to school. It was horrible; she felt like some kind of programmed automaton.

She had won one battle and that was over Freddie's school; she had said that he was not to go away to school, that Frederick had been terribly against it, had hated his own prep school, had been bullied dreadfully.

"Nonsense," Dudley said. "Happy as Larry he was, never heard a word of complaint."

"No, Dudley," she said, emboldened by the strength of her feelings. "That's not true. He told me but he always felt he couldn't tell you, he was too ashamed."

A compromise was reached of weekly boarding "next year." But they were deeply dismissive of Catherine's revelations about the bullying, clearly felt she was being naïve. Caroline's school seemed all right; it was full of rather overconfident little girls who all seemed to have ponies, but who were very friendly at the welcome tea party, at the beginning of September, two weeks before term proper began. They were due to move down on 10 September; term for both of them started a week later. Catherine had accompanied Phyllis to the secondhand uniform sale and watched her buying everything in a size too big for Caroline. "Then it will last longer—it's so expensive, you probably don't realise."

The conversion to their "flat" consisted of putting a gas ring and a sink into what had been a very small bathroom. "We'll leave the bath, as we may want to convert it back again," Phyllis said. "Dudley suggests fitting some kind of casing over it, to make a useful surface for you—such a good idea, don't you think?" And had installed a minute shower into the lavatory. "It saves expense with the plumbing, you see," Dudley had said. The children had small individual bedrooms, made by partitioning one big one, and Catherine's bedroom was even smaller, with a single bed; while she was sure there wasn't the slightest possibility of her ever needing a double again, she still felt rather written off, as she said to Lucinda.

"You're dreading it, aren't you? Poor Catherine."

"No, no, not dreading it," said Catherine firmly, for once she started to talk about her misery, she knew she would never stop. "A little apprehensive, of course. But—well, you know, it will be nice not to be so desperately worried about money and to know the children are at good schools. And I'm sure I'll make lots of friends in no time . . ."

She could hear the hollow ring in her voice now, thinking of the mothers at Caroline's school, all briskly sporty, wearing Puffas and dirndl skirts, shouting at one another about pony-club camps and point-to-points. Where among them would she find one friend, let alone lots?

"Well, you must come up for the day as often as you can and see me," said Lucinda. "Oh dear, I shall miss you."

"I'll miss you too. I was thinking about Simon . . . Lucinda, do you think he did it deliberately?" Catherine's face was very distressed.

"I don't know," said Lucinda. "It seems at least quite possible. I mean, it wasn't just the money, he'd lost his job—it was all very . . . black."

"Yes, but he was the opposite of black. Right to—to the end. Oh God, I do hope he didn't. It's such a terrible way to go."

Elizabeth spent a long, harrowing afternoon at the solicitors. The facts were stark. She had thought that because Simon had resigned from Lloyd's, when the first problems arose, his liability would shortly have ceased. "I'm afraid not, Elizabeth," John Fraser, their solicitor, said gently. "A resignation merely releases you from underwriting new business. You can still be liable for any business you've underwritten in the past."

She had stared at him, stricken.

"So we—I sell the house, give Lloyd's that money and anything else they can get their hands on, and it could still be going on, them taking money from me, in ten years' time."

"I'm afraid so, yes. It's a great pity that Simon had taken out a bank's guarantee on your house, of course. Lloyd's don't generally insist on the sale of the main residence."

"Indeed it was. But he made a foolish investment, in an overseas property business. God . . ." She paused. "So whatever I do or make, they can go on taking for as long as they like?"

"Well, no. The debts don't pass to you personally, but because Simon's estate unfortunately does, they can take everything that's in it."

She suddenly felt dreadfully sick.

"Are you all right, my dear?"

"Yes, yes, I'm fine. Thank you. Sorry."

"Don't apologise. Have some water." He poured her a glass; she sipped it and the feeling began to pass.

"Go on," she said. "I'm all right now."

"Good. Now, there is quite a lot of good news. Whatever you earn is yours. Lloyd's can make no claim on it. And there are two substantial sums that Lloyd's cannot get their hands on."

"Really? Like what?"

"Well, you have a widow's pension from the bank."

"But they fired him."

"Fact remains, Elizabeth, they are required by law to pay you the pension."

"Goodness. And . . . and how much would that be?"

"In the region of thirty thousand pounds a year."

"Are you sure? Are you quite sure?"

"Absolutely. The other sum due to you is very considerable."

"Tell me," she said. She was beginning to feel quite sick again.

"It's Simon's personal life cover. Which is written in trust for you."

"God. How . . . how much is that, John?"

"Two hundred and fifty thousand pounds. And that is tax free. So I hope that will relieve some of those middle-of-the-night fears. Grief is bad enough without gnawing financial anxiety as well."

She arrived home feeling very confused. She went straight upstairs to their bedroom, took her jacket off, lay down on the bed.

It was a huge relief, obviously, that they would still be quite comfortably off. On the other hand, it did mean that Simon was indeed worth a great deal more dead than alive. And that meant that . . .

"Oh Simon," she said aloud, looking at the photograph of him, her favourite, standing on the deck of the *Lizzie*, his hair whipped by the wind, smiling his most gloriously infectious smile. "Oh Simon, you shouldn't have done it. You really shouldn't."

Chapter 42

"My darling, you look wonderful. Positively blooming. Love the hair. Now come and sit down, let me get you something. Er . . . are you allowed—"

"I am. But this is on me. So—champagne?"

"Champagne it is. A little Bolly would go down a treat. And I won't argue, although I should as an English gentleman . . ."

The Bollinger had arrived, duly ice-bucketed. "You can't beat the Ritz, can you?" said Virgil. "I always forget how wonderful it is. We have the Plaza, of course, very similar in a way, but not quite the class . . . I prefer the Pierre myself. More discreet. Or even the Carlyle—that was Kennedy's favourite, you know. Very stylish indeed."

"Oh, I'd so love to go to New York," said Lucinda wistfully. She felt her life rather lacked style at the moment; she looked at Virgil in his pale-blue linen shirt, his black linen suit, his perfectly cropped black hair, and thought he epitomised it.

"My darling, come. You'd adore it. And it would adore you."

"Well, maybe not just now." Lucinda patted her stomach.

"No, and many congratulations on that. Is—that is, does Nigel . . ."

"Nigel doesn't," said Lucinda firmly. "I have a new—oh dear, what should I call him?"

"Beau?"

"More than a beau. A fiancé."

"How sweet. So what happened?"

"I—I just met him," Lucinda said, "and fell in love."

"Well, darling, that's very lovely. And is he another good old English toff?"

"No, he isn't. He comes from . . . from Essex. Originally."

"Essex! Lucinda, how exciting. You've got yourself a bit of rough. Well, I would never have thought it of you, the archetypal posh English rose. When you first came to work at the gallery, I really thought you were too good to be true. And when you married Nigel, well . . . How is the old fruit? Heartbroken? Or does he have another?"

"Not yet, I'm afraid," said Lucinda, "but I keep hoping."

"And you're happy?"

"Oh, so happy."

"Well, that's what matters. Nigel will get over it, sweetie. He's got lots of money, after all; some other English rose will bloom for him."

"That's the problem," said Lucinda. "He's about to be very poor, unless I can help him."

"Something tells me," said Virgil, "that this might be where I come in. And what do I come in doing?"

"Just . . . just saying something, that's all."

"Saying something. Hmm. In writing?"

"Well, yes."

"What sort of something? Go on—I like seeing you squirm, Lucinda."

"It goes something like this . . ." She told him what she wanted; he sat staring at her, then burst into peals of mirth.

"Darling Lucinda. What a glorious notion. As if you were worth that!"

"I might have been."

"Sweetheart, you weren't. Not a quarter of it."

"Oh," she said, and felt her heart literally drop. "Well . . . well, I'll have to think of something else then."

"Here. Have some more Bolly. And don't look so dejected. Nobody knows you weren't worth it, except me. So tell me what I have to do exactly. And I'll do it."

"Oh, Virgil!" She hurled herself at him, kissed him on both cheeks. "Thank you so, so much, it's so good of you."

"It is quite," he said. "It could be classed as perjury, if anyone was looking. I'm only doing it because it amuses me. And I want to hear exactly what is it about dear old chinless Nige that you want to do this for him. I long to know, darling. It sounds terribly intriguing . . ."

℘

"Mummy . . ."

"Yes, darling?" Elizabeth looked up. Tilly was standing in the doorway, very white and big-eyed.

"Mummy, I'm terribly sorry, but I just don't think I can go to my new school. I can't face it, not leaving you and Annabel and home and—" She started crying, like a small child. Elizabeth got up, went over, and put her arms round her.

"Oh Tilly. Darling, of course you don't have to go. I've been dreading it too. And worrying about you. I thought you were looking forward to it."

"Oh Mummy, no. Dreading it more every day. I'm sorry, I should have said, but I didn't want to worry you."

"It doesn't matter a bit," said Elizabeth, thinking that actually it did. Term began in two days; even a week's notice would have helped. "Now come on, darling," she said, berating herself for her selfishness, "let's see what we can sort out. The first thing to do is ring Mrs. Priest at St. Anne's. I'll do it now, while you get us a cup of tea."

Mrs. Priest was surprisingly accommodating.

"Of course I understand. Let her take her time. A couple more weeks won't make much difference, and she's a bright girl, she'll catch up."

"There." Elizabeth smiled at Tilly as she came back into the room with the tray. "They say you can take your time, start when you're ready. Isn't that good?"

"Well, sort of, but the thing is, Mummy, I don't want to go away at all. I want to be home with you, looking after you."

"Now Tilly," said Elizabeth firmly, "I can't have you, any of you, thinking you have to stay at home with me. I want everyone to do what they want, not what they think they ought to do."

"It's not what I think I ought to do," said Tilly, starting to cry again, "it's what I *want* to do. I'm scared, Mummy, so scared. It's like some monster is swallowing us up, bit by bit. I can't go away, I just can't. I want to be here, holding on to what we've got left. I feel safer here—at least I can see what's happening . . ."

And then Elizabeth was crying too, as hard as Tilly, and they sat there for a long time, holding each other. And she promised Tilly she would find her a day school.

Later, when Tilly had gone to meet Annabel, Elizabeth pulled out the *Good School Guide* and started leafing through it. A good day school, over-subscribed four times as all London schools were, that would take a child at two days' notice, how on earth was she going to find that? God, she felt so tired. So deathly, deathly tired.

ೞ

Catherine was packing rather lethargically when the phone rang.

"Is that Catherine?"

"Yes, it is."

"Catherine, it's Nigel. Nigel Cowper. I heard you were moving to Somerset and I wondered if you'd let me take you all out to tea before you went. I so enjoyed our coffee that morning at Peter Jones, I thought we could do it again. Your children are a great credit to you, you know."

"That would be lovely," said Catherine.

"So what day could you do?"

"Well, Lucinda's driving us down on Sunday. So it would have to be Saturday, I'm afraid. Is that any good to you? Of course I'll understand if it's not. You're probably terribly busy."

"What—on a Saturday afternoon? Of course not. So where would you like to go? Where would they like to go?"

Catherine suddenly felt rather reckless. After all, it was most unlikely she'd have a man asking her where she'd like to go for a very long time.

"How brave are you feeling?"

"Oh, pretty brave. I mean, I believe children like McDonald's—you know, that hamburger place . . ."

"I do know, yes," said Catherine, "but if you're feeling very brave, we could go one better. It would do a lot for their street cred."

Although, she reflected rather sadly, the children's new schoolmates would probably be more impressed by a point-to-point than what she was about to suggest.

"Oh well, I'm all for that."

"It's a place called the Hard Rock Café and it's in Old Park Lane. The children have wanted to go there forever. They do burgers, brilliant ones, and later on there's music, with DJs, rock and jazz and so on."

"I'm not quite sure I'd like that," said Nigel a little nervously.

"But not when we go, don't worry. You do have to queue, though, you can't book, it's all part of the fun."

"Well," said Nigel—and she could almost hear him taking a deep breath—"well, it all sounds very exciting. For me as well as them. It's certainly a long way from Derry and Toms Roof Garden, where I used to be taken if I'd been good."

"How grand," said Catherine, and then found herself wondering what she would wear. Which was obviously ridiculous, for Nigel was hardly going to take any notice of her, it was the children's treat . . .

Chapter 43

There she was in all the papers, crying. Because her little boy had gone away to school. Well, if it was all right for Diana to cry, Catherine thought, then she would too. Of course, Prince William was going to boarding school and Freddie would be coming home again that evening—quite late, he had to stay at school for prep—but he was still terrified, white-faced and shaking with nerves in his too-big uniform.

He had gone in without a backward glance, ushered by his form master, and in the company of a bigger boy. "Such a good system, isn't it?" Phyllis had said. "They allot seniors to take care of the little ones, as of course they would if he was boarding. Now, we've got a long drive home, Catherine. I hope you realise you're going to have to do this every day." Catherine said she did. But at least she would be driving; she actually had a car, and it promised to transform her life. Lucinda had said, when she came to collect them, that she had been thinking and that really, for the time being, she would like Catherine to have her Peugeot.

"I've got the Gti, after all, and I can't drive them both at the same time, and Blue thinks it's a really good idea." She didn't add that Blue had said that clearly the car would have been driven into several walls within the space of a week, and that he hoped Lucinda was ready to say goodbye to it. "So you take this, and—"

"Lucinda, I can't."

"Of course you can. It'll help, and make me less worried about you, down there on your own with those dreadful people. And besides, you'll be able to come up and see me more easily, think of it that way."

It seemed a very long day, waiting to collect him; all she could think of was his white face, and her terror that he might cry and be labelled a sissy.

She and Caroline spent the afternoon marking her new school uniform; it was rather nice: brown kilts, blue blouses, oatmeal sweaters, and dark brown hats and coats.

"I'm sorry it's so big, sweetie," she said, as Caroline tried it all on. "I don't think I can shorten the kilt, because of the pleats, but I can probably do the coat. Only . . ."

"It's OK," said Caroline bravely. "Honestly, I'm growing so fast, that's one thing Grandma's right about, it'll probably fit me by half term."

Catherine hugged her, thinking how brave her children were and how she didn't deserve them.

She was so terrified of being late that she was back at the school by twenty to six. The area slowly filled up with Range Rovers and Volvo Estates, with mothers shouting at one another and ignoring her.

What on earth am I going to do, Catherine thought, if he doesn't like it, if he's unhappy here? We really have burned our boats—how could we possibly move again? And she felt so sick with apprehension she thought she might follow Freddie's example and throw up in the hedge.

Endless small boys appeared, but there was no sign of Freddie; after ten minutes she was frantic; he might be inside crying, or hiding from her, afraid that she would see he was upset . . . or had he got a detention already? Or had he—oh God—had he run away again? Then three small boys came out like rockets, cannoning into her.

"Hi, Mum, this is Groom and this is Hutchings, we're all new and guess what, Mum, I'm doing soccer trials tomorrow and there's a choir, I'm trying for that as well . . ."

She stood there, smiling at Freddie, trying not to cry at the same time, and at Groom and Hutchings too.

"No problems here then," said one of their mothers, and, "Super, absolutely super, isn't it?" said the other.

However lonely she was, Catherine thought, however dreadful her in-laws, it simply didn't matter. If the children were happy, then she could stand anything else. Anything.

They drove home, Freddie talking nonstop: the other boys were really cool, his form master was great, the work was fine, he was ahead in maths even.

Phyllis met them on the doorstep, received a truncated account of the successful day, gave Catherine an "I told you so" look and then said, "There was a phone call for you. A man." Her tone carried a distinct note of disapproval.

"Oh," said Catherine. "Did he give a name?"

"Yes, Mr. Cowper, he said. He asked if you could ring him back. I said it would be better if he rang you, as it was long-distance."

"Yes, of course," said Catherine. "Thank you. When did he—that is, what time . . ."

"About six," said Phyllis. "Now I must go, I'm off to a drinks party. I'll see you tomorrow. Glad the day was a success, Freddie. What did I tell you? And if you were boarding, you'd still be there—just think of that."

"Wish I was," said Freddie.

⁓

"He loved it," said Catherine, smiling into the phone when Nigel rang later in the evening. "Of course, it's early days, but it really seems to suit him. And guess what, he said he wanted to board."

"Take no notice," said Nigel briskly. "I wanted to board at his age, and then spent the next year crying myself to sleep. But I'm so glad it went well."

"It's sweet of you to ring," said Catherine. "Thank you."

"Not at all. Nothing so terrifying as a first day at a new school. Couldn't stop thinking about him. Well, tell him well done from me."

"I will. Goodbye, Nigel."

"Goodbye, Catherine. Enjoy country life."

Well, that was clearly that, she thought, putting the phone down. Goodness, he was a nice man. And clearly still hopelessly in love with Lucinda.

❧

Debbie was actually quite enjoying her new life. Without Richard. Well, of course she missed him, she was used to having him around all the time, he was her husband, for heaven's sake; but it made a fantastic difference to how much she got done, having her evenings to herself, deciding how to spend them, being able to work if she wanted to, or watch any old crap on the telly, or have an hour-long bath and read.

The children liked it too; they liked having her undivided attention. They looked forward to the alternate weekends, but day to day, or rather evening to evening, she had never known them so biddable, so calm.

She'd found a nice lady called Jenny to look after them after school, and Richard rang three nights a week full of enthusiasm: "It's so wonderfully peaceful up here, Debbie. I feel quite different, unstressed, you know, and with much more energy, and the school's the most marvellous place—the children are all so bright and confident and really want to work and learn, and I seem to be managing. Morag's been absolutely fantastic, so patient with me, so encouraging . . ."

And Debbie kept saying good, great, that's marvellous, how wonderful, and how they were fine, but they missed him and were counting the days till half term when they were all going up there, while counting the days herself, only backwards rather than forwards, thinking, "Only two whole months left," or "Only ten weeks," and wondering how she was going to bear the ending of it. Because, of course, she just didn't want to go.

The children had all finally gone to bed that evening, and she was settling down happily to her new favourite programme, *Capital City*, which Richard would have poured great scorn on, all about the yuppies and their dealings in the City, when there was a ring at the bell. Probably Jan; it was another bonus of Richard's absence that she saw more of her now. He had been jealous of Jan and their closeness. She went to the front door, smiling as she opened it. "Hi, Jan," she said. Only it wasn't Jan, it was Joel.

"I had to see you," he said. "I couldn't bear it any longer. I'm sorry."

"Joel," she said in a low voice, "you can't come and see me at my house; the children are all upstairs, probably still awake. I'm not going to let you in. Just go away and—"

"Mum! I'm thirsty." Alexander appeared at the top of the stairs, peered down at Joel. "Who's that?"

"It's a man come to see the house," she said.

"He can't come now, we're all in bed."

"I know, Alexander, that's what I've just told him. I'll be up with some water in a minute."

"If you don't agree to see me now," said Joel, "I'll come to your office tomorrow."

"I'm not in the office tomorrow."

"OK. On Thursday in the office."

"Joel, why are you doing this? Why can't you respect what I want to do?"

"Because it's not what you want to do. And I won't let you think it. I know you're not happy—"

"Yes, I am," she said. "We're perfectly happy together, thank you."

"Bollocks," he said. "Anyway, you're much too lovely to be locked into a miserable situation and to have to spend the rest of your life in some Scottish convent—"

"It's not a convent."

"It might as well be."

"Oh, Joel . . ." But the kernel of the truth had reached her heart; she felt tears stinging at the back of her eyes.

"So which is it to be? Now, or the day after tomorrow?"

A long silence, while she fought against it. It won.

"The day after tomorrow," she said, very quietly.

☙

"All right," Flora said. "Colin, I've made up my mind. Let's do it. Anything rather than let them have this house."

"Fantastic," he said. "Look, we'd better not discuss it on the phone. Would you like to have dinner with me tonight or tomorrow and we can set the wheels in motion. I know you've made the right decision, Flora. I really do."

It was Simon's death that had determined that decision. She had gone for a long ride on Hal, thinking about this monster that had, in their own small circle, killed Simon—for she remained as sure as she could be of anything that it had been suicide—destroyed Nigel Cowper's upright, harmless life and Catherine Morgan's bright young one, and led a small boy into running away. If she could keep that monster from taking any more from any of them, she wanted to do it passionately. It was the only thing to do. Otherwise Lloyd's had won. And she just wouldn't let them. She just wouldn't.

Chapter 44

It just wasn't possible, was it? She couldn't be, could she? And if she was— well, could she cope with it? What would everyone think? What would everyone say? Did it make things worse? Or did it make them better? Two days, they'd said. That was doing it properly. Which, of course, she wanted. She wasn't going to trust some over-the-counter rubbish. Oh God. It just wasn't possible—was it? She couldn't be, could she?

Blue had gone on a two-day trip to Brussels; Lucinda had decided to take advantage of his absence to see Steve Durham, make a progress report. Now that she had given up work, it was much harder to do anything without Blue cross-questioning her about it; where had she been, who had she seen, why, what for; for some reason he probed very closely into her comings and goings, how long she had been out, how she had got there. It was beginning to drive her mad.

Blue was very patient and sympathetic most of the time, but every so often when he was tired, when he had had a bad day at work, and life wasn't easy for him, with rocketing interest rates and the country tipping fast into a depression—then he would snap if she said she was fed up, telling her she had nothing to be fed up about, constantly telling her they should have moved, that it was like living in a bloody rabbit hutch and what did she think they were going to do for space when the baby came.

And he did have a point, Lucinda thought. The little house looked like the baby department of Peter Jones, with a pram, car seat, and high chair stacked in the hall; the tiny room she had turned into a nursery only just big enough to take the frilled crib, the chest of drawers, and the changing table; and the sleek white, chrome-trimmed bathroom was filled with packs of nappies, a baby bath, and another changing table.

"We can't move now," said Lucinda, while thinking wistfully of the huge houses she had rejected, with their nurseries and en suite baby bathrooms, their huge kitchens—God, she was doing a lot for Nigel. "It's much too late. I've only got about six weeks to go—"

"Thank God," said Blue and walked out, slamming the door.

☙

"How are you feeling then?" Steve Durham said as she walked into his office. "You look wonderful."

This was so patently untrue that Lucinda felt quite cross.

"I don't look wonderful, Steve, I look like some kind of two-legged hippo."

"Nonsense," he said, and grinned at her. "Anyway, we're nearly there. Your American friend wrote a very nice letter, very nice indeed, saying exactly what I asked him to. Want to see it?"

"No," said Lucinda, "I don't think so. It would just make me cry, thinking what I might be doing, running some chic gallery in the middle of Manhattan and earning megabucks for it."

"Hmm . . ." said Steve Durham. He saw her glaring at him and gave her a quick smile. "Course. But then you wouldn't be here, wouldn't be having Blue's baby. Now, I've written back to your husband's solicitor, sorted out his questions, told him both clients are happy with it, and then we'll put it to the court, send off the consent order, and hopefully get it all done and dusted this side of Christmas. And then you can do what you like with it all. Now he has still got the farm, hasn't he?"

"Yes, he has. But it's got to go soon, he says."

"Not too soon," said Steve Durham, "or this isn't going to wash so well. You had better point that out to him, Lucinda, and best not in writing, just give him a call. Say once it's all over, it'll be fine to go ahead; in fact, it'll make it all the more convincing. Now, do you want to have a little chat about setting up this charitable trust?"

e⌢

When she got home, her head was throbbing; she lay down on the bed and closed her eyes. This was exactly what she didn't need just now: complicated arrangements and the need to remember dozens of small important things. Like . . . golly, like she must ring Nigel.

She rang his office; no reply. What was he doing, out in the middle of the day—and where was that annoying secretary of his? She dialled the home number, and when the answering machine cut in, "Hello, Nigel," she said, "it's Lucinda here. Hope you're well. I need to speak to you as soon as poss, so give me a call either today or tomorrow." And then she fell asleep.

e⌢

It was terrible. And absolutely glorious. And how had she allowed herself to do this, to get into a full-blown, wonderfully brilliant affair; and worse than that to admit what she had known all along, of course, of course: that she was in love, in love for the first time, as she could now see it was. Proper love, heart-possessing, mind-engrossing, completely obsessing love.

She'd thrown caution not just to the wind but into a reckless hurricane. She told lies to everyone: to her colleagues, to her children, to her husband, to her friends. She had to see clients, she said, she had to attend late meetings, she had to visit her dentist, her doctor—if anything really went wrong with her health it would be impossible to claim any further appointments and she would die of a ruptured appendix and it would serve her right. It wasn't just to go to bed with Joel, their meetings; sometimes it was just to snatch a coffee break, a drink after work, spending time together, talking, laughing, quite often in Debbie's case crying—it was as important as sex. The sex was amazing, flying, shouting, blazing, glorious sex; but it was Joel himself that she loved, Joel, who was funny and solemn and tender and crude and sweet and harsh, and loving and lovable. The thing that had swung it, first swung her back into bed with him, was not that he had finished with Maggie, but an unbelievable story that she had believed.

"Do you know when I realised I cared about you?" he had said at the first meeting, two days after he had come to her house. "Really cared about you, I mean. When I was in the Bahamas, fresh from you, from enjoying you, I met this girl, a model. Quite a famous one."

"Called?"

"Bibi."

"I've never heard of her," she said, cross.

"OK. She was in *Vogue* this month, she told me."

"And—"

"She came to my room. We shared some champagne, she wasn't even staying in my hotel, I met her at the other place, she'd tracked me down."

"Am I supposed to be impressed that she fancied you so much?"

"I want you to be. And then she stood up and started taking her clothes off. Well, she didn't have much on—a sort of silk tunic thing and some trousers. That was it. And she just stood there, totally sublime, this glorious colour all over—and you know what? I told her to go away. Just go away. I thought of you, with those wonderful round firm little breasts, and that flat stomach of yours, how did you ever house all those babies there, and your gorgeous thick, black bush, and I just didn't want her. I wanted you. Now you can believe me or not, as you wish, but it's the truth, Debbie."

"Did you really send her away?"

"I did."

"And was it really because of me?"

"It was. I think you're a hundred times lovelier, and sexier, and more lovable."

"You're mad," she said. "Completely mad."

"Maybe. Mad with love. Now, you going to meet me again? Like— tonight?"

"Yes," she said. "Tonight."

That was when the lying had to begin.

Annabel often wondered how she would have got through those first awful weeks without Florian. He didn't fuss much, just asked her every morning how she was, always bought her a pain au chocolat from the baker in Sloane Street on his way in, because it was her favourite, and then alternately cosseted her and teased her through the day. He didn't allow her to slack and indeed, once the first fortnight was over, pushed her quite hard; and she was grateful for that too. She was enough her mother's daughter to recognise the value of work as therapy. And then most evenings he bought her a drink on her way home, actually waiting for her if he finished before she did. They would sit in a wine bar, gossiping lazily.

"And how's your lovely little sister, out there in the blackboard jungle?" Tilly had started at the local comprehensive; none of the London independent schools could take her; Annabel and Elizabeth had seen her off the first day in a state of great apprehension at what the pupils of Cromwell Road School would make of this hopelessly posh creature with her wide-blue-eyed innocence, and in love with her pony.

"She's been there now for two weeks, and she seems OK," Annabel said. "I keep asking her if she's had any problems and she looks at me vaguely and says no, it's fine. I think it's because she's in her own Tilly world, and she just gets on with it. She comes home with two girls from the estate, you know, and they seem to really like her. They came round the other evening, one's black and very skinny and the other's white and very fat, and they all sat watching telly and giggling together. Apparently she helps the skinny one—she's called Fallon—with her homework, because she's dyslexic. And the boys all shout and whistle at her, call her Princess Posho, but nicely. You can see they think she's rather gorgeous . . ."

"And how's your mum?"

"She's back at work, although coming home quite early, which is nice. She's so brave, Florian, she tries to be cheerful with us, but I hear her crying sometimes in her room. She's lost loads of weight, and I actually don't think she's very well; she's not eating much, says she feels nauseated, and she's quite often actually sick, poor Mummy."

Lucinda woke up from her afternoon nap, it was getting dark; she looked at her watch: half past seven. Winter was clearly on its way. Well, they were nearly halfway through October: and then, goodness, only four weeks or so and the baby would be here. She realised as she struggled up from the bed that her almost chronic headache had got worse. She had been very good throughout her pregnancy, had hardly taken so much as an aspirin, but this was exceptional. She'd have to drive to the big supermarket, get something there. It wouldn't matter to Blue, he'd said it would be at least eight before he got back, and she'd got some steak for his supper, that she couldn't cook until he got home anyway . . . She picked up her keys, and went out to her car.

Blue felt absolutely shattered when he finally reached Limehouse. These trips were bloody exhausting. Well, he'd got back sooner than he'd expected at least; he was hungry though, the food on the plane had been complete crap and the delicious lunch in Brussels a long time ago.

He unlocked the front door and shouted to Lucinda that he was home: no reply. He looked in their bedroom wondering if she was asleep—she seemed to drop off at a moment's notice these days—and then went into the kitchen. There were some potatoes scrubbed lying on the draining board, and what was clearly going to be a salad, but that was all. God, things were going from bad to worse. Sex was becoming a distant memory and although he understood the reason and even sympathised, it wasn't exactly ideal, and now it seemed food was going the same way. Where was she, and why hadn't she left a note, for God's sake?

The phone rang; he was about to pick it up and then decided against it; it might be Lucinda's mother, who had taken to calling her recently. The answering machine would deal with it, and then if it was someone he wanted to talk to, he could pick up. It was Nigel.

Chapter 45

So she was: definitely. And she definitely wasn't going to have it. For so many reasons. She told her nice gynaecologist, Sarah Goodrich, when she went to see her to request a termination.

"But, Elizabeth—why, exactly?" Sarah said. "And how do you feel?"

"Dreadful," she had said. "Sick and so, so tired, all the time."

"Of course. But that won't last."

"The tiredness will. Sarah, I'm over forty. I'm not a girl. And that's another thing. Think of the risks—of a Down's baby especially. And all the other risks to my health. I can't afford that when the children need me. And I have to work, I'm the only source of income. And I still don't know how it's happened."

"Well, we took you off your high-dose pill and you had a short break from it then—"

"Yes, but that was before . . . well, before I got pregnant. And only a few days . . ."

"I realise that. But the changeover would still have been a dangerous time, in terms of conception, that is. And you know that there's an old wives' tale, that women around forty seem to have a big zoom in fertility. It's supposed to be nature giving you a last chance of motherhood. What I think is more likely is that it's women giving themselves, probably completely subconsciously, a last chance. Something has to explain all those afterthought babies."

"Well, I certainly didn't want one," said Elizabeth crossly, "and I'm not having the baby."

"Have you considered talking to the children about it?"

"No. I want to have the termination and for them never to know. They're going to find it very distressing otherwise."

"And how do you think they'd find it if you had the baby?"

"I'm pretty sure they'd find it very difficult. You know, nobody has sex over the age of thirty at the latest. And when it's your mother . . ."

"They might not feel like that. They might find it rather lovely. A positive and good thing to happen. Out of all the sorrow."

"Sarah, I'm not going to have this baby. I don't know why you're so keen on the idea."

"It's not so much that I'm keen for you to have it, it's that I think you're in no condition to decide not to. Your feelings are in chaos. And terminations cause depression. It won't help. Look—please give it a bit more time, Elizabeth—"

"I don't have much time. I'm two months down the line. I'd rather just do it, get over it, get on with my life."

"All right," said Sarah with a sigh. "I could do it next week, would that suit you?"

"Not as well as this week, but—"

"Elizabeth, we have to get a psychiatrist's signature, you need health checkups, all that sort of thing. Now how about next Wednesday? And then you come in on the Monday to see Dr. Young. He's our resident shrink."

"Yes, I think that would be all right." Elizabeth looked at her diary. "As long as he isn't going to counsel me. Oh—no. Could it be Thursday? I've got a big meeting on Wednesday."

"Sorry, can't do Thursday. How about Friday? That's my final offer." She smiled rather too brightly. "Now do take care of yourself."

"What for?" said Elizabeth rather briskly, and walked out of the office.

❧

She had reached a stage of being violently angry with Simon. For dying. How could he have done it to her, how could he? Either on purpose, or by being careless. It was unforgivable. Bastard! If he walked in the door now, she'd be so angry with him. And then she thought of what it would be like if Simon did walk in the door, smiling, calling her name, giving her a kiss, suggesting a drink, suggesting they went out for supper, sighing when she said she couldn't, that she didn't have time, had work to do . . . How could she have done that, all those hundreds of times, refused to spend so much as two hours with him . . .

"Oh God," said Elizabeth aloud, raising her arm to hail a taxi. "Oh God . . ." The anger was as much a reason as anything for not having the baby. She could see that in theory it would be lovely to have a child, a legacy of Simon, happiness coming out of the pain; but her anger was such that she didn't want that. It was too easy, too sentimental, she'd be struggling to cope when she shouldn't be struggling, the bastard had gone off without her, as he so often had, leaving her to manage without him. Of course she could have help, but those first difficult exhausting weeks, when you were worried and sore and fretful and the baby got colic or wouldn't feed, or even when it was quiet, you needed someone then as well, to share it all with you, to say, "There, there, never mind, it'll all be fine, you're just tired, and look, is that a smile? Think so. Let me get you another pillow. Are you sore, poor darling?" No. Those were not times to live through alone.

She felt sick and weary and altogether dreadfully unhappy.

Catherine knew it was terrible of her, but she was feeling increasingly resentful. Both of her children were sublimely happy at their schools and they both had large circles of friends, who invited them for tea and for sleepovers, and to play at the weekends.

Caroline's new best friend was called Jane-Anne and Jane-Anne dominated their lives: what Jane-Anne thought, what Jane-Anne said, what she liked to eat, what she liked to wear. Jane-Anne had a pony, and rode rather well.

It turned out that Jane-Anne's first pony was still kept in their stables and was very docile indeed; Jane-Anne's mother, a chatty rather sturdy lady, said that if Catherine wouldn't mind, they would be more than happy to give Caroline a few lessons on him.

"She seems terribly interested, and then the girls could come out with me sometimes, I'd love to take them. But I can see it might be worrying for you; why don't you come over one day after school and you can meet Dorcas—that's the pony—and see for yourself how quiet she is."

"That's terribly kind of you," said Catherine, "but—"

"Good. Super. How about next Thursday? I'll pick the girls up from school and if you put a pair of old trousers in Caroline's school bag they'll do beautifully for now. Time to get her kitted out if she likes it—which I'm sure she will. Jolly plucky little thing, isn't she?"

Phyllis was very excited about all this. "You do realise that Jane-Anne's father is actually the Honourable Mark Price, don't you? They are one of the oldest families in the county, and of course Mrs. Price is extremely well connected too. It's wonderful that they've taken such a fancy to Caroline."

Freddie too had a best friend, the beaming and bespectacled Hutchings; she felt easier with Hutchings. His father was a solicitor and his mother a rather worn-looking woman taking care of all the little Hutchings. Mrs. Hutchings, whose name was Miriam, was rather earnest and *Guardian*-reading, grew her own vegetables and believed in complementary medicine. She wasn't exactly a kindred spirit but Catherine was a lot more comfortable with her than with the Honourable Mrs. Jane-Anne.

Freddie and Hutchings, whose first name was Martin ("Only never call him that at school or even the gates, will you?" Freddie said rather sternly), shared several interests, including astronomy ("He's got a super telescope") and bird-watching, and would go off into the countryside together with their bird books and binoculars for hours at a time. It was all very lovely for them; but after the third Saturday in a row when she had seen nobody between the hours of nine and seven except for Phyllis and Dudley, Catherine was beginning to feel more lonely than she had ever been in her life.

And so as autumn arrived and the evenings got darker and the children's new lives developed so happily, she looked at the years stretching out ahead of her and wondered what on earth might become of her.

❧

She really should have taken Simon's advice, Lucinda thought, staring fretfully after Blue as he stalked out of the house, the door slammed behind him for the third time that week.

Steve Durham and indeed Nigel himself had both asked her repeatedly if she had discussed it with Blue, and she'd said rather vaguely that she hadn't yet, no, but she knew it would be fine, and more and more now, she found herself wondering what on earth was the point of upsetting him until she had to and the divorce came to a head. Not that she thought he would be upset; it was only window-dressing after all and he was so good-natured anyway . . .

But he wasn't anymore, he was tetchy and argumentative, and that evening she'd got back late, when he'd been to Brussels and Nigel had phoned, he'd been perfectly horrible.

"What the hell is going on?" he'd said. "What are you doing, calling Nigel, asking him to ring you? What about, for fuck's sake!"

"Well, it was about the divorce, obviously."

"I thought that's what you were paying the solicitor for, paying a fucking fortune incidentally."

"It was . . . it was just a detail," she said. "Steve wanted to know and I said I'd ask him, it was easier and—"

"Well, don't ask him about any more details," he said, "because I don't like it. I've nothing against that aristocratic waste of space that was once your husband, I just don't want him intruding into my life."

"He is not intruding."

"Oh really? I'd call it that. And finding you out of the house as well. I'd have thought you could at least have got a meal on the table for me."

"I will get a meal on the table for you. You're much earlier than you said, and anyway, it's steak. I couldn't cook it till you were here."

"Yes, all right, all right. Anyway, I call getting home to some cretinous message from Nigel asking you to call him back an intrusion."

"Does he want me to call him back? When?"

That was a mistake. Blue stood up, picked up his coat, and said, "You call him back whenever you like. I'm going out."

She had spent a wretched evening waiting for his return; at ten o'clock he did walk in, looking slightly remorseful and said he was sorry and could they go to bed, please, he was exhausted; and when he started wanting sex, in spite of his exhaustion—she didn't think he could know what exhaustion was, actually—she made a monumental effort and re-sponded, and actually it had been quite fun. But she could see she was in danger of upsetting him quite badly, and that this was not the time to get his agreement to what she was proposing. So she still had said nothing and now Steve had phoned and said he was biking over a document at the end of the day for her to look at and agree to, and if it was all right with her he'd get it over to Nigel's solicitor and they should be in business. Well, maybe it would be all right. Maybe she could get through the whole thing without ever clearing it with Blue. It wasn't as if it was going to affect him.

"Well, all right," she said, "but Steve, don't send it over this evening, make it tomorrow morning. I'm . . . well, I'm out this afternoon. I'll OK it straightaway and get it back to you."

God, she felt rotten this morning. So tired, and her head was really bad again. And her ankles were swollen, and actually this morning so were her hands; her rings were cutting into her fingers.

"I'd love to have lunch with you, yes," said Debbie, "but I can't. I've got a meeting."

"Drink after work?"

"Can't. I've used every excuse under the sun to Jenny, and she absolutely has to go home on time tonight, she's got a parents' evening at her children's school."

"Could I come to supper?"

"No, of course you can't," said Debbie sharply. She was learning that to give Joel an inch was to give him if not a mile, then several furlongs. "What would the children say?"

"You could say that I'd come to see the house again. It would be true, after all."

"I'm sorry, but you really can't."

She put the phone down. She glared at it for a minute then picked it up and rang him back. "This isn't fair. Getting at me because I can't see you. It isn't my fault. You knew—"

"Yeah, yeah, I knew you were married and you had three children. You kept on saying it, like a bloody mantra."

"Well, it's true."

"I should have listened to you," he said moodily.

"Yes, perhaps you should."

"But what good would it have done me, Debbie? I'd still be in love with you."

She was silent.

"It's bloody tough," he said.

"I know. I do know and it's tough for me as well."

"Not so tough."

"Why not?"

"Because you call all the shots. I could be with you every evening, fuck you every night. Jesus, what a thought. What a bloody thought. Do you think we'll ever get there, Debbie?"

"No," she said wearily, "we won't. And don't even think about it."

"So you're telling me there is no light at the end of this extremely dark tunnel."

"Joel, there can't be. You know. You know this is—"

"Yes?" he said. "What is it? Do tell me, Debbie, I really want to know."

She did know what it was; it was something that would wreck what was left of her marriage, was endangering her children's happiness, was even harming her career. It was completely hopeless; it could end only in misery. And yet she would not have missed it, any of it, for anything. It was rich and rare, it was happiness of the most extreme kind, it was worth whatever it cost . . .

Chapter 46

God, Elizabeth thought. Now her skirts were getting tight. It was ridiculous when the—when what was in there was only the size of an orange pip. She supposed it was hormones making her put on weight. Bloody hormones. God, they had a lot to answer for. Well, it was Friday today, she was off to see Dr. Young on Monday, and then it would only be four more days and it would be over. Sarah had booked her into the hospital, she'd made elaborate excuses to everyone, told Peter Hargreaves she was seeing someone about the inquest, told Annabel and Tilly she had to go out of town for a client meeting. It would be fine. And she'd be home next day and Annabel would be working, and Tilly might well be going out with her new friends.

"We're going down the market, Mummy," she would say, in her still-perfect accent or, "We're going up west, to Topshop and that."

Tilly had become extremely fond of Fallon, the black girl; she was very sweet, Elizabeth liked her. She had nice manners and was clearly inordinately grateful to Tilly for her help with her schoolwork; she lived with her mum and her five brothers and sisters in a two-bedroom flat in Pimlico.

"She has to share with the other girls, three of them in one room, can you imagine, Mummy, and the TV's always on. She's doing much better with me helping her, and being able to do her homework here; she's really pleased. The only thing is that Madison's getting a bit jealous now so it's rather difficult."

"It must be," said Elizabeth carefully. This unlikely scenario of Tilly being idyllically happy at the comprehensive could all go very pear-shaped indeed if she started falling out with people. "Why don't you ask Madison over on Sunday, just on her own, so you can spend some time with her?"

"I can't. She sees her mum Sundays."

"Her mum? Who looks after her then?"

"Her dad and his girlfriend. His girlfriend is really nice, Madison says, always giving her clothes and stuff, only of course Madison can't get into them. She gets so upset about her size, I don't know how to help. She doesn't eat much, she says, she's just got funny hormones."

"Oh really? So what does she have for lunch?"

"Chips," said Tilly with a sublime lack of irony, "but that's all she eats all day till she gets home. And then she has to get her own tea, because Lara, that's her dad's girlfriend, doesn't get home till late, and she says she doesn't have much then, either. I feel so sorry for her, it's so unfair."

"It is indeed," said Elizabeth, with a flash of insight into the unfortunate Madison's loveless, uncared-for life. "Well, maybe she could come over on Sunday evening, when she leaves her mum."

She thought of Tilly's friends at St. Mary's, open-faced little girls, with loving, caring parents, beautifully dressed, carefully fed, with no greater worries than whether their ponies might be missing them during the term or whether they'd manage to pass common entrance, and felt a pang of sudden rage—rage seemed to rise in her rather easily these days—at the basic unfairness of the human condition.

"That's a good idea, we could watch a video. Thanks, Mum." She gave her mother a kiss and danced off; she was much happier these days, at last beginning to come to terms with her father's death. She certainly didn't need the trauma of a new and demanding sibling and having to confront the reality of its conception.

God, she was going to be sick . . . She reached the cloakroom just in time, deposited the small amount of breakfast she had eaten down the lavatory, and was coming out, wiping her streaming eyes, when she bumped into Annabel.

"Oh, hello, darling. I thought you'd gone."

"No, not quite. You OK, Mum? Still being sick?"

"Yes. 'Fraid so. It's quite normal, the doctor says, when you're depressed. Your body gets into a state of turmoil, doesn't know what it's doing."

"Is it? Poor you. It can't help. Let me get you a cup of tea."

"No, thank you," said Elizabeth, repressing a shudder. "I'll just have some water."

"OK, I'll get you that. Sit down in the kitchen for a bit. Come on." She got a bottle of mineral water out of the fridge, handed her mother a glass. "There you are. I need to talk to you tonight, about Jamie, actually. Are you in?"

"Yes, I am. Might be a bit late . . ."

"Oh, that's all right. Florian and I are going for a drink with some friends of his. See you around eight thirty, OK?"

"OK. Bye, darling."

And she was gone. Just as well she was so wrapped up in her own life, thought Elizabeth wearily, otherwise she might start to notice—or even suspect—something.

ᕲ

"Lucinda, it's Mummy." She sounded odd, strained. "Your . . . your father's had a stroke."

"Oh God. How . . . how bad is it?"

"We don't know yet. It could go either way. The great danger, apparently, is of a second stroke. Anyway, I wanted you to know."

"Yes. Yes, of course. Oh Mummy, how dreadful. How do you feel?"

"Oh, all right. A bit . . . shocked, you know."

"You must do. I'll come down. Straightaway."

"Lucinda, I don't know that that's a very good idea. The baby's due any minute."

"Not for another four weeks. Of course I want to come, see Daddy. I'll be there at lunchtime, OK?"

Lucinda felt very upset; her father might have been frightful over Blue, might not even have been a particularly involved father, but he was still her father, and she still loved him. She packed a bag, rang Blue, and set off for Gloucestershire.

Half an hour later, a bike arrived, bearing an envelope addressed to Lucinda, and marked STRICTLY PRIVATE AND CONFIDENTIAL and URGENT.

When he found she wasn't there, as he had been assured she would be, the messenger cursed her, and then decided to push the letter through the door. It was marked urgent after all.

⁂

Half term would be a sort of rehearsal, Debbie thought. She would try and think of it like that. For the time when she would be going up to Scotland for good. Having said goodbye to Joel.

The thought of that was so frightful that it sometimes actually made her cry. The thought of a life and a world without him, for the rest of her life. If you could call it life, that is . . . Oh Debbie, stop being so melodramatic! Hearts mend, life goes on, the sun still rises and sets . . .

The children were terribly excited. They had packed their bags days ago, and were counting the hours.

Richard was tremendously excited too. "I can't wait to show you everything. I know you're going to love it here. I've done my best with the house, and Morag has been fantastic, given us lots of things like cast-off curtains—that sort of thing—keep us going till you can get it all to your liking."

God save me from Morag's cast-offs, Debbie thought; and then felt very ashamed of herself. Morag would certainly never commit adultery. Having to take a whole week off work annoyed her terribly; she was frantically trying to build up her accounts, so that Anna was more likely to let her handle at least one from Scotland, and it was difficult enough finding time for Joel without losing five whole days. But then, on the Friday afternoon, she came back to find Emma lying on the sofa, face ashen, with a bowl at her side, being sick at roughly ten-minute intervals.

"I'm so sorry," Jenny said apologetically. "It started just as we left school. And actually, I don't like the look of Rachel either. She—"

The door opened and Rachel appeared, equally ashen. She had hardly said, "Mu-um," when the inevitable happened.

"You can't take them up to Scotland like this," said Jenny, rushing for a bowl. Somehow, even when all three children were vomiting in unison, Debbie felt wildly and absurdly happy.

It was a very nasty bug, going round all the schools in the area, the GP surgery confirmed.

"Both ends too," said Debbie to Richard next morning. "And, in fact, Emma's so bad I got the doctor in. I'm so sorry, Richard, I thought I'd see how they were on Monday. Then maybe we can rethink."

"I hope so. I was looking forward to seeing you all so much and, of course, Morag will be so disappointed."

"Sorry," said Debbie humbly. He clearly felt it was her fault this had happened. She put the phone down and called Joel. "I had to let you know. Only don't you dare come round."

"I will."

"You'll have to clear up sick if you do."

"Maybe I won't," he said hastily. He was, she had discovered, intensely squeamish.

❧

Blue got in very late that night. He had taken advantage of Lucinda's absence to entertain some clients. As he walked in the door, he stepped on a letter, lying on the mat. Strictly private and confidential, it said, and urgent. It was addressed to Lucinda. He turned it over, saw that it was from Stephen Durham, Solicitor, Regent Street W1 and decided he should open it. Obviously the lazy sod had finally pulled his finger out with the divorce proceedings. He was still hoping to persuade Lucinda to at least have a civil ceremony before the baby was born; no way did Blue Horton want his son and heir born illegitimate.

An hour later, having had a cold shower, and drunk a large jug of coffee, he was in the Ferrari, headed westwards out of the city, and not sure whether rage or grief was his dominant emotion.

~

Elizabeth woke early that Saturday morning; she felt very sad. The conversation with Annabel the night before had been about Jamie: Jamie and the wretched engagement party that Frances Cartwright so wanted.

"She's suggesting early December, Mummy. I don't know how you'd feel about that. I know it's still a bit soon, but—well, it would be lovely for me. Especially as we probably can't have one here, or not for a while anyway. And I can see this party might seem a bit heartless. But—"

"But life must go on," said Elizabeth firmly, "of course."

"Anyway, it did seem quite a nice idea. To go over for the party. And then we could maybe do something here after Christmas."

"Fine. Lovely idea." Christmas! How was she going to endure Christmas? Don't think about it, Elizabeth; one day at a time . . .

"Well, the main question after that is whether you'd like to come. Feel up to it, that is."

"No," said Elizabeth fiercely, "absolutely I won't. I'm sorry, Annabel, but to see a lot of people I don't know, stay in a strange house—no, it's out of the question. Look, I'm sorry, darling, but I really do feel so tired, I think I might get an early night."

"Shall I bring you some supper up? An omelet or something like that, all soft and runny the way you like it."

The very thought of a runny omelet turned Elizabeth's stomach over. "No, thanks," she said, standing up. "Honestly, I don't want anything. Something has gone terribly wrong with my appetite. Maybe just a cup of tea." She could throw that away without Annabel knowing.

"Fine. I'll make you one. Thank you so much, Mummy."

"What for?"

"For being so understanding. You're a star and I love you."

"I love you too," said Elizabeth.

But the next morning, thinking of how Annabel's engagement party ought to be: proud smiling parents, a roomful of friends from both generations, she could hardly breathe she felt so unhappy. Or so sick. When

Annabel looked in on her, before she went to work, she saw her rushing white-faced into her bathroom, holding a towel to her mouth.

℮℩

"Right," said Blue. "Sit down." He had woken her, banging on the door just after six, stalked into the hall, his face distorted with rage.

"Blue—"

"I said sit down. And tell me what the fuck this is about!"

"Blue—Mummy will hear."

"I don't care what Mummy will hear. Or Daddy, or your fucking toffee-nosed brothers and sisters. Is he here as well? Your—your husband? I wouldn't be surprised."

"Of course he's not here. What are you talking about, what is all this about?"

"This," he said, getting the letter out of his pocket, waving it at her. "This letter."

"Oh," she said. "That." She went very white and sat down abruptly.

"Yes, this. This—document. Sent by your solicitor. I must have been insane, sending you to him. But at least it's cleared a few things up. Why you wouldn't agree to buying a house, why Nigel kept ringing you up. Jesus, you're disgusting. I cannot believe you'd have done this, Lucinda, while you're pregnant with my child. If it is my child—I'm beginning to doubt that as well. Is it Nigel's? Have you been seeing him all this time?"

"Of course I haven't. Don't be ridiculous. Of course it's your child. How could you even think such a thing?"

"Quite easily," he said, "having read what's written down here. How you don't feel totally confident about your new relationship, how you're living somewhere totally unsuitable, how you can't work because you're pregnant—nice one, Lucinda—how the thought of the house being held in trust for you is very reassuring for you under the circumstances. And I hadn't realised that you gave up your career to marry Nigel. What was that job at the publishers then? Charity work? And Jesus, what is this fantasy about the money you gave up to marry Nigel? The hundred thousand pounds?"

"It's not fantasy," said Lucinda staunchly. "If I'd gone to New York with Virgil I could easily have earned that in commission—his paintings go for millions."

· 412 ·

"Ah, Virgil. The poof. Nice little bit of fraud you've cooked up with him. I take my hat off to you, Lucinda, I must say. I didn't think you had it in you."

She was silent.

"And where does Nigel come into all this? I had no idea he'd—what does it say here—oh yes, put a brake on your career, severely limited your social life. So what were all those house parties and weddings and christenings you were going to practically all the bloody time when I first met you? And that his being so much older than you put an inevitable strain on your marriage and affected your personal life. Your personal life, God help me. Does that mean sex, Lucinda?"

"It was just something else that Steve suggested. He said it would help."

"I see. Help who?"

"Help me get a good settlement."

"Oh yes. And what is this settlement he's helping you to get?"

"Well, the house for a start."

"The house! What do you need the house for? I'm buying you a house!"

"Yes, I know. But—oh, you don't understand."

"I most certainly don't. You're hoping for some money as well, I suppose?"

"Well, yes. But— Look, please, please let me explain."

"I don't think I want you to explain, Lucinda. I don't think I want to hear anything from you ever again. I feel completely sickened by you. You can tear that nice little document up, you won't be needing it. A rather different one will be coming from me, in a very few days. And don't even think about coming to the house to get your stuff. Nigel will no doubt buy you anything you need. You still seem to have him wrapped very nicely round your finger."

And he was gone.

℮ↄ

Tilly's new friend Fallon stayed at the house on Saturday night. The girls played music very loudly in Tilly's room and watched videos. It was rather nice, Annabel thought, to hear the house brought alive again; it had been terribly quiet lately. She walked into the kitchen in the morning and found them making eggy bread, a delight Fallon hadn't savoured before, apparently.

"Oh hi," said Tilly. "You've met Fallon, haven't you?"

"Of course. Hello, Fallon."

"Hi," said Fallon. She was rather beautiful, Annabel thought. She could be a model; and then hoped no one would suggest it to her, or not for at least three or four more years. "This is a fab house," she added.

"We won't have it much longer," said Annabel. "It's on the market and we're supposed to be looking for somewhere else, I expect Tilly's told you, but . . . well, our mother doesn't feel up to it. Last thing she needs at the moment."

"Yeah, course," said Fallon.

"Poor Mummy," said Tilly, "she was being sick this morning again. It must be so horrible, she's got enough to cope with without that."

"My mum's sick every morning at the moment an' all," said Fallon.

"Oh really?"

"Yeah. She's in the club again, and not too pleased about it, I can tell you."

"What club?" said Tilly.

"Tilly!" said Annabel. "You really are hopeless. It means she's pregnant."

"Oh really?" said Tilly. "How exciting. Well, Mummy certainly isn't that. You want grated cheese on this, Fallon? It's ever so nice."

She wasn't looking at Annabel; if she had been, she would have seen her sister freeze in her tea-making and turn extremely pink . . .

Chapter 47

By Monday morning, the girls had begun to recover, and were sitting up drinking lemon-barley water and eating dry toast. Alex, however, was still vomiting. She rang Richard again. "We can't come, Richard, I'm sorry. Maybe you could come down. The children would so love to see you."

"Debbie, I can't. I'm as disappointed as you all are, but there are children still at school here. I'm really sorry. I hope you'll understand."

"Of course I do. What a shame. Bye, Richard." She put the phone down, smiling. God, she was a bitch.

By the evening the children were beginning to look more themselves, but they were still not well enough to make the long journey to Scotland.

"It's such a shame," Debbie said to Flora that evening. "They were so excited and now they look dreadful; they need some good fresh air."

"You could bring them down here," said Flora thoughtfully. "It's not nearly so far, and the weather's lovely. Better make the best of it, Debbie, the old place will soon be up for sale."

"Oh Flora, no. How horrible for you."

"Yes, it is rather. But Lloyd's are getting very heavy."

"But where will you go?" She found it hard to imagine Flora living anywhere else.

"I have no idea. Anyway—want to come? I really would like it." Suddenly it seemed like a lovely idea; to be somewhere safe, away from the whole painful difficult thing, a break for a few days at least, with nothing more emotionally challenging to cope with than stopping the children from squabbling too much and trying not to mind when Flora acted as if they were hers.

"We'd love to come, Flora," she said. "Thank you."

❧

Elizabeth hadn't liked Dr. Young, the psychiatrist, at all. He had been brusque and rather dismissive of her; he had asked her exactly why she felt she couldn't have the baby, and she had told him she would have thought any fool could see that: her husband had just died, she had three children to take care of, a full-time and demanding job. She was also over forty, her health was suffering already through the pregnancy, and she was deeply worried about foetal abnormalities.

"Plenty of women over forty have babies these days," he said, "and you seem pretty well to me. Statistically, you have a very good chance of having a completely healthy baby. And in any case, there are very good screening processes for abnormalities."

"Yes, I do know that," said Elizabeth, fighting a desire to lean across the desk and slap him, "and the one for Down's syndrome means a termination at twenty weeks if it's positive. That's hardly going to help me recover from my husband's death."

"You wouldn't have to have a termination," he said. "Down's children are very lovable; raising them can be a wonderfully rewarding experience. But—yes, all right, I am prepared to recommend a termination for you. I would urge you to reconsider, just the same. Depression almost invariably results from the process and I really don't think you are in a fit state to make this decision. Do please take time out between now and Friday to make sure you know what you're doing."

"Unfortunately I am unable to take time out," said Elizabeth. "I told you, I have a living to earn."

And now she had Fiona Broadhurst coming to see her, wasting more of her time. She had agreed to see her to discuss something Fiona had said was important; she was regretting it now.

$$\mathcal{C}\!\!\curvearrowright$$

"I really won't keep you long, Mrs. Beaumont." Fiona Broadhurst smiled her rather distant smile. "Now, I know you don't want to proceed with the lawsuit, you wrote and told me that, but I wonder if you realise that the group George Meyer was leading, together with your husband, has at least a chance of succeeding. Or so our QC feels."

"Really? From everything I've heard and read, there is precious little chance of Lloyd's ever giving up a brass farthing."

"Not quite true. Although it wasn't at all the same thing, and it was a while ago, there is a precedent for Lloyd's settling: over the Cameron Webb business—I expect you know about that?"

Elizabeth shook her head.

"Peter Cameron Webb and Peter Dixon, two very prominent brokers at Lloyd's, were found guilty of fraud. Most particularly of diverting reinsurance premiums to themselves, thus leaving their Members without adequate cover. Writs were actually issued for their arrests, but they're out of the country now, living somewhere like Miami. Anyway, Lloyd's did make a substantial offer to the Members." She paused. "The group Mr. Meyer has formed is now about a hundred strong. A large proportion of the Westfield Bradley Names—that's your late husband's main syndicate—

have joined it. And we are not alone in this case. There is a vortex of them; at least four thousand Names, possibly many more, are at this precise moment forming action groups and preparing writs. But I actually think that you probably have more than enough stress to cope with. If I were you, I would feel exactly the same.

"I shall write you a letter, absolving you from any further involvement in the matter, and of course return the money your husband deposited with us for preliminary work. Minus your husband's share of any costs so far incurred."

"Thank you," said Elizabeth.

"Now, as you know, I had lunch with your husband, the day before he died."

"Indeed? And?" What was she going to say? That Simon had made a pass at her?

"And he told me that he was still determined to go ahead. Although I had to tell him that some evidence he was rather excited about would not be admissible in court. He was disappointed about that."

That would have been Joel Strickland's tapes, Elizabeth thought.

"And that seemed possibly quite important to me," said Fiona.

"You mean as a gauge to his state of mind?"

"Yes. It seemed clear to me that he was still feeling very positive. He certainly didn't seem depressed. And of course I shall say that at the inquest. You know I've been called to make a statement?"

"I do. It was my impression too. Thank you for telling me."

Not time wasted at all; Elizabeth felt much better suddenly.

He had asked her to come to his flat. "I can't talk about this in some cruddy bar."

She agreed. "But Joel, I can't be long, I really can't."

"Yes, all right."

"You know what I mean."

"I know what you mean."

"I'll wear my tightest knickers."

"OK."

He had sounded very serious, almost strained; perhaps he had decided it wasn't worth all the agony of the waiting, the snatched meetings, the interrupted conversations. Perhaps he wanted to finish it. She shrank from the thought, while thinking that at least it would be over, resolved; she could start to recover, be living in the agony, rather than dreading it . . .

"Hi." He was wearing jeans and a white shirt, was barefoot, he had obviously just had a shower; his hair was spiky and still wet. It was all she could do to keep herself from attacking him, unbuttoning his shirt, unzipping his fly . . . She made do with a rather extended kiss, shutting the door behind her. He stood back and smiled at her.

"Phew. Please sit down. Would you like a drink?"

"No, thank you. I've got to drive and anyway, I kind of feel I need a clear head for this."

"You kind of feel right. Just hang on—I'll make the coffee."

He was fussy about coffee, about everything that was food or drink; he could no more have eaten a McDonald's meal than dog food. Good thing he didn't have any kids, she thought; and absurdly felt a pang of jealousy that one day he would, and with someone other than her.

"There. Enjoy."

"Thank you."

"Right," he said, "are you sitting comfortably?"

"Yes, thank you."

"I'm getting sick of all this," he said. "Never knowing when we can meet, never having long enough for anything, never having a whole night together, sharing you with your family, trying not to think about sharing you with him. It's just not . . . not good enough. I mean that in the most straightforward way. It's not good enough for us. For what we've got, what we feel. It was all right at first, but now I can't bear it. I love you too much, I want all of you. All the time. And all I'm getting is wretched little snatches of you. So . . ." She braced herself, closed her eyes, unable to look at him while he said it, while he said the awful, hideous ugly thing. "So I've decided. I want you to marry me. I want you to divorce your husband and marry me."

She was so shocked she felt as if he had hit her.

"I just have to, you see. I've got to have you. I'll never find anyone else, not who I love like I love you. And so I'm going to take you on. And your children, and all the complicated baggage you'll bring with you. I don't know what sort of husband I'll make, but I'll be sweating blood, I'll try so hard."

"Oh," she said. And she still felt rather shocked, but sweetly so, contentedly so; listening to this amazing thing, that Joel loved her so much he wanted to marry her, and marry her children; he wanted to be with her for the rest of his life, and the rest of hers, and wondering what on earth she did or indeed what she was that made him want that, when he could have had hundreds of girls, cool, beautiful, uncomplicated girls, and she sat there still not speaking, not moving, wanting him to go on, to say more and if there was no more, to say it all over again.

"I can't think of anything to say," she said, rather helplessly. "Except of course what I want to say is yes, yes, yes and I'd love to marry you too."

"Well, that's all right then, isn't it?" He sounded rather uncertain.

"No, Joel, it isn't. Because I can't. Because I'm already married. And I don't have any reason not to be. Not really."

"Yes, you do. I love you. You love me—or so you say. Or am I wrong?"

"No," she said, "you're not wrong. I do love you, I love you terribly."

"OK. So here we are, the two of us, loving each other. And I'm thirty-four years old now, and I have never wanted to get married. I've never wanted children. I'm ambitious and selfish and extravagant and, well—terrible husband material really. But for you I'll do it. I will take on your children—and I would love, one day, for you to have my babies too."

"Oh Joel." Her eyes filled with tears.

"I can't quite believe I'm saying all this, you know. I mean, I'm sure some of it will be complete hell, and the kids'll resent me because I'm not their dad and all that stuff. And I really don't think we're all going to waltz off into the sunset together, but the thing is I'm ready for it, ready for the hell. Just because I love you. So what do you say, Debbie? There must be something."

"There is something," she said, "of course there is. I love you like that too. But Joel . . . you've known about this for—I don't know how long."

"Oh, hours," he said, with a grin. "Possibly even days."

"Yes, well, exactly. You've got used to the idea. It's a complete shock to me, and I think it's so, so wonderful, and half of me wants to just stay here and never go back."

"And the other half?"

"The other half is scared. Of all sorts of things. I need to think, terribly, terribly hard. It's not me and it's not you and it's not even Richard I have to consider. It's the children. They love him, they think he's wonderful—I have to do the . . . the right thing."

"The right thing is to be with me."

"Well, I want to be, more than anything in the world; that's all I have to say."

"Oh, all right," he said, and then looked at his watch. "What time do you have to get back to your bloody responsibilities?"

"I said ten."

"Ten! It's already nine."

"I know. But," she hesitated, "Jan said she could actually stay till twelve."

"Right." He reached forward, put his hand inside her shirt, started to caress her breasts. "I like this Jan. She sounds like a good egg."

"She is a good egg."

She moved nearer him, unbuttoning his shirt, slithering her hand down his jeans. She felt incredible, suddenly wired, alive, every nerve on edge, on edge with wanting him.

"Bedroom then? Or in here?"

"I don't think I can wait to get into the bedroom," and then everything was confused, confused and amazing, and she could never remember feeling quite like this, even the first time with him; she seemed to feel everything at once, not knowing what she was doing, only what she wanted, and they were lying on the floor, and he was in her and it was over almost before it had begun, only wonderfully and brilliantly so, and she was sobbing and shouting and laughing with it; and then he said as she quietened, "Come on, let's go to bed now, do it properly."

It was after twelve when she got home, exhausted, exhilarated, hardly knowing who she was or what she might do. She apologised to Jan, told her they had had a lot to talk about.

"Yeah, yeah," Jan said, looking at her smudged mascara, her flushed face, her crumpled clothes. "Lot of talking you've been doing. You lucky cow."

❧

Steve Durham had been waiting in a state of increasing exasperation to hear from Lucinda. She knew how urgent the matter was, for God's sake. He wouldn't have biked the bloody document over to her if it hadn't been.

By the end of Monday, he had had enough; he had called her repeatedly during the day and left messages; the matter was too important to leave unsettled. Cowper's solicitor had his own document ready and signed; having pushed this whole thing through at his own instigation, he now appeared and felt completely incompetent. He decided to call Blue Horton at his office. It was he who had introduced him to Lucinda in the first place.

When he asked him if he knew what had happened to a document he had had delivered to the Horton household on Friday, and said that he was anxious to get it returned with Lucinda's signature, Blue delivered a pithy epithet to the effect that Steve could put his document up his arse and set light to it for all he cared, and told him to call Lucinda at her parents' house.

"And you can go after her for any money owing to you, incidentally. And tell her I said so."

Elizabeth got home feeling completely exhausted. It had been, to put it mildly, a brute of a day. Culminating in Peter Hargreaves saying almost apologetically that he would be grateful if she could possibly do the Mercers' new range presentation on Monday. Monday! She wouldn't be at her best, to put it mildly.

And the estate agent had phoned to say that the Americans had come back with an even better offer and he really thought they should proceed.

"But I haven't got anywhere to live."

"I can get you somewhere you can rent for a few weeks, until you find a property. I really think you should take the offer, Mrs. Beaumont. The market's not exactly buoyant at the moment."

"I'll get back to you in the morning," she said.

She walked into the drawing room, collapsed onto the sofa. And looked around the room and thought that among other things, the sheer hard work of moving would be incredible. They wouldn't have room for half the furniture, there would be endless decisions to make, sales to organise. And she would have to deal with all Simon's stuff; she'd put that off day after day, hadn't even got rid of any of his clothes. She couldn't face it, couldn't face touching them, holding them, throwing—or giving—them away. It would seem so unbearably, unutterably final.

"Shit," she said aloud. "Shit!"

She heard the front door open and then Annabel calling her name.

"In the drawing room, darling."

Annabel walked in; she looked very pale and tense.

"Are you all right, sweetheart? What's the matter?"

She saw her Annabel take a deep breath, then: "It's not what's the matter with me, Mummy. It's what's the matter with you. Are you . . . well, are you pregnant?"

Chapter 48

It had been such a good idea, to come down here. She felt really relaxed for the first time for—well, she couldn't remember when. There would have to be decisions made and action taken, but not yet. For now, she wanted simply to enjoy a few easily perfect days. She could never remember being so happy.

The weather had put in a last Herculean effort for them, and they had actually had a sort of picnic, a bit breezy to be sure, and they'd had to sit sheltering just in the lee of the big rocks at Mewslade, but still with the wonderful sense of being properly outdoors. She looked at the three of them, rosy again, eating for England—"Or Wales," as she said to Flora.

Flora was briskly brave about the house, full of plans. "I'm thinking of going to Scotland, Debbie," she said. "The Highlands. It's beautiful up there, even a bit like Gower, only more dramatic, and the weather won't be as nice, of course. I can get a nice little place for almost nothing." Debbie didn't like to ask her about the horses; she couldn't imagine Prince Hal travelling up to Scotland, but it might be possible, she supposed; and as for Boy . . .

"This is the first time Tilly hasn't been down for half term," Flora said rather sadly, clearly recognising her train of thought. "She says she wants to stay close to her mother for a little longer, and she's got a lot of friends at her new school, apparently. Such a relief that's worked out so well."

"Why shouldn't it?" said Debbie, feeling a stab of the old irritation.

"Well, it's a little different from what she's used to."

"Doesn't mean it's worse. And children are very adaptable."

"Debbie, darling, really! Tilly is used to extreme privilege and a very narrow social spectrum. She's unworldly to the point of absurdity; and to her new schoolmates, something of a joke, I would imagine. She could have been horribly teased, bullied even; I think it's little short of miraculous that she's adapted so well. And she does actually like it there; she wrote me such a sweet funny letter about how the boys tease her rotten and call her posho, and what she does every weekend with her two best friends, Fallon and Madison. Extraordinary."

"But don't you think it's awfully good for her," said Debbie, "seeing another side of life, mixing with real people? I mean, the sort of school she went to, it's so ridiculously privileged."

"I think you and I are going to have to disagree on all this," said Flora. "It is good for her, of course, seeing the other side, but she won't get anything like as good an education. And she'll learn a lot of unattractive things—sex, far too early, drugs . . ."

"Flora, honestly," said Debbie, and she was laughing now. "Do you really think there aren't any drugs in independent schools?"

 ❧

Debbie didn't even think about contacting Joel; it would have revived all the difficulties and the emotional discomfort; she just basked in her happiness. Richard had agreed to come down for the weekend. The thought of that was quite literally awful, she shrank from it. But Flora was very pleased. "The whole of my family together under this dear old roof," she said, "possibly for the last time." And then she turned to Debbie and said—and Debbie had never been so surprised by anything, apart from Joel asking her to marry him—"Debbie, I'd like your opinion on something. I'm desperate to discuss it, and there's no one else I trust. Simon is, well, gone, and I can't talk to Richard because it would affect him. It's about the house." She was trying to be clever, she went on, but, "I hope not too clever. I'm going to be completely honest with you, and rely on you to keep it to yourself."

"Yes, of course I will." Debbie was so curious, she would have agreed in that moment to take up hunting to keep Flora talking.

"It's a way of saving myself, and doing Lloyd's down. Anyway, I've got a . . . a friend in the property business. It was his idea. His rather brilliant idea. He buys my house—at its face value—with the land. Now the thing is, you can't build on Gower. It's all protected."

"So . . ."

"Unless you have buildings. They can be in total rack and ruin—cottages, barns, stables—but as long as they're not just sheds, you can sometimes get permission to convert them into houses."

"Ye-es."

"Right. Now Colin's plan is that I go to Lloyd's, show them the contract, say I've sold my house and I need some money and how much are they going to take? It'll be most of it. I could maybe get a tiny flat somewhere."

"Yes?" said Debbie again.

"But there'll be a second contract between the developer and another company, guaranteeing it a substantial sum of money if planning is granted within three years. To build three houses there."

"And your friend can get the planning consent?"

"Well, he's pretty confident."

"And you'd have some link with this other company?"

She grinned at Debbie. "Well, I just might. Not as a director or a shareholder, of course. Just behind it, a beneficiary. It would be an offshore company, and this would be a joint-venture agreement with the developer. My friend says it's some sort of piggybacking agreement. Even if they investigated it, I wouldn't be there. It would mean I'd still have some money, quite a lot actually, and so I could afford to buy somewhere quite nice."

"Well," said Debbie, "that does sound very clever. Very clever indeed. And, you know this person quite well, do you? I mean, you trust him?"

"Oh, absolutely, yes," said Flora. "We go to concerts together."

As if that made it all right, Debbie thought, carefully not looking at her; as it would be if he had been at Eton or belonged to the right club.

"So what do you think, Debbie? I'm not asking you what I should do, of course. I just wanted to . . . to talk about it."

"Well, your friend is clearly some sort of genius. And I like the thought of you being able to do Lloyd's down. They deserve all they get. Or all they don't get. And if it's foolproof, I mean you don't get caught or sent to prison or something—only joking, but you know what I mean— then yes. And presumably you could keep on riding, keep your horse and everything. So, why not?"

Flora met her eyes very levelly; they sat there looking at each other for quite a long time. Then: "You don't actually think that, do you? Come on, Debbie. I want to discuss it and I want an honest reaction."

"Well . . ." She looked at Flora and, for the first time in their difficult relationship, felt they were on a completely level footing. "Well, the thing is, Flora, I don't think it suits you."

"Because it's dishonest?"

"No, of course not. No, it's because I—well, it's because I can't see you agreeing to anything that would mean ruining your Meadow. And Broken Bay House, come to that. You'd never forgive yourself. At least, I don't think you would. Sorry, Flora."

"Oh Debbie." Flora looked at Debbie and then smiled at her, a very soft smile, and there were tears in her dark blue eyes. "Oh my dear, how very wise you are. Thank you for that. I'm very grateful."

There was a pause; then she said, and her tone was brusque, the familiar Flora again, "Now let's not talk about it anymore. Probably should never have told you."

"Flora," said Debbie, "I'm awfully glad you did."

⁓

Only two more days, and then she'd be feeling better. Well, she'd feel a bit worse, first, but then . . .

The atmosphere in the house was horrible; Annabel wasn't speaking to her. Tilly, clearly baffled for she had picked up on the hostility without having the faintest idea what it was about, was endeavouring earnestly to pour oil on the clearly troubled waters. Toby hadn't come home for half term, but had gone to stay with his best friend Piers Wilson who lived in

Herefordshire; she had actually been relieved when he asked her if he could go.

"Do you mind, Mum? I know I should be there with you, but this should be great; Wilson's father is going to organise a boys' shoot."

Elizabeth understood; it was not heartlessness, it was a complete inability to face the trauma, not that his father was dead but of all that it entailed. She was comforted to hear from the chaplain at school that he had talked to him a little, and that he didn't believe there was a real problem. "He just needs time. Let's try and give it to him, leave him be."

But Annabel *was* facing the trauma, and a new one too, an incredibly hard one. If only Elizabeth could have kept it from her for just a few more days.

She had guilt now, to add to her rage and misery, and of course her ill health. She had denied it at first that evening, but Annabel was sharp-eyed and sharp-eared too; she could hear the lie in her mother's voice, see the slight avoidance in her eyes.

"Mum! Come on. Grief and depression don't make you throw up every morning regular as clockwork. And your boobs have got bigger. Come on, admit it."

"Well, all right. Yes, I am."

"How absolutely lovely!" Annabel had said, staring at her, shining-eyed. "You must be so pleased. I mean, I can see it's horrible being sick, but it won't last, will it, and then—"

"Annabel," said Elizabeth gently, "Annabel, I'm not going to have it."

"What?" Her eyes, her face, her voice were all shocked. "You mean you're going to have an abortion?"

"Yes. Yes, I am."

"But you can't. It's so, so wrong. And this is Daddy's baby! What do you think he'd have said? Of course you can't."

"I'm afraid I can. And I know it's Daddy's baby, but he isn't here, and I have to look after all of us and I can't have it, not possibly."

"Mummy, you've got to have it, you've simply got to. You can't kill your baby. It's the one good thing I've heard since—well, since Daddy died. It's lovely."

"Sweetheart, I really can't. Just think for a bit—"

"I am thinking. Thinking of you ripping it out of you, killing it, what's left of Daddy—"

"Annabel, that's hysterical talk."

"Why? Why is it?"

"Listen," said Elizabeth patiently, "I know it would be lovely, if everything else was the same. But Daddy's died. I don't have him anymore. I can't bring up a baby without his help. Not emotionally, not physically, not financially. It's impossible."

"It is not impossible. You've got us, we'll help, we'll support you. It'll be wonderful."

"Annabel, listen to me. You're all growing up. And I want you to be free to do what you want. To be with Jamie. Toby will be going to university and, anyway, can you imagine how he'd feel about it—the embarrassment for him, what would his friends think and say . . . And Tilly, well . . ."

"Tilly would be fantastic. Especially now she's at home all the time. Think what a lot she could do for you, and her friend Fallon too; she seems to know all about babies."

"Tilly is just beginning to grow up, Annabel. She doesn't want to be held back by a mother with a baby. And I'm nearly forty-one. There are serious risks to having babies at my age—for the baby, that is. It could have all sorts of abnormalities. How would I cope with that? And risks to me. It's a strain on any body, never mind a middle-aged one."

"Oh rubbish!" said Annabel. "You look like you're about twenty-five."

"Not gynaecologically, I don't. I'm sorry, and I would give anything to have spared you all this, but I really am not going to have this baby. I've got a termination booked for Friday and—"

"Well, don't expect me to look after you when you come home," said Annabel. She stood up and glared at her mother. "I would never have believed this of you. And I'm sure Daddy wouldn't either. I feel—I feel ashamed of you. Really ashamed."

❧

Lucinda's father was recovering.

"I'm delighted with him," the doctor told Mrs. Worthington when she arrived on Tuesday morning. "His speech is returning and though there's some impairment of movement down his right side, and the hand is decidedly a problem with stroke cases, it's the first forty-eight hours that matter. If we get lightning, as we call it, then the auspices are good."

Lucinda received this piece of news rather listlessly; she had tried very hard, ever since Blue's departure, to be a good daughter and put her parents' problems first, but it was very difficult. She felt terribly unhappy and dreadfully anxious. Mercifully her mother, who had taken a sleeping pill the night before, hadn't heard anything of the drama and her sister had gone home for the night.

She had tried ringing him twice and he had simply put the phone down. Steve Durham, when he had finally found her, reported a similar problem, without actually spelling out Blue's words. What was she supposed to do, how could she ever explain? He was hardly going to read a letter if she tried writing one, and certainly not believe what it said. It was so dreadful and entirely her own fault; the story was so extremely unlikely, and even Steve had urged her to tell Blue what she was planning in good time. She must have been mad, she thought.

"Oh Gertie," she said to the small black-and-tan Dachshund that was her mother's rather unlikely choice of dog, "Gertie, what on earth am I going to do?" And then she heard the phone ringing, and her mother answering it, and then heard her name being called.

"Lucinda, quickly, dear, come quickly."

She thought something terrible must have happened, Blue must have taken an overdose or something, but, "It's Nigel," her mother said, handing her the phone, smiling at her. "He wants to speak to you, as soon as possible. And he asked so nicely about your father, please thank him from me."

She clearly thought they were going to get together again, Lucinda thought, and that explained Blue's absence. She took the phone and said, "Hello, Nigel," and then, as her mother hovered on the stairs, clearly hoping to hear more of a reconciliation, "I'll take this in Daddy's study."

"No need for that," said Mrs. Worthington, and went into the kitchen and slammed the door.

"Lucinda, hello. Are you all right?"

"Yes, Nigel, I'm fine. Thank you."

"Good. Only I gather there's been a bit of a problem . . ."

"With the divorce? Oh Nigel, it's so totally awful, I should have listened to you, should have talked to Blue, told him what we were doing, but I kept putting it off, you know, and now he believes all that rubbish about me feeling insecure and wanting the house and everything; he thinks I meant it and he won't listen to me, won't speak to me, and I just don't know what to do."

"Oh dear. Oh Lord," said Nigel. "I think I'd better go and see him."

Blue was sitting down to a very large whiskey when there was a knock at the door. He ignored it at first; but at the third time, he got up swearing and went to open it.

"Whatever you're selling—" he said, and stopped short. Nigel Cowper stood there, looking very determined, holding a very battered leather document case. "Good God," he said, "you've got a nerve. Just fuck off, will you."

"Absolutely not," said Nigel. "I need to come in and talk to you."

"Well, you'll have to go on needing. And if you want her back, you're very welcome. You can tell her that with my compliments."

"Of course I don't want her back," said Nigel. "She doesn't want to be with me. She wants to marry you."

"Yeah? So much that she feels—what was it? Oh yes, 'unsure of our relationship.' Wants to keep the house. Like fuck she wants to marry me."

"There really is no need to be so offensive," said Nigel. "I've come to explain. Please let me in."

"Look, mate, I don't want anyone here, least of all you. That is, with the possible exception of your wife. So just piss off to whatever gentlemanly place you spend your evenings, and leave me in peace."

"I'm not going to," said Nigel. "Not until you understand. Look, it really isn't how you think."

"No? How do you work that out then?"

"I'll tell you if you let me in," said Nigel slightly desperately.

Blue opened the door fully and gestured into the living room. "In there," he said.

Nigel looked around with great interest; he could see it had all cost a lot of money, but it looked pretty dreadful to him. Deep, deep carpets, flashy chrome furniture, an enormous television, a music centre that filled up half a wall, a large glass coffee table, a lot of very odd pictures—and not a book in sight. How did Lucinda stand it?

"Very nice," he said politely.

"Just get on with it," said Blue.

"Yes. Well, the thing is, and I did tell Lucinda she should have told you this, the whole divorce thing is a . . . a sort of front. It's something her lawyer dreamed up. You know I'm dreadfully in hock to Lloyd's? Well . . ." Nigel tried to explain; about the charitable trust, how he would be one of the major trustees, how the house in Cadogan Square would be made over to Lucinda, mortgage free, and that she'd borrow against that to benefit the trust. "Could be quite a lot of money. Or she might buy a second property, where I could live, and—"

"All right, all right. I get the drift. So Lloyd's won't be able to get hold of all this money of yours?"

"That's it in a nutshell."

"Well, I don't know," said Blue. "You could have done this anyway, couldn't you—set up all these trusts and things—without involving a divorce."

"Well, no, not at all. The thing about a divorce is that it's legally binding and the case had to at least appear . . . sound. Lucinda had to seem as if she really did need the money, that she had a right to it."

Blue sat staring at the blank television screen.

"Right," he said finally. "Right, I get it. Very clever."

"Oh good. So is that all right then? You're quite clear? No more problem over Lucinda or . . . or anything."

"Oh, I don't think I could say that," said Blue. His almost black eyes were very hard in his white face. "I'd never have believed it of her, that's the problem. The fact remains she was prepared to say all that and she never told me about it, just went on plotting and conniving behind my back, with you and that arsehole Durham. Why the fuck couldn't she have talked to me about it?"

"Well, I think she was scared to," said Nigel. "Once it had got under way, you know? It was easier to leave it and think she'd tell you . . . later."

"Very good of her," said Blue, "and how am I supposed ever to trust her now? She's a deceitful, conniving little cow and—" He didn't get any further.

Nigel stood up and said, "I really don't think you should talk about Lucinda like that."

"Oh really? Would you like to tell me why not, you public-school ponce?"

"Could you take that back, please?" said Nigel. He could feel the blood beginning to pound in his head.

"Take what back?"

"What you said about Lucinda. And me, for that matter."

"I couldn't, actually. No. It was all true. Sorry. Old chap," he added.

Something snapped in Nigel; he bent down, grabbed Blue by the tie and pulled him up to his feet.

"I said, take it back."

"I can't," said Blue, "unfortunately. She *is* a deceitful, conniving little cow and—"

He got no further; Nigel pulled back his fist and hit him very hard, an uppercut to the chin. Blue staggered backwards, hit his head against the coffee table and sank, neatly and rather theatrically, onto the ground, his eyes closed. A trickle of blood began to seep down onto the beige carpet.

"Oh my God," said Nigel, staring down at him. "Oh my God."

Chapter 49

Tilly was weeping, as only she could. Tilly had always been a champion weeper; not only did she weep loudly but an enormous amount of wetness was generated. Annabel was with her, her arm round her.

"What is it?" said Elizabeth. "Tilly, darling, whatever is the matter?"

"It's Fallon," wailed Tilly. "She's so upset! She cried all day; her mum's lost her baby—she's in hospital, she's really poorly, Fallon's there now . . ."

"Oh dear," said Elizabeth, as calmly as she could. "I'm so sorry."

"Yeah, right," said Annabel, "you would be," and walked out of the room.

Elizabeth sighed, and then returned her attention to Tilly. "Darling, don't cry. These things are usually for the best. It's nature's way of dealing with things. Most miscarriages are babies with something wrong with them."

"No, no, you don't understand," said Tilly, wiping her eyes. "Fallon's dad hit her mum—punched her in the stomach, he was so angry about the new baby. Madison is so afraid she's going to die. I just don't know how anybody could do that, Mummy, hit someone like that, kill a little baby on purpose. It's so, so wrong, don't you think?"

Half an hour later Elizabeth walked into Annabel's bedroom. She looked at her daughter rather awkwardly.

"I've decided to keep the baby," she said. "To have it. But you're bloody well going to have to help me, Annabel. I can't do it on my own."

Annabel stared at her for a while, her face very serious. Then she got up and went over to her mother and put her arms round her.

"You won't have to," she said, "I promise."

"Mummy, I've got to go to London." Lucinda appeared in the kitchen looking wild-eyed. "Blue's had a . . . an accident, he's in hospital."

"What sort of accident?"

"Um, I'm not sure, but he's been hit on the head, been concussed. I'll go there now."

"But, Lucinda—it's eight o'clock at night. You can't go driving off like that—"

"I've only got to drive up the M4 and it's practically still the rush hour," said Lucinda. "Don't be silly, Mummy, I'll be fine. I'll call you later." And she was gone.

Nigel was sitting in the Casualty Department of Barts when Lucinda rushed in. "Where is he? Is there any news?"

"I think he's going to be all right," said Nigel, "he's gone for an X-ray. He's concussed. And he lost a fair bit of blood—you know how heads bleed. But they don't think it's very serious. He'd come round even before the ambulance arrived."

"Thank goodness," said Lucinda. "Will they let me see him?"

"I should think so, when he comes back. They're talking about keeping him in overnight, whatever the X-ray shows."

"What could it show?" said Lucinda fearfully.

"Well, a clot or something. But he doesn't seem too bad; apparently he was swearing like a trooper in the ambulance."

"He swears like a trooper wherever he is," said Lucinda, "but I would say that's a pretty good sign, yes. Oh Nigel, thank you for letting me know so quickly But how exactly did it happen? I don't understand."

"I hit him," said Nigel simply.

Blue was brought back about thirty minutes later and wheeled into a cubicle; a doctor and a nurse went in after him and pulled the curtains closed.

A nurse came over. "You're with Mr. Horton, I believe," she said to Nigel.

"Yes, I am."

"And I'm his—his wife," said Lucinda. "Is he all right? Can I see him?"

"I can't give you an answer to either question for a moment," she said. "Doctor is looking at the X-rays now. He seems not too bad, if his conversation is anything to go by."

"Oh dear," said Lucinda. "I suppose he's swearing terribly?"

"Just a little."

"I'm so sorry. How upsetting for you."

"Oh, I've heard worse," said the nurse cheerfully. She looked at Lucinda, taking in her condition. "Er, you say you're his wife? He told us he was unmarried."

"Well, I nearly am. Or nearly was, I should say," she added with a sigh. "Sorry, I'm not making a lot of sense. I've just driven up from the country. Bit tired."

"Actually, she's *my* wife," Nigel said. The nurse looked at the two of them and visibly gave up.

"When's the baby due?" she asked Lucinda, reverting to safer territory.

"Not for another four weeks . . . oh goodness, here's the doctor. How is he, Doctor? Is he going to be all right? And can I see him?"

"He's going to be fine. He has a concussion but the bleeding was just from a surface wound. And yes, you can see him. But I'd like to keep him under observation."

"Yes, of course," said Lucinda. "I understand. So can I go in?"

"Well, if you really want to. I hope he'll be more polite to you than he was to us," he added.

Lucinda put her head round the curtains. Blue was lying on his back with his eyes closed, a large bandage wound round his head.

"Just piss off, would you?" he said. "I'm tired, I feel sick, and I'm trying to get some bloody sleep. What is it with you people?"

Lucinda went over to him, picked up one of his hands, and looked down at him. "I'll piss off in a minute," she said gently. "I just wanted to make sure you were alive first."

He turned to look at her. "My God," he said. "Lucinda."

"That's me. Glad you recognised me."

"Of course I recognised you, you silly cow. Christ, my head hurts." He closed his eyes again. "That husband of yours can pack a bloody punch. Couldn't believe it." There was a note in his voice she couldn't at first analyse; then she realised what it was. Admiration.

"He learned to box at Eton," she said. "People are always surprised." Blue opened his eyes and looked at her rather hazily; then he half smiled.

"Don't spoil it, Lucinda. I was just coming round to thinking he wasn't quite the idiot I'd thought."

"Sorry. And—well, what were you thinking? I mean, do you . . . think about me? If anything?" she said, and she was so frightened she could literally hardly speak. And then the words came out in a rush, and she stood there, the tears running down her face. "Blue, I'm so sorry, I know Nigel's tried to explain and I know how wrong of me it was not to tell you, but I do love you so, so much, I wouldn't have hurt you for the world, you must believe that, I'm just stupid, stupid and—thoughtless, and—"

"Just shut up, for Christ's sake," he said, "you silly cow."

"Yes, all right," she said humbly, "but Blue, I really, really did—"

"I said shut up." And then he looked at her very seriously, and she was afraid he was going to tell her to go away again. But: "It's all right, Lucinda," he said quite gently, "I'll get over it in time. In time for the boy to be born, I daresay. How is he, by the way?" And he reached out and moved his hand tenderly over her stomach.

"He's fine. Oh Blue, darling Blue, I'm so, so relieved and thankful and—"

"I tell you something," he said, and there was a new expression in his eyes as he looked at her, that she would have said came close to respect, "that scheme you dreamed up between you. Bloody clever. Wouldn't have thought it of you, Lucinda. I'm well impressed."

"Impressed! Blue, I can't take any credit for it, you know, any at all—"

"Course you can," he said. "You're obviously not quite as feather-brained as I thought you were. Now give your old man a kiss."

She bent down to kiss him and he kissed her back, quite thoroughly; he couldn't be too bad, she thought, if he could do that, his reflexes must be pretty all right . . .

Catherine had come up to London to see her solicitor and to do some early Christmas shopping. Her children had been invited to stay with friends for the night; and she had twenty-four hours of glorious freedom. She phoned Lucinda to see if she could meet her at some point, only to be told that Blue was in hospital.

"He got knocked out," Lucinda said. "I'll explain later. You couldn't come over, Catherine, could you? I'm a bit tired, and I'd love to see you."

Catherine said she'd come straightaway.

Lucinda was looking extremely tired; hardly surprising, Catherine thought, considering what she'd been through: her father's stroke, some row with Blue—she didn't expand on that—and a late-night spell in Casualty at Barts.

"But Nigel was so sweet, he looked after me. And he's been trying to clean up the carpet. He'll actually be back in a minute—he's just gone to return some machine he hired."

"Nigel!" said Catherine.

"Yes. He and Blue had a fight and he knocked Blue out. Only don't say anything when he comes back, will you?"

"Of course not," said Catherine. If Lucinda had told her Nigel had opened a gay strip joint she could scarcely have been more surprised.

"But why? I don't understand."

"Oh, Blue said something Nigel didn't like about me and— Oh, here he is now. Nigel, darling. You remember Catherine, don't you?"

"Of course I do," said Nigel. He smiled at Catherine. "In fact, we shared a very racy dining experience didn't we?"

"Yes, we did," said Catherine. She was still trying to come to terms with the thought of gentle, vague Nigel knocking anybody out. Let alone Blue. He must be still very much in love with Lucinda, she thought, and felt a pang of sadness.

"Oh, did you?" said Lucinda. "How lovely. Now let's all have some coffee and then I'm going to collect Blue. I'm not sure I relish nursing him, but still . . . no choice, I'm afraid."

"So how's country life?" asked Nigel as Lucinda disappeared into the kitchen.

"Lovely," said Catherine, and then, "Well, pretty awful, actually."

"I'm sorry. That's a lovely part of the world."

"It is, yes. But the people a bit less so. Specially the ones I live with."

"Ah. Think I can imagine. Yes. Children like it?"

"They absolutely love it," said Catherine.

"Well, that's the main thing. I mean, that's why you went, after all. And children should live in the country, don't you think?"

"I suppose so," said Catherine with a sigh.

Lucinda came back with the coffeepot. "The carpet does look miles better, Nigel," she said. "Well done."

"That's all right. Least I could do."

Catherine suddenly felt as if she was going to cry. She stood up abruptly; knocked the coffee table, and the contents of the jug went all over the newly cleaned carpet. And although Lucinda and Nigel were both absolutely sweet about it, and Lucinda said she couldn't mind less, and Nigel said that there was plenty of carpet shampoo left, so it couldn't have been more convenient, as she drove away, she did start to cry and she was still very weepy as she joined the Westway, wondering what it must feel like to be Lucinda, who had two men in love with her and literally fighting over her, and trying not to mind too much that she was returning to her Jane Eyre existence. With not a single Mr. Rochester anywhere in sight.

ↄ

It would have been over now, Elizabeth thought, sitting toying with a piece of dry toast; she wouldn't have been pregnant anymore, wouldn't be feeling sick, she'd have been on her way to feeling better.

All the good things that had resulted from her decision, Annabel's relief and happiness, Tilly's pink-faced delight, even her gynaecologist's quiet, "I do think that's wise," were over now and she was facing the reality of having a baby as a widow, of coping with it all on her own, of having no one to share it with—well, of course she did have the children, and that was lovely. But there would be no Simon to share the weariness, the anxiety, the trauma of the tests—like the amniocentesis she had insisted on.

She had taken Peter Hargreaves into her confidence; he had said how delighted he was for her, how wonderful that she would have this comfort. Comfort! But she managed to smile back and thank him.

"So are you really all right to go on working?" he had said, and, "Yes," she told him, "of course I'll be fine."

"Well, you must let me know if you're not. Immediately. I'll do everything I can to help."

"Thank you, Peter, I appreciate that. But I won't let you down."

She hadn't told Toby yet; she was waiting till he came home next rather than inform him over the phone or in a letter. Which gave her time to rehearse it.

She really, really didn't want this baby: still. She didn't sit staring dreamily at her stomach as she had with the others, thinking how miraculous it all was; she sat thinking with foreboding of how hard she would find it to cope with, to live with. She had changed her mind only because of the girls; because she could see that for them it would be dreadfully hurtful to think of their mother terminating a pregnancy, a pregnancy that would have resulted in a new sibling, the last legacy of their father. And it was going to take all her love for them to get her through it without resentment. But she could do it; and she would do it.

She suddenly stood up, experiencing a rather unfamiliar sensation; a shot of energy.

She mustn't waste it; she would make a start on the sorting for the move; go through each room methodically, making lists, deciding what to take and what to sell.

Two hours later, she was feeling very pleased with herself, having listed all the drawing-room furniture that must go, all the dining-room furniture, and the things in the front hall. And then she suddenly felt that yes, she would start—just start—on his dressing room. It had to be done, nobody else could do it—it couldn't be so terribly bad, could it? And taking a deep breath, she walked up the stairs and into it.

She started pulling down the suits, one by one: and of course it was terribly bad, for they exuded him, every one of them; she could see him in them, feel him in them, and she sank onto the ground weeping, clutching them, longing for him as she would never have thought possible, longing for him to hold her, to talk to her, to smile at her, to tell her how lovely she looked, how good she felt, how much he loved her.

And the now-familiar anger came back, and she stood up, dragging the other suits off their hangers, raging at him for daring to die, for taking himself away from her, leaving her alone with this new, unwelcome burden; and as she reached and pulled and hurled them onto the ground, she suddenly realised there was a dull but unmistakable pain, stabbing deep within her, not constant but spasmodic: and realised at once also what it meant. She was having a miscarriage.

Chapter 50

She wasn't bleeding—well, hardly. Just a few spots. But the pain was still there; quite insistent, tugging away.

Dr. Rice, who had looked after the family for years, said he would come at once. "Just go to bed and stay there. Put the door on the latch first, so you don't have to come downstairs to let me in. Any bleeding?"

"Only a bit. A tiny bit."

"Good. I'll be there in about half an hour."

She was actually in bed. Lying down, and staying there. And fearfully checking the bleeding, every few minutes. She felt rather near to tears and wished Annabel was there.

This wasn't fair. It really wasn't. Oh God, here came another pain. But—was it a bit less strong? It certainly wasn't any worse. And the doctor would be here soon and he'd give her a hormone injection which would hopefully stop the contractions. Which is what the pains were.

And realised in that moment that she wanted to keep this baby, wanted to terribly badly.

℮ↄ

Richard didn't come to Wales for the weekend. He phoned on Saturday morning and said it was essential he stayed at school. A parent wanted to consult him about his son's chances in common entrance, another about some alleged bullying . . . There was no way he could suddenly disappear for two days, he told Debbie.

"It would lay too big a burden on Morag. She's absolutely exhausted, she needs my input and support . . ."

A few months earlier, Debbie would have told him that she needed his input and support as much as Morag did. Things being what they were, she heaved a sigh of relief, said of course she understood, and then had to spend half an hour comforting the children, who all burst into tears. And if they cried because they weren't going to see him for a week-end, what hope for— Stop it, Debbie, don't. It's too soon to think like that.

℮ↄ

Colin clearly found her explanation unsatisfactory.

"Of course, you must do what you think best, Flora. But I imagined you had thought it all through a little more clearly."

"Well, I have tried, of course. But . . . well, I'm sorry, Colin. I'm afraid I must have wasted a lot of your time."

"Never mind about that," he said. "These things happen. I do hope you won't regret this, Flora. I mean, you're going to lose your house any-way, aren't you?"

"Yes," she said, "yes. But, well, Colin, there are just some things that one can't quite come to terms with. I'm sure it's happened to you?"

"Of course," he said, and his voice was very cool. "Right, I'll cancel the whole project then. If you're sure."

"I am," she said. "Quite sure." And put the phone down, hoping he would forgive her. She would miss him if not.

Chapter 51

The Sunday papers were full of it: impending drama, tragedy even, of crises and conspiracies, of stalking horses and wrestles for power.

Elizabeth, lying free from pain but still anxious, still bleeding a little, read of the unthinkable, the almost unimaginable eventuality of the departure of Margaret Thatcher from the leadership of the Conservative Party and, even more unimaginably, at the instigation of someone other than herself.

Michael Heseltine was on every front page, looking more handsome. It was all wonderfully distracting.

Joel, who had missed Debbie more than he would have believed possible, was quite relieved when Hugh Renwick phoned him halfway through the morning and asked him to do a piece for Monday's paper on the financial implications of Mrs. Thatcher's possible departure.

"A lot of it's to do with finance, after all: Lawson's resignation last year, John Major's no great shakes, terrible state of the economy, everyone going bust, negative equity, all that crap—and you could drag Heseltine's opposition to the Community Charge into it as well. About fifteen hundred words, OK? Sorry about your Sunday."

"It's fine." It would give him something to do, something else to think about.

Until he had her back again.

"Blimey," said Blue, "I wonder if the old girl's finally going?"

"What old girl?" said Lucinda. "More coffee?"

"Yes, please. Maggie. Could be on her way out. They seem to be out to get her. Heseltine and that mob. This country's in a right old mess at the moment . . ."

"Is it? Blue, I've been thinking. About Nigel."

"Oh yeah? Got some new way of giving him even more money?"

"No. Something better than money."

"Not much that's better than money, Lucy. What were you thinking of?"

"Love. All that sort of thing. Catherine."

"Catherine! What—the plain one?"

"She is not plain," said Lucinda firmly, "and I think she and Nigel could be rather good together. They're both lonely, both in need of someone. What do you think?"

"You'll have to give me a bit of time to digest that, Lucinda. Blimey, my head hurts."

"Shall I get you some more painkillers?"

"No, thanks. I've got something better than painkillers in mind. Come over here, give your old man a kiss."

Lucinda was glad he felt better enough to contemplate sex; she only wished she did. Still, she had a lot of making up to him to do . . .

❧

"Mrs. Morgan?"

"Yes?" Catherine could see that Phyllis was hanging about in the hall, pretending to be sorting through the post; she turned her back on her, spoke into the wall.

"Mrs. Morgan, I do hope you don't mind my telephoning you."

"No. No, of course not." Mind? Being called by a man—a man who wasn't Dudley or one of the children's teachers? It was wonderful, the most exciting thing that had happened to her for months.

"We met last week, at the point-to-point. You were there with the Prices. Patrick Fisher . . ."

"Yes, I remember you, of course."

"Good, good. Jolly day, wasn't it?"

It had been quite jolly. It had also been very cold and wet, and inevitably muddy, and her hands had been so frozen she'd dropped the mug

· 441 ·

of tea Mrs. Jane-Anne had handed her, but they'd been so nice to her, both of them, and it had been quite interesting, watching the races, following the Prices as they charged about in the mud, and certainly good to see Caroline so happy; and compared to spending the day with Dudley and Phyllis, yes, it had been jolly. She remembered Patrick Fisher too; he'd been about fifty, jolly himself, a bit overweight with a rather red face, dressed in a Barbour so old it was shiny and a checked cap on his head, the caricature of an English country gentleman.

"I'm having a few people over for drinks next Saturday evening, wondered if you'd like to come. I remember you saying you hadn't met many people down here yet . . ."

If Phyllis hadn't still been hovering in the hall, Catherine would have sunk onto her knees there and then and offered up a prayer of thanksgiving. As it was she said, "That would be lovely, thank you so much."

"Good, good. Now I know you've been living in London, so you may find us rather boring . . ."

"Of course I won't," said Catherine, thinking of the endless evenings alone in Fulham.

"Hope not. Jolly good. About six. Now then, address is Musgrove Hall, Upton Stratton . . ."

Phyllis was very put out. Catherine had to tell her, because she had to know if she could leave the children at home on Saturday evening.

"Yes, we will be in. You're going to drinks with Patrick Fisher? Well, I hope you enjoy it. He's very eccentric, of course. Never married. I mean, there are stories . . . well, never mind."

Catherine didn't ask about the stories, although Phyllis was clearly dying to share them.

"He seemed very nice," she said. "I met him at that point-to-point that the Prices took Caroline and me to last week, do you remember?"

"Yes, of course," said Phyllis crossly. She had found the Honourable Prices inviting Catherine to join them at the point-to-point almost intolerable.

❧

Why did they have to talk like that, Elizabeth wondered. Why? As if you were in some way mentally defective. Why couldn't they just say, "Wait over there," instead of "If you could just go over there for me," or "Please put this on," instead of "Now could you just pop into this gown." Always accompanied by that painfully bright smile. It just made everything worse. And worse—rather than better—was what she was expecting. She felt better, for a start: that in itself was worrying. If she was still pregnant, why didn't she feel sick? She was still bleeding—only a tiny bit, but—

"Mrs. Beaumont, would you like to come in now? Sorry about the designer outfit."

She stood up. "The what?"

"The robe. Not exactly Chanel, is it?"

"Mum," hissed Annabel, "don't look so cross." She had insisted on taking the morning off to come to the hospital. She said she didn't give a shit if Miki was annoyed or not. "You're much more important."

"Now, Mrs. Beaumont, if you could just pop onto the bed for me, that's right, lovely. How are you feeling?" The nurse had an Australian accent; for some reason, it made things much worse.

"Fine, thank you."

"That's great. What we like to hear. Now I'm just going to rub this jelly stuff on your tummy—sorry it's so cold. You all right?"

"Yes, thank you. Fine." What did she think, silly cow? That she was going to pass out with the shock of a bit of cold jelly?

"There. Not too bad, I hope. Now, have you had a scan before?"

"No, I haven't. They hadn't been invented when I had my other children."

"And do you know how they work?"

"I think so."

"Right, well, I'll explain. This contraption here," she waved what looked rather like a microphone at Elizabeth, "is called a transducer, and it emits and receives sound waves. Which convert into a two-dimensional image of whatever we want to see. In this case, your baby. So I'm just going to start now. If you look at that screen, Mrs. Beaumont, you can see for yourself what's going on in your uterus. Now you are . . . let's see . . . nearly thirteen weeks, so Junior is about seven, maybe eight centimetres long, and you know he's in a kind of little watery sac—"

"I do, yes, thank you," said Elizabeth. "I do have three children already."

"Three! Well, isn't that lovely. Girls or boys?"

"One boy, two girls."

"How old are they?"

"They're all teenagers."

"Teenagers? You don't look old enough to be the mother of teenagers."

Smile, Elizabeth, come on, make an effort, she's very nice really.

"They must be so thrilled about this. Now, he's bobbing around in there . . . where is he? Can't see him. He must be playing hide-and-seek . . ."

She couldn't see him, silly bitch, because he—or she—wasn't there. He'd left her, dissatisfied with the accommodation, with the negative vibes she'd been sending down to him all these weeks. She clenched her fists.

"Right. Well, no luck that side, let's have a look over here . . . there's one of your ovaries, see, and there's the other one . . . come on, little feller, where are you?"

Elizabeth thought she might scream. She couldn't lie here, listening to this drivel, feeling so terrified and so despairing, any longer. She would just—just count to ten very slowly and then scream. She shut her eyes; the radiographer, silent now, was moving the transducer over her stomach. Her flat, clearly empty stomach. Eight . . . nine . . . ten.

"Mrs. Beaumont? If you open your eyes and look now—there, see—there he is, bobbing around like crazy. I'd say you've got a real little footie player there . . ."

"Oh, my God. My God." Suddenly the Australian accent was the most wonderful sound in the world, and the girl's podgy face rather beautiful.

"So, you mean, you mean it's still—still there?"

"Of course it's still there. Set to stay for the duration, I'm sure. Is that pretty girl out there one of your daughters?"

"Yes, she is."

"Do you want me to get her in, show her her baby brother? Or sister, of course."

And so for a full five minutes, she and Annabel sat transfixed and tearful, clutching each other's hands and staring at the flickering image on the black screen, watching the baby, Simon's final legacy to them: and sharing a sense of huge relief and happiness mixed inevitably with intense sadness and loss.

Chapter 52

Well, that was a bad start. She'd managed to persuade Nigel to invite Catherine to a drinks party; in fact, his eyes had quite lit up at the suggestion, and then it turned out that Catherine was going to another on the very same day. Which was excellent, of course, it was wonderful that she was making friends down there, but: "Gosh, how annoying," Catherine said. "I'd much rather go to Nigel's. Talk about all the buses coming along at once. But I can't change it, unfortunately."

Lucinda put the phone down and sighed. It had been such a perfect occasion to get them together. And she could hardly ask him and Lucinda to cosy little drinks at their house.

❧

"Well, I'm sorry, Jamie, but you'll just have to postpone it . . . Yes, I can see that's difficult and I'm sure your mother won't be— . . . Yes, but this is really, really important. My mother's pregnant, for God's sake, and she's just nearly lost the baby. I really can't come rushing over there in a couple of weeks . . . What? . . . Oh, wouldn't she? Oh dear. Jamie, I am sorry but you must see how difficult it is for me as well. And if Tilly and Toby are going to come too, well, Mummy'd be alone. What about after Christmas? Like January. How would that be? I want to look after my mother and at this precise moment that's the most important thing! It's very hard for her, you know and— . . . Oh, for fuck's sake, Jamie. I can't take any more of this . . ."

"I just put the phone down on him," she said to Tilly later. "He's so selfish, couldn't see how much it mattered, and went on and on about what a lot of work it would be for his mother, unscrambling everything and reinviting everyone. I mean, what's that, compared to a baby?"

Jamie rang back; he was incredibly sorry, he hadn't meant to be selfish, that of course Elizabeth and her baby were much the most important thing and that yes, his mother thought January would be a better idea.

"We can wait if you can," he said.

"I can wait. Well, I can't, but I have to. I'll enjoy it much more. How is your mother?"

"She's fine. She sends her love. She says to tell you she's writing to your mother. About the baby. It must be making her feel so much better."

"Well, yes and no," said Annabel cautiously. "I think she's pretty scared. Of coping on her own, you know."

"I guess so. Well, better go, this is costing Dad a fortune. Love you."

"Love you too," said Annabel, "lots and lots. Jamie . . . could you—that is, would you like to—come here for Christmas? It was Mummy's suggestion, and it would be so nice for me and for all of us. This Christmas is going to be difficult and . . ."

There was a silence, then Jamie said, "Well, it would be great, of course. And thank you for the invitation. I'll, well, I'll have to talk to my parents. Christmas is pretty sacred here; we have terrific family traditions, you know, and—"

"Most families do," said Annabel briskly. "Well, think about it, Jamie. Bye now."

She rang off; if Jamie thought she was going to spend the next fifty years or whatever having Christmas with his family and not hers he—well he really did have another think coming.

❧

"Debbie, it's Joel. What the fuck are you playing at? It's Thursday, and I haven't seen you for over a week. What are you trying to do to me?"

"I'm not trying to do anything to you. I'm just . . . just thinking."

"Well, stop it. Or at least, don't think on your own. Let me help."

"Joel, I can't see you. Not for a few more days. I really can't. I'm—I'm sorry." And she put the phone down.

She'd thought she was doing all right, clearing her head of him, in order properly to face the future, and decide what she was going to do.

But hearing his voice was agony, a bit like pulling off a scab. Or having the first drink. Just like having the first drink. Suddenly she couldn't resist it. She had to see him. She just had to. While she could.

She rang him back. "I'll see what I can do," she said, "babysitting-wise. Tonight."

"I love you," he said. Nothing else. Just, "I love you."

"I love you too."

℮

Toby had been told about the baby—by Annabel. He had reacted exactly as Elizabeth had predicted: he was embarrassed, shocked, almost morose. He managed to come and congratulate her, but she could see he was finding it almost impossibly difficult. He had gone back to school, clearly with relief.

"Stupid wanker," Tilly said, as his glowering face disappeared into the train. Her still-perfect accent made her comment somehow all the more powerful.

"Tilly, that's not a nice word," said Elizabeth.

"Good. He doesn't deserve nice words. He's a complete pig. What does it mean, by the way?" she added. "Madison says it a lot, but I don't like to ask her."

As Elizabeth sat at her desk, writing a conference speech and feeling better and stronger than she had for months, she had a call from the coroner's office. The date for the inquest had been set: for the second week in January. January! So long after Simon's death. It would inevitably threaten her fragile recovery. She was at least surviving; surviving and functioning, doing her job, coping with her family, and that was all she could hope for, for the foreseeable future. Even the sale of the house, due to be completed two weeks before Christmas, seemed to be manageable. But the thought of going into the exact circumstances of his death: that was truly terrifying. Brave as she was, tough as she was, Elizabeth really didn't know how she was going to face it.

Chapter 53

NOVEMBER TO DECEMBER 1990

Well, was this really worse than being at home with the children? Catherine wondered. She had been at Musgrove Hall for more than an hour now, and she could have been invisible for all the notice people took of her.

Patrick had been very nice when she arrived, inevitably one of the first. "Sorry, lot of the guests have been out hunting today, sure to make them a bit late. Still, jolly nice to see you. Gin? Or Whiskey? Or there's sherry, of course. Your shout."

She settled for a gin and tonic, thinking that it would make her slightly less drunk and she could move on to just tonic; and then followed Patrick into the freezing-cold room that he described as the drawing room; no carpets, no curtains, just stone flags on the floor—she'd have to be careful not to drop anything on that, she thought. The stone fireplace contained a rather feeble log fire, but it was unarguably beautiful.

She felt rather underdressed in her black trousers and silk shirt; the two women who were already there both wore what she remembered from her childhood, cocktail dresses. Wherever could you still buy such things, stiffly skirted, three-quarter-sleeved, scoop-necked dresses—one in dark velvet, one in heavy silk—the perfect background for strings of what were inevitably real pearls and large brooches.

"Right now, this is Pattie Smithers and her husband, Paul, and this is Mo Cummings, and this useless-looking fellow is Mr. Mo, as we call him."

"Don't you dare," said Mr. Mo, holding out a clammy hand to Catherine. "Mike Cummings."

"And this is Catherine Morgan, only been here for a couple of months. These are all neighbours, my dear. Catherine's from London, so she's used to all sorts of excitement. I told her she'd find us pretty dull . . ."

"Oh no, not at all," said Catherine. "It was London that was dull. I—"

"Husband away, is he?" said Pattie, interrupting her. She looked rather fierce.

"No, he's—that is, I'm a widow." She smiled nervously at Pattie.

"Oh, sorry to hear that." She appeared neither embarrassed by what would have seemed to many a social gaffe nor in the least sorry for Catherine. "So where do you live?"

"Oh, over at Gillingham. I'm, well, I'm living with my parents-in-law. At the moment. And with my—"

"Gillingham, eh?" said Mo, her brow briefly furrowed. "No, don't know anyone there. Do they shoot?"

"Er, no. No, they don't."

"Hunt?"

"No. 'Fraid not."

"Shame. Well, jolly nice to meet you. Ah Sally, lovely to see you," and she beamed at a third cocktail-dressed lady with an even redder face.

"Good day?"

"Oh terrific, we found almost at once, and . . ."

And Catherine was spoken to no more.

Every so often Patrick would clearly remember her, drag her from one group and over to another. He was really very sweet, Catherine thought gratefully. But he must be regretting his decision, as she seemed to be nothing but a burden to him.

The talk was entirely of hunting and shooting; no one had so far mentioned fishing, but she felt that was inevitable. The drink was very slow to materialise; she supposed it was harder to remix gin and tonic than pour glasses of wine. The good news was that she was still stone-cold sober. And stone cold, come to that.

The only other topic of conversation was Mrs. Thatcher and her downfall; the general consensus seemed to be that Heseltine deserved to be strung up for setting the whole thing in motion.

"Met him once," someone said, "couldn't stand him. Bit of a cad. And that hair . . ."

"Well, at least he's been to a decent school," said someone else.

"Suppose we got Major. Dreadful fellow."

"Hurd'd be all right," said a completely bald man. "Not exactly charismatic, but—"

"I say, Geoffrey old chap, long word for you," said Patrick. "Catherine, do you know any of these dreadful politicians, as you live in London?"

Bless him, Catherine thought, he really wants to include me. "Well, I once met Neil Kinnock," she said tentatively, "but he—"

"Kinnock? The Welsh Windbag? Only thing I can say for him is he's doing a pretty good job, keeping the Labour lot out," said Geoffrey. "How on earth did you meet him?"

Catherine started to explain that he had come to her children's school, realised that must indicate being in the state system and therefore even worse, and said, with a glance at her watch, that goodness, she really had to be getting home, she hadn't realised how late it was. As it said 7:25 p.m., she could see it wasn't very convincing.

Patrick, however, appeared to find it perfectly acceptable. Clearly party regulations, like everything else, were different in the country. "I'll come and see you off," he said. "Hope you enjoyed it?"

"Gosh, yes, it was great fun," said Catherine. "Thank you so much."

"Oh, not at all. Very nice to have you here. Breath of fresh air, someone new you know, not just the old crowd. Still, they're a pretty good lot, as you'll discover. Well, see you again soon, I hope. You going to the point-to-point at Trister on Saturday?"

"Um . . . no."

"Well, look, I'm going. Should be quite a good one. Would you like to come with me?"

"Oh, gosh." Catherine felt rather confused. Was this a date? If so, did she want to accept? He might be very sweet, but he wasn't exactly her type. On the other hand, it would be lovely to be out. Except of course . . .

"It's so kind of you," she said, "and I'd love to. But I'll probably have to bring the children."

"Oh, that's all right. Seemed rather a jolly little thing, your daughter."

"Shall I bring the picnic?"

"Oh, that's jolly kind. No, don't bother, Mrs. P will do that."

"Then let me make a cake. For—for sort of teatime."

"Capital," he said. "Very good of you. See you on Saturday then."

If Mrs. Bennet had been her mother, Catherine thought, looking back at Musgrove Hall in all its Jacobean splendour, she'd be getting quite excited.

*

Debbie felt she had grown two heads. Or at least two lives. There was the familiar one, where she was a good wife and mother, much concerned with and involved in her children's lives: she delivered them to school every morning, neatly uniformed and well-breakfasted, their homework done and their projects well in order; after which she proceeded to her job, where she worked hard and did rather well, five days a week now, three of them finishing at three so she could collect the children. And then proceeded home, where she did the housework and the washing and entertained the children's friends and spoke to her absent husband on the phone, reassuring him that all was well, and asking him how his job was going: and then at night she went to bed fairly early, in order to begin the next, well-ordered day.

And then there was the other, secret life: the one in which she lied and deceived and invented meetings and set up fake interviews and spent half her housekeeping money on babysitters, and drove across London, her heart racing, her body dissolving with desire, in order to meet her lover: to spend precious, rapturous hours with him, talking to him, laughing with him, making love with him, and all the time refusing to consider the future and how fast it was rushing towards her.

If Joel pressed her in any way, she simply told him not to. "What matters is now, us being together, me loving you, you loving me; us just enjoying each other. Why spoil it till we have to?"

For it would have to be spoiled, and for many people. There was no happy ending to this story, no crock of gold, and indeed the end of the rainbow was shrouded in rain; but while it lasted, it was spellbinding and full of joy.

It was not all sweetness and light, of course. Joel sometimes grew angry, often impatient, demanding a decision, upbraiding her for failing to commit herself.

"I can't do more, for Christ's sake. I've asked you to marry me. Why won't you answer? What else can I do?"

"Nothing," she would say, kissing him, holding him, "nothing at all. Let me be, let it be, something will happen, something will settle it. Please, Joel, please wait."

The rows were worse on the weekends that Richard was coming home: when Joel raged and stormed and told her she was cowardly and fraudulent and cruel too, and that if she wouldn't make her decision, then he would do it for her. She went through those weekends (only two of them since half term, thank God) in a state of complete terror: terror of Richard growing suspicious, of the children revealing how often she went out, of Joel arriving on the doorstep, of—and this was by far the most stressful—Richard making love to her. Which he did. How she got through that, she never knew afterwards. She would compose press releases in her head, plan meetings, even think what she might wear on Monday morning. The amazing thing was that he never seemed to notice.

And Monday came in due course, after what seemed like an eternity, mostly of stories about the wonders of Morag and the joys of the new job, and she returned with a sigh of welcome to her two lives. Only she knew, deep within the heart of her, at the centre of both the lives, that she had to make the decision and she had to make it alone.

e

"Please, please Mr. Clark can you hurry it up?" said Lucinda, looking fretfully at her consultant over her vast stomach. "I'm going to burst, I think. I can't stand it any longer. Can't I be induced or something?"

"No, you can't. Induction for social reasons is a thing of the past, I'm very glad to say. You're not even due till next Thursday. First babies are generally late. And the head isn't engaged yet. I should say you've got a good week to go. At least." He patted the stomach, beamed at her. "I know it's a bore, but try to be patient. They come when they're good and ready."

She took a cab home; Blue was already there, looking slightly apprehensive.

"You're early," she said.

"Yeah, I know. Easy day. What'd the doc say, Lucy?"

"Oh dear. He said probably another week or even two. I think I'll go mad."

"No, you won't. Poor you. I got your supper ready for you, by the way."

"Blue, you're so sweet."

He looked slightly shamefaced. "Yeah, well, it's only Chicken Chernobyl. From Marks and Sparks."

"I wish you wouldn't call it that."

"What, Marks and Sparks?"

"No, Chicken Chernobyl. It's so—so insensitive."

"Sorry."

"Anyway, I do appreciate it. Thank you."

"You sit down, put your feet up, I'll bring it in."

As she sat there, trying to imagine ever having a flat stomach again, the phone rang. It was Catherine. She'd got the children sorted for Monday, was coming up to town to do some Christmas shopping. Would Lucinda like a visit?

"Oh, yes. So, so much. Come over here as soon as you can; as soon as you're shopped out."

"All right. Golly, Phyllis is calling me. Better go. Bye, Lucinda."

Blue came in with a tray, complete with Lucinda's best linen napkins and a small vase with a rose in it. She looked at him suspiciously.

"Blue, what are you up to? What's going on? Come on, tell me."

"Well, few of the lads are going over to Paris on Monday. Just for the day. Bit of a pre-Christmas jolly. I said I wouldn't go, of course. Said the baby was due."

"Well, it is."

"Yeah, but you said—well, obviously I wouldn't dream of going. Not if it's imminent."

"It isn't. Blue, you are such a bad liar. You'd better go."

"Really? You don't mind?"

"Not too terribly," said Lucinda with a sigh. "It might even bring it on."

"In that case I'll certainly go. It really is only for the day. And we're going by private plane—a client do. So all you've got to do is call me—"

"In Paris?"

"That's the one. On my mobile phone. And I'll be back before you can say contraction. Well, two hours later, max. But honestly, Lucy, I swear I won't go, if you don't want me to."

"You go," said Lucinda, "it's fine. Probably the last time you'll be able to go out for ages. But if you switch your mobile phone off, and I need you, I warn you I'll never speak to you again!"

⌒

Nigel's company was limping towards closure; if he got hold of John Major, he thought, he'd give him a very strong piece of his mind about what Major swore was a recession and which was clearly a full-scale depression. The company had a small factory in Yeovil which was running at catastrophically low production levels, and was costing him more than it earned. He decided he should bite the bullet, go down the next Friday and break the news himself.

Looking at the map, it occurred to him that he wouldn't be so very far away from Gillingham, which was where Catherine now lived. If Lucinda had been right, she was pretty lonely and might appreciate a visit. Although maybe not so lonely now, as she hadn't been able to come to his party last Saturday, which had disappointed him quite a bit. She was such a sweet girl, and pretty too. And he liked her children a lot. He'd give her a ring, see what she said. Perhaps they could all go out to lunch together on Saturday.

Catherine was very sorry, she said, but she was going out on Saturday. "To a point-to-point. With a . . . a friend."

"Oh, shame. Well, never mind. Just an idea. Another time."

"I don't suppose," said Catherine tentatively, "you'll still be down here on Sunday?" She didn't want to appear too keen; but she did like him so much, and it seemed silly to lose the opportunity to meet.

"No 'fraid not," said Nigel, and then, because he really rather wanted to know, without being sure why, he said, "This friend of yours, does she live in Gillingham as well?"

Catherine hesitated, then said, "No, but quite near."

At least it was a woman. Not a man. That was something.

"Well, nice to talk to you, Catherine. Some other time perhaps."

"Yes."

He obviously wasn't really interested in her; otherwise he would have hung around till Sunday. Damn. He was so nice, so gentle . . .

❦

It was fairly horrible, telling the people at the factory that he had to close it. He took everyone out for a few drinks at the pub, and then a few key people for a pub meal in Yeovil. They were all very good about it, said they'd been expecting it, swapped stories about the old days. There was hardly anybody young there.

He told them he'd arrange as much redundancy money as he could, left them for a rather dismal commercial hotel, and woke up next morning feeling suicidal. If only he could have seen Catherine, she would have cheered him up. And God, she'd had far worse troubles than this. Suddenly it seemed worth waiting at least till Saturday evening. Maybe they could go out for a drink or something. He could mooch around during the day, maybe visit Wells or somewhere like that—he'd always wanted to see the cathedral. He ate a fairly disgusting breakfast and set off for Wells, where he enjoyed the cathedral and indeed the rest of his day, then drove to Gillingham and parked in the lane by the Morgan seniors' hideous house—he was a little shocked by its hideousness, but told himself Catherine could hardly be blamed for it—to wait for her return from the day with her girlfriend.

And then drove away, even more shocked, and indeed saddened, after a very large and mud-spattered Range Rover had pulled into the drive and disgorged not only Catherine and Freddie, but Caroline, fast asleep and carried in the arms of its equally large and mud-spattered male driver.

Chapter 54

DECEMBER 1990

"Hello, Lucinda, how are you?"

"Oh, all right. You know."

It was so unlike her to sound down, Catherine felt quite alarmed.

"You're not—not . . ."

"God, no such luck. Just fed up. I'm so looking forward to seeing you, Catherine. Blue's in Paris and—"

"Paris!" For the umpteenth time, Catherine wondered what on earth Lucinda saw in Blue; Nigel would never have gone off to Paris the week before the baby was due, he'd have been there with her every moment, caring for her, worrying about her.

"Yes, but it's only for a day. He'll be back tonight, sooner if I need him. 'Fraid I won't though. But do come, Catherine, as soon as you can. I feel awfully odd."

"Well, I've got to do a bit more Christmas shopping, haven't got anything for Phyllis yet. I'm in Selfridges—there must be something there—and then I'll come right over."

"So how long do you think you'll be?" She sounded almost desperate.

"Let me see, about . . . an hour and a half. That should do it. Yes, by—let's see—four."

"OK. I'll try and stay sane."

"When will Blue be back?"

"Oh, quite late. He just rang, said the client wants to have dinner there. An early one, of course. I've been so bad-tempered and horrid to him all weekend, I think he'd stay the week if he could."

"I'm sure you haven't," said Catherine, who found it impossible to imagine Lucinda being horrid. "Just hang on, and I'll be there by four."

"OK. Thanks."

Lucinda did, as she had told Catherine, feel terribly odd. Not physically so much as mentally; she felt rather confused, restless.

The phone rang: "Lucinda?"

"Oh—Nigel. Oh, how lovely to hear your voice. How are you?"

"I'm all right. Bit depressed. I rang you to see if you had heard anything from the solicitors."

"Not yet, no. But Steve's totally confident. Don't worry. Um—do you want to come round, have a cup of tea, see if I can cheer you up? I've got some crumpets."

Nigel felt rather choked suddenly; she had always got him crumpets or scones, every week, and had served them with Little Scarlet strawberry jam or Cooper's Oxford Marmalade for Sunday tea . . .

"Oh, I don't know," he said.

"Please, Nigel, I'd so love to see you. I'm terribly bored and fed up with waiting for this baby. Catherine's coming too. We can have a tea party."

"Catherine? Ah, yes," said Nigel, thinking of his lonely vigil at the bottom of the Morgans' drive, and its unsatisfactory outcome.

"Yes. She's up here Christmas shopping."

Nigel hesitated, then he said, "Well, it does sound quite nice."

"Good. How long will you be? Because I was about to have a bath . . ."

"Oh, about an hour."

"That's exactly what Catherine said. Good. I'll have the kettle on."

ℰ↝

Nigel and Catherine actually arrived at the same time; they smiled rather awkwardly at each other as they approached Lucinda's house from opposite directions.

"Hello, Nigel."

"Hello, Catherine. You're looking well. Country life must agree with you."

"The life maybe," said Catherine with a sigh. "Not sure about the people."

"But you are making some friends?"

"Sort of."

Nigel thought of the large male figure, cradling the small girl in his arms so tenderly, and felt irritated.

"Well, shall we go in?" he said.

Lucinda was wearing a towelling bathrobe, and her bump looked enormous. Nigel tried to avert his eyes.

"How lovely," she said. "I am just so pleased to see you both. I'll just go and get dressed and then we can all have tea. Catherine, darling, put the kettle on, would you? And Nigel, you can find the crumpets. I feel rather perky all of a sudden. I shall enjoy our party."

"Crumpets!" said Catherine. "I love crumpets. We used to have them every Saturday for tea. With Little Scarlet strawberry jam. Frederick's favourite—mine too."

"How extraordinary," said Nigel, staring at her.

"What?"

"Oh, nothing."

Half an hour later, they were all munching crumpets when the phone rang.

"Hello . . . What? . . . Oh Blue, you are so hopeless. How could you have let it do that? He's let his phone run down," she said to the others.

"What? . . . Oh, just a couple of friends, popped in for tea. Well, thanks for ringing anyway. And no, I'm not in labour. Which is lucky for you, I'd say . . . Yes, you keep ringing me, since I can't ring you, all right? At least every hour. Bye. And don't come home drunk."

"Where is he then?" said Nigel.

"He's in Paris. On a pre-Christmas jolly. He'll be back tonight. Not late either—they went by private plane."

What sort of husband, thought Nigel, looking at her tenderly, went to Paris when his baby was due? And had to be told not to get drunk. What did she see in him, for goodness sake—what?

"Now," said Lucinda briskly, "more tea, anyone? I'll go and fill the kettle. I—goodness. Golly. What a mess. I didn't spill all that, did I?"

"No," said Catherine calmly, looking at the large pool of water that had formed underneath Lucinda, "your waters just broke."

Catherine rang the ambulance number on the telephone pad; after an incredibly long time (or so it seemed), someone answered and said they would try and get one out immediately, but they were experiencing serious delays.

"Traffic's shocking. How often are the contractions?"

"There aren't any," said Catherine. "But her waters have just broken."

"Where are you?"

"Limehouse."

"Bit of a way. Is this her first baby?"

"Yes."

"And absolutely no contractions?"

"Absolutely not."

"I honestly think you'd be better bringing her in by car. The traffic's bad going out in that direction, but it's more or less OK coming in. So just set off, I'm sure you'll do better that way. Tell your hospital you're coming so they know to expect you. Good luck."

They left a message on the answerphone for Blue and went out into the street; Nigel's Volvo, square and reassuring, stood waiting for them.

"You get in the back," Catherine said to Lucinda, "and I'll map-read."

"Oh, no need for that," said Lucinda. "I'll tell you the best way to go. I'd rather you sat next to me, Catherine, held my hand. This is rather fun, I'm enjoying it."

"Good," said Catherine, "that's as it should be. Off we go, Nigel."

Nigel was shaking so much he could hardly turn the ignition key.

They were just going over Holborn Viaduct when Lucinda gave a small yelp.

Catherine looked at her. "Contraction?"

"Yes, think so. Wasn't very bad though."

"OK. We need two more."

"Surely it'll take longer than that?" Lucinda's teeth were beginning to chatter.

"Of course it will, you idiot. But that means we can time them."

They were driving down towards Gower Street when Lucinda yelped again; Catherine looked at her watch.

"That was quick. I mean, after the last one. About five minutes. Keep going, Nigel."

"I'm doing my best," he said. He sounded very shaky.

Another contraction came in five minutes; it lasted about thirty seconds.

"You're fine," said Catherine. "They're very short."

"They may be short, but they're not exactly sweet," said Lucinda. "It quite hurt, that one. Maybe I should do my breathing. How are we doing, Nigel?"

"Fine. Much better. Don't worry, soon have you there."

By the time they arrived, Lucinda was having contractions every three minutes and everything happened rather quickly after that; a nurse appeared with a wheelchair and Lucinda was helped into it.

"Thank you so m—" she said, and then her face distorted with pain as another contraction hit her.

"How often are these coming?" the nurse asked Catherine as they wheeled her in.

"Every three minutes."

"Three! That's pretty quick. When did she start?"

"Just now," said Lucinda, "on Holborn Viaduct. But it seems to be happening quite quickly." She smiled her radiant smile. "So aren't I lucky? But I'd like to get the epidural going. Is Mr. Clark here?"

"Not yet. But he's on his way."

Nigel looked at them both hopefully. "Should I—should I go and park the car?"

"Yes," said Catherine, "but then mind you come back. We need you."

"Is he the husband?" said the nurse, looking after Nigel's tall gangly figure.

"Yes. But he's not— Oh God, here comes another. This is quite— Oh dear, oh Catherine—quite painful. Hold my hand, will you."

"I'll just go and check Lucinda's all right," said Blue. He had just had a third champagne cocktail; they were sitting in the bar of the Hotel George V in Paris, having had an extremely long and drunken lunch at the Crillon. They were all flushed, unsteady, slurred of speech, shaky of hand.

"Remember where the phone is?" asked Charlie.

"Course."

They watched him weaving off.

"Silly old fool," said Charlie affectionately. "I think one more of these all round and then—"

Blue reappeared wild-eyed. "We've got to go," he said. "Now."

Nigel and Catherine sat in the corridor outside Lucinda's room at the hospital. A rather loud groan came from the room; followed by another.

"Oh God," said Nigel. He grabbed Catherine's hand. "This is awful."

"Nigel, it's quite normal. Don't worry, she'll be fine. It does make you make noises. Lots of people swear. I did."

"I'm sure Lucinda won't."

Another groan.

"Oh, poor Lucinda. Why don't they help her?"

"I'm sure they are. They'll have the epidural rigged up in no time. Lucky her—they hadn't been invented when I had mine."

A large, rather handsome man came hurrying along the corridor, wearing a three-piece suit and a bow tie, and disappeared into the room.

"That must be Mr. Clark," hissed Catherine to Nigel.

"How do you know?"

"That's what expensive gynaecologists look like. All of them."

Sister Johns put her head out of the door. "Mr. Cowper, you can come in now. Quickly, or you're going to miss the big moment. She's doing wonderfully well."

"But—but—I'm not—that is—"

"You'll be fine," she said. "Don't worry. Besides, she needs you. Nurse!" she called into the room. "Have you got a gown for Mr. Cowper?"

"Yes, I have. Tell him to get a move on, she wants to push."

There was a loud wail of pain from the room.

"No, I can't," said Nigel. He sat down, put his head in his hands. "I really can't. I feel sick."

"The thing is," said Catherine quickly, "he's not—not the father."

"Oh. Well, where *is* the father?"

"On a plane somewhere," said Catherine.

Another wail: long and low, followed by Lucinda's voice telling someone very loudly to fuck off. Nigel looked shocked.

"Told you," said Catherine. "That's a very good sign. She's nearly there."

"She does need some support though," said Sister. "She keeps asking if Blue's arrived. I assumed it was Mr. Cowper."

"Could—could I come in?" said Catherine.

"What's your name? I could ask her." She reappeared. "She says she'd love you to come in. You'd better stay here and keep quiet," she said severely to Nigel, as if it was he making all the noise, not Lucinda.

Catherine went into the room; Lucinda held out her arms to her. "Catherine, Catherine, I'm so pleased to s— Oh shit. Shit! This is fucking agony. Tell them to give me an epidural, for God's sake."

"We can't," said Mr. Clark. "Wouldn't work in time now. Here comes another one. Push, Lucinda, push hard . . . head down on your chest . . . that's right. Good girl. Few more of those and you'll be there."

"I wish I *was* there," said Lucinda. "I wish I was anywhere. How did you do this twice, Catherine, how— Oh God. God. Shit. He-elp!"

It seemed to Nigel to be going on forever: the groans, the yells, heavy panting, like a terrified dog. How could he have even considered putting Lucinda through this? And where was Horton? Where was he when she needed him?

$\mathscr{e}$

Blue was in a plane somewhere over the Channel, silent with terror. Occasionally he said, quite quietly, that if the fucking pilot didn't get the fucking plane to City Airport in the next ten minutes, he'd fucking sue him; but apart from that he said nothing, just sat berating himself, wondering how, why he could possibly have done this awful thing, abandoned

Lucinda, leaving her alone in her hour of greatest need. God, he was a shit, a bastard. What had she done, for God's sake, to deserve him? If she was all right, if the baby waited for him to arrive, he'd join a fucking monastery. No, that wouldn't do any good, he had to support them both.

"If you don't get this fucking thing to fucking City Airport, I'll fucking sue you," he said for the fourth time in half an hour.

"Blue, calm down, mate," said Charlie. "She'll be fine."

"You don't know that," said Blue. "Anything might be happening, anything."

"Come on Lucinda, once more. PUSH." Mr. Clark was looking very stern. "And again . . . go on, harder, harder, come on, this is why it's called labour, you know . . . Now—good, good—right, big deep breath and nearly there . . . There we are. Yes! You've done it! Let's just—well done. There she is. A beautiful little girl."

"A girl! Oh, how lovely. Oh, Blue will be so cross. Serve him right, just serve him right. Look, Catherine, look, isn't she lovely, aren't I clever, aren't we all clever; thank you so, so much, Mr. Clark, sorry I swore at you. Oh, look at her, look at her great big blue eyes . . . Come here, let me hold you, you beautiful, beautiful little thing . . ."

Catherine went out of the room to tell Nigel the news and to reassure him that all was well; he was still sitting holding his head in his hands.

"Nigel, it's OK. She's fine, absolutely fine. And so's the baby—a little girl, absolutely beautiful."

"I thought—I thought she was going to die," he said. "I couldn't bear it."

And as she stood there, tearful herself, Catherine realised that Nigel was weeping, great tears rolling down his cheeks which in his turmoil he kept wiping away with his tie.

He's still in love with her, she thought, with a sense of desperate sadness. Still in love with her, and he always, always will be.

Chapter 55

Maurice Crane had finally returned to work at Jenkins and Jenkins. His leg had taken longer to heal than expected, and as everyone kept reminding him, he wasn't as young as he had been.

On the third day, Roger Spence, the managing director of Jenkins and Jenkins, called him into his office. Rather nervous, wondering if his absence had been too long, whether he was going to be eased out, Maurice straightened his tie, brushed down his jacket and went along the corridor.

"Ah, Maurice. Good to have you back. Feeling completely yourself again, are you?"

"Yes, thank you, Mr. Spence. I never thought to say this, but I was really missing the old place. Only thing is, instead of looking forward to my retirement, I'm now rather dreading it."

"Well, you've got a few years yet, haven't you?"

"Four," said Maurice; clearly Mr. Spence was leading up to an early-retirement package.

"Now, one of your clients was a Mr. Simon Beaumont, wasn't he? As I expect you know, he was drowned, just about the time you had your accident."

"Yes. Most regrettable. Such a charming man."

"He was. But apparently there is to be an inquest. Although it was probably an accident, there were circumstances which could be interpreted as being sufficient to drive him to suicide."

"I'm very sorry to hear that."

"Yes, he'd lost an awful lot of money from Lloyd's, had to sell everything, even lost his job, poor chap. Now the coroner's office is investigating the actual state of his finances, whether he had further debts and so on and so forth. Now, because you were the executive in charge of his policies, I have to ask you if you received any instructions from him, over the course of the past—what?—six months. Any changes made, any extra policies taken out, that sort of thing."

"Ah. Yes." Maurice Crane looked at his well-shone shoes. "Yes, I see."

Roger Spence looked at him sharply. "Do I take it that means yes, you did hear from him?"

Maurice Crane sighed. "Like George Washington," he said, "I cannot tell a lie. I was hoping not to be asked such a question, that I might remain silent. I think Mr. Washington would have found that acceptable."

"I think, Maurice," said Roger Spence wearily, "that you'd better tell me what you're talking about."

Maurice Crane did so; and went home feeling depressed and rather guilty.

ℰↃ

Jamie wrote Annabel a long letter, declining her invitation to spend Christmas with the Beaumonts.

I would have loved it, of course, but Mother is very protective about our family Christmas. The matriarch in her comes out.

Comes out! thought Annabel. It doesn't seem very well hidden to me.

I'm hoping that next year you'll be here, spending it with us. But we can talk then and I do send you and your brother and sister and your mother, of course, our very best wishes for a happy holiday. Or as happy as it could be, under the circumstances. Do you have any plans? I'd love to hear them. And then, darling Annabel, it will be January and you'll be here for our engagement party. You haven't told me yet how many of you will be able to join us. But actually as long as you're there, that's all that matters to me . . .

Love, love, love you, Jamie

Annabel sat for a long time, holding the letter, staring out of the window. She was thinking not of Jamie but of Christmas. It was going to be totally hideous. They were moving in another week; the house had been stripped of all the large furniture, and walls that had worn pictures for years and rooms that had sheltered tables and chairs and wardrobes and tallboys all looked not only empty but oddly shabby. It was horrible.

The house they were renting in Fulham, painted, furnished, and carpeted throughout in shades of beige, completely bland and modern, was not an ideal setting for Christmas.

Their mother was feeling well now, and almost restored to her normal energetic self, but she was very thin—apart from a very neat little bump—and her face was pale and drawn. Tilly spent a great deal of time weeping over Boy and his imminent departure from her life, the news broken to her by a distressed Flora, who now had the house on the market. Toby was breaking up in a few days; he was still edgy and down, and clearly found his mother's pregnancy deeply embarrassing.

$\backsim$

"Got a minute, Joel?" Hugh's large figure loomed in his doorway.

"Yeah, sure."

"Like a word. Maybe after conference?"

"Fine." Now what?

$\backsim$

"She's so beautiful, so bl— absolutely perfect," said Blue. He was gazing intently into his daughter's face. "I still can't get over it. It's a blooming miracle. Nine months earlier there's a bit of how's yer father and then— boom. A new person."

"I know. Haven't we done well? Here, take her a minute, I want to get more comfy."

Blue took the baby rather gingerly. "You look like your mum," he said to her, "you know that?"

"She does, doesn't she? Everyone says so. You don't mind, do you?"

"Course not. Think if she looked like me."

"Well, it would be fine if she'd been a boy. There, that's better. I'll have her back. Come on, precious, back to the milking parlour."

"The what?"

"It's what you call the place where they milk cows every day."

"They haven't half changed," said Blue, looking at the mountainous objects that had replaced Lucinda's rather neat round breasts.

"Just as well. Blue, give me those tissues, would you. Thank you. How are things at work?"

She had ordered him back to work on the second day, finding his restless, nervous presence the opposite of what she wanted; and his undoubtedly genuine remorse had become extremely irritating.

"Look, Blue," she had said as he embarked on yet another round of "How could I have done that to you," and "How are you ever going to forgive me?"—"It's all right. It happened. I said you could go, it was just as much down to me as to you. Just stop going on about it. We've got more important things to think about. Our new responsibilities."

"You're an angel, Lucinda," said Blue, kissing her tenderly. "An absolute angel."

"I know," she said, smiling sweetly. Her plans for herself and the baby were actually the opposite of angelic, but he didn't have to know that.

"Now," she said, "I've been thinking. We're coming home tomorrow, Little Miss and me—we must settle on a name for her, Blue."

"Yes, I know."

So far they had been unable to agree on anything. They had ranged from the popular Jade ("Over my dead body," said Lucinda), to the esoteric Annunciata ("You must be bleedin' joking"), and taken in the plain Jane and Anna and Caroline ("She's much too pretty") and the fashionably floral Daisy and Lily and Rose ("Because she's my little flower," said Blue tenderly).

"But anyway, yes, you can come and get me at two o'clock and then we'll be home together, a proper little family. Isn't it totally lovely?"

"It is."

"But you know something? I just don't know how we're going to manage in that house."

"Lucy, I've been telling you that for months."

"Yes, I know and I'm sorry, but at least you know why. Now I had one idea," said Lucinda, and her eyes sparkled at him.

"Yeah? Look, I'm sure she's smiling."

"No, I think it's only wind. Golly, there's a lot coming out the other end, did you hear that?" She giggled. "She farts as loudly as you do. Now you might not like my idea . . ."

"Not your mother? Please, please, not your mother's—"

"Well, she did offer. And there is lots of room."

"Lucy, no."

"Now you did promise, Blue. To make it up to me. For not being here, you know."

There was an endless silence while a series of violent and rather obvious emotions chased one another across Blue's face; then he said, dragging the words out of himself, clearly with an enormous effort, "Yes. All right."

"Or," said Lucinda, "we could go to Nigel's house. Well, my house actually."

"What? Lucinda, I can't live there!"

"It wouldn't be for long. Just till we put it into this trust thingy. I asked Steve if he thought it was a good idea, and he said brilliant, gave the whole thing a bit of credence."

"When did you ask him?" said Blue suspiciously.

"Yesterday—I rang him. And there's something else. I think I'm going to have to get a maternity nurse."

"I've told you, Lucinda, I'm not having any nannies."

"A maternity nurse is not a nanny," said Lucinda firmly. "She comes for about six weeks, until the baby starts sleeping through the night. So you can recover properly. I just think we need the help. And we can't fit her into Limehouse. And the other house is empty—it's not as if Nigel would be there. He's found a flat in Sloane Street to rent; he says the house is just impossibly big, and he feels lonelier and lonelier in it. Poor darling Nigel. I do wish he and Catherine could . . . Well, anyway, the house is empty, it's mine in any case, and I think we should go and live there for a bit. It would be so easy."

"I can't do it, Lucy, I really can't—sorry."

"Well, it'll have to be Mummy then. Oh Blue, and I thought . . . I thought . . ." She started to cry.

Blue hastily went over to her, handed her some tissues. "Don't cry, Lucinda, it's—it's all right, we'll manage somehow. Can't you get these maternity people to come in just for the day?"

"Don't be silly," said Lucinda. "The whole point is having her there at night. No, we'll have to go down to my parents'. Maybe you could stay in Limehouse if the journey's too bad."

There was a silence, then: "Lucinda, I'm not having us separated. I'm not leaving you and the baby, when I've just got you both. I just— Oh, all right. Yes. We'll move into that mausoleum. But I'm having a new bed."

"Oh Blue, thank you. Thank you so much. Of course you—we can have a new bed. And the minute I'm feeling better, we can have a new house. Oh, you're an angel. I love you, I love you so much. And you know, lots of those houses we looked at are still on the market. I checked up on that as well."

"How?"

"I phoned the agents, how do you think?"

"What, even the one in Chislehurst—with the indoor pool?"

"Even that one," said Lucinda. "Now . . ." She reached for a pen and a piece of paper.

"Lucinda, be careful, you nearly dropped the baby then."

"Of course I didn't. You mustn't mollycoddle her, Blue, it's—" She stopped. "Goodness! Maybe we could call her Molly? Molly! How do you like that? I think it's divine."

"I—well, it's quite nice, I suppose. Look, I don't care what you say, Lucinda, that baby is smiling."

"She obviously likes the idea of her new name. Go on, Blue, say you like it. I love it."

"It'll do," he said, taking the baby, stroking her small head. "It'll certainly do."

"And if you like, we can make Rose her second name. Molly Rose Horton. How do you like that?"

"Fine," he said. "Absolutely fine." He smiled down at his daughter. "Hello, Molly Rose."

The baby farted loudly again.

"There—you see? It's the only way she can show her approval at the moment. And now you'd better get going on moving all her stuff. We haven't got long."

"How do I get a key?" he said.

"I've still got one," she said, fishing the key Nigel had given her the day before out of her bag. "Here you are. And I'll make a list, to help you."

When he had gone, she looked down at the baby. "Well, that wasn't too difficult, was it?" she said. "And how lucky, Uncle Nigel having the key with him yesterday. And I tell you something else, Molly Rose, there is no way I'm going to go and live in Chislehurst. But we won't have to. Silly lot, they are, men. When you're older I'll tell you exactly how to deal with them. Now, do you want to come back into the milking parlour, or . . . ?"

But Molly Rose was already fast asleep.

"Flora? This is Colin."

"Oh, Colin. How nice."

"Yes. Well, I hope so. I'm . . . I'm sorry if I overreacted the other day. I was—"

"Colin, you didn't. You underreacted: lots of people would have beaten me up."

"I hope not." His tone was quite shocked. "Anyway, I admire you, Flora. Admire your integrity. And feel a little ashamed of my own lack of it."

"Colin!" Flora suddenly saw things very clearly, that he had actually had to bend his own principles to help her, that it went against his own rather honest grain. She felt a lump in her throat. "Colin, I shall never, ever cease to be grateful to you, for what you were willing to do for me. I do thank you from the bottom of my heart. And I feel very bad indeed for wasting so much of your extremely valuable time. Why don't you come to supper tonight and I'll cook one of your favourites. How about some nice Welsh Black beef?"

"That—that would be very nice," he said, "and there's something . . . something I was going to ask you a while back."

"Yes?"

"I wondered—well, I mean, I wondered how you'd feel about us— that is . . ."

"Colin, whatever is it you're trying to say?"

"Well, I wondered how you'd feel about us going to Salzburg together this summer. For the festival."

"Colin, I'd absolutely love it. You know I would. Why should I feel anything but pleasure?"

"Well, you know," he said. "I mean, some people might think— well . . ."

"What might they think?" said Flora. She felt absurdly near to tears. "They'd think what a very, very kind man you were and how lucky I was not only to be going, but going with you."

"Oh. Well, that's marvellous." She could hear his pleasure, even hear his smile. "In that case I'll book it all up then, the whole thing—flights, hotels, everything. Er, separate rooms, of course," he added quickly.

"Of course," said Flora, even more quickly.

Suddenly, even losing the house seemed less dreadful.

There was something wrong: Debbie could feel it. Joel wasn't properly—there. Distracted and distant, even as he made love to her: silent afterwards.

"What is it?" she said. "What's the matter?"

"Oh, nothing," he said, and his voice was cool. "I mean, it's just great, you know, what's happening to me at the moment."

"What do you mean?"

"I mean, I'm so much in love with you I've asked you and not only you, your three bloody kids, to marry me, and all I get is being told to wait. While you think. My whole life on hold, while Debbie Fielding thinks. Can't work properly, can't make any plans, everything based on the next time you might be able to see me, and all the time fucking terrified in case you say no and go off to bloody Scotland. What do you think's the bloody matter, Debbie?"

She was silent; her heart thudding so loudly she felt he must be able to hear it. She sat up in the bed, started pulling on her shirt.

"What am I to make of it, your behaviour, your inability to decide what to do? How am I supposed to believe you love me, when you throw this pile of shit at me. I'm fucking fed up with it, you know that? Even with fucking, as a matter of fact. It's all so bloody—futile. You arrive, you say you love me, we have sex, you say you haven't decided yet, you go again. I can't stand it much longer, you know."

"You won't have to," she said, very low. "In two weeks, term ends, and—"

"Well, that's very good news, isn't it?" he said, and he was up and pacing round the room now, staring at her, his face dark. "Term ends. Your

· 470 ·

husband comes home. That'll be the end of it, of us. Unless—unless you deign to say yes, you will marry me, and leave him; unless these protestations of love of yours actually turn out to mean something, instead of just being rather pretty words. Why don't you go home now, Debbie, right now, and don't come back until you've made your mind up." And confronted by the reality of it, of losing him, of saying goodbye to him, Debbie started to cry.

"Something's happened, hasn't it?" said Debbie. "Something's changed. You're not just fed up, it's something else—something you haven't told me."

"Well, yes, there is. I . . . I didn't want to tell you until you'd made up your mind. I felt it wasn't fair. But, well, I suppose you know me too well for that."

"I suppose I do."

As she did; and as he knew her, every tiny piece of her, not just her body, not even just her senses and how perfectly and exquisitely to arouse them, but her brain, how it worked, what it did, where it went. It was almost frightening: that they should be so close after so short a time, when Richard, who she had been married to for ten years, whose children she had borne, was still in some ways an unknown quantity, Richard to whom Morag was a beacon of perfection, Richard who could deceive her, lie to her even . . .

She came back to Joel with an effort. "So—what is it?"

"I've been offered a job. In New York."

"New York." It didn't mean anything to her at first; anything at all. Just as, at first, a cut—even a burn—doesn't hurt: and then the pain comes.

"Yes. Running our New York office. It would be fun, and it would be a huge step up for me."

"God. How amazing. How . . . how absolutely amazing. I'm so, so happy for you, Joel, so proud of you, I—I—" She realised she was crying again. She had no idea why, really, except that the pain had started.

"I'm sorry," he said, "I was so determined not to tell you. It's too much to put on you."

"What do you mean?"

"I mean that of course you can't come to New York. If we're together. It would be out of the question."

"Yes," she said very quietly. "Yes, of course I couldn't."

"So you'd be making your decision on the wrong basis."

"Would I?" She felt dizzy; her brain didn't seem to be functioning.

"Well, yes. I think so. You'd know you were changing my career. Stopping me from doing what I wanted to do." He smiled, rather awkwardly. "It suddenly struck me that this must seem rather déjà vu to you. I mean, it's a bit the same, isn't it, as Richard going to Scotland."

"No," she said, thinking about it. "No, it isn't. You've made me your prime consideration. You've put me before the decision. He dragged me along after it." She went into his arms, clung to him. "Oh Joel, I love you, so much, I don't know how to bear it. I'm so, so sorry that I'm so useless and selfish."

"You're not," he said, "not useless, anyway. Come here." He sat down on the bed, held out his arms. "Come and be useful. I love you so much too. Do you think I want to go away to New York without you? Do you think I want to leave you here, far away from me? I dread it already—if it has to happen. I'm just hoping and praying to a God I have no time for, as you know, that it won't."

He bent his head, started to kiss her breasts, very gently. And: "Joel," she said, still awed at her realisation of the extraordinary difference in the way she was to him and the way she was to Richard, reaching out to touch his face, "I want to be with you, I want to marry you, if you'll still have me."

"What?"

"I said, I wanted to be with you. Please. I'm sorry I've been so long making the decision."

"Oh God," he said, "oh, thank God." And she felt something splash onto her hand, and realised he was weeping.

Chapter 56

Elizabeth had received a list of names from the coroner's office of the people who would be giving evidence at the inquest. It was alarmingly lengthy, and some of the names slightly unexpected.

There was, at least, no need for the people from France to come over; the coroner's officer would read out the medical reports from France, the results of the postmortem, the pathology, the official reason for Simon's death.

There would also be a statement from his doctor in London and there would be a summary, apparently of his recent history and his financial position. John Fraser, their solicitor, would be attending. His boss at Graburn and French would also be called. Good, thought Elizabeth. I hope he can't sleep, thinking about it all.

And then came a long list of the people who had seen him, or spoken to him, the day before: "Not a lot of men, are there, Simon?" said Elizabeth aloud. "Nothing new there." Catherine Morgan, Lucinda Cowper, Flora Fielding, Fiona Broadhurst—it sounded like the roll call at a girls' school—followed by Joel Strickland. Why would he be involved, she wondered, and then remembered the article. David Green would be called, of course; and then there would be a technical report on the yacht, and another from an expert on life belts.

And then there was a name she simply didn't know. Maurice Crane, an executive at Jenkins and Jenkins, insurance brokers. That worried her: quite a lot. Of course, she had spoken to several people there, and they had all been most helpful, over the life policy and so on, but who was Maurice Crane, and why had he got to make a statement? The whole thing loomed over her life, casting a huge, heavy shadow. A shadow she had to walk through.

ℰ

Catherine was dreading Christmas. Phyllis and Dudley had told her they always had Christmas dinner at the Golf Club, and that she and the children would be very welcome; she almost felt that warming up some cooked turkey on her gas ring would be preferable. She was still pushing the whole thing as far back in her mind as she could when the Jane-Annes asked her if they would all like to go there.

"Jane-Anne would love it," Kate Price said, "and so would the boys. We've got masses of family coming—you'd be so welcome. And Patrick always comes round in the evening—loves his charades. You and he have become rather friendly, I believe," she added, winking at Catherine.

Which they had; but friendship was clearly all he had in mind. It was a relief. He was sweet and kind and rather amusing in his bluff way; but he was the opposite of sexy. And anyway, she was in love with Nigel.

Dear, bumbling, perfectly natured Nigel, with his sweet smile and his rather desperate honesty. Nigel was good: good through and through. And she loved him through and through. The only problem was, he didn't seem to be in love with her . . . He was still in love with Lucinda.

Oh well. Enough of that, Catherine. The invitation touched her immensely; she also savoured the uncharitable thought of how much it would annoy Phyllis and Dudley, to think of her spending Christmas with the Honourable Prices.

A sort of peace had descended on Debbie. Even the suggestion that they might all spend Christmas with Flora couldn't shatter it. She still had moments of complete panic, but released now from the anguish of indecision, she felt she could at least look forward, although the view was not pleasant.

She had to tell Richard. She had to tell the children. She had to tell Flora, or at least let Richard tell Flora. At the very thought of that, she literally shook. Finally, Richard had to tell Morag. It seemed to her not impossible that Morag would decide to find someone else to run the school, another family man, with a more amenable wife.

The house still had to be sold; or she supposed it would. Richard was hardly going to let her live in it on her own. They had to decide where the children would go to school, whether they went up to Scotland with him, or stayed in West London with her. In which case she'd need the house.

Decisions had to be taken about decisions. Who would decide on where the children lived and when? And would the children have a say in where they spent the term time—always supposing their father stayed in Scotland? It was all very ugly.

The children and Richard and Flora, however, had no idea about the ugliness; they were safely encased in a shiny rainbow-coloured bubble.

Debbie stood outside that bubble, and knew she had to burst it, had to tell them all these horrible things and contemplated what it would do to them. Her husband would be hurt almost beyond endurance, his frag-ile self-esteem further diminished. Her children would be grieving and shocked, the absolute security within which they had grown up shattered forever. Their loyalty would be strained. They would quite possibly think they hated her and would certainly tell her so. They would certainly hate Joel.

And the joyful, intense way that she and Joel loved each other would be dragged through the dirt of real life.

All these things she knew must happen; all these things she was afraid of. And all these things were worth her being with Joel for the rest of their lives. She had decided, after discussing it with Joel very carefully, that they shouldn't be told until after Christmas. It would be too horrible for them to bear, Christmas made dreadfully unhappy. What child deserved that? She couldn't do it; they couldn't do it.

And Joel, happily patient, agreed. He had turned down the New York job for "personal reasons," had suggested various other people to Hugh, who told him he was a fool. Joel agreed that he very probably was.

And with only two days left until Richard came home, the two of them seized and savoured whatever time they could find.

❧

Flora had just got back from taking Tilly to Swansea Station to catch the London train when the phone call came.

They had had a perfect three days together: the four of them—Tilly and Boy and she and Hal. Flora had found a buyer for Hal and invited Tilly down to spend a last weekend with Boy, hoping it would give her some outstandingly happy memories. The weather had been wonderful, brilliant and frosty, and they had ridden every corner of Gower; along the beaches, over Rhossili Down, along Cefn Bryn, through the woods at Parkmill to Three Cliffs Bay and up to the storybook ruins of Pennard Castle high above the sea. Mostly they walked slowly and chatted, long rambling conversations.

Flora spoke of the horses she had owned, from the small Shetland she could scarcely get her legs across, to her beloved Prince Hal, a present from William for her fortieth birthday. She told Tilly that she had lost lots of babies, after she had had Richard, and that riding out across the hills was the most healing thing she could do, and that after William had died she could lose her grief entirely for a few hours with long fierce gallops along the beach.

"If only Mummy could ride," Tilly had said, "but you know, I think work does the same for her, it heals her somehow; everyone keeps saying she should take time out, specially with the baby, but it would be disastrous for her."

There was an underlying sadness to her, as she talked; and on the last night she started to cry. "It's not just Boy, Flora, it's because he's so much part of Daddy to me—that sounds so stupid but you know what I mean. Daddy wanted me to have him and he was so proud of me and my riding, which is pretty pathetic really as you know, and I feel I'll be saying goodbye to both of them when Boy goes, and I can't bear it, I just can't." She cried for a long time in Flora's arms, and in the morning, pale and subdued, she dressed for her return to London and went out to the stables on her own. Flora watched her, as she put her thin arms round Boy's neck and rested her head against his neck; and then she ran her fingers through his mane and kissed his nose, and a very short time later she came in again, her small face white and set and said, "Can we go now, quickly?" And she had got into the car, her face turned determinedly away from the stables, breathing rather fast; and as they turned onto the road, she said, "Right. Well, that was all lovely, Flora, thank you," and smiled at her—a quick, brilliant smile—and then cried all the way to Swansea as if her heart would break.

The phone was ringing as Flora opened the front door, and she almost didn't answer it. It was that awful estate agent, no doubt, to say he had more people wanting to view the house; the advertisement, published the previous Saturday, had had a poor response so far. For which she was profoundly, if foolishly, grateful.

"Mrs. Fielding? Mrs. William Fielding?" The voice was not Welsh, it was rather grand English.

"Yes."

"Good morning, Mrs. Fielding, this is Bernard Edmund-Jones from Harris and Harris, solicitors. Of Cardiff."

Who on earth were Harris and Harris? Not her solicitors, not the one she and William had used; she'd never heard of them.

"Yes?"

"May I speak with Mr. Fielding, please?"

"I'm very sorry," said Flora, "but I'm afraid you can't. He died seven years ago."

"I'm sorry to hear that. Very sorry. Well, then I shall have to discuss the matter with you."

"Which matter, Mr. Edmund-Jones?"

"I have just seen the advertisement for Broken Bay House."

"Oh yes?" Obviously he wanted to buy it; and he did sound a much more appropriate inhabitant than Mr. and Mrs. Davies from Llandeilo.

"Mrs. Fielding, I'm sorry, but you can't sell that house. It doesn't belong to you; it's not yours to sell."

Chapter 57

"Well, this is it."

"Yes, 'fraid so."

"I shall miss these," Joel bent to kiss her breasts, "and this," moving lower. "Take care of it all, won't you?"

"Of course I will. And it's not for long. After all."

"It will seem long."

"Yes, I know. But then next time we're together, it'll be so different. It'll be proper."

"I don't know if I want to be properly together with you. I've enjoyed improper."

"Well, me too. But—"

"You won't forget about me over Christmas, will you?"

"Probably," she said, smiling and thinking she could never, ever forget him, even if she never saw him again; he was imprinted on her, part of her now, part of her thinking and her doing, there as she woke and talked and worked and played with her children and drove her car and cooked and shopped and drifted off to sleep at night: whether he was with her or not.

"Well, I'll try not to forget you," he said. "But it won't be easy." She hated these times, getting up, dressing, leaving him when she longed to stay, driving home too fast, suddenly fearful for the children who she was betraying, even as she betrayed their father.

"Love you. And thank you so, so much for my present." It was a mobile phone; it meant they could hear each other's voices whenever they wanted.

"And it'll help, maybe on the day. You can call me just as often as you like."

"But don't you dare use it over Christmas."

"I can't promise that, I'm afraid. Too much to ask."

"I won't take it then. I'll leave it behind."

"Well, that's really sensible. Oh Debbie, I love you too. And see you on the twenty-seventh."

That was the day they had agreed she would return to London to join him, the day she would break the news, leaving Richard and the children to be comforted by Flora.

"The twenty-seventh. Definitely hopefully."

"Don't say that, Joel. Just—definitely."

"Just definitely."

∾

Mr. Edmund-Jones had the white hair and almost transparent skin of the very old, and the hand he held out to her was bony and etched with large brown freckles, the nails long and yellowing. He wore striped trousers and a black jacket, and a slightly grubby Old Wykehamist tie. He smiled at her, showing some surprisingly good teeth, and gestured to the chair in front of his desk.

"How do you do, Mrs. Fielding. Do please sit down. May I offer you some refreshment? Some tea, or perhaps coffee—we find some of our younger clients prefer coffee these days . . ."

So I'm a younger client, Flora thought; the idea was at once both pleasing and intriguing.

"I'd prefer tea," she said, "thank you."

"Good, good. Mrs. Andrews, tea for two if you please, and do bring in the Dundee cake."

Mrs. Andrews withdrew and for a very long time there was no sign of either tea or Dundee cake; Flora wondered if she might have forgotten.

"Well, now," said Mr. Edmund-Jones, "I expect you have some questions for me."

"I do," said Flora. "Indeed, I do. Obviously, and most important, if I don't own Broken Bay House, who does?"

"A trust. The beneficiary of which is your grandson," said Mr. Edmund-Jones. "As you really should know."

"My—my grandson!" Flora said. Alexander, with his skinny legs and knock-knees, his floppy brown hair, and his high-pitched ten-year-old voice. How could he possibly own Broken Bay House?

"Yes, indeed. I do apologise for not realising your husband had died."

"Thank you."

"I really should study the obituary notices. Somehow there's never time. I'm so sorry, Mrs. Fielding. Such a charming man."

"Well, thank you. Yes, indeed he was. But how, why, isn't the house mine? I don't understand."

"Because you're a female," said Mr. Edmund-Jones.

"But why does that mean I can't own the house?"

"Mrs. Fielding, Broken Bay House is a male entail, held in trust for the eldest grandson's first grandson. I know you have a grandson, because your husband told me."

"Oh," said Flora. She felt rather dizzy. "So—so what happens to the house?"

"Well, nothing very much," said Mr. Edmund-Jones. "Ah, Mrs. Andrews, tea. How nice. Perhaps you would be Mother, Mrs. Fielding?"

She smiled at him rather weakly, and poured out the tea. He nodded approvingly as she added the milk.

"So nice to see it properly done. My mother always divided people into Mifs and non-Mifs."

"She did?" said Flora. Any minute now a white rabbit would surely run through the office.

"Indeed, Milk in First. Not the right way at all. Cake, Mrs. Fielding?"

"Er, no thank you," said Flora. The cake looked as dusty as the office.

"Very well. Now, what did you ask me?"

"What might happen next."

"As I said, nothing very much. I imagine your grandson is quite young?"

"He's ten."

"Yes, I see. Well, unless you and he are on very bad terms, I would expect him to allow you to remain there, until your demise. On his reaching twenty-one, the entail passes the house to him, subject to it passing on his death to his eldest grandson. Your grandson will be entitled to live there for his lifetime. If he dies without a grandson, it will pass to the eldest living male in the family succession." He pulled out a file from one of his drawers.

"It's all in here," he said, leafing through the tattered, yellow pages. "Fascinating story. Began with the first owner of the house, John Fielding, who had it built in 1780. John had had a bit of a ne'er-do-well son called David, a gambler, and John was afraid that he might try to sell the house at some point in the future to pay his debts. So he set up an entailed settlement cutting out David and leaving everything in trust for David's son, John's grandson, and thereafter to each eldest grandson, thus ensuring that the house could never be sold or bequeathed; only designated. That is what is meant by a male entail, and we as trustees hold it for your grandson."

"But I *have* to sell the house," said Flora, slightly desperately. "I have considerable debts to Lloyd's of London. They are insisting on it."

"Well, I'm afraid that is their misfortune," said Mr. Edmund-Jones. "Lloyd's can't lay a finger on Broken Bay House. They will have to—what is that rather vulgar modern expression—ah yes, they will have to whistle for their money. Dreadful business, that. I have several clients who have been completely ruined by it."

"So—sorry to go back over this and I must seem very stupid to you, but does this mean I can stay in the house? That it can't be taken away from me."

"Well, unless, as I say, you and your grandson are on bad terms. In which case, after his reaching his majority, he could ask you to leave. Insist on it, in fact. But I presume that is not the case."

An image rose before Flora's eyes of Alexander curled up on the battered kitchen sofa beside her, saying sleepily, "You're a really great granny, you know."

"I don't think so," she said. "No."

The first thing she did when she got home was pour herself a very large whiskey. Then she sat down at the telephone and dialled not Richard's number or even Debbie's but the Beaumonts'.

Elizabeth answered it. "Oh, hello, Flora. How nice to hear from you. Thank you so much for your note."

"Not at all. Such lovely news. How are you feeling? Tired, I expect."

"Yes, I am a bit."

"Is Tilly there?"

"No, she's not, I'm afraid. She's out with her friends. Is there something wrong with Boy, or—"

"There is absolutely nothing wrong with Boy. He's never looked better. No, I would very much like to speak to Tilly, that's all."

"Well," said Elizabeth briskly, "I could be trusted with a message, you know."

"Elizabeth," said Flora, "I know this must be hugely annoying for you, but I do desperately want to tell Tilly this news myself. It's so important to . . . to both of us. Perhaps you could ask her to ring me when she gets in. Will she be very long?"

"I have no idea, I'm afraid." Elizabeth's tone was cool still. "But not late, no. She has to be in by ten at the latest."

"Then could you please ask her to ring me? As soon as you possibly can?"

"Yes, all right," said Elizabeth. "As soon as I possibly can." Irritating woman, she thought, returning to her packing. She just had to control everything. But Simon had been very fond of her, and she had done a lot for Tilly. God, she was tired. She'd be lucky to stay awake until ten at this rate. Maybe she should leave a note out for Tilly, in case. It was only eight.

And thus it was that she went to bed early, leaving a note on the hall table for Tilly; and Tilly burst into her bedroom just after ten, her eyes shining, her pale face flushed, great tears welling in her large blue eyes, and woke her as she drifted into oblivion—and now she'd have trouble getting back to sleep, bloody, bloody Flora Fielding . . .

"Mummy, Mummy, the most wonderful thing. Flora can stay in her house, and Boy can stay with her! Some peculiar legal thing. Isn't that amazing? Isn't that just totally amazing?"

And Elizabeth was forced to admit that it was indeed totally amazing.

A lot of it had to be guesswork. She pieced the story together, with the help of such solid facts as Mr. Edmund-Jones was able to supply, and with her rather more intimate knowledge of William. He had certainly never mentioned a trust, but that was William, in every way. He had been quite a lot older than her, twenty-five years older, and very old-fashioned in all his attitudes. Flora, marrying him at the age of nineteen, highly unconventional herself, had been kept in the dark about many things, including his income and his financial status.

He had loved her very much, but he had always made it plain that because she was a woman, she did not need—and indeed should not ask for—knowledge of his affairs. Just as he did not expect her to discuss her housekeeping or maternal problems with him, he did not expect to discuss his financial ones with her.

They did not use Harris and Harris as their day-to-day solicitors; a firm in Swansea had handled all their affairs. The will had been absolutely straightforward, and everything had been bequeathed to her; he often said that he must revise it, but he had died so suddenly that any plans he might have had were not incorporated.

She also wondered if he had not entirely trusted her when they were first married, however much he loved her. And any revelations would have become more difficult to make as the years went by, as the lack of trust had to be confessed to.

And of course there was another explanation for a possible lack of trust, she thought soberly, staring into the darkness; she had always hoped and indeed had been fairly sure that he had never known of it, but what if he had? She felt a stab of remorse and then of fear; and then crushed them both. Set it aside, Flora, she told herself. As you did then.

He must have planned to tell Richard at some point, but Alexander had only been four when William had died—with a suddenness that not only had shocked everyone but had removed any opportunity for the setting in order of his affairs.

She roamed the house for a while, smiling, savouring it, savouring it remaining hers. She leaned on the gate overlooking her Meadow, and stood there a long time, careless of the cold, drinking in the great expanse of sea and sky; and then went out to the yard and told the horses. They took the news calmly. And then she went indoors and stood at the dining-room window in a state of joyful excitement, looking down at the sea and waiting impatiently for Tilly's call.

Tilly had been one of her first thoughts; that she and Boy need not be parted. There was no way she could have allowed Elizabeth to tell her; it was rarely granted to human beings to grant perfect happiness themselves, and she intended to make the very most of it.

❧

Blue was a man in love. He often wondered what on earth he had thought about or talked about before Molly Rose had been born. Lucinda, of course, and then, in descending order, his work, and his sundry expensive toys like the Ferrari and his Jet Ski; but none of them had even begun to occupy his mind in this all-consuming way. He thought of her the moment he woke up in the morning, leaping out of bed to go and gaze at her before she woke—or, more frequently, while the maternity nurse fed her or changed her, for she was an early riser—and last thing at night, as he drifted off to sleep, while listening anxiously for her cries which he was convinced the nurse wouldn't hear.

Lucinda could never remember being so happy. She had been warned so many times, by people in her antenatal classes, by her mother and her sister, by friends, by magazine articles—even by Mr. Clark—that she would have a letdown, that she would feel tired and sore and depressed, that she might have trouble with feeding, that she would be desperate for sleep: but she experienced none of those things. She glided through the days and indeed the weeks in a haze of absolute contentment. She recovered physically with extraordinary speed, and was going out for walks with Blue and the baby only a week after the birth, and even did some Christmas shopping—"Not that going to Harvey Nichols was exactly arduous"—and Molly Rose was absurdly well-behaved, slithering off her mother's breast with a loud burp when she was sated and then into a deep sleep.

She cried so rarely that when she did everyone remarked upon it, and even if she was awake, lay contentedly squinting at the mobiles which hung above her cot and her pram. Nor did she favour the behaviour pattern best known to babies of sleeping peacefully all day and commencing to scream at around six o'clock in the evening until far into the night; she lay, squinting happily, or slept peacefully on.

She was also extremely pretty, and a few days before Christmas she did unarguably smile properly for the first time. They knew it was a smile and not wind because Lucinda screamed to Blue to come and see, and although she had stopped, she did it again quite quickly. It was the usual rather uncertain, wobbly smile, the small face almost surprised by it; but a smile it was.

"She is clearly quite incredibly advanced," said Lucinda, "and you are right to be so proud of her, Blue."

"Aren't you proud too?" he said and, "Yes," said Lucinda, "of course I am. Oh look—look, Blue, here it comes again!" And indeed it did, and repeatedly throughout the evening until, quite exhausted by all her efforts, Molly Rose fell asleep.

"Isn't that lovely? What a wonderful Christmas present," said Lucinda. "I just don't think I want anything else ever again."

"That's a pity," said Blue, " 'cos I got you this. Better take it back then."

"This" was a small blue Tiffany box, tied up with a white ribbon. "Don't you dare," said Lucinda, snatching it from him, and then: "Oh Blue," gazing into it at a diamond eternity ring, "Blue, I must have been terribly good in a former life to deserve you. And Molly Rose, of course."

Nigel was going to stay with his Norfolk relatives for Christmas; the prospect was profoundly depressing, but he could see no alternative, apart from spending it alone in his new flat.

Once the divorce was through, he felt he could at least begin to look forward. The revenue from letting the house would be considerable. He still felt a degree of disquiet about the whole plan—it wasn't quite the sort of thing he had been brought up to think one did, but he would be clearing over half of his debt to Lloyd's, and whenever he felt particularly bad, he thought of poor Gillian Thompson and several of the other tragic people featured in Joel Strickland's article, and found his conscience eased. And there was Catherine Morgan, of course: her experiences had been dreadful. Who would have dreamed that the conduct of a company that had been so generally assumed to be upright and gentlemanly could have led people into such distress and, indeed, danger?

Nigel sighed. He was doing it again—thinking of Catherine; he tried very hard to keep her out of his thoughts. And failed. She was so . . . so sweet. Sweet and gentle and really rather brave: leaving London and her friends, moving to a place where she knew no one, where she would have no independence, to live with what sounded like the most dreadful people: and all to ensure her children's happiness.

He had considered inviting her and the children up for a day before Christmas, perhaps to see a show, but every time he plucked up the courage, approached the phone even, he saw that picture of the three of them going into the house, little Caroline in that other man's arms, and decided against it. He wasn't risking his heart a second time.

℮

Leaving the house hadn't actually been as dreadful as Elizabeth had expected. It had hurt, of course; but Simon was so much a part of that house, with all the contradictory experiences of living with him, being married to him, and it might be easier now, in some ways at least, to say goodbye to him, to accept that he was gone.

She had seen a house that she liked very much: smaller, of course, but charming in its own way, early Victorian, in Little Venice, close to the canal, with lovely light, tall rooms, the street overhung with trees, and a quiet green garden. She could see her new life being lived there, for it was large enough for the older children to lead their lives and entertain their friends, while small enough to contain her and the baby without a sense of being surrounded with too much space. The children had all liked it, bagged rooms, staked out their territories. The rented place was all right; they would survive Christmas in it, and then in the New Year, the inquest would soon be behind them for better or for worse. They had discussed Christmas very honestly, had agreed it was just something to get through, that they could do it together.

"I think we should go to church," Annabel had said rather unexpectedly, "on Christmas morning, give the day a focus," and the other two had agreed. They would have scruffy lunch, Tilly said, and supper in the evening. "Maybe even beef or something," said Toby, "not turkey and all that."

"Yes, good idea," said Tilly, "but I do want crackers. We can't have Christmas without crackers. And stockings."

"Stockings, of course," said Elizabeth. "But I want one too."

"Self self self with you, isn't it?" said Annabel, giving her a hug. "Never think of us having to find things for you. OK, just this once."

And then, a week before the day, she came home and said, "Mummy, don't say no at once, but Florian wondered if he could come round in the evening on Christmas Day. Just for some champagne and a chat. He's such a brilliant chatter, and I think it would be nice, give the evening a lift. Only if everyone agrees, obviously."

"Obviously we agree," said Tilly. "Don't we, Toby?"

"Suppose so," said Toby; he actually rather liked Florian. He had street cred and Toby longed for that beyond anything.

So it wouldn't be too bad. They'd get through it. As they were getting through all the rest.

Toby was much more relaxed about the baby now. The change had been wrought not by Florian but by Fallon. Fallon was becoming day by day increasingly beautiful: she had had her wild hair cropped short—by Florian, who had met her one night at the house and begged her to allow him to do it—and it clung to her head like a small black cap. She was tall, almost as tall as Tilly, and very slender, and she had begun to wear rather eccentric clothes, bought from secondhand stalls in Kensington Market—long floating skirts and loose silk blouses, rainbow-coloured sweaters and large floppy hats. Her voice was gorgeous, low and husky, and she had a deep, rather dirty laugh. Toby thought she was wonderful and had even asked her out, but as Fallon said to Tilly, there was no way she could go out with someone who looked and dressed and talked like Toby. "No offence, Til, but I'd be a laughingstock."

But she did like him and they had many long conversations over the kitchen table; and one of the things she said to him was that he must be well pleased about the baby.

Whereupon Toby had gone scarlet in the face and opened another bottle of beer and lit one of the cigarettes that Elizabeth had forbidden in the house.

"What's the matter? Did I say something I shouldn't?"

"No," said Tilly, "but he doesn't like the idea."

"Why on earth not?" said Fallon. "I mean, there's all the noise, I suppose, and the stink from the nappies and that, but you're not here that much. And I'm sure your mum will keep it nice. But they're good fun, babies are. I should know, we got enough of them."

"Yes, but you're a girl," said Toby.

"You noticed! Well done. Yeah, I know, but what if it's a boy? You can be its—what d'you call it, Tilly?—something about a model."

"Role model?" said Tilly.

"Yeah, role model. You'll be the only male in this house, and he won't half need you. You can take him off, go to the football together, all that stuff. Nah, it'll be great. Me little brother misses me big one something awful."

"What's happened to him?" said Tilly.

"Oh, Dean's gone to live with Ron—that's our oldest brother," she explained to Toby. "Dean is a lot better off with 'im 'cos he doesn't like my mum's latest boyfriend at all. Well, none of us do. But poor little Darren, he's quite lost without Dean. Nearest thing to a dad he's got."

"Yes, I see," said Toby; and then, smiling at Fallon rather awkwardly, "Well, I hadn't thought of it like that."

"No," said Fallon, looking at him almost pityingly, "I don't suppose you had. Can I have a puff of that, Toby?"

And they sat there, sharing the cigarette and chatting while Tilly endured an agony of anxiety that her mother might suddenly appear. Which she wouldn't; for Elizabeth had come downstairs in search of a cup of tea, caught the whiff of cigarette smoke, heard Fallon's unmistakable voice and Toby's laugh, and decided the best thing she could do was creep back upstairs and pretend ignorance of all of it. Certainly until the morning.

ლ

Flora was acutely excited about Christmas. To be spending it at Broken Bay, the future safe: it was truly too good to be true. She went into a fever of cooking and planning and decorating and shopping; and when Debbie and the children arrived, on the evening of 22 December, ahead of Richard, the house looked so beautiful, hung with holly and with ivy garlands, every windowsill set with candles, a huge tree in the hall, they burst into spontaneous applause.

Debbie looked very strained, Flora thought; she did too much, worked too hard. She would try to give her a happy Christmas, a rest, try not to annoy her, not to be bossy.

She had written to Richard about the house; explaining that it was safe, that she could stay there "as long as Alexander allows!," telling the story of the first John Fielding, saying that she had known nothing of the entail. Richard would find it difficult, she knew; he was stiff and proud, just as William had been, but he had to know; and he seemed to have taken it well, wrote back a generous letter—but she felt there was more to come. What pleased her far more was that Debbie had rung to congratulate her, sounding genuinely pleased.

Richard was coming down directly from Scotland; he had a lot of administration to do at the end of term, and he and Morag needed a few days of quiet together to accomplish it: "She's worn out, but she won't give in, of course."

The children were in a state of acute excitement, decorating their rooms, deciding where best to hang their stockings, foraging for holly and locking themselves into rooms with much giggling while they wrapped presents. It was all totally idyllic, Flora thought, the sort of Christmas people dreamed of.

"You've made a wonderfully happy family, Debbie," she said, as they walked out on the moor, the children running ahead. "It can't always have been easy. Well done."

Debbie said nothing; looking at her sharply, Flora saw that her eyes had filled with tears. Some instinct told her to pretend not to have noticed, and to change the subject. She hoped the marriage wasn't going wrong again; she had allowed herself to think things were better. But she was fearful for Debbie's happiness in Scotland with the much-revered Morag.

Later she said, rather casually, that she had a friend coming to supper on the following evening. "I hope you don't mind, Debbie, but it's quite a long-standing arrangement and Richard will be very late."

"Of course I don't mind," said Debbie, "and anyway, I've got to go and meet Richard at Cardiff Airport. Who is she, your friend? Have I met her before?"

"It's not a she," said Flora, "and no, you haven't. His name is Colin Peterson—the one who was helping me with the sale of the house, remember?"

"Oh—yes," said Debbie. "Of course."

Flora was clearing the table very busily; if the notion hadn't been completely ridiculous, Debbie would have thought she was blushing.

℮↻

She was getting through it; hour by hour, day by day. She did her best to close her mind to the events of the twenty-seventh, when she would talk to Richard, to the dreadful repercussions that would ensue, but it overshadowed everything she did. And Flora congratulating her on her happy family as she had today made her feel even more like a murderess, like Lady Macbeth or Lucrezia Borgia. How could she do it to them? What right did she have? She didn't know, and she had no right; she only knew she had to do it.

She drove over to Cardiff to collect Richard from the airport, feeling queasy. How was she going to pretend for—what—three more endless days? How was she going to smile at him, talk to him, express interest, affection, let him make love to her . . . Stop it, Debbie. You've got to. Just do it.

℮↻

"Debs, hello. Lovely to see you. Let me give you a hug." Well, that was all right. She could handle a hug. Just . . .

"Lovely to see you too," she said. "How are you?"

"A bit shattered. We've been working flat out, Morag and I. There's so much still to learn, you know. And she's incredibly patient with me."

"Good, I'm glad. How was your flight?"

"OK. Bit late leaving, as you know."

"Yes. Luckily, I'd phoned to check. So I've even had a quarter of a supper. What about you? Your mum's keeping something for you."

"Good. I need it. How is my mother?"

"She's fine," said Debbie, leading the way to the car. "So happy about the house."

"She must be. What an extraordinary story, isn't it?"

"Quite extraordinary. Our little Alexander, a landowner."

"Yes, well, that does seem rather absurd," Richard said stiffly.

"Anyway, I must tell you," Debbie said, "oh look—there's the car—yes, I must tell you, your mother's got an admirer."

"She's what?" Richard froze and turned to stare at Debbie. "What sort of admirer?"

"The usual sort. A man, you know. Clearly interested in her—devoted actually, I'd say."

"Devoted? Some man devoted to my mother?"

"Yes. Don't look so disapproving, it's lovely for her."

"Well, I don't know what to say. Who . . . who is he?"

"Not sure. Some kind of property developer, I think. He had been advising her over the sale of the house. Obviously he's thrilled about the way things have turned out for her. I rather like him. Anyway, he may still be there when we get back. He said he'd like to meet you."

"But what's he like? I mean, is he an old man? I don't understand why she's never mentioned him."

"I think because she was embarrassed," said Debbie, doing up her seat belt—thank God they had so much to talk about. "She was talking coyly about a friend and stuff like that, and when she had to tell me the friend was a him, she got very flustered. Anyway, when he arrived, it was perfectly obvious they were very fond of each other. They go to concerts together. He's her sort of age, and the most surprising thing about him is that he's not like the people she usually has as friends. I mean, he's—well, you know, a bit naff."

"No, I don't know," said Richard. He sounded irritable. "What do you mean?"

"Well, his clothes are a bit odd, for a start. I mean, he had a really weird cardigan on, sort of striped . . . And he's not exactly posh, bit North Country. He's perfectly sweet. He's called Colin."

"But . . . do you think it's serious? Debbie, do look what you're doing, there's a lorry coming towards us."

"I did see it." She controlled herself with an effort. "I don't know if it's serious, I mean, I presume they're not planning to get married. Or—"

"If you're going to drive in the outside lane, you really should speed up a bit. It's dangerous."

Why did she always forget the way he did this? She pulled sharply over to the inside lane. "Better?"

"Yes. Anyway, you were saying—about this man?"

"He's called Colin. Colin Peterson. Like I said, I really liked him." The other Debbie would have added, "You probably won't," but she was determined not to sound crabby. She owed him three good days. And the children. Three really happy days. And then . . .

"Debbie, please get into fifth gear. Surely you can hear the engine labouring."

Debbie pulled up onto the hard shoulder and got out.

He stared at her. "What's the matter?"

"You drive. Please. I can't cope with this." She was close to tears: all her good resolutions gone.

"Look," he said, "I'm exhausted, I've only just got off a plane, for heaven's sake—"

"Just shut up, will you? If you can't say anything nice, don't say anything at all. Let's just get home. And then you can ask Colin yourself what his intentions are."

He didn't say another word all the way to Gower; and when they reached the house, Colin's car was gone. Flora came out to meet them.

"Hello, darling. Lovely to see you. Happy Christmas."

"Yes, it all looks wonderful. You've excelled yourself, Mother."

"Well, I've had lots of help. Good trip? Come along in, I've saved you some casserole."

"Thank you, that was kind. Are the children all asleep?"

"Emma's still awake. She wants to see you."

They went into the hall; a small thunderbolt in a nightdress hurled itself at Richard.

"Daddy! Oh, I've missed you so much!"

"I've missed you too, darling."

This is why it's so dreadful, Debbie thought, staring at the two of them: Richard lifting Emma up, kissing her, her small arms winding round his neck. This is why I know I'm so wicked. This is what I've got to destroy.

She felt so bad, she drank two large glasses of wine in the time it took Richard to eat a very small supper, Emma on his knee. And was vaguely aware of Flora watching her. Oh God. God help me.

As if He would, a wicked woman like her.

Braced for sex, Debbie was spared. Richard kissed her, said he was sorry, but he was completely exhausted, and turned out the light. She lay there, looking at his back, listening to his snores, thanking God for the reprieve. And tomorrow, to quote her favourite heroine, was another day.

Chapter 58

She had watched herself go through it, hour by hour, smiling, opening parcels, saying thank you, singing carols, eating turkey, drinking too much, playing charades, watching Rachel fall asleep on her father's knee, putting the children to bed. And then sitting with Richard and Flora, drinking still more, listening while they talked and reminisced and didn't seem to notice how quiet she was. To bed, then; where Richard made love to her. She got through it somehow.

"Lovely Christmas," he said, turning away from her. "Thank you." And fell asleep. How could he not know? How could he not tell? But—tomorrow was Boxing Day. And then soon, soon it would be over. The worst would be over. For her at any rate.

Amazingly, through it all, she had still felt not one shred of doubt. She knew she was doing the right thing.

Boxing Day was cold and brilliant.

"Isn't it lovely?" said Flora. "You know what we ought to do. Walk the Worm."

"Oh ye-es!" the children all shouted at once. They had only done it once, walked along the sometime peninsula, sometime island of Worms Head, the great stretch of land that stuck out over a mile from Rhossili Bay. Named the Worm, because it looked like a dragon, lying there in the water ("wurm" being Old English for dragon), it was one of the great walks of Gower: children particularly loved it, and loved looking at it when the tide was in and saying, "We were walking there yesterday." But it could be dangerous, if not enough time was allowed for tides; and today it would be icy cold.

"I really don't think . . . ." said Debbie doubtfully.

"Now, Debbie," said Flora briskly, "you know we always have this discussion and it's always fine. The children are growing up, they're wonderful walkers"—she paused, for a notional "thanks to me"—"and it's a beautiful day. Let's look at the tides, anyway. Richard, what do you think?"

"I think it would be fun," he said. His expression as he looked at Debbie was chilly; she was doing what he most hated in front of his mother, being overprotective.

"Good. Now let's see . . . ah yes. Low tide at one thirty. So we'd be absolutely fine."

"Don't forget it gets dark at half past four," said Debbie.

"I hadn't," said Flora, "and I had no intention of going as late as one thirty. You know the tides allow us five clear hours. In fact, we could take a picnic."

"A picnic!" said Debbie, and this time she was laughing. "Flora, it's freezing out there."

But, "Ye-es!" shouted the children again.

The phone rang; Flora answered it.

"Colin! How lucky that you rang . . . What? . . . Well, because I thought you might like to join us. We're going on a picnic . . . Yes, I know it's freezing, but look at the sun . . . On the Worm. Then you could meet Richard, and . . . Oh, all right . . . What? . . . Oh, that's a good idea. Yes, come and meet us, park at Rhossili and walk along towards the Worm. At about four. No, let's say three thirty. Debbie is anxious about the tides. And the light, of course. Then we can come back here for tea. Fine . . . What? . . . Yes, I will." She smiled at Debbie. "Colin said to tell you how much he enjoyed meeting you, and how he was looking forward to seeing you again today."

"Well good," said Debbie, "and I'll look forward to seeing him." Thinking that when she did, they'd be back, warm and safe, not stranded on the icy rocks. And it would be the end of the last day. Their last day as a family.

They set out along the grassy cliff walk that led to the sea; the children ran ahead, shouting and laughing.

"They're having a lovely time," Debbie said, and meant it.

"Of course. Now, Richard, you take the rucksack, and then I can help Rachel over the Causeway. Are you all right, Debbie?"

"Yes, I'm fine. Thank you." It would be all right; they'd have loads of time and she'd already said bravely she didn't want them to go as far as the Devil's Causeway, the treacherous narrow high walkway that had to be crossed to reach the last quarter of the Worm. Richard, to her surprise, agreed.

"It is too far in the cold. And I don't want to have to carry anyone back."

Flora slightly scornfully agreed.

The sun was still high and the sky brilliant as they set out across what was known as the causeway; not exactly a causeway at all, Debbie thought, just a difficult scramble across rocks and stones. Emma danced ahead chattering to her father, Rachel held her grandmother's hand, Alex walked more slowly with Debbie. Every so often, Richard or Emma would turn and shout, "Come on!"

"Don't take any notice," Debbie said, "and don't let them hurry you."

"I won't."

They had their picnic on the grassy plateau just above the causeway; Flora had put some soup in a big Thermos jug and they dipped French bread into it, and then ate cheese sandwiches and tomatoes. It was idyllic, but in spite of the sun and the blue sky, it was very cold; a sharp wind had blown up, and Richard looked around almost anxiously.

"We'd better get on," he said. "Don't want to risk anything."

"Dear oh dear," said Flora, "you townies!"

They set off again, Richard and Emma walking with Debbie and Alex now. Flora stomped ahead, her long rainbow-coloured scarf blowing in the wind, holding Rachel's hand. Debbie watched anxiously for signs of flagging from Rachel. She was awfully little, Debbie thought, only six; this was a big journey for her. She said so to Richard.

"Oh Debs, don't be silly. She's a very good little walker and—"

"I'd feel happier if you were with them," said Debbie stubbornly, "so if Rachel does start flagging you can insist on coming back."

"Oh, all right," he said. "Coming, Al?"

"No, thanks," said Alex; he had become rather pale and quiet.

She watched till Richard and Emma had caught the others up, then said, "Alex, you don't have to do this. We can wait here for them, if you like."

He shook his head. "Granny'll think I'm feeble," he said.

"Which won't matter one bit. Well, just say if you really start to get tired. Remember, every inch we walk, we have to walk back again."

"Yes, all right." He looked up at her and smiled. "It's nice to be with Dad, isn't it, Mum?"

For you, not for me; for me it's horrible; everything about him hurts me— his voice, his face, the way he talks to me, just the way he isn't who I want him to be.

"It is, indeed."

"Soon we'll be with him all the time again. It'll be great, Mum, won't it?"

Soon we won't be with him all the time. It won't be great and you'll be very unhappy.

"Yes, it will, love. Really great. Now, shall we try and catch them up, or—"

"Mum." He stopped walking. "I feel a bit sick. Sorry."

"Don't be sorry, Alex, you can't help it. Although I did tell you not to eat so much of Granny's ice cr— Oh, Al."

He was very sick suddenly, there on the grass. Trying to comfort him, clean him up, looking after the others, too far ahead now to hear her call, Debbie wondered what she should do.

"Just stay there quietly," she said to Alex. "I'll go and tell them what's happened."

"No! Don't leave me! I'm scared."

"Lovely, there's no need to be scared. I'll only be ten minutes."

"You might be longer. I can't see them anymore."

"Oh, it's too bad," said Debbie, feeling a wave of rage. "They could have waited for us. It's just not fair."

"Yes, and look, Mum. It's getting misty."

This was true; the sea mist that the wind blew in and onto Gower was descending, grey and wet and scary; it wasn't thick like a fog—you could see perfectly well where you were going: for about two hundred yards or so. But no farther. And it had certainly blanked out the rest of their party.

"Well, what do you think we should do? Just sit here—or start going back? I think we should just wait."

"OK, but it's getting jolly cold."

"Here," said Debbie, taking off her scarf, one of Flora's thick long ones that she had borrowed. "Wrap this round you. It'll help. I'm sure they'll be here in about half an hour at the most."

"Half an hour! Mum, that's too long."

"Well, I can't help that," said Debbie.

❧

"Where are they?" said Flora. "And however did they get so far behind?"

"God knows," said Richard. He felt anxious now as well as irritated. He felt irritated with everyone, with Flora for proposing this absurd walk, with himself for not resisting her, with Debbie for not keeping up with them, even with Emma who was whining now, saying she was cold, she wanted to go back. Only Rachel was still dancing ahead, turning to beckon to them through the mist every few minutes.

"Oh, very well," said Flora, "we'd better turn back. Come on, Rachel, everybody wants to go home."

"Everybody but us," hung in the air; Rachel stood still, her hands on her hips, clearly cross.

"Come on, Rachel. We've lost Mummy and Alex, we have to go back."

"That's their fault. I don't want to go back. It's so fun being here."

"Look," said Flora, "you go back, Richard, with Emma. Rachel and I'll go a bit farther. Don't worry, we won't go near the Devil's Causeway. But she's enjoying it so much and it seems a shame to cut it short now."

"Well, it's getting terribly misty," said Richard.

"Richard! It's only a mist. It'll be sunny again in half an hour."

"It's also getting late. It's half past two, well past low tide."

"Yes, and with at least two hours when it's completely safe to cross.

Look, we'll just go a bit farther and then we'll turn round and catch you up. Well, we'll meet you on the Rhossili side. That'd be best. All right?"

"Yes, of course," said Richard, "but do be careful."

"All right, all right," said Flora. "You sound like your father."

"I don't consider that such a bad thing," said Richard slightly stiffly, and turned away with Emma.

⁓

Flora was quite right; in half an hour, the mist had gone again and the winter sunshine was back. As Richard and Emma reached the place where they had had lunch, they saw Debbie and Alex sitting and singing.

"What happened to you?" said Richard. "Why didn't you keep up?"

"Alex was sick and felt rotton," said Debbie. "We had to sit down and wait. Anyway, where are the others?"

"Oh, Mother decided to take Rachel on a bit, she was enjoying it so much. They'll be here soon."

"Hope so. Can we start to cross?"

"Yes, she said we should meet her on the other side of the Causeway."

"Good. I hate this walk, it frightens me. And I think I was right. Actually. What with the mist and the cold, and—"

"Yes, all right. Come on then, let's get started."

"I don't like leaving them here," said Debbie, looking over her shoulder. "I wish you hadn't agreed to them going on, Richard."

⁓

They reached the other side safely, although it took almost three-quarters of an hour. Alex was feeling sick again, and kept stopping, and the mist had made the rocks more slippery. Both children fell several times.

"God, I'll be glad to get safely back to the house," said Debbie. "I'm exhausted."

"So am I," said Alex plaintively.

"Well, you can have a rest now. Let's go up the hill a bit, then we can watch them coming."

They went rather slowly up the cliff path, found a place to sit, and settled down to wait.

"I'm thirsty," said Alex.

"So am I," said Emma.

"Well, you'll have to wait," said Richard.

He sounded harsher than usual; Debbie wondered why, then saw he was looking down into Rhossili Bay.

"The tide's coming in quite fast now," he said, almost as if it didn't matter.

"Hello!"

It was Colin Peterson, dressed in a virginal waxed coat and matching cap. And Hunter Wellies so new they gleamed. His voice was incredibly welcome; he was so sensible, so—so normal. What did he want to get mixed up with Flora for, Debbie wondered.

"Hello, Colin. How nice to see you. This is Richard, Richard, this is Colin Peterson."

"How do you do," said Richard rather shortly. "Sorry I missed you the other night."

"I was sorry too. But very pleased to meet you now. And this must be Alex."

"Yes. And Emma you met."

"I did indeed. How are you, Emma?"

"All right," said Emma. "We've just had a picnic."

"Only your grandmother would have a picnic on a day like this," said Colin.

Too right, Debbie thought. And where is she? And where is my youngest child?

"So where is she, the redoubtable Mrs. Fielding?"

"Oh, just coming," said Richard. "She'll be here any minute, I should think."

Only she wasn't just coming. There was no sign of her, of either of them.

It was Debbie who cracked first. "Where are they? Where are they? What are they doing? Why don't they come? What's happened?"

The tide was rushing in, up the beach; in ten minutes, Debbie thought, it would be lapping at those stones, those bloody stones, all of which had to be crossed before Rachel was safe. God, the wind was creating crosscurrents, the sea was getting up; it was horrible—her worst nightmare.

"I'm going back," said Richard, standing up. "Something must have happened."

"I'll come with you."

"No, you won't. It's dangerous. And someone has to stay with the children."

"I can do that," said Colin. "No, better still, I'll come with you, Richard. Debbie can stay with the children."

"OK," said Debbie, her teeth chattering with fright and cold. "Thank you."

"Be careful, Daddy," said Emma cheerfully. She and Alex were mercifully unaware of the real danger.

"I will."

Richard and Colin started running down the path; Colin's new cap blew off, was tossed out on the wind. Debbie watched it slowly descending into the dark grey sea, a hideous omen of what might come. Suppose they were already in that sea, Flora and Rachel? Suppose Flora had decided to explore some cliff path? It was more than likely, stupid bloody woman. Suppose Rachel was hanging on desperately to some rock. Suppose—

"I hope they'll be all right," said Alex.

"Of course they will," said Debbie. "They'll be fine." She started making bargains with God; if they got out of this, if Rachel came back to her safely, she'd give up work, she'd never see Joel again, she'd train as a teacher, she'd have sex with Richard every night—

"There they are," said Alex suddenly. "Look!"

"Oh, thank God, thank God," said Debbie, even then thinking fearfully of her bargains.

But then: "It's not them," said Emma. "There's only one. Mummy, it's Rachel—look . . ."

Well, it was Rachel. Not Flora alone, thank God. But how would she manage? She was so tiny; how had she got this far alone? But the men would reach her, surely, before the tide really came in.

She was waving furiously, trying to attract their attention; she must be so frightened, Debbie thought, so terribly frightened, she was just a dot out there, a solitary dot, moving dreadfully slowly . . . why?

Don't be ridiculous, Debbie, she's being careful not to slip.

"Daddy's coming, darling!" she shouted, while knowing it was totally impossible that Rachel could hear her.

She looked down the cliff path, realised that Richard and Colin might not even have seen her, from their lower viewpoint, and shouted to tell them, but the wind blew her voice away from them as well.

"Stay there," she said to the children. "I'm just going down to the rocks, to tell Daddy and Colin. Don't worry, I'll be back in no time."

"Don't go, Mummy, please."

"I must. I promise I won't go far."

She reached the bottom of the path, waved, shouted, but they didn't hear her. She wondered if she should go after them, but decided it would be silly, someone had to be with the children. And someone not be drowned came the thought unbidden into her head, and she went back up the cliff, to watch as Richard and Colin began to work their way, agonisingly slowly, across the causeway. The water was already creeping up over the stones.

"Oh God," she said, for Richard had slipped, fallen heavily; it took him what seemed a long time to get up again, and Colin came back to help him. This was terrible, awful. He seemed to have hit his head; she could see him wiping his forehead, look at his hand, obviously at blood. He sat down very gingerly, took something from Colin, dabbed at his head.

"Get on, get on!" she screamed into the wind. "Your head doesn't matter. Nothing matters except Rachel, don't waste time!" And then Richard slowly stood up, said something to Colin, and together they recommenced their journey. Having lost precious time.

It was very difficult to make out what was happening from where Debbie and the children were sitting. At times Rachel seemed to be going in the wrong direction, moving away from her: surely that couldn't be right. But maybe it was; maybe she could see the tide coming in, had decided to go back. She was so little, Debbie thought, looking at her, and so vulnerable in the pink anorak she had begged for and the pink Wellingtons, a tiny little girl, just six years old: battling now all alone with the sea and the tide and the wind. How could she have left her, trusted Flora to look after her, how, how?

Richard appeared to be halfway across now, and the water was well over his feet; he had boots on, but they were slippery in the water and he kept sliding sideways, just managing to right himself each time. But for how long, she wondered fearfully, and what would happen when the water came over his boots, filled them: which it would, in a few more minutes, another clutch of waves. At least he had seen Rachel now, was waving at her, and she was waving back, apparently cheerful. God, she was brave. Colin was moving doggedly forwards too, rather more confidently than Richard; he was almost level with him now. But what could they do? How could they bring a small child over, once the water was thigh-high, waist-high—chest-high on her, as it would be, and it would be dangerous, fast-running.

"Oh Emma," she said aloud, unable any longer to pretend everything was all right. "Oh God."

Emma looked at her. "Do you think we should get help?" she said.

☙

Richard was scared. He knew these seas and this crossing, he had grown up near it, knew the dangers. But Rachel was only about two hundred yards away, and still clear of the water; she should stay there, he saw with sudden clarity. It was perfectly safe there; the inshore lifeboat at Port Eynon would rescue them; and he began to wave at her, to try to indicate that she should go back up onto the Worm. But she misunderstood, waved again cheerfully; she had no real idea of the danger she was in. He went on towards her; at least he could see properly, the late-afternoon sun was brilliant, it helped, made it seem just a little less frightening.

He heard a shout, saw Colin had caught him up; he was being pretty brave, the old chap, and he'd been grateful for his help when he fell. His head was bleeding quite hard; large drops of blood fell steadily from his wound into the water, but he felt nothing, no pain, only the awful fear.

Colin was picking his way across the higher stretches of the causeway, steadily and confidently. He grinned at Richard as he drew level with him. "We're doing OK, I'd say," he said. "Nearly there."

"Hardly," said Richard. "But we should be with Rachel in five minutes now. Where the hell is my mother?"

"God knows," said Colin, managing a half smile, "and it's possible that even He isn't sure. So we're agreed, we'll go back up onto the Worm?"

"Yes. Rachel," he shouted, "go back, go back!"

And this time she did hear him, but shook her head and shouted something in reply, her light child's voice useless against the wind.

"Plucky little soul," said Colin. "Look, if we go over onto that side there, look, it's a bit higher and dryer, we'll get to her sooner. See? Come on."

He was right; it was higher and dryer. But Rachel was not coming that way, she had chosen the central route and her small pink Wellingtons were already half-covered in water. And then she stopped still, for the rainbow scarf had become unleashed, was blowing away, and she grabbed at it, almost losing her balance in the process, and it blew away into the wind.

"I'll go down and head her off," said Richard. "You carry on up to the Worm."

"No, no, I'll keep with you. We could both be needed. Oh—shit."

And Richard saw a wave suddenly break over the rocks and rush towards Rachel.

She was knocked flying by it. Screaming with fear, Debbie watched in gut-wrenching terror as the small pink figure struggled to right itself, only to be knocked sideways again.

"Do something! Do something!" she shouted to anyone or thing who might be able to hear her, and to help, but Richard and Colin were too far from her to hear and from Rachel to reach. And God seemed to have turned away.

❧

Flora surfaced again to find Rachel gone.

She had forbidden her to leave, had insisted, through the pain that kept blacking her out, that they should stay together, but Rachel had argued vociferously that she should go, that she could get help. It wasn't even a temptation to let her try, it was too dangerous, the tide would be rushing in now; when it went down again, people would be able to find them, they would be rescued. They might even be rescued before that; if Richard had the sense to get help, to ring the police. But they must stay together, she told Rachel, wrapping the rainbow scarf round her to try and keep her warmer; it would be cold and dark and boring but they would get through it, they would sing songs and play games and they would be rescued. But the third time she had blacked out, for longer than before, Rachel had simply been gone when she surfaced again.

And then there had been terror; absolute terror; for she could see, when she hauled herself painfully, so painfully and slowly onto her feet, hanging onto the rock to support herself, to keep the weight off the leg that she knew was broken, that the tide was coming over the causeway; and any chance of Rachel getting across now was being removed, yard by dreadful yard.

She had sunk down again, weeping with remorse as well as terror, for her arrogance in insisting she and Rachel went on, her folly in suggesting the outing at all, her stubbornness in refusing to listen to the voice of caution and common sense that was Debbie's. And decided that however great the pain, and impossible-seeming the task, she must make her way at least as far as she was able, so that she might have a chance of calling Rachel back, of stopping her.

She looked about her for something to support her, a stick of some kind; and a few yards away she saw a large piece of driftwood: that would do very well. But she had to get to it. Hopping was too dangerous; crawling would be easier. And so inch by agonising inch, she crawled towards the piece of wood, every movement of the broken leg agony, the other one cut and scratched by the stones, her hands too.

Dusk was settling now, removing the colour from everything: and it was terribly cold. If they didn't come and find her, if she had to stay there until the morning, might she die of hypothermia? No, don't be absurd, Flora. People survive stranded on mountains for nights on end. You'll just be cold, and serve you right . . . Ah, now here she was, at the driftwood; if she could just lie on her side, propped on one elbow, and get a good grip on it, use it almost as a lever, she should be able to haul herself up. And yes, she could, she was rising on it, very slowly, little by little, up on the good knee now, she was nearly there, yes, she was upright . . . and just before the wood slipped again and she went down with a scream of pain, she saw that the water had completely covered the causeway and that Rachel could well have drowned in it, and she was alone as she had never been in her life before, alone and experiencing a fear that was far worse than any pain she had ever known.

ℰ~

Still on the cliff path, and in a scene she knew would be carved into her consciousness forever, Debbie watched Rachel surface for the second time, saw her small arm reach out of the water, her desperate, supplicating pink arm, and thought she really could watch this no longer, it was beyond endurance; and then saw, incredulous, that Richard, up almost to his waist now in water, had managed somehow to grab Rachel's foot, and then her leg, and draw her towards him, and lift her clear of the water and into his arms, and then turn and take Colin's outstretched hand, haul himself beside him up onto a rock; and then the pair of them, Richard holding Rachel, made their way slowly and with great difficulty away from the rushing water, and Colin climbed up onto the grass and reached down and took Rachel from Richard and appeared to be setting her down on the ground. And then they all froze into invisibility as dusk settled relentlessly down.

And then Emma said again, as she had said what seemed a lifetime earlier: "Mummy, don't you think we should get help?"

There was an emergency phone on the cliff top: next to a sign that said DANGER. How could she possibly not have remembered it was there, she thought, running towards it. She should be shot, or forcibly drowned, but somehow it had been wiped out by the drama and the fear; she lifted it, gasped out her message.

$e^{\sim}$

They looked down at the lifeless little figure on the ground: only for a moment, but it seemed forever, fearing she was drowned, for she had shipped in a lot of water, or concussed by the nasty gash on her head from the rocks. Then Richard dropped to his knees beside her, turned her on her front, with her head sideways, sobbing like a small child himself, started kneading away at her back, hoping to get her lungs working. And then suddenly there was the wonderfully unpleasant sound of Rachel vomiting up a lot of water, and then she looked up at them and said, "We have to fetch Granny, we think she's broken her leg," and then she started to cry and Richard cradled her in his arms, saying, "It's all right, you're safe now," and "No, no," she sobbed, "it's Granny's favourite scarf. I've lost it, she'll be so cross."

Flora surfaced again to feel her hand being rubbed very gently, and her hair stroked tenderly back from her face; she thought she must be hallucinating, and opened her eyes with an enormous effort—for even that seemed to cause pain in her leg—to see Colin Peterson looking down at her, and to hear him saying in his wonderfully level voice, "You really are an extremely silly woman," and replying in a whisper, "I know, I know, I'm sorry," and then remembering and saying, "Rachel," her heart clutched with fear, and Colin telling her, "She's fine, she's cold and wet, but she's fine. Rachel! Over here—your granny's over here."

And by the time the wonderful rescue helicopter had arrived, summoned by Debbie's call, Rachel at least was cheerful, if cold, sitting by her grandmother and telling her everything was going to be all right, and that she was terribly sorry but she'd lost her rainbow scarf.

"I think I can just about forgive you," Flora said.

Chapter 59

Joel, back in London after a rather unsatisfactory Christmas with friends in Kent, had slept badly—and woke to the realisation that today, life properly began. It was 27 December, the day on which Debbie was telling her husband that she was going to leave him: and then she would drive to London to be with him.

He was not expecting her to arrive radiantly happy; she would be desperately upset, remorseful, guilt-ridden, and quite possibly even hostile to him. It was a horrible thing that lay ahead of her. He felt wrenched with sympathy, concern, and even some guilt of his own for her; and he wished suddenly that he could be nearer her when she had done, and that she didn't have to make the endless drive up to London alone. And then he realised that there was no reason why he should not drive down, maybe to Cardiff, and meet her there. He couldn't imagine why he hadn't thought of it before; the only problem was how to let her know.

A phone call was dangerous, even today. Even on her mobile. Anyone might pick it up. But—oh, what the hell. It was worth the risk. And she surely wouldn't leave it lying around . . .

He dialled her number: it rang and rang. Come on, Debbie, come on. I want to hear your voice, I want to tell you I'm coming to get you. The phone moved cumbersomely onto the messaging service; Joel decided it was safe. Richard was such a dinosaur, he would hardly know mobile phones existed, so he certainly wouldn't be familiar with the mechanics of picking up messages.

"It's me. Good luck today. See you soon, definitely hopefully. Ring me. I'll come to Cardiff to meet you. Love you."

℮

Colin was sitting by Flora's bed in Swansea Hospital the next morning, as she lay still groggy from her ordeal and the general anaesthetic that had been necessary to set and pin her broken leg.

She turned her head towards him. Her voice was unnaturally faint. "Could you ask if I can have a cup of tea? I'll die of caffeine withdrawal at this rate."

"I'll try. What about some more water?"

"I don't want water, I'm sick of the beastly stuff. I want something warm and comforting. Please, Colin, do ask."

"Yes, very well. But I don't think they'll agree. They didn't half an hour ago. They kept saying you'd been so sick last night."

"Yes, well, this is this morning. And I feel fine."

She felt far from fine, but it was not just the pain from her leg that was troubling her, it was a sense of dreadful shame and remorse. She had been solely responsible for risking the lives of her entire family, had very nearly caused the death by drowning of her youngest granddaughter; she had distressed her daughter-in-law almost beyond endurance; she was a stupid, arrogant woman, and if she never saw any of them again, if they turned against her and never allowed the children into her house, never mind her care, it would be absolutely fair and just and she would have no right to complain or even question it. Why was she like this? What drove her, what convinced her that she was right and everyone else wrong? Why couldn't she listen properly to people instead of simply hearing what they said and ignoring it? Somehow she must learn, even at this late stage in her life, and somehow she must do penance for this dreadful thing she had done. But how? What was she to do about herself, her overbearing, wilful self? And who would help her to do it?

Colin reappeared, smiling rather nervously. "I'm sorry, Flora. They say in another hour . . ."

"Another hour? That's ridiculous." And then she thought that this at least would be a beginning, an acceptance of a judgement of someone other than herself. "I suppose I'll have to wait then," she said, and then found herself weeping.

Colin pulled his chair up to the bed and produced a very large, very clean handkerchief with his initial on it, which he passed her.

"It's the anaesthetic," he said. "Upsets all your emotions, everyone knows that. There, there, the tea'll be here soon."

"No, Colin, that's not why I'm crying. I'm crying because I'm so ashamed of myself, I feel so wretched about what I did. It was wrong of me, I should have known better, and—"

"No," he said, taking her hand, "you mustn't feel like that. You were only trying to give your family a nice day."

"No, Colin. I could have given them a nice day perfectly well by hiking over the Bryn, or in Oxwich Woods. But I have to—to sort of show off, to be reckless. It's a terrible way to behave, it's no wonder Debbie doesn't like me."

"Doesn't she like you?" he asked in genuine surprise.

"No. And it's entirely my fault. I was never very friendly to her, and I've made it worse over the years, being so domineering and bossy, and she's just grown to hate me. I was the same with William, you know—I always had to know best. He was a very careful, rather fussy person, and I used to be so high-handed with him, ignore his wishes half the time— ride out without my hat, for instance . . ."

"That doesn't sound too bad."

"But it was, because every time I went riding he was in agonies of worry, thinking I'd be thrown. It wouldn't have hurt me to wear a hat. And I used to tease him about his financial carefulness too; do you know, he had never ever been overdrawn in his entire life, not by so much as a fiver. I was always trying to persuade him to be a bit bolder, take a few risks, buy shares . . ."

"Going into Lloyd's was hardly careful," said Colin mildly.

"Oh, but it was, or so he thought. It was his one bit of speculation and he went into it so carefully, examining all the history, went over and over it with the dreadful Trafford Smythe, making sure there hadn't been a lot of big claims—and there hadn't, of course, as you know, except that one in the sixties. Oh no, he can't be blamed for that. If anyone could, it's me."

She was crying harder now; Colin looked rather wildly round for help and saw a nurse bearing down on them with a cup of tea.

"There you are," she said to Flora, putting it down. "Little sips, mind. Now what are you upsetting yourself for—you'll send your blood pressure up. Come on, lovely, drink your tea like a good girl, there, that's right."

Ten minutes later, Flora lay back obediently, having duly taken the prescribed little sips, and submitting to being called "lovely" and "a good girl" without complaint. It wasn't easy, but she did it. It was a start, after all, on the making of a new humble, docile Flora. In time it might get easier.

"Why don't you have a little sleep," said Colin, picking up on the hospital turn of phrase and she did suddenly feel very tired.

The last thing she thought, as she smiled at him and thanked him for coming in, was that his clothes were particularly dreadful this morning: a light-green polo-neck sweater in the style favoured by Mr. Val Doonican, with contrasting blue stripes, and some ready-creased trousers. The funny thing was though that it actually didn't seem to matter in the very least.

⁓

Richard walked into the kitchen; it was eight o'clock. Debbie was sitting with Rachel on her lap, trying to keep her quiet as the doctor had said she should, and reading aloud from *James and the Giant Peach*.

"You all right?" he asked.

"Yes, I'm fine." She looked very white and drawn.

"Good." He smiled at her. "You were so fantastic last night, Debbie. Thank you for being so . . . so great. Especially to my mother. I really appreciated it. It can't have been easy. Not a word of reproach."

"Well, not a lot of choice really. And she was in a terrible state." She had been, poor Flora; in fearful pain, until they gave her the morphine injection and even then it had still obviously been agonising. But she had insisted on talking to Debbie as she lay in Casualty, waiting to be seen by the orthopaedic surgeon.

"I know you've got enough to worry about with Rachel, but if you could see her, just for a minute, please," Richard said.

ᶜ⌒ᵔ

They had rendezvoused at Swansea Hospital; the helicopter that had picked them all up, Richard, Rachel, Colin, and Flora, had radioed the police at Reynoldston, where Debbie was waiting. She would never forget that moment for as long as she lived—being told they were all safe, that Flora had a broken leg but that the others were just wet and cold. The policeman had insisted on driving her over to Swansea, said she wasn't fit to drive, that she'd had a terrible shock, and indeed, she was shivering violently as she sat in the back, one arm round each child, Alex goggle-eyed at being in a police car, and one moreover that was going extremely fast with its blue light on . . . Debbie had been touched by that, and said so. "Well," said the sergeant, twinkling at her in the mirror, "you want to get there as fast as you can, don't you? Must be terribly worried."

They'd rushed into Casualty, and Rachel had shot into her arms, kissing her, saying, "Mummy, Mummy, the helicopter was so exciting, it made a huge wind and we looked down and we could see all of Gower."

She was showing no apparent signs of distress. "That may come later," the doctor had said in a low voice, after putting a couple of butterfly stitches in the gash on her forehead.

Richard had appeared, kissed Debbie on the cheek, and asked her if she was all right, more tenderly than she could remember for some time.

"Of course I'm all right. What about you, Richard? You're soaked, and what about your head? That looks nasty."

"No, it's fine, couple of stitches'll fix it, they said."

"And I should have brought you some dry clothes—how stupid of me."

"No, no," he said. "They're getting me some hospital pyjamas."

"Pyjamas? You're not having to stay here, are you?" For some reason, she didn't want him to; she wanted him home.

"No, of course not. But it's all they've got in the way of dry clothes. That's what Rachel's wearing—hospital pj's, didn't you notice?"

"No," she said humbly, wondering what sort of mother she was, not even thinking of bringing warm clothes for her nearly drowned child.

"No, I only noticed that she was alive. Sorry."

"It's OK. She is. Very much so."

"Where's Colin?"

"Oh, in that cubicle. He got a gash on his arm, they're just cleaning it up, checking him over. They thought he might show some ill effects, but he seemed fine, said he'd enjoyed it. He was bloody wonderful, Debbie, don't know what I'd have done without him."

"I know, I could see. Bless him. So where's your mum?"

That was when he'd asked her to see Flora.

She'd looked dreadful, white and hollow-eyed with pain, but totally lucid.

"I just had to say something to you, Debbie," she said, "before they took me away."

"How—how are you?"

"I'm all right. Leg hurts a bit. But . . . I owe you an enormous apology. I am deeply and terribly ashamed of myself. I should never have done it, insisted we went, when I knew you were anxious, and as for putting Rachel in such danger—"

"Well, I'm sure it wasn't deliberate," said Debbie carefully.

"That part wasn't, of course. I simply slipped, went down with a bit of a bang. And I insisted she stayed with me, of course; only I conked out a couple of times and she took the law into her own hands, and when I came round the last time, she was gone. Oh Debbie, I'm not even going to ask you to forgive me, I'm sure you never can, but I do want you to know that I am completely remorseful—"

"Of course I forgive you," said Debbie, "don't be silly. It was—was an accident. Anyway, Richard shouldn't have left the two of you, shouldn't have agreed. It was stupid of him, he must bear some of the blame."

"But I pretty well insisted he went."

"Oh Flora, that's rubbish. Richard is thirty-five years old. He can stand up for himself. Look, I've got to go, Rachel needs to be got home, given some food and the others too. I'll see you tomorrow. But please don't feel so bad. Everyone's all right, that's all that matters. Bye now."

She kissed her mother-in-law and left. She was feeling odd, very odd indeed. She supposed it was the shock.

But this morning, if it was indeed shock, then that was only part of it. She did sleep, greatly to her surprise: a heavy, haunted sleep, filled with images of rushing water and darkness and the sound of screaming and terrible fear. But at least it was sleep. What she woke to was different and she knew what it was, and it was a revelation so inescapable and so dreadful that she couldn't face it, tried to push it away, to keep herself safe from it. Only she couldn't; it was impossible. It pursued her as she got up and went downstairs into the kitchen, and made herself a cup of tea and sat at the table staring unseeingly into the dark morning, thinking of what today would have held, and knowing that it could do so no longer.

She couldn't leave Richard, not today, not tomorrow, not ever; however much she wanted to, however much she loved Joel. Richard was who she belonged to; because he was the father of her children, their children. That was all there was to it. Together they had done this amazing thing, this amazing and yet totally unexceptional thing; they had created three people, three small people, totally dependent on them emotionally and physically. As she was in turn dependent on them. They were the centre of her life, the core of herself, and she had known as she watched Rachel in the water yesterday, possibly lost to her forever, that nothing was as important, as precious as they were, and had thought too that if anything had happened to any of them, she would truly want to die.

There was a bond between her and Richard that was steely strong, and it had been created by those children; they might be at odds with each other over many, many things, but in their love for the children they were as one, absolutely concerned, completely together. And the thought of what that meant to her was so horrible, so painful that she sat there, bent over, clutching her stomach, her eyes closed, fighting down the tears.

She couldn't start to cry, because that would do it, would defeat her, she mustn't, she couldn't, and she fought it off, pacing the kitchen, her arms still folded in front of her, but the tears were stronger than any resolve she might have and finally they broke through, great waves of weeping, each larger and more painful than the last.

She would not be driving to London this evening to start her new, joyful life; she would not be telling Richard she was going; she would not be telling Richard anything at all, except that lunch was ready, or the children wanted to play some game or other, or that there was some football on the television . . . And at the terrible, aching banality of recognising that, of looking down the drab, love-starved years, she gasped aloud with pain.

And then because the kitchen, the walls of the house could no longer contain her, she put on a coat and a pair of Flora's boots and walked out into the garden, down into Flora's Meadow, and paced round and round it, sobbing loudly, and once or twice she screamed, the sound mingling with the cries of the seagulls and the crash of the sea. And then she went finally indoors, exhausted, and lay quietly on the kitchen sofa, to contemplate her new, dutiful life: and to try and dredge the strength from somewhere to telephone Joel and try to explain.

_e_

Joel went shopping. He wanted everything to be as perfect as possible for Debbie when she arrived. He had already put fresh sheets on the bed, cleaned the bathroom and the kitchen, and filled every vase he possessed with the best post-Christmas flowers he could find. He had bought her some presents too, silly things that he knew she would love: some white lace briefs from Knickerbox (she only liked white pants, said colours were tacky), a tape of Madonna doing the songs from _Dick Tracy,_ a video of _Back to the Future,_ a box of Ferrero Rocher chocolates which she always declared naff and then consumed in vast quantities, and a framed photograph of the two of them giggling, taken by his delayed-action camera. All designed to make her laugh, make her relax, make her glad to be with him. He bought supper too; she would probably say she wasn't hungry, but it would be awful if she wanted something. Some smoked salmon, some bread, and some Brie, so ripe it was ready to walk out of the flat. And some champagne. Of course.

He took his mobile phone with him, but it didn't ring. When he got back, there was still no message on the answerphone. Well, it was only eleven, she had probably hardly started to talk to Richard. Or, as the children were there, maybe hadn't started. But she had promised that she would do so by lunchtime, that she would ask Flora to take the children for a walk, so they wouldn't have to wait until the evening.

He sat down and read the papers, and then wondered if it was too early to have a drink. It was Christmas after all; and a glass of wine might make him feel less jittery. But then if she wanted to meet him in Cardiff, he had to be very sober. He made himself a jug of coffee instead. And sat down again, by the telephone, and tried not to look at the clock.

⟨⟩

"Richard, I'm going to pop out for a bit. I feel like a breath of fresh air."

"Shall I come with you?"

"No! It looks like it's going to rain. I just thought I'd stretch my legs. Is that all right?"

"Yeah, OK. And then we can have lunch when you get back. I've found some soup in the freezer, thought we could have that."

"Good idea."

"I've got rather a dab hand at making soup myself. Morag's given me a couple of recipes. She's a marvellous cook—"

Suddenly, she could stand it no longer. "Richard, I don't want to be rude, but I'm getting just a tiny bit tired of hearing about Morag's virtues. I'm sorry. Could we give them a rest for a day or two, do you think?" She had meant it to sound lighthearted, funny even; it came out heavy and almost bitter.

He looked at her, surprised. "Oh, all right. Sorry," he said, rather more patiently than she would have expected. Perhaps he was trying to make allowances, after the events of yesterday.

"Thanks. Right—well, won't be long."

She walked out to the car as briskly as she could, in case he was watching her. Every step was a huge effort, she had to literally force herself along, one foot after another.

She got into the car, drove up to Cefn Bryn. The mobile reception on Gower was very poor, she had discovered; you had to be at one of the highest points to be sure of getting any reception at all, and even then you could get cut off mid-sentence. She had considered using a public phone, but the thought of having this terrible conversation with Joel from a

stinking call box—they all seemed to smell, a mixture of beer and pee—
was horrendous. She looked at her watch. God! It was half past one. Joel
would be expecting to have heard from her by now; would be sitting
there—she pictured him in the flat, thinking about her, happily and confidently, or perhaps a little anxiously by now—and she wondered what he
was wearing, jeans probably and a white shirt, and no doubt bare feet, he
never wore shoes in the house, and she had to close her eyes briefly, so awful was the contemplation of what she could have had, and that was now
barred to her.

A new wave of grief hit her; it was like the pain of childbirth and she
thought she must wait for it to pass, cry, release some more of it before
she started to speak to him. She couldn't break down mid-sentence. She
had to be strong. Stronger than she'd ever been in her life.

℘

This was awful. It was twenty to two. What was she doing? Keep calm,
Joel, she's probably still talking to the bugger, it was never going to be a
quick conversation. But she had promised to call him by one; it had been
one of her promises to him. "I swear, just so you'll know everything's all
right. Even if we haven't quite finished. All right?" It had comforted him,
that timetable; he had been able to get through the morning, less anxious,
less impatient.

But she—and it—had failed him now.

He'd just wait till two and then he'd really have to ring. Ring her mobile, not the house. He sat down, watched racing on the television; anything to take his mind off the crawling clock. It crawled on, and at two
o'clock he dialled her number.

She was standing by then on the moorland of Cefn Bryn, had parked
the car and taken her mobile out of her bag. And seen she had a message:
from him, about meeting her in Cardiff. The sound of his voice was almost too much: for a moment she would have gone, left everyone and
everything behind her, but then she pulled the broken pieces of herself together again. She must do it quickly, before he set out for Cardiff. What
if he already had? How would she be able to resist that, knowing he was
less than an hour's drive away? She stood there, gazing down at the lovely

stretch of wooded bay that was Oxwich, and as she did so, her phone rang and it was him.

"Oh, hello," she said, amazed that she could sound so ordinary, so cool; and then interrupted him as he started to talk and said, "Joel, I'm not coming." Just like that.

e

"Can we go and see Granny?" said Rachel.

"Of course we can. Tomorrow."

"I want to go today. I'm worried about her."

"So am I," said Emma.

"So am I," said Alex.

"Rachel, Daddy's just got back from seeing Granny," said Debbie. "She's fine. He told you."

"But that was ages ago. She might be worse. She might be lonely. Why can't we?"

"Emma—" Debbie stopped. Why not? It was moving around, distraction . . .

"Well, maybe I could take you. Daddy's very busy. Go and see what he thinks."

Emma came back, beaming. "He says it's a good idea."

"All right then," said Debbie. "Let's go. Quick, into the car." They stared at her; grown-ups usually spent hours getting ready to do anything.

"What—now?" said Alex.

"Now," she said, and she could hear the desperation in her own voice. "Yes, now."

She really wasn't fit to drive. She felt rather as if she was drunk: drunk and exhausted and coming down with some horrible illness, all at the same time. She couldn't think, either; couldn't think how to get to Swansea, even had trouble getting the car into gear. She stopped at the top of the drive, looking at the headlights of the traffic streaming along, wondering if this was actually such a good idea. But anything was better than sitting in that room, hurting, hurrying out of it every now and again to go upstairs or outside to cry. This was good, it was moving around, shifting the pain about, making it briefly more bearable. The traffic blurred;

she had been about to move forward, had to slam on the brakes until the view cleared again.

"You all right, Mum?" said Alex.

"Yes. Yes, I'm fine. Sorry. Just—just getting a cold, I think, that's all. Right. Off we go."

❧

He'd been so angry, that had been the worst thing.

"Right," he had said. "Well, thank you for telling me. I suppose I should have known better. Goodbye, Debbie."

And her mobile had gone dead. And she stood there, staring at the sky, trying to bear it; and then walked for a while, stomping along in the cold, the sheep and wild ponies which roamed the Bryn pausing in their grass-chomping to look at her, wailing and moaning like a madwoman. And then finally she felt strong enough to return to the car and go back to the life that had claimed her so irrevocably.

❧

"Darlings!" Flora held out her arms. "How lovely. How are you, Rachel, how's your poor head?"

"It's fine," said Rachel, and then clearly mindful of all the spoiling it had already brought her, said, "Well, it's quite sore."

"Like my leg. Quite sore."

"When can you come home?" said Alex.

"Oh, not for a couple of days. I've got to be able to get myself around first. They're going to bring me some crutches tomorrow, see how I get on. The minute I can sprint down the ward on them, they'll let me go."

"Sprint!" said Alex. "I don't think so, Granny."

"Oh, you just watch me. Debbie, dear, are you all right?"

"Yes," said Debbie, "yes, I'm fine. Thank you. Must—must just go to the loo. Back in a minute."

She looked appalling, Flora thought, and she had clearly been crying. Maybe she'd had a row with Richard; maybe it was just shock. She smiled at the children. "Well, what an adventure we had, didn't we? Never let Granny take you on the Worm again."

· 516 ·

"Of course we will," said Alex. "We love the Worm. It's fun."

"Well, quite fun," said Rachel. She seemed very cheerful; obviously not seriously affected, saved by the blessed resilience of childhood. Unlike her mother, Flora thought, looking at Debbie coming back now, managing to smile.

"So, what have you been doing today?" she said.

"Not much," said Rachel. "It's boring without you."

"Thanks, Rachel," said Debbie.

"Sorry, Mummy. But it is."

"How's Colin?" said Emma. "I liked him, he was so kind."

"He is, very kind," said Flora, "and I'm glad you like him. He's coming in later. You might see him."

"Excuse me," said Debbie suddenly, and hurried out of the ward again.

"I don't think she's very well," said Emma, looking after her. "She seems to have a terrible cold, poor Mummy. She was trying to be brave and not cry after lunch, but I could tell . . ."

God, Flora thought, she's been seriously traumatised by this and no wonder. How on earth are she and I ever to become friends now?

"I can hear a phone," said Alex.

"A phone? Can't be."

"Well, it is. Listen . . ."

"Honestly," said Emma scornfully, "you're just hearing things—oh no, I heard it then too. Sounds as if it's under the bed."

"Might be Mum's new mobile she got from work," said Alex. "Here, give me her bag. No, it's stopped. I wonder if . . ." He started rummaging in Debbie's bag.

"Alex," said Flora, "you shouldn't do that, handbags are private things."

"How can it be private? It's always open. Here it is. I wonder if there's a message."

"How on earth do you know about mobile phones?" said Flora.

"My friend's dad's got one, he was showing me it the other day. It's just like Mum's. It's really good, you know. It doesn't just make calls, and take messages, you can find out about the traffic on it and share prices. Anyway, yes, she's got a message, let's see who that was. Dad probably . . ." He looked up at his mother who was coming back to Flora's bedside, smiling determinedly. "Mum, your phone just rang, you've got a message." He was listening, looking mildly puzzled; then he said, "Mum, who's Joel?"

And Flora watched as Debbie's face went first white then very flushed, and she snatched the phone from Alex and ran away again, out to the corridor: but Flora could still just see her, and she was holding the phone and listening very, very intently and then she switched it off and leaned against the wall, her hand held over her eyes. It was quite a long time before she came back.

"Poor Mummy," said Emma, "you do look so sad, and why are you crying? Is it because your cold is so bad?"

"Yes, I . . . I think so," said Debbie, and her voice was thick with tears. "Children, we must go."

"You've only just come," said Flora, "don't be ridiculous. Now you three, I want you to see if you can find yourselves some drinks or some sweets. There are some machines on the ground floor, quite near where you came in, and on the third floor as well, I think. Take my purse, there's lots of change in it, and you can buy two things each. All right?"

"Ye-es!"

"Flora, they'll get lost," said Debbie. "I really don't think that's a good idea."

"Debbie," said Flora firmly, "if they can survive a picnic on the Worm in midwinter and being cut off by the tide, they can survive a walk round a hospital. Children, if you get lost, just ask a nurse or a doctor where Ward Six is, all right? And don't leave the hospital."

"We won't."

They rushed off; Debbie sat staring after them, too overcome now even to pretend not to cry, tears streaming down her face.

"Debbie," said Flora gently, "why don't you tell me what the matter is. It'll help you."

"I can't."

"Of course you can. And if it's anything like I think, then let me tell you, I won't be shocked, which is obviously what you're thinking. Not in the least. In fact, if it is what I think, let me tell you I've been through it myself."

It had been so different, listening to that message. So different from listening to him before, being cold and angry and hostile. She had played it three times, unwilling to let it go.

"Debbie, it's Joel. I'm sorry about earlier, about being so angry. You must do what you think is right, and I'll try to understand and do what you want. New York is probably a good idea, yes. I don't think I could bear to be in the same city as you and not be with you . . . But I want you to know I love you, so much, and that this time with you has been perfect. Absolutely perfect." A pause and then, his voice shaking: "Bye, Debbie. Remember I love you."

She felt she could cope now, bear it now. It would go on hurting, but it wouldn't be quite as bad.

⁓

"I'm sorry," she said to Flora. "Can I have one of those tissues?"

"Of course." She passed her the box. "Now do you want to tell me? I promise you it'll help."

Debbie shook her head. "I can't. I really can't. It wouldn't be fair."

"Not fair to who?"

"You. And—and Richard."

"Ah, so I'm right. Well, there's no need to tell me, of course. Certainly not now. Maybe another time—whenever you want to. Or not at all." She reached out, stroked Debbie's hand very gently. "But—you are staying? Staying with us?"

Debbie nodded helplessly. How did she know this, how could she? "Good. I'm glad. It's the children who bear the brunt of these things. And you've made such a happy family. Really happy. Those children are the greatest credit to you."

Debbie nodded again. "I've tried to," she said.

"And you've succeeded. Debbie, listen. I know how difficult Richard must be to live with. He's exactly like his father. Demanding and possessive. My wings were clipped quite severely in the early years. I longed to do more with my work, my photography, but William wouldn't hear of it. It was unbearably hard at times."

Debbie stared at her. "I thought—I always thought . . ."

"That I thought my son was wonderful? Yes, well I do, of course. And

I also know he's good and kind and totally devoted to you all. But I'm not one of those blind mothers. I can see how he is, very clearly." She paused, then said, "It's going to be very hard for you. I know exactly how hard, in fact. It will hurt like hell. Bit like childbirth, I thought. Comes in waves."

"Oh my God," said Debbie, staring at her. "That's what I thought too. Exactly."

"Well, there you are. You see, I do understand. But it does end. Finally. And in a way you don't even want it to. You feel disloyal, mending, starting to forget. But you will, I promise you, you won't be able to help yourself. Things, little things at first, will start to work on you. You just have to be patient. Put up with it. Because it will be worth it. I promise you that."

Debbie sat there, gazing at her, feeling as if someone had given her a powerful drug, feeling suddenly able to go on.

"You're wonderful," she said finally, "and I'm so, so sorry I've been—been—"

"Oh, now don't let's start on all that," said Flora. "I'm just glad that finally I can be useful to you. Now listen, Debbie, I'd tell Richard you don't want to go to Scotland. That you won't go."

"What? But Flora, I have to. I—"

"You don't have to," said Flora briskly. "And you need your friends, you need your work. And you don't need that dreadful woman, Morag whatever her name is."

"Have you met her?"

"No, I haven't. But I don't need to. I can tell how ghastly she is. You just tell Richard you can't go. That he can stay there if he likes but you can't."

"He'll be terribly angry," said Debbie. "And it will ruin his career. No, Flora, I have to go. It's, well, it's one of the reasons I . . . I . . ." Her eyes filled again.

"At least tell him you need another term in London. Don't rush up there. I'll talk to him, if you like, put my two penn'orth in."

"Would you?"

"Of course. I can get him thinking, to see what it's going to do to you. He should have consulted you from the beginning. I felt very ashamed of him over that, Debbie, and of myself. I really thought I should have done a better job with him. Insensitive, overbearing behaviour! But he does have great virtues, as I said—"

"Yes, of course he does. And I do love him very much, really."

"I know. Oh, the children are back, and they've got Colin. How nice. Here, blow your nose again. Colin, how sweet of you to come again. Children, how did you get on?"

"Very well," said Emma. "We've got Smarties, look, and Coca-Cola cans and Mars Bars. And Mummy, this is for you, to cheer you up. It's your favourite, peppermint cream. Is that all right, Granny, do you mind?"

"Terribly," said Flora, smiling at her.

"Oh Emma," said Debbie, holding out her arms, enclosing her daughter in them, burying her face in her shining hair. "Thank you. Thank you so, so much."

"I love you, Mummy," said Emma, looking up at her and then resting her head against her. "I don't like it when you're sad."

And Debbie remembered Flora's words, and thought that perhaps this was the very first of the little things she had promised her would come.

"Come on, children," she said. "Let's leave Granny and Colin in peace."

"But Mum—"

"No, I mean it. Granny's very tired, and Colin wants some time to talk to her before visiting time ends. Give her a kiss, and thank her for the sweets."

She watched her children—worth all of it, all the pain—watched them kiss their grandmother, suddenly and surprisingly dear to her too; she bent down and kissed Flora herself and said, "I don't know how to thank you. But . . . thank you."

"You are thanking me," said Flora simply, "by staying with us. I couldn't bear you to have gone."

Those words stayed with Debbie and comforted her, over and over again, in the weeks that followed.

Chapter 60

"This is it. You look beautiful."

"Thank you. You don't look so bad yourself."

He didn't either: in his dinner jacket—would she ever be able to call it a tux?—his fair hair, newly trimmed, smoothly back, his blue eyes filled with love as he looked at her.

"Thanks. Excited?"

"So excited."

And she was: What girl wouldn't be, the centre of attention, admired, exclaimed over, her engagement party about to begin? And the Cartwrights had all been so sweet to her: even Frances had been really sensitive about her father: "We were so sorry, we could hardly bear it for you," and about her mother not coming: "Of course she mustn't come, she has enough to cope with, and the flight might be dangerous for her. We would have loved to have her with us, but—we understand."

And they did seem to: all of them. Dana had been especially sweet, tears in her eyes as she hugged Annabel, telling her she could talk about it if she wanted, but she would "just totally understand" if she didn't. She really liked Dana; she was her favourite Cartwright, apart from Jamie. Well, she wasn't actually a Cartwright, of course. But the others had been lovely too, obviously genuinely sympathetic.

She felt more in love with Jamie than ever; he seemed to have got even better-looking. And he was so excited about the engagement, about showing her off to everyone.

"Especially my friends, they can't wait to meet you. I already chose my ushers."

"Jamie, you can't have chosen them already. We're not getting married for at least eighteen months, are we?"

"Annabel, sweetheart, those eighteen months will just fly. I remember when Kathleen was marrying Joe, one minute we were reading the engagement announcement, the next we were doing the seating arrangements."

"How is Kathleen?" said Annabel, playing for time.

"She's just fine. Mother's so excited, she has the nursery decorated already—"

"What, at Kathleen's house?" This seemed a little excessive, even for Frances.

"No, no, here. She's expecting to have the baby here a lot. Obviously. She's using Kathleen's old room for it."

"Yes, I see," said Annabel.

❧

After dinner, the night before the party, she and Dana were sitting in the snug as they called it, their shoes kicked off, watching a terrible old movie. Jamie and Bif were ensconced with their father in his study discussing some case they were all involved in.

Dana glanced at her. "Looking forward to tomorrow?"

"So much, yes."

"Good. We all certainly are," said Dana. "I'm really loving you being in this family. You're so . . . refreshing. It's not just because you're young, your attitudes are so good."

"In what way?"

"Oh, I feel you're not going to let them turn you into a Cartwright. Did I just say that? I did not."

"OK, you didn't," said Annabel, and grinned at her.

"It was the champagne talking. But—you know. They're pretty formidable. You've no idea what a hard time I'm getting over this baby thing. I'm just getting to where my work's interesting, you know? I have my own caseload, it's great. Why should I give it all up to look after some squalling brat?" She sighed. "I'm sorry. Not your problem. And very disloyal of me."

"I don't see why you have to," said Annabel. "Give it all up, I mean. My mother didn't."

"No. I remember you saying that. She sounds great."

"She *is* great."

"She must have had such a tough time," said Dana, her large brown eyes clouded with sympathy. "Not just your dad dying, but being pregnant, and carrying on with everything. I mean, is she OK? It must have been so hard on you, Annabel, as well."

"Just a bit. But we've got so close over it, Mummy and me. We help pick up each other's pieces. Some days she's worse, some days I am. She's really upset about the inquest now. It's only another few weeks."

"There has to be an inquest? Why?"

"Well, because Daddy's death was linked to an accident. And because there's some doubt over whether it really was an accident or . . . or well, suicide."

Her voice shook. Dana turned to her, put her arm round her.

"How truly horrible for you. And for her. I'm so sorry."

"Yes, it is very horrible. Of course, we all would love it to be established as an accident. It would be so much nicer for us all, so much more hopeful. But how could it be proved now? It's so terrible to think of Daddy being in such despair it wasn't worth going on."

"Poor you," said Dana. "Poor all of you."

"Anyway," Annabel said, determined not to let the evening slide into gloom, "my mother worked right through three pregnancies, three babies. And now a fourth, of course."

"I guess your dad must have been pretty remarkable. To agree to that."

"I suppose he was," said Annabel. "I mean, we had nannies and so on. But it was more that he was so supportive and so proud of her, never complained if she was out or away at conferences. God, he was special. Oh dear." Her eyes had filled with tears. "Sorry, Dana, I guess it's a bit of an emotional occasion, what with one thing and another."

"Of course. I understand."

"Thank you. But really, if you want to work, nobody these days should have to stop working just because they have a child. It's—it's archaic. I certainly won't."

"Well, good for you," said Dana. She didn't look exactly convinced. "Have you discussed it with Bif?"

"Annabel, he's opposed to mothers working, he says they should stay home with their children. And to an extent I agree, of course. In an ideal world. But then not all of us are ideal people, are we?"

"Mummy always said she'd have been so miserable staying at home, we'd have been miserable too, so it was better for everyone that she worked."

"And how do you feel about it, now that you're grown? Do you have terrible complexes?"

"Oh, terrible," said Annabel with a grin. "So terrible that I intend to do exactly the same thing."

"Did you discuss this with Jamie?"

"Not yet. It seemed slightly premature. But I will."

"Let me know what happens, won't you?" said Dana. "I might even hide in the closet while you talk to him."

She smiled brilliantly, but Annabel felt she was actually close to desperation. Which provided yet another pang of panic.

e

The party passed in a glorious blur of endless people wanting to talk to her, telling her how thrilled they were to meet her and how wonderful that she was going to marry Jamie; of Mr. Cartwright's amazing speech, saying how charming and beautiful she was, and how happy they were to be welcoming her into the family; of hearing again and again Frances telling people she felt she was gaining a daughter and in no way losing a son; of Jamie's face flushed with pride as she made her own little speech—she could see from Frances's face that she felt it was a little forward of her, that if anyone else spoke it should have been Jamie. But she really wanted to do it, to thank everyone for coming, and the Cartwrights for being so wonderfully welcoming and kind, and how excited she and Jamie were about the future . . . and Jamie made a speech too, after that, full of references to "my fiancée" (much cheering) and "my future wife" (even more). There was an amazing buffet supper; and then there was a disco for the younger guests, and she danced endlessly with Jamie and all his friends, most of whom she liked very much.

And then later still, when most of the guests had left, all telling Jamie what an incredibly lucky guy he was, she sat with the family and chatted easily and happily, and conducted a bit of a postmortem about the party, and she went over to Mr. Cartwright and put her arms round his neck and kissed him, and thanked him for the party, and for making such a wonderful speech, and then she moved on to Frances and kissed her and thanked her too. And finally, they all went to bed; and Jamie joined her after the requisite thirty minutes and made the most perfect love to her, and she fell asleep in his arms, thinking she really must be the luckiest girl in the world.

Chapter 61

"Mummy?"

Elizabeth went out into the hall, gave her daughter a hug, said it was lovely to have her back; and then realised she was crying.

"Annabel, darling, what is it? Are you just sad at leaving him, or—"

"No. No, it's not that. Mummy . . ." She stopped, swallowed hard. "We're not engaged anymore." She held out her left hand. Her bare left hand. "I gave it back to him. It's over."

"But why? What's happened to you?"

"You, I think," said Annabel simply. "You being my mother and, just possibly, Dad being my dad."

It had begun the day before; they had been having lunch alone and she'd told Jamie about her new job, at the salon Florian was opening in the Fulham Road.

"Can you imagine, Jamie, I'll be a stylist in the smartest, coolest salon in London. I can't believe it. Aren't you proud of me?"

"Well," he said, and his voice had been rather flat. "Yes, it's wonderful. Well done."

She'd said, just slightly sadly, that he didn't sound very excited, and he'd said of course he was, but . . .

"You know what you always say, Mummy, that nothing counts before the but . . . but he sees my career now as being married to him, moving to Boston, having a family in due course. And I said yes, I saw it like that too, but still having a career. And he said that was not what he'd envisaged for us at all. And I said why not, that was what Dana wanted."

That had been a big mistake; he'd said Dana was causing Bif a lot of unhappiness, that he was desperate for children and she refused to have any.

"Jamie, that's nonsense," Annabel had said. "She does want to have babies, she just doesn't want to give up her job. That's all. I told her about Mummy, about how she's made it work . . ."

"Dana discussed it with you?" he said, and his voice was harsh suddenly. "What's it got to do with you?"

"Well, she's going to be my sister-in-law, I—"

"Annabel," Jamie said, "that's between Bif and Dana, not you."

"But if she can work and have a baby, why shouldn't she?"

"Because Bif doesn't want that. Because he feels she should be at home with the children. And I agree with him."

"You don't think she—or I could do both?"

"No, I don't. What Bif does, what I do too, is very gruelling and stressful. We work long hours and at the end of the day we need to come home to—to—"

"To what, Jamie?" She could feel a tight spring of anger beginning to uncoil.

"Well, to a well-run household, and a—a—"

"A little woman in a pinny? Jamie, come on!" She'd been so sure he was teasing she began to tease him back. "Barefoot, pregnant, and in the kitchen, is that how you think we should be, us wives? With a gleaming house and a dinner ready to leap out of the oven? Sorry, Jamie, you've got the wrong girl if—"

"Don't be ridiculous," he said. "Of course I haven't."

"Phew. For a moment I thought you meant all that rubbish."

And then there had been a silence; and then he said, "I did."

After that, she said, they'd had a real row, with him shouting at her and telling her she didn't appear to know what marriage and commitment meant, and her shouting at him and telling him he didn't appear to know what the real world was like, and certainly not what she was like, that she would never agree to be a Stepford wife, her sole aim to please and look after her man. Surely he couldn't expect that. And if he did, then they shouldn't be together.

"Don't you see, Jamie, if I was like that, you wouldn't love me. I'm me, you love me, not some figment of your imagination, not a carbon copy of your mother—"

He said they should leave his mother out of it, and that he hoped Annabel wasn't criticising her; she said of course she wasn't, but that Frances was another generation, a generation that saw things differently.

"Well, I'm afraid I don't," Jamie had said. "I don't think something so fundamental is susceptible to a passing trend."

"A trend! You think women having careers is a trend!"

"No, but women having children and careers is. It doesn't work. Why do you think the divorce figures have shot up? Why children are growing up undisciplined and undirected? Why there's so much juvenile crime?"

"Jamie," Annabel said, "I'm one of those undisciplined, undirected children. I grew up in a family where children and careers were absolutely compatible. My parents weren't divorced and we're not juvenile criminals."

He'd pulled back a bit then, said he was sorry, and they'd gone home and everyone had been there, and they'd pretended everything was all right; but that night she'd slept alone—or rather not slept. "I just lay there, going over and over it in my head, thinking how important it was to me, knowing his attitude was wrong, and this morning, when he took me to the airport, I said that unless he would promise to acknowledge that my career was important, agree to my working when we had children, I didn't want to marry him. And he said he couldn't do that. So I took off the ring and said goodbye to him and went through to departures without even kissing him. I felt quite brave at the time," she added, "but scared now. Oh Mummy, I do love him so much, but—I can't marry him, can I? Not if he really feels like that?"

"No," said Elizabeth, very gently, "I don't think you can. But darling, he's very young. They're obviously a powerful clan. He's been brainwashed all his life. It's going to take him a while to learn to see things differently."

Annabel shook her head. "You've no idea how stubborn he was being. They are so different from us. I actually said, it was one of my suggestions for us being together a bit more, why didn't he come to London for a year—his father has loads of contacts in London—and he said it was the most absurd idea, that he worked for Cartwrights and nobody else, and that if I wanted us to be together then I should move over there, right away. Tell me I've done the right thing, Mummy, please."

Elizabeth hesitated. This was a minefield. "I'm very proud of you for having the strength of your convictions, Annabel. And to be honest, I had been afraid the Cartwrights were overwhelming you rather. I can see now they weren't, so that's very important. And yes, it is something you have to work out between you. Some kind of compromise . . ."

"We won't be working anything out," said Annabel. "It's over."

"Well, I think that's a terrible pity. He loves you, very much, and you love him."

"But Mummy, I can't believe you're talking like this. You and Daddy made it work and—"

"Yes, we did," said Elizabeth, "but the cost was very high at times. Daddy was wonderful, but I know there were many times when he would have longed for a Frances Cartwright waiting at home for him, asking him about his day."

"Of course he wouldn't. You wouldn't have been you and he wouldn't have loved you."

"I know that. All I'm saying is, it isn't easy. It's as hard for him to cope with as staying at home would be on you. You have to recognise that, in your discussions with Jamie."

"There won't be any discussions," said Annabel. "I told you, I've given the ring back."

"I know. But he might come round, might think about it more carefully. Shake off some of the brainwashing."

She shook her head. "He won't. He's totally stubborn."

"Well, we'll see. Come on," she said, "you look terribly tired. Go on up to bed, and I'll bring you some tea. How would that be? And if Tilly comes in, I'll tell her you're asleep. You don't want to have to tell her about it as well, do you?"

"No," said Annabel. "No, I suppose not. But I'll have to, won't I? And an awful lot of other people. Oh dear."

She started to cry again; Elizabeth cuddled her for a while, and then sent her up to bed and went into the kitchen to make the tea. She felt very sorry and sad for Annabel, but also rather relieved. Not that she had broken off the engagement but that she needn't worry about her daughter so much. Annabel knew exactly what she was doing; she could take care of herself. Whatever happened.

⌒

Two days before the inquest, Robert Jeffries at the coroner's office telephoned Elizabeth. He said he hoped she was well, and not feeling too anxious about it all; and he asked her if she had any questions.

"No, not really, except what time should we be there?"

"We begin at nine thirty. So anything between nine and nine fifteen, I would suggest. You'll have your children with you, I believe?"

"Yes, all three of them."

"We don't have wonderful facilities, but I can take you to one of the waiting rooms, and if you come early enough, I can show you the court, where you'll be sitting and so on, before everyone arrives. It helps if it's familiar. Er . . . I have to warn you that there may be some press here."

"Press! Do they have to be, can't you stop them?"

"I'm afraid not, Mrs. Beaumont. Inquests are open courts, and the press can attend if they wish. Likewise members of the public. The thing is, in this case, your husband was well known and his death was reported in the papers. As was his funeral, of course. The article, the famous one that young man wrote, featured him quite largely as well, so—yes, I'm afraid they may well be there, the press. I'm so sorry. Now we have a very nice coroner, a Dr. Holden. Very kind and calm, and very good at keeping things moving."

"Moving?"

"Yes. People can get bogged down in detail, you see. Dr. Holden won't allow that. You'll like him. Now there's one other thing. You'll give evidence first, which I imagine you'll prefer. Get it over."

"Yes," said Elizabeth. "Er—what sort of things will he ask me?"

"Oh, he'll want you to confirm that you identified your husband. All you'll have to say is yes. That's a formality, of course, but it's legally necessary. We have your statement already, so a lot of what he asks you will refer to that, how you thought your husband was, his mental state, whether he had any medical problems, whether he'd said anything to you that indicated he might be considering taking his own life."

"I see. Well, thank you, Mr. Jeffries. Thank you so much. I'll see you on Wednesday."

"Indeed. Just ring the doorbell when you get there if it's closed, and I'll let you in."

How was she going to get through this: how?

e∽

Debbie was dreading the inquest. It wasn't the inquest itself, of course, although that wasn't going to be the best fun; it was the thought that Joel might be there. He'd been pretty involved with Simon over the article, which had been published, after all, only a couple of days before he'd died. She would be sitting in the same room as he was, contained by the same walls, breathing the same air . . . How was she going to bear it?

It had worked, Flora's plan. She had told Debbie to be very straightforward about it, just say that she was very sorry, but she really couldn't go up to Scotland for another term.

"Of course he'll be furious, but he'll get over it. And if he's very bad, then I'll talk to him. OK?"

"Thank you, Flora. Thank you very much."

He had been very bad, most unusually shouting at her, rather than moving into icy rage: What would he say to Morag, how could he do the job for another term on his own, what about the various schools the children were supposed to have left, and the house, supposing they sold the house? And how did he know she wouldn't do this next term, and the next and the next?

"You don't know," she said calmly, "except that I give you my word I won't. You'll have to trust me on it, Richard, I can't do more."

She said the schools wouldn't be a problem: she'd already rung them, to check, and they'd all said they'd be happy to keep the children for another term, that although they'd filled Alex's place, it was such a tiny class—only fifteen—they could easily accommodate him. Ironically, the state school was more awkward. But in the end they said yes too.

Anna was over the moon at hearing that Debbie could stay for another three months at Know How; she hadn't managed to replace her, nor had she properly worked out which of the accounts Debbie could do from Scotland. Which just left Morag—who had been very upset, Richard said, but marvellous just the same, and understanding too. He imparted this information over supper, having had a long conversation with her; Debbie and Flora, who had come home that day, became helplessly overwhelmed with giggles.

"I don't see what's so funny," Richard said rather stiffly, and Flora said through streaming eyes, "Richard, you are obsessed with that woman. If you could only hear yourself. Do give us, particularly poor Debbie, a break. I'm sure Morag is magnificent in every way, but she does make us ordinary mortals feel terribly inferior." She winked at Debbie as she said this; she exploded afresh and then said, "I'm sorry, Richard, but it's true, we feel we simply can't compete with Morag."

And then Debbie realised that she hadn't thought of Joel for at least ten minutes, and that laughing like that with Flora had been quite wonderfully enjoyable. Enjoyable! When she had never thought to enjoy anything again. Another little thing to tick off. She was surviving. She would survive. But not if she had to see Joel.

⌒

Annabel had heard nothing from Jamie; she had been right about him, then. Pigheaded, arrogant—a true Cartwright. She was well shot of him. She didn't even feel that bad. Except first thing in the morning. And last thing at night. And pretty often in between as well. She had more or less stopped crying. Well, she was doing it slightly less often. She'd get over it; she knew she would. She'd be fine. She'd be successful. Not a corporate wife. And when she was the first woman to own a chain of hairdressing salons, she'd be able to write to him and tell him. And it would be totally, totally worth it.

⌒

The day before the inquest, several people phoned Elizabeth to check she was all right, and to wish her well. David Green, of course, who was coming up and staying with them. Catherine, sweet Catherine, and equally sweet Lucinda, who said she was desperately nervous and sure she was going to get everything wrong.

"Lucinda," said Elizabeth, laughing in spite of herself, "there's nothing to get wrong. You've just got to answer their questions."

"Yes, I know. And I never can. I've told people I don't know where

· 532 ·

Cadogan Square is when I'm standing in it, by my own front door. But I'll do my best. Lots of love, Elizabeth. See you tomorrow."

Flora phoned, said she must try not to worry. "It'll soon be over now. We had to have one for William, you know."

"Why?"

"Well, he died within twenty-four hours of admission to hospital. It was dreadful, of course, but it lacked reality in a strange way. They're much less formal than a normal court, less frightening."

"Flora, I'm so sorry. What a ghastly thing."

"Oh, not really. One survives what one has to, don't you think?"

"I suppose so. Now—how are you going to get up here?"

"Oh, my friend Colin is driving me. He's got a very sleek Jaguar, very low to the ground, I can get in and out of it perfectly easily."

"I'd have liked you to stay," said Elizabeth, "but we're living in a shoe box."

"Oh, my dear, don't be absurd. Colin has booked us into the Savoy. We'll be fine."

Separate rooms, I hope, thought Elizabeth; and yearned as she so often did, to be able to share this delicious thought with Simon.

And Joel Strickland phoned her.

"Elizabeth, hello. I just wanted to call and say I will be there tomorrow. And that I hope you're not feeling too bad."

"That's kind. Well, I'm dreading it, of course."

"Of course. But these things are much less forbidding than you might think. I've been to dozens of them in my capacity of tabloid reporter. I mean, clearly it won't be easy for you, but there's something about coroners; they're so calm and make things seem so normal. I think it might not be quite as bad as you're expecting."

"Yes, someone else said much the same thing," said Elizabeth doubtfully. "Flora Fielding—I think you met her."

"Yes, I did," he said, and there was an odd silence. "And her daughter-in-law. I believe she's going to be there."

"Yes, she is."

Another silence, then: "And is your lovely daughter going to be there?"

"All the children are."

"That's brave of them," he said, "but then I suppose they would be. They've got brave genes. Please give Annabel my love."

He was a charmer, she thought: charming and thoughtful. She did hope he had a nice wife or girlfriend.

❧

The 2:30 p.m. British Airways flight from Barbados was an hour late getting in; it was after five when Felicity Parker Jones got away from the airport, and it took an hour and a half for her taxi to navigate the rush-hour traffic around Gatwick and to reach her house near West Dean in Sussex. By which time all the local shops were shut.

Felicity was starving; she made it a rule never to eat on planes, but the fish pie in her freezer was not an attractive colour and her housekeeper had most inconsiderately been taken to hospital with suspected appendicitis. Felicity decided to go to the Sailing Club to eat and sat down in the bar for a pre-supper gin and tonic.

"Good trip?" someone asked.

"Super. Wonderful sailing. Bought myself a new baby, actually. Forty-footer. Very pleased with her. God, it's a beautiful place. Now, is David Green about? I really want to ask him something."

"No, he's gone up to London," said Brian Thomas, the club secretary, "with Andy Peasmarsh. They're giving evidence at this inquest tomorrow."

"What inquest?" said Felicity.

"Simon Beaumont's. You did know he died, didn't you—drowned—dreadful tragedy?"

"Yes, of course. I was quite upset, I have to say. But why on earth are they having an inquest?"

"Well, it could be suicide, apparently. His financial situation and so on. Nobody can say for sure, of course."

Felicity sat staring at him for a moment or two, and then she stood up; she looked rather pale beneath her tan.

"I can say for sure," she said, "at least I think I can. I must try and get hold of David Green. It's really rather important."

Chapter 62

Debbie woke very early: feeling violently sick. This was going to be tough. Very tough. But Flora would be there. She would manage. Somehow. She hoped.

Hating herself, she took a lot of trouble over her appearance. She told herself it was because it was an important occasion and she would be the centre of the court's attention, albeit briefly. And then she remembered Joel telling her, when they had discussed the inquest, that people often came to such events looking extraordinarily different. "The last one I went to," he'd said, "there was a lady about Flora's age, all done up in furs and diamonds, and a funny old chap who was a plumber wearing his overalls." Just the same she washed her hair, put on a new shirt from Gap under her black suit, and spent more time than she would have normally done on her makeup.

"You look nice, Mummy," said Emma. "Going out to lunch?"

"No. I'm going to that thing called a court—remember I told you? I've got to give evidence."

"Gosh," said Alex, "like Rumpole, you mean?"

"A bit like that," said Debbie. "Now eat your breakfast. Jenny's going to collect you all from school, as I may be late."

"I've got used to you not being late," said Rachel, giving her a hug. "It's much nicer."

Another little thing. They were becoming more frequent. She was going to need them all today.

⁓

Flora had been up for two hours before joining Colin for breakfast. She had to do her physiotherapy exercises, take her painkillers, wash herself—how she longed for a bath—and then dress. It all took forever. She sank exhausted onto the dressing-table stool to do her hair, wondering if she actually had the strength. And then told herself not to be ridiculous. As if she had anything to complain about: compared with poor Elizabeth and her children—and just possibly Debbie. She was aware that Joel Strickland might be there; and she was fearful for Debbie's fragile recovery. Odd how she had taken Debbie's part entirely in this; she supposed because she had been through it herself and understood it in its entirety, from temptation to conclusion. She would be all right; they would all be all right. Especially if Richard made a bit of an effort. She had had one conversation with him, and intended to have more. She loved him dearly, but he wasn't always very sensitive. Just like his father.

She twisted her hair into its high knot and swung herself on her crutch out into the corridor.

❧

Elizabeth also woke up early. She lay quietly, in the rather small bed, thinking of the last time she had seen Simon, in a rather larger bed, and how he had told her he loved her, and how happy she had been all the following day. For the last time in her life, as far as she could see.

"Oh Simon," she said aloud, "why did you have to do it to us? Why, why, why couldn't you stay and let us help you?"

She felt a stab of the old anger and was pleased: that was the way to get through today, she thought, being angry with him. If a verdict of suicide or an open verdict was brought in she would never forgive him: never.

They arrived at the court just after nine, the four of them in a car that Peter Hargreaves, ever thoughtful, had provided: Annabel quiet and quite calm, Tilly visibly trembling, Toby determinedly stiff-upper-lipped.

It was a lovely day; Elizabeth wondered if it helped, and decided it didn't. Dark storm clouds would be more appropriate. The building was brick with a large wooden door, probably Edwardian, Elizabeth thought—why was she noticing such things?—in a wide, tree-lined street just behind the Brompton Road. A small crowd was already waiting outside.

She rang the brass bell as instructed by Mr. Jeffries. He appeared immediately, smiled his wonderfully calm, reassuring smile. "Good morning, Mrs. Beaumont. And what a good one it is. Now you must be . . ."

"Annabel," said Annabel, "and this is my brother, Toby, and my sister, Tilly."

"Welcome, all of you. Now, why don't you have a look at the court-room, while there's nobody here." He led them along a corridor which opened into a large square hall: and through a door, which he opened with a flourish.

"Come in," he said.

"Goodness," said Annabel. "It's rather—rather nice." Somehow they hadn't expected this: a light, high-ceilinged room with rows of seats, rather pew-like; a large Edwardian fireplace; tall, vaulted windows; and very nice brass wall lights. Set higher than the rest of the room was the coroner's bench.

"Now this is where the family—where you—will sit," said Mr. Jeffries, indicating the front two rows. "And here the press, and that is the witness box, over there. Everyone else just settles themselves down. Friends probably behind you, officials of various kinds, doctors and so on, over there. There's plenty of room, as you can see. Now, do you have any questions?"

"No, I don't think so," said Elizabeth, "except—do you have a loo?" She had already been three times since breakfast. How did babies play quite such havoc with the bladder?

They drank coffee in the waiting room and heard the noise level rising as more people arrived. Elizabeth could hear Flora's clipped, rather musical tones, Lucinda's absurdly Sloane Ranger vowels (and Blue's rather different, equally strong ones), Martin Dudley's boom, and then Debbie Fielding's less-posh voice, very subdued.

And then they were ushered in by Mr. Jeffries, and the courtroom was suddenly full of familiar faces, people Elizabeth knew; it was rather like a wedding, she thought, and felt absurdly that she should rush round greeting people, or even that she should say a quick prayer for the right verdict . . .

They sat in the family pew, the girls on either side of her, Tilly still shaking, hanging on to Elizabeth's hand as if it was a lifeline, Annabel staring calmly in front of her, Toby glaring at his feet.

And then, "Rise, please," Mr. Jeffries said, and the coroner, Dr. Holden, came in from the side, mounted the steps to the bench, nodded briefly to them, and they all sat down again.

It had begun.

Dr. Holden had an extraordinarily nice voice, that was the first thing

Elizabeth noticed; educated, well modulated, and very clear without being in the least loud. It was going to help, that voice. He had fair, gently greying hair, and was wearing an extremely well-cut grey pinstriped suit. He could have been one of their neighbours in the Boltons. He smiled very briefly in her direction and then said, "We are considering today the death of a man by drowning. If we may start, Mr. Jeffries?"

Mr. Jeffries walked over to the witness box and took the oath. Somehow, in the pleasing half informality of the court, she hadn't expected that, hadn't expected all the stuff about Almighty God and the truth, the whole truth, and nothing but . . .

He picked up a sheaf of notes and started to read from it. "The deceased was identified as Simon Gerald Beaumont, aged forty-seven years. He was born on May the seventeenth, 1943, and he lived at number seventeen Bolton Place, London SW7. His body was found on the French coast, at Gravelines, near Calais, on August the twenty-sixth, where a postmortem was performed and the cause of death stated as drowning. A dry drowning—that is to say, one where the water reaches the top of the trachea and closes it, shortly after which the heart stops.

"The deceased was identified initially in France by his passport, which had remained in the pocket of his trousers, and later by his widow, Mrs. Elizabeth Beaumont. His body was brought to England and taken to the mortuary at the Kensington and Fulham Hospital.

"Until shortly before his death, Mr. Beaumont had been employed as a board director of Graburn and French, Merchant Bankers, and—"

She was losing concentration already. It just didn't seem relevant, was nothing to do with her. The body had nothing to do with Simon, or the deceased; it was all very odd. Mr. Jeffries was continuing to read from his statement; a report from toxicology stated that blood samples contained alcohol and analgesic, consistent with perhaps one or two glasses of wine and one or two paracetamol . . . insufficient to cause any loss of consciousness; there was indication of a blow to the back of the head, probably from the boom; the deceased had been wearing a life jacket but it was not inflated; there was no indication of foul play; the boat, a twenty-two-foot Seal, was found intact the following day adrift in the Channel. Mr. Beaumont had apparently been fit and well and in good spirits the day before his death.

Dr. Holden leaned forward. "Thank you, Mr. Jeffries. Perhaps we can hear now from Mrs. Elizabeth Beaumont. Mr. Jeffries, would you read Mrs. Beaumont's statement?"

She listened as Mr. Jeffries told the court that she had identified Simon's body and where, that a visit from the police had informed her of his death by drowning, that he had been in good spirits the day before . . . again she found it hard to concentrate.

"And now, Mrs. Beaumont," Dr. Holden said in his beautifully courteous voice, "would you please go to the witness box."

Suddenly it was all real again: real and terrifying. She felt sick, she felt panicky, her mouth dry, her head spinning. She stood up and stared at Dr. Holden, and couldn't move.

"Mrs. Beaumont are you all right?"

For a long time, it seemed, in that courtroom there was silence: everyone looking at her. She could see the mass of faces, some kindly, some concerned, some shocked, some embarrassed. She realised that in spite of carefully dressing in a looser jacket, her pregnancy must be obvious: she was nearly five months now and without the taut stomach muscles of her twenties to help conceal it. She felt absurdly foolish, desperately alone; the full horror of her situation hit her suddenly. Here she was, alone in a courtroom, widowed, pregnant, giving evidence about her husband. Her late husband. Who had abandoned her, abandoned her to this.

And then she saw Annabel looking up at her, standing up too, taking her hand, and Tilly also standing, putting her arm round her waist, and strength soared back into her.

"Yes," she said, with a quick smile at her two daughters. "Yes, I'm perfectly all right. Thank you."

She walked over to the witness box; Mr. Jeffries gave her some water. She sipped it gratefully, and then put her hand on the Bible.

"I swear by Almighty God," she began, and heard her own voice growing in confidence, and when she had finished, Dr. Holden smiled at her, and she felt as if she had just passed some tricky exam. Which she supposed, in a way, she had.

"Would you like to sit down while you give your evidence, Mrs. Beaumont?" Dr. Holden said, and, "No," she said, "no, I'm perfectly all right now, thank you."

"Very well. I see you live now at 14 Kensington Avenue, and you are employed by Hargreaves, Harris and Osborne, who are"—he paused, looked at his notes—"advertising agents."

"Yes, that's correct."

"And what is your position there?"

"I'm the managing director."

"I see." He looked up, just slightly surprised, and then smiled at her briefly—and it made her feel better, that reaction, slightly less vulnerable somehow, that she could still impress—and then went back to his notes.

"Now, you have moved from Bolton Place, I see. Could you tell us the reason for that?"

"Yes. We were forced to sell our house. We lost a lot of money at Lloyd's and—"

"And was the house already on the market on August the twenty-first?"

"Yes, it was."

"Was your husband distressed by that? By being forced to sell the family home?"

"Of course. We both were."

"Thank you. Now, it was you who identified your late husband's body?"

"Yes, it was."

"And you last saw him alive on the evening of August the twentieth. Perhaps you could tell us about that."

"I came home very late; Simon was half asleep. I had been working on a presentation."

"A presentation? Could you tell us what that is?"

"It's an advertising term. It describes work that you present to a client, work that will promote a product."

"I see. And did you have any kind of conversation that evening?"

"Not really, no. We were both terribly tired. We went to sleep." After making love; after making this baby. The last thing he did for me.

"And did he tell you where he was going in the morning?"

"No, he didn't. But he left me a note, to say he had gone sailing. That he'd be back probably that same night, but quite late."

"You didn't actually see him that morning?"

"No."

"And did he often go sailing? During the week?"

"Often—he loved it. He had a sailing boat of his own once, but he had had to sell it. And not usually during the week, no, but he had recently lost his job, he had been dismissed by the bank he had worked for, for twenty-five years, and—"

"Yes, we will come to that. So it was not anything out of the ordinary that he went sailing?"

"Not at all, no."

"And was he a competent sailor?"

"Very competent. He had won many races, had many trophies."

"And had he been depressed during the days leading up to August the twentieth?"

She hesitated. "Not exactly depressed. That wasn't his style. But he was worried. He had lost a great deal of money at Lloyd's, as I said. And he had lost his job. We were selling the house. It wasn't a situation likely to make him very cheerful."

"Was he inclined to be depressed?"

"Not at all. He met life head-on, always had; he was meeting this head-on—"

"He wasn't undergoing any treatment for anxiety or depression?"

"No, of course not. As I said, he wasn't inclined to be depressed."

"And were there other changes to your lifestyle recently?"

"Well, yes. We had a house in Sussex, which we sold over a year ago."

"Would you describe your marriage as happy, Mrs. Beaumont? Forgive me for asking."

"Very happy," said Elizabeth firmly. She felt suddenly acutely aware of her bump.

"Thank you. And your own employment was perfectly stable, was it? There was no question of your losing your job?"

"No, there wasn't."

"You have quite a large family. Three children at public school . . ."

"Only two when Simon died. Our older daughter had been working for a while."

"I see. Still, even two is expensive."

"Well yes. But I could pay the fees. He wasn't worried about that."

"Now I see that your husband was involved in a lawsuit with Lloyd's?"

"He would have been, yes. It hadn't begun."

"That must have been expensive."

"Yes, indeed. We were planning to invest some of the proceeds of the house in it."

"So you were supportive of him in that, were you, Mrs. Beaumont?"

"Yes. I felt at first it meant further risk, but I came to see that if we gave the money to Lloyd's, they would continue to demand more, ad infinitum. Better to let them sue us, we thought."

"I see. Thank you, Mrs. Beaumont. You may sit down. I would now like to hear from Mr. Beaumont's GP."

❧

Dr. Rice's evidence was swiftly over: Simon had been in excellent health, was exceptionally fit for his age, and had an extremely well-adjusted and optimistic outlook on life. He had never prescribed anything more for him than an occasional course of antibiotics, and certainly never any antidepressants or even sleeping pills. He had last seen him a year earlier for an annual checkup; he had passed it twenty-twenty.

"Thank you, Dr. Rice. Mr. Martin Dudley, please."

❧

Dudley was self-righteous even in his statement; on his questioning, more so. He hadn't wanted to terminate Simon's employment but had been forced to do it by the terms of his contract. Mr. Beaumont was about to be involved in a lawsuit against Lloyd's and possibly to become bankrupt, and therefore could not remain as a director of the bank. Yes, Mr. Beaumont had taken the news well.

"You make it sound as if he was grateful to you," said Dr. Holden, rather briskly. "Were there no harsh words uttered at all? May I remind you that you are under oath, Mr. Dudley."

Elizabeth wanted to climb up onto the bench and hug him. Dudley looked deeply embarrassed. "As I recall, Mr. Beaumont did say he thought perhaps I could have tried to find a way round the problem. He was quite . . . quite offensive."

"What exactly did he say?"

"He . . . he called me a miserable, mean, cowardly bastard," said Dudley with extreme reluctance.

"Anything else?"

"No. Well, he said he hoped I didn't think this was going to finish him. I said of course not."

"Did that not occur to you, though?"

"No. He was a very self-confident, competent person."

"I see. And then?"

"And then he left the building. We never saw him again."

"Thank you, Mr. Dudley. You may sit down." He watched Dudley return to his place then said, "Well now, where do we go from here?" He looked out at the court, his handsome face thoughtful. I bet he wanted to be an actor, Elizabeth thought.

"I think we should hear from the people who saw him in the two or three days before his death. Could we begin with Mrs. Lucinda Cowper."

❧

They were all wonderful, Simon's girls. They all said he had been amazingly cheerful, considering how extensive his worries were. He was fantastic, Lucinda said, "So brave and upbeat and good."

"Did you see a lot of Mr. Beaumont?" asked Dr. Holden. "I mean, was he a good friend of yours?"

"Oh yes, terribly good. We had lunch sometimes, and before I had the baby—"

"The baby?"

"Yes, I've just had a baby. Well, about six weeks ago."

"I see. Now you are still married, Mrs. Cowper?"

"Well, yes I am, but the baby . . ." God, she was making a hash of this. "I think I'd better start again," she said. Her blue eyes were huge and earnest. "Sorry. I was married, to someone who had also lost a lot of money at Lloyd's, that's how I met Simon—Mr. Beaumont—but the father of my baby is . . . was . . . The father of my baby is that gentleman over there," she pointed at Blue, who half stood up, as if ready to acknowledge any applause. "It was a rather difficult time, you can imagine,

· 543 ·

but whenever I was a bit down, I used to ring Simon for a chat, and he always cheered me up. He cheered us all up."

"And did Mrs. Beaumont know about these chats?" asked Dr. Holden. He was clearly very taken with Lucinda.

"Yes, of course she did. We all had connections with Lloyd's. And we met at Ascot, things like that."

"I see," said Dr. Holden. He was clearly struggling now not to laugh.

"Anyway, I felt a bit bad because Simon wanted to have lunch with me, the day before—the day before . . . Oh dear." She stopped, wiped her eyes. "And I felt a bit bad because I couldn't. But he said, 'Let's do it next week,' and he said he'd ring me and fix it."

"But he didn't set a date then?"

"No. No, he didn't."

"Thank you, Mrs. Cowper."

⁐

Catherine was next; she said he'd been really kind and good to her, he'd got her a job at the bank which had saved her bacon. Dr. Holden asked her to explain how at this point—"But when he was fired, they fired me too. He was very upset about that."

"In what way?"

"Well, he enjoyed being able to help people. It was important to him. And that day, the day before the accident, he came to see me with a big bunch of flowers, to say he was sorry."

"Sorry that you'd been fired?"

"Yes."

"Although not by him?"

"Well, no, but he felt responsible. He took it all on himself, rather."

There was a silence, while Dr. Holden made a note.

⁐

Where was he, Debbie wondered in an agony of tension. Maybe he wasn't coming at all, maybe he was already in New York and hadn't got to come . . . God, this was awful. Horrible. Every time the door opened, her heart quite literally seemed to stop. God, oh God—

"Could we hear now from Mrs. Deborah Fielding?" Well, at least she hadn't got to stand there, giving evidence with him watching her. She'd be able to speak, to think; just the same, she was shaking violently as she put her hand on the Bible, swore the oath. She listened to her statement. A statement from someone very calm and competent. Who would have guessed that someone had been caught up in a kind of madness—reckless, lying, dangerous, adoring madness? Ready to jettison her husband, her family, everything she had? Who would think it, looking at her now, composed, careful, neatly dressed?

"Mrs. Fielding." The coroner smiled at her; he was quite handsome, she supposed, in a middle-aged sort of way. Not unlike Simon, actually. Not unlike the Simon she had so resolutely disliked until she came actually to love him for his kindness, his patience with her, his interest in what she did, his wise counsel. Not as she had loved Joel, of course, but loved him just the same. And he was gone . . .

"Mrs. Fielding. Perhaps you can tell us exactly how you came to know Mr. Beaumont?"

"Yes." Her voice was faint now, faint with fright. The door was opening. She . . . no, it was all right, it was yet another carafe of water being passed to someone—Flora this time, thank God, thank God. "I met him through my mother-in-law," she said, her voice firmer now. "I got very fond of him and he was very, very kind to me."

"In what way?"

"He advised me on my career. He was imaginative and clever, and he loved helping people. He was sort of a family friend," she added. "I used to see him when he went to Wales with his daughter, to stay with my mother-in-law. She was looking after a horse for them."

Oh, and he introduced me to my lover. I forgot to mention that. Who might walk through the door any minute now.

"Yes, I see. And I believe you saw him very soon after he had been fired from the bank."

"Yes, that's right. I offered to buy him a drink."

"You offered to buy him a drink? An interesting way round."

"Not at all. He'd bought me drinks from time to time, and I felt it was my turn."

"Yes, I see. Well, that was very generous of you. And how did you find Mr. Beaumont on that occasion?"

"Well, he was slightly anxious, but full of plans. He was going to mount this lawsuit, you know, and—"

"Indeed. Now, this was some time before he went on that fateful sail, wasn't it?"

"Yes. A couple of weeks."

"And did you see him after that?"

"I spoke to him several times. Including the day before he died."

"And how was he that day?"

"Well . . ." she hesitated. "He was a bit subdued."

"Could you define subdued?"

"He was less . . . less cheery than usual. But far from depressed."

"And what was the purpose of his phone call?"

"Oh, just to have a chat. He was at a bit of a loose end. And to ask me to lunch."

"Really? And did you agree?"

"I said I couldn't, that day." She'd said worse than that, she'd said she was too busy to talk. Suppose that had done it? Suppose it had been that, that had tipped the balance? "But he said another time, maybe next week. He said he'd be very much around."

"Right. Well, thank you, Mrs. Fielding. And now I see we have another Mrs. Fielding. Mrs. Flora Fielding." He looked at Flora as she stood up, assisted by Colin. "Are you able to get up into the witness box, Mrs. Fielding?"

"I most certainly am."

She heaved herself across the court on her crutches and was helped up into the box. She stood there looking magnificent in the blue velvet jacket that she'd worn the very first time she'd met Simon. She'd worn it deliberately, in his memory, the better not to let him down.

"May I tell you before you ask me any questions," she said, having taken the oath, "the last thing I said to Simon Beaumont was, did nothing ever get him down? And he said, 'Not much.'"

"The procedure of the court is for me to ask the questions, Mrs. Fielding," Dr. Holden said briskly, "which you are required to answer. Please observe that."

"Very well."

"Now how was his mood that afternoon? When you had the lunch referred to in your statement."

"Well, he was very upset. Briefly," she added hastily, "and more angry than anything."

"Why was that, do you think?"

"He'd been involved in getting this lawsuit together. Against Lloyd's. It was only in the planning stages, but he was trying to gather evidence . . ."

"Ah yes. I see we have a statement from Miss Broadhurst, of Evans Dixon Campbell. Perhaps we should hear from her next. Anyway, was this evidence forthcoming?"

"No, it wasn't. I felt my Members' Agent at Lloyd's might be able to provide some information that would be helpful. But he couldn't."

"I see. And Mr. Beaumont had set great store on this information, had he?"

"He was very hopeful about it, yes."

"So would you say he was very disappointed?"

"Well yes. Yes, I would."

"How did you and he meet, Mrs. Fielding?"

"At a Lloyd's meeting. Or to be precise, a meeting of Members of our main syndicate at Lloyd's. We became friends; I was able to look after one of his daughters' horses at my house in Wales."

"He must have been very grateful."

"He was indeed."

"So you were a victim of Lloyd's? And—forgive me—have you come out of it unscathed?"

"No, not really. My house has been saved by a legal loophole. But at that point, I did think I would lose it. Mr. Beaumont was very upset about that also."

"Why particularly?"

"Well, because of his daughter's horse, which was being stabled by me. I clearly couldn't keep him in a flat in Swansea."

"Indeed not." Dr. Holden twinkled at her, and then said more soberly, "So more unhappiness, more worry for Mr. Beaumont."

"Well yes, but I'm sure he would have worked something out. He was a very, very resourceful person."

"I'm sure. Let me just ask you again, when you parted on that afternoon, was he visibly upset?"

"Well, he was," said Flora, "but as I told you, he was still in positive mood."

"Thank you, Mrs. Fielding. You may sit down."

She'd failed him. She felt terrible; she'd made a complete hash of it, barging in like that, speaking before she should have done, bossing everyone about as usual, even the coroner. And damaging Simon's cause. She felt suddenly near to tears and nudged Colin to give her a handkerchief. He looked at her alarmed as she wiped her eyes; such weakness was very unusual.

⁓

Fiona Broadhurst took the stand. She looked very self-assured, very cool. "Do you frequently go to lunch at the Caprice with clients, Miss Broadhurst?" Dr. Holden smiled at her, an almost conspiratorial smile.

He likes her, Elizabeth realised, likes what she represents, literally law and order.

"No, not very often. But Mr. Beaumont was very generous—"

"Despite being virtually penniless?"

"I don't think being penniless changes a personality," said Fiona coolly.

"It seems not. Go on."

"He wanted to tell me something important, he said."

"And what did he want to tell you?"

"That he had what he hoped was some evidence—tape-recorded evidence. I had to tell him it wouldn't satisfy a court, as the person talking didn't know he was being recorded, although a judge might consider the contents as background evidence."

"Indeed," said Dr. Holden. "Quite correct."

Fiona gave him a very cold look.

"And how did Mr. Beaumont take this news?"

"He was very upset. His confidence had obviously taken a beating."

God, thought Elizabeth, this isn't helping—we don't want to hear this.

"We've heard a lot about this confidence of Mr. Beaumont's. You are the first person to imply today that it might have been shattered."

She was silent.

· 548 ·

"So then what happened?"

"He said he still wanted to go ahead with the lawsuit."

"And was he disappointed about your reaction to his news?"

"I would say so, yes."

"I see. And did you discuss it any further after that?"

"No, we didn't. He said he would tell the others involved himself. And then we talked of other matters."

"Legal matters?"

"No. More general ones."

"And there were no other conversations in the restaurant that day? No one came up to the table?"

"Well . . . I went to take a phone call, outside in the street. And as I came back, I saw him talking to someone."

"Just exchanging a greeting?"

"No. They were—she was . . ."

"She? This was a lady?"

"Yes, it was."

"A young lady?"

"I would say she was in her late thirties, early forties. She gave him a card, and then she went back to her table and they didn't meet again."

Elizabeth felt herself tauten: the old familiar fear surfacing.

"He didn't tell you who she was?"

"No."

"Thank you, Miss Broadhurst."

He turned his brief, charming smile on the court. "So here is a man with good reason to be depressed, a man who logic tells us should be depressed, and yet who, by all accounts, was not depressed at all. Very admirable. He was obviously a very strong character indeed. I think we should take a break now, stretch our legs. I would also like to hear evidence from the journalist, Mr. Strickland. Has he arrived yet? I know he was going to be late."

How could they say his name like that, Debbie wondered, give this desperately crucial information about him while sounding perfectly normal? How could she still be sitting here calmly, looking up at the bench, when she wanted to jump up and down and scream?

"I'm told he's on his way now, Dr. Holden. Hopefully within the next half hour . . ."

Definitely hopefully, thought Debbie, almost his last words to me, the last time we were together. They shouldn't be using those words here, they belong to us.

"He was out of London last night, working in Liverpool, and the train was very badly delayed."

"How very unusual," said Dr. Holden with a smile. "Thank you. Well then, let us reconvene in fifteen minutes exactly."

Mr. Jeffries said, "All rise," and Dr. Holden stepped down from the bench and disappeared, and life briefly became itself again.

$$e \sim$$

Toby was very angry. "He's just setting out to trip everyone up, make them say Dad was depressed when he wasn't."

"I know," said Elizabeth wearily. Who was that woman who gave Simon her card? On the last afternoon of his life. How dare he? How dare she, indeed . . .

$$e \sim$$

Debbie left the courtroom, went to one of the officials. "I've given my evidence," she said. "Is it all right if I go now?"

"I should think so. I'll go and ask Mr. Jeffries."

Be quick, Mr. Jeffries, please be quick. I have to get away from here before . . . before . . .

"Yes, that's fine. Is there a number where we can get you if we really need you? Very unlikely, but . . . you're not leaving London, are you?"

"No, I'm not, and I have a mobile phone. The number's here, look, on my card."

"Right, well, I'll give that to them but I don't suppose we'll need it. Thank you for coming, my dear."

She started to run down the corridor; she'd have to say goodbye to Flora later, phone Elizabeth, hear the verdict, but she had to get away now, at once, quickly, before . . .

She shot out of the door into the brilliant sunshine; slightly dazzled by it, she saw a taxi had pulled up across the street. No, no, please no—yes, yes, please yes.

He stood there, ten yards away from her, perhaps less, stock-still, just looking at her. And she stood, stock-still also, frozen in time and fear and longing, looking at him.

Who she loved more than anything in the world—except, except—who she had wept over, longed for, dreamed of literally, night after night, remembered him loving her with such force it shook her physically at times, wanted it still so, so much. There, standing there, real, hers for the asking. And she stepped off the kerb and started to walk across the road towards him as if compelled by something outside herself, and he did the same, their eyes fixed on each other, held absolutely, her own filled with tears.

And she might even then have gone, forgotten all her brave good resolutions, gone with him, into happiness; but the cab hooted and the cabbie shouted, "Another fiver mate, please," and he turned briefly to look at him, and as he did so her strength, her own will came back to her, and she ran, ran faster in her high heels than she would have thought possible, gasping, fighting for breath, away from him, away from all of it, terrified that he would follow her, speak to her, touch her, longing for him to follow her, speak to her, touch her.

Only he didn't; and after five minutes she felt safe, and walked on very fast for what seemed a long time and then found she was in a McDonald's—and sank down on a chair and sat staring, staring out of the door, still afraid he would come in; and then she started to cry, quite gently, when she realised he wouldn't.

Chapter 63

Joel had given his evidence: Elizabeth felt close to despair. It had been yet another story of disappointment; of Simon's excitement, of his conviction that Joel had delivered him the smoking gun: only to be told by Fiona Broadhurst that it was of little use.

Joel looked very shaken as he walked into the court. Obviously the trauma of being late, of the delayed train, had taken its toll. As he sat down again, he very briefly buried his face in his hands. And then sat back, smiled at her and at Annabel, but rather wearily, and fixed his eyes very firmly on the witness box.

❧

The next witness was David Green; and his session in the box took a long time. Every detail from when Simon arrived at the Sailing Club "later than he said he would—about half past ten or even eleven" to when he had untied David's boat around an hour later, saying he would be back in five or six hours.

"And how was he?" Dr. Holden asked. "How was his state of mind?"

"Extremely cheerful. Almost excited, I'd say."

"Really?"

"Yes, indeed. He insisted on ordering a bottle of champagne which he shared with me before he went off."

"He didn't tell you why he was excited?"

"No, he didn't."

"Would you say he was in any way overexcited?"

Elizabeth felt Toby stiffen, put her hand over his and pressed it gently.

"No," David Green said. "He was just as he always was when he was feeling particularly cheerful."

"And he was sailing your boat, Mr. Green? You'd lent it to him?"

"That is correct."

"Are you in the habit of lending your boat to people?"

"From time to time, yes. Especially to Simon. He had been very upset when the *Lizzie* had to go, naturally, and I said if he was ever desperate for a sail, he could take mine."

"And did he say where he was going?"

"He said he had wondered briefly about going over to France, and staying the night there if necessary, at a small hotel in Saint-Vaast, a few miles south of Cherbourg, that we often use, but that as he had a lot to do, he'd almost certainly be back by evening."

"And when he left, the weather was good?"

"Yes, it was. Fine, with a lovely breeze. The last thing he said to me was"—he paused, blew his nose—" 'This is going to be a perfect sail. One for the archives.' That was an expression he often used."

A pause; then Dr. Holden said, "And what of the weather forecast?"

"There were warnings of fairly stiff breezes mid-Channel. Nothing to worry about, just enough to make things a bit more exciting."

"I see. So then he went straight off?"

"More or less. I walked him over to *Princess Charming* on her mooring. He had his life jacket with him, actually put it on while I told him a couple of things about the boat."

"What things did you want to tell Mr. Beaumont about your yacht?"

"Oh, that I'd had a new radio fitted—ship-to-shore variety, that is—showed him how it worked. Basically it was a modern version of the one I'd had before."

"He wouldn't have a problem with it?"

"Good Lord no. And I said there were some beers stashed away in the locker. Oh, and he asked me if there were any paracetamol in the locker, that he had a bit of a headache. I told him he shouldn't drink champagne at breakfast time, and he said it was a good idea to drink champagne any time. And then—well, then he said—he said goodbye."

"What were his exact words, Mr. Green?"

"He said, 'Cheerio, David, and thanks again. Wish me luck.'"

"Why do you think he wanted you to wish him luck?"

"I have no idea."

"Was that something he often said?"

"When we were racing, yes. Not normally, no."

"So why do you think he said it?"

"I think he was just excited, looking forward to the day, dying to get out there . . ." His voice trailed away.

"Right. And when did you first suspect something was wrong?"

"Well, I was vaguely uneasy when he didn't come back at sundown. And there had been reports of a really nasty squall in the Channel."

"But you weren't worried about him, even then?"

"Not at first, no. I thought he'd probably decided to stay the night in France after all."

"Did you try to make contact with the boat?"

"I did, yes. As the evening went on, I radioed constantly, but there was no reply. And if he had docked in France, he wouldn't have heard it anyway. So I was a little worried, but not seriously. Simon was a superb sailor. There were very few situations he couldn't have dealt with. But of course one never knows how bad these squalls are going to get. And a Seal isn't a very big boat really. The *Lizzie,* that is to say Simon's boat, was a Contessa, quite a bit bigger, and he was used to sailing her, so he could have found himself in more trouble than he might have expected."

"Yes, I see. And then, when did you get the first report that your boat had been found?"

"Not until the following morning. It was drifting, south of Calais; the mast was slightly damaged, but otherwise it was completely unharmed."

"And did you think, immediately, that Mr. Beaumont must have had an accident?"

"Yes, I'm afraid I did. So I called the emergency services and . . ."

e͡

Dr. Holden called another break after that: an hour for lunch.

e͡

Elizabeth and her children were brought sandwiches, and more coffee, while everyone else went off to find food. Except Joel Strickland; he stayed, sitting quietly, in the other, larger waiting room. Annabel saw him when she went in search of more coffee.

"Hi, Joel, nice to see you. You OK?"

"Oh—yes. Yes, thanks." He appeared to be only half with her, his mind elsewhere. After a moment or two he smiled at her and said with an obvious effort, "Is your mum all right?"

"I think so. She's holding herself together with safety pins. She'll be better when it's over. Obviously we're all praying for a misadventure verdict. It will help her so much. But not sure we'll get it. Somehow the evidence that it might be . . . well, not misadventure, is stacking up. Which will be very hard for her. For all of us, really."

"Of course." He sighed heavily, forced a smile at her. "Well, we must all just hope. He's a good bloke, Holden. Very thorough. Well, nice to see you, Annabel."

As if it was nice to see anyone at the moment. Even stunningly beautiful girls like Annabel. He wanted to be with a girl who wasn't really beautiful at all, who was a bit too skinny, and had a smile that could light up England, when it came, which it didn't unless she really meant it . . .

Flora appeared in the doorway. "Hello, Joel. So glad you got here. How are you?"

"Oh, I'm fine. Yes. Thanks. I'm off to New York in a couple of weeks. To run the *News* office there."

"Oh, how marvellous. What fun. So good for one, a complete change of scene. It gives such a boost."

"Well, hope so."

"You missed Debbie," she said. "She had to rush away."

"Debbie?" he said.

"Debbie, yes, Joel. She's been a bit . . . low recently. But I think she's beginning to feel a little better now. She's been very brave," she added. "I've been so proud of her. And so sorry for her too."

"Er—yes."

She smiled at him suddenly, a very sweet smile, reached out and patted his hand. "Goodbye, Joel. Take care of yourself. Enjoy New York. You will, I promise you. Even if you don't think it now."

"Goodbye, Mrs. Fielding."

"Flora, please. Well, I'd better get back. My escort will think I've done a runner. Let's hope for a good verdict. A correct one, that is."

"Yes, indeed. And—thank you."

What had she been on about, he wondered, watching her hobble off on her crutches. Was she trying to tell him she knew? That she understood? Surely not. But it was possible. She was an amazingly nice woman. He'd always tried to persuade Debbie of that. And then because even thinking of Debbie that much was excruciatingly painful, he went out of the building and walked very fast down the street. He found a pub, downed half a pint of Michelob—would he ever be able to hear that word again without wanting to start blubbering—and then went back to the court.

&

"Now Mr. Phillips. You're from the Royal Yachting Association and, as I understand it, something of an expert on life jackets. Mr. Beaumont's was not inflated when he was found. Does this mean that his jacket failed him? That it was faulty?"

"No, certainly not. It was a nonautomatic type. That means, you have to pull a cord to inflate it. A lot of people don't trust them: but then an equal number don't like the automatic sort."

"Why would that be?"

"Well, they have a habit of overinflating if they get wet, in heavy weather for instance, and once inflated they become very cumbersome."

"But safer?"

"If you go overboard, yes, providing they work. As I said, you can't always rely on them."

"Have you examined the life jacket Mr. Beaumont was wearing?"

"I have, sir, yes."

"And was it faulty in any way?"

"Absolutely not. It just hadn't inflated."

"And what could explain that, do you think?"

"Well, my theory would be that Mr. Beaumont had this blow to the back of his head from the boom—they come at you very hard, booms do—and he would be momentarily stunned."

"But why should the boom be swinging about? I thought it was central to the control of the boat."

"Of course it is. But Mr. Beaumont had clearly run into this storm, worse than he had anticipated; it's a lot to handle on your own. You've only got to get out of control for a few seconds, you know. Everything goes haywire very quickly. So he'd have got hit on the head, fallen into what would have been pretty rough water, and it's easy to imagine that he wouldn't have been able to find the cord. Underwater, as it were."

"Yes, I see. Have you heard of other instances of people not opening these life jackets?"

"It's unusual. But it does happen, yes."

"And why do you think people continue to use them?"

"As I said, the automatic variety can be cumbersome. And unreliable."

"I see. Thank you, Mr. Phillips. I—"

The door of the court had opened and a clerk came in, spoke under his breath to Mr. Jeffries.

Mr. Jeffries followed him outside and shortly afterwards, and looking distinctly ruffled, reappeared with a note which he passed up to Dr. Holden. Dr. Holden read the note, nodded to Mr. Jeffries, who issued the now familiar exhortation to them all to rise. Which they did, and Dr. Holden left the bench and indeed the courtroom, having announced a short break. The whole thing was a bit like a courtroom drama on television—as Annabel whispered to Elizabeth.

Proceedings recommenced with some very tedious evidence on yachts and their seaworthiness, which lasted for about half an hour. How much more of this could she take? Elizabeth wondered. Did it really have to last so long? Surely—

"I would now like to hear from Mr. Maurice Crane," Dr. Holden said, "of Jenkins and Jenkins, insurance brokers. Mr. Jeffries, could we have Mr. Crane's statement, please, and Mr. Crane, would you please go into the witness box . . ."

Elizabeth heard Mr. Jeffries reading out Mr. Crane's statement, that he was employed at Jenkins and Jenkins as an insurance executive, that Mr. Simon Beaumont had been one of his clients, how he had consulted him on the morning of 20 August about his insurance policies . . . she had the feeling something crucial had been said, but couldn't think what it exactly was . . .

"So, Mr. Crane, you were quite possibly one of the last people to speak to Mr. Beaumont?"

"Yes, sir."

"And he telephoned you in your office. Do clients often telephone you about your policies?"

"Yes, sir. If it's something that requires an immediate answer."

"Yes, I see. And Mr. Beaumont telephoned you to ask you what, exactly?"

"It was about . . . about his life policy."

"His life policy?" said Dr. Holden. "And what exactly did he ask you, Mr. Crane?"

"He asked me if his life policy was—well, safe."

"Safe? You mean was it still viable? That is what I could not ascertain from your statement."

"Well, not exactly viable, no. He was concerned that in the event of his death, the policy might not benefit his wife and family. That it might go to Lloyd's, as part of his estate."

There was an absolute silence in the courtroom. Nobody moved, nobody looked at anyone else. Down in the street, Elizabeth could hear a police siren wailing, and a lot of cars hooting and a burglar alarm going off somewhere, and she thought that she would never be able to hear such things for the rest of her life without reliving that moment. That moment when she knew, for a fact, that Simon must have gone out deliberately that morning, to drown. To leave her forever and not tell her about it. He had told her he loved her, made love to her indeed, and then left her for all eternity. The bastard, the absolute bastard.

"And what did you tell him, Mr. Crane?"

"I told him that the policy was in trust for his wife. That Lloyd's couldn't touch it. Ever. That it was safe. As I said earlier."

"I see. And was that the end of your conversation?"

"Yes, sir. He thanked me, he was a very courteous gentleman always, and then rang off."

"And what time was this?"

"About half past ten, sir."

"So, shortly before Mr. Beaumont arrived at the Sailing Club. Did he sound in any way distressed or anxious, Mr. Crane?"

"No, sir. I would say he sounded more excited than anything."

"Excited! I think that was how Mr. Green described Mr. Beaumont's mood as well. Thank you, Mr. Crane." Dr. Holden paused. "That would have concluded the evidence. However, we have another witness, who has arrived unexpectedly, with some new facts about Mr. Beaumont's last day. I have agreed that we should hear it."

And into the court, mounting the steps to the box, came a blond woman, wearing what the initiated could see was a Chanel suit, and the uninitiated could just see was a very nice one, in pink tweed, the lapels in slightly lighter pink silk, the hemline just above the knee to show superb legs. She was tanned, and her long blond sun-streaked hair was held back loosely with a black ribbon, her shoes were brilliant pink, and extremely high-heeled, and as she looked round the court, her eyes finally settling on Elizabeth and the children, she gave the touch of a smile.

"Miss Parker Jones, thank you for coming today. Mr. Jeffries, perhaps you would read Miss Parker Jones's statement."

And so they learned that Felicity Parker Jones was a divorcée, that she lived in East Sussex, that she had spent the last four months sailing in Barbados, and that she had met Simon Beaumont several times at various regattas and sailing events. That she had actually sailed with him on several occasions; and that she had seen him on that fateful last morning and that they had met at the St. George Hotel, Arundel, to discuss a proposition. She had heard that he had drowned, but no more details, and had not realised that there was to be an inquest until she arrived back in England the evening before.

"So, Miss Parker Jones, you last saw Mr. Beaumont before that, on the twentieth of August. Where was that?"

"At the Caprice restaurant."

So that was who it was, Elizabeth thought, but not Her, please don't let this be Her, this overconfident, tough-looking woman.

"He was having lunch with someone and we talked briefly. He told me he was no longer employed and I said I could have a proposition for him. As I was leaving for Barbados the next day, we agreed we should talk sooner rather than later. He told me that he was going down to Chichester the following morning, and we arranged to meet at the St. George Hotel in Arundel, as I said in my statement."

You bastard, Simon. You knew you were going to meet her, and you didn't tell me. Just went off and didn't tell me. Well, a lifelong habit dies hard.

"And what was Mr. Beaumont's mood when you met him that morning, Miss Parker Jones? Was he cheerful, buoyant?"

"Very cheerful. And pretty buoyant, yes. Of course, I knew about the Lloyd's thing, everyone at the Sailing Club did; it was so terrible when he had to sell the *Lizzie,* but of course he wasn't the only one—lots of friends have gone under. Simon always seemed to me to be taking it so much better than most people; he was so—so positive about it, and—"

Keep going, Miss Parker Jones. This is better, much more helpful. I might even forgive you at this rate and him as well.

"Now Miss Parker Jones, this proposition. Would you like to enlarge on it?"

"Oh yes, of course. I've got two yachts, one I keep in Barbados—just a cheap little thing—and then another, much bigger one which I joint own with my father. He always does the Atlantic Rally in it."

"The Atlantic Rally, could you tell us what that's about?"

"It's a race from the Canaries to Saint Lucia."

"I see. That's quite a long way, I would think."

"Yes. It can take anything from two weeks to a month. It's a great race, any size of boat can enter, from twenty-seven to fifty-five feet. It's very exciting, and huge fun. Anyway, we were looking for a fourth crew member. I asked Simon Beaumont if he'd like to join us."

"I see. Tell us about this race, Miss Parker Jones. When does it take place?"

"In November."

"And it's a favourite, is it, in the sailing calendar?"

"Yes, it is."

"And is it dangerous?"

"Well, it's like all sailing—it can be. On the other hand, it sometimes isn't dangerous at all. It's all down to the weather."

"I see. And what would most people's reaction be, to being invited to crew in such a race?"

"Well, I think I could say that most people would be thrilled."

"And was Mr. Beaumont thrilled?"

"Absolutely. He said it had given him a real motive for going on, getting the better of bloody Lloyd's, all that sort of thing. Yes. But—"

"But?"

"Well, he said he must talk it over with his wife, obviously. That he would do so that night, and let me know."

"Did he say anything else?"

Such a silence there was then: time itself seemed not just to stand still but to freeze.

Lucinda gripped Blue's hand; Flora, Colin's; Annabel, her mother's. Fiona Broadhurst held her hands together as if in prayer; Catherine bit her lip so tightly that afterwards it was quite swollen. Every eye, every muscle of every face, was concentrated on Felicity Parker Jones.

"Well, then he said that one thing would be very important as the race was potentially dangerous, and that was his life policy. He would need to check it out, make sure that the money was safe for the family, that Lloyd's couldn't take it. He said his wife would obviously need to be reassured on that point. And he said he might as well do it straightaway, so that at least was out of the way . . ."

Half an hour later, Dr. Holden finished his summing up. And then he said, and he looked at Elizabeth and smiled, just very briefly, before he said, "On the evidence before me," and then he paused, "I am satisfied that this death came about by misadventure . . ."

Elizabeth burst into tears.

Much, much later that evening, when Elizabeth had gone exhausted—but happily—to bed, and Toby had gone out with his friends and Tilly with hers, and the phone had finally stopped ringing, and Annabel was sitting in the kitchen, trying to concentrate on a very tedious old film, and wondering if she would ever feel properly happy again, there was a knock at the door. She thought it must be Tilly having forgotten her key as she so often did, and went to open it, mildly, no not mildly, very irritated.

"You really are a complete idiot," she said, as she pulled it open.

"I know I am," said a voice: speaking rather humbly. Only it wasn't Tilly. It was Jamie. Jamie, looking slightly pale but very determined, in the light of the porch. "Do you think I could possibly come in?" he said. "I need to talk to you about something."

'And as she stood there, only half able to believe he wasn't some figment of her imagination, he said, "Annabel, I've left Boston. I've left Cartwright and Partners. I told Dad if working for the firm meant living in some kind of fifties time warp, then it wasn't for me. I can work here as a lawyer, for God's sake. I love you and I want you to have a career if you want one, and I want to marry you. If you'll still have me."

And Annabel, amazed and moved beyond anything at this demonstration of courage and determination, and indeed of love, said she most certainly would and that yes, he had better come in.

"I told Dad all I wanted was to come to London to work for a year, so we could spend some time together, get our lives figured out, that there was no reason why not, the firm hardly depended on me, and that you had your career to consider as well. And of course he said your career should be taking care of me and our children, and I told him you felt that you could work and do that, and he said he didn't want anyone in the family who felt that way. So I said I was going to come over and see you anyway, for a week or so, that we had to talk, and that was when he got really angry and said he didn't want me back in the firm if I came at all."

"But you did, just the same."

"Yes, I did," he said staunchly, and she thought that nobody who hadn't spent time with the Cartwrights could ever know what courage that had required. And realised also how much he must love her.

"Oh Jamie," she said, "I love you so, so much. And I'm sure your dad doesn't mean it. And if he does, I can think of a dozen firms that would be thrilled to have you join them. Mummy knows lots of lawyers."

"Really?"

"Really. Now let me tell you what happened at my dad's inquest today. It was truly amazing . . ."

"Oh God," he said. "I forgot, I'm so sorry."

"Don't be. Just listen."

Epilogue

She made the most extraordinarily beautiful bride. Everyone said so. The blessing had been lovely, and as everyone also said, virtually indistinguishable from the marriage service proper: she had swept down the aisle in a cloud of white silk and pink roses and happiness, to join her fiancé who was so overwhelmed by this vision that he walked up to greet her.

There was an exceptionally large group of bridesmaids and page boys, including the bride's nieces and nephews, and the children of friends, but none so excited and proud as Caroline Morgan who, when she heard she had been granted this great honour, dropped the glass of Ribena she was holding onto her grandmother's spotless white carpet. Her mother reflected rather sadly that she had clearly inherited more of her own genes than the ones responsible for Caroline's brown eyes and hair, and that her pretty hands—also an inheritance—were going to drop a great many more things before very long.

The chief bridesmaid, Miss Molly Rose Horton, wasn't actually up to most of her duties, and certainly not capturing the heart of the best man, but she did succeed in looking absolutely ravishing—carried in the arms of Catherine Morgan, who had, after all, been present at her birth—

beaming toothlessly on the congregation, wearing a dress made of the same material and as closely as possible in the same style as her mother's and, her large blue eyes wide with wonderment, watched as her parents exchanged their vows.

The bride's mother had smiled graciously at the congregation as she entered the church on the arm of her youngest son, and at her husband as he rejoined her after giving the bride away himself. There was a sharp social divide in the church; the bride's side brayed, as Blue put it afterwards, while the groom's whooped; the only visual difference was that the morning suits on the left were a lot older and shabbier than those on the right: and many of the whoopers were not in morning dress at all, but rather sharply cut suits.

Lucinda had carefully chosen hymns that everyone would know—"It's like listening to Songs of Praise," Mrs. Worthington hissed to her elder daughter—and Lucinda and Blue left the church smiling with such patent joy it made even Mr. Worthington smile back; Blue was carrying Molly Rose who by now had fallen so thoroughly into the spirit of the thing that she performed her latest trick, which was waving to all and sundry, greatly encouraged by all and sundry waving back.

Mr. Worthington found himself actually rather enjoying having Mrs. Horton on his arm; she was a pretty woman anyway, and dressed entirely in varying shades of pink, the skirt of her dress being short enough to reveal some very good legs; she put Mrs. Worthington, in her rather weary wedding navy, distinctly in the shade. Mrs. Worthington took Mr. Horton's arm rather gingerly, as if it might suddenly sting her, but when he told her in a stage whisper that he thought Lucinda was a dead ringer for her mum ("May God forgive me," he said, recounting this later to Mrs. Horton), she inclined her head to him graciously and started smiling almost as broadly as Molly Rose.

The reception was at the Hortons' new home, a large and impressive mansion in St. George's Hill, Surrey; Lucinda had managed to steer Blue away from Chislehurst, but she could see that unless she made some concessions, she was going to find herself unmarried again, and that she should bid farewell to any ideas of Georgian or even Victorian houses in London.

The mansion, called Hedges on account of some splendidly tall and thick beech hedges which surrounded it, was one of St. George's finest, boasting not only a swimming pool, a three-acre garden, and six bedrooms all with en suite bathrooms, but what the estate agents described as "a small ballroom." This, extended by a large marquee, formed the reception area; where the bridal party stood in line to receive their guests. Of which there were two hundred and twenty.

Flora, accompanied by Colin, was greatly enjoying herself. She was wearing a silk dress in darkest blue, with an embroidered red silk coat over it, a red hat with a display of osprey feathers that would not have disgraced the Queen Mother, and some very high-heeled red boots.

Colin was wearing a morning suit that was not as new as he would have liked; he was all set to have one specially made for the wedding, but Flora had managed to persuade him against it.

"That one is so nice," she said, pointing to the one hanging in his dressing room, to which he had summoned her, the better to discuss the matter. "Why do you want to get a new one?"

Colin said the old one was at least ten years old, and he really thought the occasion demanded something a bit more special, as he put it; he'd been to a wedding recently where one of the guests had had the lapels of his coat piped in a much lighter grey, to match his trousers.

Flora hoped he hadn't noticed her shudder and told him that she really thought his old one was fine and that he should leave such refinements to the bridal party. Colin rather reluctantly agreed, but said that at least he would get a new top hat—which sounded perfectly safe except that he had had a dark red band put round it, to match his waistcoat.

They had had a rather good lunch on the way to the wedding, and she was already feeling slightly tipsy; that, combined with the sunshine and the emotion of the day, and her own great new happiness, suddenly overwhelmed her and she reached up to kiss Colin.

"You look very, very nice," she said. "Really handsome."

"Well, thank you," he said, "and you look absolutely beautiful. You must bring that outfit to Salzburg. Not long now."

"No, indeed," she said. "And that reminds me, Colin, there's something I wanted to say to you about Salzburg."

"Ye-es?" He looked rather wary.

She smiled and kissed him again. "It's all right," she said. "All I wanted to say was, could you change the booking slightly?"

"I'll try," he said. "What would you like me to change?"

"Well," she said, smiling at him and thinking how even the hat wasn't too bad, "I really would rather we weren't in separate rooms. If it's all right with you."

❧

Annabel Beaumont was attracting a lot of attention. Dressed in a sliver of palest blue silk, with extremely high-heeled silver sandals, her hair scooped back in a waterfall of curls, she looked almost as ravishing as the bride herself: indeed, Lucinda hissed at her as she embraced her in the receiving line, she made her feel like a fat old bat.

"Lucinda, I don't think so. You look about seventeen, maybe a bit younger, doesn't she, Jamie? Lucinda, this is my fiancé, Jamie Cartwright."

"Oh, how lovely to meet you," Lucinda cried. "Blue, darling, this is Jamie, Annabel's totally handsome fiancé—he's a lawyer from the States, you know. Lucky you to be married to a lawyer, Annabel—wish I'd been, saved me a lot of trouble."

And Jamie kissed Lucinda's hand and shook Blue's and said how extremely generous of them to have invited him to their wedding, and Annabel thought not for the first time how charming he was, and how he really was rather like her father.

Jamie was still an associate of Cartwright and Partners, but he was to move to London for a year, to work for a firm in Lincoln's Inn with which Cartwrights had an agreement. After that, he and Annabel had agreed, they would decide together where they would settle permanently.

This had not been arrived at without difficulty.

Elizabeth had managed not to display any great surprise at Jamie's presence in the house the day after the inquest and kept carefully out of the whole thing for the next twenty-four hours, merely greeting Jamie with affection. Later, when she was told that Jamie and his father had made up their quarrel and that Jamie was going to be allowed to spend a year in London, she was more relieved still, and any anxiety she had felt for Annabel joining the Cartwright clan diminished considerably.

"The old bugger actually said," Annabel told her, "that he could see Jamie was going to be an excellent lawyer, having demonstrated an ability to stay cool in a—a standoff situation. And Jamie's going to work for some firm where all the partners are his best friends."

"Well, it's lovely," said Elizabeth carefully, "and I'm very happy for you. The only thing I would say, darling, is that you must make some concessions too."

"Mummy," said Annabel indignantly, "do you think I'm stupid or something? Of course I will." Adding that if Jamie thought she was going to move to Boston when she had Florian's salon to work in, then he had better change his mind pretty quickly.

"Annabel," said Elizabeth warningly, and Annabel looked very discomfited and said, "Well, not till we're married anyway."

And now Jamie was in London for a year, and they were looking for a flat—"But very, very near, Mummy, I promise you. You don't have to worry."

"I'm not worried," said Elizabeth, while thinking that this was what she had predicted would happen when she had agreed to have the baby, and that Annabel's life would of course take precedence over hers, and that that was precisely what she wanted for her.

℃

Elizabeth was not at the wedding; she had been invited, of course, but as she was now eight and a half months' pregnant she said that she was sure Lucinda would understand and forgive her.

Every day now she felt happier, stronger, more able to cope with what was a fairly daunting future. She had found a nanny, a stalwart Scottish girl called Tess, who was clearly going to fit into the household extremely well—not least in that she was very pretty and Toby approved of her.

Elizabeth had insisted that they all interview her; and Tess had liked that very much, said she always knew there would be trouble when she'd only been allowed to meet the mother.

℃

Nigel was not at the wedding either; Lucinda knew he wouldn't come, nor even want to, but she felt that he would be very hurt if he wasn't invited, and so sent him one of the somewhat excessive invitations. He had looked at it through slightly blurred eyes while wondering even then how Lucinda could have become the sort of person who added pink ribbons to a wedding invitation, but after that he did feel much better, as she had known he would, and put it on his fireplace along with some more sober ones. He ordered a pair of bay trees for a present, to be delivered to the house on the day of the wedding, and then found it surprisingly easy to regard the whole thing with equanimity. He supposed Catherine would be at the wedding; unless of course she was in Somerset with this man. If he hadn't feared rejection so, he might even now have tried to see her. But it was all a bit depressing.

He tried to think what he might do with the day. In the end he decided to stay in London; he had a few houses to look at—one in particular, a pretty little terrace house in Ovington Street. That would be a positive thing to do on such a day, and then maybe he'd have dinner at his club. The day would pass, and then—well, then what? A lifetime of bachelorhood, he supposed. There were worse things. At least you could do what you wanted.

❧

Toby was at the wedding, and looking forward rather desperately to the wedding breakfast when Fallon was arriving, to help in the kitchen. Lucinda had told Tilly she could bring a couple of friends if she liked, and Tilly had asked both Fallon and Madison, but Madison, who was very shy anyway, said that it would be too much of a temptation with her diet—at Tilly's instigation she had joined Weight Watchers, and already lost two stone—and Fallon said she'd feel like some kind of freak at a fair, unless Tilly could find her something she could actually do. It turned out that the caterers were two short on the washing-up front, and Tilly had volunteered Fallon: "And then we can maybe have a bit of a bop at the end of the evening."

Fallon said pigs could maybe fly, "And certainly not with that brother of yours, bet he's a sight on the dance floor."

Tilly told her rather stiffly not to be so rude, and Fallon, who genuinely adored Tilly, told her not to be so silly and that actually she thought Toby was pretty good-looking really, and if he'd only unstarch his neck and learn to speak properly, he could look quite fit.

⟁

Debbie and Richard weren't at the wedding; they had hardly known Lucinda. In any case, Debbie couldn't have gone as it was a Friday and Friday was the day she wrote and filed her copy for the *Daily News*.

Joel had done something wonderful for Debbie before he left for New York; he had taken Nicky Holt out to lunch and asked her if she "or one of your mates in that silly business of yours" could possibly give Debbie a chance to do some writing.

"Debbie Fielding's a PR," said Nicky witheringly. "You fancy her or something, Joel?"

Joel said of course not, but: "She writes really nicely and she's funny and she's just desperate for a break. Please, Nicky! I'll buy you dinner at the Pierre next time you come to New York."

"You do fancy her, don't you?" said Nicky curiously. "Yeah, OK, I'll try and think of something. I'm setting up a panel testing various products each week—how'd that be?"

"Great," said Joel.

And Debbie, managing somehow to function more or less normally—how did she do that, how, when she felt increasingly she was going mad—was telephoned one morning by Nicky and asked if she would like to join her panel of guinea pigs. "I'll only want about two hundred words each week—could you manage that, d'you think?"

"Of course I could," said Debbie. "I'd love to." And within four weeks, she had so impressed Nicky, her two hundred words being much sharper and funnier and better composed than any of the others, that Nicky asked her if she'd like to extend her testing to various health clubs and spas—"that sort of thing."

She was now writing a regular review—literally a column running down the right-hand side of Nicky's Monday pages, of such places; she'd turn up incognito, stay a day, and then deliver copy so well-honed, and so coolly to the point that within weeks she had a modest fan mail. Nothing could have soothed her pain, eased her loneliness, restored her sense of optimism more efficiently and quickly than that column. She could even listen to Richard telling her how wonderful Morag was without wanting to scream. And the best thing of all was that when she moved to Scotland in the spring, she could just carry on doing it. It meant being away overnight once a week, but that was wonderful; she told Richard it was the least he could do for her, and slightly to her surprise he agreed without any argument. She wondered if Flora, her newest and greatest ally, had anything to do with it, and decided she probably did.

She still missed Joel with a savageness that was physically painful, she still cried at least once a day; she still woke up from dreams that he was there—but she was surviving. The first dreadful days, when it had hurt so much she was actually frightened, had passed; she managed from time to time to enjoy things, her children, her job, the contemplation of her lovely new house. And one day, she could see, she would be properly happy again.

☙

Elizabeth hadn't mentioned a terrible headache to Annabel as she left for the wedding, or a feeling of distinct dizziness to Tilly when she came to kiss her goodbye, and obviously neither of these things to Toby. She knew if she did, they would all have refused to leave her. But once they had gone—soon after midday, for they all had much to do, not least Annabel who was assisting Florian on the bridal hair—she phoned Mr. Taylor, her obstetrician and reported these things to him.

Within thirty minutes she was in a private ambulance on her way to the Princess Diana Hospital, where a rather worryingly large committee was waiting for her, headed by Mr. Taylor, looking stern.

"I think," he said, after checking her blood pressure, and both their heartbeats, "it's time we got that baby out. Your blood pressure is extremely high, you're only two weeks away from term, and there's no earthly reason not to. I'm going to do a section, so we don't waste any more time."

"Oh God," said Elizabeth, feeling fear literally clasping her heart, longing for Simon more than she could ever remember. "Oh Mr. Taylor, is it going to be all right?"

"Of course it is," he said. "The baby's heartbeat is extremely strong.

It just wants to get out. Now try to keep calm, I'm going to get that blood pressure down a bit, and we'll do it late afternoon. You haven't had any lunch, have you?"

"No. Breakfast though. And a cup of tea about—oh, about one." Her mouth felt very dry; she was shaking violently, her teeth chattering. "I— I want—" she said, and then started to cry, for she knew she couldn't have what she wanted, what every woman in labour wants, her husband with her.

Mr. Taylor was very sweet; he sat down beside her, took her hand and said, "You're going to be fine, Elizabeth, just fine. And so is your baby. Now, is there anyone you'd like to have with you, who could come and be with you for a bit?"

And, "No," she said, and that made her cry harder than ever, her aloneness spelled out by that small, awful word. "The children are all at a wedding and I don't want to spoil their day."

Mr. Taylor looked at her and smiled. "Elizabeth Beaumont," he said, "you are a trouper. World-class. And you'll just have to make do with me."

❧

Nigel was about to have a bath when the florist phoned. They were simply devastated, but it appeared that the pair of bay trees, destined for Weybridge that afternoon, had not after all been delivered.

"Well, do it now," he said, and they replied that they couldn't because their drivers had all gone home, and would the morning do? He had been about to say yes, when he thought he really did want them to arrive that day, he had envisaged them at the entrance to the marquee, had indeed written that on the card, giving him some kind of presence there, and thought then that it would only take him an hour at the most to drive them over himself; no need to go in, or to announce that he was there, he could deliver them and then drive away. And when the trees arrived by taxi at his flat, in square white wooden tubs with large white bows tied around the trees—"We might remove those, I think," he said to the totally disinterested cab driver, "bit vulgar"—he put them in the back of his Volvo and set out for Weybridge.

❧

Catherine wasn't sure if she was enjoying the wedding or not. Of course it was all very lovely, and Lucinda looked gorgeous and so did the garden and the house and the marquee; and the string quartet was playing the most delicious music, and everyone was being very nice to her, and Caroline and Freddie had both been extremely good—although they were now being slightly less good and haring about the garden shrieking with Lucinda's nephews and nieces—but the fact remained that she did feel very lonely. Again.

The wedding was accentuating that, rather. Everyone was in couples, not just the young ones, and halfway through the reception, and before the meal, she began to feel tearful, and decided to go for a walk round the garden. She was looking rather hopelessly for Freddie and Caroline and consequently not at where she was going; and managed to walk straight into one of the waiters, his tray laden with glasses of wine.

Catherine looked down at her pale pink suit, now liberally spattered with red, tried not to cry and fled up to the room where she had got ready. She would just have to change; she had a linen dress with her, it was hardly festive and a bit creased, but it was at least all one colour and didn't smell like a winery.

She put it on, trying to keep positive—all would be lost if she gave in to self-pity now—and was just reapplying her makeup when she saw in the drive what looked remarkably like Nigel's Volvo. And not only did it look like it, it was Nigel's Volvo, and what was more, he was getting out of it and removing first one and then a second bay tree from the boot and handing them over to a man in charge of the gate.

Catherine watched him, as he looked up at the house rather wistfully, all on his own, as she was, not dressed in wedding finery as she no longer was, and knew with absolutely clarity what she had to do. She leaned out of the window and waved and shouted, "Nigel! Nigel, wait!" He didn't hear her.

She raced out of the room, down the stairs, out of the door and down the drive, through the gate: to see the Volvo moving away, quite fast down the tree-lined road.

"Oh Nigel—oh God, no," she said, and because it really did seem like more than she could bear, she sank onto her haunches and started to cry, her head buried in her arms.

And then suddenly she heard him say, "Catherine? Isn't it?" He must have reversed up the road, for she looked up and saw him, leaning out of the window, clearly very concerned.

And, "Oh yes, it is, it is Catherine," she said, grief and relief making her stupid; and he got out of the car and came across to her and squatted beside her and put his arm round her.

"Whatever is it? What's the matter?" he said, and she really started crying then, sobbing quite loudly, and he stood up and helped her up too and led her across to his car and put her into it and drove very slowly down the road, away from the house and the noise and the curious eyes.

"Now then," he said finally, pulling to the kerb and turning off the engine. "Now then, tell me what the matter is. Thank goodness I spotted you. I can't bear to see you like this, Catherine, I really can't. Has someone upset you?"

And Catherine looked at him, at his face, even more mournful than usual, his pale-blue eyes full of concern for her, and said—because she had to know that first—"Nigel, are you . . . are you still in love with Lucinda?"

And when he said, Good Lord, no, no he wasn't, not at all, thank goodness—although he was still very, very fond of her, of course—she said, "Because you see, I think . . ." God, this took courage, huge courage, she felt terrible, so scared and so foolish, but it was her last chance, she knew, and a chance she wanted so much, "Nigel, I think I—I might be in love with you."

And after that it all became very simple.

℮〜

At roughly the same moment, Mr. Taylor was stroking Elizabeth's hair back gently from her face as she surfaced from the anaesthetic, and smiling down at her—really he thought he might be a little in love with her himself—and telling her that she had a very fine and extremely noisy new son.

℮〜

The meal had been wonderful, the speeches very funny—especially Charlie's—and the dancing had begun, when the maître d' walked up to

Lucinda who was chattering at one of the tables, and whispered something in her ear.

Whereupon she said, "Oh my God!" and began looking wildly round the room. And then ran over to Toby, who was dancing, really rather badly, with a ravishing black girl, who was dancing rather well, and said, "Toby, Toby, she's had it, your mother's had her baby, it's a boy!"

And was alarmed to see Toby standing first stock-still, completely emotionless, and then bite his lip and his blue eyes, so like his father's, fill with tears.

And then he punched the air with his fist and shouted, "Yesss!!" and Tilly came rushing over and Annabel too, and they all three stood there, hugging one another, crying and laughing at the same time. And then Annabel said, "We must go to her at once, can someone get us a cab?" and the maître d' said he would, right away.

When they had gone, Lucinda, quite tearful herself, suddenly said, "Has anyone seen Catherine? I hope she's all right."

"Oh yes, sorry," said Caroline, "we were meant to tell you. She's gone off with Nigel to have dinner, she hopes you won't mind. She'll be back later."

"Nigel!" said Lucinda. "My goodness, how wonderful."

And, "Blimey," said Blue, "any more dramas at this wedding and I'm going to the office, get a bit of peace and quiet."

❧

In their mother's room at the hospital, Annabel and Toby and Tilly stood by her bed, smiling down at her as she said sleepily, "Didn't we do well?"

"You did, Mummy," said Annabel, and, "Darling Mummy," said Tilly, and, "It's great," said Toby, "I'm really pleased." And then the nurse brought the baby in, still yelling. "I'm afraid he's going to be a rather noisy addition to the household," Elizabeth said, taking him in her arms—and they all gazed at him, in absolute awe, and Tilly spoke for them all when she said, quietly but quite happily, "How pleased Daddy would be."

"He would indeed," said Elizabeth, and she said it quite happily too.

They left not long after that—for she was very tired, and the baby wouldn't settle—promising to come back in the morning.

"You know what?" said Annabel, as they sat in the kitchen, toasting the baby with tea. "I just had a rather good thought."

"What's that then?" said Toby.

"Those beastly people didn't beat us, did they, not any of us. They didn't win. We did."